The Hatchling

Rev. Paul V. Beyerl

The Hatchling

A Unicorn and Her Humans

First Edition

by

Rev. Paul V. Beyerl

published by The Hermit's Grove

Cover illustration by Michele Dennis

Other works by the author:

The Master Book of Herbalism
© 1984 Phoenix Publishing Co., Custer, WA

A Compendium of Herbal Magick
© 1998 Phoenix Publishing Co., Custer, WA

A Wiccan Bardo
© 1989 Prism Press, Bridport, England

A Wiccan Bardo, Revisited
Revised Edition © 1998 The Hermit's Grove, Kirkland, WA

Painless Astrology
Revised Edition © 1996 The Hermit's Grove, Kirkland, WA

The Holy Books of the Devas
Fourth Edition © 1998 The Hermit's Grove, Kirkland, WA

Gem and Mineral Lore
First edition © 2005 The Hermit's Grove, Kirkland, WA

The Symbols and Magick of Tarot
First edition © 2005 The Hermit's Grove, Kirkland, WA

The Hatchling

published by:

The Hermit's Grove

An educational subsidiary of The Rowan Tree Church
P O Box 0691
Kirkland, Washington 98083-0691

Dedicated to the four pillars of medicine:

Dedication to the Joy of Learning
A Knowledge of the Psychology of Astrology
Skill in Herbal Medicine and Alchemy
Commitment to a Virtuous Life

Library of Congress Control Number - 2007932537
ISBN 978-0-9655687-5-3

This edition published by The Hermit's Grove

The Hatchling

It was in the Candlemas, 1995 issue of The Unicorn that the first episode of The Hatchling was published. The Unicorn is a newsletter I initiated in 1977 and which, despite the internet, remains in print as a published-on-paper newsletter sent out eight times a year to coincide with the eight seasonal Wiccan Sabbats. In the 'old style,' it continues to be distributed through the postal system. Are unicorns part of our past, ancestral myth? Or are they part of our present and future reality?

The Unicorn has grown into its own. It all began with my work in the theatre department when in University in the 1960s. Through that I met my first unicorn, Tennessee Williams' glass unicorn which belonged to Amanda in his play The Glass Menagerie.

We have had Unicorns within our Wiccan Tradition of Lothloriën for many years, now. How did this come to be? Goodness, that's a long story, one which goes on for several pages in our booklet, The Unicorns of Lothloriën.

When the series The Hathcling debuted, the following appeared in the opening letter by our newsletter's own resident Unicorn, Andrius: "It is with unabashed excitement that we present a new series of stories beginning in this issue. The Hatchling is an exciting story, one which fits the times. You humans who read The Unicorn are very important. Our Mother Earth is facing an assault. Over the past decades we've been fighting hard to preserve the rain forests, to provide flowing rivers for the salmon, to keep those with greed for oil and lumber from wreaking even more destruction. Now we stand on the threshold of a new political era and it has become a very real possibility that commerce will win over sacredness."

What was I thinking? I did not realize that it would be twelve years before the series would reach a conclusion. Twelve years! Writing fiction is far more challenging than writing non-fiction has ever been for me. When I write non-fiction it's simply another form of teaching: I'm talking on paper. But when I write fiction there are characters to keep track of as well as dates and events and the geography of the story. With nonfiction I'm simply expressing the facts with a goal of helping the reader learn what it is I am teaching. With nonfiction there is no controlling the characters. They must have the freedom to move forward with their own lives. When Ollis Piper appeared I had no clue that he would return and win Flying Raven's heart.

And I certainly did not suspect that Gino would be married and a father by the time the series ended. At one point I made just the slighted suggestion to the readers that there might come a time when the series would end. Annette in New York, one of our faithful readers and supporters, wrote that I could not just kill them all off! And how true that proved. It had taken very little time before the events and personalities of Merrydale took on a life of their own.

As the characters and the story lines created their own reality, I was merely the instrument recording what was taking place. I would spend days and days (sometimes weeks) attempting to understand what the plot and events of the next installment were becoming. As the author and editor of these individuals who seemed to have free will and lead their own lives, quite often I would begin an episode only to discover that it was heading off in a far different direction than I had anticipated,

The Hatchling includes names and activities drawn from current global events, from the warming of our planet to political strife and even war as we encountered it in this new century. There is one reference to history, based upon records which indicate that Genghis Khan halted a major invasion of the Kwarazmian Empire. Some reports indicate that the Mongols had seen a unicorn and I have seen another version of this story indicating that Khan had a dream which included a unicorn. That event led him to call off the invasion. If some of the major forces for war in today's world could but dream of a unicorn!

Other aspects of the story involve the Wiccan beliefs and practices of my own Tradition of Lothloriën and the activities of The Rowan Tree Church. A number of the personalities in the episodes began their appearance in The Hatchling based upon real people and some evolved into unrelated beings. For many episodes, the events followed real life.

In fact, with the first earthquake in the stories already planned, just as the first episode was being mailed, The Robinson Point earthquake shook us on January 28th, a magnitude 5.0 temblor, definitely enough to get one's attention. Us? Over thirty years ago a Unicorn - named Andrius entered my life. Not only did I learn to share publication space with this creature but he changed my life as well and has become a major influence in my Wiccan Tradition - The Tradition of Lothloriën. In March of 1993 ce I met my beloved partner, gerry, who is the Holly to my life as an herbalist. We live here at The Hermit's Grove, with 45,000 square feet of gardens which include our ritual spaces, one of which is back in the woodland garden and is a Stone Circle. If you ever visit us to see the hundreds of species of herbes which grow here, you will see that we clearly live with unicorns. We live in multiple realities.

Perhaps the question posed by this series is this: Can a dream or vision coexist with real life? As I wrote these episodes, The Hatchling was not simply a work of fantasy. It was also our reality. My own magickal evolution has shown me that dreams and real life are not separate. If we but believe in our dreams with enough passion, they will manifest. I personally know that Magick (along with some unicorns) have certainly brought all of the dreams I once cherished into manifestation. And now, the publication of The Hatchling is yet another.

Rev. Paul Beyerl
The Hermit's Grove
July, 2007 ce

With special thanks to my much-loved partner, gerry,
to Andrius, the gentle blue Unicorn who shares our lives,
to Annette, an angel in the Unicorn's world,
and to Cat J., who proofread all these many pages…

The Hatchling

I - The Discovery

Candlemas. Yes, it was true, the days *were* growing longer. It was no longer dark when they sat down to their evening meal. And the bulbs! Oh, yes, the winter had been warmer than usual which was a blessing when it came to heating their cabin, but the spring bulbs were impatient. Daffodils had stretched their leaves up to the winter sky, crocuses had long been showing their green and little catkins grew long and thick from the hazel. The gardens wanted to believe it was spring. Throughout the woodland the devas were filled with hope.

But even as the Eve of the Waxing Light neared, there was a darkening cloud spreading throughout the land. Those who believed in preserving the Devas had been scorned. The voice of the salmon was no longer heard. The music of the pines was being threatened by the sickening shriek of the saw. Far away, beneath the great dome, secret meetings were being held and the word was spreading throughout Lothloriën. The political tides had shifted and the growing darkness was not that of the Wheel of the Year, but that of fear. The great House, the political battlefield where the laws were made, was now overrun by the Users. The Users did not love our Mother Earth. Their gods were those made of coins and of personal power. Now a minority, the Preservers felt a growing dread. Years of work to save the forests, to protect even a few of the smallest species, were now in peril.

Arnica looked out the window. He felt old, this day. "Old bones," he thought, remembering an earlier Candlemas, nearly twenty years ago. But this was not a time for reverie and he sighed, long and deep. Arnica had worked with Holly for many years to preserve this small woodland, a safe and sacred space for the Devas. The firs were tall and strong, creating a home for the hawk. The gardens were ready for spring, the buds on the fruit trees were strengthening. And the Wheel was ready to be turned once again.

"How come you with the tools, my sweet?"

Holly called back from the kitchen sink, "I'm just drying the last one." The wondrous chalice, over a century old, was polished and shone as bright as a silver diamond on the Lady Moon. The blades were sharpened, the metal bright and gleaming. The crystal of the goblet was as clear as the stars on a cold winter's night. "Have you the fuels?"

"Yes the old fool's ready," Arnica said, chuckling. The lifeblood of the cabin was often stirred with endless hours of puns and word games.

Holly filled a large, woven basket with the ritual tools. The athames and chalices, their wands set in so the ends would come out at the crack of the lid. A small jar of salt, the ground herbes and censer. Holly packed all that they would need for their Candlemas Eve Ritual. Arnica's job was to gather the candles which would light the cardinal stones, safe against the winter zephyrs in their little glass shelters. Two more for the stone altar. Then the cauldron and a large flask of fuel for the Candlemas Fire.

Only that day had the Politicos declared that the Devas would no longer be protected. With more and more people crushing the Earth, the demand for food and

1

lumber was higher than ever. After many years in which the salmon had been returning to the streams, their numbers growing, their spirits protected against slaughter. The Earthkin had grown fearful. The Descendant Tribes had been drumming and dancing and calling upon the Great Mother to give them help. Arnica was not of the Descendant Tribes. He and Holly worked with the Renaissance Tribes, a new people who returned to the Earth during the Changing Times. Their work was always difficult, for the Changing Times brought greater peace and greater war, balanced plague with miraculous discoveries. And the stress of change left the greater peoples vulnerable, willing to grasp for security at any straws offered by the Users who promised short cuts and wealth for all who gave them power, caring little for those seeking to preserve the Mother.

They walked along the path and, as they entered the woods, patches of light frost kissed the moss of the trees. Arnica held a lantern, its light beaming along the wet carpet of leaves.

"Oops!" Holly tripped over a root. After so many years tending the trees, Holly was easily distracted, looking everywhere but the path, checking to see that each of the saplings was growing strong.

Arnica and Holly reached the stone circle. What comfort was here! Sheltered beneath the soaring arches of fir boughs, the huge rocks had been carefully laid in place. Mother Earth had stretched out Her loving fingertips of moss and the small gems and crystals set about by the couple and by their Renaissance friends sparkled bright in the night. Slipping their concerns about politics into the dark recesses of their minds, they set thinking, itself, aside and moved into their ritual form.

The Circle cast, the candles flaming. They sang their songs and chanted the sacred poetry of Lothloriën. Calling upon the four Guardian Unicorns, their forms emerged from the astral, each taking the proper place at the great, Cardinal altars. As they invoked the Goddess, Her power rose up from within the Earth and the very air within the stone circle seemed to shimmer with Magick. When they invoked the Horned One, an owl cried into the night, the trees shifted their branches and the wind played the music of pipes - but only the trained ear heard it.

The cauldron filled and set in the Circle's center, Arnica and Holly held hands and danced the Rune. Suddenly the flames spiraled up from the cauldron, far higher than their heads. Just as their hearts panicked in fear for the trees, the flame shot down. The cauldron was instantly dark, but the soft loam beneath the cauldron was glowing gently. Arnica stepped to the Circle's edge and reached beyond the stones for a fallen stick. Hooking it in the handle of the cauldron, he pulled the warm vessel aside. No, the soil was not glowing but there was a light coming from beneath its surface.

Holly began digging gently, fingers moving decaying needles and bits of soil they had gathered from sacred sites from Circles throughout the world. And then it happened, Holly's fingers uncovered the glowing, smooth surface of some unworldly treasure. They worked together, recalling the days they had struggled to dig up huge rocks left from the last glacier as they made beds for herbes and homes for the Devas.

As the form was revealed, it was obvious that it was shaped like an egg. Warm and radiant, it was so magickal that Holly stopped unearthing it. "What should we do?"

"Touch it with me," said Arnica. They laid their hands upon it. Just the slightest rhythm could be felt. "Listen," said Arnica, and Holly got down upon the earth, an ear held just at the shell's surface.

"A heartbeat!" Holly whispered in excitement.

How could it be? Arnica sat, quietly. The arthritis in his old bones ached and he rocked back and forth, moving through the pain until he sat in the Crone's arms. Holly sat quietly, one hand upon the glowing Warmth, one extended with the palm against Arnica's heart, joining in spirit to help Arnica find the answer.

Arnica's eyes opened. He spoke slowly, "We must leave it here until Eostara. We have been asked to give it protection. Andrius has sired a Unicolt, and ours is the job of giving it shelter. It must grow strong that our Mother Earth will be protected."

They gently pushed the soil back over the egg. Unsure if the Cone of Power would provide enough warmth, they laid their robes over the Circle's heart. The desire to stay here was so great but they padded barefoot back to their cabin. The Wheel was turning and the work ahead left them quiet and ready for sleep.

Later that night, as dreams wove themselves into their magick, Holly cried out into the dark. Arnica woke, his arm pulling Holly close. "It was horrible. I saw the Earth's crust crack open..."

"Quiet, sweet thing. Breathe slow and feel my love. Sleep, my sweet." And they did.

II - The Earthquake

Arnica's fingers were brown with Spring mud. He and Holly worked the soil around their stone circle, preparing the site for tomorrow night's ritual. They'd been here as much of their time as possible in the weeks since Candlemas. The memory of that night was never far from their minds. Circling within the stones, the candles flaming, the image of the fire as it spiraled up into the Universe was a recurrent theme as they pondered over the strange and wonderful event. A warm, egg-shaped object had begun to gently emerge from the earth, right at the center of their Circle. It was no wonder Arnica and Holly spent all of their free time working the soil around the stone circle. Arnica's vision told him it held a Unicolt, offspring of their Unicorn friend, Andrius. The egg was never far from their minds and this year's gardening was taking place around the stone circle where they could observe it and watch for changes. Their gardens between the cabin and the woods, and there were many, seemed to be doing a good job of tending themselves.

The first day of Spring was nearly upon them. In two days the Sun would move into Aries and all of Nature would pivot on the precarious balance between winter and spring. The gardens would be at the midpoint between the shortest day and the longest day, between winter and summer. It was warmer than usual, this year. Indeed, the thermometer outside the greenhouse had recorded warmer temperatures for this season than either Arnica or Holly could remember.

And they were glad. What was a faint heartbeat in the egg, barely audible last Candlemas had grown to a healthy pulsing. They no longer kept the egg covered with blankets and robes. It stayed warm to the touch, seeming to generate its own heat no matter how cool the air at night. Just as the woodland flowers were sending up their early shoots, as the bulbs were stretching in March exuberance, was the life within the sacred egg growing strong as well.

"Look," shouted Holly with excitement, "a trillium - the first!"

Trilliums were one of their sacred flowers. When they first walked among these trees there were but a few of the wildflowers so loved by the Devas. These they nurtured and gave space, clearing the brambles and invasive weeds, singing songs and giving the trilliums love. Several times at the market they had seen other trillium species offered for sale. Arnica would slip his fingers into his money pocket and count the coins by touch. There were always enough. This first trillium was white, but between Eostara and Beltane there would be some yellow, some deep red and even a few nodding trilliums to bless their magickal woods.

The spotting of the first trillium was always a time for giving thanks. Holly went to get Arnica. The mud wiped upon their pants, they held hands and walked along the path to the stone circle. Usually they would move into the very center, there to kneel and offer their blessings to Mother Earth. As they neared the moss-covered stones, their hearts quickened.

A beam of sunlight slipped between the firs, tall overhead, and came to light right upon the egg. Arnica breathed deeply, glad he was not superstitious. This was such a dramatic image that one could easily believe that the egg was being touched by the hand of the Sun God. Arnica squeezed Holly's hand tightly and they began walking around the stones, pausing at the East and the other three cardinal points. Then, rather than kneeling in the center, they moved so that the egg was between them.

Without a word, they simultaneously bent over to listen.

"Can you hear it?"

The heartbeat had grown stronger - but the rhythm had changed. As motes of dust and early pollen danced in the sunbeam, it was as if a silent song danced to the rhythm of the natural wonder. And just as quickly, a cloud passed overhead and they were shaded. Holly's jaw dropped. The egg, which should have lost its glow, continued to radiate light.

"What do we do now?"

"I'm not sure. It seems to have grown larger as well. Maybe we should cover it. The nights can still be cool. Help me gather fir needles to cover it like a blanket."

They worked quickly, bringing handsful of needles until the egg was left safe and warm. Arnica and Holly gathered their tools and called it quits for the day.

The Moon shone through their window. Her light gave shape to the two forms snuggled against each other beneath their quilt. A long day's gardening tired Arnica's old bones. A hot, soaking bath helped, but he was more than ready to sleep. His arm held Holly close, their dreams interwoven with images of the magickal egg and the stone circle, images of weeding, digging and working the soil.

At an instant, they both sat up. Within a moment the sound of the Earth's bones cracking came roaring up and caught their cabin, shaking their bed. The sound of glass breaking upon the floor as their bed tossed like a leaf brought them wide awake. Almost as quickly the earth's trembling subsided.

"Actually, that wasn't too bad," said Holly, breaking into relieved laughter.

"Wow," Arnica answered, stretching his arm out to turn on the bedside light. "Four-thirty. I bet Mars has just risen in the East. Let's get up."

Donning their shoes, they went into the kitchen. Only a couple of glass jars which had been left on the counter for recycling had broken. A few things had come down but their earthquake proofing was reliable. Holly swept up the glass as Arnica checked everything thoroughly. As he knelt in front of their altar, just for an instant he thought he saw something reflected in the large, crystal ball - but nothing was there.

The image was clear in his mind and he felt a sense of urgency as he hurried into the kitchen to Holly.

"Holly, do you remember that dream you had last Candlemas?"

"Yes, how could I forget. I think that's what had my heart going when it first hit."

"There's something about your dream I can't quite put my finger on. I just saw something in the Orb. I can't explain what but we've got to get dressed and go out to the stone circle."

"Now? In the dark?"

"Trust me, sweet thing. I can't explain why, but this is important."

Dressed warm, their flashlights played beams about in the dark. First coming outside they'd stopped to pick up some clay flowerpots which had fallen unbroken from the potting bench. Others, shattered, would wait until later in the day.

They walked the path carefully. Over the years they'd experienced other temblors. There was a wry amusement in seeing damage only where humans had been building. The forest always seemed untouched, other than dead branches having been brought down.

As they neared the stone circle, Holly played the light about. Twice before, a few mossy stones had been dislodged when the earth quaked, but they'd been replaced and reinforced. But Arnica moved directly to the egg and gasped loudly.

"Look!"

The shell was badly cracked. As they knelt, both felt sickened, thinking this damage caused by the quake. But right before their eyes, the shell cracked further, and the delicate point of a spiraled horn poked through.

"I can't believe it!" Holly was so happy, the words could barely come out.

It took nearly an hour, but the Unicolt had broken free. Arnica took off his warm coat and they picked up the hatchling. As Holly held the flashlights, Arnica carried it back to their cabin. Stepping carefully over roots, they were too awed to speak.

Reaching the cabin, Holly stepped up to the door. Before opening it, he turned to look at Arnica. Just then the Unicolt's head stretched up, and it's tongue gave Arnica a big lick. Holly bent over and kissed the Unicolt right on the nose. And to think, that tonight was the Eostara Eve ritual, when the birthing of the seeds would be honored!

III - The May Horn

Arnica walked carefully past the potting bench. Small bits of orange clay pots could be seen upon the ground beneath, remnants of the earthquake which happened the morning of Eostara Eve, more than a month ago. The grass was fresh-mown and the herbe beds freshly weeded, the dark soil worked deeply. The gardens looked ready for Beltane. Clumps of iris sported proud blooms, raising themselves proudly up to the

Goddess Isis. Beneath the lilac a bleeding heart arched tender stalks, each strung with a row pendant pink flowers dancing with early morning dew. Beltane Eve would be celebrated this very night in a ritual circle of grass surrounded by small, standing stones. A patchwork of beds spread out from a sacred site, beds of herbes and perennials. And right there, cutting across the beds, through the soft soil, was a trail of cloven prints leading right to the garden Circle.

"At least she didn't step on any plants," Arnica grumbled affectionately, for there stood 'the munchkin' nibbling on the grass in the Circle.

This still-awkward unifilly which had been hatched in their stone Circle had come to be called 'the munchkin' because she just *loved* to munch the grass in the large garden Circle. She looked so pretty, munching away. Whenever Arnica and Holly wondered where she was and went looking for her, this lovely, young Unicorn was usually found grazing inside the circle or just sitting there, looking young and so sweet. She obviously knew that it was sacred space.

Shortly after her birth, one of the first mornings the unicolt had wandered off, only to be found in the Circle. It was remarkable. Even though Holly fed her bottles of warmed goat milk, she had begun to munch sacred grass within a week or two of her birth. There was a precocious quality about her which could only be a gift of the gods; that, and having a father like Andrius! The first time she was found with tiny wisps of new grass tucked in her mouth, "you must have at least a trace of munchkin blood," Holly teased her, scratching her soft ears, and she had been called variations of munchkin since. Arnica's intuition told him that she had been named even before birth and that her name would be revealed to them 'when the time was right.' In the meantime, they had to call her *something*, and she responded to her nickname. Holly could stand by the open kitchen door and call out, "hey, munchie," and she'd come trotting up within a minute or two.

Arnica walked over toward the beds with the tell-tale signs of unicolt trespassing. As he suspected, not a plant had been touched. He got down on his knees, trowel in hand, and began working the soil around the dicentra. "Aha," he said, spotting a tiny pair of bright green ears coming up through the soil. Moving over to that spot, he began digging deeply, going after a piece of dandelion root which had sent up new growth in search of sunlight. More than three years since they'd put in this bed and buried pieces of weed roots which escaped at the time were still appearing now and then. "Look at that, over a foot deep," Arnica said to no one, his voice filled with wry admiration for the stray dandelion root's tenacity. The munchkin whinnied in response, to Arnica's amazement.

Munchie trotted over to the edge of the garden Circle, staying carefully on the grass and began making sounds at Arnica. She cocked her head to one side, as if exasperated with this old human who was unable to understand her. Arnica looked at her and began laughing, then decided that he ought listen to her more carefully. He sat back on the soil, tucking his legs beneath his body, carefully (he had 'old bones' in his back) and began to slow his breathing and relax. He looked at the munchkin and extended his thoughts and emotions to her. As if she understood (and she may well have), she sat down and looked right into his eyes, then jumped up and began trotting out of the Circle. Arnica rose, and now knew that Holly wanted him to come to the house. He gathered his tools and began heading up the path.

Putting the garden tools away in the shed next to the potting bench, he sat on the back steps and removed his garden shoes. The munchkin dashed about, smelling a flower here, chasing a butterfly there. "If only I had her energy," Arnica thought, but realized that his youth had not been wasted and his age was a great treasure, one he wouldn't trade for anything, not even restored youth!

He stood, turned around and reached for the kitchen door when it suddenly opened and Holly jumped with a loud, startled sound. "I don't know how you do that!"

"It wasn't me this time, it was our muncher," Arnica said. His intuitive sense of timing was the source of teasing between them.

"Well, it's time for lunch," Holly said. "I thought we should eat early so we can complete our preparations for tonight's ritual."

The munchkin leaned forward and nuzzled Arnica in the back of the neck and this time it was Arnica who jumped, much to Holly's glee. Lunch started off with lots of teasing and giggling to stir their appetites.

The sun was soon to set. The woods were filled with twilight but in the gardens there was plenty of light. The Maypole was set in the center of the garden Circle, long ribbons hanging down to the grass. Set toward each of the four directions were symbols of the four elements and candles. Toward the north side of the Circle was the altar. The delight of magick was in the air as Arnica and Holly scurried about like elves. Gathering the needed herbes from the closet, the cauldron from the temple, chalices and ritual blades and all sorts of ritual tools, Holly carefully set them into an old woven picnic hamper he liked to call his 'Wicca basket' and placed it just outside the door for their next trip out to the Circle.

"What robe should I wear?" Holly asked Arnica.

"You know I like it best when you don't wear any robe at all," Arnica teased as he tried to make his face look like a leer.

"If you weren't so full of the Horned One, you'd be a dirty old man," Holly joked. "I think we've got enough for this trip. Let's carry things out to the Circle."

Arnica picked up his staff and opened the door. "But where are they, Holly?"

"Right there, can't you see them?"

"No, I can't. They're not sitting on the porch like you said."

Holly came to the door and, to his surprise, the basket was missing!

"I wonder..."

They walked out the door and looked down, toward the Circle. There was the munchkin, just as proud as she could be, carrying the basket, its handle in her mouth, as she walked toward the Circle with a cocky strut to her gentle gait.

"Well, I'll be an old salamander," Arnica said. "Something tells me this will be quite the night. Let's head out to the Circle."

Just at twilight their closest friends began to arrive. Phoenix and Pearl, a Pictish couple who lived on the other side of the village, came dressed in matching gold-toned robes embroidered with bright patches of flowers. "Quite stunning, the Mother will be honored" said Holly with admiration. This couple was known for their skill with needle and thread!

A few minutes later Amethyst and Crystal came chattering their way around the corner of the house, busily talking about the latest foolishness the Politicos were trying to foist upon the Tribes. There was a movement in the great House. The Users wanted to outlaw all religions but those which accepted *their* god and considered the massive Book of Doom to be the only book of religious myths to follow. The Earthkin were doing their best but many were beginning to worry and a few talked about retreating, moving away to the mountains to live in hiding. The village commons in Lothloriën were filled with much talk these days.

Amethyst shook her long, dark hair. It had ribbons and beads strung throughout it and looked like a work of art. Crystal's fair hair was cut very short. She had just completed a long, personal vision quest which included offering her hair to the Goddess. As he saw them, Arnica thought to himself, 'what a fun couple they are.'

"Jewel and Lotus called and said they can't make it. They tried calling you but you must have been out in the gardens. Jewel thinks she may be having a Beltane baby although she's not really due until the Full Moon next week."

"How will we dance?" asked Pearl, even though she knew that they could do the round with six. Eight was their usual number.

"Patience, bright one," said Arnica. If his intuition was flowing well, he knew the answer would soon be arriving. "Let's just move into our places as we normally do." He took Holly's hand and they kissed, lightly, then entered the Circle and moved to stand before the North altar. Amethyst and Crystal headed toward the East, for they worked together to invoke Air and the couple clad in gold started crossing the Circle toward the South. The munchkin whinnied in her curious way, and pranced into the Circle and went to the West where she stood poised. No one could say anything.

Holly held forth the large gong they had found years before at the bazaar and Arnica, striking it with the felt hammer chanted, "Let the Rite begin..."

From the time Crystal spoke the first word until the moment the element of Water was to be invoked, all had moved into their ritual mindset, focused only upon their individual work, upon the verses and the images and the element each was working. As they turned to the West, they saw munchie kneel, bowed before the basin of water, and then, wouldn't you just know it, a familiar large, blue unicorn came leaping over the munchkin's head, turned smartly and took his place alongside his unifilly. "Andrius," chuckled Holly, "why didn't you tell us?"

"He did," whispered Arnica...

The weaving of the Maypole was never so festive. Unicorns could dance with greater agility than humans, but they certainly took up more space! The pole was not woven as tightly as usual, but there was more laughter ribboned into place than ever before.

When it was time to close the Circle, Andrius and the munchkin began to frolic about. Andrius snuck up behind Pearl and, with his long, silver horn, snatched Pearls' braided crown of flowers and tossed it across the circle where it landed, perfectly, around the munchkin's horn. The Circle dissolved quickly into complete silliness. Andrius had crowned his daughter as the 'mayhorn!'

IV - A Midsummer Night's Dream

Holly had noticed a definite change ever since the unicolt had been crowned by Andrius. Although she was less than three Sabbats old with many years' growth before she reached maturity (for a Unicorn), there was a maturity about her. When working about the gardens, Holly would look up and there she'd be standing, her head tilted just a bit as she watched him closely. Their eyes would meet and Holly's mind could still see the crown of flowers circling the unifilly's delicate horn.

She was quite precocious, although neither Arnica nor Holly had even a clue about the nature of Unicorns. Andrius had come into their life many years before, but he was already full-grown, his personality developed (even if not quite matured around the edges). Perhaps the munchkin was no different than other Unicorn young? Well, there was no way of knowing but she certainly made day-to-day life more interesting.

"I certainly wish she could develop a taste for dandelion and cat's paw flowers," Arnica mused as he sat back on his heels, a bemused smile on his face. "Not that I begrudge her the borage blooms..."

"Mother knows there are plenty of them," Holly responded, laughing.

Arnica and Holly shared a running 'garden joke' about this year's borage. As the Wheel of the Year turned past Eostara, no borage had been found sprouting in any of the garden beds. Arnica and Holly had relocated many of the beds and reworked others yet not found even one seedling borage.

Borage was an essential herbe in Arnica's pharmacopoeia and the thought of there being none at the Harvest Days was unsettling. Many of the Earthkin families came to Arnica for herbal remedies and borage was much used during the winter. Borage was useful when the children ran mild fevers during the virus season. Holly enjoyed using the pink and blue blossoms in salads. Every year borage brought fun, for there was a sense of joy watching the seedlings appear here and there in the gardens, as if having chosen their growing sites the year before.

Holly called up Jewel to see how *their* borage was growing. "Oh, it's up about four inches and it's just wonderful," said Jewel. She was happy about everything in life since her baby was born at the Scorpio Full Moon, just a week after Beltane. "Why don't you come and get some and then you can see Dagon. He's just the cutest baby I've ever seen but I know that's because he's my first!"

And so Arnica and Holly went in to the village to buy a small, silver bell for the baby Dagon. Going to town was increasingly unsettling. The cute, little shop once known as Amber's Crystal Emporium was changed. Since their last trip to town, Amber, daughter of the Loon Tribe, had closed up her shop and moved to the River Mountains to be near her peoples of the Descendant Tribes. One time too often a wife of one of the Politicos had come into the Crystal Emporium, making rude comments about the lovely gems and crystals being tools of the darkness, according to the Book of Doom. Now Amber was gone, her little store having become yet another real estate office selling off many of the properties once owned by the Earthkin who had since left under growing ecological and economic pressure from the Politicos.

The bell delivered, the baby adored, a large pot of borage now sat in the greenhouse awaiting planting and here it was, Midsummer Eve. It was unlike Arnica and Holly to let plant babies sit so long but borage had begun to appear everywhere in the gardens, dozens and dozens of plants! There must have been a lot of borage seed in the compost turned in this spring, and just as Arnica was beginning to think they'd need to start weeding out the excess, they found the hatchling was supplementing her diet of her favourite grass from the garden Circle with mouthsful of borage blossoms! And there were so many seedlings coming up that no matter how much she munched, they were assured of a plentiful harvest.

The hatchling began dancing about the paths and grass, pink and blue borage blossoms peeking out from her mouth. Arnica gave up. Setting down his garden trowel, he gave himself over to laughter. There was not enough laughter these days and it would be wonderful Magick to bring to tonight's ritual!

Holly took advantage of the situation. With Arnica doubled up, laying on the grass laughing, he pounced on his older lover like a cat and the two of them tumbled together, amid tickling and laughing until the munchkin tried to jump in as well.

"It's time," Arnica said, "we're ready, now, to begin preparing for Midsummer's Eve," and off he and Holly went to their cabin to take their ritual baths. Little did they know that the hatchling knew she must prepare as well.

Midsummer's Eve. This was one of Holly's favorite Sabbats which led him to make elaborate preparations! Although twilight lasted very late into the night, Holly had lined the path into the woods with little candles, set safely in jelly jars, to guide them all the way to the stone circle. The Circle, itself, was set. A silk scarf lay upon the altar stone, the chalices and candles waiting. Arnica had made as many trips as Holly, and as Holly brought candles and jars, Arnica brought vases filled with flowers to set on just about every stone of the circle capable of holding a vase upright. It was beautiful and easily moved their emotions and minds into a completely different world.

They knelt before the altar and readied their thoughts. So focused were they that they didn't hear the hatchling come quietly down the path and lay down to watch, just around the turn. It seemed she blended right into the foliage. They kissed, sweetly, then Arnica stood and, drawing his ritual blade from the scabbard hanging from his belt, walked around the altar to the East. Carrying it around the Circle he called upon the Guardians of the Fir Trees to keep this sacred space protected, always, even as the Changing Times moved about them. As he passed the north stones and came to the northeast portal, his intuition took over and, contrary to his conscious desire, his blade created an opening. Arnica was so focused that he didn't realize what had happened as he returned to join Holly at the altar.

As their Midsummer's Eve ritual progressed, the woods seem to darken with the deepening twilight, each little candleflame growing in brightness. This was surely a night of Magick! As it came time to give honour to the Mother of All, dozens and dozens of tiny fireflies began to flit about the trees and as Arnica invoked the Horned One, an owl sang into the night, causing tiny shivers to dance along his spine.

Holly met Arnica at the center of the Circle and they lit the Midsummer fire and began dancing around the cauldron, their voices chanting into the night. This was the night when dreams were called forth, when the Earthkin would commune with the realm of the faerie. Dancing to part the veils, Arnica and Holly lost track of conscious thought. The flowers around the circle blurred into a mist of nature and the fireflies danced with the stars until all around them was a spiraling Magick. Just as the two were about to move into ecstatic reverie, the munchkin leapt right through the northeast portal. In one more leap, she jumped right through the cauldron's fire! A portal opened in the great tree which stood just outside the circle, showing a descending spiral of stairs and down she went, into the underworld just as Holly and Arnica lowered themselves to the ground, the vision of the hatchling blending itself with the Magick of the Midsummer dreams as they moved into the realm of the faerie as well.

When the morning sun stirred the trees overhead, Arnica was wakened by a cramp in his elbow. "Sweet thing?" he asked.

"I'm here," Holly answered, waking.

It was dawn, the candles having finished their brief life during the night. At once both remembered the hatchling's disappearance and sat up at once. But there she was, lying near their feet, sleeping in the Circle just as sweetly as Dagon slept in Jewel's arms. But there was something different about the Hatchling, nothing Holly could put his finger on, but it was obvious she had spent the night touched by a very strong Magick!

V - Harvest Days

"Jewel said she's bringing Dagon along. Lotus made a small cart for Jewel and Dagon to ride in so they can make the journey easily." Holly was excited. "I love Harvest Days. It's one of my favorite Sabbats."

"Hah," snorted Arnica, "they're almost all your favorites!"

"I think you're right," Holly agreed, "although this is the most fun for the gardens."

"There'll be a good gathering this year," mused Arnica, as he sat back on his heels, trowel in hand, rubbing the old bones in his elbow. "Amethyst and Crystal are coming. Even Amber's coming down from the River Mountains. She said she was going through the cartons of things from the old Crystal Emporium and found something she 'must' bring for the Harvest."

"Look, there she goes again!" Holly exclaimed, excitedly. The hatchling was playing in along the garden paths, stopping to smell a flower here, taste an herbe there. She had become quite graceful but every so often she'd dash off, friskily, her mouth full of borage blossoms.

The munchkin continued to change and the transformation was both subtle and overpowering all at once. Arnica and Holly talked about it, but many days life just slipped past, the wheel kept on turning and they lived in their new reality. The hatchling had been with them only since Eostara, her egg cracked open during the earthquake. She was no longer a unicolt, but was maturing. Holly commented that it seemed as if she had been with them always.

"Perhaps it's my age," said Arnica, "but it's as if we were placed into a different dimension after she came into our lives." Arnica enjoyed using his age as an explanation for having slippage of his memory.

"How long does it take a unicolt to mature?" asked Holly.

"I don't know," answered his older lover, "I once thought Unicorns aged like horses. I've known Andrius for years but he moves in and out of the Eldritch so easily that I was never quite able to tell. His horn was well-spiraled when first we met... Just look at that - there's borage everywhere!"

Holly laughed. The joke of the summer was their having 'borrowed' a pot of borage seedlings from Lotus and Jewel. Still sitting in the greenhouse at Midsummer, within less than a week of the longest day their garden was a profusion of borage plants. It seemed the old compost must have been rich with borage seed from years before and there were dozens of borage plants coming up in the most inopportune places. In many of their herb beds borage was growing so profusely that it was necessary to remove it to protect the herbs for which the beds were created! Borage, borage everywhere...

Harvest Eve was upon them. All the herb gardens had been readied and were mostly weeded with the soil freshly turned. Holly had brushed the unicolt thoroughly until her coat shone like the finest silk while Arnica set out the candle lanterns which hung along the paths and around the Circle. An altar had been set near the rustic cabin at the head of the path, the censer and chalice polished, the wand and athame filled with Magick.

"Hello you two" called a voice filled with music. Amethyst came first through the gate and held it open for Crystal who carried a huge basket filled with goodies. Amethyst loved to bake. "Guess what we've got?"

"Chocolate chip cookies," both Holly and Arnica answered in unison, then broke out laughing. Andrius' long-established love of chocolate chip cookies was near legend. Although they often brought nice, esoteric ritual cakes made with anise and other carefully selected herbes, there was nothing like a good, old-fashioned chocolate chip cookie!

"But that's not all," said Crystal, removing the lid of the basket. "We brought a Grain Man made from the rye we planted last Eostara. These past hot, sunny weeks helped the grain ripen and mature. We cut it after making love in the gardens at the last Full Moon."

"Crystal," said Amethyst, blushing.

"Well, they're friends and we all know that 'blessing the crops' is an important part of our work, whether we're Descendant or Renaissance peoples! But guess who's coming down the lane?"

"Hello," called out a strong voice. "Blessed Harvest." Lotus came through the gate, giving Crystal a hug and kiss.

"I brought him," Jewel said as she followed Lotus through the gate. She held baby Dagon in her arms, a bright blanket with golden threads woven through it keeping him safe.

As they gathered about the baby and exclaimed over his good looks and healthy growth, a loud voice came from the other side of the closed gate. "Come on, dear ones, move it. You're blocking the path of the Goddess."

Laughter bubbled over like the sound a flock of birds makes when stirred into action. They quickly moved into the yard freeing the space before the gate as it swung open and a tall, handsome woman came through. Her raven-colored hair was braided tightly and she wore a loose, earth-colored frock brightly embroidered with symbols and designs.

The Hatchling

"Amber," Arnica said, "you made it. How happy we are to see you." And he moved to embrace her with the enthusiasm only friends kept apart can share.

"Let's get on with things," Amber said, "I have much to tell you about the Politicos but I refuse to mention a word until we've celebrated Harvest Eve."

They worked a beautiful procession. Arnica led them, his old, bamboo staff held high with its crystal glimmering almost like a star. Holly danced around his partner, aspurging the path with sacred water from his cobalt blue chalice. Phoenix and Pearl followed, playing their flutes as Amber's voice led the melodies and chants while she scattered tiny gemstones and minerals. Lotus carried the censer as Jewel carried Dagon in his first Lammas Procession. Amethyst, costumed as Mother Nature, led Crystal, who carried the Grain Man. They danced and processed until every herbe bed had been blessed. Then they moved toward the garden Circle to begin the Harvest. There, her mouth filled with the bright, cobalt blue flowers of borage tops, was the hatchling. Their laughter punctuated the evening as the unicolt tried to whinny her delight through her mouth of borage.

They all moved to their respective places about the Circle. Arnica took his harvest scythe and carried it around the perimeter. As he completed the Circle in the East, all breathed a quiet sigh of relief. The tension in the valleys was growing. Old friends were tumbled from office as, throughout the land, Conservers were voted out and the Politicos took their place. Laws were being rewritten every week and the changes created great stress. Their countryside, once considered sacred and preserved by law, was now being placed in the hands of corporate heads, Users who professed their religions but believed it their right to clear the land of all trees, dam the rivers for utilities, and fill every space with factories and houses. But thoughts of the times were now safely kept outside the Circle and they were safely within this garden temple.

As Jewel began to call upon the Creatures of Air, Dagon's little voice cooed and chortled and their hearts felt again light and joyous. After Amber drew down the Great Mother, Arnica brought forth his sacred blade and began the Lammas Walk. He headed toward the East, where grew the bright yellow mullein spears. Lovingly, he cut three of them. Holly brought forth the Lammas basket and they were laid within. In the South, stalks of crimson monarda were cut, their scent strong enough that it quickly filled the Circle. In the west, where a deep pond held fresh water, Arnica knelt on the soft soil and, reaching forward, dipped his blade into the water where he cut loose a single, blue lotus bloom. In the north he cut some ivy from a tall tree.

As remarkable as it seemed, the hatchling sat near the northeast portal, watching with wide eyes. They had never seen her so still yet so alert. The Harvest now begun, it was time to give thanks with the ancient custom. Amber brought forth the large cauldron and Phoenix filled it with fuel from a large flask. When Holly lit it, flames shot skyward. Amber took the Grain Man and told a story of ancient customs. At the end, she held the woven 'man' just above the fire until it burst into flames as she let it go. The hatchling was uncomfortable. She remained sitting upon her haunches, but her quiet whinnying indicated her distrust of fire and uncertainty over this symbolic sacrifice of the woven dolly.

And then they broke into song and rang bells and began to take turns dancing around the Circle to leap over the cauldron in the center. Now the hatchling thought

13

things were more fun and her curiosity won out. She joined in, prancing around but staying close to Jewel. There was always some affinity between babies and animals and the hatchling appeared to be completely fascinated with the human baby, just as Dagon was with her. Her fear of the fire soon passed and then, much to everyone's surprise, there went the munchkin, leaping right over the cauldron.

"Well, my friends," said Arnica, "no matter what's going on in the world, the Mother of the Harvest has shown us that the coming months are ours! Let us break bread and celebrate!"

VI - The Harvest's Weight

"Where's the bag of dried borage flowers?"

"Over here by the comfrey root. How many bushels of apples did we count?"

"I think it was 76, no 67... Rats, I can't remember," said Arnica, "but I wrote it down someplace and the slip of paper is on my desk."

"Do you mean by the paper we wrote the measurements of our land on?"

"Yes, I think it's in that stack of records we have to take with us."

"You know," said Holly, stopping the scurrying pace which had dominated their lives increasingly every day since the Lammas Harvest had begun, "I don't like this, I don't like having to do this at all."

"Easy my sweet," said Arnica, "in principle this isn't so bad a deal. Some of the tithe will go to fix our road out in front and some will go to build a new schoolhouse."

"I know," Holly responded, a bit petulantly, "but in principle it doesn't seem fair that we are required to tithe to a government that is trying to destroy our Motherland. The Politicos have voted to begin cutting down the trees of Merrywood. I don't like it at all."

Both Arnica and Holly had been a little tense since Amber's disheartening news at Lammas. The Politicos had found it necessary to increase their available revenues in pursuit of their plans to remove vast areas of trees and replace them with commercial ventures. The Politicos saw the earth only in terms of usage. Forests were to be cut down for factories and then more woodlands cut down to build more homes. Recognizing that most of the Earthkin peoples did not use money, they devised their taxation carefully. Produce which people grew for their own use was not to be assessed, only what was grown for trade. As a result, people were to measure their harvests and take their counts in for recording. At that time they were to be prepared to pay a tithe on the portion of their harvest grown for trade.

Arnica knew that this year's crop of ginseng and echinacea was outstanding and was preparing to pay their tithe with these roots. It was more than they could carry by themselves, for their herb gardens were what supported them, and Arnica had been thinking of ways to carry the dried roots in to Merrydale. Just then, the hatchling came up behind him and demonstrated her newest trick. She was growing unusually fast in so many ways, even for a Unicorn. Stepping slowly and carefully, she could sneak up behind Arnica without him hearing her and then, ever so carefully, raise up on her hind legs and, with the tip of her horn, knock Arnica's hat forward so it would fall on his nose.

"Munchie, is that you?" Arnica laughed, and just like that he had the answer. "Holly, run to the herb closet and let me know how much male fern we have."

Holly's mind was filled with unasked questions. A tingle danced up and down his spine, a sure indication that Arnica had been touched by the Mother's inspiration. He quickly returned, breathing heavily. "The jar... is two-thirds full... from last year's... harvest... looks good..."

"We can do it," shouted Arnica, jumping up in glee so surprisingly that even the hatchling was startled in a delightful turn-about.

"Steady, steady," Arnica cooed to himself as he poured a little of the liquid through a glass funnel into a beaker.

"Oh, it looks wonderful," said Holly, trying to keep his excitement under control.

"Now, get me just the tiniest measure of powdered jade."

"There isn't any powdered... should I mill some?" asked Holly.

"Yes, do, love. Now, what is it I'm missing?" Arnica went to the shelves and took down the dark green jar of black hellebore. Coming back to the work table, he opened the jar, quietly saying his magickal verse to the hellebore deva. Twice dipping his measure into the chopped herbe, he mumbled "I sure wish we had some growing here. It's better when gathered fresh but this is better than naught."

The sound of Holly pounding and grinding the small chips of jade was like background rhythm to the counterpoint of their voices. Holly was chanting the Rune in rhythm to his grinding. Arnica was thinking out loud as he worked on the magickal concoction.

"Now with the male fern," he said, "and are you done with the jade?"

"Yes, here..."

And Arnica placed all the ingredients, two gems, four herbes and a pinch of powdered gold, into their best mortar, one handed down from his great-great grandmother. Picking up the pestle, he mused "we must put our best energy into this. Help me, Holly."

And together they chanted, Arnica circling the pestle and Holly with his hands on Arnica's back and heart, moving energy into his partner. "Now, now..." said Arnica.

Holly grabbed the hot mitt and took the kettle of boiling water off the stove. He lifted the lid and Arnica poured the mix into the steaming water. Holly quickly put the lid on. "Fifteen minutes by the Mother," said Arnica, "then it gets filtered and poured into the extract."

"Will it work?" asked Holly, knowing what Arnica will say.

"Only the Mother knows, and She isn't telling."

"Oh, no, it's fading, no, I mean it's *not* fading... the, the horn, I can see it again and oh, I'm just so..." Holly sounded like he was about to cry, the despair in his voice betraying his confidence in the power of Magick.

"Hush," said Arnica impatiently. Holly's anxiety would only cloud his access to the Mother's lore. Arnica *knew* that they could render the munchkin's horn invisible long enough for her to go to town and back with them.

The magickal potion all complete and cooled, they had tested it. The hatchling was brought into the cabin, to sit in the center of their temple. Oh, and how she loved the attention! "Quiet, now, Munchkin" said Holly. Dipping his index finger into the jar, he helped Arnica rub the liquid into the hatchling's horn. Within a couple of minutes, it began to fade from view and become invisible. The problem had been that the invisibility spell only lasted about ten minutes, not nearly enough.

"If we had *fresh* hellebore..." Arnica sighed but then... "I've got it! Holly, can your young legs fetch about thirteen of the best fern fronds from near the north altar of our garden Circle?"

"Oh, yes," said Holly, as if he'd heard the thought emerge into Arnica's mind, "And I'll bring some bindweed to tie them."

"Bless you, that'll be perfect."

The streets were dusty and the town of Merrydale seemed a little noisier, a little more tense since they'd last been here. Many were carrying large bundles or huge baskets filled with grains, nuts or other produce. One elderly woman was struggling with her crutches as she tried to carry a cage with two roosters. And all were heading in the same direction.

"Look, there's The Crystal Emporium and it's been sold again! We'll have to remember to tell Amber when we see her."

"Ugh," said Holly, "it's been bought by the Users. The windows are filled with the Book of Doom and replicas of the cross of blood. How sad."

"Hush, my sweet," responded Arnica, "this is neither the time nor the place. Turn your mind to getting us out of here quickly."

They walked along the street, the munchkin laden with bags of herbs. The hatchling was unaccustomed to such chaos and her eyes were very wide although she easily carried her packs.

"What a pretty horse..." said a young lad, "may I pet her?"

"Yes, if you walk along with us," answered Arnica, "we're on our way to the Tithing Office as is everyone."

"Oh, let me show you a shortcut," the boy offered, his freckles shifting as his face broke into a great smile. "I can save you a lot of time!"

"Thank you, mother," Holly quietly prayed.

They paid their tithing without incident. The Politico in charge of recording the harvest's weight was too overwhelmed with the enormity of his task. A few things he muttered quietly did not escape Arnica's ears. The man was not happy with the new laws being pushed through by the Users, nor was he happy with the tree cutting. It was nice to know that not all Politico's sought to destroy the beauty of Mother Nature.

The day had passed well, despite the crowded tension in Merrydale. The hatchling's horn remained unseen throughout their journey, although Holly thought that the boy, Gino, may have sensed it. And once he said to the hatchling, "you are so beautiful, you look just like a Unicorn I've dreamt of." When Arnica learned that the boy's mother was an Earthkin of the Descendant Tribes, he told the boy he was welcome to come out and visit them at their herb farm. It was nice to make new friends.

The hatchling's horn began to emerge from the veil of invisibility as they left the last valley of the Merrywood and saw the lane leading to their cabin. "Go, munchkin!"

cheered Holly as she ran on ahead, frisky and eager for the safety of their own woods. Holly and Arnica walked quickly but their legs were too tired to run.

"We're home," they both said at once. The hatchling was already laying on the grass near the garden Circle, her horn fine and bright as she tried to munch a few flowering stalks of borage, but they could see her eyes slipping closed. Their Unicorn was having difficulty staying awake. Holly and Arnica set aside the empty bags as they went into the cabin for their evening meal.

VII - Depths of Darkness

"Look at her frolic in the leaves," Holly said, laughing so hard he dropped his rake.

The hatchling had been unusually frisky since the first frost had changed the leaves seemingly overnight into a rainbow of golds and reds and oranges. The sweet gum trees added their deep burgundy and purple and almost-blue shades and the unicolt would race through the leaves leaving them swirling in her wake, then turn, cock her head (her horn catching the sunlight), and dance back through them, prancing and pirouetting. As Holly and Arnica raked them into a large pile, she discovered that she could run toward the mound of colour and jump with all four legs right into its midst. She was having so much fun it was difficult to feel any irritation at the scattering of their many hours' work. Instead Holly and Arnica found themselves working fast to pile up the leaves as high as possible so the munchkin (as they liked to call the young Unicorn) could have a safe landing.

"O.K., loved ones," said Arnica, "it's time. We must stop our play and begin preparing for the Feast of the Dead on this Hallows Eve."

"I'll set the candles," offered Holly. "I'd like to use that new oil we made and prepare the candles for the altar and Circle first, then I'll set out the candle lanterns all through the woods along the path back to the stone Circle."

"Wonderful," mused Arnica. "I wonder what herbes should be added to the bread dough for this Dark Night..."

The hatchling said nothing, but trotted off quickly and soon caught up with Holly, her basket hanging from her mouth. She had learned that she could help by carrying the basket so that herbes, candles or ritual things were more easily transported. Before either Holly or Arnica had begun anything obvious in setting the garden Circle for the last New Moon, the hatchling had appeared at the back cabin door, sitting there holding the basket. For a unicolt only five sabbats old, she was both wise and precocious well beyond the turns of her horn. She would make many trips back and forth from the cabin to the stone circle before this night's ritual would begin!

Arnica and Holly stood ready in their warm, wool robes. Holly was holding a lit, wax taper with flame gathered from the hearth. Arnica held forth the open lantern so the candle within it could be lit. The sun long set, they would enter the Hallows Circle alone this night. Jewel and Lotus were home soothing Dagon who was cutting his first tooth. Yes, it was early but this was an unusual baby, to say the least. Amber was uncomfortable making the trip from the River Mountains through Merrydale during this Sabbat, Phoenix and Pearl were staying at home. Gino, the boy who helped Arnica and Holly in Merrydale this past Autumn, had begun learning the old ways and Phoenix and Pearl were the ideal teachers. Amethyst and Crystal had taken a journey east to assist Crystal's great grandmother in letting go of her dying body and passing over with grace and love. The candle was lit, the little door to the lantern closed. They set forth quietly, followed by the hatchling.

Candles along the path lit the way. The night was cloudy as if the Mother had pulled a comforter over her, keeping her warmer until morn but it shrouded the stars and made the darkness more mysterious. If it wasn't for the candles, they would not be able to see. Moving deeper into the woods they felt the presence of the trees whose spirits were always more evident during the night. A few more candles lit the path back to the stone Circle. Pausing at the entrance to this temple beneath the tallest firs, Arnica felt a chill run down his back and he shuddered.

"What is it?" asked Holly.

"Nothing," answered Arnica, "just the night."

Holly stood poised at the East, chanting the song of Air. A breeze stirred and the wind chimes hanging in the cedar stirred, waking their tones to life. As the last note drifted across the stones into the night Arnica's athame flashed bright as he lit the South candle and began singing the song of Fire. It seemed noticeably warmer within the Circle. The cool damp air was no longer a distraction.

"Greatest Goddess burning bright... Dance around the fire bright..." As Arnica chanted and the small fire pot flamed with abandon, Holly moved around, behind Arnica and stationed himself in the West. Arms raised, he picked up the last note from Arnica and began singing to the Waters as Arnica quietly moved around to the North.

The elements present, the four directions in balance, the walk continued. From the time they stepped into the Circle every step was known, every pattern traced by their feet as they had done so many nights as the Wheel Turned, as the Moon shone down upon them and on those nights when the Sun and Moon were hidden, far beneath the Earth. Their choreography was a simple design, but one they knew well. The hatchling had taken her usual place at the Circle's centre, watching them in their sacred dance as they censed and aspurged, lit elemental candles and followed their ritual forms.

When the Goddess was called forth, the hatchling rose to her feet and as the presence of the God was called her tail flicked in anticipation... but of what? The energy within the circle of the stones shifted dramatically as Holly and Arnica set the cauldron in the centre of the Circle. The hatchling moved over to the altar to watch them as they lit the fire then danced and chanted.

"Gone to the Summerland, distant shores grown past;
Winter draws upon us now, summer didn't last..."

Arnica and Holly were dancing the Circle, now, gathering all the energy and images of the ritual into a grand swirl of energy.

"Near we now the gates of death, on this fearsome night;
We'll call lost loved ones from within, to join us on this night..."

And at this, the Goddess, Herself stepped into the Circle from within the great tree, the ancient sentinel which stood tall near the northeast portal.

"I go now," She said to the hatchling who bowed before Her, trembling. "I must leave you, for I descend into the Underworld to keep My rendezvous with Death."

The hatchling whinnied, and tears came to her eyes.

"Cry not, for I shall return. I give you My word. You are My chosen and you are the hatchling not only of the great line of Unicorns, but you hold within you the promise."

Arnica and Holly could not see the Lady but they felt Her presence and Her voice was clear and spoke directly into their hearts. As the hatchling watched, the Mother raised Her arms to the heavens and, as She spoke, wind moved through the trees and even the earth seemed to tremble.

"I am the beauty of the green Earth,
And the white Moon among the stars
I am the Mystery of the waters
And the desire within the hearts of humans..."

When She finished, the Circle was quiet. Nothing moved but the flames, dancing in the cauldron. Holly and Arnica held their scrying stones, gazing through their clear crystals into the fire. The Goddess put her hand on the hatchling's neck and said, lovingly, "Look, gaze into the fire. There will you see into the future."

As the hatchling looked deep into the flames, a vision formed. She saw the Goddess descending spiral stairs deep within the earth, coming to a large, wooden door. The Lady raised her hand and knocked three times upon the door. When the door opened, an ageless male figure with large, stag horns upon his head stood there, wearing robes the colours of the shadow. The Lord knelt before the Lady, kissing Her feet as he said, "Blessed Be Your feet, which have brought you through the Gates of Death..."

Just before the vision faded, Holly and Arnica saw the Goddess as She spoke to the unicolt.

"Remember, little hatchling, you hold the promise. The nights grow dark and death will be prowling the land but you are My dark star. I will be with you at Spring..."

And the flames went out, the cauldron dark. No one moved, neither Arnica nor Holly, and the hatchling sat there as if entranced. Holly first moved, whispering "Dark Star..."

Arnica rose, silently taking his athame and beginning to close the Circle. The ritual things were carried back to the cabin in silence. Not a word was spoken although both Arnica and Holly would whisper the hatchling's new name when emptying the basket.

That night all three slept restlessly and all shared a dream unremembered in the morn. The earth was seen shrouded in darkness, trees hewn, streams empty, voices wailing and pleading with their gods, asking for light, for a sign. As this dream faded, another replaced it, this one to be remembered. Not even images, it was like the memory of the Goddess, with Her voice speaking to the hatchling. "You are My dark star... I will be with you at Spring..."

VIII - Dark Star's First Yule

The air was filled with the sounds of humming and singing, of scissors and paper, of the rustle of dried herbes and clatter of containers. Arnica and Holly were sitting at the kitchen table making Yule baskets for their friends. The kitchen counter was filled with jars of berries and dried herbs, bowls of apples and nuts, dried flowers and evergreen branches and spools of bright ribbon in all the holiday colors.

"Dance 'round the Yule this night, as the fire blazes bright..." sang Arnica. He picked up a basket and checked it carefully. There were different shapes and different sizes and different colors. Arnica and Holly collected baskets throughout the year, usually bringing one or two home each time they went to market or attended a fair. "Love, what do you think of this one for Amethyst and Crystal?" Arnica held up a wicker basket the colour of a feisty dragon.

"Oh, that's wonderful," said Holly. "It will make my peppers look like they're glowing." Holly held up the red and orange string of peppers he was threading with a needle. Holly loved making strings of dried peppers to hang in the kitchens of their friends just as Arnica liked stitching bay leaves into wreaths. This year there were small jars of bay leaves but their tree had been lightly nipped by a late frost last spring decreasing the harvest of the pungent laurel.

"Dance until the Sun comes in," sang Arnica

"Sing a song and raise a din," Holly chimed in.

And just then a loud whinny from Dark Star left them almost falling off their chairs in laughter. What a beautiful unicolt she was.

"Listen to the munchkin," Holly exclaimed, his words coming out midst his glee. "I think she likes our song."

"Here, Dark Star," said Arnica, offering her a handful of hawthorne berries to eat. "You know, I'm still having to adjust to calling her by her name. When I see her face I still think of her as our hatchling, but she has been touched by the Goddess and I know that her role in life will be much more than in our quiet lives here with our gardens."

The hatchling looked at Arnica. It seemed her eyes grew deeper in color. Although she was usually frisky and filled with the never-ending curiosity of a unicolt, since her encounter with the Goddess at Hallows there were times she seemed almost touched by the threads of sadness. She turned and went in to the altar room to lay near the fire.

"There, this one is done," said Holly with obvious pride in his voice. He held up a two foot length of bright, dried peppers, their hues shiny and bright. At the top he had fashioned a blue ribbon with tufts of holly leaves. Holly liked their pointed green shapes and used them in many of his gifts.

"Can I use it in this basket for Amethyst and Crystal," asked Arnica. "I've got the apples and nuts put in it, and seven jars of greene herbes for their kitchen. Let's see, there's sage and thyme, rosemary, rue and dill, and one each of oregano and spearmint. And I've put in a jar of horseradish and packets of mistletoe and holly berries. There's just room for a jar of your preserves and a pepper string."

"Here it is." Holly handed it to Arnica. "It will look beautiful."

Together they wrapped the basket in clear cellophane and tied a bright ribbon on it next to the tag. Holly set the basket in the front room on the altar next to the two baskets already finished. There was a green, woven basket for their Pictish friends, Phoenix and Pearl and a lovely straw basket for Gino's mother. The lad's father had found it necessary to leave Merrydale and travel far over the mountains, hoping to find work in Mill City, where much of the grain from the upper plains was ground for the bakeries. Since Gino's father had voiced his displeasure to the Politicos over their plans to cut down more trees, he had lost his position as town warder and Gino's mother was usually so busy taking care of her neighbor's children to earn a little money, both were grateful to Phoenix and Pearl for the attention they gave the boy. Arnica had been pleasantly surprised to learn that Gino's parents believed in the old ways and were quietly supportive of the Renaissance Tribes.

"I'm bushed," said Holly. "My fingers don't want to push another needle."

"There's just one more," said Arnica. "We ought finish the basket for Jewel and Lotus. All our other gifts have been delivered and tomorrow being Yule Morning, I'd rather get them done now and be able to relax. Tonight we will do our Yule Eve Ritual alone, with just the three of us and tomorrow morning is our Feast and we'll be giving the baskets from our altar."

"You're right," Holly sighed, "let me light a candle and try a verse. 'Fill the forest with the Sun! Let Pan rule so winter's done. Bring Him to this holy night! Start us now to summer's rite.'"

As their voices blended in harmony, Holly's fingers moved lightly as the string of peppers quickly grew. Arnica finished working on the deep, blue basket for Jewel and Lotus, an extra large one with room for some little poppets they had made for Dagon, stuffed with chamomile and herbs to protect the toddler in his sleep.

"There, we're done. Let me blow out the candle and let's sit back and enjoy this magick."

Holly and Arnica sat down on the floor near the fireplace where Dark Star was laying. Arnica picked up the brush and started on the hatchling's coat. What a color it was. In some lights it looked blue, a hue reminiscent of the unicolt's father, Andrius, but not nearly so strong a color. But in other light it looked the same colour as the seapinks growing in the rockerie. There was an iridescent quality to it just as there was to her horn. Sometimes her horn looked like pale gold and at other times like pale silver.

As Arnica brushed, Holly scratched her ears and chin. What a contented unicorn this hatchling was. Her eyes grew heavy and soon her head was laying happily dreaming in the warmth of Holly's lap.

"What do you think about tonight? Do you think she'll be able to stay up until dawn to see the first sunray over the eastern horizon?" Holly bent over and kissed the tip of her horn.

"If we sit here long enough, she'll have quite a nap. This will be her first Yule Eve. So far she's done well with ritual. She seems to understand the magick as well as any human. I can't believe she's only been with us since Eostara. Look how she's grown."

And Arnica set down the brush and they sat there, warm with the hatchling, as the fire danced and sparkled in the late afternoon.

The scent of snuffed candles still floated in the air, along with frankincense, Arnica's preferred incense for Yule Eve. Dark Star seemed restless. She enjoyed spending time in the warmth of the cabin but even on a crisp, clear night she usually wanted to go out and romp about in the clearings, check the gardens for tasty leaves and dance with the stars. The cabin seemed empty whenever she was let out but they knew that the time would come when she would no longer be a unicolt and their cabin would be too small for a growing unifilly.

Arnica stood at the sink washing the chalices while Holly put away the censer. Their Yule Ritual was done, the baskets blessed and the glass ornaments hung on the Yule tree in anticipation of the morning's first ray of sunlight. As they did their work in the kitchen, the final stanza of the Yule Song filled the air.

"From this night He grows to full... Heed His throne and feel His pull..."

Holly took down the large stockpot as Arnica opened two large gallons of his best home-made cider. They went to the herb cupboard and brought forth cinnamon and allspice and other mulling herbs.

"You know what I'd like," said Holly, "some mulled wine."

"My sweet, it always puts you to sleep and this is the night we stay up until past sunrise."

"But it's the holiday and I think it would be just fine."

And so a second pot was set with wine to mull as they finished touching up the decorations for the morning, put away the ritual things and prepared the cabin for their guests.

"Dancing 'round the Yule Tree... Dancing for eternity..."

The wine ready, they filtered off the herbes, set the cider to spend the night bathed in the moonlight drifting through the kitchen window and took their glasses to sit before the fire, sip their wine and feel their love. And before they had even emptied their glasses, both were sound asleep on the soft rug as the fire sparkled into their dreams.

"It's morning!" Arnica's voice was loud with surprise. "We must get up and ready ourselves."

"Oh, no," Holly said laughing, a touch of sleep in his voice. "The sun's already risen. See Him shining through the window? Our tree is bright with His promise." The ornaments all caught the sun's reflection and the tree looked as if it had brilliant lights tucked all about.

Just then there was a loud knock at the door.

"Hang on, I'm coming," said Arnica and he scurried to the door, tucking his shirt back into his trousers. He pulled the door open and, much to his surprise, Dark Star scampered in, snowflakes stuck to her coat and mane, a small clump of mistletoe attached to the tip of her horn. Her eyes were wide open and she looked filled with excitement.

The hatchling shook all over with bits of snow scattering all over the room. Some flew right into Arnica's face. They laughed.

"Wait a minute, something's wrong here," said Holly, and he went to the door and opened it wide. The sky was clear blue, the sun just reaching over the gardens but there wasn't any snow to be seen and it was too warm. "Where did the snow come from? Dark Star, how did you get snow on your coat?"

And the hatchling whinnied lightly, nudged Holly in his tummy with her horn and seemed to chuckle as if she had a secret. Obviously, Dark Star was the only one to witness the birth of the Sun Child.

IX - A Feast of Candles

"Do you think we need to put jade on our shopping list?" asked Holly. "There are only a few pieces left in the jar."

22

"It might not be a bad idea. We have quite a bit of elixir stored. I don't know how long the potency lasts. Your idea of growing hellebore in the greenhouse this winter was wonderful. This batch should be even better than what we made last Lammas." Arnica was pouring the warm elixir into small vials and sealing their glass stoppers with wax.

"We could use some more amber pieces for our ritual incense as well and a couple of boxes of charcoal. With Dark Star we can bring more back from Merrydale and save a trip this spring." Holly was adding items to the list they were taking with them. "What do you think is in the parcel Amber sent us?"

"Candles, I think. The postmarm said it was heavy, but not too large. Put down a half pound of dried boneset, would you? We're running low. I've given out quite a bit already and we're not even in the midst of the flu season yet. This year seems worse than usual. Did you hear? There are two deaths in Merrydale and three in Mill City. This year's influenza is worrisome. But so far, not one person taking my tonic has even caught a cold. Amethyst said we're 'lucky' but I think it's the magick of the herbes in our gardens."

"Ouch," Arnica exclaimed with humor. Dark Star had poked him right in his buttock with her horn. "Yes, munchkin, I'm sure it's your magick as well! Look, Holly, her horn is completely invisible. Let's get our walking shoes and jackets on and be off. It's a beautiful day and Merrywood is already showing the signs of renewed life."

"The bulbs are up early this year. I sure hope we don't get a late freeze." Holly buttoned his jacket and laced his hiking boots. "I'm ready... let's go, munchie!"

And Dark Star walked to the door, her hooves sounding sharply on the floor.

Dark Star did not like this part of their journey. The road through Merrywood was fun. At times she'd run ahead and duck into the trees, jumping out to startle Holly and Arnica who feigned great surprise. The woods were filled with the scent of new life, for the growing sunlight was causing the trees to bud and mosses to green. Bulbs were pushing their leaves through the damp, brown leaves and life was returning. But here she was, tied to a post in front of the apothecary just like a horse. Yet the hatchling knew the dangers should anyone realize that she was a Unicorn.

"Hey there, Dark Star... Are Holly and Arnica in shopping?" Gino's freckled face was warm and loving and he began stroking her neck. Dark Star no longer felt frustrated. Gino's touch was so calming and she was glad to be right where she was.

"Gino, what a treat!" Arnica was backing out the door with three large parcels in his arms.

"Here, let me help," and Gino ran quickly to give his older friend a hand.

"Look who's here. Gino, have you grown since Yule?" Holly's compliment brought just the slightest blush to the lad's cheeks.

"I've got nothing to do this afternoon," he said. "Can I help you carry these things back to your cabin?"

"Bless you, boy," said Arnica "you're strong for your years, Dark Star will be so happy to share the walk back with you and I've got a fresh apple pie waiting in the cooler. Can you stay for dinner?"

"I'll need to call my mother when we get to your cabin. I'd have to borrow a lantern for the walk back."

"What about staying the night? You can snuggle up with a blanket next to the hatchling and you could join us for Candlemas Eve if you'd like. Pearl said you've been doing well in your training and Phoenix believes you're ready to start joining us in Circles."

"Oh, Arnica, do you mean it? Can I really?"

"And I've got a robe you can wear. It's a little small for me and I've been thinking you'd look pretty fine in it," said Holly.

Just then darkness fell upon them as a man strode purposefully up to them. They fell silent and drew their energy in, even without wanting to. Shadows seemed to spread from his black cape and frowning face.

"I know who you are," he said lowly. The hair along the hatchling's neck showed her nervousness but she did her best to look 'horse-like.' "And I know why you're here."

"Good morning, Pastor Dolorum. How is your mother? I heard that she has had difficulty recovering from her stroke." Arnica spoke carefully, shaping his words into a soothing sound so that their vibration created a sphere of protection about them.

Dolorum, the new minister hired by the Church of the Martyr was a 'New Priest.' Holly had heard he was very popular among the Users and was known to quote from the Book of Doom in ways which caused the Politicos to give him considerable support and tithing.

The man stepped closer to Arnica. Holly wanted to back away but forced himself to move closer to his partner. He slowed his breathing and focused his mind to wrap Arnica with his love.

Pastor Dolorum spoke quietly.

"I do know who you are. I understand more than you may realize. We each have our own calling. While at my morning prayers I sensed that you would be here but I also have my ways. Here," he said, reaching into an inner pocket of his heavy cape, "this is for my mother. Could you please bless it in your rites this night and secretly return it to me?"

"Yes, we would gladly do that," Arnica said kindly. Gino exhaled loudly but he pretended to have not heard. "We would be honored. It may be that Gino could drop it at your mother's door tomorrow morning."

The dark man's face brightened. "That would be a blessing. Thank you. Don't think badly of me. We are not all the same."

Arnica placed one hand on the man's shoulder and extended the other. They clasped hands and the Dolorum seemed visibly moved. "But I must move on. You do understand."

"Oh yes, I do." Arnica's voice suddenly grew louder. It was his 'public' voice, one which could freely be heard when they were in the village. "Please give your mother our best." And they parted ways, Dolorum heading toward the village square and Dark Star, Gino and the men quickly carrying the packages back toward Merrywood road. They were anxious to be back home.

"Oh, it's so beautiful. I never could have imagined. Why, it's like magick." Gino was stunned. He stood upon the back stoop wearing his 'new' robe. The path through the gardens back to the stone circle was lined with small votives in clear, glass holders. Earlier he had helped unpack the box of hand-made candles Amber sent from the River

Mountains. It was a large carton, for she sent enough for all of her kindred of the Loon Tribe. Baskets of candles were waiting to be blessed, then returned so they could be burnt throughout the year. Gino held his candle in his hand, a beautiful work of art with many colours banded throughout the wax. His father sent it from Mill City, hand-carved by an artisan who worked alongside him in the flour mills. So many of the Renaissance men found they had to turn to hard labor to support their families. The Politicos saw that most moneys went to the factory owners and their wealthy friends. There was a growing inequity in this country that worried Arnica. At least they were safe here at the Grove during these Changing Times.

Arnica came out of the cabin in his winter robe, his staff in hand. "Look how clear it is," said Holly following behind, holding their most sacred chalice aloft, it's crystal as clear as the night sky. And they set off down the path. Dark Star was waiting for them in the woods.

The stone circle was ringed with candles of all shapes and sizes. They were set to flame on this night of the Waxing Light, one by one to represent the subtle shifting of the tides, the growing amount of sunlight which blessed their days and which would carry them to Eostara. Many of these were the stubs from the previous year's rituals, many were new, sent by friends who could not be here in person.

The baskets of new candles had been anointed with oils and blessed with incense. The cone of power had been raised and they quietly spread small rugs and the three sat in a three-pointed circle, forming a triangle with their hands as they moved into trance. Their thoughts merged and mental pictures melded. Holly's eyes closed, his mind saw Gino's mother. Her face looked strangely different and he realized that this was how Gino saw her, not the way she appeared to Holly. Gino was imaging his mother and asking the gods to bless her candles.

The energy shifted. Individual blessings done, they now began to draw down the Goddess. No matter that the Moon was just a slim crescent hanging low in the sky, together they imaged a Full Moon directly overhead with a beam of radiant light rising from deep within the Sacred Earth upon which they sat. Despite the brisk air, they were warm within the stones. Dark Star was quietly walking deosil around them. They began breathing as one, moving the energy through the candles, then slipping into deeper meditations so they could themselves be filled with Her awesome power.

"What?" Holly was pulled out of his trance by a slurping sound. All three opened their eyes and looked about.

There, in the west, stood Dark Star, bent low and drinking from a small pool of water just outside the west altar stone..

"I don't believe it," Holly said in wonderment. "There was no water there. Am I awake or am I in a vision so real I'm confused?"

"No, you're awake," Arnica responded. "We all are and somehow, when we thought the legends of the Mother renewing Herself at Her sacred well before She returns as the Maiden, we now have a sacred spring."

"Can we wash our faces in it, just like the Lady does?" asked Gino.

"Oh, yes," said Arnica. "Look at her." And the hatchling, a few beads of water dripping from her chin, looked at them. Her eyes twinkled. She knew more about this gift than they could ever have imagined.

"I'll start," said Holly, who knelt alongside the west stone and dipped his hands into the water. "This is so wonderful," bathing his face with the sacred water.

Gino's first ritual had brought him a rare experience. These candles would be some of the most healing, ever. All done at the spring, they gathered the ritual tools and candles and headed back to the cabin. The flames would safely burn themselves out through the night as they settled into dreams. Gino yawned, a basket in each hand, as he walked along the path. He was eager to snuggle up with Dark Star and feel her warmth. His first ritual! What a Candlemas Eve this had been.

X - Eggs in the Trees

"Be careful, you'll fall," Holly said with more than a trace of anxiety in his voice. Arnica was high up the ladder propped against the branches of the hawthorne. Holly could tell that Arnica's legs were bothering him a bit and it was a bit windy out today. The branches, the ladder and Arnica all moved gently in the breeze.

"I'm almost done with this one - hold the ladder steady." And Arnica began slowly lowering himself, rung by rung. 'Old bones,' he thought to himself. A new set of wind chimes had been hung high in the tree in anticipation of Eostara. A loud whinny set both men to laughing. Dark Star had been pacing nervously about ever since Arnica had climbed up the ladder higher than her head. Apparently she did not think humans belonged in trees!

"Holly, you should have seen the view from the top of the hawthorne! It looks as if Merrywood is under attack. I could see plumes of smoke and it looks like many acres of trees have been cut down."

"Oh, Arnica, no!" Holly was on the verge of crying. He always felt so deeply for the trees. Arnica knew that Holly held some type of spiritual kinship with the tree devas.

"Don't let your fear and pain become part of our magick, my sweet," answered Arnica. "Just remember to increase the magick of your morning devotion. I think it's time to move forward with our plan."

"Hello, is anyone there?" A voice called from the other side of the gate.

"It's Amber," said Holly with excitement. "Dear lady, I'll come and open the latch," and off he went running toward the side of the cabin.

In moments a flurry of voices was heading back toward Arnica who was hanging more Eostara eggs from the lower branches of the hawthornes around Circle in the gardens. Holly was carrying a large traveling bag and Gino and Amber were both carrying baskets filled with goodies. "Amber, you look lovelier than ever! How lonely my arms have been for one of your hugs." And they embraced warmly, as old friends do.

"Look what I've brought with me," Amber said. "It was a blessing that Gino was able to come with me from Merrydale. Phoenix and Pearl sent this one," and she reached into the basket and brought forth a large egg, decorated with the most delicate of miniature needlepoint runes and sigils. Her silken, black hair spilled over her shoulder as she leaned forward.

"How do they do that? It looks as if they made the egg itself with their magick needles," Gino asked. This was his first Eostara and he'd never seen anything like this before.

"Pearl learned this art from her grandmother, Lady Ellhorn," Arnica explained. "I'm not even sure that Phoenix understands how she does this, even though Pearl taught him how to hold the Circle around her while her stitching transforms the egg. Oh, Amber, how are they doing? Does Phoenix look well? Have they decided?"

"Yes, they have. They're moving," Amber said, quietly. Holly and Arnica both sighed, for there were no words. "Phoenix looks well enough but he needs a change of climate. Lady Ellhorn's house is large, with many empty rooms and no one to help her tend it. And she's getting old - she's almost eighty. Phoenix will be able to live more restfully and he'll be closer to good healers in Cloverville. It's a good-sized city."

"Where's Cloverville?" asked Gino. His freckled smile was so sunny and he loved asking questions. "Phoenix said I can come and visit him if I can reach my Initiation with you, Arnica."

"I was there once," said Arnica, "many years ago. Pearl had been here to attend the Beltane Faire when she met Phoenix. It was pure magick, so much that the morning of Beltane she decided she would come and join him here in his work. I went with Phoenix to help him move Pearl. Lady Ellhorn is wonderful. She's so beautiful and I'm sure she'll be glad to have Pearl and Phoenix home again. When I saw Phoenix last week he said that the pain in his bones is worse and some days he's no longer able to go up and down the steps even to reach their gardens. It's warmer and dryer in Cloverville. Oh, Gino, I'm sorry, my mind was wandering. Cloverville is far to the south, about seven days by carriage from here, in Sagaireau Province. It's a different climate and Phoenix can grow his roses year 'round."

Amber held up the egg. "Pearl sent this. It's been prepared and filled and she asked that you bury it back in your woods near the stone Circle. She said that she can journey easily if it's here and she'll be with you at all the Sabbats, carrying the healing back to Phoenix."

"We'd better keep going," said Arnica. "We've got more eggs to hang in the trees."

"But where's Dark Star," asked Gino, his voice raised in youthful hope. He so loved the young Unicorn. They had bonded quickly and were quite a pair when they were together.

"She was here when we heard your voices," Holly said. "I was so distracted by the news of our Pictish friends' move that I don't know. Where could she be? Dark Star... Munchkin..." he called out, but there was only silence.

More and more the hatchling was wandering off on her own when she felt the need. Arnica no longer worried about the Users spotting her in the village for she'd learned well how to render her horn invisible, blending in and easily moving about. Holly and Arnica had learned that, despite her frisky demeanor and her fey, eldritch soul, she was highly skilled in working within the mundane world.

"She'll be back before the eve," said Arnica. "She's been preparing for this celebration for weeks. I expect she's going to have one of her surprises for us."

The torches were set along the path through the garden and candles were lit around the garden Circle. Arnica seemed restless. He'd gone to the window frequently but trying to do so in ways no one would notice. Holly was doing the washing up. Amber's long journey and Gino's hunger (a boy's hunger, Holly thought) meant a nourishing meal was essential before their Eostara Eve ritual. It was just a year ago that the hatchling was born. Holly was always amazed at much their lives could change in a year. Arnica was definitely able to stir the cauldron of change and now, with Dark Star in their lives... Living in both worlds, she matured at her own rate and in twelve, short months it now seemed like she'd been in their lives for a long time. And perhaps she had.

Holly's train of thought was interrupted when Arnica called out, "she's here," trying to downplay the fact that he'd been more anxious than Gino. "And look, who's this with her?"

They gathered, all cozied together in the kitchen as Dark Star stood in the doorway, half in and half out. An elfin-looking man stood there shyly, not knowing quite what to say. His face looked as boyish as Gino, his eyes sparkled with a wisdom as old as Arnica. Despite his reticence, a smile of pure glee lit up his face.

"I'm, um, my name is..." his words stumbled softly into the room. "Actually, I don't have a name. I mean I've had lots of names... I've been living with the dryads since before the Changing Times began and trees don't use names but I've lost my home, you see, they cut down the trees near Fern Hollow and all the creatures had to flee quickly and find new homes and I was wandering in Merrywood when she came along and she told me you needed me here and..." He stopped in mid-sentence, his face blushing brightly.

"I'm Arnica and this is Holly. This is our home and we welcome you." Arnica reached forward and took the man's hand. How small and gentle it was. "This is Amber. She's here all the way from River Mountains - a two days' walk. Amber's of the Loon Tribe." Amber smiled warmly. "And this is Gino, our young friend from Merrydale." Gino stepped forward and spontaneously hugged the man, who was not that much taller than Gino!

Now they all felt better.

"Thank you," the man said. "Actually, I don't have a name. I've been living in both worlds. The Mother blessed me with the gift of shape. When I'm with the trees, I can dance through the woods looking like an image of leaves. And here, where I'm safe," at this the man blushed ever so slightly, "I can look like my parents. My mother was of elven stock and met my father - an Earthkin Priest - at the Sabbat. When I was born on Midsummer's Eve it was in the realm of the faerie and I was given this gift. My job has been to move in and out of the village to let the nature creatures know what's taking place. When I'm in Merrydale, I look like a puppy and no one holds back when I'm around. But I need a new home and Dark Star told me I was her birthday present."

A loud whinny demanded their attention and they all looked at the hatchling. It was obvious that she was ready and her hoof pawed at the wooden porch to let them know she felt it was time.

"She wants us to begin the Ritual," the man-puppy said. "My mother sometimes called me Poppy and I've been in Circle many times. Dark Star and I speak without words."

"Then, let us begin," said Arnica. "We've got eggs in the trees and it's time to turn the Wheel. Last year at Eostara Dark Star was brought into our lives and now we have Poppy. Oh, Amber, I'm so glad you're here to share this with us. O.K., my loves, let's hold hands and breathe as one, settle our thoughts quietly before we carry the cakes out to begin the Circle."

And so they did. Dark Star looked quite pleased with herself. She loved surprises. Ever since her earthquake birth she'd enjoyed shaking things up just a bit... She reached forward and took the handle of a basket in her teeth and followed the procession out along the garden path.

XI - Dance of the Devas

"What flowers should I pick?" mused Holly. He was weaving circlets of Beltane flowers from the gardens with bright-colored ribbons. "Dark Star's horn will be filled with the magick of our gardens!" and he began weaving the columbine from the basket at hand.

Poppy, Dark Star's new friend, was off with the hatchling. They were dancing through the gardens, Dark Star with a basket handle in her mouth, Poppy with small, garden scissors, gathering flowers for Holly. There were lilacs and daisies and wild dicentra and bleeding hearts and ajuga and the list went on as far as the edge of the gardens!

Arnica was working with the crystals. Four wonderful new specimens had arrived with Gino from Crystal. Holly thought that it was great fun calling them 'Crystal's crystals.' Crystal's gifts included a large, yellow topaz for the East altar; a surprisingly large piece of red garnet for the South altar; a blue tourmaline for the West altar; and a beautiful chrysophase for the North altar. Around the Circle Arnica was setting a mandala of their temple stones upon the large, granite rocks: a large piece of nacre, a jade carving, amber and onyx. Next was a brilliant iridescent crystal cluster no one had quite been to identify. Then were set thirteen ivory carvings brought back from another land by a distant ancestor which had been in the family for generations. Upon the next stone was an amethyst cluster, then a topaz (this one almost golden in color), a ruby, a blue sapphire and a green emerald. These would set the pattern of energy in motion linking the Circle to the faceted crystal set in his bamboo staff. When the Circle was cast for Beltane, Arnica would carry his staff slowly around the perimeter of the garden circle setting the energy in motion, all linked to the radiant crystal in his staff, to be carried to the Beltane 'tree' which had been fashioned from a straight cedar branch Crystal had carved from a straight, slender limb which had come down in the woods the previous Hallows. There would be six of them this Beltane Eve to dance the ribbons 'round the pole, weaving the magick of the gardens' exuberance into a dance which would last until the first killing frost.

"Oh, look," cried Holly, "they are beautiful!" Poppy and Dark Star had just brought him a basket with lilacs, both pure white and deep purple. "There are enough to make circlets for everyone."

"Let me take my staff back into the cabin and give you a hand," Arnica offered, and headed up the path to their little house.

"Would you bring some more spools of ribbon?" asked Holly. Arnica paused, his silver-grey hair catching the sun.

"Any particular colors, my sweet?"

"What about blue for Amethyst and white for Crystal? And I think a bright green for Gino would be just perfect! Poppy, do you have a favorite color?"

"I think a golden color would suit me," Poppy said. "I've been 'retrieving' all afternoon."

They all laughed at this joke. Since Dark Star had brought her new friend home, a changeling of Elf mother and Earthkin father, the young man who shape-shifted into a puppy whenever he was near human civilization, had enjoyed teasing them all with his 'canine humor' as he called it.

"Golden it will be - as wonderful as the warmth of the Sun," Arnica said and turned toward the cabin.

"Holly, they are so beautiful," said Poppy. "Can I try mine on?" Holly handed him the ring of bright daisies with golden ribbons. It was stunning. "Look, it fits perfectly. Dark Star, do you want a turn?" Poppy tossed it to the hatchling and it landed, perfectly around her horn. The hatchling whinnied in pure delight. She loved this curious fellow a lot, even though he had been in her life only a matter of weeks.

Dark Star lifted her head and turned her neck as if to say, 'catch me.'

"You're on," said Poppy, and the two of them went scampering about the gardens.

"It's not fair," Poppy cried, "you leap right over the large beds and I must run around and stay on the paths." He was a bit breathless from the chase, and landed upon the grass.

Dark Star knew her cue and she turned upon her hooves and came right up to him. Kneeling down, she lowered her horn and the flowered hoop landed right on Poppy's tummy. His laugh spilled into the afternoon air like the sound of the many wind chimes hanging in the trees.

Now that the scampering was done, Arnica and Holly brought the garden altar from the storage shed next to the greenhouse. It was a fine old desk with the legs removed. When it was sitting in just north of the garden circle's center, it was a wonderful piece of furniture. They carried it through the lattice archway at the Northeast portal and set it in place. Holly opened one of the drawers to bring forth the altar cloth and together they spread it carefully over the walnut altar top. They worked so well together, knowing just what the other would do. Poppy had found this a constant source of amazement. Sometimes Arnica and Holly seemed to share their very thoughts!

Arnica had opened another drawer to bring forth the altar stones. He wanted to be certain the cloth would not be carried away in a flirtatious afternoon breeze before they set the altar early this evening.

"Bring them all here, Poppy, would you please?"

The man-puppy loved 'fetching' in any form. He jumped to his feet and strung the circlets upon his left arm. One each for Crystal and Amethyst, one for Arnica and one for Holly. He put his upon his head, Gino's in his left hand. The last one, the best, was Dark Star's and he carefully laid it around her horn and they both went into the garden circle.

Holly and Arnica took the ribboned hoops and laid them lovingly upon the altar, then all went into the cabin to rest and meditate in preparation for the evening.

A gentle knock at the kitchen door announced the arrival of Crystal, Amethyst and Gino.

"Look who we met on the way. Did you get the parcel?" asked Crystal.

"Oh yes, and wait until you experience them tonight in the Circle. The mandala has grown and should be quite amazing," answered Arnica.

They hugged and talked a bit as they changed into their ritual robes. When all was ready they embraced as one and sang a song together. Then Arnica picked up his cobalt blue chalice and aspurged the path before them as they sang their way through the gardens into the circle.

Holly removed his athame from its scabbard and scribed the Circle as Arnica lit the two, white altar candles. Gino stood at the center, his gloved hands holding Arnica's powerful staff. Poppy sat near his feet and they turned as each of the other four invoked, in turn, their respective element. Dark Star moved from one to the other as each of the four cardinal directions was set in motion. Crystal was very pleased. The stones she had sent integrated their energy and evoked a very strong magick.

Now the Circle was prepared. Arnica took his staff and walked carefully to the East. Holding it out so that it's crystal crown extended over the perimeter of stones (upon which were set the mandala of crystals and gems), he moved slowly. One by one the crystals and gems seemed almost to change hue, as if glowing from within. All the gardens and trees outside the Circle seemed to move a bit into the distance, as if a sheer veil was being dropped from the starlit sky. As Arnica completed his walk around the Circle, Crystal set the Beltane pole in place, right at the center of it all. Arnica walked in a spiral, bringing all the magick together and then, at the climax, touching it to the pole.

"Oh," they all gasped, sounding as if fireworks had been set off, for at the very top of the pole appeared the most beautiful flower. The magick had worked and the pole had been transformed into the Beltane Tree. The others stood, transfixed, as Arnica and Holly moved the altar to the north.

"Is it now?" asked Poppy.

"Oh, yes, we may begin," answered Arnica. Holly placed the circlets of flowers upon each person's head. Dark Star stood in the archway, right in the northeast portal and waited as Holly took hers to the altar, blessed it with sacred water and incense, then set it over her horn. They stood, then, around the pole, each taking in hand their ribbon.

"Blessed Be the dance of May," they began, as the chant grew and the dance started. Holly, Crystal and Poppy danced deosil as Arnica, Amethyst and Gino moved counter. They wove in and out until the pole was braided with ribbon and the Circle was filled with glowing Magick.

Arnica went to the altar to get the silver chalice and Poppy stood up, proud.

"I wrote an invocation," he said. "May I say it?"

They nodded, and Arnica set the chalice back down so he could listen carefully.

"Blessed Be the stars in the night skies.

Blessed Be the Moonbeams surrounding us.
Blessed Be the God and Goddess here in our hearts, Their spirits divine.
Dance in the Circle and give Them honor
Up in the Astral they do outshine.
Heavenly parents, we invoke you for blessings here in the Circle, scribed for you tonight.
Shine in our lives so all can be arisen.
Blessed Be the Child of Light, for he is the master of heavenly flight."

And with that a loud sound, almost like thunder (but the sky was clear) shook the very ground upon which they stood. There, next to Dark Star, was the Goddess, looking beautiful and wild all at once. She looked upon them and spoke. "It is time. The changeling must come with me. His mother cries for she misses him. Poppy, as they call you, you may no longer wander in this world but must return to your own."

Dark Star neighed loudly, her cry of anguish tearing at everyone's hearts.

"Dark Star, you above all must understand that he cannot remain here. He is of elven blood and he must return to his own world. Take his place Dark Star and dance, all of you dance now for the Magick is upon you."

And they did, unbraiding the Beltane Tree then winding it up again before they stopped. And when they did, a voice called out from the distance, "Blessed Be the Child of Light..." and there, just outside the edge of the Circle's stones, the devas, spirits of the flowers, were seen dancing on this Beltane Eve, a vision none had ever before seen and one which none would forget. Poppy's spirit would always be there, among the dancing devas.

XII - Jewel and Lotus' Surprise

Summer was arriving in the gardens and grove. The first firefly was spotted just a few nights ago and the borage continued to brighten the gardens with a multitude of five-pointed blue flowers. Dark Star, last year's hatchling unicorn, had discovered just how tasty borage can be.

"It's a good thing, too, for it's coming up everywhere," said Holly. He and Arnica had been encouraging Dark Star to carefully reach and pluck all the borage she could find growing everywhere but in the new borage bed. After dealing with last year's borage 'experience,' they decided to create one large bed for the borage and declared 'that's it.' Borage found growing any place else would have to go. Dark Star didn't seem to mind one bit!

"Remember a year ago Midsummer? That was when Jewel and Lotus first brought baby Dagon here. He was so tiny then," Holly mused, pausing while dead-heading the brilliant red Chinese poppies.

"Yes, I remember well," answered Arnica. "He's certainly grown fast. We should polish his bell and ring it tonight. He's so quick for his age I must believe that he would recognize the sound." Last year at Midsummer a silver bell was hung for Dagon. In fact, the trees around them contained numerous bells and wind chimes sent by friends and students scattered all throughout the lands. Some were hung so that their music would remember the birth of a baby, some for the passing of a loved one, some to remember a singular event and others just for the pleasure of their sound.

"Dear Sirs, may I take the candles?" Gino's face was radiant with freckles and his ever bright smile. He had become an apprentice to Arnica, learning all there was to know about herbs and magick. His special relationship with the hatchling had grown since he first saw her horn despite the powerful herbs which led all others to see her as a horse.

"Yes, son," answered Arnica kindly. He had grown very fond of this lad. "Take them and set them out with love and song."

Last year they had used votive candles placed in jelly jars to line the path from their cabin through the woods to the stone Circle. But this year would be different. A week after Beltane a huge carton arrived. Their friend Amber, now living in the River Mountains, was dating a steelsmith. Together she and the man (what *was* his name, Quicksilver?) designed and crafted a set of twenty-four wrought iron hooks to set into the earth. At the top end each hook curved like a shepherd's crook to hold the hangers for the candles. Amber had also sent a set 24 glass bowls to place in the hangers. How beautiful this would look. Gino would need to make many trips.

As the boy went along, setting the candles every so often, he stopped to offer a simple blessing for the redbud which Holly had planted several years before. Further along, he gave honor to the rowan, a sacred tree of Arnica's. It looked to be recovering. It had provided its first growths of leaves for the deer family. The gardens around their cabin and grove had been visited by the deer often this year, for they had lost their feeding ground when the trees at Fern Hollow had been cut down. In fact, the deer had done serious damage to the dogwood and to the prized pussywillow last Eostara but now, at Midsummer, everything looked to be doing just fine. The last candlestake placed, Gino went to tell Holly that the path was readied.

Now it was Holly's turn to prepare the stone Circle. He carried a large basket with their ritual tools. A small jar contained fresh-dried salt sent to them from Cloverville by Pearl. In her last letter she wrote that Phoenix' health was somewhat improved but that he still had bad days. The Pictish couple had been well known among the Earthkin for their skill with needle and thread and she had sent the salt jar in an embroidered bag. Holly set the salt bowl, water chalice and censer upon the altar.

Then he brought forth the crystal chalice. Every year it would appear clear at Candlemas but now, for Midsummer, it shone with a golden glow to honor the Sun as He neared His zenith. Holly carried the chalice slowly around the Circle and offered a prayer for Weaver, whose cremated ashes were buried beneath the great cedar just east of the stone Circle. Then he went to the west to honor Ladstar, whose ashes were placed with his athame where the two firs grew from a single root. Both were now guardians of this sacred space.

The chalice set upon the altar, Holly unpacked the incense and thurible and carried them to the south. Holly sighed, gazing beyond the south altar stone. How he loved the trees, and how deeply it pained him to see the loss of these elders. The Politicos still held the majority vote in Parliament and, at the Users' urging, more and more of the protective laws for the woodlands and forests were being voted down. Rumor in Merrydale was that they wanted to cut down even more trees and sell the lumber for more houses. The

Earthkin people were increasingly upset. At the last election two Politicos lost their seats, replaced by Conservers, but it still wasn't enough.

"Houses," Holly snorted, "there are too many people moving here. Holy Mother, please do something..."

Holly was nudged out of his reverie by a wet nose at his ear. Dark Star had come to get him and they headed back to the cabin. Tonight would be a night of magick!

Holly adjusted Arnica's robe. They were gathering near the cabin, preparing for the night's journey. Jewel was adjusting the straps on the baby basket which Lotus wore upon his back. Jewel wore daisies woven into her rust-colored hair and looked so lovely as she fussed with the straps. Lotus stretched and moved, adjusting to the weight and checking to make sure that Dagon's carrier was secure.

Gino toyed with Dagon, keeping the baby happy and occupied. Gino looked so fine in his new, first robe. Although he had studied from her only briefly, Pearl remembered him with many gifts. Hand-stitched of cloth she had woven herself, Pearl had dyed the fabric a medley of colors from dyes she made of flowers grown in her southern garden. She felt it was time for her former student to have his first robe. Gino was excited to be part of this year's ritual held back in the stone Circle. It was to be a smaller procession than usual, for Amethyst and Crystal were unable to attend Midsummer with their friends. Their lives were busy and they often had to be there in 'spirit' only.

"Are we ready?" asked Arnica.

Everyone nodded and Holly rang his ritual bell once, then set it carefully in the pocket of his robe as he took up the censer.

Arnica took his staff and led the procession along the path. "And the Goddess breathed gently into the void, behold, the gentle breezes caressed the soul of the Universe ..." Holly swung the censer gently as they passed the entrance to the woods. Their voices all blended in a chorus so gentle that not one bird stopped its chirping.

The chanting continued along the path and the Circle was cast in a flowing choreography of sound and imagery. As the time neared for the Midsummer invocation of the realm of the faerie, fireflies began to dart in and among the trees around the stone Circle. As Jewel walked to the center of the Circle to invoke the Mother Goddess, Lotus set the baby Dagon in his wicker carrier upon Dark Star's back.

Jewel's voice sang out into the dusky sky. Although only two hours until midnight, the sky was still light. "Call unto thy soul, arise and come unto me...."

At this the portal to the Realm of the Faerie opened. It first appeared as a hazy mist at the northeast edge of the Circle. Everyone felt uneasy and thrilled at the same time but just then, Dark Star started and leapt right through the portal, baby, basket and all, and disappeared into the mist as the portal closed quickly behind.

They were stunned, but before anyone could speak Jewel was transformed. A tall woman to begin with, she seemed to have grown in stature and it was not her voice at all which spoke: "Patience. He will return." The Goddess, Herself, was speaking through Jewel.

And just as quickly the sacred presence left and Jewel fell to the pine-needled floor of the Circle as Lotus rushed to her side. Holly quickly closed the Circle.

"Hurry, bring me valerian and scullcap," Arnica told Gino who ran off to the cabin. As Lotus held a sobbing Jewel, Arnica and Holly comforted both, reminding them to trust in the Goddess.

XIII - The Rhymer

"Do we have any more baskets?" Holly called to Arnica, who was tending the plants growing in their small greenhouse.

"Did you check the potting shed? What about the closet in the temple room?" Arnica answered, the snipping of scissors making rhythm as he pruned the rose geranium.

"I guess that's it. We should have enough baskets for everyone. This will be a large gathering, won't it? It's been quite a few years since a Council was called." Holly was stacking all sizes and shapes of woven baskets just outside the cabin.

"Hasn't it been wonderful spending time with Wren and Robin?" asked Arnica. "They are so connected with the earth. I hadn't realized how much I've missed them since they moved to their property in Highland. Let's see, it's been almost a handful of years since we last heard the music of their laughter!"

"That reminds me," interjected Holly, "I want to have the seastones here for the 'harvest.' Each person could choose a couple of the stones we brought back from ocean. Wasn't that a fun journey with them? Watching Robin dance in the wet sand as Wren played her lute was such a wondrous event!"

"Oh yes, do set the stones out for our guests. What a wonderful idea!" Arnica set aside his pruning scissors and walked over to Holly and the baskets. "Just look at this. What a Harvest celebration this will be. I only hope that this Sabbat will see the return of our hatchling and baby Dagon."

They fell silent. Despite their gardens being more lush than ever, despite the victories won by the Earthkin which preserved one more tract of trees in Merrywood, there was a shadow in their hearts. Automatically their minds formed images of Jewel and Lotus. Jewel had been having a rough go of it, struggling to accept the wisdom of the Mother while agonizing over the absence of her baby. Arnica and Holly had been carefully working with the image of Dark Star - oh, how they missed their unicolt - seeing the hatchling come dancing back through the portal of the stone circle with Dagon safely upon her back. These past weeks had been very difficult for all of them.

Their reverie was suddenly set aside with the sound of bells. Holly almost ran into the baskets, he was in such a hurry to get to the front path. "It's the Rhymer!" he shouted, the joy in his voice matched by the fleetness of his feet.

Arnica's old bones moved pretty quick, even for the hermit. "Rhymer," he said as he came around the corner. "It's been far too many years," and he embraced the tall figure draped in a deep, green cloak.

"Ah, many years but you know how little I enjoy traveling." The Rhymer's voice was like music dancing through the air. He and Arnica were of the same generation, Elders of the Renaissance tribes and they had been ritually bonded together long ago. "Take me to the Circle and tell me the details."

"There's not much to say," Arnica mused. We were doing our Midsummer Ritual, opening our Circle to the magick of the devas and, as Jewel was invoking the Goddess, a

The Hatchling

portal to the eldritch opened and Dark Star - the hatchling unicorn you've been hearing of - leapt right though with the baby Dagon upon her back."

"And the Goddess manifested through Jewel and said we must have patience," Holly finished. Holly and Arnica were such a pair that they could not only finish each other's sentences but often knew each other's thoughts.

"Let me set down my harp and books, then take me to the Circle." They walked the Rhymer into their cabin, deep in conversation, before taking him to the site of last Midsummer's amazing event.

The sun had not yet set but the nights were surely coming earlier than they did at the last Sabbat. They were gathering in the grassy area near Holly and Arnica's greenhouse. Lammas was a celebration of the Harvest, usually conducted with a procession through the gardens as herbs were cut and the first grains harvested. This year their hearts were hoping to bring back an even greater 'harvest.'

Jewel's russet-colored hair was tied back and, despite the smiling, brave face she presented to all of them, her eyes showed the traces of many days of weeping. She turned to Arnica and said, "I want to thank you for asking us to make the grain man. It helped us more than you could imagine."

"There is much magick in this bread," Arnica said cryptically, "and it was only fitting that you should make the offering for tonight's ritual."

"You should have seen the love and tears which went into this loaf," added Lotus. "Look. I took these weeks and watched this staff emerge." Lotus held a beautiful wooden staff with leaves and flowers carved from near the base up to the head of the staff, which emerged as a sculpture of the Goddess, Herself. "She will lead us, no matter what loss life may bring."

"Lotus, you are truly growing wise." Arnica put his arm around the younger man.

"Oh, Lotus, that's beautiful!" Wren's voice shimmered in the air like music. "Why, I have a line in my new song that describes a staff so much like this...

'See the sacred staff which guides the way
To bring us forth to hear our Mother say
These are my herbs, my flowers, my love
And these my stars and mine the Moon above...'"

Robin had started dancing to the lines of poetry, taking Gino by the hand, encouraging the boy to express his creativity through movement. They were dancing around Crystal as Amethyst stood by, laughing at the joy.

"Blessed Be!" A new voice broke into the merriment. "I see I made it here in time." A stately woman came through the gate. "I was beginning to wonder." Flying Raven was Keeper of the Archives for the Renaissance Tribes and lived far across the mountains and plains in the Mothervalley. Walking directly to Jewel, she embraced the woman and said, "I'm known as Flying Raven and you must be Jewel. My children are long grown but I understand well the depths of a mother's love," and their arms held one another for many minutes as they shared the mystery.

"Where is Amber," asked Robin, "I haven't seen her since we were maidens."

"She's in the cabin helping the Rhymer with his robes," answered Crystal. Her hair looked flaxen in the evening sun. She had kept it very short since last Hallows, having pledged to wear it cropped for a year and a day as part of her work to help her departed Grandmother prepare for a new birth.

"Arnica, I'm ready." A voice that calmed and quieted the group in an instant spoke the appearance of Rhymer.

"I'm carrying the Rhymer's harp."

"And I have the basket of seastones." Holly began walking among them. "Please select one. We picked these with Wren and Robin just the other day, choosing only those which spoke to us. These will be laid back at the stone circle with your other gifts."

A bell silenced them. Arnica raised his boline. "Let Lammas Eve begin."

Wren set her lute near the north stone. She had sung her new song as the procession left the gardens, their baskets filled with flowers and herbs and fruits and grains, guiding them with her voice beneath the trees. Wren's skills as a Bard were growing and her music set the patterns for the Rhymer.

Amber smudged the site with sage hand-picked by her sisters of the Loon Tribe, then Holly and Arnica cast the Circle. Gino lit the candles at the four elemental stones. This was the first time he had performed an active role with guests, and he moved carefully. How proud Pearl would be to see him in the robe she had embroidered!

The Circle prepared, the patterns in place, they set their offerings around the perimeter of the circle. The seastones were laid about as were bunches of flowers and herbs and the best fruits of the harvest. Jewel moved to the center. They stood around her, holding hands in a Circle. Only the Rhymer moved between the circle of stones and the circle of loving friends, the brilliant purple of his harpstrap a bright swath against the green of his robe. The Rhymer's voice began singing to the notes of the harpstrings. Jewel's arms reached up to the sky, her voice intoning, "I am the beauty of the green earth, the white Moon among the stars..."

None would remember the Rhymer's song yet every soul would carry that melody deep within as a Mystery. Their eyes all created a focus upon Jewel as she set aside her mother's ego and gave herself over to the Goddess. The last words of the Charges slipped into the dusk, and they stood silently as the Rhymer's harp created visions. By now the Elderbard's voice was singing a tongue which spoke only to the eldritch and they felt, as one, a shift in time or gravity or something which they felt right in their stomachs as if their Circle has suddenly moved into a different dimension.

The green-cloaked Elder, whose harp was now slung across his back touched Lotus upon the shoulder. The young man bent down and picked up the grain man loaf which waited at Jewel's feet and handed it to the Rhymer.

"Sing."

It was more than a command. As he took the loaf, the Rhymer handed his harp to Wren. Wren's eyes alone indicated her amazement. No one else had ever been allowed to touch the Rhymer's harp, but this was not the time to think. Wren slid the harpstrap around her shoulder and her finger touched the first string. A note danced forth and from that moment no one quite remembered just how the magick progressed.

The Rhymer walked the Circle behind them but they were oblivious. Wren's fingers moved of their own. She knew her lute, but had rarely played a harp yet the words and music emerged as if from the Rhymer's soul. Images of their dreams, visions of their hopes were like a tapestry of light. Only vaguely did they sense that the Rhymer was no longer there but now their visions were touched by the voices of the devas. Plant spirits were laughing and singing and they could hear the life forces of Nature as if the gate between worlds had not only opened but embraced them.

"I am here." The words shook them back, a strength behind them which broke through their collective reverie. "I am *here*," the Rhymer's voice commanding them to turn, seeing that the portal which opened to the Realm of the Faerie was again open. In one arm slept the baby Dagon and the other arm was loosely draped around the neck of Dark Star.

Jewel cried out and she and Lotus rushed forth to claim their baby, just in time, for the Rhymer fell to his knees exhausted, the harvest a success.

XIV - The Gates of Death

"I miss his quiet stories."

"I miss listening to his harp," Holly responded to Arnica's comment.

The Rhymer's visit for Lammas remained a vivid memory. His journey into the Realm of the Faerie had taken a physical toll upon him, but Jewel and Lotus were grateful that their baby Dagon had been brought safely back to their arms. Holly and Arnica were glad to have Dark Star back, although they knew well that their Unicorn hatchling was bound to be off in all magickal directions at any time. The Rhymer had stayed two more fortnights at the cabin, resting and regaining his strength from the arduous task before starting out on his long trek home.

Every few days Jewel and Lotus would come out to sit with him until, as his body regained its tone, he would walk with them in the gardens. Soon they were learning the Bardic Mysteries from the Rhymer and they would wander back to the stone circle every two or three days where they would sit upon the soft ground to listen to the Rhymer teach them through the music of his harp. When the dusk was just right, music seemed to emerge from the trees that sounded much like Wren's lute. What an event was Lammas, with Wren and Robin here from the Highlands and the Rhymer all the way from Loriën.

Dagon would quietly crawl about but often would sit and watch the Bard's slender fingers pluck such music as had never before been heard. Although not much more than fourteen months old, one was certain that somehow, Dagon understood what the Rhymer was teaching. Despite his gurgling speech, Dagon's eyes shone with a curious type of wisdom ever since his weeks spent in the Realm of the Faerie. If there was any way to describe it, Dagon *listened* differently and seemed aware of all aspects of his surroundings. When the Rhymer held Dagon, kissing the baby goodbye, the others noticed a strange exchange between the two, for they communicated with their eyes.

"He's not been gone that long," mused Arnica. "Can you lift that basket of grapes by yourself?"

"But I miss him... Of course I can," Holly said, struggling with a huge basket holding more than two bushels of fresh, concord grapes. "Maybe you should lend a hand, after all. I wouldn't want my pride splattered on the floor beneath these beauties!"

Arnica chuckled. They could both be stubborn at times but they adored each other and offered thanks every morning that the Universe saw fit to let them share their work. Holy had been running the fruit steamer since sunrise (although sunrise was so much later than at Midsummer!), creating jars of pure grape juice.

Arnica was working at the table in their small kitchen, figuring the tithing crops they would need to take in to Merrydale. "Do you have enough herbs?" In addition to the jars of juice, every thirteenth was set aside with herbs for ritual drink for the coming year. The last jar of the season was to be created specifically for Hallows, steeped with herbs which would open the Gates of Death.

"I believe so. The back arbor has been all harvested and the front holds about two more baskets when these are done... Let's see, I've got three, four dozen jars..." and Holly's voice drifted off in counting.

"Three pounds of ginseng, one of goldenseal..." Arnica continued working on the harvest tithe.

"If I put in two measures of herbs into each thirteenth jar..."

"And our apples did not bear well this year so one less..."

"Four, five, and there must be more than six measures in the bowl..."

"Eight, nine, the tithing can go in tomorrow as planned." Arnica began laughing. "You know? It's almost like music in the room with the counterpoint of our counting!"

"Yes," Holly laughed also, "but you're the only person who doesn't distract me when we're both counting out loud! I know what you're counting and keep track of it and yet keep track of my numbers as well. It's just like being in ritual with you when our minds follow their mandalas."

"How is the steamer doing?" Arnica asked, "Do you have time to help me prepare the herbs to open the Gates?

"Oh, yes. Can I light the candle now?" Before he'd even lit the fire beneath the steamer, Holly had set up the small kitchen altar. Sitting over the still-empty jar designated to hold the Hallows drink was a wonderful, crocheted doll. "Pearl's jar-dolly would be happy with some incense as well." The 'body' of the jar was the jar, with the torso sitting upon the lid. The head was hand-stitched to represent the Goddess Who guards the portal to the Underworld and sent to them from Cloverville so that Pearl could participate long-distance in the Autumn rite.

"Yes love, it's time." Arnica opened the pages of his herbal grimoire, in which he kept the recipes as they marked the turning of the Wheel of the Year. "What I need from the gardens are six aconite blooms and thirteen holly berries. The rest of the herbs are in the cupboard." And off they went to collect the herbs and finish up the day's canning.

"It certainly seems, well, *loud*, doesn't it?" Arnica mused out loud.

"I like it. It's exciting," piped Gino in his young voice, "but I like staying at your home too. It was just a year ago I met you in Merrydale and I've certainly had some amazing adventures since then!"

"No one even noticed Dark Star when she was tethered to the hitching post at the apothecary's," Holly commented.

"Did too," Gino parried, "I saw the preacher stroking Dark Star's head. And she licked his face and he laughed, right out loud!"

"Pastor Dolorum? I haven't seen him since we blessed the charm for his mother. You know, I used to think all Politicos were bad, but these are curious times, aren't they, Arnica?"

"I must say, it's not nearly so stressful an election campaign as I had expected. I had expected some pretty intense fighting ever since the trees at Fern Hollow were cut down," Arnica answered. As he walked, he adjusted the cloth bags of herbs and provisions which were borne upon Dark Star's back. She whinnied lightly and slowed, an opportunity to munch some late season mulberry leaves which stretched over the road's edge.

"I was pretty shocked to learn that Pastor Dolorum told his congregation to join the march. Who would have thought Iris would have become such an activist? Gino, were you there?" Holly turned to the freckled boy.

"Oh, it was something, all right! There were only a few dozen people at the village square and the postmarm sounded a little discouraged. She had just begun her talk when we heard some noise around the corner and then, there he was! Pastor Dolorum brought almost fifty people, some of them the most upright Users, and they were even carrying their Books of Doom. Dolorum, he called out, 'Iris, we're here to join you. My mother used to take me to Fern Hollow for picnics when I was a lad and these fine people believe that the trees of Merrywood are part of God's work. We're going to join you in your fight.' Well, you could have knocked the postmarm over with a flower!"

"I know that the balance in Parliament may change this election. Too many people are unhappy with the way the Politicos have tried to bring in more mills and cut down trees." Arnica had spent many restless afternoons walking down the road to look at the raw damage at Fern Holly, coming home to quietly offer prayer in the stone circle. "Dolorum's unexpected involvement made people very aware of how painful it is for Merrywood. I don't think the Politicos stand much of a chance in the election, but we've still many weeks to go."

"How did things go in the tithing office?" asked Holly.

"The tithing agent was less harried this year. He took our figures and tithe without question but Mr. Pounds quietly said to me that he's thinking of voting with the Conservers this year. I know he was a bit unhappy last year with the Politicos but I didn't expect this, since the Politico candidates have softened their rhetoric."

"My mother said they don't want to upset the applecart," Gino chimed in. "And can we have apples tonight at the ritual feast?" And they all laughed as they walked along the country road. Dark Star seemed unusually quiet as the two men and boy chattered busily along the lane.

"Where's Gino?" asked Holly, coming through the door with his arms full.

"He's in the front room, already sleeping next to Dark Star." Arnica continued with the washing up. There were many goblets and plates and ritual things from their Autumnal Rite. "They're both curled up in front of the fire. Interesting timing, isn't it? This being Autumn Eve and it's the first night so cool we've had to light the fire."

"Dark Star has been quieter ever since her weeks with the Faerie, hasn't she?" Holly said, setting down the candle lanterns on the pantry shelf.

"Yes, but she goes out running more, also, which tires her out. Her young muscles are growing and wanting hard exercise. She's still quite young but my, can her legs go.

What did you think of the ears of corn that Amethyst had braided? Weren't they beautiful?" Arnica was drying their best chalice.

"When she knelt before Amber - wasn't that great that Amber made it down from the River Mountains? She's staying in Merrydale until Hallows before heading back... when Amber was the Goddess and Amethyst knelt, offering the corn, it was so beautiful!" Holly's voice climbed in excitement.

"Careful, you'll wake Gino," Arnica hushed.

"I don't think *anything* could wake him tonight!" Holly said, but more quietly.

"Well, love, the harvest has been blessed and prayers offered for the election. I wonder what this winter will bring. Amber said the mountain birds portend a hard winter this year."

"We're certainly ready. The gardens are harvested, plants cut back and the soil turned. The grapes aren't done yet and already our cannery cupboard is full. We've got foods for us and our guests. I feel so blessed."

"And I feel tired." Arnica tipped the pan and let the water spiral itself down the drain. "Put out the lantern, sweet, and let's take ourselves to bed. Tomorrow is the new season and my bones feel old."

XV - Face to Face With Death

Life had seemed quiet as Holly and Arnica went about preparing their gardens for Hallows. Most of the herbs and flowers had ceased their life cycles, turning brown with death to indicate that it was time to cut them back so that their underworld life within the roots could be renewed during the winter months. The leaves had drifted slowly off the trees, sometimes coming down in a thick flurry when the wind shook them loose and, all about them, it appeared as if Mother Nature was truly preparing to descend into the Underworld.

The old, cut-crystal jar of herbal elixir designed to part the veils between the world had sat upon the altar since Autumn, kept protected by the hand-stitched 'jar dolly' sent them by Pearl. The aconite blooms and holly berries were steeping in its wine, along with mandrake root and mistletoe berries gathered and dried last Yule. Two Full and one New Moon had come and gone and at each ritual the small bottle was kept central upon the main altar, becoming a focal point for the special magick brought forth as the Circle was worked. Although their friends had been present at Lammas and Autumn, as Hallows neared it appeared that this Sabbat Holly and Arnica would work alone.

Some were traveling, taking the high passes before winter began to make the River Mountains impassible. Amber had planned to stay in Merrydale until Hallows, but it had begun snowing in the mountain passes and it made her anxious to return to Quicksilver the steelsmith, who was becoming an important man in her life. Jewel and Lotus were among the travelers. They were traveling with Amber to the River Mountains. The couple wanted to take their baby Dagon to spend some time playing with the children in the mountain village where Amber now lived as it was untouched by the illness spreading through the lands of Lothloriën. They hoped to join in the drumming and dancing which was being done to shift the political tides in the upcoming election. A growing number of people were alarmed with the destruction of the forests and the attempt by the Politicos to outlaw all religions which did not accept their Book of Doom nor worship their cross of blood.

Even young Gino was gone, off to spend a fortnight with his father in Mill City, taking a large hamper of herbal mixtures which Arnica had prepared, complete with instructions. There were a growing number of men from the Renaissance Tribes who had found it necessary to turn away from their gardens and crafts to take jobs in the mills during these difficult times. Although the illness had not reached Mill City, Arnica knew that his herbal tonics could keep them safe. Despite his youth, Gino had been given his first task as Arnica's apprentice.

Over the past weeks, Amethyst and Crystal had been trying to put a new thatch on their roof, working on it after long days at their regular jobs until Crystal, herself, took ill with the virus. Iris, ever-healthy Iris the postmarm, came over to help and the roof was soon done but all three were very tired and Crystal was not well. All of the close friends had decided to meet with Holly and Arnica in the astral temple, meeting in spirit since few could be united within a Circle for the Hallows Sabbat. October had not been an easy month. As the days grew dark, so was a darkness falling upon the land.

"They said that seventeen people have died in the past weeks. Oh, Arnica, that is so many. When I posted the letter to Pearl and Phoenix, Iris looked tired but well. Mr. Pounds the tithing agent was in the postal shop and he did not look at all well. And Pastor Dolorum came up to me on the street, openly and asked if you might know of any herb for his mother has caught the virus as well. She has been so frail since her stroke and he fears she hasn't the strength to make it through the fevers." Holly was sitting on the floor, deep in thought, his hands going through the motion of combing the hatchling's mane. Dark Star was laying with her head across his lap.

"Oh, it's so hard," answered Arnica. "I've gazed into the Orb so many hours this past month," he said, turning toward the crystal ball sitting upon their altar. "Even if the Conservers do take back a majority of seats in Parliament, the lands are becoming so crowded, so many trees have been hewn to death... I fear that the Mother is trying to bring things into balance and it will be a painful process for so many."

"Will we work in the stone circle tomorrow night?" asked Holly.

"No, I think not. It is just we two and I think our bones would rejoice to part the Gates of Death in here with the fireplace to keep us warm."

"What is it, munchkin?" Holly asked of the hatchling. Holly had developed the ability to communicate with the unicolt. Dark Star turned her head toward the orb and lowered her horn. When she sent her thoughts through the crystal ball toward Holly, her horn paled to its silver color. Holly quickly moved his body into a trance-like state and sent his mind into the Orb to seek her voice... "Dark Star said she'd prefer being out in the brisk air, but she wants to attend the Circle with us. She feels that it will be important for her to be with us." Holly did not hear the hatchling speak in words or sentences, but was learning to put his impressions of her energy into his own words.

"I've felt that as well. It would be easy to wonder whether we're just nervous with this sickness bringing so much death but I feel there is something else. The other morning when I removed the jar dolly, I thought I saw an image moving in Pearl's needlework but when I blinked my eyes, there were only the intricate designs. This morning, when I worked magick with the jar of elixir for the Hallows Ritual, I felt cold... but hot at the same time. It makes me think that this sacred Eve contains both fire and ice."

Holly did not answer. Arnica's words moved something within his own being. His hand picked up the brush again. Dark Star laid her head back down quietly, her horn now its natural hue. The three of them remained quiet for more than an hour as they contemplated Hallows Eve.

Working indoors meant first carrying the Feast of the Dead out to the stone circle. Food was set out for Weaver and Ladstar. Weaver had passed into the Summerland many years before and Ladstar's cremated remains and athame were placed just two years ago. The friends respective ashes had been placed on either side of the circle. The stone circle was not only the place for their more private rituals but also a memorial for those remembered with bells and crystals in this wooded glen.

The temple in the front room was warmed by the fireplace, burning quietly in the south, its mantle providing the South Altar. Other than the fire, there was no light other than the small flame from a single, black candle sitting upon the main altar. Dark Star took her favorite position, sitting in the northeast portal, staying out of the way as the two men walked the Circle.

"One lone candle lights this night..." The words chanted, the Circle was begun. Soon the other candles were lit and the four elemental directions honored. In time the entire room had been transformed into a magickal circle.

The cauldron brought forth and placed in the center of the room, Holly and Arnica sat down and the Hatchling moved forward. The fire was lit and the ritual chanted...

"Near we now the Gates of Death, on this fearsome night..

"We'll call lost loved ones from within to join us in this rite..."

Holly was startled. His eyes closed during the chant, Dark Star had whinnied gently, the way she did to greet their friends.

There they sat, the three of them, seated around a much larger cauldron and joined by all those of their coven: Arnica and Holly, and then the Rhymer in his green cape. Wren was there with her lute, and Robin seated just behind her. Flying Raven was making notes on parchment with her quill. There, why there was Poppy! They hadn't seen him since Beltane when he was called back to the elven land. And there was Iris! Her image looked quite strong. Why, she must be working the rituals of the Renaissance Tribes... They hadn't thought her to be practicing the old ways. Perhaps they should invite her to become part of the working group.

Gino's energy looked bright. Behind him were two shadows. Those must be his parents who encouraged his beliefs but who had not joined the Earthkin. Jewel and Lotus sat cradling their baby, Dagon. Dagon looked quite fey in the astral! Near them was Amber. Behind her was a faint image of a man. Was that Quicksilver? Would he be joining their Circles in the coming year?

Amethyst was sitting next to Holly, but Crystal was lying down, her head in Amethyst's lap. At least Crystal was there: that meant she was healing. But where were Phoenix and Pearl? They should have been present as well...

The notes from their voices cried out into the darkness as they began the litany: "Come dear Goddess, come this night... Join us in this fearsome night..." Line after line of invocation was chanted. Suddenly the flames in the cauldron flashed high, startling everyone.

"She is mine this night." The Goddess had appeared, large and mighty, her arms holding the limp body of Mildora Dolorum, the pastor's elderly mother. "I shall take her through the Gates." And she opened her arms and the woman's dead body fell down into the cauldron.

And Her voice shook them again. "He is mine this night." The Goddess stood tall, holding an emaciated corpse in Her arms. "It is time for him to enter the Summerland."

"It's Phoenix," Holly said, "something's wrong with Phoenix."

"He's dead." Pearl entered the circle from the Northeast, her image cowled in a black robe. "His body could take no more. Thank the Goddess for Her arms. I could take no more."

They turned, again, to look at the image of the Dark Goddess.

"He is mine this night," She repeated, and let her arms drop Phoenix' body which disappeared into the flames. "He is but one of many. Each of you, look at Me." Their heads turned to gaze upon Her. "I am the face of Death and I am walking the land. Weep not, for behind My scythe's reach comes the light."

And She disappeared as the cauldron went black.

Holly and Arnica sat there, stunned. Dark Star edged closer. The room was quickly cooling. The fireplace, itself had gone dark. All the candles, save the black one in the center of the altar, had been extinguished.

Hallows Eve had come and gone.

XVI - Merrydale's Surprise Yule Tree

Iris stood at the table, the thick braid of her hair draped over one shoulder. "Should I light the candle," Merrydale's postmarm asked. "Are we ready to begin?"

"Aye," answered Pastor Dolorum, minister of the Church of the Martyr. It was Dolorum who had asked for this secret meeting. His brow was furrowed as he spoke of how essential it was that the Politicos and Users knew nothing of this meeting. These arch-conservative factions within the Kristos religion had grown in political strength and were attempting to impose their intolerance upon all peoples.

"Pastor, would you bless this flame?" asked Holly. Holly and Arnica sat next to each other across from Dolorum. Arnica knew there was value in keeping this meeting secret even from the Earthkin. Many would not understand an alliance with what they perceived to be the 'enemy' and others would be too quick to talk, letting their love of gossip be the downfall of this friendship.

"Why, thank you, Holly. I would be honored." Dolorum rose to his feet. Holly and Arnica quickly stood and all four held hands around the table. "We ask of the Father that this light..." Dolorum colored a bit and stumbled on his words. "We ask of the Father *and the Mother* that this light be both inspiration and birth." Three 'Blessed Be's' were a counterpoint to Dolorum's 'Amen.' No one said anything, but Iris and the two men were visibly touched that Pastor Dolorum had given an inclusive blessing. The warmth among the four grew and they sat to get down to business.

"Friends, I asked for this meeting. There are many risks, as you will soon learn." Dolorum looked at Arnica. They had shared a bond since last Candlemas. Dolorum had asked Arnica to bless a candle in the old ways for the Pastor's mother. No Renaissance peoples attended Mildora Dolorum's funeral last month. Although many knew the elderly woman loved the earth and was sympathetic to their religion, it would have created a ruckus among the Users. Dolorum cleared his throat and continued.

"The Politicos have decreed that Merrydale must have a creche scene. They are determined to create an image that everyone within miles of Merrywood follows the Book of Doom. You may know that my own mother's great grandmother, may God bless her, was of Descendant Tribe blood."

Arnica and Holly were visibly startled by this. Iris interrupted the man, "That explains why your mother was sympathetic to the Earthkin?"

"Yes," answered Dolorum. "I tried, tactfully, to mention that there are many peoples of many religions here, but Hatchitt began quoting from the Book, out of context, but in such a way that no argument could avoid getting quickly out of hand. I spent a night in prayer and found my answer. This is why you are here and also why I asked for complete secrecy. There is much to risk. Should I lose my position at the Church of the Martyr, and Hatchitt would like that, their Elders would hire a new minister who would help them with their desire to eradicate all traces of the old religions."

Arnica looked at Dolorum with new respect and admiration. "What, my friend, can we do to help?"

"You know that I am bound to the decree. But I believe that, if handled the right way, we can integrate many of your customs and further strengthen the bond between the Earthkin and the Kristos. Since Iris' march to Fern Hollow, many of the Kristos see a common concern for the ecology to be more important than a focus on religious differences. I believe I have a plan which can work, but only with your help."

With that they began talking quietly, passionately. Holly made notes and Arnica made lists. They knew there would be some way to present the real nature of Merrydale without excluding the Kristos nor angering the Users and they believed that their completed effort would bring the Earthkin and Kristos together to share in the true joy of the season, no matter how the concept of rebirth was observed.

There was much excitement building. Dolorum had been very creative, convincing his church elders to fund a framework with large canvases so that the site was kept hidden from view until the Sunday morning before Kristmas. How interesting they found this! With Kristmas on a Friday, this year the actual solstice was within an hour of day break *on that very Sunday morning.*

Rather than placing the creche in the center of the town square, it was decided to place it just north of Merrydale at the edge of the wood. It took some fast talking by Pastor Dolorum on this one, something about the Kristos walking from the Church of the Martyr and arriving just beyond the town and how that would be like the wise men arriving at a stable. "They bought it," Dolorum said, excited just like a boy, when he told Arnica the news.

During the day there were the sounds of construction. Three men from Dolorum's church volunteered to do the carpentry. They were building a facade of a stable. When Hatchitt insisted that it look like a church and have a large cross upon it, Dolorum countered by reminding the politician that Jesus' stable would have looked quite rural. "You mean ... pagan?" teased Iris.

"Well, 'rural' allows us to follow through with out plan," said Dolorum. They had never seen him look so radiant and happy with life. This entire project was, without saying a word, in memory of his mother.

At night, when the workers had gone home, Arnica and Holly's Circle emerged from the woods. Unseen by the village, they moved the workers' ladders to the trees and did *their* work. Lights were to be allowed. Whether or not to allow lights had been a contentious point among the elders of the Church of the Martyr. When they balked at the idea (thinking it too pagan), a deft comment by Dolorum pointed out that the church in Mill City went all out with their decorations. "Why, the Cathedral of Thorns had so many show up for their Kristmas services that they paid off their new bell tower," Dolorum mused. Despite Hatchitt's objections, the potential for increased donations won the elders over and yes, there could be colored lights and an aura of festivity.

Dark Star, their hatchling from less than two years ago, had grown strong and she proudly carried the baskets of decorations along the path through the trees of Merrywood. Unable to climb ladders nor wield a hammer, mostly she had to stay out of the way although she was quick of hoof to scamper over and pick up something with her mouth to help out. Dark Star's work was to help tote things to the scene late at night and walk back even later with the tired men. Arnica's old bones did not take well to late nights.

"Get down from there," worried Amethyst. Crystal always did have a streak of tomboy in her and there she was, perched by one leg on the high rungs of the ladder, happily hanging small, ivy wreaths by red ribbons.

"Hey, Amethyst, I'm just fine. Reach over there and throw me up another bunch of circlets. How do they look?" Crystal loved physical work. She had already worked with Lotus to string thousands of lights in the trees. When they got the huge carton of ivy wreaths, she stepped forward to volunteer to hang them in the trees. The wreaths came from Amber, over in the River Mountains. They were made by the Descendant Tribes in a great ceremony. There was one for each day of the year which had been blessed with drumming and smudging.

Iris had worked on the star. It was to be a large pentagram. Five-pointed stars made no one uncomfortable during the holiday season. Just the most subtle colors brought together the four elemental arms and legs of the star to merge through the top point as spirit. When the workers returned the next afternoon, they were surprised to see the star poised up above the false roof of the manger but, surprisingly, they simply accepted all the changes and seemed to assume that Dolorum had a crew of workers there every morning.

The days passed quickly and soon the site had grown into a marvelous creation. On Yule Eve Arnica and Holly did a simple ritual in their Garden. Then, they snuggled up with Dark Star in the front room near the fireplace to sleep the night. Early the next morning, Holly brought the small bottle of elixir, the one made of powdered jade, black hellebore and male fern which made the hatchling's horn invisible to any but the most magickal. The bottle safely in the pocket of his robe, they set out early in the morning to do the Yule blessing at the creche site at the moment of the Solstice.

It was a perfect morning. There was snow in the mountains and the skies showed the promise of sunrise. Dolorum met them near the manger scene.

"I feel good about this," he said. "We've made it to the opening day without arousing any suspicion. You did good work."

"Thanks," answered Arnica. "Your design for the stable is wonderful. It truly captures the humble beginning of that birth. You don't think the multitude of lights and colored ornaments will be too much?"

"In my sermon this morning, I'm going to tell the parishioners that the lights in the trees are a metaphor for the wonders of the Universe - which they are," his eyes twinkled at Iris. "And tonight, at 8:00 sharp, the canvasses will be removed and *everyone* is to be invited. This may be the largest gathering of Merrywood folks to all come together in Merrydale at once, perhaps ever."

"We've spoken to the Earthkin and they'll be attending, bringing fruits and breads to share. The word is out that this is to be an ecumenical gathering and all the Tribes will go out of their way to avoid creating dissension. We feel good about this. And you are to be thanked."

Pastor Dolorum didn't know what to say. He looked down.

Arnica went on, "You know, it's been wonderful sharing these past days with you. I am grateful to know you better and to have had this time."

Both men felt a bit awkward, for there were no words.

"It's time," said Holly. Dolorum needed to go to his church for the 'final' sermon before the unveiling and Arnica and Holly had the last work to do. Just as Dolorum was about to depart, Dark Star trotted right up to the man and licked his cheek. The laughter was like music among the trees.

The sky was dark, save for the spangling of brilliant stars. The Church of the Martyr had asked everyone to bring candles and the gathering of about two hundred people was a-glow with the radiance of candles.

Dolorum stood on a small platform before the crowd. He spoke about promoting love and joy among all peoples during the Kristmas week. Arnica and Holly could not see - they were behind the canvas and would be out of sight just in the trees where the cables from the generator met in a large box before threading their circuits up overhead, into the trees. Dolorum spoke about this being the first day of winter and shifted so easily into the growth of light that Earthkin and Kristos alike felt he was speaking right to them.

As Dolorum asked everyone to blow out their candles, the notes of a harp began to dance through the air like the wings of a bird. Holly had set up a small player with a recording of the Rhymer playing his harp. The Kristos silently sang *their* words and the Earthkin silently sang *their* words and everyone was happy as the darkness spread. The old carol ended and the silent signal was given.

The canvases fell away and there was the scene. For just a moment there was but a sole candle lit near the crib and then everyone gasped as the trees were filled with the sparkling of thousands of lights. There, before them, was the entire scene: a family dressed in the ancient Israeli ways with the baby Dagon laying in the crib, playing with his toes. And there were animals from the woods, squirrels and several deer off to the side. And birds flying in and out of the trees, sheep and goats from a local farm, and there, next to the crib, a beautiful 'horse' named Dark Star.

XVII - A Candle for Pearl

"Steady, now," soothed Holly as he positioned Dark Star's head. The Unicorn's mane had been carefully braided to keep her long hair out of the way. She looked almost comical, her concentration was so intense.

"O.K., now dip," said Arnica. He had hung a loop of cotton string hanging straight with a small, round weight at the end from Dark Star's gold-hued horn. Holly gently stroked the unicolt as she lowered her head, the string dipping into a tall kettle of melted wax.

"That's good, sweet hatchling," crooned Holly.

"O.K., now up," encouraged Arnica. "Now hold it while we count..."

"Darksome night and shining moon, east then south then west then north..." Arnica and Holly chanted the first stanzas of 'The Witches' Rune' which were just enough for the layer of wax to set.

"O.K., now dip..." And Dark Star carefully lowered her head. Her cobalt blue eyes were focused upon the candle they were making for Pearl.

"Now up..." And the chant began, the words crafting the Magick the two men and their beloved unicorn were placing into the candle. Pearl was a lovely woman, her slight build showing her Pictish heritage. Her deep, red hair was like her Scorpio personality: concealing a fair-skinned vulnerability.

"Just a few more times," said Arnica, "Now dip..." As Dark Star lowered her head, the candle grew one more thickness. Pearl was having difficulty with the loss of her lover, Phoenix. Holly had spoken with her just after Yule to see how she was doing.

Lady Ellhorn, her grandmother, had answered the call and told Holly that Pearl was ailing. "Why, the poor thing seems to be losing her will to go on," said the Lady. "Phoenix had a good passing. Pearl worked the Circle and the elementals came in to carry his spirit to the Summerland. But since that night, last Hallows, she's not done much. At first I figured it was just the time she needed but more weeks pass and she's not even picked up a needle so I know something's wrong."

"Thank you, Lady, for your insight," said Arnica. "I think I'm ready to speak to Pearl now. I know what to say."

"O.K., now dip..." Another layer of wax, made magick with sacred herbs, was added to Pearl's candle.

"Now up..." And they chanted again. Dark Star could only whinny softly, but her eyes remained focused upon the candle hanging from her horn, right before her youthful unicorn face.

Several more times was the new candle for Pearl dipped into the melted wax. Dark Star looked so mature when she was helping on an important magickal project. Sometimes it was easy to forget that she was not even two years old.

But once the cord was removed from her horn, Holly opened the cabin door so she could trot out into the gardens and romp and play. The men knew that she needed to stretch her neck so it wouldn't be stiff the next day. "Young muscles are much more supple than our old bones," said Arnica, laughing. They watched the unicolt leap and frolic, chase imaginary butterflies and smell imaginary flowers. The gardens were still dormant, waiting the spark of Candlemas.

"Look, aren't they beautiful?" exclaimed Holly. He had just unwrapped a set of ribbons from Amethyst and Crystal. Amethyst loved to braid ribbons. There were several colors, carefully selected to give Pearl hope and courage. Crystal had taken very small gemstones and set them at the ends of the braided ribbons.

"The note says that these are to be tied around the candle as we raise the Cone of Power during our Candlemas Ritual," read Arnica. "They'll not be coming to Candlemas but hope be here the following Sunday. Amethyst has a concert scheduled. How exciting for her to be performing at Merrydale Center. She said they'll think of Pearl, sending her as much of the energy from the theatre as they can."

"Where should I put them," asked Holly, holding the ribbons up to the light, their colors shimmering as the stones glistened like wee stars.

"Right on the altar, next to the smudging sage that Amber sent," answered Arnica.

"How did you do with the song that Wren sent?" Holly's voice was bright, as if he was twenty years younger. He truly loved preparing for important rituals.

"It works well. My fingers don't seem to move quite quick enough for one line in the second verse, but I'll have it down in a couple of days. I sent copies of the words to Iris and Gino so they can help weave the song into the Circle." Arnica paused, remembering Wren's visit this past summer when she and Robin made the long trek from Highland. "It's quite amazing how easily she wrote rhyming words for Pearl's healing, using our Candlemas myth to weave Pearl into the magick!"

"How fortunate we are to have such a group of friends. Let's hope that we can reach Pearl and touch her heart," wished Holly.

And so their days passed as they prepared for Candlemas Eve. Ever so subtle morning came earlier and the sun set later, little by little.

Why, just the day before Arnica and Holly were touring their gardens, taking delight to discover that the peonies had new shoots up through the soil. It may be January, but their gardens are eager and waiting for Spring!

They wore warm, woolen robes even though the fire was blazing brightly. Many years Candlemas was celebrated in doors but this night was important. To be truthful, since the hatchling's egg first appeared (just two years ago this Sabbat) it was difficult to think of Candlemas being anywhere else but in the stone circle. The cauldron was set at the center of the circle and the five of them formed the points of a pentagram. Arnica and Holly sat bundled in matching deep-green cowled robes. Arnica was wearing gloves with the fingers snipped off so he could play his dulcimer.

Iris pulled her rust-colored robe about her. Down her back hung the point of a very long hood, reaching past her waist. It was a new robe, one sent all the way from the Mothervalley as a gift from Flying Raven. The Keeper of the Archives knew a weaver who lived at the river's edge who used wool from local sheep. Flying Raven had made certain that the hood would hang long enough to accommodate Iris' beautiful, long braid of hair. Right from the tip of the hood hung a new bell. Iris loved to adorn her ritual robes. Her oldest robes were a wondrous array of mementos of the most important rituals!

And there sat Gino. The young lad was the only one with his hood pulled back. "Typical boy," thought Arnica, smiling at the freckled face. Gino was snuggled into an old robe of Holly's. Still new in the Craft, he had but one ritual robe, a beautiful work of art hand-stitched by Pearl, herself. Phoenix and Pearl were his first teachers. Although but for a few Sabbats, he had bonded deeply with them.

The fire danced brightly, keeping their front sides warm. Dark Star completed the group. Now and then she would stay settled down so as to actually attend a ritual. Usually she loved the ritual dancing but often grazed upon the grass around the garden Circle. She was growing, however, evident in the way she helped making the candle for Pearl. Who knew what wonders waited in this unicorn's future?

Very focused, their voices chanted in unison. The fire not only kept them warm but served to help them focus their minds into the creation of single images. It was time to invoke the element of water...

"From the deep waters of Her eternal wisdom, brings She forth the Mysteries of Life..."

Their voices faltered as they were distracted by the gentle sound of bubbling water.

"It's back," whispered Gino, pointing toward a spot just beyond the west stone where a small spring of water had appeared. Just last year Gino joined them in ritual for the first time. They were startled out of their visioning by the sound of Dark Star drinking water from a small pool they'd never before seen! And there it was again, bubbling forth with a gentle sound.

They continued chanting, creating a web of images all about them. Soon they were in a sphere of Magick, protected against the weather, warmed by the cauldron but also by the power of the Universe which flowed through them.

The Circle almost prepared, Dark Star sprung to her feet. Arnica had hoped she would stay focused, but she was, after all, just a unicolt. The older man almost started chuckling out loud but remembered to remain focused. They would soon be consecrating Pearl's candle and her health was more important than his humor!

Suddenly, a voice broke the stillness. "I am the beauty of the green earth and the white moon among the stars."

Not a one of them spoke. They knew the words. In fact, they were soon to begin the Charges of the Goddess, but there, Her hand resting upon Dark Star's neck, was the Goddess, Herself.

Something splashed in the small pool. Instantly, four heads turned to look and She continued. "I am the Mysteries of the deep waters..." Her words brought them back, turned toward the cauldron and to Her. "And the desire in the hearts of humans. When you have need of anything, call unto Me, for I am always here."

Arnica began rising to his feet. His movement brought them all into motion. He held the new candle. It's iridescent colors radiated the fire's light. The miniature stones sparked with brightness. "I understand," spoke the Lady. "Phoenix is resting with Me. He has found that there is peace, freedom and reunion with his ancestors and his loved ones who have come to join Me in the Otherworld. He sends his love and he asked Me to offer My hand to Pearl. Give Me the candle. This will be My last act before I seek renewal."

Arnica offered it to the Goddess. When She took it, he could feel the slightest touch of Her skin. It was like being kissed by the purest of Magick. The Lady took the candle and walked around them to the East stone.

"Lords of the East, creatures of air, come! Watch this rite, fill it with air!" Her voice called out strong as she invoked all the facets of elemental air. A large, pale yellow unicorn flew down, out of the night. As it knelt before Her, it gently folded a pair of gossamer wings. The Lady held the candle up high and the ribbons swirled in the breeze.

Dark Star could stand it no longer. This was the first other unicorn she had ever seen, not counting her father, Andrius. Astral though he was, they were kin, nonetheless. She impulsively danced right over and as the Goddess finished Her invocation, the hatchling touched noses with the unicorn known as Raphael, Keeper of the Breeze.

As the Goddess went to the other three cardinal directions, each brought forth a wondrous, elemental unicorn and Dark Star was a sight. Her reaction to other unicorns was a delight. Her curiosity at life's wonders was the very magick Pearl needed to begin moving forward with her own life. As the Lady and Dark Star finished their work in the north, the fire in the cauldron seemed to burn brighter, the flames dancing higher. The Lady turned to them.

Instantly, the fire went out. "Take this," She said, handing the candle to Iris. "It is in your hands now. Send it to the woman and she will heal quickly. Now I must go. Spring will soon be coming and I am tired. I have not yet rested since the birth of the sun child and I am weary. Turn your eyes, for I will bathe in your western pool."

They all pulled into their robes, the hoods drawn over their heads and their eyes closed. The fire out, they even pulled back. Only Iris' fingers were extended, holding the candle for Pearl. A loud splash of water, and somehow they knew they could open their eyes and would find the Circle dark, the Lady gone.

XVIII - Blessing the Seeds

"Are you alright?" Holly asked Arnica. Climbing up and down the ladder, garlands of ribbon draped over his shoulder, Arnica occasional verbalized the sound of his old bones.

"I'm fine," Arnica answered. "My knees will do better once we're into Spring and I'm out gardening in the sun. My joints will get their summer blood. What do you think?" He held a long trail of ribbon high above the altar.

"Oh, dear One, it looks so beautiful in here. Maybe a bit to the sunward side so the ribbon clears the candles. You know we must have candles upon the altar for Dark Star's birthday!" Holly's eyes sparkled with humor.

"Lots of candles!" Arnica laughed. "It may be only her second birthday. I don't think she'd be thrilled with only two upon the altar. What adventures we have had these past two years since our hatchling came into our lives. My beard has more gray, but it's not been caused by Dark Star."

The Hatchling

"So much has happened. Do you think Pearl will be back in time for the party?" Holly was setting up the temple for the celebration. "And what do you think about our hatchling? She's growing, quickly it seems, will the day come when she no longer fits into our cabin?"

"Hopefully she will not grow faster than a colt but I think about that as well. She's still small and, if the gods are willing, she'll always have a place in our home."

A small celebration was planned to honor Dark Star's second birthing day anniversary. Just two years ago the morning of Eostara Eve, the large egg discovered right in the center of the stone circle had hatched, bringing Andrius' daughter into their lives. What a beautiful unifoal she was.

"I'm here," a voice called out into their kitchen. "Have you a cup of coffee for a cold postmarm?" Iris, now a member of their Circle, was a frequent guest. Her face was glowing for it was a cool walk from Merrydale this year. She tossed back the hood of her woolen cloak, her long, thick braid tumbling out.

"Iris, you're the first and yes, we've a cup of warmth for you. Give me a hug," greeted Holly. "What's this?" he asked, seeing a wrapped parcel in her hand.

"It's a small, carved quartz egg. When you hold it up to the light the natural pattern inside the crystal looks almost like a little Unicorn. I thought of her when I found it... guess where? At the apothecary, of all places."

"Dear sister," said Arnica, coming quickly into the kitchen to embrace his friend. "We're so glad you could make it. We sent Dark Star out into the woods to search for the first trillium."

A knock at the door interrupted their greetings. "Better step out of the way," Holly suggested. And the door opened as Amethyst and Crystal came into the cabin.

"We're here, we're happy and Spring is almost upon us!" said Amethyst, always cheerful in her outlook. Amethyst's hair was growing longer, braided with ribbons and shells.

"Merry Meet," cheered Crystal, her short fair hair mussed by the wind.

"I thought you were going to let your hair grow," commented Iris to her friend.

"Well, I was. My vision quest bade me keep my hair short for a year and a day. My time was ended last Beltane," said Crystal, "but it's so comfortable that I've left it as it was."

"Hello?" a voice called out, the sound of a gentle rap at the door.

"Come in," they all called out at once, causing the cabin to be filled with laughter. "Pearl!" they all shouted, again as one.

"I'm here. I'm back. I've finished my promise to Phoenix but for one thing: I have some of his ashes to strew back near the stone circle." Pearl entered the cabin wearing a beautiful, embroidered cape. She was well-known for her skill with needle and thread and the fabric draped around her small, Pictish body. "I lit the candle you made for me last Sabbat... and I realized that my place was back here in Merrydale with you, my friends. Lady Ellhorn sends her blessings and wished I would stay but I've promised to visit her and I found a young woman to help her with her house. She's a proud old woman and I'm so glad I had those months with my grandmother. I don't think I could have endured Phoenix' last days without her strength."

"Oh, my friend, let me get my arms around you." Arnica held her close. He had not seen her since she took Phoenix to Cloverville, hoping that the warm, dry climate would provide a cure. Arnica and Pearl had written often and, since Phoenix' passing last Hallows, they had spoken often.

"Is Gino coming?" asked Pearl. The boy had first begun his studies with her and Phoenix a year and a half ago and she had missed him.

"Any minute," answered Holly, "and he said he can't wait for you to see him wearing the robe you sent him. He's grown."

There was another knock at the door.

"Come in," called Holly.

Nothing happened. The knocking repeated itself.

"Come in," Holly called, louder, which only led to more knocking. He went to the door, wondering who it could be!

"Dark Star!" Holly burst out laughing. There she stood, the first trillium of Spring hanging from her mouth as she'd carefully brought it from the woods. She'd been knocking with her horn!

The six of them raised a party of noise as they brought the hatchling into the temple to begin the celebration of her birthday. Later that evening the rest of their Circle would arrive.

Just a year ago, eggs hung from the hawthornes. But as Eostara Eve arrived with the softness of a dark, star-filled night, the temple was lit with candles, the ritual Circle prepared. They sat upon the floor busy at work. Arnica and Holly in their matching robes with white cowls emerging from richly sewn overlays sat just east of the northeast portal, the gateway to the 'Otherworld.' At Holly's left sat Gino, quietly focused upon the handwork before him taking great care to avoid soiling the beautiful hand-stitched robe made by Pearl, who sat just to the left of Gino. In front of each was a hard-boiled egg and each member of the circle was focused upon decorating an egg which would represent the seed of one's desires for the coming growing season.

It was, for Pearl a joyful event but one which reminded her that the last time she sat in circle with her friends, Phoenix was yet alive, there as her ritual partner. Her slender, Pictish fingers moved quickly, applying small daubs of paint, creating intricate designs. Iris sat to Pearl's left, just in front of the south altar. Working with colored pencils, she worked designs collected from her astral journeys upon the hard-boiled egg held before her.

Next were seated Amethyst and Crystal both in robes of a deep purple interwoven with silver threads. They were creating magick upon their eggs with glue, adding tiny sea shells and a few tiny semiprecious gems amid small bits of glitter and ribbons and thread.

The surprise of the evening was Pastor Dolorum, himself. Increasingly active in his sympathy toward the Earthkin, since the secret meeting before Yule at which he invited several Elders of the Renaissance Tribe to assist in the creation of Merrydale's creche scene and 'Yule' tree, he had begun to recognize his own heritage. Arnica looked over in amazement, remembering it only a matter of months since Dolorum had told him of his own Descendant Tribe blood, passed down through his great grandmother and mother. And here he was, having asked to learn more of the Renaissance ways. Dolorum seemed a bit nonplussed, for the ritual symbols were still a bit foreign to him but he seemed intent upon working his needs for the coming growing season into his egg. Why, he would certainly lose his position at the Church of the Martyr were any one outside their circle to know Dolorum was seated there - among *pagans*, no less - wearing one of his clerical robes. He was too new to have a ritual robe of his own.

Continuing deosil, to Dolorum's left were Jewel and Lotus. Jewel worked hard upon the decoration of her egg. She was not yet accustomed to leaving Dagon with a sitter. In another Sabbat and a few days Dagon would be two and Jewel wisely knew her toddler needed to begin establishing his independent identity. Her tweed robe was tucked around her as she wrote her wish upon the white shell. Lotus, a skilled carver, had brought a small but fine knife with him and a dark black marker. First coating the egg the color of midnight, he was etching away his design so that it shone white through the black.

And next, just on the other side of the altar, in the northeast portal itself, lay Dark Star. She was not quite so fidgety as she was during her first rituals. Unable to use her hooves to decorate her own egg, she kept one close to her which Arnica and Holly had decorated the night before as she carefully watched.

"A sigil to keep our hatchling safe from any harm," said Holly using a small quill pen and magickal ink to mark the egg before handing it to Arnica.

"And the symbol of the Goddess Who has taken you on many journeys," added Arnica, then marking another design. And so it went, with their quiet, private wishes. Dark Star looked from one man to the other, feeling truly grateful to have been born on their land and becoming part of their lives. Who would think that humans could be so wonderful?

When everyone had finished their work, all the eggs were set carefully upon the altar. Holly had removed everything but the candles and set a serving tray in place. No one wanted *their* eggs to roll off upon the floor. They stood quietly, adjusting their robes and preparing for the chant.

"No room to dance the Rune tonight," mused Arnica, and he began singing the chant. One by one the voices chimed in as they wove a spell with the words. As they began the chant for the third time through, Dolorum's voice grew stronger as he had quickly picked up the words, finding them strangely familiar.

The chorus of voices built a strong, cone-shaped vortex of energy and in an instant, they stopped, moving not a muscle but holding the magick strong within the center of the temple. It was palpable, so strong no one dared move and then, as she would, Dark Star bent low and touched the tray of eggs with her horn as if blessing them with her magick wand. Everyone broke into fits of laughter, releasing any extra energy and grounding their auras.

Now it was time to carry them out into the brisk night air and plant them deep among the trees so that their dreams would come true.

XIX - Ribbons From Her Horn

All was quiet in the cabin. Holly was in the temple with Dark Star, working with his orb. Since last Hallows when he discovered that he could 'hear' her speak while gazing in the crystal sphere, he had been working to develop his skill during his quiet times. Holly experimented with different techniques, holding the orb to his ear, to the center of his forehead, even placing it against Dark Star's forelock. The hatchling thought that was funny and whinnied almost like laughter.

Arnica was quietly working at his desk, planning this year's herbal crop which he hoped would be mature in time for the market later this summer. Dark Star had developed quite a taste for borage. Whether it was the beautiful, blue pentagram-shaped flowers or simply the magickal property which brought courage, all Arnica knew is that he'd better add at least two new beds simply for the hatchling's favorite herb!

It was so quiet in the cabin. The only sound in the little office was the sound of the pen scratching upon the paper. Holly was quietly 'listening,' exploring Dark Star's thoughts. Holly was perplexed. He scrunched up his blue eyes and looked at the unifoal with big questions in his mind. Why was he seeing a storm cloud? He opened his mouth to ask the hatchling why he was picking up this odd image when the peacefulness of the cabin was shattered by a frantic knocking at the door. The sound pierced the late night.

"Who could this be at such a late hour?" asked Arnica, all but running to the door. Turning the latch and pulling it quickly open, he saw a distressed-looking Pastor Dolorum. "My good man, what can be wrong?"

Dolorum, his dark face pale and his body speaking of anxiety, quickly stepped into the cabin. Holly and Arnica had not seen him look so stricken since the death of his mother. In fact, since Dolorum had begun exploring the practices of his Descendant Tribe ancestry (and even attended ritual!), he had never looked so at peace with himself.

Dolorum was trembling and his face ashen as he spoke. "It's the new bishop. I tried reasoning him but he looked at me so intensely that I was fearful he would know that I walk in both worlds. He... he..." And his voice broke off.

Holly stepped up to the man and embraced him. "My friend, calm down and feel this warm hug. It's safe here in our cabin."

Dolorum calmed considerably and his breathing slowed. "They've banned all Maypoles. It's now a felony offense to have one on public or on private land anyplace within the districts of Merrydale and Merrywood."

"But why? Why would they do that?" asked Arnica.

"The bishop appointed two more Elders to the council at Church of the Martyr, both of them staunch members of the Politicos and supporters of the Users. They've been alarming the other Elders with insidious comments about the pagan origins of some of the Kristos customs which we've used for so long no one can remember. May I sit?" The three men sat down around the small kitchen table and Pastor Dolorum continued. "Not all of the Politicos reacted. A couple of them even tried to defend these customs as highly desirable but the new Elders questioned their faith... and you know in these times that such a public accusation has no defense other than submission. So I tried meeting with the bishop in private. I questioned whether it was reasonable to impose the Kristos beliefs upon the Earthkin peoples in our districts. His face grew red and he jumped to his feet.

Staring me right in the eye he said, 'and I've been wondering about *your* faith, Dolorum. Seems to me you might not be a good representative of our faith.' And I mumbled something about asking permission to rethink my position and quietly left."

"No Maypoles? No Maypole in Merrydale?" Holly was shocked. "Why there's been one every year for the children."

"But even ours would be illegal," Arnica thought out loud.

"But no one would have to know," offered Holly.

"It's too risky," said Dolorum. "Why, this Eostara was only my first Sabbat. I know it was good. For the first time I felt the thread of connection that my mother learned from her mother and her mother's mother. I know that I can continue as the priest for the Church of the Martyr, that I *can* bridge both worlds and that no one has to know. But the new appointees to the council were talking about the bishop beginning to use informers and spies. He would just love to find out that I have become part of your Circle. We don't know who they are, but if they found out that you had a Maypole here that information could be used to ruin your herb business. You *know* how they are."

"Yes, I do..." Arnica was quiet. They all felt silent. Holly and Dolorum could tell that the old herbalist was thinking. Just then, Dark Star trotted into the room with a garland of flowers around her horn.... "Dear man, are we 'allowed' to gather with friends for a picnic which just happens to be the last day of April?"

"I don't see why not," answered Dolorum.

"I'm very sorry to say it, but it might be safer for you if you do not attend our Beltane Eve celebration. Be with us in spirit... Would you get for me some lengths of ribbon?"

"Why, of course," Dolorum answered. "How long do you want them?"

"Oh, maybe three to four feet long."

"Should they be any special color?"

"Whatever you want. And, is there by chance a length of ribbon which might have belonged to Mildora?"

"Why, there must be. I still have my mother's sewing things and she used ribbon. But why?" asked the Kristos minister.

"If we can't have a Maypole, then I will transform us into Maypoles," Arnica answered. Holly laughed out loud. "Certainly there can be nothing wrong with someone wearing a garland about their neck. Look at the Hatchling - she brought me a clue." Oh, she looked so proud as the three men turned their gaze to Dark Star and to the ringlet of dried flowers.

Holly got excited. "I can see it! We'll attach the ribbons to the garlands and then we can each 'be' a Maypole and dance freely. But why do you want a ribbon from Mildora?"

"Beltane may be a celebration of fertility, of the union of the Earth Mother and Sun Father, but it is also directly across the Wheel of the Year from Hallows, which observes death."

"I understand," said Dolorum. "I feel much better. You are correct, I must be very careful. Some days it is very tempting to abandon my work at the Church of the Martyr but I believe I can reach more people and help keep their minds from closing. And I do believe in the goodness found in the teachings of the Krista. It's just that I don't think it's the only way and I believe that the Kristos Conserver Party folk need my help. The two seats they gained in Parliament could easily be lost if there was a scandal ... or if I was replaced by a priest who supported the Users. I'll send the ribbon and a letter to you through Iris. It's the safest route. Everyone loves the postmarm and she has good reason to be in contact with *everyone* in the district. I'd best head home, now, because it's very late." Dolorum rose to his feet.

The three men all moved to the kitchen door and embraced. As the three stood there, breathing in unison as they visualized a healthy, growing tree, they were interrupted by the nudging of the hatchling's horn and the room was filled with laughter. Dolorum went back into the dark night with his cares eased and his heart lightened with song.

"Guess, guess, guess what I brought along?" Amethyst was so excited, she was just like one of the children she taught at the Merrydale school. "It's bells, bells, bells. They're so cute. We can stitch one to the end of each ribbon. There's a whole bag just filled with little bells. I can't stand it," she laughed, "this is so much fun. I feel like a little girl." And she went dancing off to the garden circle, her long dark-brown hair itself braided with ribbons and bells.

"Can you believe it?" said Crystal. "She's been like this all day long ever since she found all these bells at a yard sale. She's been giddy... and it's wonderful." Crystal was sitting upon the mown grass, sewing ribbons onto her neck garland. A straw hat, the same color as her short hair, shaded her eyes from the afternoon sun.

"Who sent that ribbon?" asked Gino. And before Crystal could say a word, the freckled boy's enthusiasm spilled right over. "Look at this one," he said, holding up a narrow ribbon of brown velvet, "it's from my *father*. He sent it express and said he went to the best store in Mill City. Oh, I'm sorry..." Gino's head bowed.

Crystal laughed. "It's from Amber. It was made from hand woven fabric. She asked two ladies of the Loon Tribe to weave a narrow strip, just for me. Isn't it beautiful?"

They sat about the yard, laughing and sharing stories about their ribbons and sewing them onto the rings of lace and cord and flowers which would fit about their necks. The growing difficulties in the local councils brought them all together. The topic was divisive in Merrywood and sure to be addressed in Parliament, but for now, they were happy to be preparing for Beltane and realized they didn't need a Maypole to celebrate, after all.

Jewel and Lotus loved the idea. Arnica's plan was for each to wear a garland from which hung ribbons gathered from friends and loved ones. After the Circle was prepared, they would dance around the garden circle and along the paths between the herb beds. This was something that the toddler Dagon could try. Since his time in the Realm of the Faerie when just a couple of months old, they'd waited to see him in his first ritual and this was perfect. No prouder parents could be found anywhere. Their ribbons included many which Lotus gathered from the folk for whom he'd carved ritual items. He was well-known for his ability to work with wood.

Iris and Pearl were sitting over near the hawthorne, sewing and quietly talking. Iris' involvement in their circle had really begun while Pearl was away at Cloverville and they discovered how much they enjoyed each others' company. Iris was known for her wit and earthy humor and it helped Pearl heal from Phoenix' death. Pearl was sewing a long teal-blue ribbon sent to her by her grandmother, Lady Ellhorn, as Iris fell back and lay on the grass, laughing aloud as Pearl talked about the way in which some of the older Kristos women referred to her as a *widow*. The very connotation of that phrase put sparks in Pearl's eyes!

Arnica and Holly sat over near the greenhouse. The gardens were filled with bloom and the yard was full of laughter. Why, this might be one of the best Beltanes they'd ever had. Dark Star danced about, running the path back to the stone circle, then prancing among the friends. How excited she was. After the ritual dancing tonight, the circlets would be placed upon her horn and she'd be sent off on a mission: with ribbons streaming from her horn she'd run through the night to a select list of houses to hang one of the magickal wreaths from each person's door. Arnica added a pair of cobalt blue ribbons sent to him from the Highlands by Wren and Robin. Why, Wren's music could be felt almost vibrating in the satin! On the other side of the same circlet Holly was sewing a jade green ribbon from the Rhymer. As others laughed and joked and had fun, they worked quietly, sewing magick into these ribbons. *This* wreath was for Dark Star to hang upon Pastor Dolorum's own door!

XX - A Warning From the Faerie

It was a quiet, late-spring evening. The sky was so clear that one could peer deep into the Universe. The gardens were covered with a cool dew as the night air condensed. Holly sat in the rocking chair with a log gently burning in the fireplace to keep away the damp inside their cabin. Rubbing "Holly Oil" into his staff, the scent of this special oil permeated the front temple. 'Holly Oil' was the source of jokes between the two men. Arnica had made the oil in stages, gathering the hyacinths at Eostara, the hyssop blooms at Midsummer and the hollyhocks at Lammas. And yes, there were some holly flowers in the oil as well. All the herbs began with the letter 'H' for Holly!

As he sat and worked the oil into the long staff with his fingers, Dark Star, their Unicorn hatchling now two years and almost two Sabbats old, lay with her head across his right foot. The cabin was so very quiet. Arnica was in the kitchen making a tincture of *Digitalis purpurea* to send to Lady Ellhorn, grandmother of their friend Pearl. The Lady lived far to the south in Cloverville, a seven day journey by carriage but Iris, the postmarm in Merrydale, could get a parcel sent express reaching Lady Ellhorn while the tincture was still fresh.

Arnica was gently stirring a beaker of flowers and chopped root, his eyes focused upon the candle-lit photograph of Lady Ellhorn lent to him by Pearl. His voice, barely a whisper, chanted the words to a healing ritual as he balanced the tincture to the natural powers of the Universe. There was no sound in the front temple other than the quiet, rhythmic sigh of the floorboards as Holly rocked, his mind beyond words as he was both working the oil into the staff from the outside but had placed his awareness within the staff, experiencing the warmth of his fingers as if he, himself, was the sacred wood. And the hatchling? Well, if you listened close, you could just barely hear her snoring, she was so at peace with the world.

Just then there was a light 'tap-tap-tap' at the door. Not disturbing, yet clear enough that Holly began readjusting his mind as he heard Arnica's voice fall silent as his partner's footsteps walked across to the kitchen door.

Arnica opened the door and there stood Wren, wearing a long, green Novice Bard's cape, carrying her lute case in one hand and a traveling bag in the other. "I'm here for Midsummer," she said simply. "The Rhymer told me I was needed here."

"Ah, come in," said Arnica, caught a bit by surprise. "I knew *something* was likely to happen, but I didn't know we'd be so fortunate to have you here. What a blessing. Where's Robin?"

"Robin's still in Highland. She's all caught up working on a special project for her former employer. When the Rhymer told me I must open the portal to the Realm of Faerie this Midsummer, I asked her if she couldn't take a break to come here with me but she has so much work to do and this also guarantees that our gardens will be watered while I am here. I brought my lute," she said, holding up the case, "but I guess you can see that. Did you know that Echo is to be here as well?"

"Echo?" Arnica was pleasantly surprised. "No, I didn't expect this at all. We had planned a quiet Midsummer, working our ritual back in the stone Circle. Recent political activity has given strength to the Politicos, you know."

"Ah, it's been the same back in Highland, as well. The Kristos have spearheaded a drive to force the Politicos to pass a law making the only legal union one conducted in a Kristos church between a man and a woman. I don't think it stands much of a chance, but their very audacity is alarming." Her luggage set down, the door shut, Wren removed her cape and she and Arnica wrapped their arms around each other and held a warm embrace.

"Wren!" exclaimed Holly. "How fun! You'll be here for Midsummer's Eve?"

"Oh, yes," Wren's gentle voice warmed the room. "In fact, that's the nature of my visit."

They talked late into the night, even though Arnica had to rise before the sun, a mighty early hour this time of year. Wren explained to them that the Rhymer was journeying into the Eldritch and visiting the astral Gardens of Lothloriën when something alarming happened. Out of the mists stepped some of the faerie with a very clear message. "A Bard must be waiting at the hour on Midsummer's Eve. A message awaits." And that was it.

The Rhymer gave serious thought to making the journey to Holly and Arnica's stone circle himself. He knew that it would be best if a Renaissance Tribe elder entered the Realm of the Faerie. But the journey from Loriën was long and difficult and the Rhymer travelled only with great difficulty. He called Wren and told her that she was ready, that this was her journey to take. Wren, having played the Rhymer's harp only last year at Lammas, was now ready for her first walk into the astral as a Bard. The Rhymer knew that Arnica's training as a Renaissance elder would provide her with all of the additional support she needed for this perilous quest.

As a crescent moon lit the woodlands and gardens with a soft glow, all turned in for the night. Although Arnica's sleep would be but a few hours, the energy permeating their cabin was intense. All three knew that there would be little sleep until the Midsummer's journey was complete. All but Dark Star. She was already sound asleep in the front temple. Wren laid out her traveling bed next to the hatchling and soon the entire cabin was sharing the same dream...

"You all know that the portal to the Realm of the Faerie is open this night," Arnica was speaking to their circle of friends. Heads nodded, but Jewel and Lotus knew only too well that the portal would be open. The memory of their baby Dagon, only one year old, being carried into that Realm upon the Hatchling's back still woke Jewel. It was difficult for her to learn to let Dagon out of her sight and it took her some time to calm herself for a rare night such as this when Dagon would be left in someone else's care.

"Dear Sirs," asked Gino, "do we have anything to fear?"

"Not a bit," chuckled Holly.

"It's just that this is serious business. We have been asked to bring back an important message and there are, for she who must pass through the portal, certain risks. Once touched by faerie, one is never quite the same. The Rhymer, you know, is a bit other-worldly."

"And Dagon," Lotus interjected, "his eyes bespeak a level of wisdom beyond his years." Known for his woodcarving skills, Lotus was nonetheless a proud father. "Already he's begun to speak and I *know* that he thinks about things almost like an elder."

"Friends," Arnica tried to bring focus back to the temple, "please let me bring us back to the ritual we are about to begin. Once the Circle is cast in the garden Circle, I will take Wren by the hand and guide her back to the stone circle."

Holly let out a quiet gasp. Why, he and Arnica were never separated during ritual. Together they worked the polarities and kept the energies in balance.

"I will be carrying my staff, the one Lotus made for me some years back, with the large fluorite set in the top. You will all continue working the Circle except for Holly, who will take the very center and remain there, moving into a trance and working to create a link between the ritual's energy and my staff. And I will make that energy available to Wren. When all is done with the Circle, keep the energy flowing through Holly. Keep it strong until we return." The room fell silent as they suddenly realized the import of this Midsummer's Eve.

Arnica stood at the northeast portal, Wren and her lute just behind him. Holly was at the Circle's center holding his freshly oiled staff. Dark Star was sitting back, her horn constantly pointed to the top of Holly's staff. For a hatchling, she had become skilled in taking her part as a unicorn in the ritual world of humans. Pearl and Gino stood at the East in beautiful hand stitched robes. Lotus and Jewel were kneeling in the south, tending the fire in the cauldron. Iris was at the west, gently pouring water into the basin, the sound dancing through the circle in a gentle music in counterpoint to the crackle of the fire. Dolorum knelt in the north. A Kristos' minister here in secret, he felt comfortable kneeling when giving honor to the Earth. Helping him with the element of earth was Echo, an infrequent guest. She was much-loved for her slightly bawdy songs and hearty laughter, but this night she was still and focused.

They walked slowly, Arnica and his staff leading the way. Wren strummed her lute as she walked. Words from the ritual followed them as they moved through the trees. "Oh thou Circle, be thou a meeting place of love and joy and truth..."

At the entrance to the stone circle, Arnica stood aside as Wren stepped to the center of the circle and sat, moving into a Bardic trance, letting the magick of the trees bring the music through her fingers. More than an hour passed. Arnica could feel the pulsing of the energy coming through the giant, arching firs and directed it from the fluorite to Wren's seated figure. Her body moved with animation as if she was carrying on a conversation with an unseen presence. Arnica remained just outside the Circle. This was not his to see on this magickal Eve. And then she stood, her eyes shining bright, reflecting the visions she had witnessed.

"They have spoken." Wren sat with her back to the altar. The eight friends sat upon the grass so that they completed a Circle with her. Dark Star lay in the center, her nose nuzzling at Wren's hand. With one hand Wren felt the Uni-kisses helping her return to the manifest world and with her other hand she caressed Dark Star's forelock.

"Their kindred are threatened and they need help. Vast numbers of the faerie are dying. The safe, dark places of the world are being destroyed. Thousands of their sisters in the rain forest have lost their homes. Now, a highway carries heavy trucks and noise and pollution. The elders among the trees in the River Mountains are losing their homes to poisons which come with the rains." Dark Star looked at Wren, a tear running down her cheek.

"Yes, even the unicorns will be in danger if we cannot turn the tide."

"But what can we do? We are so few and those in power do not listen to us." Dolorum was ever ready to quietly attempt to turn his congregation to doing good works although he was increasingly frustrated that he was unable to bring enough change. Of late he'd had to pull back from some of his activism, having attracted too much attention from some of the Politicos.

Wren was silent for a moment, then spoke. "The Faeries warn us that time runs out. It will not be gone in a human lifetime. Indeed, while time is perilous and short for them, in human years there is enough that too many can coast in their complacent attitudes. But we, those of the Earthkin, are being given direction. You, Iris... I am to tell you that your path is to become an Initiate of the Renaissance Tribe. Echo, you also. Madrona, Faerie Queen, said I must tell you that you have too long held yourself back but that you must become a Priestess. And I..." Wren's voice faltered and her eyes closed.

Dark Star shifted her four legs forward until her head was laying in Wren's lap. Her ears were up and attentive, waiting for the words. Suddenly Wren's voice came through strong and clear. "They brought me to meet my soul and they embraced my heart. I - I am now a Bard," and she began crying, the sheer intensity of the experience now bathing her in tears.

Wren slept very soundly that night.

XXI - The Sanctuary

"Iris, could we open a window?" asked Holly. "I think there's too much smoke in here for Dark Star"

"Do you know what?" laughed Amethyst with a toss of her long, blond braid. "We're sitting in a smoke-filled meeting just like the Politicos do when they're making an economic deal with the Users."

"Only this is from smudging, not cigars!" Pearl was almost back to her former laughter. Being back in Merrydale with her Circle was so good for her. She continued to do ritual for Phoenix since his passing the previous Hallows, but now it was a weekly working, not daily.

"I'll do it," Gino offered. His freckled face radiated such happiness. He loved being with these magickal people. Although still in middle school, his parents were grateful for the changes they saw in their son as he grew from his studies with Pearl and with Arnica and Holly.

"Are we ready now? Can we begin?" Iris looked at the group of friends gathered in her living room. It was a full room and this was the first time they'd all met in her home. Maybe she'd smudged just a little too much? But the times were dire and this was such an important meeting. No, things were just fine.

Arnica stood to begin the meeting. Everyone grew quiet. A light summer breeze wafted through the room. The room calmed, he sat back down again and said, "let's hold hands and begin with our chant, but quietly for the words of Magick can carry easily to reach the wrong ears.... Breathe deep..."

"Rowan tree, blossom and bloom..." Their voices blended together in a chord which wove sounds and notes together. "Willow tree, put down roots..." Dark Star, the unicorn colt, lay in the middle of the room. Forming a circle around here were Arnica and Holly at his left; then Iris, the postmarm. "Hawthorne tree, blossom and bloom..." To her left were Pearl and then Gino, teacher and student.

Amethyst and Crystal were seated on the floor and snuggled together in an oversized chair behind them were Jewel and Lotus. Lotus, known for his skills at carving wood, was holding their two year old baby, Dagon. "Holly tree, bring forth fruit..." Next was Amber, representing the Descendant Tribes, here all the way from the River Mountains. A long, raven-colored braid draped over her shoulder and landed in a coil on the floor between her crossed legs. Their voices wove a sound every bit as thick as the sage smoke was earlier, filling the room with a gentle intensity.

To Amber's left was Dolorum, a dark man who walked in both worlds. A member of their Circle since Eostara, the rest of Merrydale knew him as the Pastor of the Church of the Martyr, a respectable man despite his occasionally being a little too concerned about ecological matters. But he seemed like a good Kristos man. And, at Dolorum's left, completing the circle was Echo, still here from Red Mountain Plateau. Echo lived near the Highlands but was spending two months in Merrydale, completing an important part of her studies. The group of friends were happy, for Echo's sense of humor brought much laughter into the world.

"Holly, would you describe what we were told by Wren at Midsummer?" Arnica turned to his younger partner.

Holly moved to the center of the room and sat on the floor next to Dark Star. Leaning over, he nuzzled the hatchling's nose with his own. Holly was such a gentle spirit that it was painful for him to think of innocent beings dying.

"When Wren was brought back from the stone Circle, she brought the message from the Realm of Faerie. There is much cause for concern. Over the coming decades, unless the world civilizations begin a dramatic change, more and more species will be lost. The faeries are losing their homelands and each time a species of plants becomes extinct, a Deva is forever lost. The message given Wren is that even the unicorns are in danger because of what is taking place on our planet. Many of you were there. Am I missing anything?"

Jewel's russet-colored hair was pulled back, her arm around Lotus. His lead was leaning upon her shoulder as the baby Dagon slept in his lap. "I remember that part of the message seemed to stress that it is very important that we, as individuals, work hard to learn the Mysteries and to bring them into the world." Jewel's voice was like gentle music. "Iris, you were urged to seek Initiation, weren't you?"

The postmarm, always uncomfortable being the center of attention, nodded. "Yes, and Echo as well. Madrona, the Faerie Queen, said we were to complete our pathworking and become Initiates of the Renaissance Tribes."

"But those are long-term goals. What about the Devas who are in danger now, this very summer? What can we do?" Dolorum looked at Arnica.

All eyes turned to Arnica. His eyes, in turn, moved to Holly and Dark Star. He smiled, then spoke, "My friends, I have given this much thought, and I have a plan... In the past we've celebrated the Harvest Days sabbat by blessing our gardens and ritually gathering certain herbs and grains and fruits to begin the harvest season. But this year we're going to extend our Harvest Days ritual out into the trees and meadows of Merrywood." Arnica turned to Echo.

"Over the past months Wren and I have been making music together," Echo said. "She would play her lute and I would sing. We were working on some new songs for our rituals but one evening she played a new melody and I mimicked it and one thing led to another and soon we began this sort-of game in which Wren would play a melody on her lute and I would imitate it with my voice."

"Tell them what you and Wren did before she returned to Highland." Holly was very excited and his eagerness quickly caught everyone's attention.

"Well..." Echo loved sharing a good story. You could hear her love of the dramatic. "As a Bard, Wren can hear the music of the faeries. Wren stayed for a fortnight following Midsummer and the afternoons and evenings she and I would go walking. Wren carried her lute and every so often she'd sit and let the plant spirits move through her. As the notes danced into the air like bright gems, I worked to imitate the sounds so that the shape and color of the melodies was clear. These songs will help lead us to the more endangered of the species growing within walking distance of the cabin. Wren's music has woven a map and I can sing my way through it."

"This year," Arnica said, "to bless the beginning of the harvest season, we're going to begin rescuing the Devas and providing them with sanctuary here in our gardens. Bring your gardening tools to our Harvest Days ritual!"

And so they did. They looked quite a sight, gathered in the garden Circle. The just-risen sun was filtered through the slightest mist and leaves in the early morning. There were no robes worn to this ritual. Garden shoes and garden clothing, long sleeves to protect against mosquitos, straw hats for the sun made them look anything but a Circle of friends, well-trained in the rituals and beliefs of the Renaissance Tribes, dedicated to preserving the sacredness of the Earth. Only the simplest of ritual tools sat upon the altar. There would be no candles, for they were working their Harvest Days ritual early in the morning and it would last for many hours. Unattended candles were hazardous.

The ritual tool of choice was the boline, traditionally a white-handled knife used for digging and cutting. Each had brought a small collection of blessed gemstones, small trinkets and things of beauty and value to leave behind. They all knew that one must never take from the plant world without leaving behind a gift. And they carried botanical identification books, trowels, spades and flower pots, all to be blessed before setting out. Dark Star had a pair of baskets hanging across her back. She thought this was great fun. Her young unicolt legs were happier walking and running. Although she loved participating in the rituals, an adventure was far more appealing.

"Mother of the Harvest, Goddess of the fields...

"You Who bring our dreams to ripe, You Who bless the yields..."

They finished invoking the element of Earth and then set off on their Quest. Echo carried a staff to help her walk. Walking long distances was not easy for her and her friends would be scattered over quite a distance. But her name was a reflection of a gift she had, able to transport her singing to a distant tree or hill and have it reverberate back. The others would be able to follow the notes she would sing even if a mile or two away! Echo offered a silent prayer of thanks to the Goddess before she led them out of the garden Circle. As Dark Star followed Arnica and Holly, she stopped and looked up at Echo. The hatchling formed her thoughts for Echo to hear, but Echo was not trained to hear a unicorn's thoughts as Holly and Arnica were. Realizing that this wouldn't work, Dark Star's tongue gave Echo a big lick and she followed her two men off to the trees. The first sound to permeate the meadows and valleys of Merrywood was the laughing sound of Echo's pure delight!

Hours ago, when they left the Circle, they looked bright and alert. Now as they straggled back, they looked happy, but their knees were muddy, their fingers tired. Some had walked as many as fifteen miles, carrying their tools and increasing weight of plant species. The clear morning air had allowed Echo's voice to carry a great distance and the natural magick of the Sabbat gave Echo's legs more strength than usual. They knew that this was only the first of such plant gathering rituals they must do over the coming years.

Iris arrived with a plant in a pot. "The last of its kind," she said. "I don't know exactly what it is - some type of arum - but I heard its spirit talk to me. I was led there by the sound of Echo's voice. It was as if her singing was softly coming right from the flower. Look at the faint striping on the flower. Isn't it simply beautiful? And I have four other plants as well."

"This is a seedling from a small grove of trees." Dolorum held up a heavy, two gallon container holding a baby tree, no more than a foot tall. "I thought I heard Echo singing in a small grove and, upon moving into their midst, the elder trees told me that this one seedling was the only one to survive. Seven elders, now past the age of bearing fertile seed, they're the only ones of their species left. Remember that large tract of trees cut down a year ago last Eostara? It was their homeland and hundreds upon hundreds of them were killed."

Each one of them had stories. A few knew the names of the species they had rescued. They wrote descriptions and locations and had made notes to provide as much information as possible. Amber was very skilled with her pen and colored pencils and had taken the task of collecting seeds. On the outside of each envelope she had drawn a beautiful and accurate depiction of the flowering plants.

Arnica and Holly had led Dark Star over some rough terrain. They had found an endangered reed, *Papyrus merryvar*, alongside a stream. Two pots held bronze oaks. There was a golden-hued trillium which they would never have found but for Dark Star leading them through much foliage to the small patch of three trillium leaves, now dying back for their seasonal hibernation.

"My friends, what a great work we have done today. All together we must have nearly a hundred species which we can plant and preserve. In future rituals we'll be able to dance with the Devas and know that the Realm of Faerie has been strengthened." What Arnica didn't say out loud (but Holly knew what his friend was thinking) was how much work it would take before these plants were safely planted in new beds!

XXII - Tithing Echinacea and Goldenseal

It was unusually warm for this time of the year. The equinox was nearly upon them yet it felt like early August. Only Gino didn't seem to mind the heat. It was nearly two years ago that he had come into their lives. Now twelve years old, his bright smile and eager ways were always welcome at the cabin. A large bucket of soapy water sat upon the grass as Gino used a sponge to wash down Dark Star in preparation for the trek into Merrydale. The hatchling, now a most handsome young unicorn, returned the favor, taking an occasional lick at the youth's freckles.

The sight caused much laughter around the potting shed where Arnica and Holly were taking down bunches of echinacea and goldenseal roots. Using a soft brush, each root was given a light scrub to remove any dust. Spirits were joyful around the gardens, for this was an exceptional harvest and the prices for both herbs were at an all-time high on the market. It was going to be far easier to pay the tithing this year. Despite a movement by two of the Politicos to increase taxation, the rate had remained the same.

"Do you remember when we..." began Arnica.

"First saw Gino in Merrydale?" Holly easily finished Arnica's thought. The two were inseparable and each usually knew what the other was thinking. "I was just thinking about that. Well, almost. I was wondering if you had enough of the potion for Dark Star's horn."

"I checked earlier this morning. There is more then enough. Either this batch was stronger than usual - which is possible given the potency of the black hellebore this year - or our hatchling's horn may be developing the ability to remain invisible on its own." Arnica enjoyed working with the herbs. He was considered one of the more knowledgeable herbalists in the land, even though he was not so public about it. "Here, I think this is the last of the echinacea. Eighty bundles, just think of that!"

"And look at all the goldenseal! This is the first year we've harvested it and there are sixteen more bundles than we had of ginseng for last year's harvest." Holly always felt a sense of relief knowing they would do well at the herbal market. "It's good that we can give the ginseng a rest. I bet we'll have a great harvest next year."

"Well, gods willing, but Dark Star will have to continue growing strong. I don't know just how we would have gotten this year's harvest to market without her," Arnica began chuckling, looking over at the antics of the hatchling and the freckled lad.

"Aren't they a sight?" asked his partner. "What a blessing it has been having Gino in our lives."

"She loves him, doesn't she? Well, sweet one, let's take the garden inventory and then begin packing for the trek into town."

The walk into town was uneventful. Here and there they commented on locations from which they had collected endangered plants, bringing them back to plant in the sanctuary of their gardens. What a Lammas they had celebrated with Echo, their friend from the Red Mountain Plateau. With her voice guiding them, they had located nearly a hundred species of plants, some already believed extinct. Nearly all were thriving in the loving environment of the gardens. Many mornings Arnica and Holly would rise, look out a cabin window to see the hatchling carefully making her rounds of the gardens, checking the new plants out. There was a relationship between the young unicorn and the plant devas which was beyond the human realm. Although they did not understand, they were grateful for Dark Star's attentiveness and the love with which she helped the plants take root. Only a couple had not made the transition.

"There, just a mile through the woods, is where we found the *Papyrus merryvar*, a type of reed found no where else," Arnica told Gino.

"What a hike that was," Holly added. "We had some steep hills and a lot of brush to get past before reaching the stream. It's one of the plants that didn't make it, isn't it?" Holly's voice grew quiet.

"Yes, that and the one type of bronze oak. But there is more *merryvar* and we'll bring it back and give it another go in more suitable weather. I'm so glad Echo came all the way from the Highlands to help us find our deva friends."

"Look," exclaimed Gino, "we're almost there. I can read the sign from here. And look at all the people at the crossroads." Their country lane was soon to merge with two more-travelled roads. There were many people, some with horses and carts, most carrying bundles and all wearing fine, bright clothing. The visit to the tithing agent would set the great market in motion with its fair atmosphere. The increase of population in Merrydale and even in the wooded areas of Merrywood was making the equinox more and more of a festival.

Their journey to the tithing office was most enjoyable. Although known as hermits, Arnica's herbal skills were well known and Holly's cheerful demeanor and ability to remember everyone's name and personal history meant that many sought them out. It was Gino's role to stay close to Dark Star. Despite the popularity of the men, it would be dangerous if people realized that Dark Star was a unicorn. To their eyes, the magick potion upon her horn allowed them only to see a lovely horse.

As they entered the tithing office, Mr. Pounds left his desk and went to the office door. "Folks, I hope you won't mind but I have to ask Arnica about some herbs for an... um-mm. personal matter." The people waiting in line tittered in amusement, enjoying Mr. Pounds' embarrassment.

The door safely closed, the government official spoke in a subdued tone. "Sit down, my friends, there is something I must relate to you."

The sudden change in Mr. Pounds' demeanor quieted Arnica and Holly. They sat there, expectantly. The portly gentleman walked around his desk and sat down facing them. Once well known as a Politico and supporter of their ways, Mr. Pounds was appointed to his office. He was well liked at the Church of the Martyr and each morning read from the Book of Doom as did all faithful Users. But there were lines of anxiety in his face. Arnica knew that Mr. Pounds had quietly shifted his vote to the Conserver party.

Pastor Dolorum was one of the few whom the agent could trust. Both of them remained prominent and seemed strong Politicos in the public eye, but both Dolorum and Pounds no longer trusted the goals of the Users and were growing increasingly alarmed at what they saw taking place throughout the land.

"Something has happened," the man said simply, drawing a white handkerchief from his suit-coat pocket and dabbing at his brow. It was obvious that he was ill at ease. "I knew I had to speak with you, knew that you are aware of my growing sympathy and support for the Earthkin despite my need to keep it very secret. My subterfuge was the only way we could speak in private without drawing attention. I'm asking you to mumble something about me having hemorrhoids after you leave the office. Public embarrassment and humor is safe. What I have to tell you is very dangerous."

Holly's hand reached over to take that of his partner. Arnica said gently, "Go on, Mr. Pounds," his voice weaving a cloak of secrecy about the small office.

"There are reports." Pounds was edgy. This was not good news. "Government records indicate that the ocean temperatures are the highest in recorded history. The media is talking about the *el nino*, but it may be more than that. The Politicos still hold control in Parliament and the Committee for Internal Affairs has yet to accept a Conserver. The Committee is trying to keep the reports and studies hidden from the public. Despite their efforts, news of the deteriorating ozone layers continues to be leaked to the press. I suspect that one of the Politico committee members has grown sympathetic and intentionally is trying to alert people."

"I watch and read all the news I can," said Arnica. "I've suspected as much. I don't think that this would come as a surprise to most people, even though we've had some successes in preserving Merrywood."

"Well, the Users are all in denial," answered Mr. Pounds. "They still believe they can continue to plunder the earth's resources as they wish with no regard for the future. Sometimes I believe they've replaced the Cross of Blood with a money bag as their sacred icon. It scares me, sometimes. Reports which have not been leaked to the media indicate that it is likely the global temperature will be running three to five degrees higher for the next ten or more years."

"Is that so much?" asked Holly.

"Oh, yes," Arnica said with a sad note running through his voice. "It's enough to turn Cloverville back into a desert. It's enough to cut the harvests east of the Red Mountains down to half."

"And with the growing population, this is cause for grave concern," added Mr. Pounds. "And that brings me to my news. A developer, I have not been able to learn his name, is trying to purchase all of Merrywood. He's begun and bit by bit has already amassed eight parcels of land. It's not much, but it's all done in secret. He has employees who are trained to act as if they are Earthkin, who purchase land from the elderly who are retiring from the land. Rumors I've heard around the inner Politico circles of Parliament are that the developer intends to acquire the entire tract of Merrywood, cut all the trees and sell them for wood, and turn the land under. Here the rise in temperature would be hard on the crops during the summer, but during the winter we'd still be growing. Much money would be made supplying food and fiber to the rest of the country."

Arnica suddenly sat upright. "You mean there's a plot? The environmental reports are being kept secret so some of the Users can turn a huge profit?"

Mr. Pounds said nothing. The sadness as he sighed an assent told it all. Then he raised his head and said, "we must open the office and go on as if you've talked about my embarrassing condition. For now, this cannot go beyond your inner circle."

Holly colored slightly. They had thought their circle was a better-kept secret. But certainly the gathering of the same small group of friends on the Renaissance Tribe religious days would make anyone who is aware begin to add it up.

"Just remember to make suppositories of the slippery elm," Arnica said as if in private but just loud enough to be heard by the first eight or nine people in line. Mr. Pounds did his part and blushed. How did he do it? What a marvelous job of acting. By the time Arnica and Holly reached Gino and the hatchling at the post office just two blocks away, they could be certain that everyone waiting in line (and many others as well) already knew that Mr. Pounds had 'secretly' sought Arnica's advice for hemorrhoids.

"Iris, we must hold a highly secret meeting. And I must ask you to quickly begin work sewing this year's corn dolly." One final jar of herbs each year was covered with a doll and skirt to represent Mother Nature. "Watch and listen for any news related to the ecosystem, the environment, and in particular anything related to the sale of any parcels of land within Merrywood's district."

Iris tugged at her long braid. She couldn't put her finger on it but this confirmed her intuitive sense. There was definitely something afoot. With her left hand she took Holly's right and with her other, she took Arnica's hand. Gino completed the circle with Dark Star's head leaning over the lad's left shoulder, as if intent upon every word being said. None of them had yet guessed the hatchling's role in the events of the next two years! The energy surged through them, then they stood quiet. A few hugs, and the men and boy were on their way, quietly walking their 'horse' back to the cabin in the woods.

XXIII - The Jar Dolly

Iris sat at her kitchen table, her fingers nimble yet showing a life of hard work as they plied the needles. Working the magickal colors of yarn, Iris was knitting the jar dolly for the Hallows ritual. A custom of the Circle, the jar dolly covered Arnica and Holly's jar. Iris paused and looked at the jar, sitting upon her altar flanked by a pair of candles. The facets of the cut crystal sparked in the light. It was very old, having been passed down from Arnica's grandmother. Arnica's mother presented it to Arnica and Holly at their Handfasting.

'The return address says it all,' Iris thought. Her forehead showed the signs of worry. Ever since Wren brought back the message last Midsummer's Eve from the Realm of Faerie of the dangers from the plunder of the forests and rivers, Iris had watched the mail pass through the Merrydale post office with her careful eyes. Something was definitely going on. Her fingers continued to knit the basic form of the dolly. She tried to keep her mind centered within the interior of the crystal jar, but thoughts from the outside world continued to distract her.

'Arnica was definitely agitated after he and Holly came from Mr. Pounds, the tithing agent's office. What happened? Our Circle's energy has shifted since then. What can it be?' Then she took control back of her thoughts. Reaching over to a small shell, she took several beads sent her by Amber. Good friends, they were allies in Merrydale. Amber's Crystal Emporium had been a gathering place for many of the Earthkin, but now she was back in the River Mountains with her Loon Tribe family. Amber and several of the women of her Circle had made these beads during the dark of the last new moon, fashioning them of clay and of blood and drying them in a small kiln set over the open fire. Their energy was so strong that Iris put two of them back, wanting to place only one at a time over the needle to be knit into the jar dolly. 'What powerful magick,' she was thinking. Knit-purl, knit-knit, Pearl... 'Pearl?' Iris thought, 'What does Pearl have to do with this?'

And then, out of nowhere, the answers to her worry became clear. Why, the Society for the Forest, an organization which recently began sending out mailings from Mill City had the same, the very same address as the Cathedral of Thorns! And old man Hatchitt, that red-faced angry man who carried his Book of Doom with him, had brought a sheaf of flyers for the Society right into the post office, demanding that she hand them out to all the patrons. Why, Hatchitt was one of the strongest and most vocal figures of the Users, the radical, right wing faction of the Politicos. When Iris declined, saying that the government office could not do that, his face darkened and he threateningly said, "We'll see." 'They're all connected,' Iris realized. 'I must complete this jar dolly and get it to Arnica as quickly as I can.'

Just then a loud knock at her door startled her so that the next bead slipped from her fingers and rolled across the table, coming to rest right against the shell, safely. Iris rose, her back a bit tired from the long hours at work, and went to the door. She was not prepared for the two figures standing there in the night.

"Gino! Dark Star! Why, what are you two doing out so late at night?"

"There's no school tomorrow, Iris," answered Gino. "Holly was working with his orb, practicing listening to Dark Star when suddenly he stood up and called for Arnica. The hatchling was telling Holly something about Iris discovering the answer."

Dark Star whinnied in her unicorn manner and moved closer to Iris, leaning against Iris' arm and looking into the postmarm's eyes as Gino went on with his story. "After hearing what Holly had to say, Arnica asked me to come into Merrydale and tell the Circle that you must all come to the stone Circle in the woods, but you must take the secret path through Merrywood and only Amethyst and Crystal can come together and Jewel and Lotus and..."

"Slow down, young man," Iris began laughing. This was just what she needed to put things in perspective. A late evening surprise from Gino and the hatchling. "Dark Star, I can almost see your horn." Iris looked at Gino.

The freckled lad smiled broadly and reached into an inner pocket of his jacket. "See? Arnica trusted me with some of the elixir made with jade and secret ingredients. The jade is the only one I know. Oh, no, I said it!" Gino was obviously very excited to be trusted with this mission.

Iris sat the boy down and made him a cup of warm tea, setting a plate of ginger biscuits on the table. "Dark Star, I have just the treat for you," and Iris brought out a small bunch of borage blooms. "Guess what? These grew protected by my little greenhouse. They're the last of the season and just for you." Iris knew Dark Star simply loved to munch on borage blossoms. As soon as Gino was warmed up, she sent them on their way. They had several other stops before Gino would head to his mother's home and Dark Star would take a fast trot back to the cabin where Arnica and Holly were waiting. Pearl's house would be next and now Gino had messages from both Arnica and from Iris!

"Holly, we're supposed to be serious for Hallows," Arnica's graying beard trembled as he laughed at Holly's antics. Wearing his new long johns beneath his robe for this brisk night, Holly said something about them being a little tight in personal places and then began dancing about the cabin, trying to stretch them out. It was a pretty amazing sight, to be sure.

"There, I think that's better. It's so important to concentrate on this night and I know I can't be scratching during those parts of the ritual," Holly said. The affection between the two men filled the cabin with warmth. "Did Dark Star head back to the stone Circle?" asked Holly?

"She's restless tonight," Arnica said. "As near as we can figure, there are seventeen species of plants which have been lost. Their devas are out crying for help, their voices mingling with those of the human dead."

Holly's face was instantly somber. "And I spoke to Lotus. Dagon is two, now, and Lotus took him to a barbershop for his first haircut. Actually that part was sort of funny, Lotus joking about it being a male rite of passage. But Lotus said he overheard a local Kristos man in the shop quietly talking to one of the Politicos, saying something about the frogs on his farm hatching with deformities. Arnica, things are getting worse. Sometimes I feel frightened."

Arnica's arms embraced Holly and they stood there, quietly for a few minutes. "Go get your Wicca basket," Arnica said, with a twinkle in his eye knowing well how Holly enjoyed that pun. Holly's 'Wicca basket' was an old picnic hamper he had fixed up for toting ritual tools back into the woods.

Soon they were walking through the gardens to the woodland path. Arnica carried the large cauldron, filled with ritual things which would be used on this sacred night. Holly carried the Wicca basket, in which was carefully packed the best chalice, over a century old. It was made of an unknown crystal, one which seemed remarkably similar to that found in one of the steps leading to Lothloriën's astral gardens. Capable of changing colors, it usually ranged from crystal clear to a golden color for the sun. But tonight it seemed darkened, a color which neither man had previously noticed.

After walking the path through the trees, the stone Circle became apparent by the glow. Extra kerosene lanterns had been set about to keep the chill at bay. It was quite bright within the ring of stones. Some of the others were already waiting, hooded and quiet. No one was talking, now, each having begun their solitary work. Since Arnica and Holly's woods had become a sanctuary to shelter some of the species from extinction, each ritual, each Sabbat seemed more important and more intense.

Hatchitt's rumblings in Merrydale had not gone unnoticed. Almost each day every home's mailbox carried unsolicited flyers and letters which *seemed* to support saving Merrywood but the Earthkin shared news whenever they met. Someone important in Parliament was suppressing news about the environment. The Committee for Internal Affairs maintained that trees could be harvested without ecological damage, that the odd reports about the ozone layer, about *el nino*, about things too disturbing to talk about were simply flukes and the wild imagination of radical Conservers. Everyone was growing more tense. Meeting in public in Merrydale meant speaking in quiet, hushed tones. And there were rumors about what might be happening in Parliament in Mill City.

Dark Star was sitting on the ground, looking lovingly at Pearl who was caressing the hatchling's horn. It was just a year ago that Phoenix left his pain-torn body for the last time. Tall, lean and wearing his best black cape, Dolorum, pastor of the Church of the Martyr, was lighting the charcoal so it would be ready for incense. No one outside their Circle knew that Dolorum, appearing to be an upstanding Kristos was now active within the Renaissance Tribes and expected to communicate with his mother this Hallows. Lotus, hand-carved staff in hand, was setting up the south cauldron. His fame as a wood sculptor growing, his partner Jewel had stayed home with Dagon, now two and a half and a bit restless in adult Circles. Gino was playing in the water, watching the candles and lantern light dance in the glass ewer which would be poured forth into the basin as the invocation to the west was read. And Iris, the quiet tinkling of bells hanging from her rust colored robe, was quietly meditating upon the element of earth in the north. Arnica and Holly were setting the altar tools upon the altar. Just as everyone finished, something shifted and silence permeated the woodland.

Hands clasped, they formed a dancing circle as the movement of their bodies and the power of the ritual caused the flames to spiral upward from the cauldron in the center of the Circle.

"Summer's warmth has come and gone, let us light the fire,

"Call our friends form Avalon, If they so desire...

"Near we now the gates of death, on this fearsome night, we'll

"Call lost loved ones from within, to join us in this rite!"

Just then the flames burst forth. Hands parted as each stepped back, startled. Standing in the midst of the cauldron's flames was.. Phoenix ... at least an image of Phoenix! "I'm not lost and I did desire to be called." Phoenix had his wry humor with him even from the Otherworld. "My love," Phoenix' voice reached toward Pearl.

Shaken, Pearl's arms were wrapped around Dark Star's neck for support. "Iris has told me," Pearl answered, "and I am prepared. There is no one I trust more than you, my love."

Turning toward Gino, Phoenix' voice was at once the sound of thunder and the gentle music of a baby bird. Later, when trying to describe it, not one present could find words. "Son, have you what Pearl needs?"

"Dear Sir, I gave Pearl the pocket watch my father gave to me. He'll know to trust her if he sees that." Gino was fascinated. He was too young to realize what it took for an incarnate human to move through the Gates of Death and back. Not wanting to frighten him, Pearl had said nothing. Arnica and Holly wondered if even Pearl knew the risk.

Phoenix reached forth his hand, Pearl took it and just like that the flames disappeared, and so did Pearl. Dark Star pawed at the ground near the cauldron, then turned to Holly. "She's worried," Holly said. "Our hatchling believes she should have accompanied Pearl to Mill City."

"Now our vigil begins," Arnica's voice was quiet. "We must keep the Circle vibrant until Phoenix brings Pearl back to us. Gino, I only hope your father will understand what is happening to him." No one spoke. They sat upon the damp grass and pulled their robes about them to ward off the chill night air. This was a Hallows none would forget.

XXIV - Birthing the Light

It was quite an amazing sight. Dark Star, laying on the floor near the fireplace, was having a wonderful time with some scones Pearl had made just for her (with no sugar) which had been spread with borage jelly! A hard freeze a few weeks before had claimed all the remaining borage plants. Pearl knew that borage blossoms were Dark Star's favorite and she had devised a jelly recipe. Dark Star was in unicorn heaven.

The cabin was filled with nearly all of their circle. This was the first time some of them had even seen Pearl since her Hallows adventure. Not only did they want to hear of her astral journey to Mill City but they wanted to meet Lupine as well. The cabin was filled with the most delicious scents, each household having brought their favorite food for the potlatch. Arnica provided warm mugs of his 'Magick Tea,' a recipe kept secret in his grimoire.

The Yule Eve ritual complete, the sharing of food was a wonderful way to celebrate the birth of the sun and take time to socialize. The ritual working completed the decoration of the Yule tree which looked quite stunning with the hand-made ornaments including Holly's new strings of bright peppers, a striking red against the dark fir.

Jewel and Lotus shared a chair, their plates perched upon their knees. Now twenty months old, Dagon was playing on his rug near Dark Star, his favorite toys a chalice and a toy athame carved from ash wood by his father, Lotus. Jewel's corn bread, bean and walnut casserole was very popular this evening. Lotus stood, bending his lanky frame to kiss Jewel upon the forehead. "I'm heading to the kitchen for more of your dish before it's gone." They would not be spending the night out in the stone Circle. Jewel knew that Dagon would undoubtedly waken them before sunrise!

When Gino learned of Lupine's return, the lad Arnica and Holly met a year ago this past harvest was first concerned that his role in their lives might be diminished. But he learned that he had actually gained a new friend. The freckled boy was so proud of the role his father, working for the flour mills on the other side of the mountains, had played in Pearl's adventure. The pocket watch was almost never out of Gino's sight. Gino's plate was full, it seemed so much for such a small frame, yet this was already his second serving of everything and he showed no signs of slowing!

Iris sat across from Pastor Dolorum, both in animated conversation with Amethyst and Crystal. In their midst was a basket filled with fresh currant muffins, chocolate chip cookies and apples from Holly's autumn harvest.

Arnica caught himself yawning. It was getting late and Gino had school the next morning and it was a work day. Arnica stood up with a slight groan as that of a fine, wood floor. He sometimes made noises when his 'old bones' shifted postures. Holly nodded to Dark Star who, in a quick motion, raised her head, her horn sweeping across a small set of wind chimes which had been hung conveniently at hand, or would that be 'at horn?' The room quickly grew quiet.

"Dear ones," Arnica said, "we have much to cover and time grows late. With sunset so early, we easily lose track of the night hours. Dark Star is older this year and should have less difficulty staying up until sunrise. A few of you must leave (Gino groaned - he had school the next day) but the rest of us will soon be heading back to the stone Circle where we'll spend the night with mulled cider and a fire in the cauldron, waiting for the first ray of the new sun. Stay the night with us among the stones, but dress warm. There's sure to be a nip in the air this year." Arnica looked toward Pearl, catching her eye to see if she was ready. Her small, Pictish features were always striking candlelight. Pearl turned toward Lupine, indicating that she wanted him to speak next.

"Dear Lupine," Arnica said. Holly squeezed Lupine's hand, a gesture of a deep, brotherly love. They smiled at one another and exchanged a gentle kiss. Lupine rose and went over to Arnica. Arnica's arm went around the young man's shoulders. "We first met Lupine," Arnica said, "some years ago. Lupine was just a pup, learning of his interest in the Earthkin. One night he saw a vision in Merrywood of a wolf which howled at the Lady Moon and the next day the Mother sent him on a learning quest far away, all the way to the east where he was led to gaze upon the great waters of the Atlantikos and gather vials of sacred water from south to north. Next he was led to Heartland, still far east from the Highlands, where he had to complete his karma and prepare himself for initiation into the Renaissance Tribes. Holly and I are very pleased to welcome him into our home and our family, for we have missed him."

A loud whinny from Dark Star caused the room to instantly erupt in laughter. She thumped her front hoof upon the wood floor twice to make sure no one missed her assent.

"That was to make sure you all know that our hatchling believes that Lupine has a long future with us, Holly?" Arnica turned toward his companion of many years.

Holly scooted over on the floor, his fingers playing in Dark Star's mane and, with his other hand, scratching her under her chin. The unicolt *loved* her chin scratches! "Our hatchling told me that long ago while in the Bardo, even before she was brought forth in the egg she had a vision of a lean, dark man who looked much like Lupine. In her vision she saw him knocking at a cabin door. There were the sounds of joy and laughter and the Three of Cups, only with male figures. It was the arrival of Lupine."

"My friends," Lupine spoke. He had a calming, deliberate voice. "I am grateful to be so welcomed into your Circle. During the many, long years of my quest I kept a watercolor image of Arnica and Holly with me. My journey took me to such distant places that although I fantasized that some day I might be returned here, to Merrywood, I did not believe I would ever again see this cabin. In my deepest dreams did I desire to apprentice myself to Arnica, to share my work and love with my soulbrother Holly. I have been accepted for training into the Renaissance Priesthood and I give to each of you my sacred word that I will do my best." Lupine suddenly sat down, unaccustomed to such a public declaration.

"Lupine, thank you for your candor," Arnica's voice settled the energy in the room. Still speaking to the young man, Arnica continued. "When you arrived just a few days ago, I told you that I would explain the work which we have been sharing. Last Autumn when we went into Merrydale to pay our annual tithing to the government, Mr. Pounds, the tithing agent, told Holly and me in secret that he had learned of a conspiracy among Parliament's Committee for Internal Affairs. Despite the growing crisis, global warming, the continued destruction of forests world wide, even the growing violence among the crowded cities, the Politicos refuse to confront the issues. Rather they are concealing reports from the public and secretly selling off public lands to be bulldozed for commercial and industrial development. Last Midsummer Wren, our dear sister from the Highlands, went into the Realm of the Faerie where they warned her that more and more of the devas are dying."

"But we've saved many of them, turning our land into a sanctuary," Holly added. Holly's thick moustache turned up as he smiled, proud of their success to date.

"And just before Hallows," Iris' resonant voice caught everyone's attention, "I put two and two together. Sometimes the Politicos are simple minded, not realizing that some of us actually *read* a return address." Iris was much loved in Merrywood as the postmarm. Only those in their circle knew that she was now an active priestess of the Earthkin. "There's an organization called the 'Society for the Forest' in Mill City. Turns out it's a front for the Users, the most right wing factions of the Kristos, working through the Cathedral of Thorns. We believed that they were trying to delude the public and, if successful, we believed they would be turning large areas of Merrywood into open pit mines for low-grade ore, the type which is highly polluting yet could turn many of them into millionaires."

"But what to do?" Arnica said. This was amazing to Lupine, the way in which they all shared the telling of a story so fluidly, as if they'd rehearsed it. Why, this must be the result of working together in a coven so well. Pearl stood and Lupine's eyes were drawn to her. She was so lovely!

"I never expected to see Phoenix at Hallows. Oh, you know we *believe* that our loved ones will step through the veil, but I'd just begun to get on with my life. Phoenix had been dead just a year, so I hoped I would have something, but suddenly, there he was speaking to all of us, *and we all heard him.*" Pearl now stood, feeling stronger. This was an emotional speech for her.

"Phoenix asked me for my pocket watch," Gino's voice, filled with excitement, took its turn, "and I gave it to Pearl."

"And Dark Star and I took it to Gino's father in Mill City. I, who had never before moved within the astral! I must have seemed like a waking dream when he saw me, but he recognized the watch he'd given Gino. 'He is fine and well, he's a good son,' I said, to assure him that I was not bringing fearful news. I spent nearly two hours talking with him while Dark Star moved about the city. I was exhausted when I returned, but I felt so good. I know that Phoenix is waiting for me in the astral temple, and that we'll be joined again." Pearl pulled her embroidered dress about her and sat. The stitchery of the new design shone in the light, one which depicted symbols of her journey. Pearl's needlework was a thing of magick: her wardrobe told the story of her magickal history. Still emotional over having spent time in the Bardo realm with Phoenix, Pearl looked pleadingly at Arnica.

"Thank you, my sister," Arnica's voice soothed her, and he continued the story. "Gino's father has been working in the offices of the Mill and one of the men sharing his apartment works for the cathedral. Although he leads the choir, he shares office space with the administrative offices. We'll soon have verification that a faction of Users within the Kristos is perpetrating a fraud upon all the people of Merrywood."

The room quickly filled with voices until Dark Star whinnied loudly and the tension was dispelled with laughter. Goodbyes were given, embraces exchanged, and Gino set out with Jewel and Lotus back to Merrywood. The others took up their ritual tools, Holly and Lupine carrying the great cauldron, and headed to the stone Circle in the woods.

"Oh, look!" Iris sat upright. She was more weather-hardy than the others, having spent much of her life hiking the hills and spending many nights with little more than a blanket while on long quests. Holly and Lupine were wrapped warm in a thick quilt, leaning against Arnica. The elder man had been gazing into the cauldron fire but was transported into the land of dreams right out of his meditative trance.

Iris nudged Dolorum. Not asleep, but so swaddled with his hood and his wraps (the Kristos minister was not yet acclimated to the Earthkin rites!) that he'd been focused only upon staying warm and was not paying attention. Amethyst and Crystal had brought a double-sized sleeping bag, zipped themselves up and were sleeping like spoons upon the pine-needle floor of the stone Circle.

But there, dancing by the east altar, were Pearl and Dark Star. Hanging almost from the tip of Dark Star's horn was a bright bauble. Pearl must have hung it there in the early morning light. The first rays of the sun had crested the distant hill and were filtered through the boughs, catching the ornament so it gleamed as of Yule fire.

Arnica added a couple of logs to the cauldron fire and suddenly, everyone was renewed by the reborn sun. "Blessed Yule," everyone shouted.

XXV - The Note In The Candle

Holly sat upright in bed. It was the very middle of the night and something was very wrong. He blinked his eyes, adjusting to the dim night light. Arnica was not in bed and Dark Star was not sleeping upon her rug. Holly climbed out of the warm bed and padded barefoot across the wood floor. As he stepped into his woolen slippers he took down his robe from the peg, quickly wrapped himself in its warmth, and headed out into the cabin.

There sat Arnica in his chair before the fire. Holly's companion was holding his large, crystal orb in his hands and he and Dark Star were gazing intently into its depths. Without even moving his eyes from the quartz Arnica spoke, "Something is not right... can't quite tell..." Holly walked over to the fire and quietly stood there, quickly shifting his mental processes so as to assist Arnica.

"Hello," a quiet voice heralded Lupine's walking softly into the front room.

"I just came out to find Arnica sitting here scrying," Holly said. "Why are *you* up?"

"I was wakened by a strange dream." There was an odd tone in the younger man's voice. "It left me feeling oddly frightened." Holly was about to ask a question but Lupine sensed it. "No, I can't recall how many years have passed since I had a bad dream."

Dark Star whinnied softly. The Hatchling saw something, of that they were certain.

"Water... water..." Arnica's quiet voice gave only the slightest hint of what he was experiencing. Stroking his greying beard, Arnica sat up, set the orb down and said, "we'll know before lunch."

"Brother, tell me of your dream." Holly's arm went around the dark-haired Lupine and they both sat next to Dark Star on the hearth rug. Lupine's fingers casually braided the hatchling's mane and the unicolt, looking up at Holly, swabbed his face with her wet tongue. The tension in the room was dispelled and Lupine felt ready to speak freely. Arnica sat quietly, listening intently.

"There was a body floating face down in a large pool of water. Some type of wheel was turning and water was splashing about. I don't know what took place before then. These images were so shocking that I awoke, trembling, and all the earlier memories from the dream were gone in an instant." Lupine turned to Arnica. "What did you mean by water?"

Arnica rose from his chair, stretching slightly. His back was no longer young. "I don't know exactly what has happened but Lupine, your dream is speaking of events either taking place or already passed."

Dark Star, now standing on all fours, was maturing yet still had to look up into their faces. She looked anxious. Her horn began nudging at Holly. "What is it, my hatchling?" crooned Holly.

"I think she wants to speak to you through the orb. Dark Star may have seen more than I, for certainly she is closer to the astral than any of us. Here, sit in my chair." Arnica stood aside. Holly began to protest, wanting to care for his partner's back, but Arnica insisted and Holly sat, holding the ball of crystal so that he and the hatchling could both gaze into its depths.

Holly's voice began quietly, speaking from a near-trance as he 'heard' Dark Star speaking to him through the orb. "It's Gino. No, not Gino... maybe his father? Dark Star, is Gino's father in danger? Not seriously... but he must come back to Merrydale soon.... That's it, that's all she can tell us."

They talked for some minutes, but it was growing late. Arnica and Holly went to their bedroom but Lupine decided to roll up with his blankets and pillow and sleep next to Dark Star. Soon the cabin was once again quiet.

The news came the next morning. None of the men were surprised, but it answered their questions. They sat around the kitchen table listening to Pearl. Her dark hair combed back, her fine, Pictish features were striking in the morning light.

"They found Kalven this morning, dead, floating in the mill pond. It's been ruled an accident, but Carlos is unsure. I spoke to Carlos when he called to reassure Gino that everything was fine. Gino had a nightmare last night about his father. It was so disturbing to him that he called me very early and asked me to come over." Pearl chuckled, the sound a welcome music in the midst of this dire news. She looked at Holly and smiled. "Gino's mother was quite taken aback when I showed up at their home at six this morning. She was still in her robe, making her morning coffee. Gino hadn't said anything to his mother, not wanting to worry her and still uncertain whether his dream was to be taken seriously or not. I was there when Carlos called. He asked to talk with me so I could let you know this news."

"What did he say?" Holly's voice was anxious.

"Kalven was at the Cathedral of Thorns, ostensibly working on choir music. Once he found the papers linking that 'Society for the Forest' and sent us photocopies, he was unable to simply let it go. Kalven had felt that working for the Kristos had been an opportunity and did not compromise his sympathy with the Earthkin, but discovering how powerful that secret group of Users was in the administration of the Cathedral gnawed at him. He kept hoping to find more information."

"What then?" asked Lupine.

Pearl's voice lowered. "He never came home last night. None of the men, Gino's father shared the apartment with three men, even noticed until it was time for them to leave for the Mill. Usually Kalven had come out of his room to join them for coffee. One of the men knocked and when there was no answer, they opened the door and found

Kalven's bed empty. It was only moments later the police came by. Carlos told me that he had nothing to go by, but he feels that they will all be under surveillance, that this was his last chance to speak freely by telephone."

"How is Gino taking all of this?" asked Arnica. "Does he know his father is in danger?"

Pearl's face paled. "What? Carlos is in danger?"

Arnica explained the visions and dreams which had wakened the house. "We must let him know at once. Carlos must quit his job at the mill and come back to Merrydale at once."

"But he wanted to earn enough money to buy a house for his family," Holly worried. "Do you think he'll understand?"

It was decided. Arnica wrote a note on a small piece of heavy parchment. Written in Ogham, it was simple and to the point. "Grave danger. Must move back to Merrydale at once. Delay threatens your life." Lupine and Holly brought out the mold and melted several old candle stubs. A candle was made with the parchment message secreted in the wax. Pearl volunteered to have the candle sent by courier across the mountains. With luck, and if the weather held out the pass would stay clear, Carlos would have the candle in a day. Her message was clear and would not be misunderstood. Pearl would say the candle was to be burnt that same night for Kalven's soul, saying something about how terrible the accident was. She knew Carlos would find the message as the candle burned down and, after reading it, burn the parchment in the same candle flame. It was an old custom used by the Earthkin in times of danger when messages needed to be secretly passed on and Carlos would remember.

After Pearl left for Merrydale, the men began preparing for Candlemas Eve, just two nights away. Their minds were very preoccupied.

Gino sat on a kitchen chair wearing the lovely robe Pearl made for him back when she was living in Cloverville, before Phoenix' passing. Dark Star was sitting up on the kitchen floor, her lead laying upon Gino's lap. No one had told Gino that his father was in such danger, but Gino knew something was up and was having difficulty preparing his thinking for the evening's ritual. Pearl was helping Lupine set small bundles of candles all about the temple. Dolorum had brought two good-sized baskets of candles. Iris had been quietly collecting them at the post office and was bringing a third basket of candles local Earthkin wanted blessed at their Circle's Candlemas rites. Few knew that they worked as a coven although some may have suspected. They only knew Arnica and Holly as herbalists and healers.

Dolorum was in the pantry with Arnica mixing the ritual water. Over the years, bottles of water had been collected from sacred sites near and far, from both mighty oceans and from all continents save Antarctica. A large basin was filled with rain water into which measured quantities of each of these sacred waters was added. After the Circle was closed, each covener would take home a bottle which they would add to their ritual water for use throughout the coming year.

Finally all were robed and the temple was prepared. All of the Circle were present and now standing snug in the cozy kitchen, holding hands. They calmed themselves and stood quietly. Their breathing gradually shifted until, as one, they drew air together and exhaled together in preparation for the intoning which would prepare them to enter the

The Hatchling

Temple. No one noticed that Dark Star was not focused with them. Their eyes closed, they could not see that she had turned and was looking out the window.

A tentative knock broke their reverie. Startled, Arnica went to the door. Opening it, there stood Carlos.

"Come in, quickly," welcomed Arnica.

"I came here directly. Pearl," he said, looking at the slender woman in her robe with its embroidered patterns of green silk, "your message reached me in less than a day. The gods blessed us and I was able to catch the train leaving at sunrise."

"Daddy," Gino's voice betrayed his age and he ran to the entry to throw his arms around his father. Part of him was yet a boy and he was so relieved to see his father safely, he had no words, just a warm hug. Gino had grown much since his father went to Mill City to work and had seen Carlos very little. That was now changed.

"I want to thank all of you," said Carlos. "I haven't yet been home and Gino's mother is waiting. I borrowed a horse from a friend and rode here directly. No one else in Merrydale knows that I've left Mill City. There is much I must discuss with you, Arnica, before I make my presence known."

Arnica turned to his friend, the postmarm. "Iris, could we hold a quiet meeting in your home under the pretense of dinner?"

"Say no more. All of you, please come." Iris was one of the most hospitable and gracious of friends. "Carlos, bring your wife."

"My friends, may you be blessed. Gino, I'll see you later tonight." Carlos turned to go out the door.

"Welcome home, Daddy," Gino radiated a joyful energy. "I'll hold you in my heart during our ritual. Tell Mother I love her and I'll be home before too long."

Carlos turned back into the night and the group of friends began their chant.

XXVI - An Egg for the Cathedral

"Look, aren't they beautiful?" Lupine carried a vase filled with tall daffodils, their glowing yellow vibrant against the cobalt blue. His black hair, pulled back into a braid, contrasted with his pale skin as striking as the daffodil and the cobalt.

Holly was kneeling before the main altar preparing for this evening's Eostara Ritual. The crystal chalice, treasured throughout his relationship with Arnica, had begun to emanate a soft, golden glow in harmony with the waxing sun at this solar Sabbat. Holly had set a small glass stand to hold the goblet in the center of a large, crystal bowl where floated a number of bloodroot blossoms.

"El nino was good to our gardens," Holly answered. "I don't recall such beautiful hyacinths in years." Lupine had brought in several hyacinths, yellow upon the east altar, red in the south and blue in the west.

"I can believe it," Lupine answered. Breaking into laughter he said, "I keep wishing there were green-colored hyacinths to complete the cardinal set." He looked to the potted maidenhair fern sitting upon the north altar, then walked over and knelt next to Holly. Resting his head gently upon Holly's shoulder so as not to interfere in his new brother's work, he asked "Where did that chalice come from?"

78

"Why, Arnica had brought it back from the land of Loriën decades ago. It was hand-carved by gnomes from the same crystal which forms the last step leading to the Temple of Loriën."

"There is so much to learn," Lupine sighed. "Sometimes I think I shall never learn it all."

"Patience," soothed Holly. They both laugh. "That's Arnica's word for just about everything, isn't it?"

"I do hope he'll be home soon." Lupine smiled. "I've been looking forward to our ritual bath, all three of us together in the hot tub." His voice had a mischievous twinkle.

Just then, Arnica wished he was back at his cabin, safely surrounded by tall fir trees. It was as if he could feel Holly and Lupine wishing him back. The undercurrents of growing political tension had taken away some of the joy from his trips into Merrydale. Arnica told people he was in town planning a 'birthday party' for the hatchling, Dark Star. Three years ago the morning of Eostara Eve a moderate 4.6 earthquake had rumbled through the region. It was then that the large egg hatched, having mysteriously appeared in their stone Circle weeks before as they did their Candlemas Eve ritual.

Dark Star had quickly worked her way into everyone's hearts. What a wonder to have a unicorn living with them. Andrius still came and went, but he was mostly astral, more than able to slip through the veils of reality. Dark Star had substance. It hurt when she accidentally stepped upon your toe with her hoof! A Unicorn was pure magick. Arnica and Holly instinctively knew her true identity should not be known outside their coven. Dark Star had come into town with Arnica, but as always, he had rubbed the elixir into her horn. Made of two gems and four herbs with a pinch of fine gold dust, her horn was now invisible. No one thought twice about the 'pony' other than to note her unusually intelligent eyes. Dark Star was laying upon the living room floor in Gino's home. Gino, a bright lad, was now a coven member. He recognized the hatchling as a Unicorn on their first trip into town, when Dark Star was but four Sabbats old.

Magenta, Gino's mother, was clearing the dishes. Gino got his freckles from her. Quite an interesting lunch, Rosetta was thinking. Here was Arnica, famed Renaissance Tribe herbalist. And sitting next to him was Pastor Dolorum, Kristos minister from the Church of the Martyr. If it hadn't been for the strange events of the past weeks, she couldn't believe this herself.

Over the past two years Gino had been spending more and more time out at the cabin. Carlos had been gone, living in Mill City to earn money to support them. There were few jobs in Merrydale and the big factories were built in Mill City. She and Carlos considered moving but liked Merrydale. "Yes," Rosetta thought, "wouldn't Mrs. Busynose next door just be wondering about both Arnica and Pastor Dolorum here in my house for lunch?"

"That was an amazing memorial service for Kalven," Carlos looked at both men, his voice quiet and deep. Gino's father was glad to be back in Merrydale.

"Kalven provided us with a rare opportunity," said Dolorum. "In confidence, I have been working with Arnica for over a year. You can well imagine the stir this has created even though we are discreet." Dolorum looked, as usual, quite serious.

"I miss him," Carlos mused. "The four of us shared that apartment and travelled back and forth to Merrydale carrying parcels from each other's children and wives. In the past two years we worked and lived together and had begun to feel like brothers."

Kalven's death continued to be the source of much speculation. Despite the 'official' word that the man had slipped and fallen into the mill pond, no one believed it, least of all those in this room. Kalven's job at the Cathedral of Thorns led him to the papers which proved the 'Society for the Forest" was not conservation-oriented but was, in fact, a front for a faction of the Users hoping to bulldoze Merrywood and turn it into a pit mine.

"I admire the work you're doing," Carlos said to Arnica. "Until Kalven made a comment one day, I had no idea that the Users were becoming so powerful. It's difficult to understand their desire to destroy our forest, to take it through deceit. And you, my good man," he said, looking now at Pastor Dolorum, "how can I thank you for finding me a good job."

"It was in my own best interests. I'm under increasing pressure at the Church of the Martyr. The last election of Elders increased the strength of the Users. They've been unhappy ever since I encouraged the congregation to join in Iris' march to Fern Hollow calling for protection of our trees. An ally on the staff would be a blessing."

Gino was getting restless. He took out his prized pocket watch, the one given him by his father. "Dear Sir," he said to Arnica, "I'd like to go to the cabin and help Holly and Lupine prepare for tonight's ritual."

"You're right, lad," Arnica said. "Just one more thing." He turned to Carlos. "We're preparing a traditional Eostara egg but instead of it being hollowed and filled with delight and festivity, information is being inserted that uncovers the Society for the Forest. The egg will be blessed and placed so it reaches the Merrywood Gazette where it will surely be picked up by the wire service."

Stopping at the postmarm's to send a parcel of herbs to a friend, Arnica heard the news. Amethyst and Crystal were there. They looked a bit frazzled.

"Arnica," Crystal's face, usually smiling with its halo of short, fair hair, looked troubled. "We're moving."

"I know it's unexpected," said Amethyst. "I was offered a job in Cloverville. It's a good offer and..." Tears came to her eyes. Amethyst knew that this meant leaving her coven.

"What Amethyst hasn't said is that there's growing pressure at the school." Crystal was a writer for a large magazine. She could work from anywhere. It had been easy for her to move here four years ago to be with Amethyst. "Several of the Users on the school board are trying to have her fired because, well, because we're lovers. And if it comes out that we're not only lesbian but active with the Renaissance Tribes, we're sunk."

Arnica's arms embraced Amethyst. This was hardest on her. Crystal was the stronger of the two women and had been wanting to move to a larger city. Amethyst had belonged to the coven for many years.

Arnica took a deep breath. "Will you tell Holly yourself?"

"We called him earlier. That's how we thought to meet you here at Iris's. We're going to stop by tomorrow for lunch on our way."

"I'm surprised yet not completely," Arnica said. "I've known something was taking place." He looked out the window. Gino was petting and talking quietly to Dark Star. "You'll miss her party?"

"Yes, but here's a present for her. And we're bringing borage cookies with us tomorrow. You know we love you all so much." Amethyst was close to tears.

"O.K., my dears, I've got to be going. Take some time tonight when we're in Circle and be with us in spirit."

Gino thought Arnica strangely quiet as they walked the road from Merrydale to the cabin. Arnica was processing the realization that the persecutions had begun again.

The ritual candles put away, the friends sat about the kitchen. Dark Star sat upon the floor at the table. A large carrot cake sat there, made of shredded carrots pressed together with a little egg and decorated with borage flowers and three lit candles.

"Where did you get borage flowers?" Dark Star questioned Holly in her mind.

Holly, ever more able to understand the hatchling, laughed out loud. "Where did we get the flowers? It's *a mystery.*" The phrase, often used among the friends, caused them all to laugh. Dark Star snorted - a unicorn laugh - so hard that all three candles went out.

Everyone cheered and laughed. The cabin was filled with joy. Dark Star looked so lovely. Three years old. How their lives had changed since the unicolt became part of their household and an informal member of their coven. They feasted on carrot and helped Dark Star open her gifts. She got borage seeds (her favorite herb) and a beautiful, embroidered harness. Pearl's needlework was among the best of the region! Amethyst and Crystal, known for their gems, had found a perfect, egg-shaped geode with an opening. Inside among the little crystals was a tiny, silver unicorn statue.

Dolorum and Iris went to get their woolen capes. The nights were still brisk. "Is there something between them?" Holly wondered. He was certain that Iris called the clergyman 'Dolly' once during the evening.

As Dolorum fastened the buttons of his black cape he went over the plan. "It will be easy for me to place this egg in the mailbox at the Gazette office. They'll find it in the morning. At least one of the staff remembers the folk custom of written wishes in eggs for Eostara so I'm confident it will be opened and the truth found."

"We did our part," said Iris. She felt good about the evening's ritual. "I feel like we've prepared an egg for the Cathedral."

"Well, the 'secret committee' at least will have egg on its face," Lupine rejoined.

Knowing that they were about to fall into a whole series of egg jokes, Pearl and Gino got their wraps as well and soon the night ended. Pearl and Gino walked back to town with animated, quiet conversation. Dolorum and Iris were quiet, their hands almost touching.

Back at the cabin, Holly, Arnica and Lupine were snuggled beneath a large comforter and Dark Star, well, Dark Star was much too happy. She was still in the kitchen, gazing into the geode and asking all of her astral kindred to help bring peace to her loved ones. "When this news reaches the people," she thought to herself, "there will be a lot of political tension," and she didn't want that for her human friends. Not at all.

XXVII - The Maypole Conflict

"Look, Dark Star, Dolorum's growing borage in his garden." Holly's voice was bright as the late April sun. Lupine was down upon his knees to smell the bleeding hearts. Lupine loved smelling every flower he saw!

Arnica, Holly and Lupine had brought the hatchling into Merrywood to have lunch with Pastor Dolorum. He was still in his study working at his desk so they were passing time in the garden which his mother, Mildora, had kept until she passed into the Otherworld a year ago last Hallows. Her passing had opened the older Mysteries to Dolorum who now, despite his working for the Church of the Martyr, secretly had become part of the coven which met at the cabin in the woods.

"Go ahead, Dark Star, you can have some of the borage." A voice laughed through a window as Dark Star was caught completely by surprise. The look on the three-year-old's face left all four men laughing. "I'll be done in a few minutes," said Pastor Dolorum, closing the window to return to his work.

For the next ten minutes Holly and Lupine picked borage blooms and played with Dark Star. Lupine would toss one in the air, one at a time and the unicolt would catch them with her tongue. Arnica sat on a bench at the edge of a garden, deep in thought. Watching the flowers, he noticed that here, too, there were less bees. Merrydale was a wonderful place to live and others thought so too. Despite all their efforts, Merrywood was losing some of its trees to make space and materials for new homes. 'Change was inevitable,' Arnica mused, 'but did it have to be so hard upon our Mother Earth?'

Arnica set the letter down upon the coffee table. Without thinking, he rubbed his fingers upon the fabric of his pants as if to clean them from the words printed upon the paper.

"What thoughts do you have?" asked Dolorum.

"It's obvious that the bishop is determined to stop you from having the Maypole for the children of your parish," said Arnica. "Do you know Carlos, Gino's father?" Dolorum nodded. "He told me that a friend of his in Mill City overheard the bishop speaking to a group of mill owners, telling them that allowing Maypoles will encourage people to work against The Society for the Forest."

"Well, there's truth in that," Lupine's dark braid was dancing behind him as he and Holly played with Dark Star. The hatchling looked quite at home in Dolorum's study. It was safe here and her horn was visible. The men were very careful to rub it with Arnica's magickal formula. Over the past three years, only Gino had ever seen Dark Star to truly be a Unicorn.

"What will you do?" asked Holly. "All the children would be sorely disappointed."

"So would many of their parents," said Dolorum. He turned to Arnica. "Have you heard nothing about the article in the Merrywood Gazette? Has nothing reached Mill City?"

"It certainly was major news here in Merrywood, but nothing seems to have much happened in Mill City. We're dealing with a large consortium of wealthy Users. Only two years ago the Politicos were passing laws allowing more and more of the woodlands to be cut for lumber. We've seen it happening. There is a lot of money to be made. Locally people now know that the Society for the Forest is actually a front for wealthy lumber barons who want our trees, but they control so many aspects of life in Mill City that it's easy for them to suppress the news. Each day in our morning ritual we offer blessings to any brave journalists who might be willing to take the Gazette's exposé and uncover these wrongs."

Dolorum turned to Holly and Lupine. "So, for now, our Maypole goes on but the truth is, the bishop can stop me from having one and he can have me removed from my church. Sometimes compromise is what allows us to get greater work done over a longer period of time."

It was a quiet trio of men who were about to tether the hatching to a hawthorne tree behind the postmarm's. The work they'd done at Eostara to bring the truth to the people had not worked as they'd hoped. A bell tinkled, the sound of the postmarm's office door. Iris came running toward them as a wave of excitement rolled over them.

"Have you seen it? Look!" Iris' eyes were bright. Her hair, usually neatly braided, was loose and free like the postmarm's energy. "I can't believe it. I've been checking every issue of the Mill City News and for weeks there's been nothing, then this!"

"What is it?" asked Arnica.

"We won this victory," said Iris, almost breathless. "This young journalist saw the article in the Gazette last March and she's been researching and collecting data. Not only that but she got a camera and another reporter from the Mill City television station to go with her when she went to the bishop's office with her facts." Iris held up the paper. The words of the banner were clear: *Friends of the Forest Outed: Bishop Denies Knowledge.* "Not only that," Iris continued, her voice filled with the edge of excitement, "but the Committee of Internal Affairs, almost all old Politicos, is being forced to conduct a hearing. It's likely that a couple of the old-boy Politicos will find themselves out of Parliament before this is done."

Dark Star was very excited. She began prancing about the yard, her hooves light as a child's feet, as she danced in circles about the hawthorne.

Holly began laughing. His long months' training to learn to 'hear' Dark Star speak through the crystal orb was paying off. Sometimes he simply knew what was in the hatchling's mind! "Dark Star knows that Merrydale will have its Maypole. She's also hoping that we'll have one at the cabin just for our coven so she can dance as well."

"Hooray, hooray for the first of May," sang Lupine, already feeling the exuberance of Beltane. "We may have April showers left this month, but this is such wonderful news!"

"I must go in and call Dolorum about this," said Arnica.

"Beat you to the punch," Iris said quickly, blushing lightly. "You had just left his home when I rang him up. He feels certain that the bishop will be more than distracted in the coming weeks and plans to move forward with the children's Maypole." Iris was certain that Arnica had seen her blush. She and Dolorum were in the very early stages of discovering their attraction to each other.

Arnica acted as if he hadn't seen. The spark between them was still more apparent to others than it was to the two of them. Iris was well-known for her activism. People remembered Iris for the march to Fern Holly she organized nearing two years ago. 'Why,' Arnica thought to himself, 'I wonder if the seeds of their attraction date back to that September when Dolorum brought his congregation to join Iris' demonstration.'

"Hey, you," Iris said, poking Arnica in the shoulder. "Did you even hear what I was saying?"

"I'm so sorry. My mind was wandering." Arnica deftly covered his mind's tracks. "I was remembering the march you organized to Fern Hollow and thinking about how things have changed in the past two years. Amethyst and Crystal have moved away to Cloverville. You've become like a sister and are part of our coven. And Dolorum! Who would have thought?" Arnica quickly lowered his voice. "I knew his mother, yet not even in my dreams would I have imagined him being part of our coven. There's much magick about in Merrydale, Iris, and like it or not you have been the catalyst for it. I've often thought that the town post office is the true heart of our village."

Iris didn't know what to say. She often had trouble with compliments. She turned to Holly and Lupine, both still rolling in the grass with Dark Star. 'There was still a touch of boy in both men,' she thought to herself.

"Holly, Lupine," she called to them. "I have some things to send back to the cabin with you. Could you bring them from the back porch? And there's also a plate with some cookies - made with honey, not with refined sugar - on my kitchen table. Grab a couple for each of you."

Dark Star trotted up to Iris, snorting and whinnying like a child begging for a cookie.

"Silly hatchling," Iris laughed. "You can have all the borage flowers you want but cookies are simply not good for your diet and I love you too much to give in to your teasing." Dark Star nuzzled Iris' hands and waited for Holly and Lupine to fasten the baskets to her back for the walk back to the cabin.

The cabin is quiet, save for the occasional pop of a log in the fireplace. Dark Star is laying on the floor before the fireplace, all the ribbons from this year's Maypole attached to her horn and draped loosely around her neck like a rainbow-colored garland. His arm around her neck as well, Lupine is snuggled against her, his face smiling at some wonderful dream. Both share the same quilt which will keep them warm after the fire tires. It will not be long.

Several candles sit upon the table in the kitchen, warming the room with a gentle glow. Holly and Arnica sit on their chairs, sharing a cup of late-night tea.

"It's good to share this peace," mused Arnica. This past week had been a flurry of excitement. Pastor Dolorum's 'ecumenical Maypole' had done well. As expected, the bishop was too busy with his own travails to worry much about Merrydale. He was trying to put out a political fire on the other side of the mountains.

"I liked the way Dolorum presented the Maypole to the town," Holly offered, raising a pottery mug of chamomile and peppermint to his lips. The scent was heavenly. Nothing had been mentioned about a Maypole being an old pagan tradition. All Dolorum said or wrote was that it was 'a holiday custom your grandparents may have loved.'

"Did you hear what he said this evening before the ritual?" asked Arnica.

"No, what was it?"

"When I made a comment about the success of his project," the memory brought a smile to Arnica, "he said it was ecumenical 'more than they knew.'"

It had been a lovely evening. Their Circle was joyful this year. Jewel and Lotus left Dagon with his grandmother. Imagine! Dagon would be three years old in a couple of weeks. They looked good. Parenting brought a wonderful quality to them. Pearl had begun to teach needlework classes at the Community Center. To her surprise the classes were attracting younger, school-age women and girls. Very gently she was weaving in concepts of living in harmony with the earth, of the sacredness of all things. Pearl was a wonderful teacher and her new life was growing with beauty.

"Gino's getting older," Holly commented. Arnica nodded in agreement. Gino had grown a lot in the past three years. He was growing into a young man and looking more like his father. Learning the ritual disciplines and religious philosophies had given him many skills which carried over to school. His mother was so proud of his grades, which had so improved, as well as his growing self-confidence which gave him social skills he'd not had.

Arnica picked up a candle snuffer and handed it to Holly. "Well, I think they've done it," he said, carrying the tea mugs to the sink to rinse.

The light began to dim as Holly put the candles to rest. "They looked wonderful," he answered. As the kitchen settled into darkness, their hearts felt warmed remembering the look on Iris and Dolorum's eyes as they sat in Circle, openly holding hands. The discovery of love was a sure sign of Beltane.

Soon the cabin was quiet. Dark Star slept before the glowing embers. Did you know that a unicolt can snore? Very gently, however. It's a most magickal sound. Lupine had stirred and brought his blanket to bed where the three were sleeping in the large bed. Beltane Eve was turning into morn and everything seemed at peace with the world. Yet, on the other side of the mountains, there was trouble afoot. Merrywood was not yet safe.

XXVIII - What The Devas Said

"Look at all the apples," Holly mused. He was thinning the apples on their trees, leaving only one fruit from each cluster of blossoms.

"We have bees everywhere. Despite the difficulties in the bee populations in parts of the country and what seemed like a late start here, we've an abundance of bees. Why, there must be at least fifty on the small patch of creeping thyme by the fruit jar shed."

It was true, there were bees everywhere. Dark Star, the unicorn hatchling, seemed to enjoy them. More than once they'd seen her gently lift a bee from a flower with the tip of her horn and carry it to another bed, as if showing the buzzer additional sources of nectar. To their amazement the bees didn't mind at all and made no attempt to fly away.

"I read Lady Ellhorn's letter." Holly's voice quieted.

"It's frightening, isn't it? There are major fires throughout many of the warm climates of our planet, in all hemispheres. To think that there is so much smoke it's drifting all the way into Cloverville, over eight hundred miles to the north!" Arnica was concerned about the global changes impacting the planet's climate. "Catch..." and he tossed a handful of borage flowers in the air.

Dark Star loved this game. Nibbling at borage blooms was her favorite garden pastime. Each flower was like a cobalt-blue, five-pointed star. Perhaps the borage flower was a symbolic connection with her name? Or perhaps it was just one of those 'unicorn things.'

Holly had taken a bowl of tiny apples to the compost bin. Knowing that Dark Star was distracted by Arnica and the borage flowers, he snuck up behind her and pounced and soon Holly and Dark Star were rolling in the grass as if they were a young boy and a puppy. Arnica sat back against a tree and laughed so hard his stomach muscles began to hurt.

Just then Iris came through the gate. "What is going on here?" She was not accustomed to seeing Arnica doubled over with laughter. The very sight of the two men and their unicolt left her laughing.

Holly, breathless, said, "oh, nothing. We're just playing."

Arnica rose to his feet, giving the postmarm a warm embrace. "It's true," he said. "You should see the two of them. There's still a lot of boy in Holly."

Holly laughed and hugged Iris. "You're early, aren't you? We haven't even begun to set the outdoor circle for tonight's Midsummer's Eve ritual."

"Yes, I am," Iris answered, "but I thought you'd want to see this." She opened up the newspaper which she'd brought with her. The headline was dark and loud: *Bishop Decries Earthkin, claims their destructive ways blind him to God's work.*

"Let me see this," Arnica said, a tone of alarm in his voice. Iris handed him the paper and he began reading aloud. "The Bishop met with reporters late yesterday. When asked about his involvement in the now-dismantled 'Friends of the Forest,' Bishop Miter, his wife at his side, offered his explanation. Claiming the increase of non-Kristos in our cities and rural areas is causing an erosion of family values, he said that he sincerely believed leaders behind the Friends of the Forest had good in their hearts. Bishop Miter called for new laws aimed at defining religious rights more closely and called for classes in religion in school. Miter claims that it was a secret pagan and homosexual agenda which eroded prayer in the classroom. Miter, his voice heavy with emotion, told us 'any politician who deserves to remain in office would make it illegal for homosexual and other sick people to worship the devil and dance around their May poles.'"

"Don't read any more," Holly said. "You told me the other week that you expected this type of backlash."

"It's absurd. Hatchitt's investigation into Kalven's death has been set aside. Instead he turned his committee of Politicos to the 'Friends of the Forest' and says he can find no wrong. And the Bishop?" Arnica's emotions were strong. There was too much injustice.

"Innocent, of course. And his church is behind him 100% and that's enough!" Iris grabbed the paper back from Arnica and stuffed it into her nap bag. "Now it's time to prepare for ritual. Look, Dark Star, I brought you a treat from town." The hatchling perked right up. Not all that interested in listening to human's politics, she was watching the butterflies and the birds in their flying dances about the gardens but now she was watching Iris intently. Dark Star *loved* treats. Iris reached into her bag and brought out a beautiful crown made of fresh flowers...

The coven sat around the circle in the gardens. Candles flamed at the quarters and upon the altar. Lamp beetles flew among the hawthornes, their night lights flickering on and off and on as they pursued their Midsummer mating quest.

The dance was completed, the cone of power raised and the veils separating them from the Realm of the Faerie were opened. Midsummer's Eve was when they sought visions of wisdom from the realm of the plant and forest spirits. They sat about the Circle, quiet, as each worked to further enter a deeper level of awareness. Music began to drift through the trees, as if a dance for the lamp beetles. Why, it sounded just like Wren's lute!

There was a soft intake of breath as the coven saw the lights come together forming a small sprite.

"Tonight's the night for Deva sight, we're out this night to bring you light. Messages of news I bring and Music to your hearts I sing." The little being looked quite pleased with her own rhyme. "I am the Deva of the Elfwort. Last Beltane I was crowned Queen of the Garden and it is my role to come to you and speak." The tiny, glowing wings moved quick, like those of a hummingbird as the Elfwort Deva hovered above the center of the Circle. Turning toward Arnica and Holly, as she spoke again the notes of the lute spilled out of the trees like stars in a sky. "Gentle herbal gardeners, we thank you for providing safe haven for all the Devas. Be warned: dark forces would see your gardens and woodlands taken from you."

"We do know," answered Arnica. His arm held Holly closer.

Holly loved Midsummer. It had long been one of his favorite Sabbats. "Dear Deva," he said, "we ask that you and your kindred lend your strength to our work."

The spirit did not answer Holly but moved toward the West altar where Iris and Dolorum sat next each other. "Dolorum, why have you not spoken your heart? Bind your love then prepare for the fight. She will join you" Iris blushed. Did Dolorum as well? Everyone knew what was asked by the first question. The fight? They knew the Bishop was not pleased with Pastor Dolorum's liberal views.

"You, young man," the Deva speaking to Gino now, "you must be discreet. Speak no magick outside this Circle. It would be best if your parents knew not that you were here but this cannot be. Be careful."

Gino was sitting next to Pearl, his first teacher. He pulled his robe about him, the lovely, hand-embroidered robe Pearl had sewn for him. Still a year short of his teens, Gino was a mixture of wise, young man and frolicsome boy, not always understanding how the changing political tides could impact his future and endanger his family.

Now the sprite flitted close to Jewel and Lotus, who were seated together near the South altar. "Dagon holds promise, but his future is not what you expect." Now *that* was a cryptic comment!

Flying quick across the circle toward the north, the Deva stopped near Lupine, seated upon the grass with his arm around Dark Star. "Lupine, you must return. You know what you have left behind and you cannot move forward until you face your past. You cannot hide any longer."

"Look!" Iris pointed up at the sky where a dazzling meteor shot like a star through the heavens. And just like that the Deva was gone and the Midsummer rite was ended.

All the ritual things were put away and the candle lanterns were hung back in the storage shed. Their friends gone, Dark Star was sitting upon the kitchen floor. She leaned her head from left to right to left to right. The circlet of flowers which Iris had sewn together slid from one side to the other. The sight of their hatchling playing filled the room with joy. And yet...

Lupine's aura had become like a cloud filled with impending rain...

"What is it, Lupine," Arnica asked with concern. Lupine had come to them last winter seeking training for the Renaissance Priesthood. Having completed his quests which sent him to Atlantikos and then to Heartland, he was well liked by those in their circle and filled a niche in their simple cabin. Lupine fit well into Arnica and Holly's family.

"I hadn't told you before. I was afraid you wouldn't accept me for study," Lupine said.

"What is it, my brother?" Holly quickly came to his dark haired friend and put his arms around him.

"Arnica, I'm sorry. My being here has not been in Perfect Trust and the gods have brought me face to face with my karma. I must return to Heartland. I have not paid my tithing for several years and my moving about was an attempt to avoid facing my debts. I realize now that I can never have freedom if I do not embrace my responsibilities. I love being here and perhaps I can return once again, but tomorrow I will pack my things and catch the afternoon coach back to Heartland."

Arnica and Holly understood. This answered an underlying sense of unease which was becoming apparent to them. All was not right with Lupine. The Deva had spoken.

Tomorrow would be the first day of summer. The days would begin growing shorter and changes would be coming. Would the Politicos be successful in clearing the forests? Would the Earthkin lose their freedom? Tomorrow Arnica and Holly would turn to their gardens. Working among the Devas was where life made the most sense.

IXXX - The Lammas Fires Burn Bright

Tongues were busy in Merrydale. Politics topped the list. The scandal which broke last winter over the 'Society for the Forest' had not quite died down. Bishop Miter was diverting attention from his own involvement by blaming the Earthkin for a list of purported evils, even insinuating that it was the Earthkin's acceptance of racial and sexual diversity which was causing global warming. But there was more. The new sapphire on the postmarm's finger had been noticed. The residents of Merrydale thought highly of the pastor from the Church of the Martyr, quite liberal in his views for a Kristos minister. Iris, although a government employee, was a known activist for Merrywood ever since organizing a public march to keep Fern Hollow from having its trees logged. Although no one really *knew*, everyone assumed that she was of the Earthkin. What would Bishop Miter think of one of his clergymen actually *marrying* outside his religion? And to an Earthkin no less?

"Oh, Dolly, the ring is so beautiful." Iris sat in a large wicker chair on her back porch, Pastor Dolorum in a chair at her left. She held her left hand so the sun sparkled upon the faceted stone, her right hand idly scratching Dark Star's ears. The Hatchling was spending a couple of days with Iris while Arnica and Holly were at Mill City, attending a press conference called by Parliament. She looked at Dolorum. "I'm sure everyone knows we're engaged. But what will your parishioners say?"

Dolorum took her hand and held it. "My people have known where I stand on things. Fifty of them came with me to march with you to Fern Hollow two years ago. You know, since seeing the fire in your eyes and your passion for the trees there has been no other woman for me."

"But what if Miter has a fit over your marrying me?" Iris knew that their marriage could end Dolorum's career as a Kristos minister. Bishop Miter was not a tolerant man.

"Iris, I'm not that concerned." Dolorum's voice was gentle.

Sensing that the energy of the situation was changing, Dark Star stretched herself up and took a few steps and sat herself in front of Dolorum. She laid her head in his lap. Her horn was becoming visible and she needed Dolorum to rub Arnica's magick ointment upon it. Merrydale was not ready to discover a unicorn in its midst. Dark Star loved her privacy.

As he gently rubbed the ointment of male fern and powdered gems into her horn, Dolorum spoke to Iris. Tending the hatchling made it easier for him to speak. He breathed slowly and deeply, his finger counting the spirals of Dark Star's horn. Already three and a half turns. At Lammas in just two days, Dark Star would be three and a half! Dolorum's gaze turned to Iris.

"I think of myself more as Dolly, now, than as Pastor Dolorum. The passing of my mother nearly two years ago opened many doors for me, the most important of which brought me to Arnica, Holly and the Grove. It's not easy for me living this double life. The part of me which is increasingly filled with joy is the man who sits in Circle with you. My religious life in our coven is more important to me than that of my former Kristos beliefs."

"I've wondered," Iris murmured.

"My work as a clergyman allows me to reach people. And I know I've made a difference. But it's become more and more clear that I can help my people just as much - perhaps more - if I set aside my Kristos' robes and make a public statement. If Bishop Miter acts against me, it may set me free but certainly cannot harm me."

Dolorum's talk was interrupted by the bell.

"Excuse me," Iris said, "Someone's at the post counter." The post office was attached to the front of her house.

Dolorum sat there, sharing thoughts with the young unicorn. No words were exchanged, but he felt assured by Dark Star that what he was saying was a *truth*. What Dolorum must do was beginning to take shape in his mind.

"Dolly," Iris said, coming back through the door, "look who's here."

"Pearl," Dolorum and Dark Star both jumped up. They were both delighted to see their Pictish friend. Although small in stature, Pearl was a dynamo of energy.

"Have you heard?" Pearl said. "Parliament has decreed that there are to be no Lammas fires this year. Holly called early this morning and told me they're on their way home. He and Arnica will be back late this evening."

"What?" Both Iris and Dolorum were shocked. This was a strong political move and sure to cause civil upheaval. "Sit down, please," Dolorum said.

"Weren't you sitting there?" Pearl was always gracious, her manners as fine as her skill with needle and thread, for which she was well known.

"I can sit here by Dark Star," he offered, sitting on the porch near Iris.

"Now that's a thought, having my husband-to-be at my feet," Iris started laughing. Dolly only blushed. "But tell us, Pearl."

"Word is spreading fast. The Politicos majority maintains that our constitution makes us a Kristos country. A battle of words took place in Parliament with the Conservers losing. The more the Conservers spoke about religious equity for all peoples, the more riled up the Politicos became. The Users have been gaining strength and are using Bishop Miter's current plight to build support. Fear is a powerful weapon." Pearl fell silent.

"You know there will be fires despite any decree," Iris mused.

Dolorum was silent and deeply troubled. It was obvious that Miter was a major force in this decision. The Users had been growing in number and organizing to pass laws to make it increasingly difficult for the Renaissance and Earthkin Tribes to practice their own religions. If the Users had their way, they would outlaw not only all other religions but probably the liberal Kristos churches as well!

Pearl spoke again. "Arnica said that there are plans for a very large, highly visible fire where the trees in Merrywood were clear cut. It's safe yet also highly visible. Once lit it can be seen by everyone but no one will be needed to tend it. On my way over I stopped to talk to Carlos. People are talking about 'fighting fire with fire.' Many will be lighting small fires in front of their homes on Lammas Eve."

"That's what I will do." Dolorum spoke suddenly, obviously thinking out loud.

"I must head home. I'm still sewing the grain man for Lammas Eve. I think I'm going to place some extra magick into it this year!" Pearl kissed Dark Star on her horn, then hugged Iris. Dolorum was still sitting upon the porch, completely lost in thought.

"They've taken the majority of the school board and Dad said they're going to require we take an oath of allegiance to country and to their god before we can register for school." Gino had been helping haul branches all day, packing them on Dark Star's back and taking them to the growing pile for the great fire. "Arnica, can they do that?"

Arnica was gently packing their ritual things into a basket to take back to the stone circle. "Morally, no. Legally? It's possible but will take a challenge in the courts. You hauled a lot of brush, my young friend."

Gino's face looked bright. He was very proud to be treated like a young man at the Grove. "We got the entire pile of last winter's pruning. Poor Dark Star, she was tired... But I'm not," he added a bit too hastily.

"Why not go over and hold her for a bit. See if you can merge with her unicorn dreams to prepare yourself for the ritual." Arnica knew what he was suggesting. It would be only a few minutes and the lad would be sound asleep with the hatchling beneath the lilac.

"Open." Holly came up with a large, juicy strawberry in his hand. Arnica opened his mouth and Holly popped it in.

"Almost as good as a kiss," Arnica teased.

"Hey, that *was* a kiss," Holly responded.

Energy was very intense for this Sabbat Eve. All the plans were in place. Their coven ritual would begin late. At sunset the great fire would be lit. Carlos, Gino's father, had volunteered. He said he wanted to do it for his friend Kalven, who had been working at the Cathedral and was about to make public information he had uncovered. Kalven's body was found in the mill pond last winter.

The Wheel would definitely be turned this Sabbat!

Robes and bare feet dancing about a cauldron of flame, they held hands and raised the cone of power as the fire swirled up into a spiral. At the very height of the chant, Pearl held the grain man above the cauldron until the dried straw caught some flame. She dropped it into the fire below and they all sat upon the soft fir needles in the stone circle.

Even through the trees they could see the glow on the hill a few miles distant where a large bonfire raged against the Politicos' decree. Jewel's russet hair spilled out of her hood. Lotus had stayed home to sit with Dagon. A toddler now, they felt it best on this night of fires to keep Dagon at home. There was no telling what might happen with such tension in the air. Gino sat by Dark Star. The nap had done both the boy and the young unicorn some good and they were enjoying being in the stone circle on this night. The brightness of the fires was exciting but they were little concerned with the political ramifications.

Iris leaned her head against Dolorum's shoulder. She would be attending his church this Sunday. Dolorum was going to take a public stand, announcing his engagement and offering his resignation. He wanted his church to know that the fire burning in a large cauldron in front of the Church of the Martyr had his support. "People have taken note," his sermon would say. "I believe people should be judged by their actions, not their words. I urge you to take a stand for equality. "

"Over forty fires around Merrydale alone," Holly mused. The response to the decree was amazing.

Arnica was quiet. Would it take fire to save the forests of Merrywood? Although the ruling party in Parliament was hoping for the upper hand, what they may have done was to empower all who felt close to the earth. This would not be an easy autumn.

XXX - Of Harvests and Hearings

Holly and Arnica were in the gardens, preparing for the Autumn Eve ritual. Dark Star, their unicorn who had magickally appeared in their lives three and a half years ago, was lolling about, nibbling at the late borage blooms, her favorite herb. Just then, a large 'V' of geese flew overhead, their honking cutting through the quiet glade where the two men grew their herbs. It was a joyful sound but an odd quality echoed with it.

Arnica looked up. "The geese portend some major changes."

Holly looked startled. "Could you hear that in their calls?"

"No," mused Arnica, pruners in hand as he cut back the towering elfwort stalks. The herb's seeds gathered, it now was ready for its winter dormancy. "I'm not logically certain *why* I said that, but I know it to be true."

"Haven't we had enough excitement?" asked Holly. The younger man was digging iris to transplant to a large, new bed. Holly sat back and reflected. "Ever since Dark Star came into our lives, it's been one adventure after another." At the sound of her name, the hatchling's ears perked up, she nimbly leapt to her feet and trotted over where she licked Holly right on his ear. Laughing, he wiped his ear dry as Dark Star dropped to the ground and lay her head right in his lap.

"But we're in for more. It will take many years for this political climate to settle down. The Users are in control of most of the Kristos churches and hold the majority of the Politicos seats in Parliament, even though the Conservers did gain some. A growing population, the instability of the world economy and the changing climate make people very nervous. The Users would like nothing better than to prey upon people's fears so they could impose their sense of order upon as much of the world as possible."

Holly looked pensive. "We've a long struggle in front of us, don't we? It was just two years ago that Iris organized the march to save Fern Hollow as Dolorum offered his support and mobilized much of his congregation."

"Well, those trees were saved but it came with a price. Honestly, my love, I don't see Pastor Dolorum continuing at the Church of the Martyr much longer. He's publicly come out in opposition to many of Bishop Miter's views, his religious views could be perceived as increasingly Earthkin..."

"Well, that Kristos clergyman *is* part of our coven," interjected Holly laughing.

"And once the word spreads beyond Merrydale of Dolly's engagement to Iris ..."

"Do you think a public Handfasting could happen?" Holly was having fun with this.

"There's such a growing fear among the Users. It's common knowledge Carlos' friend Kalven was murdered to protect the Users. We don't know what information he found while working at the Cathedral, but it had to have been very important. And when there's fear..." Arnica's voice drifted off as his mind sifted through the events.

"Do you think the school board will enforce that damnable oath?" Holly wondered aloud.

Meanwhile, Gino was again at his school, trying to enroll for the coming year. This was to be his first year in Merrydale's junior high school. Gino, the youngest member of the coven, had grown more confident since his mother allowed him to begin studying the Renaissance traditions from Pearl. Gino spent a lot of time with Holly and Arnica and had become a very good friend with Dark Star. In fact it was just three years ago that he recognized Dark Star to be a unicorn even though Arnica had used his herbal potion to keep her horn invisible.

The school board, under great pressure from the Politicos and Kristos, had adopted an oath of allegiance. Gino heard about this just before Lammas, but had forgotten. When the counsellor asked him if he believed in the 'one true god,' Gino was visibly upset and excused himself, saying he needed to go home and get his mother. They sat there in the head principal's office.

"What do you mean, he can't register?" Gino's mother was very uncomfortable dealing with authorities. Her fingers nervously twisted the handles of her bag. She wished Carlos was here, but he was up on a large farm in the upper plains, helping with the wheat harvest.

"Ma'am, I did *not* say he could not register." The administrator was frustrated. His face was flushed, looking as if his starched collar was too tight. "But the school board passed a resolution that every student must take an oath of allegiance to God and to Country. After all, we live in a Kristian land."

Rosetta quickly stood up. Her usual shyness flung aside. Gino stared at her with his mouth agape. "Sir," she said, " This country may have been founded on Kristian principles but those founding fathers from the Old World offered us a country with *religious freedom*. Gino, come with me. You deserve a better education than this."

As mother and son abruptly left the administrator's office, the man offered a quick prayer. He knew the school board's decision would provoke controversy and in his heart he agreed with the boy's mother. Yet, he could not defy the order of his superiors. He hoped that this would not be the worst year of his career.

They were seated around several portable tables set next to each other and covered with several large tablecloths. Bowls of grapes and apples were the harvest from Arnica and Holly's gardens. Ears of maize and strawberry corn were braided together, adorned with spears of millet. Each centerpiece was decorated with small corn dollies. The conversation was intense and lively, yet frequently punctuated with loud gales of laughter. These people truly loved being together. All the humans were upon chairs and Dark Star, the unicorn gaily trotted about enjoying each one of the guests.

Arnica sat at one end of the table. To his left sat Iris, Merrydale's postmarm. Her long, thick braid lay over her left shoulder, small bright marigolds woven into the dark hair. At her other side sat Pastor Dolorum, although the title 'Pastor' was likely to soon be deleted. Dolorum (Iris calls him 'Dolly' and the nickname was catching among the coven) was dark complected. They were a very striking couple and obviously very much in love.

"I know my mother, Mildora, would be so proud of us." Dolly's eyes sparkled as he looked at Iris.

"We've talked about it," said Iris. "It's going to be a Handfasting, but not open to the public although we are certain that they *will* learn about it."

"I've been at the Church of the Martyr nearly three years. It's not a long time." Dolorum's dark countenance had led many to believe he was a puppet of the Users but he had proved to be a renegade. During the months his mother lay at home dying, he discovered his Descendant Tribe heritage and just the year before last he worked with the Earthkin to mount a wonderful Yule/Kristmas celebration. The people of Merrydale had grown to love him but his superiors found him unwilling to accept the increasing dominance of the Users, the right-wing faction within the Kristos which was trying to take control of the Politico Party.

A sound like many little bells filled the late-afternoon clearing. Dolly turned the crimson color of embarrassment. The tinkling of silverware against the water glasses grew louder. Finally Iris rose to her feet and the bell sounds were silence.

"My friends," she said, "why we're only making *plans* for our wedding. This isn't fair."

"Bless the crops for us," Lotus called out. Seated near the other end of the tables, he held Dagon on his lap. Dagon was just over three years old. Jewel, her russet-colored hair perfect for Autumn, tugged at Lotus' sweater.

"Sweetheart," she pleaded, "you're embarrassing them."

"You win," Dolorum said. "And I'm trying to relax my old Kristos ways." And with that he took Iris in his arms, swooped her backwards and gave her a long and passionate kiss. The gardens were filled with cheers. Dark Star began trotting around them all. As the couple came up for air, Dark Star nuzzled up to them, wanting something.

Holly's face always looked ready to smile. "Dolly," he asked. "Tell us all about the Synod. We've heard the rumors."

Dolorum's energy quieted as Iris sat back down. "My friends," he began, accustomed to speaking before a congregation. "As you know I have been called before a Synod. Bishop Miter has recommended that I be fired. Several members of the congregation have been asked to testify as well and a ruling will be issued sometime next month."

Carlos leaned over to Rosetta. "I knew about the Synod, but not that old Miter would be so foolish." Carlos and Rosetta thought highly of Dolorum.

Dolly cleared his throat quietly which brought everyone to attention. "What Bishop Miter doesn't know is that my resignation will be read aloud tomorrow morning at Sunday services. This will be my last 'duty' as a Kristos minister. I cannot ethically allow this to happen." Considering the gravity of his statement, Dolly and Iris looked positively radiant. Dolorum turned toward Pearl. "Pearl, would you please make the announcement?"

"First, Arnica, I want to thank you for a beautiful Harvest Ritual this afternoon. What a joy to be in your gardens. Holly, this year's fresh grape juice is the best ever. What magick have you put in it?" Holly laughed. Pearl looked at her coven mates and the other friends and guests. "Now you know. Dolly will be pastor no more after tomorrow. But other events have happened as well. Near three years ago I accepted a young lad as a student. That was before I took Phoenix to Cloverville for his last months. Gino is now old enough to begin junior high school but not even Rosetta could convince the school to let him register unless he took that oath."

Dark Star snorted her displeasure bringing welcome laughter to the group.

"Many of you may not know it, but I have an education degree. Until I met Phoenix I had once hoped to teach school. Dolly and I intend to begin with a home-schooling program this year and possibly expand it into an actual alternative school where children are taught to respect our Mother Earth and where Earthkin ways are considered as healthy as any religion."

Pearl's voice was lost amid the cheering. As she sat, Carlos stood up. Had his dark hair not been cut so short it would be quite curly.

"Pearl, Pastor Dolorum, friends..." Carlos was an outgoing man and loved this moment. "Arnica, thanks for letting us come to the celebration. My wife and I have learned a lot from Gino and we're very comfortable with the Renaissance Tribal ways. You may not know it but Rosetta and I have been talking to many of our friends in town. I don't know if you can handle it or not, but among our friends are seventeen children, grades three through ten, who would be in your school as quick as you open a door. And we would all pay for the privilege of getting our young ones a real education!"

"I don't know if we can handle that many," Dolorum said.

Just then, Dark Star, who had trotted off to the gardens, came back now with a couple stems of bright blue asters. She laid them on Holly's lap. Everyone turned to look at Holly. He stood to take his turn speaking. He was so loved and people easily smiled in his presence.

"Arnica and I have been talking. You know that I once taught third grade, long ago, until the school board was infiltrated by Users. It's time for me to come out of retirement. If there's a need, I've kept up my certification." Holly reached over and took his partner's hand.

Arnica rose to his feet. "Dear Ones," he said, "I've known this to be happening and we've been doing some checking. There's a building available which meets the code. It could be converted into as many as four classrooms although right now we have three of our coven who are certified as teachers: Holly, Pearl and Dolly. I know that we could accept as many as twenty students but this move will bring controversy to Merrydale. It's a small town and we'll be more conspicuous than we've been to date."

"Dagon will be ready for your school in just a couple of years." Jewel said. "Let us know what we can do." There was a rush of excitement throbbing around the tables.

"Trust me," said Arnica, the serious tone in his voice bringing people back to realty, "we will. There's a meeting here in three days, for we must be completely organized and legal before any public announcement can be made. We'll finalize our decision at that time. Dear friend Dolly, thank you for all you are doing. Our blessings will be with you tomorrow. And now, it's time to play ring toss!"

Loud cheering filled the gardens. Dark Star was so excited and danced back and forth. Ringlets of leaves would be tossed at her horn, the 'winners' given one of Dark Star's kisses and the hatchling getting a borage treat in return.

Much fun would be had by all.

XXXI - The Bishop's Revenge

"You can't be serious?" Dolorum was kneeling next to the elfwort, its tall, eight-foot stalks holding fading leaves. Dark Star stood just at his right, playfully nipping at the upper leaves as they danced from Dolorum's touch.

"It's a *perennial*," Arnica said, his face gathered up in amusement. "It's trying to completely die down so that next spring it will start all over again from its root system." It was a beautiful, late-October day. Arnica felt some conflict. The sunny, warm days allowed him to make great strides with the gardens yet there was an undercurrent of uneasiness as he wondered if this might not be part of the global warming.

"That's amazing," Dolorum mused. "What would happen if you just left it?" he asked, taking the clippers to the thick stalks. Dark Star quickly stepped back.

"Slug heaven," Arnica answered. "It would all die down quickly and be a decomposing feast for garden pests."

Dolorum, having recently resigned from the Church of the Martyr, was enjoying his new freedom. No longer held to the demanding schedule of the church, he was able to expand his Earthkin roots. It was nearly two and a half years ago that Mildora Dolorum had passed over. Dolly, as Iris like to call him, had taken a position in Merrydale so he could be there for his mother in her final years. Little did he know of his Earthkin heritage, nor could he have imagined that he would leave his Kristos ministry and take great joy in belonging to Arnica and Holly's coven. Here he was helping Arnica prepare the gardens for Hallows and next year there would be a public Handfasting, conducted in the Renaissance Tribe ways. It no longer mattered if people knew or not.

Dolorum stood up, his arms full of elfwort stalks. "Where do these get thrown out?" he asked Arnica. One slipped loose and Dark Star quickly lowered her head and picked it up with her teeth.

The Hatchling

"Not quite thrown out," Arnica said kindly. "See that large bin over at the edge of the woods? That's where we place all the garden plants which are cut back. It will take them much longer to compost than the scraps from the kitchen or the refuse from canning our fruits. But give them enough time and they'll provide the gardens with rich humus."

The hatchling, her horn bright in the sun, pranced over to the bin. *She* knew where the various types of compost went. Dolorum followed her. "Ashes to ashes and compost to compost... " he chanted in the autumn breeze. Dolly loved this work. "It looks like the gardens are being touched by Hallows" he called to Arnica.

"Yes," Arnica raised up to his knees. "It's truly a joy to live with the changing of the seasons and there's nothing like a garden to bring full awareness."

As Arnica and Dolorum worked in the gardens Holly was in Merrydale, sitting in Pearl's kitchen around a very large table. Iris was there. The post office was closed for her lunch. After the school board, now run by the majority vote of the User faction of the Politicos, voted to require an oath of allegiance, the decision was made to establish an Earthkin school.

"We're going to volunteer our services," Carlos said.

Rosetta, Gino's mother, nodded in agreement. "I've sort of held back," she said. Her dark hair framed her lovely face. "I've watched how Gino has grown and changed since he's had the guidance from you, Pearl. He's growing into a fine young man and I know it's because of the extra education he's getting from your coven. We've talked," and she looked at Carlos. He nodded at her. "I'd like to volunteer to fix the noon lunches for the children. It will give me a chance to be involved. Gino is old enough - and independent enough (she laughed at this) that I need something to do."

Carlos picked up her train of thought. "She's too modest to say so, but Rosetta has cooked for large family gatherings of fifty or more and she's wonderful. Those young ones will eat well if she's in the kitchen. And there's more. I'd like to offer my services for remodeling and maintenance."

Pearl looked as if she didn't know what to say. Just weeks ago they were hoping to have perhaps twenty students but the word was quietly circulating among other Renaissance peoples. Parents from other villages had contacted them. Even some of the native Descendant peoples let them quietly know they would prefer an Earthkin private school to the increasingly Kristos dominated public schools.

"We're going to need this help," she said. "Carlos, between you and Rosetta, it appears that we can pay for one full-time position. It's not a lot but..."

Carlos interrupted her. "But we don't need much. We live simply. Over the years I worked in Mill City we put half of every paycheck into savings. Rosetta's so good with our budget that we're nearly two years ahead in house payments. Please, let us help you get this school established."

Holly took a turn speaking. It was obvious Pearl was very moved, emotionally. "Carlos, it's been quite a year. Since Kalven's tragic death last Candlemas, I've come to know more about Gino's parents. It will be wonderful working with you both and getting to know you. Gino's quite a fine young man, a reflection of your parenting. I know you'll both be a good influence on the young ones." Holly raised his cup of cider. "To Carlos and Rosetta. Welcome to our staff."

Dark Star lay upon the grass, soaking up the warm rays of the sun. Dolorum lay upon his back, his head resting upon her flank. What a picture they made.

"Gardening's hard work, but it feels wonderful," Dolorum said.

Arnica was digging among the honeysuckle vines, pruning and setting them in place to withstand the winter wind. "It's different than writing sermons, I'll wager."

Laughter danced through the gardens like the breezes among the wind chimes.

"Dolly," Arnica asked, using Iris' pet name, "what *is* your first name? For so long you were known as 'Pastor Dolorum' by everyone. Even after you became active in our coven we called you Dolorum like everyone else. Until you and Iris, that is..."

Dolorum blushed slightly. "Good timing, Arnica," he answered. "I've been thinking about this. You know, all of Merrydale still thinks of me as the Kristos pastor associated with the Church of the Martyr. If I'm to stay here and have a new image, it's time to claim the rest of my name."

"Which is?" Arnica paused in his work and turned, attentive, to the dark man.

"It's Deodar." Dark Star raised her head and looked at him at the sound of his name. "My mother's mother named me. Deodar means 'timber of the gods' in Sanskrit. I never really thought about it until this past year. My Earthkin heritage is stronger than I had realized. Once I began public school I was simply known by my surname. We lived in a small town, Spencer, in very conservative area and my father was pushing for me to go to seminary so I was cultivated for a Kristos lifestyle. I don't think my mother objected for she knew it would bring me a better education than I would get in Spencer. And she was right. Seminary training gave me my master's degree. And after my father died my mother left Spencer far behind. I was here in Merrydale for nearly two years before I fully realized why she chose it. I thank her every day in my morning blessings. Yes, it's time for Merrydale to know me as Deodar Dolorum."

"Deodar." Arnica said the word several times. "How fitting that the principal of the new school is named for a tree of knowledge. You will do well, my friend."

"Who's going to be at tomorrow evening's ritual," asked Deodar. Certainly, he thought, this year should be much calmer than last year, when Phoenix appeared from the Otherworld. What a series of events followed Pearl's moving through the veil to take that message to Carlos!

"Amber is in town and she'll be here. She's one of the few daughters of the Loon Tribe who seems to thrive on our Renaissance ways."

"Didn't she own a little gift store?" recalled Deodar.

"Yes, the Crystal Emporium was a joy for Merrydale." Both men fell quiet, reflecting on the store's present incarnation. 'Tears of the Savior' attracted many right-wing Kristos. Users drove for many miles to buy religious books and gifts. Amber was quite furious to see what had happened to her magickal location. Arnica picked up the story. "She'd been seeing a steelsmith but after two years, the relationship hasn't worked out and she wanted to take a break from the River Mountains."

"I've heard much about her. I'm looking forward to being in Circle with her." Deodar rose to his feet. "Well, back to work!"

Iris had left to return to work, Carlos and Rosetta had gone home. Holly and Pearl sat there, engrossed in their first 'curriculum meeting.'

"I could teach grammar, writing and literature. I taught language skills, in fact, for a couple of years before switching to third grade." Holly had thought about this for weeks. Holly and Pearl were trying to settle some important issues. At first the thought was to teach the middle grades, but there were concerns about the challenges students would face when they returned to public school. Holly and Pearl were working to see if an upper school might be the answer.

"My degree is in arts and music," Pearl commented. "Dolorum has the credentials to be principal and to teach the math courses. And I bet we could get him to offer a course or two in philosophy and ethics!" Pearl was probing the recesses of her mind. "Wait, what about Flying Raven? Do you think we could get her to come here and teach science? She could keep her home in the Mothervalley. I think she'd be a wonderful teacher."

"And Amber," Holly was growing very excited. "Let's ask Amber if she wouldn't consider taking the history and social studies. I know she taught those classes for the Loon Tribe schools before she moved here to open her store. I wonder if she'd come back to Merrydale."

Just then Iris dashed into the kitchen unexpectedly. Why, the postmarm must have closed the office early.

Iris looked at them both. "I just heard," she was breathless. "Bishop Miter got his cronies to push through legislation. They're going to try and outlaw any private school which isn't based upon Kristos principles."

"Isn't that against the constitution," asked Pearl.

"It is," answered Holly, "but you don't know Miter."

The room fell silent.

"And he doesn't know us, either." Iris was a strong woman.

Seated upon the floor in a circle, the bright flames from the cauldron threw odd, dancing shadows about the room. The Circle had been cast and each was in rapt silence in communion with their ancestors.

Suddenly, Dark Star sat up trembling. She looked at Holly sitting next to her, her eyes showing fear. Holly, who had learned to hear her thoughts, quickly put his arm around her and pulled her head down upon his shoulder and listened.

"A death," he said. "Not one of us, but the news will be like an earthquake."

No one spoke another word.

XXXII - The Tower Card

Although the concept had arisen just this past Autumn, progress was being made toward establishing an Earthkin school in Merrydale. The coven, the unofficial board of directors, had decided that the school would include grades 8-12. With seventeen students ready to sign up last autumn, there were now fifty. Parents were pooling their resources and making donations. Textbooks were being ordered and a building a block south of the post office had been given to the school. Just like that! It was a two-story building of large offices around a courtyard which could be converted into as many as ten classrooms. It even had a kitchen for one of the businesses once renting there had been a restaurant. The cost of converting the building would be minimal and a large parking garage could be converted to recreational and exercise spaces. And the school mascot had been chosen. Naturally, it would be a unicorn!

Gino and Dark Star, the hatchling, were at Pearl's house. Faced with the new requirement of an oath to 'the one true god,' Rosetta kept Gino at home. He was being home-schooled under Pearl's tutelage and making excellent progress, but it was difficult for the young teen to not ask "when will the school be ready?" Today, although cloudy outside, the kitchen was warmed with the rich scent of pumpkin pies. Dark Star was curled on the floor beneath the table. During all this school excitement, she was spending time both at Pearl's during Gino's schooling and back at her home in the cabin with Arnica and Holly. Dark Star seemed to thrive in the bustle of activity surrounding the creation of the school.

The corporate charter had been filed with the District of Merrydale. There were no difficulties with the local administration. Trillium School received a provisional charter. But it was not so easy with the parliamentary educational office in Mill City, over on the other side of the snow-covered mountains.

Bishop Miter, still smarting from Deodar Dolorum's resignation and the exposé of the Society for the Forest, was a force unto himself. Even his attempt to ban Maypole's was not successful. Realizing that his right-wing religious movement was losing political power, Bishop Miter appealed to the media. "God will punish evil," he lectured, his face reddening. Miter ranted on, stirring hysteria against "pagans, heathens and other cults" and called upon politicians to protect the children against those who were anti-Kristos, thundering that allowing *them* to have their own schools would foster sexual perversion. Miter's plea that Parliament investigate the teaching staff at the proposed school did not pass but was currently stalled in committee. Although still the minority party, the Conservatives were able to raise the constitutionality issue and a growing number of Politicos were sensitive to growing public sentiment favoring an Earthkin school. Meanwhile, Miter was making segments of the population uncomfortable at the new school in Merrydale. Taking advantage of these threads of fear of the unknown, "God will punish evil" was the bishop's slogan. His supporters were waiting to see if the Bishop was truly a prophet.

During one organizational meeting, Pearl did a Tarot reading to see how things would turn out. The cards were turned one by one. Although the final card was the Four of Wands, certainly a reason to feel joyful, the fourth card was the Tower Card.

"The news will be like an earthquake," Arnica said, quoting Holly's message from Dark Star at the Hallows Eve ritual.

The kitchen was filled with the scent of cinnamon cookies. Rosetta was creating a new recipe for the school. Gino sat at the kitchen table, happily eating those cookies which didn't turn out 'perfect.' It was a tribute to his mother's baking skills that there were very few, indeed. Carlos was out in the front room creating pages and pages of plans and tools and materials needed to convert the new building to a school.

Pearl and Deodar were both on their way to the postal shop to meet and share lunch with Iris. It was a lovely day, cool but clear. In the distance were the snow-topped mountains. Iris had called both of them that morning, saying that she had news. What Iris was eager to share were the letters from Flying Raven, who lived far away in the Mothervalley. Her children long grown, she wrote that she was ready for a change and would rent out her house and come to Merrydale to teach at the new school. And did they know of a little house for rent? The other letter was from Amber, a daughter of the Descendant Tribe. Amber was up in the River Mountains with her people but since her brief relationship with Quicksilver ended, she was ready to return to Merrydale. Both Amber and Flying Raven expressed great delight for now they would be in Merrydale when Iris and Deodar Dolorum were Handfasted.

Arnica and Holly were hanging ornaments on the tree and decorating their home in preparation for tomorrow's Yule Eve Ritual. The scent of apple cider was in the air, as heavy as incense. It was Arnica's special recipe. In addition to the cloves, allspice and cinnamon sticks, he also added anise stars and a couple of 'secret' ingredients. Presents littered the house, wrapped in bright paper, filled with wonderful home-made treasures for their growing list of friends and coven mates.

Dark Star was sitting next to the fireplace. She had tired herself out with a good romp that morning. Coming home from Merrydale, as the invisible powder began to let her horn show again, Holly told her to hurry home and see what Arnica had waiting. Dark Star loved surprises. She was panting hard when she found Arnica in their small greenhouse. She was rewarded with some December borage blooms which Arnica had nursed and coaxed into doing well, just for their unicorn hatchling.

Life among our friends was very good when the news came, shaking the entire District of Merrydale like a fair-sized earthquake.

"What? Are you serious?" Arnica had answered the telephone.

"What is it?" Holly asked. Dark Star sat up, her ears turned toward the men. She sensed that this was the premonition she felt when the veils were parted this past Hallows.

"He's dead, Bishop Miter fell dead while giving one of his sermons this very morning!" Arnica's hand over the phone, he could not believe what Iris was telling him.

"That's amazing," Holly said. In his mind he wondered about Miter's predication that his 'God will punish evil' then shook his head. No, he could not consider Miter 'evil,' even though the man's fears and lack of enlightenment surely brought much harm to many.

"Thanks, dear one, we'll see you tomorrow." Arnica hung up the phone. The cabin was quiet for a time, until the dust of the unexpected news had settled. Arnica and Holly were quieter as they went about the cabin, transforming it into a temple for Yule.

The air was holiday-scented. In the front temple, Gino sat on the floor, Dark Star at his side, carefully looking at each of the dozens of drawing pens. One by one he would take one out of the finely-crafted box and try a few strokes on the first page of a thick drawing pad of excellent paper.

"Just you wait, Dark Star," his freckled face turned toward the hatchling. The unicorn was his favorite friend. "I'm going to draw pictures of you."

The temple air wafted the remains of the Yule Eve ritual incense, the slight smell of wood smoke from the fire and the light yet pungent scent of the spruce, all decorated up as the most honored guest of the ritual.

The adults were all in the kitchen. Isn't it amazing how the kitchen is where friends gather, no matter what size that room?

"Dolly said we could be Handfasted at Beltane." Iris blushed, quickly acting a bit distracted by playing with her long braid.

"That's true," said Deodar. "And Arnica, what would you think if we held the ceremony in the courtyard at the new school?"

"What a splendid idea," said Holly. The last time I was there, watching Carlos at work, I spent some time in the courtyard and thought about our Circles, once Flying Raven and Amber are both living here. We may not all fit into our cabin!"

"When do you think it will be ready?" asked Iris. Wearing her robe with it's little bells sewn on, Iris was their strongest activist for ecological concerns. An active, outdoor woman, until she met Deodar (who was then still known as Pastor Dolorum), she had no interest in marriage and everyone took great joy in her happiness.

"The building," answered Arnica, "may be ready by mid April. Carlos told me that over a dozen of the fathers and also a couple of the mothers have considerable skill at construction and repair. The faculty? We're working on it."

"I've ordered the books for the faculty." Pearl paused and laughed lightly, her voice like the sound of bells. "I haven't adjusted to being *faculty* again! Not that my work with Gino hasn't brought me great blessings as a teacher."

"I propose a toast to our new principal, Deodar Dolorum" Arnica raised his mug of mulled cider. "Blessed be your feet for having walked this long path which brought you to Merrydale and the Church of the Martyr and now to our new Trillium School."

Voices cheered out, the soft clink of glass mugs punctuated the air.

"And I propose a toast to Arnica and Holly. You can't imagine how wonderful I will feel to have you conduct our Handfasting." Iris, said, radiant with her joy.

And so went the evening. When the coven finished laughing and joking and dreaming out loud about the changes as Trillium School took shape, they woke Gino, who had fallen asleep with his arm around Dark Star. Soon all were off into the night.

Arnica and Holly did the washing up and put things away. Even though it was late, they enjoyed their quiet time together.

"Go wake Dark Star and we'll be off to bed." Arnica kissed his partner upon the forehead.

Holly went in to wake the hatchling. "Dark Star," Holly whispered. He stroked her mane and scratched her ear. "May the new Sun God bless you as much as you have blessed us."

And then, the lights out, the cabin itself seemed to sleep.

XXXIII - It's In The Paint

"I'm grateful for a comfortable season," Arnica commented to Holly as they walked toward Merrydale.

"I am too. Did you see the new peony shoots? Candlemas just here and you can already see them hinting at Spring?" Holly loved the peonies.

"The gardens are a better herald of the waxing sunlight than the dozens and dozens of seed and garden catalogs." Arnica pulled a fresh sprig of borage from a bag slung from his shoulder and turned to Dark Star, "Here's another." An experiment this winter had proven successful. Arnica had been growing some borage in the greenhouse just for the hatchling. Dark Star walked leisurely along her humans, a woven basket of candles for the coming year's rituals hanging from her back. They walked along quietly, then Arnica mused, "It's a blessing that the weather for our gardens has been so temperate."

"Amber said she barely made it through the pass from the River Mountains." Holly's arm stretched out so his fingers could scratch Dark Star's ears. How content she was, padding along the road to Merrydale with her two humans. "All the snow seems to be falling east of the Red Mountains. It's as if the north wind Boreas lost his grip for a bit and the arctic cold has slipped loose." As they made their way, Holly adjusted the straps on the hatchling's carry-all bags. One of them held his 'Wicca basket' which contained their best ritual tools. "Do you think this is part of global warming? Or maybe the shrinking ozone?"

"I don't know," answered Arnica. "I can say with certainty that our Mother Earth is suffering greatly from the growing population and the destruction of her resources. We know so little about our planet and her weather that unfortunately, those in power are unlikely to believe it's time for a course of action until it's too late." Arnica gently stroked his greying beard. "But isn't it wonderful that our main topic of conversation is the weather?"

Life everywhere in the land seemed quiet since the passing of Bishop Miter. Miter had become a spokesperson for the Users, the right wing of the Politicos. The Politicos were pro-business, seeing forests and minerals as theirs to be exploited, frequently quoting from the Book of Doom, their religious book, about the earth being theirs to develop for the glory of their god. But greed and spiritual imbalance had taken their toll and their movement began to unravel following the death of an Earthkin man, Kalven, in Mill City. Events reached a climax when Miter, bishop of the Cathedral of Thorns was preaching "God will punish evil" and fell dead right during his sermon. At least for the present the Users were quiet.

Despite the earlier legislation passed in Parliament requiring an oath which was clearly sectarian favoring the Kristos' god and the recent inquiry instigated at Miter's request, the educational office in Mill City had quietly approved the corporate charter for Trillium School. The District of Merrydale had offered no opposition and the Merrydale Council, for the village, realized that the town would have not one school but two. Earlier fears of a loss of enrollment in the public system were quieted when the Merrydale principal spoke on their behalf.

The coven, having celebrated their Candlemas Eve at the Grove, enjoying their intimacy in Arnica and Holly's cabin, were looking forward to a Candlemas Day celebration being held at the school. At Arnica's suggestion it was 'by invitation only' limited to the new faculty, staff, students, their parents and the families of those directly involved. Despite the recent political calm, all were in agreement that keeping the ritual low key was wise. Some voiced the opinion at the last school meeting that they didn't want to have curiosity seekers or any radical member of the User party arriving to create a disruption.

At last everyone was gathered in the courtyard. Once again they were blessed with good weather, a benefit of being on the west side of the Red Mountains. Chairs from the classrooms had been brought in and the people formed a loosely-shaped circle around the new central fountain. And what a fountain!

Lotus, known for his skill as a wood carver, had tried his hand at sculpting with a mixture of cement and other substances. Lotus had created a beautiful fountain, about five feet across at the widest, shaped like a large scallop. In the center was a small jet of water, just enough to provide the sound of running water throughout the courtyard. Carlos had done the plumbing.

Arnica, the much loved elder of the local Renaissance Tribes, was the obvious choice to lead the blessing of Trillium School on Candlemas Day. As he walked to the center of the circle to stand next to the fountain, the small crowd burst into applause, laughter and cheering. Holly's eyes opened wide: why, Arnica actually blushed!

"Dear Ones, as the President of Trillium School's new Board of Directors, I welcome you." Arnica's voice brought quiet to the courtyard, "This is quite an occasion. We will begin the blessing of our school with this fountain. Lotus..." Arnica's voice was drowned out by the sound of bells. Each person had brought a small bell to ring and the joyful tinkling was to celebrate the craftsmanship of the wood carver. The sound filled the courtyard like a wave but quickly ebbed when Arnica raised his hand. "Thank you," he said. "and thank Lotus. It was his work which brought the fountain into manifestation." Arnica waved his hand in his friend's direction.

Lotus stood shyly with all the attention, then quickly sat down to the joyful clamor of bell ringing.

Arnica continued, "There is much magick in the air surrounding Trillium School. And there is much magick in the waters of this fountain. We have collected sacred and special waters from everywhere, all of us. Tomorrow, after Iris and Flying Raven finish their sunrise smudging of all the rooms, Carlos will begin painting. We chose a water base paint so that as he mixes the colors, some water from the fountain will be added to every bucket of paint. All of the magick we set in motion will become permanently bonded to the school." There was a murmur of pleasure at this wonderful idea. "And so, should anyone ask you why Trillium, the first Earthkin school in our country, seems to have so much magick, you know what you can say: It's in the paint!"

Laughter filled the room like the heady scent of a warm garden. Holly stood, beaming like a ray of spring sunshine. "Let me introduce our teachers for you. Our math teacher, Deodar Dolorum." Holly's eyes shone with a mischievous twinkle. "Also known as the former Kristos minister of the Church of the Martyr, now liberated as the Earthkin's first school principal."

Cheers and bell-ringing filled the room. Dolly stood at the fountain, pulling one small bottle after another from various pockets and emptying them into the fountain. "I collected water from my nomadic years as a missionary when I was young. I also thought about a bottle of holy water from the Church of the Martyr but thought better of it and emptied it into the Merrydale pond." A rustle of just a slight disappointment at the latter brushed through the room. "Next, your teacher of arts and music, Pearl Lamina."

"This is water my grandmother, Lady Ellhorn, sent from an artesian well near Cloverville." Pearl emptied a small bottle of water into the fountain. The gentle splashing could be heard throughout the courtyard. "And this is a small vial of water from the Passing ritual of my late partner, Phoenix." Finished pouring, she added, "And next,

Flying Raven, who has moved here from the Mothervalley to become your science teacher."

Tall and a bit stately as she walked to the fountain, Flying Raven realized her natural stature might seem too imposing. As she drew a bottle from an inner pocket she quickly did a few silly dance steps which filled the courtyard with the laughter of adults and giggles of children. "Water from the Great River of the Mothervalley." Parents and students alike knew that Flying Raven would be a much loved teacher.

Amber was next. Already well-known in Merrydale from her years owning the Crystal Emporium, she had many small vials and little bottles of water of the most *interesting* shapes. "This is from our tribal collection. The Elder Mothers each sent some of the most sacred waters collected over many generations." The people were very proud that Amber, a daughter of the Loon Tribe, was moving back from the River Mountains. Everyone believed that the presence of a teacher from the Descendant Tribes would maintain a healthy balance. Amber would be the history and social studies teacher.

Holly was next. He carried a large, glass jug of water which Arnica, Holly and the coven had mixed last night at the Candlemas Eve ritual. "Let's see, there's water from the Grotto of Our Lady from across the great sea in land of Bavaria from the magickal spring dedicated to Pan a millennium ago."

"And water from the many years of our collection," Arnica added. "For anyone who might not already know, Holly will be your language arts teacher."

"I like the water from the Great Chasm and from the Bear Valley we collected from the geysers," Holly added.

Gino's parents were next, Carlos and Rosetta. Rosetta, the new cook for Trillium School, spoke softly, "My mother brought this over from our homeland. This is from Astarte's Well near the ancient ruins of Italica." Carlos couldn't help himself. He reached into the water to check his plumbing work.

Representing the Board of Directors, Iris brought water. Lots of water. As postmarm, she had put out a call and had been receiving two or three parcels a week from all over the world, it seemed. Jewel and Lotus brought water which they carried up with their toddler Dagon, soon to be four years old. The water was from his Wiccaning.

Water was brought forth by many present. Wren and Robin sent water from the Highlands plus some they had gathered from their trip to the ocean with Arnica and Holly three years ago this coming summer. The Rhymer sent very precious water, gathered from the Realm of the Faerie. Echo sent lake water from the Red Mountain Plateau. As it trickled into the water below, the story teller's laughter seemed to take life in the fountain.

Many of the parents and new students brought water. There were the Croffy twins, who would be in the same grade. Last was a short, dark man named Shadow Tail, recently moved to Merrydale in order to begin studying the Earthkin ways from Arnica. Shadow Tail was a member of the Loon Tribe who lived in the Lower River Plain south of Amber's homeland. A quiet sort, some of Merrydale's residents had noticed curiously that the town squirrels behaved quite differently when Shadow Tail walked through the town square.

All the water added, Arnica asked that everyone bow their head in thanks. He offered a prayer to the Mother of the Earth and the Father of the Woodlands. At a nod of his head, Carlos flipped a switch and a stream of water rose up in the fountain's center to splash down, mixing all of the waters together along with the music of the chanting.

As everyone focused upon the wonder of it all, what should happen but Dark Star, trotting up from a corner of the courtyard. Gino, the youngest member of the coven, quickly ran up to her. The people, quite accustomed to seeing this small but very curious 'horse' were very amused. As Dark Star bent forward to drink from the fountain, the jet of water came splashing down, catching her head, horn and all. As Gino watched in shock, the young unicorn's horn became visible.

Gino pulled her back and looked in panic at Arnica. Reaching quickly into his pocket, Arnica grasped a handful of a magickal herbal dust he had prepared just in case of emergency. In a quick movement he spread it into the air, spoke a word no one could understand.

The room quickly filled with the sounds of awe and amazement as everyone began talking about seeing a horn quickly appear and disappear on the colt's head. With Trillium School's mascot having earlier been announced as a unicorn, Arnica's magick worked and everyone but those in the coven were certain that they had witnessed the most marvelous optical illusion created by the magick of the waters.

Arnica aspurged water to the four corners of the earth as people offered blessings and invocations. The final act of the ritual was to carry water to a bucket sitting upon Carlos' workbench which had been set up as a carpenter's 'altar' with his new tools.

"It *will* be in the paint!" Arnica said. Trillium School was filled with cheering and chanting and the ringing of bells. There was much joy in Merrydale this Candlemas Day.

XXXIV - Handfasting Plans

"Look at those wild plum blossoms! Aren't they something?" Holly, Arnica and Dark Star were walking in to Merrydale. The March sun bright, Dark Star's coat was sun warmed beneath Holly's hand.

"The forsythia that Pearl brought to Eostara Eve last night was certainly a joy, wasn't it?" Arnica wore one of his straw gardening hats. "Ours is about a week later than the forsythia in Merrydale. I buried my egg by the forsythia just below the blueberries, in case you weed there this year."

The coven celebrated Eostara Eve by decorating hard-boiled eggs and writing their desires for personal change and growth upon them. Holly, with his ability to 'hear' Dark Star in his mind, created an egg for her. But what a curious message it was. *Something blue* was what Holly interpreted it to be and the hatchling seemed to be content with that message. Holly wrote Dark Star's message and Arnica went with the young unicorn and buried it for her. The hatchling led the older man to a spot out in the stone Circle, just about where her egg first appeared. It was four years ago this Sabbat that Dark Star had hatched from the large egg, a very momentous occasion.

They walked along in thought, just the sound of Dark Star's hooves striking an occasional rock and the quiet sound of Arnica and Holly's soft shoes.

"Did you see the look on his face?" asked Holly.

Arnica knew his partner was remembering the District Inspector's tour of Trillium School. It was quite an event. "I don't know what he was expecting..."

The Hatchling

"A cauldron..." Holly said, laughing. Even Dark Star snorted at that one, turning her head toward her humans as they walked along the road into the town.

"It certainly wasn't what he was expecting. Carlos has worked so hard, even the kitchen was approved. How amazing to get the permits and pass inspection in but a matter of months!" Arnica knew it was a culmination of hard work, commitment and magick.

And Holly, knowing just what his love was thinking remembered how they consecrated the paint for the school building with sacred waters at their Candlemas Ritual. "It's in the paint!" he laughed.

The murmur of voices in the school's courtyard echoed the sound of water in the fountain, ornamented with laughter and the melody of people exchanging pleasantries and sharing news. Dark Star found a quiet corner. Even within the sacred space of an Earthkin school Arnica and Holly didn't want anyone outside the coven recognizing Dark Star as a unicorn. Life was safer with everyone thinking her a pony, even if she was the most amazing little colt ever seen, and there was still some talk about the 'image' of a unicorn's horn appearing last Candlemas. Fortunately, the idea of it being 'group imagination' woven out of enthusiasm for a unicorn being the school mascot was a most satisfying explanation.

Someone rang a bell. The sound cut through the festivity leaving a quiet in its path gently coddled with the soft splashing of the fountain. Arnica, the elder of the Earthkin community, went to a small dais. He thanked everyone for joining them. There was much applause. He shared the events when Trillium School passed its inspection. There was more applause and considerable laughter. Then Arnica called upon Lotus, the coven's wood worker. It was Lotus who created the fountain.

Lotus brought forth the egg which would serve as the time capsule. It was beautiful, a large egg over a foot tall carved from two pieces of madrone. There were madrone trees growing in a few magickal places. A large branch of the oldest of the *Arbutus* had been felled in a storm. Local Earthkin often called it the Mother Tree and the crew cleaning up after the storm brought the largest segments of the branch to Lotus in whose hands they knew the wood would continue to
have a long life.

Holding the two halves the egg, Arnica placed a small collection of papers and items into the hollowed out madrone which would serve as a time capsule for Trillium School. There were copies of the deed and the front page of the newspaper. Only the coven knew the time capsule also contained magickal script designed to protect the school, written upon a piece of ancient parchment and tied into a scroll with seven braided hairs from Dark Star's tail. The hatchling was very happy with these events. She had seen her humans work through some harrowing politics before reaching this day. All of Merrydale was buzzing with excitement over the new school. Not even the more self righteous Politicos could avoid the contagious pride. Trillium School was the first Earthkin school ever chartered by the government. Dark Star knew that her presence was part of this magick, for that is why unicorns come to earth. She was able to sit quietly with her young friend Gino, knowing that treats were waiting for her as soon as the parents and children finished the ceremony and celebration.

Although it took longer than they hoped, eventually the Earthkin of Merrydale left for their homes, their hopes and dreams for the next generations vigorous on this special day. A few town officials had come as well, including the mayor. Despite an attempt by some of the Users, the right wing faction of the Politicos, to describe Trillium School as subversive and evil, all of Merrydale saw this as a great asset which enhanced their town's esteem.

The coven and a few staff and close friends sat about. The unofficial board of directors and trustees of the school, they were the mainstay of the local Earthkin and had worked the hardest.

Deodar Dolorum sat on the floor playing with Dagon, Jewel and Lotus' toddler. Iris looked over at her lover and smiled. He was so good with children. How she looked forward to her handfasting with Dolly at the next Sabbat.

"Jewel," Iris said, "how old will Dagon be?"

"Four just after Beltane," Jewel answered.

"Could he scatter the flower petals for the Handfasting?" Iris asked.

Dagon stopped playing with his 'Uncle Dolly' and answered, "yes, I can." Terribly precocious, ever since Dagon had slipped into the Realm of the Faerie at Midsummer three years ago he was wise well beyond his years.

"That reminds me," Pearl called across the staff and teacher's lounge to Iris. "Lady Ellhorn asked if you would like to wear her wedding dress. It's 75 years old and was hand-beaded by the last Elvenkin Priestess who had emigrated from the Otherlands."

Iris was visibly moved. Although known for being strong willed and forthright, the postmarm had to collect herself and wipe a few tears with fingers. "Dearest Pearl! Your grandmother's wedding dress? Oh, what an honor. Do you think it would fit?"

"My eye says it's so close only minor adjustments would be needed." Pearl's reputation with the needle was well-known.

"Something borrowed..." Holly sang out.

"I still need something blue," mused Iris.

"What about Dark Star as a ring bearer," offered Arnica.

"That's perfect. Oh, I'm so excited." Iris and Dolly were a wonderful couple.

Arnica stood up. Raising a glass of grape juice he and Holly had canned last autumn, his voice charged the room with energy. "My friends, an Equinox toast." Arnica looked about the room. "Holly, where's Dark Star?"

Just then the hatchling walked in, a yellow daffodil in her mouth. She trotted over to the elderly herbalist and raised her head high, joining in with the toast. They all knew she preferred borage blossoms but the surprise daffodils which had appeared in the courtyard were a gift to them all from previous tenants of the building which was now Trillium School.

"We have done well. On Monday the home schooling class will begin here." Arnica's eyes sparkled toward Pearl.

The Pictish woman, slight of build, raised her glass. "Gino helped me finish moving my books on Thursday. I'll be happier when the other teachers have students in their rooms but I'm so very honored to be the first."

Gino raised his glass. How proud he was to be the very first student. He had worked so hard with his magickal training and was doing well with the home schooling. Gino felt he could have much better grades this fall when school started for good.

Deodar got to his feet. "The plans are nearly set. Parents were told they can begin enrolling their children for the summer session. This will give us an opportunity to make everything work. We'll have just enough students for all five of us to get our educational programs in gear."

Dolly looked toward Gino's mother as Rosetta raised her hand. Still a bit shy, the dark-haired woman looked first toward Iris and then Deodar. "If the two of you would accept it, I would like to prepare the feast for your Handfasting. Several of the mothers approached me about this. It's something we would like to do to honor you both." Dolly and Iris looked at each other. It was such an offer, they didn't know what to say. Seeing their hesitation, Rosetta added with enough hope in her voice, "It would allow me to give the new kitchen a test run."

Gino was caught by surprise. "Mom," he said, "that's really neat!" Everyone laughed.

Soon it was time to close up the school and head home. There was the usual teasing of the engaged couple, asking them how ever they could wait past Beltane Eve. Iris was able to kid them back. Only the twinkle in her eye let them know she loved the teasing. But Deodar! Dolly blushed so bright. Sometimes his old Kristos' background left him at a loss with his new freedom.

Everyone hugged everyone else. Dark Star gave Gino a big wet lick across his face. Arnica and Holly took the hatchling and headed out into the woodland as the others turned toward their homes. Spring had arrived in Merrydale.

XXXV - The Surprise Guest

The sun shone brightly on Beltane morning. There was not much time left for quiet reflection. Arnica and Holly were walking in to Merrydale. Gino, the youngest of the coven, was with them, skipping and dancing along, filled with the exuberance only a teen could have on such a Beltane morning. Dark Star was wearing the most beautiful garlands of spring flowers. Holly and Gino had braided bells into the hatchling's silver-blue mane and tail, and with each graceful step of her small hooves, Dark Star carried the music of the devas with her. Her horn was sure to remain invisible. Arnica had altered the herbal formula which he rubbed upon her horn so she appeared no more than the most wonderful, small pony which was the most curious pet. A small cart wheeled behind the hatchling in which were the ritual tools Arnica would need for the Handfasting, their ritual robes, and a brightly colored parcel which carried their gifts for the couple's public ceremony. As its wheels turned Arnica reflected upon the turnings of the wheel since the hatchling had come into their lives.

Life at their cabin had changed little, although their coven had felt the wheel's turn. Pearl's partner, Phoenix, had passed over just two and a half years ago but Pearl had created a new life and was doing wonderfully. Four years ago at Beltane Amethyst and Crystal were still with them but they moved to Cloverville a year ago and already were so busy with their new lives that they rarely had time to stay in touch. Together they were the Three of Swords, Arnica reflected. And into their coven had come Gino, and Iris and Dolly. And with the new Trillium School, their lives were changing.

Although it was still out of sight, Arnica could sense that Merrydale was bursting with Beltane magick. Earthkin families felt the rising energies of spring within their homes. Not only was Trillium School becoming more functional every week, but Iris and Deodar were the talk of the entire region. Today Trillium School would be filled with guests as Merrydale's postmarm and Deodar Dolorum were joined in Handfasting. In truth, not everyone was as happy as the Earthkin. Although the anti Earthkin had quieted down since the death of Bishop Miter, there were still some individuals who bore a strong resentment over Dolorum's resignation. Miter who worked with the right wing Users faction of the Politicos party died unexpectedly last winter just after he had ranted that his "god will punish evil." The controversy over this and over Dolorum's earlier resignation from the Church of the Martyr in protest last autumn were now quieted. For most people, including the Kristos, a marriage (even an Earthkin rite) was a sacred event and Merrydale was bursting with smiling faces and the bloom of flowers everywhere.

The binding of Iris and Dolly's wrists had been done with a more private Handfasting last evening at the coven's May Eve observance. After Pearl drew down the Goddess and Arnica brought forth the Poetryman, Holly opened the portal. Dark Star guided the newly blessed couple down the path toward the stone Circle, the very site where her egg had appeared four years ago this past Candlemas. Candles placed in glass jars safely lined the path and created the most magickal of sights. Iris and Deodar walked together, their robes the color of the blossoms of Beltane, soft pinks like the apple blossom, pale creams like the cherry. Patterns and designs of flowers and of sigils were embroidered in the colors of the first rhododendrons and azaleas. Dolly and Iris looked radiant and their love and desire for each other heightened the glow of their auras. Earlier they had followed Arnica around the quarters, to Gino in the East (so proud that he now had an 'adult' role in the coven. Lotus greeted them in the South where he held one of his prized staffs, beautifully carved. Tomorrow they would be surprised at their public Handfasting when it became a gift! Holly invoked the element of water in the West and Flying Raven, discovering how pleased she was to be back in Merrydale, held her station in the North. Jewel sat just outside the Circle where she played a small harp, one of her new interests now that Dagon was old enough that she had some time for herself.

The coven waited in the Circle as the strains of music from Jewel's harp danced through the dusky light like delicate flying creatures. Suddenly the sound of hundreds and hundreds of tiny bells began ringing out from the woods. Dark Star came trotting back toward the Circle, blushing as much as any human! The hatchling had gotten the Faerie and Devas, her Otherworld friends, to ring small bells at the moment of the consummation.

But it was a Mystery. As far as anyone knew, Iris and Deodar had not noticed Dark Star's effort nor taken the music as anything other than the ecstatic crest of their passion. No one ever told them and Dark Star's 'gift' to Iris and Deodar would not manifest until Candlemas!

Trillium School looked little like a school. The townspeople of Merrydale had placed streamers and bouquets of flowers at the doors and windows. The gardens in front had been beautifully planted. Shadow Tail, staying temporarily with Arnica and Holly, had taken a position working at the school with Gino's father, Carlos. The men quickly determined that the grounds were best left to Shadow, who was studying herbal magick from Arnica.

Iris was in her bedroom dressing for her Handfasting. Pearl was fastening the silver clasps of the hand-beaded wedding gown which her grandmother, Lady Ellhorn, had worn just 75 years ago. One of the last garments made by the last of the Elvenkin Priestesses to emigrate from the Otherlands, it radiated with its own energy. Iris looked so beautiful. Today there would be no postal service in Merrydale. The mayor had declared a town holiday in honor of the village postmarm's Handfasting. Just a few rooms away was the attached office. Iris and Dolly would be living in her house.

Deodar Dolorum was dressing in a handsome robe. He was in 'his' home which he had inherited when his mother, Mildora, had passed away. The former Kristos clergyman was moved to his soul upon feeling such fulfillment and joy. All that he had sought through mainstream religion was being fulfilled through the Earthkin. Dolly was the new school's principal, he had been joined with the most wonderful woman he'd met last night in vows taken before the coven, and now the community of Merrydale was gathering to celebrate his marriage and the new school. Never had he felt such love from so many people. He looked around his mother's house. Dolly had never quite felt it was his and was more comfortable in Iris' home where he'd officially be living starting this very afternoon!

Deodar and Iris knelt before the altar in the school's courtyard. There were people sitting in the classrooms looking through the open windows! It seemed as if all of Merrydale was here. Marking the separation between the sacred circle and the space for guests were a multitude of flower petals. Dagon, just four years old, had scattered them as Arnica scribed the Circle. Jewel and Lotus' little boy carried a basket Amber brought as a wedding gift. Woven by her sisters of the Loon Tribe, it had husks from maize to bring the couple fertility in their Union. Bleeding hearts, primrose petals, violets, some roses (from the greenhouse) and tulips (from the higher elevations) created a wonderful medley of Beltane color.

Arnica stood behind Iris and Deodar, looking handsome with his greying beard and best Wiccan robe. Holly stood over by the fountain, his arm around Dark Star. Dark Star was to come in at just the right moment carrying the ring. Holly had been very honored to 'give Iris away,' which (or course) led him to making all manner of jokes. When Holly asked Iris about her father, she reacted strangely. A quick cloud passed over her shading her smile. Iris looked a bit sad and said she didn't know where he was but that it was o.k... and quickly changed the subject.

Arnica looked about. He stood a bit taller and waited until the small crowd grew very quiet. He gathered their energy and brought it as the bud of a flower, planted between Iris and Deodar, and then he began reading the Charge of the Beloved from the Handfasting Ritual:

"Beloved, I seek to know of you and ask of the Gods and Goddesses that I be given the wisdom to see you as you are and to love you as a Mystery.

"I will take joy in you, I delight in the taste of you. You are to me the whispering of the tides, the seduction of Summer's heat.

"You are my friend, my Lover. Grow old and wise with me and I'll the same with you: A life before us of rainbows and sunsets and a willingness to share those things of sadness.

"I love you. I adore you."

Gazing into each other's eyes and hearing the words from each other's souls, Iris and Deodar were momentarily lost in their love. Many of the guests, including the men, quickly wiped away a tear. Arnica paused, waiting for everyone's attention, then nodded in the direction of Dark Star so she could bring in the ring.

Dark Star didn't move but remained next to Holly. What could she be doing? Arnica maintained his composure and then, over by the passage to the street, a small commotion began. Why, here came Andrius holding a small, silver basket with the two ring boxes. Both unicorns looked as pleased as they could be. What a trick they had played on their human friends. And Andrius' horn was quite visible. Voices were buzzing. Just last Candlemas some thought they saw a horn on Dark Star's head.

As he strode past the first rows of guests, Andrius paused and looked over at a stranger. A dark man, sitting quietly and not really part of the celebration, Arnica noted the object of Andrius' distraction. Who is the man in the corner? Then, to keep the Handfasting moving, Andrius came in with the rings and the Handfasting vows were exchanged. Andrius stood there, definitely looking more 'unicorn' than the public 'horse' image. He was pleased. His daughter, Dark Star, had made secret arrangements so that the 'something blue' would be quite a surprise for everyone. Then, the Handfasting done and kisses exchanged, the courtyard bubbled over with the ringing of bells. Some said they could hear them ringing far beyond Merrydale's boundaries!

The guests piled into the school's new cafeteria where Gino's mother, Rosetta, had prepared the feast. This was the school's first major test of its kitchen. Rosetta and the volunteer mothers did well. As people congratulated Iris and Deodar, Arnica and Holly looked for a quiet table, more than ready to rest their feet. As they sat down their plates of cake they looked out the window. Andrius and Dark Star were trotting back to the cabin but there was that man, walking down the street. "Who could he be?" they both wondered in unison.

XXXVI - That Dark Stranger

Life in a small town among the forests of Merrywood was usually quiet. The scandal surrounding the mysterious death of Kalven, a friend of Carlos, in Mill City a year ago Candlemas culminated in Bishop Miter's untimely death shortly before last Yule. The political environment had calmed. Over the past four years there had been enough excitement to last a lifetime for the local folk of Merrydale. The threat to their beloved forest when the Bishop tried to influence Parliament to allow commercial interests to clear the trees was the first in this chain of events.

Walking about with an eye to the sky, the weather was the major concern of the folk. La Niña continued the unpredictable cycles of spring like some mischievous weather deity, following unseasonable, cold deluges by bursts of Lammas heat, quickly drying the fields. Fortunately, the primary topic of conversation was of good news. People were still talking about the joyous Handfasting just last Beltane. Such an intricate tale. Iris had been the local postmarm for many years. She was loved but also respected, the first to take a public stance and organize a march to save Fern Holly just three years ago. Her love of the wilds created the impression that she was active in the Renaissance Tribes, but her popularity kept her from the subtle political pressure by the extreme factions within the Kristos.

Iris had looked so beautiful. Her long braid plaited about her head, a halo of flowers which were tucked throughout it. The gossips of Merrydale had *never* thought she'd marry, much less to Deodar, who arrived in Merrydale five or six years ago as minister of the Church of the Martyr. Standing up to Bishop Miter, Pastor Dolorum resigned his ministry. Unknown to the locals he had become involved in the coven. They sometimes called themselves 'Friends of Dark Star.' Deodar was now the principal of the new Trillium School, the pride of Merrydale for it was a quality school and the first Earthkin school chartered in the District. Secretly the older gossips wondered how long it would take before Iris was pregnant. "You know what they say about those Earthkin men," voices whispered as the threads were pulled taut in their needlework. "And who is that dark stranger Nettie saw walking with that science teacher from the new school? You know, that woman who just moved here from ... where is it? ... the Mothervalley?"

Holly and Dark Star were playing around the garden Circle. Dark Star was carrying a basket, the handle gently held in her teeth. It was filled with multi-colored bells, each attached to a long ribbon. Holly was opening and closing a tall, lightweight ladder. It was the hatchling's duty to hold the basket so Holly could select a bell to tie to a branch of the tree. Dark Star loved to tease him. You could tell she had Andrius' blood in her! She'd be really good for a few bells as Holly repositioned the ladder for each and then she'd play.

Just as Holly would reach for a bell, Dark Star would move the basket just out of his reach. The sound of a unicorn giggling is amazing. She'd neigh with her teeth holding the woven basket handle, the sound making Holly laugh as well. He'd hold tight to the ladder so his laughter would not cause him to tumble. Holly tried to act stern but Dark Star knew better. One time as he was climbing up toward the large hawthorne, she actually nipped him in the back pocket. Quick as a finch, Holly jumped down and the chase started. Dark Star's lead would gain because she could jump over the borage bed but, once on the grass, Holly would catch up because she couldn't run fast without spilling the bells from the basket.

Arnica was doing his 'garden inventory.' With the weather so erratic, he wanted to feel secure that the harvest would be adequate for this year's tithing. With a loss of fifty students to the new Earthkin school, the Merrydale School District would be increasing their taxes to cover a loss in government allocations and the need to rearrange some of their classes. Arnica had been encouraging all of the Earthkin to accept the District's needs without creating friction. It was important that Trillium School foster only the best of energy.

"The raspberries are terrific this year and the grapes are outstanding. As usual we have so much comfrey that we'll offer a couple dozen bushels free to the local goat farmers. I'm not sure if we can take up any Solomon's seal root or mandrake this year but we have enough goldenseal that, with the current market, we'll not only easily pay the tithing but will also be putting a good sum into our savings."

But Holly was off chasing Dark Star again. Unicorn and man romped along the paths until both tumbled into a heap upon the grass up near the cabin. Arnica was still counting out loud and making notes as Holly and Dark Star worked to slow their breathing and cool down.

"Did you know that Flying Raven has gone out twice with that dark stranger?"

Suddenly Holly sat upright. Arnica's running inventory of the gardens was like the chirping of the birds. Holly heard his partner's voice, but wasn't really listening. This, however, came through with startling clarity.

Flying Raven was in her new science classroom. Hoping to be making progress on her lesson plans for the coming school year, she found herself gazing through the window at the school's courtyard. The fountain was on and the splash of the water played music in her mind. But it wasn't the melodies of her ritual songs she heard. Little ditties spun through her mind like a small swarm of bothersome gnats. 'Ollis,' she muttered to herself, 'why did you have to go and tell me your secret?'

Her children grown and on their own, Flying Raven had thought herself too mature to become caught up in romance. The dark stranger who appeared at Iris' and Deodar's Handfasting was, in his own way, quite attractive. Certainly he was mysterious and Flying Raven knew that the talk of the town was that she and the man had been seen together. They'd had dinner and gone for a couple of evening walks. She was flattered that the man sought her attention, that any man found a woman in her upper forties to be a desirable companion.

Last night he asked her if he might confide in her. Now she knew his secret and didn't know quite what to do. Logically the science teacher could understand why Ollis carried this knowledge as a personal burden but why had it become hers? 'Ah, Goddess, I don't understand.' The problems wasn't in the secret itself but in her having promised to say absolutely nothing to anyone. Ollis had caught her off guard. Flying Raven had not imagined that his secret had anything to do with any of her friends. Tomorrow was the Midsummer's Eve ritual. How could she go into the circle with her friends? How could she express Perfect Love and Perfect Trust without being open about what she knew? If she absented herself from the coven's sabbat questions would be raised and she couldn't answer them.

For a blessed few moments Flying Raven's mind merged with the sound of the undines playing in the fountain and she was given relief. If only she could find a solution to her dilemma in the water's music.

"How many Midsummer Eves have you celebrated here?" Gino, the youngest of the coven at 14 had begun developing a curiosity about the history of their Circles. Arnica was not certain why, but it seemed to arise just after the incident at the old school last Autumn when Merrydale School District began requiring an oath of allegiance to the Kristos god. Gino's mother allowed the lad to be home-schooled, all of which led to the opening of Trillium School. Watching the course of local history change before his eyes had brought maturity to the freckled youth. Gino was brushing Dark Star's coat. Dark

Star loved Midsummer's Eve. Having been conceived in the astral, Dark Star had a strong affinity with the world of the faerie.

"Oh, Gino, it's been since long before you were born." Arnica, sitting on the grass near the greenhouse reading through the ritual script for last minute changes, was stalling. He really couldn't remember. He looked toward Holly.

"Well, do you mean those before the coven began? Or just those we've formally worked together. Our coven was nineteen years old last Hallows. I just came across an entry in an old diary at the last New Moon." Holly was filling a large basket with little sweet breads, two large jars of home made grape juice and unbreakable mugs. Holly loved preparing the ritual feasts.

"Can we come in?" Iris' voice called from the other side of the gate.

Knowing the answer was yes, Deodar opened the gate for his new bride. Despite the newness of their relationship, Iris and Deodar worked so well together they seemed to have been a couple for a good many years. Deodar's dark hair was growing longer and had just gotten to the length so as to be pulled back. "Guess who was coming down the lane behind us," he said, and in came Pearl.

"Dear Lady!" Holly jumped up to give Pearl a welcoming hug.

"Pearl," Arnica called from where he sat near the greenhouse, "do you remember our first Midsummer here?"

"You know, dear one, I was just thinking about that the other afternoon," she answered. "I was sitting on my porch watching the bees among the roses and thinking about Phoenix. I miss him so and yet my new life is so busy! I was reflecting upon my old life when I spent most of my time sewing. In my 'new' life there is so much to prepare for my art and music classes. And I've had good practice home schooling my favorite pupil." Pearl's kindly eyes looked toward Gino who blushed right through his freckles.

"Is Flying Raven here yet?" Iris asked. "Something's up. She came in to post some letters yesterday but seemed anxious to leave. I had asked her to stay for tea. I was due to close for my morning break in but a few minutes."

"I heard that she's been..." Pearl was about to mention the Merrydale gossip about Flying Raven and the dark stranger but hellos from the gate distracted them.

"It's Jewel and Lotus. Dark Star, here comes Dagon!" As Arnica walked quickly to greet his friends, he remembered how, three years ago, Dark Star and Dagon, then only a year old, had slipped through the portal into the Realm of the Faerie. Jewel was emotionally devastated but had since come to realize what an honor it had been for her little son.

Lotus set his beautifully carved staff against the fence (he was now a master carver) and lifted Dagon up so the child could sit upon Dark Star's back. The hatchling and Dagon had a special relationship, having shared an adventure which remained, to this day, a great secret between them.

"Is everybody here?" asked Jewel, her russet-colored hair braided with beads which matched her ritual robes. "Are we late?"

Arnica gave Jewel her welcoming hug. "We're ready to begin the procession down the path to the woods. It's only a matter of a few minutes before the sun's rays shift into twilight."

Holly cheered, "We're off to give thanks to the devas for blessing our gardens."

Dark Star shook her head gently, ringing the three sweet sounding bells attached to her young unicorn horn.

Iris adjusted her ritual necklace and, as she and Deodar began walking with the others, leaned toward her new husband and quietly whispered, "Where is Flying Raven?"

XXXVII - Reconciliation

"And she still doesn't know who you are?" Holly was incredulous yet spoke quietly.

The dark man slowly shook his head, his voice barely audible. "No, I've not told her."

Holly's hand gently stroked Dark Star's neck. The hatchling sat next to Holly. She was intently listening to all that was being discussed. This was a facet of human behavior completely new to her. The young unicorn, now four years and three sabbats old, was fascinated by her existence. Living with Arnica and Holly in the cabin with their gardens surrounded with forest had proven to be a fulfilling manifestation. She thanked her father, Andrius, nightly as she settled into the dreaming.

During Dark Star's first year, life was quiet, although the increasing power of the Politicos and their right wing movement was threatening the forests of Merrywood. It was then that Iris, the postmarm, came into her life. Dark Star loved Iris. With her long, thick braid and willingness to stand up for her rights (Iris had organized the first march to Fern Hollow), the hatchling thought Iris one of the most remarkable women of the human species! Now, with an Earthkin school soon to open, Dark Star thought herself the most lucky of those unicorns allowed to incarnate in the world of humans. Arnica and Holly had about them the most wonderful circle of friends. The young unifilly was daydreaming, remembering the first time she met Dolly, when his unhappiness as a Kristos minister left her wishing she were safe at the cabin. And now Dolly was active in the coven, and she would be dancing with him and the other friends at Lammas!

But what was the dark Piper saying? Dark Star realized she had missed some of the man's tale.

"So you see," the Piper looking toward Arnica, "I felt that I had no choice."

"But you see things differently, now?" gently asked Arnica, his fingers toying with the graying hairs of his short beard.

"Oh, yes." Piper looked into Arnica's eyes. The dark man's soul was visible through his dark brown eyes, shaded by his near black hair. He still carried much pain with him. "Why hoping that I might see Iris some day was all that kept me going. I wanted to find her right after my release, but it took time to be able to find employment and to learn how to adjust to being out in the real world again. It wasn't easy."

"You did well, my friend." Holly reached over to console the man and put his hand on his shoulder, leaning across Dark Star's neck. Holly was ever kind to people and much loved in Merrydale.

Dark Star's ears were a-twitch. On such a hazy summer day, the hot sun left her wanting to trot back into the woods to play in the stone circle. The borage was in bloom and she'd love to head back with a large mouthful and sit and munch and wait for the devas to come and visit her, something which rarely happened when humans were around. But what is this about being released? Where had this man been kept? And was that a monarch butterfly over there landing on the borage? Dark Star could not control her impulse, jumping up and trotting off to check her favorite garden bed. The men left behind were laughing, grateful for a break in their otherwise serious conversation.

"Just a year ago?" Deodar Dolorum looked at the others. "How can it be possible that a year ago I was newly engaged," he turned toward Iris who, despite her strength and will, still blushed just the slightest. Dolly continued, "And I was still a Kristos minister. Now, look at me! I'm actively involved in your coven. My mother must be very pleased, Goddess bless her. And I'm the principal of Trillium School, the first Earthkin school ever. So many changes and yet, had I not studied for the ministry and come to the Church of the Martyr, I would never have reclaimed my heritage from my great-great-grandmother, who was a daughter of Silverwing, a Descendant Tribe people of the Great Plains." Not usually the most talkative, he looked about the room, then lapsed into silent wonder gazing into the small fire.

It was a cool, rainy evening. Dolly and Iris had come out to the cabin to finish their part in the coven's plans and preparations for the Lammas Eve ritual. Last year, under the late Bishop Miter's (the most prominent of the Users, the right wing faction of the politicos) urging, Parliament passed a bill banning Lammas fires. At the time, the Users were growing in strength, but that promoted great cooperation among the Renaissance Tribes and the native Descendant Tribes and many others who believed in the freedoms of religious expression. When Bishop Miter died unexpectedly, the radical right had taken a hard blow. Although no one had gotten around to changing the law, none of the Earthkin planned a large, public fire. Arnica and Holly would have a small Lammas fire for the coven on Lammas Eve, but locally everyone was far too involved in the opening of Trillium School to worry about lobbying for the repeal of a law they knew would not be enforced. Politics could wait until winter.

"Gino and Pearl are in charge of the harvest part of the procession?" asked Iris.

"Have you noticed? Gino's shot up this summer and he's taller than Pearl now!" Holly was fond of the young teen. "Gino's mother is sending along the grain man. Carlos has the new ovens working in the school kitchen and Rosetta felt that this would be the best way to bless them." Gino's parents were so proud of the progress he was making. Since beginning his studies with the coven, his grades in school were straight A's and Gino's parents were thrilled that both were now working for Trillium School.

"Flying Raven will be here, won't she?" There was a slight edge in Iris' voice.

"Oh, Iris, I forgot to tell you." Dolly reached over and took her hand. "Flying Raven called me at the school office and asked if we could come over tomorrow evening. I checked our schedule and said yes and promised I'd get back to her if you'd already scheduled something. With so much going on it slipped my mind."

"Did she say why?" asked Iris with emotion beginning to shade her voice.

"She wants us to meet... What's his name? Piper," answered Dolly, "Piper, like the botanical name for pepper...."

"She's been acting so odd when she's around me," Iris said, trying to conceal the threads of hurt.

"Why," soothed Arnica with just the quickest of glances at Holly, "we spoke with her and Piper just a few days ago, and I can assure you that Raven's reticent behavior has nothing to do with you. By Lammas Eve, I trust that everything will be resolved."

Iris looked at Deodar. "Yes," she said, "we'll go. It will be an important part of my ritual sweeping for Lammas Eve." Iris bent down and scratched Dark Star's ears. "My lovely, I'll not see you until the ritual. You be a good hatchling and I'll bring you a treat." Dark Star *loved* treats!

They sat around the square dining table, Iris nearest the window looking into the garden and to her right, Dolly. Across from her sat this man Piper. She didn't know quite what to think of him. Something inside of her wanted to dislike him, yet another part of her very much wanted to like him. Some of his mannerisms reminded her almost of herself, but she didn't want to think of that. Tomorrow was Lammas Eve and she was having a wonderful time. It had been a wonderful meal. A fresh strawberry cobbler and coffee brought the evening full circle.

At Iris' left sat Flying Raven, closest to the door leading into the kitchen. Certainly it *seemed* as if everything between the two women was normal. Iris helped in the kitchen and they laughed and giggled as they hadn't in some time. Raven looked younger than her years. Iris found herself looking at the school's new science teacher in wonder. It was difficult to believe that the older woman had children in their twenties! And yet, there was some worry about her eyes. Just as Iris was looking toward her friend, Flying Raven interrupted the casual conversation of the evening.

"I'm not comfortable doing this but..." Raven fidgeted a bit with her napkin, looking from Piper to Iris. "I invited you here," she looked at Deodar and then at Iris, "because I know you think I've been acting a bit funny. And I have. You see, I have been spending some time with Piper and..." Flying Raven stumbled for words.

"Please," Piper moved his chair back a bit and leaned forward. The other three looked toward him. His voice spoke quietly yet with strength. Obviously, this was important.

"Iris," the man said, "when I was young, younger than you are now, I met a beautiful, sweet young woman. I fell madly in love with her and when she agreed to date me, I couldn't believe my good fortune. You see, my life had not gone well. I was very immature, had trouble holding a job, was doing poorly in keeping my life together and this woman.... Why, she was like and angel and somehow she thought she saw good in me."

Iris closed her eyes. Something within her began to sense where all of this was leading.

"When this goddess of a woman told me she was pregnant, I didn't know what to do. I had no money, no prospects. I had no self-esteem and I was certain I wasn't good enough for her, much less capable of being a father. So what did I do? I ran away and enlisted in the merchant marine." His emotions were so close to the surface that Piper was visibly trembling, his eyes unable to look at anyone.

"You're trying to tell me that you're my father, aren't you?" Iris was visibly shaken. Her face had paled and her hands tensed around themselves.

Piper looked down. "Yes." The word slipped out like a wisp of candle smoke. Then he looked up and at Iris. "I got out just a year ago and I worked very hard to find you. And I looked for your mother as well. Actually, it was she I first tried to find. I had saved over half of every paycheck and had intended to give your mother all the financial support which she should have had. But..." Piper began crying. Flying Raven reached over and took his hand.

"She died, not knowing." Iris finished the sentence. A multitude of thoughts, of memories of her mother working long hours, remembering how her mother went back to school and made something of herself and was a proud, single mother. Iris had been raised to harbor no ill feelings toward the handsome man who won her mother's heart briefly and who, as Iris' mother put it, 'gave her the gift of sunshine.' Iris had been her mother's pride and joy.

The room was so quiet Iris thought they could hear her breathing. Everyone waited for her to say something. "Piper, my mother was my joy. I hold no ill feelings toward you. I'm not ready to have a father. I've lived my life well without knowing if one even existed. Sometimes when I was a child, I imagined that my mother had slipped into the Realm of the Faerie and that my father might be of another world. That was a good belief then and may even be the best now. I'm happy that you have brought some joy to Flying Raven." Despite the seriousness of the moment, Raven even blushed. "But I must be honest. At this point in time, you're not my father. You are the handsome man in my dear coven sister's life."

Iris took Dolly's hand. "We must leave. I'll need some space and some time."

Everyone understood. The men shook hands. Iris and Flying Raven embraced. Iris did not move toward Piper. Instead, she looked about the room just before the newly-married couple departed. "Oh, my, tomorrow we celebrate the harvest. I did not expect it to include a father."

No one said a word, but everyone was aware that Iris had acknowledged the dark stranger as her father.

Later that night, Iris slept peacefully, yet in the morning, she was taken aback at remembering a vivid dream. In the dream, she was lounging upon the grass, leaning against Dark Star. A tiny baby was held in her arms, nursing, and nearby sat Piper, the dark stranger, singing them all a lullaby. This dream was not for telling. She kept it as a quiet secret to take to Lammas Eve. Let the Goddess interpret it, Iris though to herself.

XXXVIII - Of School and The Equinox

It was a beautiful, near-Autumn day. The sun was shining bright and warm and the students, although they were thrilled with their new school, had difficulty paying attention in their classes. The Equinox was this weekend, the first Sabbat for the Earthkin school. Trillium School had begun classes on the first Monday in September, the new Virgo Moon. The third week was coming to a close and the school was filled with energy. Deodar, the new principal, sat in the teachers' lounge talking to Pearl, the art and music teacher. Even though the new ethics class had only three students, the young folk were very adept and Dolly (as he was called among his friends) was finding this class a greater challenge than his seminary years. Pearl was capable of great insight which Dolly found reassuring. And yet, Pearl thought, there was something which was troubling the former Kristos clergyman. Since his embracing of his Renaissance Tribe beliefs and joining the coven, the dark man could not easily hide his feelings from his friends.

Arnica was meeting with a small group of students in Flying Raven's science room. Six students would be making a field trip to the herb gardens as part of their studies in natural sciences. Arnica and Holly loved sharing their gardens at the cabin. He had not planned on joining the faculty but as he worked with Raven he was drawn more and more into the botanical and herbal aspects of her science curriculum. Arnica was pleased to be involved. He liked walking to Merrydale with Holly. It was good having Flying Raven here in Merrydale. With her living in the Mothervalley it seemed there was never enough time together for the distance was so great. Now they would have the school year. Flying Raven would head east to her home for the holidays and summers. She had rented it out but kept the small studio behind the house so she could tend to her gardens and keep her hands in the Mothervalley's soil.

Dark Star, their Unicorn hatchling, was even happier. She *loved* going to school. The walks with Arnica and Holly were great fun. Some mornings she wished Arnica would teach every day. She missed Holly when he was gone. Yet going to school meant having to have Arnica's invisibility formula rubbed into her horn and she didn't always like that. Unicorns are proud of their horns and Dark Star was no exception. Granted, her horn was little more than four turns long and she thought lolling about in the courtyard with the young folk was great fun. But she understood that the life she shared with Arnica and Holly and the members of the coven would be forever changed - and not for the better - were the general public to realize that she was actually a unicorn and not a young, pretty pony. As the thought moved through her head she snorted at it, and rolled over in the sun.

All of the students were in classes. Amber was teaching an eleventh grade social studies class, relating the events of the past few years so that the students better understood how life in Merrydale was affected by the Changing Times and how social classes reacted and affected the balance of power in Parliament between the Conservers, the more liberal political group who found great support among the Earthkin and the 'other' faction, the Politicos, who favored business and economic growth even when it meant cutting down forests. Holly was sitting in the faculty office, grading the first tests he had given in the language skills classes. The school was a hive of learning.

Carlos was helping his wife Rosetta clean the school's kitchen. Carlos had never been so happy. Their son, Gino, was growing into a fine student since he had begun studying with Arnica and Holly's coven. The ninth grade curriculum suited him well and Gino's freckled face seemed always blessed with a smile.

"Carlos!" Rosetta acted startled and a bit horrified when he snuck up behind her to put his arms around her and hold her seductively. "We're in the school!" But she was pleased, and Carlos could tell. Rosetta had always been a bit shy and the many months he worked in the flour mills on the other side of the mountains in Mill City had been difficult for her.

"They're all in their classes," he whispered into her ear.

"Are you well?" Arnica was expressing concerns to Iris. "Dolly sent Shadow Tail over this morning to get some stamps for the school but when he came back, Shadow said that the post office had the 'temporarily closed' sign in the window. He's been a little troubled all day."

"Oh," Iris said, coloring slightly, "I didn't think anyone would notice. I should have known."

"Are you feeling alright?" asked Holly.

Iris looked away, gazing out the window. She was not quite comfortable with their questions. "Well, to be honest," she said, her fingers reaching up to fidget with her braid, "I made a quick dash for the back porch and tossed up my breakfast."

"Dear sister," both men said simultaneously...

"That's right," Iris joined in... "morning sickness."

They laughed as all three had chimed the last two words in perfect unison.

"Does Dolly know?" asked Holly.

"Not yet. I didn't even know until this morning," answered Iris. "I had a dream last Lammas about a baby but I thought it had to do with meeting my father. It wasn't until this morning's near disaster that I realized that I had not cycled in the past two months. You know me, I've always been physically strong, enjoyed hiking and never had much patience with pregnant women and their complaints."

In spite of himself, Arnica laughed.

"Now I am one," Iris jokingly wailed until the laughter took over. "Will Dolly be home soon? I had wanted him to be the first to know but my priests and brothers... Well, we've been friends for so long I guess it's fitting that you're here."

"He was in the school office talking to Shadow. I think Shadow Tail is going to become the school secretary." Shadow had begun studying herbal magick from Arnica.

"Dolly could use the help. There's a lot of paperwork involved in just the administrative aspects. It's how we spend most of our evenings." But not all, she thought to herself, thinking of the growing fetus in her belly. Iris blushed.

"Shadow's a good worker," Holly added. Holly had begun to think of Shadow Tail as a brother-in-spirit.

The men left to head back to the school and get the hatchling. The herbal potion on Dark Star's horn would soon be fading. Still warm from the circle of hugs the three had shared, Holly and Arnica agreed to avoid the school office. It would be best if there were no chance at all for Dolly's intuition to extend itself toward their secret.

"A Beltane baby." Iris had, by far, the best news to share for a personal harvest. The coven was sitting in the garden Circle, giving thanks to the Harvest Mother. This year the Harvest Mother was a maiden, in a manner of speaking. Dark Star took her role very seriously. She had shared long conversations with Holly in preparation for her first major role in a ritual, communicating thoughts with Holly through his crystal orb. "In just the past two days I have come to realize that I've wanted to bring a baby into the world more than I had told myself. And now I have the man in my life who planted the seed." Iris tossed a handful of borage blossoms into the silver bowl and looked to her left. Dark Star, as was her right as the Goddess, scooped them up with her tongue and ate them as quietly as she could.

Deodar was speechless. He'd been attending the coven's Circles for just two and a half years at this very Sabbat but sometimes the candor of the Earthkin caught him off guard. Dolly took a slow, deep breath, feeling the earth beneath him. He drew up strength and calm into his being and let his spirit speak for him. "Last year at Autumn I was a single man, struggling to maintain balance in my life as a Kristos minister. I resigned my position, no longer able to believe that I could accomplish the work before me in the Church of the Martyr. Since then I have been blessed as the principal of the new Earthkin Trillium School. And I live with joy now that Iris and I have been made Handfast. And..." Dolly blushed, visible even in the twilight, "I'm to be a father." Dolly tossed a handful of deep red snapdragon blooms into the bowl. They didn't last long.

Gino was sitting deosil to his favorite teacher. *School* teacher that is. Pearl was Gino's favorite teacher of the coven's magick. "Well," the lad began, "last year I didn't have a school to go to." When the Users pushed through legislation requiring an oath of allegiance to the Kristos god in every school, Rosetta transformed from a quiet, shy mother into a strong-willed woman. She withdrew Gino and he was home-tutored by Pearl. "This Autumn harvest has brought me a school where I can go and be proud of the magick I'm learning. I can be myself. My mom is the cook and my dad works there too. All of you, all of my friends are involved. I'm just really happy. And Dark Star, you're my best friend!" And rather than flower blossoms like the adults, Gino slipped two borage-mint cookies into the bowl. Dark Star whinnied gently in pleasure and the adults acted as if they hadn't noticed, allowing Dark Star and Gino to share their moment.

Pearl's harvest blessing was simple. "Teaching art and music at Trillium School is like a dream come true," and she tossed a whole handful of borage blooms into the basin. The hatchling turned her head and looked toward the Pictish woman. How *did* she hide so many fresh blossoms in the pocket of her ritual robe? Dark Star was sometimes quite amazed at the creative minds of her human friends.

"Well, I guess my blessing is living here, now," offered Shadow Tail. Shadow didn't like speaking in public, even in a group like this. "I'm a little new, but I'm pleased to do the office work at the school and happy to be studying with Arnica." Shadow's offering to the 'Harvest Mother' was more borage but also a couple of late rose buds and one strawberry, perhaps the last of the season!

"I'm happy to be here." Flying Raven had been a solitary back in the Mothervalley. "I miss my home and my gardens. And yet, although we are taught that astral connections are such a blessing in life, being here with you and having 'real hugs' is the greatest. I love my students. It's good, here." Flying Raven brought forth a small paper packet. "Look," she said holding it up to the hatchling as she opened it... "Candied borage buds." Dark Star's eyes opened so wide. This dear woman surely knew the way to a unifilly's heart!

Jewel and Lotus expressed their harvest blessings at having found a house to buy and having an occasional baby-sitter. Dagon was four and, despite his magickal heritage and trip into the Realm of the Faery with Dark Star when little more than a year old, he was growing into a child and ritual left him restless. Arnica and Holly both mentioned Trillium School as their blessing. They were pleased that their Circle had grown. It seemed full and complete.

As the ritual things were gathered from the garden Circle and hugs exchanged, when Holly embraced Jewel, something felt just a bit amiss. He couldn't put his finger on it. Lotus, one of the best wood carvers in the region, was fine. Later that night Holly intended to ask Arnica if he had noticed anything, but a long day's work dropped them both quickly asleep. Dark Star slept at the foot of the bed on Autumn Eve and as they slept, the Wheel turned again.

XXXIX - Jewel's Crisis

It had been a tiring Sabbat cycle. Jewel sat in Arnica and Holly's greenhouse, sipping a cup of herbal tea. Dark Star was sleeping at her feet. Arnica had made the infusion for her using herbs selected to bolster her emotional system and provide herbal support for the chemotherapy. Jewel was still feeling quite low but taking an occasional 'day off' was important. Trillium School, the first Earthkin school to receive a charter, was quickly growing into a community center for the Renaissance folk, followers of the old, earth-centered religious ways. The school principal, Deodar (until recently Dolly was a Kristos minister!) was also a coven mate of Jewel and Lotus. At Dolly's insistence, Dagon was spending the day at school, providing the older girls with an opportunity to learn about child care and education. Jewel and Lotus' young one, almost four and a half years old, was unusually precocious in matters magickal. Dagon's first adventure with Dark Star when he was little more than a year old took him into the Realm of the Faerie. At first uncomfortable with leaving her son at the school, Jewel had come to value these days.

It was just after Autumn that Jewel discovered the lump. Holly suspected something was wrong. He sensed it as they closed the Autumn Eve circle, but had been unable to figure out just what it was. It took Jewel a couple of weeks before she could bring herself to go to the doctor, in part because she, like many Renaissance people, preferred herbal medicine, imagery and natural healing and in part, she now recognized, because she had difficulty believing it could be true.

It was the beginning of October when Jewel went to Merrydale's medical clinic for a mammogram. Her russet-colored hair, often tied back, was flowing freely. Some of the oaks hinted that their leaves would soon be similar in color, glowing in the sunny days of autumn. And yet, at Hallows Eve most of the region's deciduous trees would have shed their leaves, leaving the look of death about the forests. The sun, warm upon Jewel's shoulders, helped her draw upon the Mother Earth's strength as she walked toward the clinic.

Merrydale Clinic was a friendly environment and she knew the nurses and the few doctors who worked there. Merrydale was not a large town but the District of Merrydale brought many people from the region for shopping and other services, such as medical care. People felt fortunate to have an excellent clinic. Jewel's intuition led her to ask if she could wait for the results. The doctor, not unaccustomed to the ways of the Earthkin, agreed to Jewel's request. She took the reading well, although she felt emotionally devastated. A biopsy was done that same day by needle aspiration. Jewel told Lotus that night. Although her husband expressed some concern that she'd not said anything before, both of them worked with visualization and he suspected that she wanted to believe it was nothing in the hopes that it would be nothing, and he understood.

Arnica stood at the door to the greenhouse. He said nothing but watched Jewel in silence. She looked well enough, but tired, probably just from the stress and anxiety. The malignancy was strong and Arnica knew that a mastectomy was the best option, although a frightening choice for a young woman barely 30. The older herbalist's hand petted the grey in his beard but his mind was working Magick, surrounding the young mother with healing, protective energies. Just then Dark Star raised her head, nudging Jewel's hand with her horn. Dark Star was very attuned to the humans who were part of Holly and Arnica's coven. Jewel began to pet Dark Star. Arnica sensed that Dark Star was taking her turn with providing healing magick and he quietly slipped away to leave them, sitting among the tropical plants with the statue of Eir, goddess of healing gazing at the woman and the young unicorn.

They sat on small pillows in a large circle. The basement room was large and dark, cool at this time of year. The coven was meeting at the home of Jewel and Lotus. Jewel had protested, insisting that she and Lotus would come to the cabin out in Merrywood but Arnica and Holly would have none of it.

"What, and deprive Dark Star of the opportunity to prance through Merrydale 'disguised' as a unicorn?" teased Holly. That did it. Jewel knew she could not counter that argument.

Lotus was excited, this being the first ritual in their home. The large room had been mostly unused, catching a few boxes and items here and there, providing unintentional storage. With only a week remaining, Lotus insisted on painting the walls and buying a large area rug. The others tried to convince him otherwise, reminding him of the Hallows Eve ritual some years back out in the garden when the temperature began to drop as quick as the sun in his descent beyond the western horizon, or the time working ritual in the stone Circle during an unexpected yet gentle rain.

But they did not press too much, knowing that this preparation was part of Lotus' healing. They loved the wood carving gentleman and recognized that this was part of his healing. Lotus was devoted to his wife. Being young, it had never occurred to him to face their mortality. Even when Dagon disappeared through the Midsummer veil into the Realm of the Faerie, his training with the Rhymer helped him accept the strange will of the Universe.

Arnica brought forth the cauldron and set it in the Circle's center. Holly uncorked the bottle and carefully poured the alcohol into its depths. Gino reached into a pocket in his robe, brought forth a prized lighter (one given him by his father, Carlos) and lit a wax taper the size of a fireplace match. As it was lowered into the cauldron the flames burst into dance.

"Gone to the Summerland:
Distant shores grown past;
Winter draws upon us now,
Summer didn't last..."

Arnica and Holly were leading the Circle. As was the custom, each covener held a crystal ball, used as a focal point to open the portal through the cauldron. Dark Star was not with them this evening, which was unusual. The hatchling was up above them, listening carefully but giving her attention to Dagon who was amusing himself in the playroom, drawing his own version of tarot cards with, wouldn't you know, lots of unicorns! Dark Star felt quite grown up in the role of babysitter. She and Dagon held a special bond ever since their Midsummer adventure!

Gino sat at Arnica's left, between his mentor and his teacher Pearl. The new art and music teacher at Trillium School, Pearl was momentarily distracted, looking at the altar where Arnica's herbal elixir awaited their journeying. The glass flask was concealed beneath the corn dolly Pearl had fashioned for this year's altar. It was just three years ago she broke through the veil to tell the coven that Phoenix had passed over. She and Phoenix had gone to live in Cloverville with her grandmother, hoping that the change in climate would help, but it was destined that Phoenix pass through the Gates of Death and not return.

Shadow Tail sat at Pearl's left. Shadow was still learning the ritual ways of the Renaissance religions. There were similarities but also many differences from those of his people, the Loon Tribe. Ancestral worship on this date was a common theme among nearly all people, and Shadow looked forward to communing with his forebears. At Shadow's left sat Flying Raven. It had been years since she'd sat in Circle with her friends. She sometimes missed her gardens back in the Mothervalley, but more and more was enjoying her new life in Merrydale.

Next sat Iris and Deodar. Iris looked quite radiant, even in the cool, dark basement. The four walls painted in deep, earth-toned shades of the cardinal colors, Iris fairly glowed. The postmarm was leaning against the shoulder of her husband, the school's principal and proud father-to-be.

"Though the Maid has gone away,
She'll be back again;
She has gone to grow to full,
The God-child is within..."

Although Iris felt a deep level of care for Jewel, the knowledge that she was due to give birth at Beltane, directly across the Wheel from this very Sabbat Eve was a profound knowledge. How her life had changed in just a few years. She would never have imagined that the Kristos minister would convert to Renaissance ways and that she would be Handfasted to the principal of the new Trillium School. Having been a student of religion for so many years, Dolly was learning and growing in ways he'd never imagined.

"Sleeps She now within His arms,
The Child is in the womb;
The Magick that is loose this night
Has opened up the tomb."

Jewel looked intent. Lotus knew he was having difficulty setting aside his ego. His arm provided warmth around his wife's waist.

The coven chanted the remaining stanzas of the Hallows Chant and the flask was brought around. Jewel drank deeply, knowing that she needed to seek advice from the other side. Lotus declined, believing that his strength was needed. He sat there, quietly, providing support for Jewel as she placed herself into a trance and moved her will into the cauldron's fire.

"T'will be the blade when the Moon is in the breast..." Jewel's eyes opened and the remnants of the advice from her spirit guide were at her lips. She no longer felt frightened. The others were returning from their passages beyond the veil of death. Jewel turned to Lotus. "Dearest, I want the surgery to be the first morning following the Full Cancer Moon as it begins the waning. I'm ready."

XL - Presents for All

The winter rains splashed onto the greenhouse windows and then slid down, washing their way across the panes of glass. It was only another week until Yule, but the climate was more like wet autumn weather. Holly sat upon a small, wicker stool next to a huge aloe, several feet tall. Dark Star was sitting back upon her hind quarters, which placed the young unicorn at eye level with the man. Between them, on a pedestal, sat Holly's crystal ball.

"Snow..." Holly was translating the image he received. "You want snow, Dark Star?"

The hatchling nodded her head, her horn bobbing brightly. She loved to play in the snow. She could run and romp and play hard without becoming overheated. The young unicorn lowered her head and focused her gaze into the clear orb.

Holly tried to relax. He remembered a saying he saw in his first year as a magickal student: "the art of trying is the art of not succeeding." He took a deep breath, feeling the flagstones beneath his feet and drawing upon the calm of the earth's energy.

"I want you to come and play with me in the woods. I want Gino to take me to the mountain to play in the snow." Holly looked up from the globe, startled. "Dark Star, you poor, neglected hatchling..." Holly quickly stood up, leaned over and gave her a big kiss on the tip of her horn. "You wait here."

Holly, gentle-featured and sprightly, picked up his orb and ran into the cabin to tell Arnica that he was taking Dark Star out to play.

Dark Star loved Trillium School but she missed having Holly and Arnica around. The children were wonderful and she loved playing in the courtyard of the schoolhouse, but she was ready for the winter break when her beloved men would both be home every day and Gino would be out of school and able to come and play with her. After all, the hatchling was not even five years old and she could be coltish now and then.

Arnica was sitting at the kitchen table, gazing out the window. He didn't turn his head when he heard Holly come through the door. Holly kissed Arnica upon his balding head. He could tell that his partner was distracted with thoughts.

Arnica's fingers mused in his graying beard as he spoke. "They got it all. The chemotherapy and herbal combination worked. The tumor had shrunk and the surgery was successful."

A deep sigh seemed to arise from Holly's toes, relaxing his entire body. Everyone in the coven had been a bit on edge since Jewel's diagnosis. Jewel and Lotus had been part of the coven since before their young Dagon was born, just four and a half years ago. "And Lotus?" Holly asked.

"Crying," Arnica's voice was soft. "Tears of relief. I think he'll begin carving a healing wand for Jewel from that cherry branch he took home a few weeks ago."

"I came in to tell you that I'm heading out with Dark Star."

Arnica looked at Holly quizzically. "Heading out?"

125

"She's feeling neglected. Since school started this fall we've all been so much busier. She's still just a unifilly and we've forgotten that she needs to romp and run and play."

Arnica's face crinkled up around his eyes. He realized that the hatchling was speaking for them all. "Snowshoes?"

That one word conveyed many images of memories from earlier years. Holly's eyes opened wide. Dark Star had never even seen her men with their snowshoes! "You bet," he said.

"I'll meet you in the greenhouse in ten minutes," Arnica said. "I've got to put on some thermals before we trek up into the mountains." Sensing the hatchling's youthful impatience, both men hurried off to collect their gear. Dark Star would have a great time in the snow!

The Yule log was burning bright in the fireplace. Added to their annual mantle decor were some beautiful pine cones brought back from last week's trek to the mountains. Arnica discovered that his knees were a bit older than the last time he and Holly went snowshoeing but they had a terrific time.

The altar put away, coven friends lounged about the cozy room. Holly was serving the last mugs of spiced cider which Arnica ladled in the kitchen. Dark Star was near the fireplace, enjoying the attention of her human friends. One of her favorite human customs was only minutes away.

Soon Arnica settled into his chair. Holly snuggled down on a floor pillow near Arnica's feet so he could play with Dark Star's ears.

Arnica slipped a hand behind his chair and held a brightly wrapped small package toward Holly.

The room burst into cheering at the signal and the cabin was filled with the music of human laughter and words as suddenly everyone was bringing forth Yule gifts. Colorful packages were handed about, names called out and soon each person was surrounded by a small pile of festive parcels.

Arnica looked to his left. Iris, seated in a large, upholstered chair, was nearly five months pregnant. Merrydale's postmarm was much loved in the village. Even the more conservative Kristos seemed more than willing to plant a tree. At first shocked when Pastor Dolorum resigned from the Church of the Martyr, it was a good-natured scandal when it became known that he and Iris, an environmental activist had become an 'item.' But both were well-loved and much of Merrydale turned out for their Handfasting, held in the courtyard of the building being restored as Trillium School.

Merrydale was a small village and Iris, as postmarm, saw almost everyone nearly every day as they came to pick up their mail. People were constantly asking what they might do to be of help. "Plant a tree," Iris answered. "We must have trees for our children's future. We lost so many trees three years ago when they began clearing Fern Hollow..." A painful memory for all the locals, for not only was Fern Hollow seriously damaged as trees were cut, but those events were connected with the curious death of Bishop Miter, struck dead during one of his brimstone sermons as he was ranting that 'God will punish evil.' In this midst of the chaos the union of Iris and Deodar and the creation of Trillium School was a blessing of stability and joy.

Deodar, a strikingly handsome man with his dark features ('Dolly,' to his friends), was helping Iris open their gift from Pearl, known for her skill as a seamstress.

"Look, everyone!" Iris said as Dolly set aside the wrappings. "Pearl made us a Wiccaning gown." Iris held up a beautiful crocheted and embroidered baby gown of an iridescent blue, actually quite reminiscent of the color of Andrius, Dark Star's father.

"Pearl," Deodar quizzed, "How do you know blue is the right color?"

Amused yet prepared for the question, the slightly-built Pictish woman looked about the room, catching everyone's attention. "Why," she said knowingly and looking at Dark Star, "a very kindly, older unicorn told me." Dark Star blushed just a bit at the mention of her father.

Pearl turned toward Jewel. Lounging on floor pillows and leaning against her husband, Lotus, Jewel was holding a large square, flat parcel.

Her mobility somewhat constricted, Jewel was unaccustomed to being held back. Not completely comfortable at needing to leave Dagon with a sitter (although Gino's parents were more than happy to have a young one about their house), Jewel could not move her arm freely without pain. She asked Lotus to open her gift for her.

His fingers, adept at transforming a piece of wood into the most extraordinary carving, quickly removed the paper. Gino, the coven's young teen, reached over and helped Lotus hold the matted design up for Jewel to examine. It was a striking pattern, a mandala created with a stylized drawing of Jewel's totem animal.

"Do you know what it's for?" asked Pearl.

Jewel's laughter, like little holiday bells, danced into the room. What magick! Learning just after Autumn Eve that she had breast cancer, Jewel had gone through a dark period before embracing Saturn and electing for a mastectomy just a week ago, eight days into the waning Moon. "Well, since you ask, now I'm not sure."

Everyone looking at Pearl, she raised her hands and everyone said at once, "It's a tattoo!"

Flying Raven, Trillium School's science teacher, offered an explanation. "When I was visiting Amber not long ago, she was telling me what one of her Loon Tribe sisters did."

Amber, her raven-colored hair held back with a red bow, had brought each a small pouch of crystals she'd brought back from a dream quest taken in a secret cave in the River Mountains. She leaned over, caressing Jewel's knee with her finger tips.

"Lynx Daughter, my mother's cousin, had a breast removed two years ago," Amber related. "The following summer she went to visit her son who lives near the Highlands and, when she came back, she proudly showed us a tattoo she had done right upon her chest where the breast had been. It was of the lynx spirit. Lynx Daughter has been transformed into a skilled medicine woman."

Jewel's hand reached up to gently cradle her missing breast. "A tattoo," she wondered aloud. "Yes, it can be a work of beauty..."

The room fell silent for a few moments.

"How long must I wait?" It was apparent that Jewel was very taken with the idea.

"Autumn would be ideal. Midsummer if the healing is quick. Hallows at the longest." Iris had discovered that she had a very strong desire to acquire some tattoos of her own.

Just then, Shadow Tail, the newest coven member, brought in a tray of borage cookies, Dark Star's favorite, and began singing the Yule round. The cabin was filled with much love and joy and voices singing together:
"Bring the sun king, bring the sun king, watch him grow..."

XLI - The Dark Pain of Prejudice

It was just days before the Candlemas Eve observance was to be held at Trillium School, a lovely winter day. A light snow had fallen the night before followed by a crisp, sunny morning. Arnica was hurrying into town. Dark Star, her horn quickly fading from sight pranced along. The hatchling knew that something was bothering Arnica, ever since Holly called from the school.

Sparkles of sun danced on the fresh snow as it clung to the fir boughs. The young unicorn ran about, always invigorated when there was fresh snow on the ground. Arnica was glad for the distraction. This was *not* how he had intended to spend his day. He looked over to his left and saw the thickening catkins on the hazel trees and let memories come forth...

It was five years ago on Candlemas Eve. Arnica and Holly were in the Stone Circle and the flames in the cauldron spiraled so high that they were frightened. And then, the soil glowing with light, they discovered the egg, which they protected until Dark Star hatched at Eostara!

Dark Star's horn had spiraled nearly five times. She loved her two men. Arnica and Holly provided her with a loving household and certainly, this life she had among mortals had been anything but dull. She looked to her left. Arnica was certainly distracted. The hatchling could tell that he was thinking about that telephone call again. Well, she had her ways.

"What?" Arnica started laughing, his arms flailing to stop the snow from falling right onto his head. Dark Star had jumped up and, with her horn, bumped a fir bough laden with snow. As her human friend wiped the moisture from his glasses, she looked up at him, gazing into his eyes with her most innocent expression. Who could be mad at such a lovely unifilly? "You're right, munchkin, my mind was lost."

Feeling refreshed, Arnica began humming the melody to the chant they would be singing at Candlemas Eve. As the herbalist walked along, only his hand indicated his concerns as his fingers tugged at his greying beard.

Nearing Merrydale, Arnica's hand stroked Dark Star's mane. "I'm going to leave you with Iris," he said.

Dark Star liked Iris and was fascinated with the postmarm's belly. Nearly six months pregnant, Dark Star like to lay her head on Iris' belly and listen to the growing life inside the warm darkness. This manner of human birth may have seemed somewhat normal to her human friends but to the hatchling, it was nothing short of a miracle.

It was a quick walk from the postal shop to Trillium School. Arnica walked purposefully, consciously placing his thoughts toward Jewel's healing. Jewel and her son Dagon were spending the morning with Iris. The tissue from Jewel's mastectomy was healing quicker than the doctors had thought possible. With Dagon nearly five, Jewel was going to manage the postal shop for a fortnight while Merrydale's postmarm became a mother for the first time. There were such joys among their coven!

'And now this,' Arnica thought to himself as he entered the school.

The school's courtyard was beautiful. A couple of small gardens plus the fountain that Jewel's husband, Lotus, had built lent an air of serenity. The courtyard was a place for students to rest their minds. And there, on the long wall in garish yellow spray paint like a vile scar tearing at the gentle fabric of the school, was the message: "I hate loons."

John Trouver, Merrydale's constable, was there taking photographs. Deodar Dolorum, the school's principal was talking to Carlos Santo, who stood near a couple of pails of water. There was no one else in the courtyard which indicated that something was very wrong.

"Arnica," Dolly (as Deodar was known among his close friend) said, "Holly said you would head right into town. I didn't expect you for another twenty minutes."

The older herbalist gave Dolly a quick hug. "Carlos, my friend." Carlos was a good friend. His son Gino was doing well studying with the coven. Carlos and his wife, Rosetta, had done much to help bring the Earthkin school into being but Carlos was more comfortable with a warm handshake.

"Hello, what's this?" Trouver was crouched down near a bay laurel, holding something in his hands. He was soon surrounded by the curious men. Rising to his feet, the constable was opening a small wallet. The courtyard was quiet without even the sounds of Trillium School, subdued by the racist vandalism.

Arnica, Dolly and Carlos watched without speaking. Their emotions were strong. There was sadness and anger that this had happened at all, fear that the special magick of Trillium School might not be enough to protect the students. But there was relief that whomever had committed this graphic violence was careless.

"I know this lad," Trouver said, turning to the three. "His father was active in the Users Party and the boy liked to echo the Users' extremist dogma simply to get attention. His father is still a strong Politico but no longer part of that right wing faction. He's actually grown increasingly open-minded. He's going to have a fit when he sees what his Billy has done."

"Wait," said Arnica. "What if you don't tell his father right now but speak to the boy directly. Do you think that knowing he got caught and that charges could be pressed at any time might convince him to take a close look at where his life is going?"

"I like your idea," Deodar added. "John, can we talk about this?"

It was a good discussion. The men sat in the courtyard nearly an hour. Holly was on break between classes and came out to talk with them and then sought out the view of the other teachers. By the time the impromptu meeting was finished, the situation had been nearly resolved and the energy of the courtyard was again that of Trillium School.

Many of the students and their parents were at the school this crisp morning. Each person had brought a candle to be lit as soon as the first rays of the sun could be drawn down. A touch of frost was in the air but it was early. The sun was just barely rising in the distance over the mountains. In less than an hour it would make its presence known to those in the courtyard.

129

The friends were standing in a circle about a temporary altar set in the center of the courtyard. Arnica, loved among the townspeople of Merrydale as an herbalist stood with his partner Holly. Holly's ability to teach the students their language skills amazed the parents of his students. Last week the principal of one of the largest public schools came to observe his classes for a day!

Next stood Deodar, the principal and former Kristos minister, and his wife Iris. Iris' role in the school was through her husband. Dolly's becoming principal after leaving the Church of the Martyr and now expecting a child with Iris (both much-loved among the townsfolk) had been one of the most newsworthy events in town history.

Pearl, the art and music teacher, had made them all new robes for this ritual. The coven was so glad she had moved back from Cloverville after Phoenix' passed away. Her gentle, Pictish ways were part of the coven's balance. Flying Raven, who moved this past summer from the Mothervalley to teach science, completed their circle.

Last night at their coven ritual, they remarked about how they could not have expected their role as a group to have expanded to include a new school! Jewel and Lotus sat with Dagon near the fountain. Lotus' work in building the fountain was skilled and artistic. Few realized how much magick had been worked into the sound of the splashing waters! Dark Star was laying next to Gino, Arnica's formula keeping her horn invisible.

The last of the coven, Gino, sat at the courtyard entrance. His classmates would have asked too many questions had he been part of the Circle. His parents, Rosetta and Carlos did the welcoming and guided the students, their parents and some of Merrydale's finest to their seats. In the few months since Trillium School had been opened, the number of locals who were rediscovering their Descendant tribal roots or talking about an interest in the Renaissance Tribe was turning Merrydale into a center of Earthkin activity. When the last of the Candlemas participants arrived, Gino rang a small bell to signal Arnica.

The simple sound began to quiet the gathering in the early February morn. Dressed warmly in their finest, forty or so students and adults were vibrant in the brightening dawn. No matter the hour, it was a lovely time of day.

Arnica and Holly purified and blessed the entire courtyard, creating a large Circle. The first ritual work was to wash the graffiti from the wall. Water was ladled from the fountain into a bucket. At an earlier ceremony Arnica and Holly had added dozens of samples of water from the small bottles of water kept safe in a closet in their cabin, waters collected from sacred sites representing many religions from all over the planet. The bucket was handed to the principal.

The courtyard filled with a gentle yet vibrant energy as voices wove the magick together, "... like a drop of rain, flowing to the ocean..."

Deodar knelt before the wall and, with a large sea sponge, began to wash the wall where the painted words spelled their hateful message. To everyone's surprise, including Deodar's, the paint began to dissolve.

And now, the high point of the Candlemas Morning ritual: Dark Star watched closely as Shadow brought a large ladder and set it toward the west side of the courtyard. Wearing his Loon Tribe ceremonial garments and carrying a magnifying glass, he climbed the ladder to the top.

The chanting continued as voices began to weave counterpoint and harmony. Shadow Tail, unassuming of stature and quiet by nature, looked so proud and so regal.

Holding the glass in one hand he focused the first rays of the sun upon a votive candle sitting in a glass holder, nearly the same iridescent blue as Dark Star.

A tiny wisp of smoke and then the wick burst into flame as those below broke into cheers of joy. Shadow was almost giddy with happiness, this being the first time he'd taken a public role in a ritual. He carried the flame down the ladder and to Arnica, and kissed his herbalist friend on the cheek. Arnica lit a taper from the candle and carried the sacred flame to the left altar candle, to represent the waxing Sun then handed it to Holly who used it to light the right candle for the Moon.

The darkness washed away, soon the flames spread throughout Trillium School's courtyard as each candle was lit, dispelling fear as warmth and the promise of waxing light filled every heart with joy. Dark Star's candle was lit for her. Watching how these humans had transformed a frightening event into healing was very powerful. A tear formed in the hatchling's left eye and began its downward descent but caught Gino's eye. Her young friend leaned over, wiped it with his finger and kissed her.

"I love you, munchkin," Gino whispered in her ear.

XLII - Where Are The Seeds?

"No, you don't need to come into town," Holly said. Troubled, he called his partner Arnica to discuss the curious situation. "I just wanted you to know that the baskets of seeds we brought in for the Sabbat ritual are missing."

Arnica and Holly were the donors of several small baskets of assorted seeds from their magickal gardens for Trillium School's celebration. The weather unusually warm and dry, three baskets had been placed on an outdoor altar built by their coven member Lotus, a skilled woodsmith. That morning when Holly was about to lead the first group of students in a morning invocation for blessings from the Universe and adding good wishes to the seed baskets, they discovered them missing.

"Missing?" Arnica couldn't help repeating the word, his mind mulling over the curious situation. "I'll set some extra seed aside. We have enough." It seemed their gardens always produced an abundance of fertile seed.

"I'll keep checking," Holly said. "I just don't feel that anyone's done anything. The school was locked all night. Since Billy's vandalism last January we're very careful about that."

"My sweet, I'll come in with Dark Star and meet you when school's out."

"How is my munchkin?" Holly asked. He loved the hatchling.

"Dark Star's over there getting in Gino's way. I must give him credit. Other boys might think of this as time away from school but he's taking his horticulture project very seriously and working very hard. I'll see you later."

The missing seed was a distraction for Arnica. Things didn't quite add up. Arnica fussed with his greying beard and headed out to check the new bed.

Gino, who would be fifteen this year, was the youngest of their coven. His school project was to set up a new bed for growing borage - one of Dark Star's favorite herbs. Having cleared a site, he dug down a couple of feet, preparing the earth, removing the roots of all weeds and former plants and working in the composted fertilizer he'd prepared over the past year. 'Unidoo,' he called it - composted unicorn manure. The coven knew it would be very good for the herbs grown in Arnica and Holly's gardens. In writing his paper, however, Gino had to refer to it as colt manure. Despite Trillium School having a 'unicorn' as its mascot and a few who somewhat wondered what there was about Dark Star, her horn was visible only to the coven, thanks to Arnica's formula.

Iris' laughter danced from the back porch out into her small, back gardens. She was on her afternoon break, the post office closed for afternoon tea. The postmarm's belly was quite large. The doctor had told her that her baby was quite large and very healthy. As Merrydale's postmarm and the new school's principal, the expectant parents held everyone's attention. The Beltane baby would be a big event! Arnica and Iris were talking about the coven's Sabbat Eve ritual this Saturday. This was the last Sabbat before Iris was due.

"Can you believe it?" Iris was saying to Arnica, "the men at the auto garage have a lottery! We're not supposed to know, but they're taking bets on just when I'll have the baby!" She laughed so hard she startled the young unicorn, who was trying to rest her ear against Iris's full belly. Dark Star *loved* listening to the growing baby. Humans were capable of such miracles!

"I saw Billy," Iris said. "He looks quite changed."

"Constable Trouver's 'sentence' was a good one. Billy seems quite past his prejudice toward the Earthkin."

"His parents have seemed genuinely friendly and interested in the baby when they come in for their mail," Iris said. "Their son's vandalism against Trillium School shocked them. They pride themselves on being law-abiding, Kristos-fearing citizens. Like so many of those right-wing folk, it's difficult for them to realize the prejudice they create."

"Billy's come by once or twice with some leaves carefully collected from Merrywood," Arnica related. "He's making great progress with his community project of taking a census and identifying all the plant and tree species to help protect them. And he's come to love being so connected with the woodlands. It's changing him."

"Ow," Iris jumped. Dark Star, startled, clambered to her feet. "Baby feet," she said, catching her breath after being kicked.

The hatchling's eyes were so wide. You could see the puzzlement on her face. Dark Star could not believe that the baby growing inside Iris' womb could actually kick.

Arnica reached into his sweater pocket and took out a small cosmetic jar he had recycled into a magickal container. The herbalist carefully massaged some of the ointment into Dark Star's horn. Even though it had been invisible the entire time they were in town, the coven knew this was a secret best kept.

A warm hug with some more humor. It was increasingly difficult to give Iris a hug. There was so much baby in between! The postmarm scratched Dark Star's ears and reached into her apron pocket.

"Look, munchie, I've got a borage flower biscuit for you!"

The hatchling's eyes were filled with awe. How did this woman find such a treat for her when borage blooms were completely out of season!

Arnica and Holly were talking very quietly to each other, not wanting to disturb Shadowtail. Arnica related his conversation with Iris, telling Holly that her father, Ollis Piper, was coming to Merrydale for the baby's birth.

Meanwhile, Shadowtail moved carefully about, drawing upon the tracking skills he learned as a child. Boys and girls alike were taught by their Loon Tribe elders the art of tracking animals.

Arnica was fascinated. Shadow wasn't using his eyes to explore the school's courtyard, he was *listening*. Moving silently about, Shadowtail would pause and stand there completely still. His hand would slowly raise, his fingers grasping the handle of a dried gourd. Ritually painted with a rainbow, Shadow would gently shake his rattle with closed eyes... and then listen. The small dark man was in a meditative state, in complete harmony with his environment.

Arnica and Holly were now rapt, watching their friend. The voices of young students as they left the school seemed to pass into another dimension. Just as the men felt themselves caught up in the trance, Shadowtail stopped, looked directly at them and opened his eyes but didn't see the two men. Shadow began rattling the gourd, creating a soft yet insistent rhythm with the sound. There was a pattern to the sound of the shaken seed, but not one rising from human experience.

"Skoros," Shadow breathed the sound. He appeared to be invoking that name.

"Skoros," the name spoken so softly, yet emerging from the rhythm of the rattle. Soon a scampering sound as a squirrel scrambled over the edge of the school roof and down some vines, only coming to a stop when it was still, looking directly at Shadowtail. "Skoros," Shadow said with satisfaction.

The rattle's pattern changed and blended with some soft chattering from the squirrel. Arnica and Holly seemed to barely breathe, so enchanted were they with what was unfolding. The squirrel looked at them and scampered away, soon out of sight beyond the roof.

The rattle stopped. It's silence brought them back to consciousness.

"It was the squirrel. *Skoros*," said Shadow. "He thought the seeds had been placed out for him, for the squirrel gods. I assured him that they were."

Arnica laughed, knowing that there was no other answer.

Shadow continued. "In thanks for the seeds the children of Skoros will watch the school. Surely they can be as effective an alarm as any other!"

It was a great story. The Sabbat Eve ritual complete, the seeds planted in the greenhouse pots, the coven sat around the cabin drinking hot tea made from fresh mint picked that afternoon. They were all there. Deodar and Iris were uncertain whether they would be at Beltane. Only the Goddess knew just when the baby would be ready. Gino sat by the fireplace, leaning against the sleeping hatchling as if she were a pile of pillows. The young unicorn and Gino were great friends. Pearl was putting the finishing touches on a large wreath which would be hung on the school doors to welcome guests to the public ritual in the school's courtyard. Her Pictish fingers moved quickly as she sewed forsythia and pussywillow branches into place.

Flying Raven, the science teacher, asked Shadowtail to pronounce the word *skoros* again. The older woman was fascinated and wanted to learn how to communicate with the squirrels and with other species as well.

"What if you're late," Jewel asked Iris. "Your baby could be born on Dagon's birthday!"

"I hope not," Iris laughed. "I'm ready."

Lotus was showing Deodar a new staff he was carving.

Arnica and Holly were in the kitchen, starting the washing up. They were pleased when their cabin was warmed with their friends. Tomorrow would be another Sabbat morning with the ritual at the school. Working a public ritual every Sabbat for the students and family of the Earthkin's first school was a lot of work. The older men knew that when their friends were gone, they'd be sleeping as sound as Dark Star.

XLIII - The Curious Procession

The cabin and gardens were filled with activity. Almost the entire coven had arrived in the morning to prepare for that night's Beltane Eve ritual. The cabin, set in the clearing of Merrywood Forest, was blessed with the scent of baking. Flying Raven was given the realm of the kitchen. She was making borage cookies for Dark Star (Gino was working hard to keep the hatchling in the gardens and out of the cabin!) and 'just in case' a double batch of chocolate chip oatmeal cookies. Everyone knew they were Andrius' favorite and he was due to turn up unexpectedly one of these warm Sabbats to surprise his offspring, Dark Star. More and more, Flying Raven was glad she'd accepted the invitation to move back from the Mothervalley to teach science at Trillium School. Her own children grown, she welcomed the family atmosphere of the coven and loved the stimulation of a classroom filled with eager, young minds.

Holly and Arnica were tending the seedlings in the greenhouse. Arnica was nursing several pots of mandrake seed, which were particularly challenging and Holly was busy thinning the love-lies bleeding. The younger of the two, Holly had sown the seed far too heavily and now much thinning was needed. The two men often worked nearly as one, their lives so closely entwined, and would finish each other's sentences without anyone even noticing.

The newest member of the coven, Shadow Tail was weeding around the bleeding hearts. He loved the dicentra, including the wild species growing near the giant-leaved maple along the path to the stone circle. "Look at this," he called to Pearl. Despite his darker skin from his Loon Tribe heritage, Shadow was wearing a large, straw garden hat to protect his ears against sunburn.

Pearl was working nearby, tending to the trilliums. The large, native white species had been open for weeks but the more exotic red trilliums which Arnica had brought in from a nursery, were only now preparing to open their buds. Pearl stepped lightly, her small Pictish frame not much larger than a girl's. "What do you have?"

Shadow pointed to a few small leaves. The seedling looked to be a tiny bleeding heart. "Do you think they've had an offspring?" Shadow asked?

"Does Arnica know?" Pearl asked, her mind distracted as her mind created patterns of embroidery she'd like to stitch onto Shadow's hat. He preferred it plain, even though Pearl's were the best hands with a needle to be found in the land.

A short walk away, young Gino was carefully weeding the borage bed. The borage seeds had not yet sprouted and Dark Star, the resident unicorn hatchling, was watching Gino *very* closely. She had a tendency to forget that they're a late-sprouting plant and every spring was a little concerned that her favorite herb might not begin growing. Gino and Dark Star had become great friends since they met. How their lives had changed since that important day! They looked forward to the Lammas Sabbat which would mark their fifth year. How young Gino was then, just a boy of ten but now a vital member of the coven.

Off in the woods, Jewel and Lotus were cleaning up winter debris in the stone circle, preparing it for Beltane Eve which would be the first Sabbat ritual in the stone circle. Their youngster, Dagon, was growing quickly. Born at the Scorpio Full Moon just after Beltane five years ago, in another year he would begin first grade at Trillium School. Now and then, watching Iris' belly grow full with child, Jewel found herself wanting to be pregnant again but she and Lotus wanted to do their part to protect Dagon's future. The planet's population was growing at such an alarming rate that they vowed to be wise in this matter and not allow their personal desires to take precedence over the survival of all species. Jewel had been helping Iris at the postal shop and would take over after the baby's birth until Iris could resume her job.

It was a beautiful afternoon. The air was heavy with the Beltane song of birds, the buzzing of bees gathering nectar and pollinating flowers. Everyone was busy, this one of the rare days when the entire coven worked together in preparation for the Sabbat.

Everyone, that is, except Iris and Deodar. Dolly, as the Trillium School principal was known among his friends, insisted that they stay at home until time to leave for the ritual. Iris was restless. This past week she'd done little more than make small talk with the folk coming in to pick up their mail and buy stamps. Jewel was a great help and managed just fine. There was little for Iris to do other than sit around and feel pregnant.

And she felt very pregnant. Her was time near and the Earthkin know that Moons and Sabbats can bring forth the baby! Dolly was painting some trim on the back porch, enjoying working out in the sun on this fine spring day. Iris couldn't take being restful any longer and decided to go clean the postal shop attached to their house. She got up and started toward the storage room to get cleaning cloths.

"Dolly!" Iris' voice cried out with the piercing timbre of surprised alarm. "Quick, call Arnica. Call the midwife. Call Ollis." The contractions had increased and this was no time to be cleaning. The baby was coming for Beltane.

What a curious procession walked along the road to Merrydale! All the friends wanted to go with Arnica and Holly and Dark Star knew that *she* wasn't about to be left behind. They barely took time to wash the fertile-scented garden soil off their hands, grab a few things and head down the road through Merrywood. In fact, Gino was rubbing the special ointment into the hatchling's horn as they made their way. Arnica was certain that Dark Star's horn would become invisible before they were in Merrywood. Dark Star would sit back upon her hind legs and Gino would rub the magickal balm onto her horn. Gino's freckled face was beaming with pride. He was so pleased that Arnica trusted him with the ointment. Gino knew it had jade and even gold powder in it but only Arnica, Holly and Dark Star knew the actual formula. But Dark Star was impatient and Gino wouldn't get very far and the hatchling would scramble to her legs and trot up to join the rest, Gino running after her. The birds of Merrywood filled the trees with song and the group of friends created an aura of laughter and joy as they walked.

Arnica and Holly were talking about the birthing process. Dolly's message didn't say anything about the midwife and, although the men preferred the birth be handled by a midwife, they had the knowledge if need be. They took turns carrying a satchel containing jars of herbs, bottles of tincture and a small Book of Shadows which contained the coven's baby blessing ritual

"It's a good thing I'd just taken the cookies out of the oven! The rest of the dough can sit in the refrigerator until we return" Raven's own children long since grown, she had not only given birth three times but had been present for four of her six grandchildren's arrivals as well. Jewel and Lotus walked with Flying Raven just a bit behind the couple. Jewel was glad that Dagon was in town, today, playing with a neighbor child. The adults were wasting no time and the extra trips walking back and forth between Merrydale and the cabin would leave the child too tired to enjoy staying up for the Sabbat.

Pearl had never given birth. Jewel's russet-colored hair shook in surprise upon learning that Pearl had never even witnessed a baby's birth!

"I'm much more the godmother type," Pearl laughed in response. Although old enough to be a grandmother, she still embodied the maiden aspect of the Goddess in so many ways.

By now Dark Star and Gino had finished their game with the ointment. The horn was nearly invisible and they trotted and skipped along with Arnica and Holly. At times like this Gino was much more like the boy they met, but Arnica knew their friend would be wearing his 'young man' personality as soon as they were in Merrydale.

"What if the baby's born before we get there?" asked Gino with his boyish curiosity.

"Patience, it won't happen until we're there," Arnica answered, with good humor.

"Um," Gino couldn't help himself, "how do you know?"

"It was in my dream last Full Moon," Arnica said, matter of fact. And that was enough said for the young man.

Shadow Tail and Lotus walked at the rear, talking about Trillium School. Lotus was preparing a wood-working and shop class and had many questions for Shadow, who was helping Carlos with the maintenance and assisting with office work. Both men were somewhat quiet by nature and they enjoyed this opportunity to talk.

Iris lay in her bed, with Dolly kneeling on the floor so he could whisper encouragement, generally words of love, talk of their dreams for the future, all interspersed with the regular "push," echoing the midwife.

Arnica was assisting the midwife, occasionally opening a small vial of herbal oils. "Breathe deep," he'd say to Iris. And she did. Raven and Jewel had both told her that the labor pains were intense and, of course, nearly every mother in Merrydale offered advice when they came into the postal shop, but the reality was stronger than her expectation.

Just through the door in the living room the coven was conducting - not their Beltane Eve ritual as they had planned, but the ritual which accompanied the birth and blessing of a baby. Holly was working at Dolly and Iris' home altar and the coven was standing in a circle around it.

Ollis Piper was not completely comfortable with the Earthkin traditions, but he would not miss the birth of his first grandchild. After all, he'd missed most of Iris' life, showing up just for his daughter's Handfasting. But he found the words soothing and beautiful. When he abandoned Iris' mother, he left behind his childhood religion as well, rebelling against guilt and a dour future. The Kristos church his parents belonged to damned all of his desires. Ollis was beginning to sense why Iris had taken up the Renaissance beliefs. Meanwhile, he was busy with his camera. Iris would be so happy to have photos of this event!

"I light a candleflame blessed by the Moon. She'll keep you safe at night, within Her boon. Soft lullabies for dreams Her love will croon..." Holly lit the second of the altar candles. The coven filled the room with a gentle chant, its music drifting into Iris' bedroom like the sweet scent of incense.

"Let water wash away your baby tears..." Holly was aspurging the Circle. "These droplets pure will banish all your fears."

As Ollis kept his camera busy, Holly took Pearl's hand and led her to stand behind the altar. As Pearl drew down the Goddess this Beltane Eve, the words seemed so very powerful. "Open your heart to My words, for I am the very Soul of Nature... It was I Who blessed your mother when she birthed you..."

And the cry of the baby taking it's first deep breaths filled the dusk. Sounding like a bird, a music more of song than that of an unhappy wail. And then, Dolly's voice, "It's a girl!"

"I am the beginning and I am the ending..." Pearl continued as Holly supported her arms. Her voice reached out to embrace the baby, and Iris and Dolly and also Arnica. "I am with you in your dreams... And I love you at all times."

XLIV - It's A Girl

Arnica and Holly were working along the path which led from their gardens to the stone circle. Dark Star lay near a huckleberry, having carried a small basket of half pint jars. It was a warm, sunny day and the young unicorn enjoyed being in the shade of the trees. Holly was placing a votive candle into each jar and setting one every several feet on either side of the path to light the way for their Midsummer Eve ritual. May and June had brought more than average rainfall so the woodland would be safe for this evening's candles. The moisture had been welcome and the green things thrived. Arnica, his pruning shears in hand and candles crooning to the spirits of the shrubs so that they would not feel pain, was cutting back a branch here and there to keep the path more open and to ensure that no branches might hang too close to them as they walked to Circle.

"Remember?" Both voices spoke at once. The men laughed. They had been together many years and even looked much alike. Although never confused in Merrydale, people in Mill City thought they looked so much alike they were usually considered brothers, sometimes even twins! Arnica and Holly would laugh, but they enjoyed knowing they had such a strong, magickal bond.

"Amber's store was gone when we went to get the bell." Holly was setting the candle jars along the edge of the path which was lined with large rocks and moss-covered logs. Five years ago they hung a bell to commemorate the birth of Dagon.

"So much has passed," Arnica mused as he clipped a berry branch which stretched across the path and could easily draw blood if it scratched someone walking the path. "Five years ago the Users were growing in power. The Crystal Emporium had closed. But then Carlos' coworker died mysteriously in Mill City and then Bishop Miter died in such an odd way..."

"And now we have Trillium School..." Holly walked over to the hatchling to get more candle jars from her basket. Their minds moved in the same direction, thinking of how times change. These days people were less caught up with fears promoted by the Users, the right-wing faction of the Politico Party. The people of Merrydale were far more interested in the new school's principal and his wife's new baby! Iris had been the town's postmarm for many years and their lives were more relevant to local people than the corporations of the big cities.

Most of the coven was out at the grove, helping prepare for the evening ritual. In Holly and Arnica's cottage, Amber worked in the kitchen with Flying Raven, teaching Raven how to make bread in the traditional Descendant Tribes way. They were mixing the dough which would soon be baked in a temporary, stone oven. Raven marveled at how easy it was for Amber to find stones and set them in place. How she wished her grandchildren might someday see this. As they mixed the dough a candle sat nearby burning brightly. Raven's contribution to the Midsummer bread was providing the fire to be used in the outdoor oven. She had, just that morning, drawn down the sun using a magnifying glass! The two women enjoyed working together and getting to know each other better this past year through the school and Coven.

As they worked, they talked about the new tree, a weeping goldenchain tree, [a *Laburnum alpinum* 'Pendulum' as Arnica called it] which had recently been planted in a small park just across from the postmarm's office. Carlos and Rosetta, Trillium School's custodian and cook, had managed to take up a collection from school parents without Iris and Dolly knowing a thing about it! When Mr. Pounds, the tithing agent learned about the collection, he approached Merrydale's mayor. Although usually been sympathetic to the Users, the right wing of the Politicos (the mayor was instrumental in the decision five years ago to allow a section of Merrywood to be cut down for lumber), the mayor surprised Mr. Pounds and not only made a personal donation but offered to let the tree be planted in the small park. It had been a wonderful event. The tree would do well in Merrydale's climate but was very uncommon and had to be shipped in from hundreds of miles to the south.

Like sisters, they would suddenly shift topics, talking personally. Amber found she still needed to talk about the demise of her three year relationship with a steelsmith named Quicksilver and Raven reminisced about her late husband and the brief romantic encounter with Iris' father, Ollis, last year. When they talked about past lovers, their voices were soft and healing for each other like butterflies but when they spoke about the new tree, the kitchen was filled with the music of their words.

It was just a couple of weeks ago when the small crowd gathered outside of Iris and Dolly's home - the postal shop was in the front of the house. The couple came out to see what was going on and discovered the school faculty and staff, the Mayor, even Arnica and Holly all gathered to plant the tree in honor of the baby Diana's birth. It was an old custom, planting a tree when a baby was born. It went back in time way before the Kristos religion and had survived the cycles of many different religions.

Gino, now 15, was helping Shadow Tail put the finishing touches on a new shrine built at the base of a huge, old cedar. Shadow was smudging the area with a thick braid of artemisia from the Lower River Plain. Shadow's branch of the Loon Tribe lived further south than Amber's. The shrine was very handsome, handmade by Lotus. Lotus was the true craftsman of the coven, easily able to transform a stick into a stunning staff. Lotus had also built the beautiful fountain for Trillium School's courtyard. That evening a small bell would be hung in the shrine as it was dedicated to the goddess Diana.

Lotus and Jewel had asked to provide the bell, for it was just five years ago that a small, silver bell was hung for Dagon when their baby just weeks old, as he was brought to the circle for the first time.

"How did everyone know I would name the baby Diana?" Iris asked, turning to Pearl. She couldn't figure that out.

Pearl smiled. She had walked over to Iris' home to fit a Wiccaning gown she had embroidered and to give Iris a hand. Iris was glad for the help. Pearl had many years' experience with the coven and understood how they would know such things.

It was a beautiful day in Merrydale just as it was at the Grove. It had been a remarkable five years between the two babies, their lives changed in so many ways. Even life at the Grove, with the wondrous gardens, have been profoundly changed, not so much by the political events, the marriages and births and the founding of Trillium School, but by the arrival of the hatchling, just five years ago this past spring.

Dark Star was so excited. She would trot from the front of the cabin back to the gardens, then quickly run along the path beneath the trees to the stone circle... Then she'd trot back again, stopping for a quick munch of fresh borage from her favorite bed in the gardens.

Iris and Dolly had just arrived in a horse-drawn lorry! Pearl had paid for the rental, assuring them that it was because the statue of Diana weighed far too much for anyone to carry (which was true). Pearl, the coven artist, had ordered this from a sculptor friend of hers in Cloverville and had it shipped in. Pearl had seen the Diana in his studio before she moved back to Merrydale and called to see if it was available. It was such a perfect gift for the shrine. Pearl sensed that it had been created just for this purpose, even if her artist friend did not realize it at the time.

But more, despite Iris being a very athletic woman, Pearl did not want her to even *consider* walking to the cabin from Merrydale, even though the baby was still so tiny! Deodar was carrying their tent and sleeping things back to the stone circle. When Dagon was born to Jewel, the entire coven spent the night in the stone circle to commune with the Devas but not this year. Their coven had grown in the past five years. Iris was now an active member and her husband Dolly was then Pastor Dolorum. Dolly had left the Church of the Martyr. Free to pursue his deepest beliefs, Merrydale had never quite recovered from seeing the young clergyman transform himself, marrying the local postmarm and becoming the Earthkin principal of Trillium School! And Gino, the first in Merrydale to recognize Dark Star's unicorn nature. And Raven, now living nearby after spending her married life living far away in the Mothervalley! No, there were too many of them now for sleeping in the stone circle. Shadow Tail worked with the coven as well, although he had been talking about returning to the Lower River Plain later this summer.

After the blessing of the Diana shrine and the Sabbat Eve, after they shared their evening stories and feast, Arnica and Holly would turn to their bed. Arnica's 'old bones' as he called them didn't enjoy sleeping on a pad beneath the trees as much any more. Pearl, whose Pictish ancestry gave her a delicate appearance, felt that she and the older women, Amber and Raven Hawk, would do better in their own homes back in Merrydale and would be riding back in the lorry.

Dark Star was torn. She'd never had much time to play with a horse. He was so very *interesting* but, although quick witted, didn't seem to know how to *communicate* with her like her humans did. It was like a festival. The hatchling was having so much fun. She would sleep in the gardens with Gino, who was setting up his small tent (just big enough for the lad and a young unicorn!) near the borage bed. Dagon was old enough to help carry things but young enough to be fascinated by the baby. The gardens were filled with the colors of Midsummer robes, blankets spread out for babies and for a picnic-style potluck feast. Dark Star discovered that the horse preferred hay to borage. This was reassuring, although she didn't really mind sharing! And, of course, the center of attention was baby Diana. Iris and Dolly were very proud parents!

Late that night quiet filled the cabin and gardens. Dolly was putting out the candles one by one, the small flames disappearing in the night as Iris carried the baby Diana back to their tent in the stone circle. The candle-lit path among the trees seemed to be taking itself back to the sacred stones.

Little peepers, tiny green tree frogs, filled the night with their songs. The faeries and devas, welcomed by the coven's Midsummer's Eve rites, danced and played in the woodland and among the gardens. In the distance the sound of laughter and voices began to fade. Jewel and Lotus walked along with the others who were heading back to Merrydale that night, Dagon snuggled up in a blanket in the lorry, sound asleep. Shadow and Amber were sharing memories and comparing similarities and differences in how their own families observed the Loon Tribal ways at Midsummer.

Arnica and Holly stretched out in their bed, enjoying the coolness of the sheets as a night-scented breeze drifted through the open windows of their cabin.

Dark Star snuggled up against Gino. The lad was so fond of the hatchling. He rolled over, half sleeping, and pulled her close to him. Life for all, this Midsummer, was very good.

XLV - A Troubling Harvest

Arnica and Holly were sitting on the wood floor of the new drying shed. It was a nicely built structure, simple yet practical. Sitting near the greenhouse and potting shed, it was about eight feet tall at the center and had no windows. Lotus, their wood carving friend, and Carlos, Trillium School's maintenance man, had put it up in a day. It had air vents which could be opened and closed to keep the warm darkness from becoming too hot during the sunny heat of the Lammas season.

The door to the shed open, the first bunches of herbs were tied tight and hanging from the ceiling rafters. Feverfew, meadowsweet, yarrow, celandine... The celandine would dry quickly as would the feverfew blossoms. The warm, shaded air was scented not only with the dozen or so different types of herbs but still smelled like fresh lumber, a scent Arnica particularly loved.

"Wouldn't this have been terrific for the rose buds and the peony petals?" Holly leaned back looking up at the herbs, his head resting against Arnica's shoulder.

"It's definitely a blessing," Arnica responded. Always organized, Arnica determined that the best way to hang herbs in the shed was to hang the roots and those which took the longest to dry along the walls and those which went quickly, the flowers and thinner leaves, in front of them. "It's a blessing that we won't have to worry so about spiders and other bugs!"

"I saw another monarch yesterday," Holly mused. The men were pleased that their showy milkweed was in full bloom. This was the third year since they had planted it and it had taken this long for the herb to mature.

"But only that one hummingbird." Arnica finished the thought for Holly. A week ago a hummingbird had been sipping the sweet nectar from the milkweed blooms.

"Is Dark Star," Arnica began his question about the hatchling.

"In the borage," Holly finished. They chuckled and, despite the harvest warmth, snuggled closer. Their many years of ritual work and garden labor together had greatly empowered their relationship.

"It's me ..." Iris' strong voice sung through the gardens. The postmarm had taken the day off. Iris and Jewel found it worked wonderfully over Midsummer when Jewel managed the postal shop. Merrydale residents loved Iris as their postmarm but were pleased this morning to find Jewel. They knew Iris deserved time off during the birth and an occasional day to relax as all new mothers need. Dagon was over five years old and quite content sitting and reading as his mother sold stamps and discussed the weather and news as the locals came for their mail.

Iris imagined the excited discussion in the postal shop today but knew she needed to take the day off and visit the Grove with the news. She had tried to call her friends earlier but, as usual during the growing season, there was no answer. Her long braid was pulled over her shoulder and the baby Diana was sound asleep in the back sling. Trying to calm her nerves, Iris asked "Where's Dark Star?"

"She's out playing in the woods," Arnica answered almost lazily. The older man was known for his never-ending work ethic and, to be honest, Iris was not accustomed to see him sitting back and just relaxing in the summer's warmth with Holly.

"Dear Iris, if you could have seen her!" Holly sat up, energized by the memory. "There were two viceroys around our milkweed and the hatchling was so entranced that when they drifted with the breeze off into the woods, she followed them."

"She followed them?" Iris echoed, feeling quite unsettled.

"Iris," and now Arnica sat up, sensing that things were not quite right, "why are you here? Why aren't you at the postal shop?"

Quickly Iris told the men the news which brought her from work out to the Grove. It seemed that just last week a local farmer was out harvesting his early grain when he discovered several dead animals. A couple of chickens and, worst of all, a puppy and a house cat. Immediately he and his neighbors concluded that this killing was the work of a predator coming out of the woods, possibly a fox or a wolf. Within days a small group of hunters, all known for their dislike of conservation laws and their liking guns just a little too much, had formed a sort of vigilante group and had begun searching Merrywood for the marauding predator. It was common knowledge although there was no *proof* that beer was being combined with the bullets. Most of the locals were strongly opposed to this but a few, all of the Users faction of the Politicos Party, supported the posse's actions just as they opposed any type of gun control laws. Iris told Arnica and Holly how heated some of the discussions in the postal shop had become. As she related the news Diana began making hungry baby noises.

Events had come to a head this morning. Mrs. O'Realy lived just a half mile from Merrydale on two acres of land. An elderly widow, she supported herself by sewing during the winter and selling eggs and fresh cream from her two Brown Swiss cows. This morning when she went out to milk her cows she found them both shot dead. The veterinarian extracted several 30 caliber bullets, those used in deer hunting.

"But Arnica," Iris said, now nursing the weeks-old baby, "they're still out tromping through Merrywood with their guns and their beer!"

Arnica sighed, "Dark Star..." his voice trailing off. "Holly, quick, get your crystal ball." Arnica knew they could best call the hatchling home if Holly focused their desire through the quartz orb.

Before walking back to town, Iris took some turquoise beads she'd had for many years and walked back to the new goddess shrine. She knelt beneath the great cedar with Diana in one arm as she set the beads at the feet of the statue of the Goddess Diana. "Bless us all," she prayed quickly, then went back through the gardens for quick hugs before walking back to Merrydale. Baby Diana, well fed, slept contentedly as she rocked gently in the warmth of her mother's back. Iris knew the hatchling would be fine and looked forward to Lammas Eve the day after tomorrow.

The gardens were a surprise to all the coven and their guests. This was the baby Diana's first Sabbat. Shadow Tail was leaving in a couple of weeks, returning to the homeland of his Descendant Tribe. And Trillium School would be open before the next Sabbat! Holly and Arnica surprised everyone with dozens of paper lanterns hung in the trees, each with a small bulb and all connected to a small solar transformer which had gathered the sun's energy into a compact battery.

Lammas Eve was celebrated early while the sun still shone upon the gardens. Arnica and Holly conducted a 'Drawing Down the Sun' with Gino holding the magnifying glass. This flame was used to relight all pilot lights so that the Harvest Sun would bring his flame to their homes and carry his energy to the ritual candles in the coming months.

Although not coveners, Carlos and Rosetta brought the grain man bread for the Lammas feast. Gino, their only son, was now fifteen years old. When he joined the coven he was a boy but now he was definitely a young man. Gino loved the hatchling dearly. The freckled lad was playing with Dark Star. None of the adults were quite certain what the 'rules' were to their game but Gino and Dark Star would take turns chasing each other up and down and around the garden paths.

Iris lay on a blanket, playing with Diana's toes. Jewel sat on the blanket as well. Dagon, now five, was no longer a baby and, to be honest, she was thrilled to have a baby in her life again. Rosetta was stretched out on the grass nearby. Was Gino ever so tiny? She knew he was but it was so long ago...

Amber and Flying Raven sat nearby in lawn chairs, large clipboards on their laps. Pearl was animated, her hands moving in colorful gestures as she discussed the curriculum. Arnica looked toward the women. Pearl spoke about her plans for the art and music classes at Trillium School as they discussed their plans for the courses they would teach this coming year. Amber taught history and social studies and Raven was the science teacher.

"I have an idea," Amber interjected excitedly. The Sabbat inspiration was obvious. Amber's shiny black hair was coiled above her head. "I'd like to see Iris offer some material on Merrydale's history and politics. We could even get Mayor Browning to come in once or twice." The women were immediately taken with the idea but, before they could continue with their comments Amber added, "And that's not all. Rosetta, I don't see why you could not teach a class in cooking. All of our students, boys also, should know the basics of being able to prepare their own meals before they leave Trillium School."

Deodar, new father and principal of the school, was talking with the men. Lotus would be teaching wood-working this year. Although their goal was to complete the scheduling of the various classes the seven teachers would be offering, the topic kept returning to what had happened early this morning. Carlos had been downtown and saw it for himself.

The five 'hunters' who had been out gunning for the wild predator had been the victims of 'cow karma.' From what Carlos overheard and pieced together with a later discussion with the town constable, John Trouver, the posse had been crossing a pasture, which was posted with 'no trespassing' and 'no hunting' signs when one of the men stepped in a fresh cow pie and slipped, shooting himself in the foot. To make matters worse, when the five men drove back into Merrydale speeding and somewhat intoxicated, they took the last curve too fast and drove into a tree. Carlos saw them as they limped into town carrying their friend. The injuries, including the gun shot, were all quite minor but enough of Merrydale had seen them that the men were quite humbled. Merrywood was again safe for all creatures, including those which kept the food chain active. And John Trouver now had enough evidence to guarantee that the widow O'Realy would be more than repaid for her cows.

Shadow told the men that he had seen some tracks and believed the killings to be the work of a coyote. The unusually dry conditions in the River Mountains must have brought the coyote down to the low elevations in search of prey.

The gardens were buzzing with conversations. Gino and Dark Star lay dozing together. Gino looked more boy than man as he curled against his unicorn friend. A bell rang to catch everyone's attention.

"The sun sets earlier, now." Arnica was bringing Lammas Eve to a close. He knew that everyone still had a good walk back into town. "Tomorrow is another full day. Our Lammas Day feast at the school starts at noon but we must be there by ten o'clock to finish setting up the class schedule for the coming year." The harvest season was now underway. It was fitting that the staff and faculty would meet before the harvest feast in Merrydale.

Dark Star slept well that night, her dreams of running through fields of borage with Gino interspersed with visions of being able to wander through Merrydale and Trillium School with her horn visible to all.

XLVI - Knocking At Trillium School's Door

It was a beautiful September afternoon, the sun shining warm through the trees. The gardens were no longer lush. Most of the herbs had long since been harvested. The perennials were cut back and run through the shredder. Most of them lay moldering in the compost bin. Open jars of seeds continued to dry in the cabin and the roots of dandelion, aconite and a few other herbs hung in the shade of the drying shed for the afternoon. The nights were now cool and the roots could easily attract dampness. Arnica moved them into the kitchen every evening.

It was the afternoon of Autumn Eve and Trillium School was holding its staff meeting at the cabin. The gathering was casual for the faculty was nearly the same as their coven! Dark Star loved company. The hatchling was prancing about, running back into the woods along the path where Gino, the coven's teen, was setting lanterns along the path's edge to the Stone Circle. Then she'd run out into the gardens, her iridescent coat a lovely blue flash in the sun as she raced up to Holly who was harvesting concord grapes from the arbor. Dark Star would gaze at him longingly and laughing, Holly would hold a couple in his hands.

A look of pleasure on the young unicorn's face, she would trot to the large wicker basket where Diana Dolorum, not yet five months old, lay cooing in the shade of the large rowan. And then the hatchling would go running back to Gino in the woods. The gardens were filled with merriment!

The baby's parents sat nearby on a blanket with mugs of fresh herbal tea. Iris' long braid hung down her back as she took notes. Dolly, the school's principal, was thinking out loud, exploring the topics in need of discussion. On another blanket right next to them Jewel was softly reading a story to Dagon. Five just after Beltane, Jewel was home-schooling his preschool studies although Dagon, having been through the portal into the Realm of the Faerie with Dark Star when a year old, was very precocious. It was believed that he would grow up to be a highly skilled Bard as an adult.

Arnica was picking apples, wrapping each in paper and setting them into flat boxes for their winter stay in the root cellar. Arnica was the elder of the group and he and Dolly spoke back and forth as they went about their work.

There was talk of new classes and whether they should begin next year or at the next semester. The first classes had begun just a year ago with fifty students. This year there seventy-one students.

"Seventy-one, and there would be more if we could accommodate them." Deodar shook his head in wonder. "Where are they all coming from?"

Iris looked up from her note-taking, "Merrydale may seem like a village but there are many families in the school district tucked in and among Merrywood."

"And it's a good school. We have experienced teachers." Arnica wrapped an apple, bright green with a blush of red. "And the Earthkin like the idea of having a school where their children can learn to love and care for the Earth."

"Did you hear about the Loon School?" Amber called over from the table. A folding table had been set up not too far away. Pearl, Flying Raven and Amber were talking with Gino's mother, Rosetta. They were planning a new class to be offered starting the first week of school. Amber was from the Loon Tribe in the River Mountains. During the summer when she visited her people she sat with the committees who were working with the first indigenous people's school. "Even the Descendant Tribes see our Trillium School as a role model!"

"What are the results of the voting?" Pearl, small and delicate of build, taught art and music. An earlier discussion led her to create a ballot which was sent to all the students.

"Let's see," Flying Raven said adjusting her glasses. The coven's scribe had tallied all the voting. "There's definitely a majority of students who feel that cooking should be required although most of the girls felt that the class should be only for them." The ladies murmured quietly at the expected news. "But listen to this! All but two boys indicated that the class should be required for everyone - even the boys!"

"Boys?" Rosetta gasped. She was already intimidated at the thought of teaching cooking, even to the girls but the others knew she'd do well. They remembered how Gino's mother stood up to the principal of Merrydale's junior high school upon learning that Gino wouldn't be allowed to register unless he told them he believed in 'the one true god.' Rosetta was a very capable woman.

"I got a post card from Shadow Tail," Amber said. The women knit their voices together like a multicolored shawl. Shadow had recently moved back to the Lower River Plain, just below the River Mountains. His studies with Arnica and the year he spent helping out with Trillium School were excellent experience and his new skills were much in demand as the Descendant Tribes worked on their plans for their own school.

Dagon's father, Lotus, and Gino's father, Carlos, joined their family and friends. They had been in Arnica and Holly's tool shed, sharpening the spades and hoes for next year's season.

"That cheesecake was so good," Holly smiled at Flying Raven, "I think I'd better go stretch or I'll never be able to make it through tonight's ritual!" Holly had been unable to resist Raven's secret recipe for chocolate cheesecake. He sat on the nearby grass and did some simple yoga to help his body recover from the huge, family-style picnic lunch.

"Everyone's here?" Arnica looked around. It was time to get on with the meeting. Just as the herbalist was about to call for attentiveness, Dark Star quietly stepped up behind him and nuzzled him in his grey beard, catching him quite by surprise which filled the gardens with laughter. Arnica laughed as he and the hatchling tumbled to the grass.

And then, just as sudden, he stood up and handed Gino a basket. "Young man, would you take this frisky filly through the gardens and collect the fruits and flowers for tonight's ritual?"

The freckled young man had grown so since Carlos and Rosetta gave him permission to begin studying with the coven. He was getting tall and looked so proud at having this responsibility.

"Dolly?" Arnica turned the focus over to the school principal and sat down next to Holly, leaning affectionately against his partner's shoulder.

"Rosetta is ready to start the cooking class."

Gino's mother looked doubtful but everyone knew her well. Six or seven voices all chimed in at once, "Yes, she is."

Rosetta laughed. "I am."

"It seems that every day I'm in the office someone's knocking at the door asking if they can register their offspring at Trillium School." Deodar was actually very proud of the school. "Yesterday I had to turn away three families. That would have been seven children. And they weren't even Earthkin. I knew them when I was still at the Church of the Martyr."

No one was surprised. Nearly all of Merrydale loved Dolly. He and Iris were the center of spells and prayers and the baby Diana was the star of the town this summer.

"Lotus, did you make arrangements with your job?" Arnica asked.

"Yes, it's worked out just fine." Lotus, young Dagon riding on his shoulders, would be working at the school one day a week, helping Carlos. Lotus' carpentry skills were going to help the school adjust to its growth and, next semester, he would be teaching a class in wood working.

"Iris will also be starting the new social studies class next semester. Jewel will watch the postal shop one afternoon a week. We haven't decided what to call this course." Dolly and Iris were thrilled to be able to work together.

"I talked with the mayor," the postmarm said, "and he's willing to come in a few times and talk about the town government. He thinks he knows at least one Representative who will come to the school next year and talk about Parliament."

They spoke about the school lunches, about new books. Carlos and Lotus had built new shelving for the new school library. They joked about names for Iris' course in citizenship. Arnica spoke about a letter he received from a coven in Mill City who wanted to visit the school later this semester in order to consider building an Earthkin school. Dolly asked them to start thinking about furthering the athletics and exercise program.

"Can you imagine," he said. "In a few years there might be games with other Earthkin schools!"

Then, with the business complete, the afternoon in the gardens was great fun. Carlos and Rosetta went back into town and the others, the coven, finished preparing for the Autumn Eve ritual.

The coven stood around the inside perimeter of the stone circle. With the few candles and the waning sunlight, their earth toned robes blended into the woods and they looked the part of woodland dryads and elves.

Amber held a thick braid of mountain sage. The artemisia family plant had been picked by her Loon sisters beneath a recent full moon and ritually dried and bound in the sacred lodge. Amber called upon the Great Mother and the Great Father in the words and tongue of her peoples and then passed it to Holly as it began its path around their Circle.

Each would bless it and fill it with love. On Monday morning Amber would smudge the school with it just before the doors were opened for the first students.

Dark Star whinnied gently. She was laying at the center of the circle at Arnica's feet. He stood holding his staff high. "Now do I prepare to enter the dark half of the year. I know the Mystery of Autumn: that *I am the harvest*. I carry with me the seeds of my future and seek the blessings of all which the Cardinal Four bring to me. Now it is time to step beyond myself and enter the realm of the sacred. Let me become as the autumn tree, setting free the leaves of my ego. Let me shed into the wind all that which holds me back. Let me become as the autumn flower, my seeds ripe and ready to be sown at the slightest movement. Let me prepare to join the Mother at Hallows and give me the strength to do what I must in the coming weeks to prepare for the descent into the dark. As the Sun sets into the Autumn sky, I shall carry His light around the Circle and ask for blessings of Mother Earth before She descends to the Underworld. Let my voice speak for all of the Devas..."

XLVII - Spirits From the Past

The people of Merrydale were not really comfortable talking about it and yet an undercurrent of rumor and speculation had permeated local life. No one was certain just when anyone first noticed and no one was even sure what it *was* that had been noticed.

Arnica first learned about it when Iris called him. Although he was always warmed by his coven sister's voice, her news was disquieting. Iris was calling from the postal shop, talking quietly, not wanting to be overheard. She wanted to know whether Arnica might know anything as she had begun to notice the townspeople of Merrydale whispering and acting oddly as if they didn't want anyone to see them.

This morning Maude Graves had asked Iris directly if *she* knew anything about the ghosts. Iris didn't visibly react. "But inside I was shouting 'ghosts? what ghosts?'" Iris laughed quietly.

"The ghosts?" Arnica was incredulous. Surely Hallows was nearly upon them but he'd never heard any talk of ghosts in Merrydale or even within the district!

"Yes," Iris continued louder, now alone in the postal shop. "Apparently over a dozen people have heard things or seen things. People are quite certain there are some ghosts around Merrydale and they don't know what to do. They're becoming afraid and that's not good."

Arnica was troubled, believing there must be an explanation behind all of this. He knew well that Merrywood was filled with countless nature spirits. But ghosts?

More information arrived a few days later when Merrydale's police officer came to the cottage. Constable Trouver wanted to talk to Arnica. Holly was at the school and, frankly, Arnica wished he was there as well. Holly would have enjoyed this discussion.

Dark Star had quickly trotted out toward the stone circle. Trouver had seen her in Merrydale only when she was wearing the magickal ointment which kept her horn invisible. The hatchling thought she'd go play in the woods. Dancing with the dryads seemed much more fun than pretending to be a pony for a Merrydale official!

"Now look here, Arnica," ... said Andy Trouver, "I know you're well versed in Earthkin lore. My mother has come to you for herbal information and you helped my Aunt Tibby put her husband's soul to rest when he was unable to let go." Trouver was clearly uncomfortable. His rounded face blushed. He preferred to deal with straight-forward difficulties such as the spray-painted vandalism at Trillium School last January.

Arnica sat the man down and, over steaming mugs of fresh herbal tea, they pooled their information. The autumn haze burned off as the sun warmed the gardens. A light steam rose from the potting shed roof as the early sun melted the frost. Hallows Eve was but a few nights away!

As an hour passed their conversation meandered through an array of Merrydale topics from the new school to the widow Morgan's desire to have a stop sign in front of her house to slow traffic. But when they shook hands near the greenhouse, little more was known about the ghosts other than repeating what others had been saying.

It had taken several phone calls, but Arnica and Holly were able to cancel the faculty meeting at Trillium School for the evening. Life at the cabin had been unsettled ever since the Constable's visit.

When the hatchling came back from her trot out into the woods, she was very skittery. Arnica knew something was wrong. Cleaning up the old rhubarb leaves, he was bent over the garden working, musing over his conversation with Andy Trouver when he heard Dark Star come trotting up. She looked nervous, uncertain and rubbed against Arnica almost like a puppy until he rubbed and petted her. Arnica could tell that she wanted reassurance and, although he could usually understand what she wanted, all he knew is that something was wrong. Dark Star never let Arnica out of her sight the rest of the day.

The cabin was warm and bright, the fire burning cheerfully. Holly sat on the rug before the fireplace, Dark Star laying at his feet. Holly's crystal ball sat on its stand where they could both gaze into it and share their thoughts. Arnica carried a censer around the room. The cornflower and horehound, both freshly dried from this year's harvest, with a few crystals of camphor not only cleansed the space but would make it much easier for his partner to commune with the young unicorn.

"Dark Star," Holly coaxed aloud as his mind formed images, "what did you see?"

The hatchling was not quick to answer. She was still a little nervous and the images in her mind seemed scattered. But when the room was censed, Arnica sat next to her and stroked her neck and quietly soothed her. This time Holly's question brought an answer.

"Shadows? Shades?" Holly asked. "Two ghosts..." Holly tried to stay focused upon the quartz sphere but he glanced quickly at Arnica. The old herbalist's eyes had widened as he watched Holly and the hatchling.

"One looked human, like an old woman," Holly translated from the images he saw in the sphere. "The other? It was not human. Dark Star wasn't sure what it was... By the stone circle, gesturing."

"Ask Dark Star if the woman was trying to say anything," Arnica urged.

Dark Star seemed restless. The young unicorn had never seen creatures like this, not even when she wandered through the realm of the faerie. But try she did, remembering in her mind what had happened and trying to see her memories without feeling so startled.

"The woman wants to... She has a message," Holly was almost in a trance, trying to absorb the information from Dark Star. "Morningstar, Rebecca Morningstar needs to speak with you, Arnica."

The coven was gathered in the stone circle. The night would be cool and they wore their wool coats. Dark Star, sitting near the Northeast portal, had difficulty sitting still. She was wearing a beautiful piece of midnight blue wool which draped across her back and was gathered at a silver clasp beneath her neck. Beautiful magickal sigils were embroidered upon it. This was Dark Star's first ritual robe and she was so proud. Pearl, the coven seamstress and Trillium School's 'arts department' had used metallic threads which gently caught the candlelight. Dark Star was *so* proud!

This was to be a very intense working and they were all gathered. Gino, their teen member, sat on a small rug next to his hatchling friend. He had never before seen a true calling of the dead. Iris and Deodar, Merrydale's postmarm and their school's principal, were next. It hadn't been easy for Iris to leave their baby, Diana, behind but Iris knew that Rosetta was a great baby sitter. Iris had watched how Gino's mother handled the Trillium School students (Rosetta was the school cook) and she was very wise in the ways of raising children. Why, look at Gino! He'd been part of their coven for some years, now.

Pearl sat on a small rug she'd hooked by hand. Her small body looked quite at home among the trees, quite other-worldly in the Circle. Flying Raven sat next to Pearl. Raven was a lovely woman, a grandmother and nearly matched Arnica's age. She was very pleased to now be living here in Merrydale. Although she missed seeing her children and grandchildren so often, she felt reborn with her new life teaching school and having an active role in the coven. Reading about it in letters was not nearly so fulfilling!

Jewel and Lotus had left Dagon with Rosetta as well. Dagon was five and a half and very aware of Hallows' magickal meaning. Dagon had taken his crayons and sketch book, wanting to draw pictures of his ancestors! Amber, the remaining covener, sat very still. Daughter of the Loon Tribe, she had come back to the stone circle an hour before the others to smudge the space and sit quietly. When Arnica and Holly came back with their ritual tools, Amber was so quiet a chickadee was actually sitting upon Amber's knee, preening its feathers!

Arnica was sitting upon the ground at the circle's center as Holly prepared the cauldron, pouring alcohol into it for the fire.

All were mindful, recalling what Iris had read to them that afternoon. It had taken some doing, but Iris had found Rebecca Morningstar in the community records but the information was suspiciously lacking: "Rebecca Morningstar was the first schoolteacher in Merrydale, back when there were only a dozen or so cabins. Miss Hirsch arrived by horse and wagon having emigrated from Europe. She taught in her cabin which was at the edge of the woods. She departed unexpectedly, possibly eloping with John Drover, a miner."

"We'll call lost loved ones from within to join us in this rite..." The coven voices joined in harmony as they chanted the '*Hallows Chant.*' Flames flickered in the dark. Holly sat across the cauldron from Arnica, watching his partner carefully to provide a safe and watchful balance.

Suddenly the cardinal candles went out. It was a startling thing, yet no one moved. Even Dark Star remained quite still. The flames on the altar candles had not even flickered.

"Rebecca?" Arnica's voice was soft.

"I am here," a voice answered. "I am here with Elstrum."

"Rebecca," Arnica had leaned forward as the flame in the cauldron stretched up to the sky. "Rebecca, why have you come back?"

"I am here to tell my story. It concerns you."

"I was hung for witchcraft." Although not one covener said a word, there was a silent gasp at the implication of Rebecca's statement. Someone killed for witchcraft here in Merrydale? As the voice continued, the shadowy image of a woman dressed in early settler clothing was almost visible.

"The spirit from the large oak, the hanging tree, tried to protect me but, unable to work its magick against the angry men, the dryad suffered terrible pain. Together we have waited until the time was right. Now a new tree has been planted in Merrydale. Whether you know it or not, the weeping goldenchain across from the postal shop is nearly on the same site as the oak once stood. My dear tree friend has been homeless since it fled the oak many years ago and a dryad without a tree becomes a wandering spirit."

Slowly the image of a willowy shadow emerged from the darkness of the trees to stand next to Rebecca's spirit.

"I am at rest," Rebecca said. "I've watched the Earthkin suffer terribly at the hands of those who bring darkness and I've watched the Earthkin emerge strong. And now you have a school where our ways are kept sacred. You do not know the joy I feel. But I cannot leave Merrydale in peace until Elstrum might also know rest. This dryad has asked me to appeal to you asking permission to enter the new tree. The moment it steps completely within the bark of the goldenchain, it will be reborn and have a new life as a *Laburnum* dryad."

"Iris and Dolly," Arnica spoke softly. "The tree was planted for your baby, Diana..." His voice was hushed.

"Oh yes," they both said, nearly in unison.

"So mote it be," Rebecca's voice was now strong. "I will take my tree friend there. After wandering these woodlands and watching Merrydale grow for over two hundred years, we are ready for some rest. But I'll not be leaving you for I will become a guardian spirit for Trillium School and now that I can rest peacefully, you'll never again feel my touch nor hear my step. But if you are very attuned, you will feel my blessings."

Rebecca vanished and the candles were relit in a moment. It was as if all had been dreaming and yet they knew this was true. In the weeks to come people began to comment that no one was talking about the 'Merrydale ghosts' any more and before long, only the coven would remember.

Now and then they would pause at the fountain in Trillium School's courtyard and extend a blessing to Rebecca for they felt certain she loved the sound of the water.

XLVIII - The Sun Baby

"Be careful." Holly knew that Arnica would be careful but the words were a reflex.

"I am." The response just as automatic, Arnica was several steps up the ladder setting the old, glass ornament atop the Yule tree.

"Are you ready for more?" Holly asked. They were hanging the ornaments on their Yule tree.

"Almost." Arnica snugged the glass spire down. It was fragile, hand-blown and had belonged to Holly's grandmother. She had brought it with her when she set sail for the new land, a journey of many days across the ocean and weeks across the raw, still-forested land. "There," he said, now with both feet and both hands upon the ladder.

"Here they come..." Holly took a red ball from a box, attached a hook and then carefully hung it from a loop attached to Dark Star's horn.

The hatchling carried it carefully over to Arnica and then stretched her neck carefully up toward her herbalist friend. Arnica easily took the ornament and hanger and placed it upon the tree.

This was Dark Star's first season helping to trim the tree. Arnica and Holly had talked about it a few weeks back.

Laying quietly in bed and whispering softly so she wouldn't overhear, Arnica had told Holly, "I think the hatchling is old enough to participate in decorating the tree."

Holly was intrigued, snuggling closer, and they whispered quietly before their dreamtime. Arnica had asked their coven sister Pearl to knit them a miniature stocking cap shape with a metal ring hanging from it which could be slipped over Dark Star's horn.

Now, with the Full Moon Eve tomorrow night and Yule less than a fortnight after, a new tradition was emerging in their home. Dark Star was having a wonderful time. She'd carried baskets with ritual tools in them, but this was delicate work and she was very proud.

And yet, although she was old enough for this 'grown-up' work, there was still some unifilly in her. Every ten minutes or so she'd get just a bit restless and trot over to the large doorway into the kitchen where she'd try to look innocent, as if she'd just happened to be standing beneath the fresh mistletoe hanging from the red ribbon. Wren and Robin had gone out harvesting mistletoe from an oak grove in a valley near the Highlands and, just as the Sun was direct over head (Robin, an astrologer who teaches math would be very precise about this), they cut a beautiful clump of mistletoe with a silver boline to send to their Earthkin friends in Merrywood.

This was Dark Star's first year with mistletoe. Holly, who bestowed most of the kisses (Arnica was on the ladder and usually had his hands full), knew that the mistletoe was probably going to be the hatchling's favorite part of the holiday.

Yule Eve had been joyful. Despite several inches of fresh snow, everyone had come out to the cabin for the ritual. It was a perfect Yule Eve afternoon. The sun was shining and yet it wasn't all that cold. The snow packed into snowfolk and an occasional snowball.

Eight months old, this was Diana Dolorum's first Sabbat. Her beautiful, dark eyes didn't miss anything. She was always very aware. Her proud parents Dolly, the principal of Trillium School, and Iris, Merrydale's postmarm, had decked her out in bright, warm clothing and took turns carrying her in a beautiful, wool sling. Pearl, their gentle Pictish friend, had woven the fabric in a hand loom. Deodar and Iris were still unable to believe how Pearl managed to do this as part of her art classes at the school without either of them having even the slightest idea. Obviously the mystery of secrecy, highly valued among the Earthkin, was understood even by the students!

Flying Raven was enjoying being back in the climate. With her children grown and scattered, now even her grandchildren were moving into their own lives and Raven loved once again having such a strong sense of family she found here with the coven. Raven had purchased new snowshoes and attached bells to them adding music to the procession of friends. It was at Amber's suggestion. Amber and her Loon Tribe sisters would often snowshoe off to a hidden cave for rituals of women's mysteries at the lunar times. Amber was very happy to be able to share shoeing with her coven sister.

What a sight they must have been walking from Merrydale to the cabin! Dagon, now five and a half (can you imagine?) would run ahead, throw himself into the snow, flail his legs and arms, then run back to walk along. As they'd near his spot of merriment, he'd tug on Jewel's sleeve, "Look, mother, a snow faerie must have been here." But the fresh air and excitement wore him down and Dagon finished the trek riding on Lotus' shoulders.

The only coven member missing was Gino.

Holly and Arnica were snuggled under their down comforter. It seemed they had been asleep for only an hour. Their coven family had returned into the night, gaily riding in a large sleigh they had hired to come out and take them home. Singing the Yule chant, they were bright of heart as the driver took them back to Merrydale behind two horses, one white and one black "just like the Chariot Card," Dagon cheered. Pearl took Gino's present for the youth and, when in the kitchen with Arnica, softly mentioned that she'd heard that Gino had been seeing Jenny Flower. Jenny was also in the ninth grade but attended Merrydale Junior High. Her parents were strict Kristos.

The presents had been opened and the ritual things put away. It was a late night when the men kissed Dark Star goodnight as she lay sleeping by the warm fireplace. Holly's head rested on Arnica's shoulder and they were sharing dreamtime, their astral beings literally dancing together in their stone circle, anticipating the Yule morning Great Rite.

Suddenly they were pulled back into their bodies by a loud knock at the front door. They groaned and stirred from the warmth of the bed, stretching their legs and trying to regain their mental balance.

"What time is it?" Arnica asked, sleepily.

Holly looked at his bedside clock. "Why, it's only seven thirty."

"What could she be doing?" Arnica wondered, thinking the sound was Dark Star.

"Why, I bet she's planning on watching the sun rise."

"I wish she'd be a little quieter about it."

Just then the hatchling, herself, came into the room. The men, now fully wakened, immediately sensed that something was wrong.

Dark Star seemed stressed. Something was troubling her. Whinnying, looking toward the front room, the hatchling nudged at them with her horn. Climbing out of bed, they grabbed for their robes, slid their feet into slippers and followed a troubled Dark Star through the cabin. As they padded through the front room, a hint of last night's incense still in the air but the altar set back in its place against the wall, Holly noted the mantle clock. It was 7:56 a.m., the exact time of sunrise.

By the time the men reached the door, the hatchling was sitting by it, restless and quite distressed. The sound of a baby quietly crying could be heard through the oak door.

Holly opened the door quickly.

The men gasped softly.

There, in a lovely, woven basket covered completely with a yellow, pink and blue quilt was a crying baby. It was a frosty morning. Whoever left this baby had great faith that Arnica and Holly would answer the door.

And there, pinned upon the quilt was this note: "I am the Sun baby. I need a home."

XLVIIII - Seeking the Light

The sun shone bright. A few, filmy white clouds slid over a bright blue sky. It looked like a typical, spring day in the cabin gardens and was a beautiful gardening afternoon. Arnica and Holly were working in the same garden, Holly climbing up and down the ladder as he pruned the plums, Arnica carefully weeding around his bed of prize belladonna from which he created tinctures used for colitis. Despite the bright day there were gathering dark clouds in the hearts of the coven.

"I like working in the soil but this is *January*," Arnica said. He moved the weed container, then gently worked the soil's surface with his garden trowel. Despite Arnica's enthusiasm to work hard, he sat back, distracted by the bright yellows of the weeping willows and the reds of the dogwood and an ornamental maple. "Candlemas is showing in the bark." Arnica returned to the soil.

"It's a good thing the trees' cycles respond to sunlight and not warmth," Holly said snipping off the long shoots of growth from last year, the same pruning done to their apple trees a few weeks before. "And there are a few tiny creatures flying about, maybe gnats or flies."

"Did you read Shadow Tail's letter?" Arnica asked.

"Yes," Holly answered. Standing on one foot he stretched out to snip off a long shoot.

Both men fell silent. Although many folk seemed quite happy with the dry, sunny days this winter, the coven was seriously troubled by the weather. Not only were the tree spirits beginning to sing of thirst but their friend Shadow had written that the snow levels up in the River Mountains were much lower than usual.

Despite the worrisome dry winter around Merrydale, Lady Ellhorn wrote her granddaughter Pearl of the unusual snows they were having in Cloverville. And Flying Raven's children, who lived far to the east in the Mothervalley District, had experienced blizzards the like of which hadn't been seen in more than fifty years

The District of Merrydale's weather was affected by the ocean. Most of the yearly rain came in from the great sea, stored in the mountains as snow to provide water and energy throughout the year. Just this morning Holly checked their rain gauge near the greenhouse and marked yet another week without precipitation.

As they worked, they continued to talk about the weather. Comments were sprinkled among the sounds of Arnica's trowel and Holly's pruners.

"At least our hatchling hasn't been tracking in mud..." Arnica added with good humor.

"Just yesterday Dark Star asked me if the borage would soon be sprouting." Holly and Dark Star had been 'talking' through the large crystal ball which is kept upon the main altar.

"Where is she, anyway?" Arnica asked.

"This morning she was frisky," Holly answered. "She whinnied something I understood to mean she needed to tend to something in the woods and then trotted off along the path toward the Stone Circle."

The men worked again in silence, their minds repeatedly drawn to recent events.

"We should be rejoicing about the growing light but we're having to worry about darkening shadows," Arnica mused out loud.

All of Merrydale seemed to be talking about the darkening shadows. In honesty, there were Politicos in Merrydale but these were generally more moderate folk who, if the truth were known, were more comfortable with their Earthkin neighbors than they would be with the User extremists who lived in other parts of Lothloriën. More than three generations had passed since any of Merrydale's folk had made their living as loggers and in this District people valued their life among the forests. And yet the recent election brought the Politicos into power and on January 2nd Henly Schrobbe was appointed the new Premier. Schrobbe was known to cater to the right wing factions of his party and the Users did not hide their desire to slash many of Merrydale District's forests.

"Sunna's quite a light," Holly paused, "isn't she?"

Arnica and Holly had been quite startled Solstice morning. Roused from bed by Dark Star, the discovery of the basket with a baby had certainly changed the coven's lives.

Jewel's russet hair was shorter these days. Seeing the baby in her arm brought back memories. Arnica remembered how she looked holding Dagon when he and Holly went into Merrydale with a silver bell for the baby. Jewel's richly-colored hair was long enough, then, to be tied back. Dagon, now five and a half, was in a pre-school program. Jewel sometimes wished aloud that Trillium School would grow until all ages could attend.

Holly reached over with a finger and wiped a few drops of baby drool from Sunna's mouth. "This Sun baby certainly seems quite elven to me," he said.

Jewel laughed, "Well, she certainly fills her diapers like any human child!"

Dark Star was basking in the sun. Her eyes rarely left Sunna. Like all creatures, she was fascinated with babies of any species. The hatchling's horn had been massaged with Arnica's formula of jade, male fern and powdered gold. In the sun a couple of dust motes were settled upon it, Dark Star sat so still. If it weren't for those, her horn would be undetectable even to Arnica and Holly!

"How old do you think she is?" Arnica asked. Although widely known as a healer, he was not a midwife and trusted a mother's opinion.

"Rosetta, Flying Raven and I were talking about that yesterday." Of the coven, Jewel had the most free time and missed having a baby around. "She must be around two months."

"A Hallows baby?" Holly liked that idea.

"If she's truly from the Realm of the Faerie," Arnica mused, "it could well be. But why would she be brought into the outer world?"

"The girls think that she's for the school!" Jewel laughed. "We've had to explain to them that there's no guarantee she will even end up with an Earthkin family, particularly with this new Politico administration."

"Hello," a voice called out. They recognized Iris' voice.

"We're fortunate that Iris is nursing Diana. The girls at school were quite amazed! They'd never seen a baby nurse before." Jewel rose, needing to go watch the postal shop while Iris fed the Sun baby.

It had been quite an event the first time the baby was at the school. Iris, who had just begun teaching citizenship, used this as an opportunity to talk about adoption and child custody laws. It was good for the girls to learn about babies. Although their Kristos neighbors did not believe in their schools providing education about human reproduction, Earthkin families encouraged their sons to attend the two afternoons that Jewel brought Sunna to the school.

"Have you kissed her yet?" Holly couldn't resist teasing their young friend.

His freckled face blushing brightly, Gino looked down to hide his embarrassment. "Not yet," he answered honestly, "but I sure think about it!"

Dark Star, laying near Gino's feet (she adored her teenage friend), reached up and licked him on the mouth.

The men laughed. Arnica teased, "well there's a kiss for you!"

Gino had asked if he could talk to Arnica and Holly. He'd had a lot on his mind and hadn't been out to the cabin in a month. The youngest of the coven, he'd never before missed a Sabbat nor a Full Moon.

The boy looked at Arnica. "What bothers me is that Jenny isn't really *lying* to her father but she can't be honest, either." The study of ethics was a cornerstone of Gino's training as a novice.

Holly knew there wasn't an easy answer so he diverted the conversation. "How'd she like the baby?" Jenny's mother had let her visit Iris with Gino.

Mrs. Flower was more accepting than her husband. She remembered when she was but a teen, herself, the summers she spent with her mother's sister, Juanita. Her aunt was well-known in the mountain village for her herb garden. One day she told Becky how to make wishes with a columbine. Becky picked the flower and walked off to sit beneath the comfort of a huge tree. She did just as her Aunt Juanita had told her, wishing that the new boy who had just moved to Merrydale from Highlands would notice her. Philbert Flower did notice her and a year after they both graduated, Philbert proposed.

"I really *like* her," Gino said. "I know we're only fifteen. Neither of us has any experience with romance. This is our first relationship and we're learning so much. Jenny is really *special*," he added. "She adored the baby. She'd love to offer to babysit but Mr. Flower should be back next weekend." Gino's voice said it all. His fingers scratched Dark Star's ears. The hatchling rubbed her head against the boy's leg.

The Hatchling

Philbert Flower was away at Mill City. Slade Hatchitt had recommended Mr. Flower to be the new Deputy of Water. Although a strict Kristos, Flower was not always comfortable with the extremist User faction of the Politico Party. Part of Hatchitt's plans called for a new dam as part of Schrobbe's energy platform. A new dam would provide electricity without pollution.

"Well, my friend," Arnica said, "just be careful. Phil Flowers wasn't pleased when Trillium School got its charter. He's a good man and well-meaning but not very open-minded when it comes to religion."

"I know," Gino said. "Jenny told me that Mr. Flower would be happier if she was attending the Cathedral of the Thorns' school in Mill City." Gino started to scratch the hatchling's jaw. "I'll be there for Candlemas Eve," he added. "I promise."

Five days later the coven moved quietly among the trees. They'd created sacred space in the Stone Circle and lit their lanterns from the altar candles. Now they walked carefully through the light fog, following an easily missed path to Fern Hollow. Iris and Arnica led the way. It wasn't the best night for a long walk in Merrywood.

When they neared the Hollow they stopped. The fog had settled into the valley. Young trees were everywhere, only a few years old. It was five years ago this spring that all the trees on this ridge had been clear-cut. Iris remembered the march she organized. And now Hatchitt wanted to see all of Fern Hollow clear-cut and then flooded. There were dark shadows of fear. The trees *knew* they were seriously threatened.

They descended into the Hollow. This would be an all-night ritual, for they would be seeking wisdom from the trees, themselves. Dark Star trotted ahead. It was obvious she knew where she was going. The coven felt good about this. The hatchling could bring them to the most wise of all the tree devas. By morning they hoped to have communed with the dryad of Fern Hollow.

L - Eggs, Petitions and Prayers

"And he said I should tell you," Iris slightly emphasized the word you, "to write your wishes upon your Eostara eggs so they can be planted near his roots."

The large room filled with gasps and giggles. The Earthkin parents living around Merrydale were eager to bring their young ones to Trillium School. Now in its second year as a private school which included the teaching of their earth religion lore, the parents looked forward to a time when the school might include the early grades as well, and maybe even a kindergarten!

This was Iris' day at school. Word had spread quickly and nearly every local Renaissance family was represented. Most of the Descendant Tribes who lived in the area were here as well. Their elders had long sung the legends of tree spirits and when they heard that Iris, Merrydale's postmarm and the wife of the school's principal, was inviting them all to hear the message from the dryad of Fern Hollow, the word quickly spread.

It was a busy spring for the postmarm. Her baby would be a year old this Beltane and Iris had been helping care for Sunna, the baby which had been abandoned at Arnica and Holly's door on Yule morning. Jewel and Lotus spoke about adopting the foundling as a baby sister for Dagon, soon to be six years old. Amber, daughter of the Loon Tribe, was even more wary of the new administration and felt that Sunna might be more safe with her Loon Tribe sisters in the River Mountains. Amber's people and other Descendant Tribes had not always been treated well by the Politicos, whose party seemed too easily persuaded by money at the expense of Mother Earth. Just days before, Iris, who is now teaching the Citizenship classes at Trillium School, had addressed the students and faculty. That had been quite a presentation.

For months everyone in Merrydale was talking politics. Throughout the Land of Lothloriën people were increasingly polarized. The last election troubled the people. It seemed that the Politicos worked more openly to favor industry and were proposing legislation to allow corporate cutting of vast areas of forest. The Conservers had not fared so well and no longer held a majority.

Iris brought an experienced view to her talk. Last Tuesday, all the students were gathered in the large hall. Its usual function was as a gym but today the students were seated about the floor, some in beginner yoga positions, others sprawled about on pillows. Here and there a few couples sat lounging together. Their interest in what Iris had to say was strong enough to keep their youthful passions in check even though the room was darkened save for the light above Iris' head.

The faculty (most of whom were the coven) enjoyed having a break from their classrooms. Deodar, Iris' husband and the school principal was enjoying watching his wife. Although she insisted she didn't like public life, the activist in her was lively and wonderful to watch.

Gino sat over near a window. The hatchling was at school today. Many of the girls liked to tease Dark Star, telling the hatchling that they wanted to make a unicorn horn in Pearl's art class and dress her up like a unicorn. Even though Trillium School was a safe Earthkin space, only the coven knew that she was a unicorn. The ointment Arnica made left her horn invisible. Only Gino had ever guessed and he was the young member of the coven.

Gino had difficulty paying attention to Iris. It was fortunate he knew the political history well and could pass any tests in his Citizenship classes. Gino's mind kept thinking of Jenny. They were old enough to begin dating but Jenny Flower's father would never approve. Gino would soon be sixteen and Jenny was just a couple months younger. They had gone for an occasional walk together, holding hands. He'd kissed her on the cheek a couple of times. No one knew that but Jenny and Dark Star. Gino could tell the hatchling *anything...* But their young romance was clouded by the worry that Philbert Flower, the new Deputy of Water for the Politicos, would find out. Mr. Flower was a strict Kristos. If he learned that his only daughter was seeing an Earthkin lad he would send Jenny away to school.

Iris was standing so that the seventy-one students could see her. Merrydale's postmarm was long a town favorite but when she and Deodar Dolorum were Handfasted she became far more public. When Dolly resigned from the Kristos ministry, married Iris and then became the principal of the new Trillium School, Iris' life was forever changed.

"How did the school get involved in this?" Iris repeated a question one of the 10th grade girls had asked. Although Iris was to begin teaching Citizenship this semester, the recent election was reason for the faculty to decide to introduce the postmarm in her new part-time role. Iris began the story:

Although the Conservers had made some gains in recent years, the last election left the Earthkin unsettled. Although the Districts of Merrydale and the Mothervalley had elected Conserver majorities, too many voters had been swayed by the interests of commerce and the Politicos were now in the majority. When Parliament convened on January 2nd the Politico majority elected Henly Schrobbe as the new Premier. Schrobbe was known to have received large financial contributions from the Users, the right wing of the Kristos, who in the past had pushed hard to convert the forests and sacred lands of Lothloriën to industrial use and it was widely believed the new Premier needed to appease the right-wing coalition of the Politicos. Without the Users, Schrobbe could never have won the election.

Although cause for concern, the balance of votes was so close that Schrobbe might be held back from damaging Lothloriën. But just the other day news quickly spread that Schrobbe had appointed Slade Hatchitt as Minister of the Lands. Hatchitt was well known to the coven. Hatchitt's appointment caused deep concern in the District of Merrydale where local folk remembered three years ago last Hallows. Hatchitt, one of the bellicose leaders of the Users, was found to be the connection between the Cathedral of Thorns and a curious organization called the Society for the Forest which promoted the "safe harvesting" of Merrywood's trees in order to protect the forests. Although Hatchitt's attempt at the time to promote commercial logging of Merrywood's large reserve of old-growth trees seemed to fade, it was now apparent that the Users had merely changed their tactics. The following year Hatchitt was connected with the "Friends of the Forest" which grabbed headlines when the late Bishop Miter tried to gain power for the Users by claiming that the Earthkin were at the heart of a secret pagan and homosexual agenda which had caused the decline of family values.

Iris explained the political history well and the students found themselves fascinated.

The postmarm adjusted the long, dark braid of hair and continued. Facing that crisis, the people had rallied. Lammas Eve fires were lit throughout Merrydale District. The students cheered and broke into laughter. They remembered that Lammas Eve.

And yet, despite Parliament's lean to the right, Trillium School's charter was approved. This was a great victory for the Earthkin but made the Users increasingly anxious. It seemed that the political divide in Lothloriën was growing toward a crisis when Bishop Miter died unexpectedly, but then things seemed quiet. Many Earthkin did not realize that the Users had quietly been organizing for years so they could take control of Lothloriën's government.

Iris spoke about her organizing the march to Fern Hollow four years ago last autumn and explained how her growth as an activist for the trees was related to her embracing the Earthkin religion. As she recalled her part in this history, she told the students how Hatchitt wanted to place the flyers for his organization in the postal office. Slade Hatchitt "was one of the strongest and most vocal figures of the Users, the radical, right wing faction..."

Iris had declined, responding that a government office could not distribute the flyers. Hatchitt was furious. "We'll see." he said... Years had passed and now it might just be possible that the Users could change the laws of Lothloriën and the man would get his wish.

The room had grown so quiet Iris was able to speak as soft as their voices were as the coven approached the sacred tree last Candlemas Eve.

Arnica had joined her. Iris wanted the Elder of the coven to describe the ritual process used when Arnica invoked the dryad. Although the families of the students were Earthkin, not many of them had been trained in the rituals and mysteries of their religion. Arnica's mention of the secret herbal formula stirred the youthful imaginations. Skilled at story telling, he held them in mystical suspense, the darkness of the forest night as they waited to light the first candle. When Dark Star stepped quietly up near Iris and Arnica, a candle lantern hanging from her mouth, the quiet tension of the room bubbled over with the relief of laughter.

Later, some of the students were certain that they could almost see a unicorn's horn on the young colt. Trillium School's mascot was a unicorn and when these times happened that the hatchling's horn was returning from between the worlds, it was easy for the coven to keep Dark Star's mystery.

"Bring me the eggs of your desires," the dryad had spoken. "And an egg for the baby tree... One egg... And hang your wishes for the forest for all to see."

Iris finished the story by telling the students that a magickal egg had been safely planted among the roots of the goldenchain tree, the one planted across from the postmarm's office. This was a special tree, a gift from the school parents to honor Deodar and Iris' new baby.

Their Eostara Eve's ritual done, Gino sat on the floor near Dark Star, running the new comb across her body. The hatchling *loved* it and gazed adoringly at Pearl. There had been presents for this Sabbat was also the hatchling's sixth birthday - in human years, that is. Pearl had sent away for a beautiful currycomb. Dark Star was in unicorn heaven.

Arnica, Holly and Deodar were in the kitchen, working on the plans for Beltane. Written prayers and bells would be collected from all the Districts of Lothloriën. Those who called themselves Kin of Mother Earth must now begin to put their politics where their words were. Eggs would be planted at the base of the great tree. Dolly (Iris' pet name for him) was worried about Iris' job as postmarm but they had enough savings to get by even if this organized protest led to retaliation from the Politicos.

The work before the coven was serious, indeed.

LI - The Trees of Beltane

They were a little tired when they first gathered at seven in the morning but Arnica brought some hot spiced ginseng tea and they were soon bustling about. It had been a late night. The coven had observed Beltane Eve in Fern Hollow, honoring the tree where the dryad had delivered his message to them last Candlemas. The three days leading to the

Sabbat were joyous, indeed. Arnica and Holly were first. The next night Jewel and Lotus left Dagon with Iris and on the third night the school's woodcraft teacher and his wife watched Diana when Iris and Deodar headed to the tree.

Their ritual last night was intense, the Great Rite having been consummated joyously and threefold leading up to the Sabbat. Gino, who recently turned 16, longed for the day when he, too, might explore the Mysteries of the Great Rite and secretly hoped that Jenny Flower would continue to be the girl of his dreams. Last night Gino scribed the circle for the coven with his athame. Holding the symbol of the God's phallic power he could feel the seeds of manhood growing strong within his young body.

Pearl, Flying Raven and Amber called upon the Great Mother, protectress of the forests. This was not a typical Beltane for the forest was imperiled. Henly Schrobbe, Lothloriën's Premier, continued to cater to the right wing faction of the Politicos known as the Users. It was their intent to clear-cut the forests around Fern Hollow, a project the Users tried to put in motion five years ago. At that time Iris organized a protest march which was successful. Now the Users were trying again.

The coven had talked well past the closing of the Circle. Originally they were like most Earthkin groups, celebrating the Sabbats and studying so they could better understand the Mysteries. But in the recent years their goals had changed. The coven had established Trillium School and it seemed they were constantly battling to save their beloved Land of Lothloriën, if not from the greed of the Users who desired to overrun the wild areas in the name of corporate profit, then from the ever-growing dangers of pollution from the major industrial areas of the world.

It was nearly two in the morning when they snuggled into their beds, Arnica and Holly in their cabin as Dark Star lay upon her favorite rug in the next room, the others in their homes in Merrydale.

The capital of Merrydale District had never seen such a parade! Word had spread quickly. The coven had never anticipated that so many would participate. Arnica had come to trust in the dryad of Fern Hollow. The message from the oldest tree last Candlemas Eve was clear: they were instructed to hang their wishes for all to see, and so would it be.

The coven had done its work. The parade was organized through Trillium School, still the only Earthkin school with a charter. Word had spread quickly. Gathering at the school, not a student was absent. Their families were there as well: sisters and brothers, parents, cousins, aunts and uncles. Neighbors and grandparents were there as well. Nearly all of Merrydale had turned out to show their support for saving the forests of Merrywood.

People throughout the District of Merrydale had rallied and some even made the journey from other Districts within Lothloriën. Wren and Robin had come in from the Highlands and were able to join in last night's Sabbat.

The parade was to begin at Trillium School with a few short speeches (Arnica insisted they be short) and the invoking of blessings for their work. Mayor Browning would open with a brief welcome, for the event had grown far beyond the realm of Trillium School. A number of politicians were there, driving over the mountains from Parliament in Mill City, and would be walking as well, some enjoying the opportunity to oppose the Users and garner favor among the Renaissance and Descendant peoples for the next election. Others, solid members of the Politicos, were obviously a bit uncomfortable being present at an event obviously inconsistent with the larger goals of their party. And yet, their 'political genes' (as Arnica called them) won out. They were unable to resist such a strong, local issue and had turned out to participate in this cause so obviously dear to the local voters (and future voters).

What a wonderful assortment of colors and sounds. Many were in masks, and some wore home-made costumes representing the forest creatures. There was even a walking tree! The elders from Restful Pines were sitting in nearby shade, some in wheelchairs, others on comfortable seats which had been provided them, their walkers nearby. Those not participating in the walk stood along the sidewalks, many taking photos.

Merrydale High's marching band was there, dressed in their bright uniforms and eager to participate. Only four absences were noted, young musicians whose families were strongly conservative and whose parents were very troubled that this protest against their political party had grown from an *Earthkin* event to a great gathering for all of Merrydale.

The throng stretched all the way to the small park across from the postal shop where the weeping goldenchain was growing, the tree planted by the local folk to celebrate the birth of Iris and Dolly's baby.

The procession to the elder tree of Fern Hollow even brought together Trillium School's first musical group. Four of Pearl's music class students carried large shamanic drums, gifts to the school from Amber's Loon Tribe brothers. Several art class students had made rattles from gourds. The all-percussion group had melody, however. Marco, a friend of Amber's cousin, had travelled up from Azteca, the country south of Lothloriën's border, to participate in an international bagpiping contest recently held in Verdeville. After winning a silver medal he was visiting friends in the River Mountains. Marco was highly skilled and was wearing some of his medals upon his plaid sash. The girls in Trillium's percussion group considered themselves very lucky. Marco was handsome, from a foreign country and far more interesting than the politicians!

Dark Star was very excited. She'd never been around so many humans all at once and at times the sounds and sights nearly overwhelmed her. But she steadied herself with images of the Mother and one of her father, Andrius' lessons about being calm.

Holly had been worried about the hatchling's horn being visible and Arnica was doubtful that his herbal formula would hold up throughout the day. It was Pearl, the coven seamstress, who had a great idea. Dark Star was wearing a 'fake' horn - a papier maché horn which fit right over the hatchling's and, with very obvious ribbons, tied beneath her chin. Trillium School's mascot was a unicorn and this way Dark Star would be safe with her loved ones.

Iris and Deodar stood nearby. Diana, just a year old this very Beltane, was a happy baby bouncing in the carrier on her father's back. Dolly, as school principal, would be giving a brief welcome before Arnica offered a blessing and invocation for the forests.

Dolly's short talk would thank his late mother, Mildora, whose great grandmother had some Descendant Tribe blood. What changes he had made! Since resigning as the Kristos clergyman of in the autumn two and a half years ago, he'd blossomed and become a very public figure for the Earthkin.

Iris, the postmarm, was tying some ribbons onto Dark Star's mane. Iris wore an identical backpack. During the walk she and Dolly could easily take turns carrying Diana and, to keep the baby happy, behind Iris was a large, stuffed bear that Diana called "Booby."

Pearl carried a large basket filled with many spools of ribbon. Her coven sisters did the same, so that ribbons could be tied upon trees from Merrydale all along the route to Fern Hollow. The goal of the gathering was to bless as many trees with ribbons as they possibly could.

Gino was radiant. Holly knew that the masked girl on his arm was Jenny Flower. Her father, was the new Deputy of Water, appointed by Slade Hatchitt. Philbert Flower definitely was *not* at this parade.

Flying Raven helped Dagon with some helium-filled balloons. Almost six and unusually wise, Dagon knew well what this excitement had as its goal. Dagon's parents, Jewel and Lotus, were helping keep the crowd quiet for the blessings.

The blessings had been read. To everyone's surprise, not only Arnica, the unofficial clergyperson for the Earthkin read a blessing, but the new pastor for the Church of the Martyr who had replaced Deodar Dolorum, read one as well.

And then they began. The marching band played a rousing number and the people remaining behind on the sidewalks cheered. As the music ended, a woman's voice began chanting "the Earth is our Mother... we must take care of her." Other voices joined in and Trillium School's musicians drummed the rhythm. Before the parade had gone its first kilometer, the chanted melody was echoed by the Merrydale High musicians and by Marco on his bagpipes. As the throng moved forward, every tree within reach had colored ribbons hanging from it yet there were many baskets with more than enough ribbon. When the day was done the Land of Lothloriën would know that these people expected their politicians to save Merrywood. Their message, this Beltane, would be hung from the trees.

Not everyone from Parliament was here but even those politicians at home in their own Districts had heard of the march. The Users were not pleased yet even Henly Schrobbe could do nothing. There was far too much publicity.

LII - Dark Star Dreams of Andrius

Midsummer's morn dawned early at the Grove and soon after Arnica and Holly, their breakfast finished, went out into the woods to dig out the stray brambles. Last night was the coven's Midsummer's Eve ritual and, with school out, it lasted late.

How joyful they were last night, the entire coven present. Arnica and Holly lived at the Grove and had founded the coven many years before. Deodar Dolorum, once a Kristos minister, was now principal of Trillium School and called Dolly by his wife. Iris Dolorum was the proud mother of Diana and Merrydale's postmarm. Pearl, of Pictish descent, teacher of music and arts was there with Flying Raven, who moved from the Mothervalley to teach science. And Amber as well, the only member of the coven who was of the Descendant Tribes. Jewel and Lotus were there, both again active in the community and school now that their young one, Dagon, was six. And Gino, their young friend, just sixteen this spring, had begun working with the coven five years ago.

"He's certainly growing up," Holly mused, "Isn't he?"
"A junior this fall," Arnica said. "And the year after a senior and graduation."

Arnica had been roused out of bed at sunrise. Despite their late night, Iris had heard news which could not wait. Philbert Flower, a local conservative and politician and newly appointed Deputy of Water had announced that he would no longer be aligned with the Politico Party.

Slade Hatchitt, one of the more vociferous old-guard members of the right wing of the Politicos known as the Users, had worked hard to get Flower the Deputy appointment. Iris said that Hatchitt was *furious*. Parliament was unlikely to rescind the appointment.

"Did you see Dark Star's hooves sticking through the tent flap this morning?" Arnica chuckled at the memory.

"Good morning, sleepyheads," Holly called as he pushed the spade deep into the soil to loosen a blackberry root. Gino and the hatchling came along the path on their way to the Stone Circle. Dark Star had the wicker saddle bags on her back which Gino had filled with his ritual tools. Today would be a great day for Gino - he would be leading a simple Midsummer's Day Circle for a group of his classmates.

"Morning, my Dear Sirs," Gino answered.

Dark Star, Gino's leather-wrapped athame held between her teeth, looked at them. It was obvious she was tired but yet happy. The young unicorn loved Gino.

"I imagine they were up until near dawn watching for the Devas" Arnica mused.

"What did Iris tell you of Flower's announcement?" Holly asked.

As Postmarm, Iris had access to the news few others in Merrydale imagined. The local folk often forgot that she was a public official. Iris had seen a copy of Flower's speech.

It was just a few days after the "Great Treewalk" as the media dubbed the parade. The coven organized the event to bring public attention to the threatened trees of Merrywood.. Although he had spurned the protest, Philbert Flower was hiking through Merrywood at his daughter's insistence. The Politico did not know his daughter Jenny had been seeing one of Trillium School's favorite students. Philbert did not approve of the Earthkin school, either, and had sent a strong letter complaining that Merrydale high's marching band was in the parade. Merrydale's public school students, however, responded with variations of 'get over it.' They were proud of the local Earthkin school, some more than a little envious of the educational freedom their friends had. Mr. Flower adored his daughter, however, so despite his misgivings he went walking among the trees with her. Philbert suspected Jenny was following the parade route to the old tree spirit. Here and there ribbons were tied to the trees. When he'd see an egg, one of those pagan customs, he'd scowl and mumble a brief Kristos prayer.

Jenny asked her father if they could rest a minute and they 'just happened' to be beneath the shade of the dryad of Fern Hollow, an elder of the tree spirits.

"Wait," Holly interjected, "you can't mean that Flower wrote *that* in his speech?"

Arnica laughed. "No," the herbalist answered, "I know that from last night. While you were talking with the ladies about Sunna, Gino shared with me some of what Jenny wrote him in a letter. Did you know she writes him almost every day?" Jenny's father enrolled her as a summer page working in Parliament over in Mill City on the other side of the River Mountains.

"Well, letters are safer," Holly answered. So many teens Gino and Jenny's ages were sexually active these days and the older men were not completely comfortable with the newer morals.

"Shush," Arnica whispered, "here they come again." On this trip Gino and Dark Star were taking candles and altar cloths to the Stone Circle. Arnica continued with the story.

"Philbert Flower said that something moved his soul and describes it as similar to the two times he felt the Voice of God when he was in the Church of the Martyr."

Holly started laughing. "You mean the dryad spoke to him?"

"Well, *spoke* might be strong," Arnica surmised. "But his view changed and I give him credit for standing up for his beliefs, even when it means confronting Slade Hatchitt."

"Next we'll learn that he wants Jenny to date an Earthkin boy," Holly joked.

Gino and Dark Star had finished setting the Stone Circle and helped the men clean up their work and put away their tools.

In the early afternoon sun, the Grove was buzzing with activity. The beds of thyme, from the soft and fuzzy creeping thyme to the stately bushes which looked like elders, were all in bloom and the bees loved thyme. Hundreds of bees enjoyed rush hour on the carpets of purple flowers.

The drying shed held comfrey and German chamomile, the latter scenting the warm, dry air. Rosetta, Gino's mother held the baby Sunna on her lap. Rosetta was proud of her son's accomplishments and had seen him grow in maturity and take on many responsibilities since his training with the coven began.

Rosetta, Amber and Flying Raven were running an informal summer program in baby care and family studies for a few of Trillium School's teens, four girls and a boy the faculty felt were most in need of learning about birth control and sexual responsibility. The students' parents were all strongly in approval. Although the Earthkin religion felt strongly about "all acts of love and pleasure," they also felt that young people needed to learn responsibility and to protect their own freedom of choice to pursue education. That freedom was too quickly lost when young girls and boys became parents not through choice but through failing to use control methods.

Arnica was walking six interns around the paths of the gardens, explaining to them just the simplest concepts about the mandala the paths created. The herbal students were fascinated yet, being young, they were distracted with the scent of borage cookies and chocolate chip brownies Holly was baking in the cabin's kitchen.

Dark Star carefully followed behind them, step by step. She was so pleased. With the interns and childcare students sworn to secrecy about her horn, it was not necessary to wear the special formula. As one of the boys put it, "no one would believe it anyway" if they said Dark Star was a *real* unicorn.

One of the girls, who felt her attraction to other girls was more than a phase, put it differently. "Frankly," she said, "it's like coming out gay. Those who can accept it already 'know' and everyone else would deny that the hatchling's horn existed even if they saw it with their own eyes!" They'd all laughed over that. And the fact was, to the Merrydale High teacher, a kind and open minded (yet Kristos woman), Dark Star was just a wonderful small colt.

But before they'd finished walking the mandala of all the garden paths, Dark Star knew she needed a nap. She'd hoped to follow them to the Stone Circle. None of Gino's classmates knew he'd been studying in the coven but they did know he'd spent many summers out at the cabin learning about herbs. He'd worked hard to prepare for the afternoon ritual, a simple introduction to the four elements and the magick of Midsummer.

She jumped across a small bed, ambled over and lay down in the filtered sun beneath a huge, old lilac. A viceroy butterfly landed on the tip of her horn. Andrius held his left finger up to his lips to keep the interns quiet and, with his right hand, pointed. Dark Star hadn't even noticed. She'd fallen sound asleep, napping in the dappled sun.

Andrius nudged the hatchling with his horn. Dark Star felt herself waking and stretching, then realized her body was still laying there asleep.

"Wake up, little one," her father said. "I've someone I want you to meet."

Dark Star shook her astral head, clearing her sense of vision. There sat a beautiful elder, one of the most beautiful unicorns she had ever seen. And her horn! Why, it had so many turns in it! She must have seen the wheel turn many times.

"This is Lillian, your grandmare," Andrius said, then slipped back between worlds to leave them alone.

"Why do you no longer trot upon the Earth?" Dark Star asked. "Why have I never seen you?"

"Once I did," Lillian answered. "I had a human family and they were wonderful, just like yours. But this was many, many years ago and the times grew dark." It was time for the hatchling to learn about the Burning Times.

Small tears, like tiny quartz jewels, slid down the hatchlings cheeks to the violets below. Lillian finished her saga. "My little one, the burning times for humans were a terrible holocaust. But now we face a burning time for the forests. Many here in your beautiful land of Lothloriën want to cut the forests down, but Mother Earth needs them for her health. Smoke hangs over the rain forests where the Mother's loved ones die terrible deaths in the burning trees. Your work here in the coming years will be so very important. And that is why I want you to know that my love is always with you..."

They held each other as Lillian faded into the Otherworld. Just then, the students came walking along the garden paths back from the Stone Circle back among the trees.

Holly was setting up the fresh-baked treats with a large pitcher of lemonade flavored with fresh mint.

The older women brought Sunna out so the child care class could do their work. The Merrydale High teacher, not yet ready for an Earthkin Circle, had stayed with them and was ready for a break.

As the garden party bubbled over with laughter and talk Arnica came out of the cabin.

"I have an announcement," he said. "There's more news. Henly Schrobbe, the Premier, has announced that he will make some concessions and that there will be no logging on public lands. This will protect our trees ..."

Loud cheering, plus the whinnying from one unicorn, resounded throughout the gardens, interrupting Arnica. He raised his hand to quiet them. "However... and this is important, Schrobbe will be working to change the laws. He's still a powerful man and the Users are angry to have lost.

It was that 'however' that kept them from feeling as joyful as they wished.

LIII - Sunna's Crisis

Arnica and Holly were picking raspberries. There were two long rows about fifteen feet long, one of black raspberries and one of red raspberries. The men were working back to back, Holly picking the black and Arnica the red. Their fingers were nimble as they worked through the thorny canes, plump fruit dropping into the berry buckets attached to their shoulder harnesses. On the other side of the black raspberries Dark Star lay upon the grass in the sun, watching her men intently.

Every now and then Holly would reach into his apron pocket and toss a couple of blueberries over the top toward the hatchling. Dark Star never missed one. Dark Star had many favorites from the gardens. The borage was in bloom this time of year (and she *loved* borage) but she also loved blueberries.

"Do you think it will rain?" Holly was thinking about the forest fires burning off in the distant mountains.

"They're predicting a light rain for tomorrow," Arnica answered, his fingers quickly collecting ripe, red raspberries. "But you know what happens to rain during a drought."

The air was so dry the rain evaporated long before reaching the thirsty plants. Without a word both men extended their consciousness to their gardens. They worked well with the earth and their compost-rich gardens and perennial herbs could tolerate fairly dry weather when necessary.

Holly tossed four blueberries up and over to the hatchling. Dark Star caught every one of them. She whinnied softly in thanks making both men laugh. There was nothing like the laughter of their young unicorn.

"Did I tell you I spoke with Shadow Tail yesterday?" Arnica related their friend's phone call. Shadow had lived with them for a time, learning about the Earthkin's school. Now he was back on the other side of the mountains helping with the Loon Tribe's school plans. "He said there wasn't much fire danger in the Lower River Plain but said he can often see the haze of smoke drifting from the fires in the River Mountains." The River Mountains were the dividing line between the District of Merrydale and the District of Grainland.

"Amber said the same," Holly commented. He popped a succulent black raspberry into his mouth and continued. "She talked with her Loon Tribe sisters. They have been doing ceremonies for any animals caught in the fires. And Amber's cousin is a firefighter so Amber's been a little worried."

It was a bad year for fires. Arnica felt certain that the climate changes over the past years proved with certainty the reality of global warming, yet there were too many Politicos in office who protected the interests of big business. Henly Schrobbe, the Premier, represented the Users, the right-wing faction of the Politicos. Fortunately the Politicos didn't hold a large majority. The Conservers gained just enough to stop them from cutting down large areas of forest. Holly bent over and tossed three blueberries *under* the blackberry canes. Dark Star didn't miss a one.

"Some fires are burning even as far east as the Red Mountains." Arnica added. The Red Mountains were a range much further east, separating the Districts of Grainland from the Districts of the Four Deserts and the Red Mountains. "Wren and Robin said that a fire passed within a half mile of their mountain cabin. Several deer and even a bear were spotted running down their street right there in Red Mountain Plateau. They were heading toward Highlands." Highlands was a good-sized city, almost as large as Lothloriën's capitol of Mill City. Red Mountain Plateau was next to the foothills but the creatures would have to have fled through two miles of suburb by the time they passed Wren and Robin's home.

The couple's garden talk was a quiet sound with the hatchling's occasional soft whinny a loving counterpoint to their voices. The breeze caused the leaves to rumor themselves softly. The sounds of the bees and other flying insects were as loud as the two men and their unicorn. Unexpectedly the sound of a loud bell cut through the summer morning.

"Dear Sirs," Gino's young voice called out and he burst into view riding a bright, red bicycle. "Look what I bought," and he rang the bike bell again. Despite his enthusiasm and haste, he carefully parked his brand new bike to avoid its first scratch.

Just finishing picking berries, Arnica and Holly were quite ready for a change. Dark Star loved her young friend. She jumped up and trotted over as quick as a hopper. Soon all four were gathered around the shiny new bicycle.

"And Pearl bought me saddlebags so I can carry things back and forth from Merrydale." Gino was quite excited.

Dark Star snorted at this. The hatchling thought carrying things was *her* job and she loved the woven bags Arnica placed over her back. But the young unicorn knew her job was secure and she sensed that this might mean Gino could come out to play with her more often.

"And munchkin," Gino said as if reading her mind, "I'll be able to ride out more easily than walking and can bring you fresh treats from your favorite kitchens." He scratched her ears and got a big uni-kiss across his nose from Dark Star's tongue.

Gino, his energy quite wound up from riding fast along the country road from Merrydale to the cabin, was still talking equally fast. "And I have this message for you from Iris," pulling a letter out of his pocket. Iris, covenmate and wife of Trillium School's principal, was also Merrydale's postmarm and at the hub of all news circulating about the region. "I think Sunna's in trouble." Sunna was the sweet foundling baby left at Arnica and Holly's cabin door this last Yule morning.

Arnica opened it and, after a quick glance, sent Gino off to play with the young unicorn until lunch. He wanted time to discuss the matter quietly with Holly.

"Well," he began, "they're at it again." Arnica paused, drank some of his herbal tea from a large mug, and began to tell Holly about Sunna's crisis.

No one knew where the Sun baby had been born. Dark Star roused her men from bed and brought them to find the baby at the front door just at sunrise. The hatchling felt an affinity for the baby, for the little human had also arrived from unknown places to appear in the lives of the men at the cabin. The coven believed Sunna was a Hallows baby, perhaps even from the Realm of the Faerie. Jewel and Lotus, whose own Dagon was now six, wanted to adopt Sunna as a baby sister for their son. But Amber, who spent most of her life on Descendant Tribal land felt Sunna would be safer living with her Loon Tribe sisters. With the Politicos now favored in Parliament, Amber's distrust of the government was stronger than ever.

"Slade Hatchitt must have heard about Sunna." Arnica set Iris' letter down. "He's referred the matter to a Politicos committee he created to study 'family values.' Our Conserver politicians have filed complaints that it's really a Kristos organization and violates the separation of church and state, but Henly Schrobbe voided the complaint which, unfortunately, is his right as Premier."

Holly, Arnica's lover of many years, was torn. The coven and Merrydale had weathered many crises to date but somehow life in Merrydale District seemed protected and the Goddess had always protected them. And yet, Slade Hatchitt had been relentless in his attacks against the Earthkin. Hatchitt believed that the vast forests of Merrywood were a resource that his lumber baron friends 'needed' for the economic growth of Lothloriën. And Hatchitt's anger continued to simmer, having lost a couple of major battles over control of Merrywood's trees and the very existence of Trillium School, the first Earthkin School to ever receive a charter, was a constant thorn in Hatchitt's paw. Holly realized that this could be serious.

"Hatchitt's committee has recommended that Sunna be placed in Kristos Arms, the orphanage run by the Cathedral of the Thorns in Mill City." Arnica looked out the window. Dark Star gleefully trotted after Gino who was running from her, a bunch of fresh borage in his hand.

"But that's a Kristos place," Holly's voice barely contained his outrage. "How can they do that?" But both men knew full well that politicians were well-schooled in swaying opinion and right now Hatchitt's committee was making loud noises about a foundling being raised by 'heathens.'

"Tonight..." Arnica said, and both men felt temporary peace, knowing that Lammas Eve could help them find an answer. Lammas began the harvest not only for the fields and gardens but could also gather other joys into one's life.

"We'd better start the Lammas bread," Arnica said, smoothing his greying beard.

The coven gathered at the cabin, their robes bright in the early evening sunlight. Sunna's future was their main topic but their conversations also turned around the school year. Trillium School would have 87 students this year when it opened just thirteen days before the Equinox. Lammas meant not only the harvest but started the preparations the faculty and staff must make.

Gino would be in the tenth grade. His parents worked at the school and Rosetta, his mother, also taught cooking. Gino hoped that he'd be old enough that he could begin dating Jenny Flowers, the lovely (but Kristos!) girl who held his interest.

Jewel had brought Sunna, carried in the woven baby sling she'd used when Dagon was a baby. Her russet hair was growing quite long and, on the occasional day when she helped Iris at the postal shop, always brought compliments. Jewel's heart ached to adopt Sunna.

The other eight adults of the coven were the remaining faculty of Trillium School. Originally Lammas Eve was planned to invoke blessings for the school but Sunna's crisis was reason for a last-minute change.

Dark Star sat on the grass attentively. Near her was the reed basket holding the grain man bread for the ritual. The hatchling would carry the basket by its long handle during the ritual. Dark Star loved being able to participate with her human friends at the Sabbats.

Amber, who taught history and social studies, held up a large, woven sheaf of grain and explained. "See how they've woven it? Sunna will fit safely right in here and can be carried right into the harvest. She'll reap all the blessings from the grain mother."

Lotus, holding his son Dagon's hand, spoke softly. "I'm carving a statue of the grain mother. Each flake of wood I cut away from the large cedar is an offering."

Jewel's hand brushed away a tear. She had cried a lot in the last couple of days.

But then, Holly rang the bell and they began their procession through the gardens. Every so often Arnica would cut an herb, using his sacred, silver harvest scissors. A stalk of comfrey for Gino's basket, a stem of yarrow for Pearl's.

Soon they were gathered in the Stone Circle, each holding a basket filled with herbs and flowers. A bowl of fresh berries sat upon the altar along with an ear of early corn, tomatoes and other produce. Dark Star carried the grain man right to the front of the altar where she sat, surrounded by the music of the coven's voices as they began the Harvest Chant.

LIV - Family Values

Trillium School had begun late this year. The third Monday was the New Moon, an excellent time for new beginnings. Two years ago Trillium School opened its new doors to 50 students. This year there were 87 students. If growth continued at this rate, in a few years too many students would create a shortage of Earthkin teachers in Merrydale and cause the newly remodeled facility crowding.

Heartened by their friends' success, an Earthkin coalition of Renaissance and Descendant Tribes was working to open a sister school in Lothloriën's capitol. Mill City was a good-sized town and many of the Descendant peoples lived on tribal land in the nearby River Mountains.

The success of Trillium School, the first Earthkin school chartered in Lothloriën, encouraged the two lineages of Earthkin. In the District of Grainland the Descendant Tribes outnumbered the Renaissance Tribes (the new 'old religion'). Everyone was excited when one of the Renaissance covens proposed the name "Loon School." A building was now waiting and all legal paperwork prepared with thoroughness, submitted to Parliament well in advance of the deadline.

But not everyone saw the emerging earth religions schools with enthusiasm. "Right here in the capitol of Lothloriën?" the ultra-conservative, Slade Hatchitt had roared.

Autumn fell on a Saturday. Trillium School, normally quiet on a weekend, was bustling with activity. Merrydale, known for its rustic quiet, hadn't seen so much traffic since the big parade held last Beltane to save the trees of Merrywood. Trillium School had certainly stirred up Merrydale on a number of occasions. Today the school was holding a meeting to discuss the political difficulties which beset Loon School.

There was standing space only in the school hall. Only a few years ago the building was a large garage but it had been remodeled extensively for Trillium School. Parents were holding young children on their laps. Some couples (including some of the romantically-inclined teens) used lap seating as well. People talked among themselves and the hall was filled with conversations like the sound of dry leaves rustling in the wind past a microphone.

Nearly every parent of a Trillium School student was present, only four were missing due to illness. One father was out of town on business but his wife and brother-in-law were there. Several large vans were parked out in front. Shadow Tail, a friend of the coven, had organized carpools from Mill City to make the journey east over the River Mountains, glad that the mountain passes would remain free of snow until Hallows or later.

Dark Star had not gone into town. Arnica was uncertain that the invisibility ointment could keep her horn from showing. The meeting at the school was too open, could last too long, and it remained important that people outside the coven not learn that a unicorn now lived in Merrydale. The young unicorn had trotted beneath the soaring arches of firs to the stone Circle, a ring of huge, mossy rocks. Her iridescent blue coat shimmered with the dappled sunlight filtering through the trees. Dark Star calmed herself like she'd seen Arnica teaching the coven and called out to the spirit of her grandmare, Lillian, for guidance.

Back at the school, the hatchling's closest friends were stepping up onto the large platform. Lotus, teacher of wood working, had set up a temporary stage so that everyone could see the speakers. Arnica, coven elder and unofficial elder of Merrydale's Earthkin walked to the front of the stage. As he lit a large, white candle the hall became as quiet as a clearing in the depths of a forest on a still day.

Arnica placed a small handful of herbs into a large burner. Smoke plumed upward and the scent drifted through the hall. The elder led the gathering first with a prayer of thanks that the summer's drought-encouraged fires were tempered with cooling weather and some rains which seemed to be gifts from the gods. Next, as he stroked his gray beard, he led an invocation for peace, wisdom and a solution which would be best for the Earthkin, Children of the Earth and then introduced Deodar Dolorum. The one-time Kristos Minister, now one of the most public figures of the Earthkin as principal of Trillium School, walked to the front of the stage. A tall, dark man he once looked unhappy and intimidating. Now married to Merrydale's postmarm, openly Earthkin and the father of a 17 month-old daughter, he was a joyful man whose very presence made Merrydale folk feel better.

Deodar spoke about Loon School and how the staff at Trillium School had hoped their sister school in Mill City would be opening. When he teased that, when Loon

School opened Amber would be chained to her desk, everyone laughed. Amber, a daughter of the Loon Tribe was the only Descendant daughter among them. It was not uncommon for those of the newer, Renaissance beliefs to feel a strong affinity for the native religions. The Renaissance and Descendant Tribes worked together to protect the Earth. When the Politicos party, who had a grudging respect for the land but usually voted for clear-cutting and corporate profit, had become dominated by the Users, the right wing (and usually fundamentalist Kristos) the two Tribes had sworn religious oaths of kinship and became commonly known as the Earthkin.

When Deodar (called 'Dolly' by Iris and the coven) explained that the Loon School's seventeen page application for a charter had been held up by Slade Hatchitt's "family values committee," the adults in the hall were visibly agitated. A couple of younger men booed.

"Why can't something be done about Hatchitt's committee?" a voice called out.

"Iris?" Dolly turned to the postmarm. Iris was one of the few in Merrydale who held a government job. Last year she began teaching a course in government and citizenship at Trillium School and people respected her understanding of how politics worked.

Dark Star's prayer to Lillian had brought an answer! The hatchling trotted quickly along the path back to the cabin. She grabbed the door pull with her teeth, and went to the crystal ball sitting in the temple. She wanted to send a message to Holly.

"As you know," Iris began, "Slade Hatchitt, sort of a perpetual nemesis of the Earthkin, formed this committee. It is not really *fair* for all of its members were appointed from the Politicos and are very conservative. They believe that the Land of Lothloriën would function better if it was run by a government following the Kristos belief system. Because this violated our two-party system our Conserver Party filed a complaint but when Hatchitt's PR men began touting 'family values' to the press Henly Schrobbe, our elected Premier, decided to void the complaint and let the committee stand. Loon School will be delayed for a year or longer. We can only hope it can get a charter in time for next year."

Jewel stood up to speak. A little shy by nature when outside her circle of friends and coven, Jewel had grown in confidence while helping Iris in the postal shop. "Hatchitt's committee heard about Sunna," Jewel said. Sunna had been left at Arnica and Holly's cabin door just at sunrise this past Yule morning. The identity of Sunna's mother was still not known but Jewel wanted that role. The emotions she felt were giving strength to her passion. "That man's 'family values' committee recommended that Sunna be sent to Kristos Arms, the cathedral's orphanage. But the gods were with us."

She paused, looked at the many faces. She caught Gino's eye and he blushed brightly. Sitting next to him was Jenny Flower, the daughter of a Politico official, one who did not approve of Trillium School. Philbert Flower did not know his daughter had been seeing Gino. Although both were tenth graders, their lives seemed very different. Jenny spent the summer as a page in Parliament and Gino spent much of his summer working in the herb gardens at the cabin and continuing his studies in ritual forms and magick. Gino had been in the coven for five years and his knowledge set him apart from the other Earthkin youths his age. Jenny appeared to be excited and Gino was trying to listen very intently.

Parents sat up, shifting in their seats. Murmuring filled the hall as people oohed and a-ahed. Flying Raven walked across the platform holding Sunna. Jewel's face glowed. She and Lotus still hoped to adopt the baby girl as a younger sister for Dagon. As Jewel took Sunna from Raven's arms, the people rose to their feet. Loud applause and cheering filled the hall and soon the sound shifted into the singing of "We Are the Earth People," a song which had been adopted as an anthem by both Descendant and Renaissance Tribes.

The people gone, the coven sat around the school's courtyard. They spoke quietly, the sound of the water trickling in the fountain off to the side helping them ground the tremendous energy which had been generated during the morning meeting.

Plans were being made to raise money. It would cost a tidy sum to hire a barrister to bring a petition before Parliament to override Schrobbe's voiding of the complaint. Enough publicity and skilled legal training could do it.

Arnica and Holly would be offering a fourth of this year's harvest of fruits and herbs. Maude Graves volunteered the storefront she owned. It had been empty for two years but she was comfortable, not needing the income. Pearl would provide needlepoint and some hand-sewn garments. Lotus said he would be hand-carving Yule ornaments.

Amber was quite pleased. She'd missed the store since closing her Crystal Emporium over six years ago. At the time she was tired of the Politico pressure and the public demonstrations held by a few of the more vocal Users who carried signs outside the Emporium, calling it a "tool of darkness." The site was bought out by a group of Users who tried to run a religious goods store for the Kristos but many of the locals had liked Amber and the religious store was never able to turn a profit. A year after it closed the building's owner, Jinko Graves, passed away and left it to his daughter Maude.

But the proposed fund-raising store was only one of the topics for the coven.

"I don't know what she means," Holly explained. By the time the hatchling was two, Holly had developed the ability to communicate with her through their crystal ball. About the time Jewel was talking, Holly felt that Dark Star was sending him a message. "I had images, autumn leaves falling from trees, Dark Star hiding behind the Dryad tree of Fern Hollow, and," he looked toward Gino's freckled face, "Jenny. She's part of the message as well."

LV - The Falling Leaves

"No, I haven't seen her lately, either," Holly said, a bunch of large grapes in his hand as he turned toward Gino and Arnica and looked down from the ladder.

Gino, growing into a handsome young man, had joined the coven with his parents blessing five years ago when he was eleven. His magickal training and the opening of Trillium School, the only Earthkin school to have a charter from the District of Merrydale had given him confidence. His parents, both now school employees, did not have a desire to join one of the covens of the Renaissance Tribes. They preferred a simple life but had recognized Gino's talents at an early age.

Gino had come out to brush the hatchling and enjoy a beautiful autumn day. He had some completed assignments to give Arnica. Gino had begun studying herbes from the coven elder.

"When did you see her last," Arnica asked his partner.

"She nipped at my pocket when I was getting out the ladder." Holly climbed down the ladder, handing a basket filled with grapes to Arnica. "Our munchkin saw the sprigs of borage I had tucked in my pocket for her. That must have been around eight fifteen."

"I saw her dancing around the yard, filled with a restless energy that reminded me of Eostara," Arnica mused, "but I haven't seen her since. That would have been near nine."

The men were so busy with this year's abundant grape harvest that they hadn't realized that the hatchling was missing until Gino showed up and asked the whereabouts of Dark Star.

"I checked in the cabin, too," Gino said. His freckles no longer looked so boyish. "All I found was the steamer, cooking away. The grape juice smells wonderful," he added.

"What time is it now," Arnica asked.

"The last time I peeked into the cabin it was eleven thirty," Gino said. Arnica handed him some deep, purple grapes. Their scent and succulence made the boy's mouth water even before he popped them into his mouth.

"Why, it's heading toward lunch and she *never* misses lunch," Holly said. Holly taught language skills and grammar at Trillium School. If he said 'never' then that was true. Holly didn't use words carelessly.

"Let's check the stone circle," Arnica said, pushing down a feeling of concern. His intuition didn't indicate anything wrong, but there was a sense that *something* was going on.

"Checked it," Gino said, popping a few more concord grapes into his mouth.

"Let's do it anyway," Arnica responded. "You never know..."

It was a great lunch, one of the last they might have sitting out beneath the sun until next year. They talked about school, the plans for the coven's Hallows Eve ritual tomorrow night, and carefully avoided voicing how uncomfortable they were without Dark Star sitting near them, the way she'd always tease them for borage, add affection to their lives. It was more than six and a half years ago since Dark Star's egg appeared in the stone circle, hatching after a very rare and minor temblor the morning of Eostara Eve.

But something was definitely amiss.

"She has been acting a bit mysterious of late," mused Holly, standing near the pantry.

"Of late?" Arnica's fingers mused in his grey beard. "I think it goes back almost to Autumn."

"Mysterious or not, she's *never* missed lunch," Holly said, trying to not feel anxious and bringing a touch of humor to this conundrum.

Arnica finished rinsing the last of the lunch dishes Gino handed him and then, the washing up to wait until after dinner, he turned toward Holly. "Go check the orb," he suggested softly.

Holly knew just what to do. He and Dark Star had learned how to communicate, directing the images of their thoughts into the large crystal ball which Holly and Arnica had used in many years of rituals.

Sitting in a half lotus before the altar, Holly relaxed his mind. Arnica sat quietly behind him, opening his thoughts to create a sheltering sphere around his loved partner. Gino sat quietly off to the side, his eyes and mouth both open. He'd never seen the men doing this type of work, a much more advanced level of Magick than his young years had yet witnessed.

The first images were from weeks ago. Dark Star, spending a quiet autumn day home alone is restless. Her men are at Trillium School.

It is the Saturday of the meeting when Earthkin from many areas gathered to talk about the unfair tactics of the "Family Values" committee set up by Slade Hatchitt, known as a User (the far right of the Politicos Party). The committee was trying to wrest Sunna, the baby left at the cabin door last Yule morning, to put her in Kristos Arms Orphanage. Amber, Trillium School's social science and history teacher, arranged for Sunna to stay with her Loon Tribe sisters in the River Mountains. Generally, Parliament did not have much political control over the lands held by the Descendant Tribes.

The hatchling had gone into the woods to the stone Circle and sought guidance from her grandmare, Lillian. It was then she sent images to Holly of autumn leaves, of Dark Star and of Jenny in Fern Hollow.

Holly brought himself out of the trance. "You don't suppose?" His voice was soft and still connected to the orb.

"Gino," the herbalist said, turning toward his favorite student, "what do you know?"

"Well," the boy responded, searching his memories, "do you remember when Dark Star went with me into Merrydale?" The men nodded. "When Jenny came over to see us at Iris' and Dolly's house, Dark Star was very eager to nuzzle Jenny ... and the other day Jenny told me she's had several dreams about Dark Star... Do you think it could mean anything?"

"Let me go again," Holly whispered. "Having found the past I feel I can locate the present."

Gino sat motionless.

Arnica silently moved his hands to shape the egg of energy surrounding Holly.

Slowly the images began to form. Holly's voice began relating his vision.

"I see Jenny. She's walking on autumn leaves. The firs look dark alongside the crimsons and golds ... The sound of leaves rustling behind her. Is it Dark Star? ... No... It's her father." Holly leaned forward to see more clearly even though his eyes were closed. He was watching his vision from the center of his forehead.

"Philbert Flower carries a conflict in his heart. He's very happy to be walking near Fern Hollow with his daughter. His job as Deputy of Water has kept him in Mill City too much. But he's anxious. They're nearing the Dryad tree... It's where he heard it ... He believes it was the voice of his Kristos god asking him to protect the trees... but he's had nothing but turmoil since he quit taking orders from the Politicos..."

"I see Jenny again... And she *is leading him to the Dryad tree*... She's up to something."

Gino squirmed. Oh, how he wished *he* could see whatever was going on in the globe. Gino was still a Novice and knew that he was watching a skill he wouldn't be capable of learning until he'd worked several wheels as an Initiate.

"They're nearing the tree... Jenny is holding her father's hand and they're talking but I can't hear anything they say. I can see the tree, now. Why, I can see the Dryad very clear..." Holly's voice was filled with wonder. "But they don't... The Dryad has the oddest smile on his face... Jenny and her father are talking. I can't tell but I think he's telling her about the voice he heard... *It was the Dryad...* Arnica, you were right!"

When Arnica first heard that Philbert thought he heard the voice of his god, the elder knew instantly it was the Dryad of Fern Hollow.

"Oh!" Holly was startled but he didn't let go of his vision. Arnica and Gino held their breath, waiting to hear what had happened.

"It's the hatchling... She's come out from behind the tree and Philbert can see her horn. He's sitting there but Jenny has her arm around him, comforting him. He looks shaken. And Dark Star... she's sitting down, now, next to him, nuzzling him... and starting to talk. Now he looks calmer. I think he believes.. he believes..."

Holly drifted back from his trance. This was intense and long.

"I'm going to head into town." Gino intended to ride his bicycle fast and be waiting at the Flowers' home. He needed to see Jenny and it didn't matter if her father didn't approve of Gino being Earthkin. The two had been dating secretly since last school year and he knew she needed to talk to him. "I'll be ready." Gino was very eager for the scrying at the cauldron fire, having seen what Holly could do with the crystal ball.

They quickly hugged. Arnica headed to the bathroom to begin running hot water. He knew a long soak in the tub with home-made herbal suds would restore Holly from his journeying. Both men could feel Dark Star romping through the woods, trotting in joy on her way home to her humans.

LVI - The Yule Star

Arnica and Holly were sitting on the floor of the front room, talking about the events of the past weeks as they wrapped presents for tonight's Yule Eve ritual. There was extra excitement in the air, including some from the hatchling, who had been told to stay in the kitchen as they wrapped her gift. Dark Star was impatient. She *loved* the human custom of gifts! She expected some variation of her usual present - borage flower cookies, one of her favorite treats.

"O.K., munchkin," Holly called out, "you can come back in now." Her gift was now safely wrapped. They knew Dark Star would be quite surprised when she found a hand-hooked rug with the design of a blue unicorn looking like her father, Andrius. For some years, now, Dark Star had been sleeping on an old rug near the fireplace.

Dark Star stepped around the corner, pretending to look slightly put off at having been asked to wait but her eyes sparkled so bright it was easy to see that she was happy waiting, knowing she'd have a fine gift waiting beneath the Yule tree.

The talk turned to the anticipation for tonight's ritual. The men were still checking the sky every night and yes, it was still there...

The star had appeared... Dark Star found it during the Geminids meteor shower, the night before the New Moon. She was so excited she trotted back into the cabin, even though her men were sound asleep, and jumped upon their warm bed and nudged them awake with her horn until they pulled on warm robes and went out to see the new star shining bright on a frosty, clear night. Arnica and Holly had expressions of joy on their faces as Holly's fingers tousled the hatchling's mane.

This was Gino's star. After five years of study with the coven, he was now readying himself for Initiation. Gino, 16 last April, had submitted his petition to Arnica, the coven elder. The young man was so excited when the red feather arrived in the mail: it was time for his Quest. He chose the night carefully, having decided to seek his voice from the Dryad Tree in Fern Hollow.

Arnica and Holly finished wrapping the gifts they would be giving the coven. There were so many packages this year. The coven members would be giving Gino some of the items needed for his Initiation, even though it would not happen until Candlemas was nigh.

The small package wrapped in soft, golden paper from Trillium School's art teacher waited. Pearl had woven three cords for Gino from hand-spun wool. Pearl knew that this was one ritual for which he'd not need one of her hand-embroidered robes! The wool had come from Amber's Loon Tribe sisters in the River Mountains.

Amber, the only Descendant in the coven, also taught at Trillium School. Her gift for Gino were two herbal dyes, one from *Baptisia australis*, called false indigo by the New People, as the old ones of the Loon Tribe called the early pale skinned settlers. The other was a beautiful red dye made from a mixture of rare, red clay and the powdered, dried fruit of the bloodberry tree. Gino's coven training taught him how to bleach the third cord white.

Dark Star, although eager to bring in *her* present to be wrapped was distracted as she listened to her men talk about Gino's Quest...

The Dryad Tree held special significance for the tenth grade student. His sweetheart, Jenny Flower, was the daughter of the Deputy of Water, appointed by the Politicos - that faction of politics most prone to policies which favored business over the environment. Jenny attended Merrydale High and the two had to keep their budding romance from her father. But just after Beltane, Philbert Flower thought he'd heard the 'voice of God' from the Dryad Tree. He then announced his resignation from the Politico Party. The party heads were very angry but could do nothing due to the publicity any negative action would generate.

The day before Hallows Eve, Jenny took her father walking near the Dryad Tree. She told him what she'd learned last summer, working as a page in Parliament. Slade Hatchitt didn't know she was in the next room and she was shocked by what she heard. Hatchitt, one of the most powerful of the Politicos, was proud of being a User, the extreme right of the conservative party. Openly anti-Earthkin, he felt that everyone in the Land of Lothloriën should embrace the Kristos religion and worked to legislate the Earthkin out of existence.

Hatchitt was increasingly volatile, angry over the success of Trillium School and the public's positive feeling over the Earthkin's endeavor. But Hatchitt won a victory when his Family Values Committee delayed the Loon School charter decision by a year and he expected to success with his goal of placing Sunna, the foundling who appeared at the cabin door last Yule, in the Kristos Arms orphanage in Mill City. This had only brought the Renaissance Tribes, who followed their ancestors' 'old religion,' closer to the Descendant Tribes, who were native peoples of the land of Lothloriën.

Holly told Arnica once again what he had seen imaged in the orb by Dark Star after her Hallows 'appearance.' As Jenny told her father what Hatchitt had said, Philbert, his anger growing, was stopped short when a vision of a unicorn appeared and spoke to him. "The solution will be found through a calm mind," the hatchling advised, quoting her grandmare, Lillian.

Hearing Arnica mention her name as he and Holly once again sorted through the events caused Dark Star to jump up and trot out to the pantry to retrieve what she'd been hiding. The hatchling wanted them to wrap her present for Gino before they put away their paper and ribbons.

Neither Holly nor Arnica were surprised when she jumped up and trotted out. Although the hatchling was now over six years old, she was small as unicorns go (so Andrius said) and still quite coltish and frisky.

But when she pranced back into the front room, her hooves tapping lightly on the hardwood floor, they were stunned. Dark Star held an orb gently between her teeth. It was smaller than the crystal ball on Arnica and Holly's altar and radiated a soft glow. It was obviously not of this world. As Dark Star carefully laid it in Arnica's outstretched hand, the herbal priest could feel the energy it contained. Arnica had felt this once before when his teacher had sent him a small stone to be buried in their stone circle.

"You got this from Andrius, didn't you?" he asked.

The hatchling whinnied in the affirmative.

"Wow," Holly said, "that's some gift, but I have no doubt that Gino will be able to use it." The sphere looked almost like it was made of opal but yet it didn't, at all. "Will Gino be able to share images with you in here like we do?" Holly was curious.

Dark Star looked toward the altar, gazing at the crystal ball.

Holly translated, "Not the same, but he will learn to communicate with the unicorn realm. My elders saw the star and they know that this orb has been waiting for Gino."

Gino was the only person outside the coven who perceived Dark Star's unicorn self, despite her horn being invisible at the time. Among the hatchling's astral friends, even Gino's attraction to the pretty Kristos girl had been part of the myth, as well as her father's disapproval... Dark Star thought about Jenny's father...

No one knew what Philbert Flower said to Slade Hatchitt. Mr. Flower would not even tell his wife, Becky. After Jenny told her father what she'd heard and Dark Star leapt out from behind the Dryad Tree, Philbert experienced an epiphany. But before he and Jenny left Fern Hollow to return home, he asked her to make an oath upon the tree that she would tell no one of Hatchitt's secret nor of Philbert's 'vision' of a unicorn.

Dark Star had no oath. She shared the secret with Holly, imaging into the orb later that night as Holly described the images for Arnica. They were stunned and yet not surprised. The two men laughed with glee as Dark Star provided them with the picture of her waiting to leap, of Philbert's wide-eyed gasp and of Jenny trying to act as if she didn't know the hatchling.

Arnica remembered Iris' phone call. Merrydale's postmarm, their coven sister always knew the news first.

As Holly found a box and Arnica began cutting wrapping paper, Dark Star looked at the presents from the Dolorums. Iris' gift sat in a cardboard tube, wrapped with hand-colored paper. Her baby Diana was now 19 months old and Iris found bits of time for her skills. She'd brushed up her calligraphy skills and had created the certificate the coven would present to Gino. Dolly, her husband and the school principal, had his gift in an envelope. It was a job offer. Deodar Dolorum would offer Gino a paid position during summer school, teaching the Earthkin ways at the summer preschool.

Although a government employee, the postmarm was always a renegade. The Politicos didn't know how to deal with her because the people of Merrydale loved her dearly. If Slade Hatchitt could have, she'd be out of a job. He'd never forgiven the postmarm for foiling his plans to sell the harvest rights for Fern Hollow's trees.

When Iris heard the news, she called Arnica as soon as the postal shop was empty. Hatchitt and his wife appeared together at the press conference. She was almost never in public. A good User's wife knew her place was in the home. Hatchitt made the quick announcement that his secretary, a very attractive young woman from Highlands, was unexpectedly called home and - this is what was sensational - his wife, Glenda, would be taking the position. There was no question of nepotism. The fact that a right wing Politico would allow his wife to take a prominent role outside the home meant that the Conservers had no disagreement at all and the appointment was approved.

Gino caressed the tree. He had spent occasional nights sleeping in the stone circle, but always with Dark Star. This night he was to remain alone and focused. He was to keep his thoughts within his ritual, not even thinking about Jenny.

When Arnica had read Gino's petition, one of the questions was whether Gino thought he could manage a fortnight of celibacy. Gino blushed, his freckles lost in his red cheeks. He and Jenny were barely at the kissing stage.

On his knees, Gino kissed the earth around the roots of the Dryad Tree as he began his ritual, asking that the Ancient Ones would bring the star he needed for his quest.

Tonight the cabin would be filled with mirth. Lotus had carved wooden covers for a Book of Shadows, filled with pages of hand-made paper which Jewel lovingly pressed. But they were home this night, tending Sunna who would be celebrating one year with the coven tomorrow morning. Dagon, just one Sabbat younger than Dark Star, was still too young to attend without his parents.

Gino would be riding out with Flying Raven. Her gift was the elixir and cake recipes which had been handed down in her family for many generations.

This would be a Yule Eve Gino would not soon forget.

LVII - Upon This Blade

He shifted a little, the wooden chair seat increasingly cold against his bare flesh. Why had he turned down Holly's offer of a chair cushion? Deprived of sight by a scarf folded into a band then tied snug around his head, Gino's thoughts were turned inward.

Now and then he would hear one of the coven members walk past, a clink that sounded like something just barely touching glass. Something on the altar? Once Gino thought he heard the sound of charcoal lighting. There wasn't any word for that sound, he reflected, thinking of what he would need to write later in his ritual journal. "It's pretty distinctive," he mused.

Gino was no longer teased about being the youngest member of the coven. Only eleven when he attended his first ritual at Midsummer, his birthday would be two months and a day following Candlemas and he would be seventeen. He was in the tenth grade at Trillium School. With its charter as a religious school (the first in Lothloriën), Gino was relieved to be taken out of the public school when the majority party in Parliament had required oaths of allegiance to the Kristos God. It was this local political crisis that led to Trillium School...

A bell shook Gino from his reverie. He stretched his hearing but no other sound met his ear. "This must be the *first bell*," he thought, recalling his instruction to begin reflecting upon the steps of his Pathworking which had brought him to this day.

There was the memory of Dark Star, the day he had difficulty reciting the Charges of the Goddess by memory. As he stood before the altar in the cabin, Arnica sitting in a half lotus quietly behind him taking notes, the energy of the Goddess would begin to shape itself into the image of Jenny Flowers. Gino and Jenny had been working on a friendship and trying to date although Jenny attended Merrydale High and her father was a fairly conservative member of the Kristos faith. Each time Jenny's smiling face appeared in his mind, or thoughts of the warmth of her maturing body, Dark Star would scuffle her hooves on the floor, able to sense at a moment Gino's lost train of thought. Gino passed that part of his oral exam, but only with the Hatchling's help.

Dark Star again, this time standing at the door to the cabin's ritual room. She was holding freshly nipped borage flowers (her favorite to eat) from the garden and held them out for Gino to congratulate him on having completed his performance of the coven ritual by memory, without any mistakes.

Another image of Dark Star, wondering where she was right now. Gino could 'see' her in his mind, the shiny, silver amulet around her neck. Gino had made it in school in the Tools Class taught by Lotus. It was a small silver case. Gino had tooled it, engraved it, set two gemstones upon it. It was filled with the powder Arnica used to make Dark Star's horn invisible...

Gino was recalling the first time he'd met Arnica and Holly. It was six years ago last autumn. The men had gone into Merrydale to pay the tithing on the harvest. Most of those who saw the well-known herbalist and his partner knew them as Earthkin Priests and wondered at the unusual iridescent sheen of the 'pony' walking with them.

This time the bell brought Gino sharply back to the chair. He shifted again, his bare bottom sliding on the wooden seat.

Gino heard Arnica's voice as he called upon the gods, lighting the left altar candle... "that this altar is bathed in light, that the Seeker will find the Path." And then, Holly's voice and the right candle was lit.

Time moved so slow that Gino could hear every step taken by a bare foot walking the Circle on the cabin floor. And time moved so fast that later, his memories were a blur.

It seemed as if the past six years had taken forever. Back then he was young ... but thought he was pretty mature for his age! Gino almost chuckled out loud at the thought when he felt ritual water sprinkled upon his feet. The Circle was being aspurged "that it make sacred this Rite of Initiation..."

"*Initiation,*" Gino thought... "*my* initiation!" He'd needed his parents permission to join the coven. Now he was on the verge of being a man. Sitting on the chair, unclothed as he had come into the world, Gino wore only his cords.

Pearl taught art and music at the school but in the coven was known for her sewing skills which she had learned from her grandmother, Lady Ellhorn. As one of the projects to finish as a Novice, Gino had to have three unbraided cords. Pearl taught Gino about fibers, showing him how to work with flax and wool and cotton. Together, Pearl and Flying Raven showed Gino how to create dyes from herbs and other natural sources. It had taken some doing but Flying Raven knew more about natural chemistry than the students at Trillium School could guess. Her grandmotherly demeanor was not the image of a trained scientist. It was with Raven's help that Gino was able to fix the natural dyes so that his blue, white and red cords wouldn't eventually fade into each other creating a sorry violet shade!

The cords brought him back to reality. The white cord was wound around his right ankle. It had been bleached by the sun and by hydrogen peroxide. One time he even tried lemon juice. It looked pretty good. The blue cord had been looped around his waist. It had been difficult to get an herb for blue dye as there was none growing in Arnica and Holly's herb gardens at the cabin. Gino had tried blueberries but the color was far too purple to be a convincing blue. Amber contacted her Loon Tribe sisters and got a packet of woad. And Lady Ellhorn sent a small amount of indigo plant. The cord now at Gino's waist had come out a beautiful shade of blue.

Red was another difficult color. Why not green or yellow or orange? Although Gino had studied the metaphysical properties of these three colors, red proved to be the most difficult. Most of the reds he tried from the fruits and gardens produced colors that looked more brown. Gino remembered his excitement when he opened the small Yule gift from Amber. Inside the little box was a bottle of cochineal, the powder of insect bodies. Amber wrote her cousin, the one married to a lovely man of a Descendant Tribe. She had moved with her husband to his homeland in Azteca, a country just south of Lothloriën, where the *Dactylopius coccus* was ritually gathered. Amber taught Gino how to use alum to create a bright red dye for his cord.

A difficult color and the challenging cord. One end circled Gino's wrist, then travelled up his back and around his neck before reaching down where it was tied to the other wrist. Arnica and Holly had told him this part would be difficult and somewhat uncomfortable.

A bell struck.

Gino shifted on the chair, his hands clasped behind his back. The constraint of the red cord was, he knew from his lessons, to keep him mindful that he was experiencing the constriction of rebirth for he would emerge from this ritual as an initiate of the coven.

A sharp sound tapping against wood startled him but Gino quickly realized that it was Dark Star's hooves on the cabin's wood floor.

The hatchling was moving around the Circle (always deosil, thank you!). Dark Star was in charge of the feast. The past two nights she had gone out to the Stone Circle and slipped through the portal into the Otherlands. The young unicorn needed instruction from her father on how to gather the Initiation Ritual's Magick with her horn and channel it into the borage cakes waiting for the feast. Andrius, now a wise, older unicorn, was so proud of his offspring.

The hatchling took her place, sitting on the floor in a corner next to a low table, laden with goodies. Most of the feast had been prepared by Rosetta. Gino's parents were so proud of him. They were the only people outside of the coven who knew of this great event. Most of Merrydale knew that Arnica was an elder of the Earthkin but the coven practiced the old ways and kept their inner work within the veil of secrecy.

It had been a challenge for Gino. There were times he was bursting with news, so proud of a new accomplishment as he completed the requirements for Initiation. Once in a while a topic would come up at school and it was hard for his boyish ego to keep his own Mysteries. But Gino was learning. There were times he'd had difficulty keeping his focus on school but one of the conditions of his Initiation was maintaining his grades. He'd had nearly a 4.0 in Trillium School. Not even Jenny knew. She was very proud of Gino. She knew something was going on but her Kristos upbringing kept her from asking.

"How loud it is," Gino thought to himself. The silence was so strong, it was palpable.

The coven sat waiting. Although many had given him their gifts to help him complete his work toward this day, a few were waiting. Iris, Merrydale's postmarm, had hand-lettered a beautiful scroll in the Theban alphabet welcoming Gino formally into the coven as an Initiate. Standing by her ready to share in the manifestation of the Watchtower of Fire was Deodar. Her husband, Trillium School's principal, had a written job proposal, offering Gino a summer job with the school's new children's program.

Jewel and Lotus were at the north. Without Gino ever knowing, the school's Tools teacher made a matching silver capsule.

Pearl and Flying Raven shared the west, a cobalt blue glass pitcher of water waiting. Amber placed some incense upon the burner at the east altar. The smoke silently curled up.

Arnica and Holly walked as quiet as possible around the altar to the northeast portal. As Holly rang a bell with an urgent sound, Gino stood right on cue, showing how well he had studied. At that moment the blade of Arnica's athame touched him sharply near his heart.

"Have you the courage before this blade of truth? Tradition says 'twould better be to rush upon this blade and perish, than to join this ritual with fear in your heart.'"

LVIII - Plant the Seed Slowly

"I can see him walking through the gardens." Holly and Arnica were cleaning up a bed, removing the leaves from the trilliums who poked up their first green like curious Devas. The man, handsome with his shaved head, had been walking the garden paths for hours. He'd spent the night before in contemplation in the Stone Circle, seeking guidance from the Devas.

"It will be quite a journey for him to take," Arnica answered. The man's journey would be bringing some joyful changes to Trillium School and to the coven.

It was Candlemas Eve when the coven conducted Gino's Initiation and just two days later a letter arrived. The man was called Honey and he was Adelle Amberson's son.

Arnica had known Adelle many years ago when they were both students at Mill City College. Arnica was studying botany and taking pre-med courses, the best which could be found for a budding herbalist in those days. Adelle was unsure of her major, instead relishing the freedom found in the 'big' city. Her parents attended a very strict Kristos church in a rural area of the District of the Four Deserts.

During their third year of college a Bard came wandering through the Land of Lothloriën studying from the very few Earthkin teachers which could be found, spending time living with some of the Descendant Tribes and seeking out the new Renaissance peoples like Arnica. Adelle was a beautiful, young girl with pale, golden hair and brown eyes. It was love at first song. The young couple eloped and moved to Eastborough, a large metropolis in Atalanta.

Rennie, Honey's father, was lost at sea. He was on a quest to Astarte's Well in Italia far across the Atlantikos hoping to study with a famous bardic teacher in Keltavia.

Wiccaned Thurifera Amberson, Honey was now an adult and had been following his father's footsteps as a performer, even making quite a name for himself in Eastborough. But having emerged from his Saturn return, Honey wanted more in life. Honey Amberson wanted to return to Lothloriën, more specifically to Merrydale, where his grandmother had lived until her passing. He had come to realize that it wasn't the *performing* so much, but his father's love of the Earthkin ways.

Honey wrote to Arnica asking if he might pursue study with the herbalist. The arrangements were made and Honey arrived to spend a few days. Arnica and Holly liked the man immediately and quickly took to his nickname, "the same color as amber," Honey said.

"I wish to study toward Initiation," Honey said. He was seated in a half-lotus upon the grass. Dark Star had followed him about and sat nearby, intently gazing at this intense man. The Hatchling had spent the night in the Stone Circle with him. She loved it when humans spent the night in a quest, so near to the astral gardens of Lothloriën where her sire, Andrius, trotted about with the Mother.

"Priestly studies will help me continue my father's work," Honey said. "And I know that my grandmother would be thrilled to know that I was back in Merrydale. Did you know the house is still in my family?"

"We knew it was a rental house," Holly said, "but we don't know much about real estate in Merrydale. Is it available for you?"

"The current renter's lease is up this summer and she told our agent that she's being transferred to Cloverville and wouldn't be renewing it." Honey smiled warmly. He *knew* that this was good.

"Let's have lunch, then," Arnica said. "We have a big afternoon." Arnica was taking Honey in to visit Trillium School. With this interesting turn of events (which surprised Arnica not at all), perhaps the school might have a program in theatre arts as an adjunct to ritual.

It was a warm, sunny Saturday afternoon, one which held the promise of summer's maturity. But it was spring and clusters of naturalized daffodils greeted the men when they walked into Merrydale on their way to Trillium School. Dark Star was on another journey. By spending the afternoon with Gino she would not have to wear the invisibility ointment on her horn. It worked well and she *loved* going in to town, but it was better for her horn to be natural.

Gino and Jenny were out for a walk with Dark Star. They had gone into the woods hoping to find several cones from the Dryad Tree which might provide seeds for Eostara. Jenny had been raised in a strict Kristos church. Her father had been prominent in the Users, the right wing of the Politico Party, which once sought to clear-cut this entire woodland. The Politicos believed in the sublimation of nature to the commercial needs of humans.

Jenny Flower was glad to have time with Gino. Over the winter he was spending a lot of time with his studies. She knew he was working toward goals within the Earthkin religion and was respectful of whatever it was that her sweetheart was working on. She still prayed to the Krista but more and more found comfort in praying to the Krista's mother and was coming to better understand the concepts of the Earth Mother. One afternoon, when talking with her mother about these issues, Becky Flower told her daughter that her Aunt Juanita believed that any "God the Father" had to have a "God the Mother" and preferred offering her prayers when she was in her gardens.

The Flowers had experienced political changes over this past year. Appointed Deputy of Water, Philbert Flower began his office loyal to the fundamentalist views within his Politico Party. Arnica thought it might have been the connection with water that led the man to visit the Dryad Tree with his daughter last autumn. There Flower heard a divine voice. Shortly after he resigned from the Politicos but still held his office. More and more the Flowers questioned their beliefs. Still, Jenny did not tell her father that she'd been dating an Earthkin boy for a year.

Sitting against the Dryad tree, the hatchling's head laying on Jenny's lap as she gently scratched Dark Star's ear, the two young lovers felt the warmth of the sun upon their bodies, the rising warmth within the bodies as well. In the weeks following Gino's initiation, his voice deepened and a youthful beard and moustache had begun to appear.

Now Gino was studying the Mysteries of the Great Rite. He knew that his next Initiation would be a Sacred Marriage with the Land of Lothloriën and he felt the rising tide of spring within his body as surely as the sap rising with the tree behind him.

The young sweethearts turned toward each other and kissed gently. But their desire had been growing. The sun's heat, the rising sap, their young passion kissed again. Within them the yearning to come together was growing. Jenny's breasts grew taught and Gino could feel himself growing hard. Their minds wanted them to wait but their bodies and their longing ached with desire.

The hunger of the kisses that followed did not escape Dark Star. The mating love of humans was not her realm but she knew that they were not ready to plant Gino's seed. The hatchling raised her head and licked Gino's freckled cheek. The lovers broke into silly laughter, relieved at their passion held in check through such a loving gesture by Dark Star.

Brushing the woodlands off their clothing and pulling some needles off Dark Star, they all rose and began their walk back. Several cones had been found, now safe in Gino's pocket. Their seeds were yet intact.

The Coven sat within the Stone Circle, grateful for a warm and dry Eostara Eve. At the center the flames of the cauldron both warmed them and brought its own Magick.

Holly and Arnica had cast the Circle. They so looked forward to another spring. Arnica felt his 'old bones' did better when he worked in the gardens more regularly. Holly knew that spring meant the school season was moving forward. He loved teaching but, truth be known, missed sharing the work at their cabin and in the gardens with Arnica.

Amber and Pearl had invoked Air. Holding the tray of clay pots aloft, they had asked the sylphs to bless the seeds so that the Dryad Tree would have new offspring. Amber, with desert sage from her Loon Tribe sisters, had smudged the pots before the seeds were planted in the potting shed before their procession back to the Stone Circle. Pearl concentrated. She wanted to look at Honey again. The coven's robe mistress, she could already see the robe she would sew for him.

Iris and Dolly Dolorum invoked fire. As they faced the south, Dolly's dark braid was yet much shorter than Iris' but they looked quite the couple. Merrydale's Postmarm and Trillium School's principal. To think that just a few years ago Deodar Dolorum was a Kristos clergyman. They drew upon the manifested changes in calling forth this element, as well as the endless energy of their toddler, Diana, who would be two at the next Sabbat.

Diana was spending the night with her 'coven grannie,' Flying Raven. Although she has six grandchildren of her own, they lived far away in the District of the Mothervalley and she saw them less often since moving to Merrydale to teach in the school. Raven was tired this spring and offered to care for the young ones. She was joining them with astral work as the young ones slept in her bedroom.

Jewel and Lotus sprinkled water upon the pots when they called upon the west. Lotus had brought some of the water from the school's courtyard fountain. It had become a custom in Merrydale that travelers would bring back a little water from wherever they'd traveled and add it to Trillium's fountain. There was also water sent by relatives and friends from sacred sites around the world.

The Hatchling

Their 'baby,' Dagon, would soon be seven years old. Although he loved rituals, he was at the restless age but would be starting first grade this autumn and that would bring about many changes. Dagon was quite precocious and before going to bed, he had read Raven a story!

Gino was very proud. Although not quite seventeen and in the tenth grade, he had coached Honey before the Circle and the two men (for Gino was definitely embracing his manhood this spring) invoked the spirits of earth.

As the coven gazed into the fire, silently passing the pots of Dryad seeds around, Dark Star moved up behind Gino. The young man had difficulty keeping his mind completely within the Circle. If Jenny were of the Earthkin, they could pledge their love, they could even contemplate manifesting their love with sexual joy. Although too young for marriage, they felt certain that their future lie together.

"Plant the seed slowly..."

Gino started just a bit, not enough to distract anyone else. He'd heard the hatchling's thought quite clearly. His hand reached back and pulled Dark Star's head close. Yes, this was the work at hand and sitting between the worlds with these adults reminded Gino that he and Jenny had many years before them.

LIX - Beltane Dreams

It had been a wonderful Beltane Eve at the grove. The scent of incense lingered in the gardens and the cauldron, still in the center of the stone circle, retained warmth from the ritual fire. Arnica and Holly's cabin and gardens were the coven's 'home' and this evening's ritual left Beltane ribbons hanging from the trees along with many from years past. A new visitor to the grove was always entranced by the lovely ribbons, even those slightly shredded as their threads flew off with birds for nest-building each spring. The other coveners, all but young Gino, had returned to Merrydale after tying up their ribbons, the final gesture of the evening's ritual and festivities.

It was now nearly two in the morning. A few candle lanterns continued to light the paths through the garden. In the cabin, Holly lay snuggled in Arnica's arms. Although many years had passed since they'd first shared their Beltane lust, the two men had been well-stirred this evening by the bonfire and slept soundly after some athletic joys. The hatchling was spending the night in the stone circle and they could growl and roar and shake the bed in joy.

Back in Merrydale, Iris and Dolly were almost asleep. Their daughter Diana's second birthday awaited the morning. A Beltane Day baby, she already knew what this day represented. The couple stayed up late wrapping gifts for Diana to give her friends at the party. Their hearts had been willing and their thoughts embroidered with sexual fantasy but the realities of life were theirs as well. Iris' role as postmarm provided her with access to news about Schrobbe's plans. Schrobbe, current Premier of Lothloriën appeared to be quietly moving to legislate action favoring his business friends, a move which would undo years of environmental protection. Iris was a strong and visible environmentalist within the District of Merrydale. And Dolly was tired from his work at

Trillium School. This was the ending of the school's third year. It was the principal's role to administer the new standardized testing. It had been a challenging April.

Pearl, the coven seamstress, had quickly gone to bed after reaching her home. Her partner, Phoenix, had passed over five years ago last Hallows and at some Sabbats she missed him with a deep, painful heart. But the gods were kind. Pearl was dreaming that she and Phoenix were making love. It was five and a half years since he'd passed over and as their joyful passion swept up like a cone of power, Pearl's dream became more lucid and she realized that Phoenix would be moving on toward his next incarnation. Perhaps not until the life after next might they again be lovers. It was poignant, yet Pearl was also ready to move forward with her life.

Although a grandmother of six, Flying Raven was young at heart and occasionally entertained thoughts of romance. As some of her covenmates slept in their homes, Raven sat at her desk by the front window of her apartment grading science papers. Now and then the candle would flicker on the nearby altar (Raven had an altar to the Mother in every room). Distracted, Raven's thoughts drifted back to the brief but romantic adventure she'd had with Ollis Piper three years ago this summer. She recalled the warmth of his embrace and her body's longing. "Piddle," she thought to herself, turning back to the papers, "I'm a *grandmother!*" The Goddess, however, knew that Raven was in her mid-fifties and not old.

Amber was in the sweat lodge behind her cottage, deep in trance, sharing with her Loon Tribe sisters the sacred workings of the Descendant Tribes. She loved her work at Trillium School, teaching history and social studies and she felt close with the coven and the other Renaissance Tribe peoples. But there were times when she needed to walk between the worlds with those of her own blood, sharing the visions the Loon Tribe had found in this land long before the first settlers had arrived .

Jewel and Lotus were not asleep. The couple was still making love with great abandon. Lotus had surprised his wife on her birthday (Jewel is an Aquarius) by getting a vasectomy. Lotus could feel the horns of Pan upon his brow. Jewel's body ached with the passion of many Goddesses. Their bodies had barely erupted when they heard a noise in the next room. Dagon was stirring in his bedroom, just through the wall.

"Do you think," Lotus said, interrupted by Jewel who finished his sentence.

"We should start looking for a larger house?" She often finished his sentences. Their ritual work together provided them with a strong bond at all levels of being. Lotus finished Jewel's sentences as well. Strangers sometimes had difficulty with this, looking quizzically from one to the other. Later the couple would chuckle, enjoying their private joke.

With Dagon turning seven on his birthday ("May 14th," he proudly reminded them every morning for two weeks!), their son was enrolled to begin first grade this fall. The couple wanted more privacy. Jewel and Lotus had sometimes fantasized about a larger bedroom so they could savor the Great Rite within a circle cast around their bed. Now and then Dagon might hear, but Earthkin children were taught from the beginning that sexuality was a sacred joy bestowed upon all by the Goddess and God.

And despite their plans to have just one child of their own, Jewel had great hopes of their family growing. Only days ago the woman from the Children's Office in Mill City called to schedule the adoption hearing for Sunna. The baby Sunna had been left at

Arnica and Holly's door a year ago this past Yule. Just when Jewel thought they were making progress last autumn, the Earthkin's nemesis, Slade Hatchitt, the head of the Users (the right wing faction of the conservative Politicos party) attempted to convince his "family values" committee to have Sunna placed in a Kristos orphanage. Sunna was spending the night with Gino's mother, Rosetta, who had a wonderful gift in her heart for children.

It didn't occur odd to either Jewel or Lotus that they had to go to the capitol in Mill City rather than the local office in Merrydale. No one in the coven had ever adopted a child before and they were so relieved to learn of the hearing they simply said yes and began making plans to drive over the mountains to Mill City. The meeting would be just three days before Midsummer.

And the hatchling? In the stone circle at the grove, back in the wooded area, Dark Star lay with her head against the north altar stone. She loved her men. Stirring in her sleep her unicorn spirit reached out to Arnica and Holly, but young Gino and Dark Star shared a special friendship. And this Beltane Eve as the clock danced a slow minuet well past midnight, Dark Star was dreaming of a handsome unicorn stallion. The hatchling was coming of age. In human years she was seven but in unicorn years it was time to dream of a Beltane mating. And this dark-maned male was very handsome. But what would her sire say? Able to dream and think at the same time (unicorns worked on many levels), Dark Star found herself wondering. She hadn't spoken with her father, Andrius, in a several moons. Would he approve of this 'Dark One?' She wanted to tell him of this dream.

The two peoples within the Land of Lothloriën who see the earth as divine enjoyed turning the Wheel of the Year. To the Descendant Tribes, the original peoples, this was Mating Day, honoring the arrival of the bees and the mating dances of their animal kindred. Their storytellers would sing of the days before the New People came in their great boats, crossing the Mother of Waters. In those ancient days young men hunted deer and helped their fathers hunt bison by their thirteenth summer and it was not long after that they coupled with the young women whose wombs could now nurture life, sharing the Mating Day songs with the furred and feathered ones. But the times had changed and, like the Renaissance Tribes, they now entered their unions later in their teens.

The Renaissance Tribes were of the New People, those for whom the monotheistic and puritanical beliefs of the Kristos did not work. The conflict of these beliefs with their souls had caused them to seek the ancient ways of their ancestors from the olden times before their forebears had crossed the Atlantikos. These were the ways of the Gods and Goddesses, persecuted as the Kristos religion fought many wars and claimed nearly all of the Old Country.

The Earthkin religions respected sexuality as a healthy and sacred aspect of life for all creatures. The Earthkin believed sexual education combined with safeguards against pregnancy would allow a young couple, if emotionally mature, to achieve their educational goals and settle their lives before embracing the responsibilities of parenting. It was not uncommon for a young Descendant Tribe couple in their teens to be bound in marriage by a tribal elder and even Arnica conducted Handfastings for young people if they completed their counseling, had above-average grades in school and the approval of their parents.

Gino, recently initiated just this Candlemas, was wrapped up in his sleeping blanket near the center of the stone circle, his body enjoying the lingering warmth of the cauldron. Now 17, Gino looked forward to the eleventh grade. Two more years of schooling. So many changes had happened since he met Dark Star seven years ago this summer. Now he was an initiate! And going to Trillium School, the first school ever for the Earthkin.

He knew that he was no longer a boy. His body reminded him of that. He was seventeen and his body was maturing. Gino knew two boys who would be Handfasted this summer. Gino and Jenny, his sweetheart, had often discussed the differences between their peoples. Although nearly the same age, Jenny's Kristos upbringing left her with very different values. Kristos morals imposed great burdens of guilt upon the young. Jenny's body and heart wanted to be joined with Gino but she struggled with the threat of damnation she'd so often heard from the pulpit.

Gino was dreaming. Once again he and Jenny were back sitting against the Dryad Tree, enjoying the sunny spring day just before the Equinox. Gino's hand began to caress Jenny's breast. A breeze blew through her hair, wisps of it caressing his face.

"Plant the Seed Slowly," the Sabbat theme from Eostara was the melody in the breeze.

Gino's mouth hungered to kiss her again, passionately with the lust of a thousand male species eager to impregnate their chosen mate. A sense of weightlessness borne of an astral experience caused his body to stir. The gods of the dreamworld gave him permission and their hunger grew. Gino dreamt that he would be entering her.

Dark Star and the Dark One are romping through Merrywood, in a wonderful mating chase through the trees. As they near the Dryad Tree, she slows, looks over her shoulder and allows the stallion to draw near. The sun sparkles on his silver horn. The vibrant male unicorn prepares to mount her. "Is this how my mother conceived me?" Dark Star wonders.

Jenny is sound asleep and dreaming. Her parents are still downstairs talking, but she doesn't hear. Gino's mouth is upon her breast, his erection pressing the warm fabric of his pants against her thigh... Suddenly, the antlers of a deer crash through the trees. A gun fires. Jenny sits up, her heart racing, too afraid to cry out.

Gino hears laughter. He grabs at his trousers.
"Jenny, we must..." he begins to warn the dream image and then sees a chain saw ripping through the Dryad Tree.

Dark Star's grandmare, Lillian appears in the hatchling's dream. She whinnies, wakes...

Jewel who had just drifted off to sleep, hears Sunna crying. She sits up, and rushes to the other room. Dagon is safe. But what about Sunna? She can't call Rosetta at this hour of the night. Lotus is snoring lightly, as only a man who has just spent his seed can do. Jewel snuggles up against him but the hours will pass before she sleeps.

Arnica and Holly are dreaming together. A summer storm has begun to brew.

LX - Deception

Arnica and Holly were in the garden, picking strawberries.

"Three for the bowl," Holly sang out, "and one for ... Dark Star!" He set three of the bright red fruit into the crockery bowl and tossed one to the hatchling. The young unicorn was sitting nearby on the grass. The borage was not fully in bloom yet (borage flowers were among her favorites) but fresh strawberries picked by her humans were a fine consolation.

Arnica laughed. Dark Star's lips were tinted a bit pink from her morning feast. "Gino expects to be here for the Eve." Arnica referred to Midsummer Eve which would be the night after tomorrow.

"Just think," Holly mused, his fingers carefully picking more red berries, "Gino's first coven ritual was six years ago.... He was only eleven."

They shared mental images of the boy, freckle-faced and able to completely charm the hatchling, thinking her a young horse at the time. Now 17, he was a handsome, young man. Although he had two more years of Earthkin education left at Trillium School, it was clear that he would be a much-loved priest and leader as the years passed.

"Is Carlos meeting him at the train?" Arnica tossed a strawberry to Dark Star. She'd had quite a few and the sun, now shining upon her iridescent blue coat, was making her a bit drowsy. She almost missed catching the fruit.

"Tomorrow just past noon," Holly answered.

Gino was visiting his sweetheart in Mill City, over the River Mountains to the east. Jenny Flower, the daughter of Kristos parents, was working in Parliament. This was her second year as a volunteer page. Her father, Philbert, Deputy of Water, was once strongly committed to the Politicos, even active in the Users, the more right-wing faction of this conservative political party. Over the past year or two several events caused Mr. Flower to question things and he was now increasingly protective of the forest lands.

Jenny did not want to be away from Gino but her parents did not yet know she was seeing an Earthkin boy and she and Gino had more freedom by her spending the summer away from home. This fall, as a Junior at Merrydale High she felt it was time to tell her parents she wished to make a commitment to this wonderful young man.

The Circle would be smaller this Midsummer. The coven, who practiced the traditions of the Renaissance Tribes, was pretty much the faculty of Trillium School and now had much time together. In many ways, the school year was like an extended ritual. For some, their 'other' families (their blood relatives) had found it difficult to adjust to these new schedules. Flying Raven, the school's science teacher, was spending some time back in the Mothervalley. She had not seen her grandchildren in a year and her children had planned a family reunion in a beautiful park settled beneath the bluffs of the Genetricia River.

The Hatchling

Pearl, the small, Pictish coven member, taught art and music. She had never been that far east and wanted to collect some water from the sacred river to use when setting the dyes of her home-spun embroidery threads. She travelled with Raven and planned to spend the time during Raven's family reunion touring several of the fine art museums in Verdeville, the seat of Mothervalley.

Amber taught history and social studies at Trillium School. She was the only Earthkin of the Descendant Tribe among the coven and faculty and brought a sense of the true evolution of Lothloriën to the students. Amber drew upon her tribal myths, helping the students recognize that the Land of Lothloriën was older even than the Descendant Tribes. She also taught them to measure government not simply by the standards of the dominant political powers but to make decisions based upon what is best for all species at all times.

Amber's people were not at all comfortable with the current administration. Henley Schrobbe was too willing to appease the leader of the Users faction, Slade Hatchitt. The Descendant Tribes did not trust these men, fearing for their forests and for the future of the waters. Amber was joining her sisters and would be drumming deep in a cave known only to a few women in her tribe. They would fast and drum and sweat for three days, calling upon the Earth's spirit to protect their lands.

Iris and Dolly would be there. They had plans to leave Diana, now two, with Gino's parents, Rosetta and Carlos. Iris had news the other morning when Holly took some parcels to mail. The postmarm couldn't wait to tell him that Rosetta would be baby sitting and, she added, "Rosetta wants to borrow one of my books about the Goddess!" Could it be that Gino's mother wanted to become more learned in the Earthkin ways? Rosetta was the school cook, even teaching a cooking class, and Carlos had taken on the job of school maintenance after losing his job in the flour mills of Mill City several years ago. They had seen what Gino's studies had done for their son and were very pleased.

Jewel and Lotus would attend Midsummer's Eve as well. Their son Dagon, now seven, had been carried into the realm of the Faerie just seven years ago this Sabbat. What an adventure for Dark Star and the baby! Dagon definitely had 'the gift,' already reading and showing an understanding of the Mysteries. Dark Star had assured her men that she would *not* be passing through the portal. Dagon was now old enough that he and the hatchling would be working a simple 'magick' in the gardens while the adults were in the Stone Circle. Jewel and Lotus were in Mill City as well and would be taking the train back tomorrow, riding with Gino. Dagon was with them and they planned to leave Sunna with Rosetta. Sunna was a foundling who had been left at the cabin door. In the past year and a half there had been a tug of war. Jewel wanted to adopt Sunna and the local Earthkin thought it possible that one of the new baby's parents might have been from the Realm of the Faerie. But the Politicos did not like the idea and tried to turn the baby into an 'issue.' Just last autumn Slade Hatchitt had spoken publicly. The User decried allowing the baby to remain with 'such people,' touting his 'family values.' Jewel knew that she was an excellent mother and there was no man finer than Lotus. Fortunately, all of that had been laid to rest. The adoption papers would be signed this very day.

And Honey. The newest member of the coven had visited last winter and recently made a long journey, leaving behind his old life in Eastborough and now establishing himself in Merrydale in order to learn all he could from Arnica. Honey was temporarily staying with Jewel and Lotus but expected to be renting a little cottage behind the home of one of Trillium School's families.

Dark Star was sitting up now. Some images had passed through her reverie as she'd dozed in the sun. She was a little unsettled.

Arnica placed a handful of berries into the bowl. "Six strawberries for the bowl..." The herbalist paused. The hatchling fidgeted. *She* knew what was coming next. "And *two* for Dark Star." The hatchling's eyes opened wide as did her mouth. *Two* berries at once. Could the summer get any better?

But just then, the berries not yet savored, the hatchling looked puzzled, quickly got up and trotted off to the cabin in a hurry.

She came back, a troubled look on her face, and tugged at Holly's sleeve with her teeth.

"She needs to communicate," Arnica said, but Holly was already off with the hatchling, heading to the cabin. Arnica quickly followed.

They sat in the front room which also served as the coven's temple during the cooler months. Centered between the two men and Dark Star was the large, crystal orb.

"Wait for the telephone..." Holly had moved his mind into the orb to retrieve the images Dark Star was moving there.

Ring. Ring. The telephone rang and even though all three *knew* it would be ringing, they all three jumped.

Arnica unfolded his legs from the lotus position and quickly reached the phone.

"You've got to help!" Lotus was frantic. "Jewel's hysterical."

"Breathe." Arnica used the voice, the same tones when guiding someone deep into trance.

Holly sat close by, extending his hearing and the munchkin went to the orb, gazing into its crystal depths so she could know the conversation.

Lotus calmed himself. "We reached the Children's Office early. Jewel was nervous and we thought if we had a little time to settle down before the meeting ..." He took another deep breath. "Mrs. Miniver, the woman from the Children's Office, had assured us that there would be no difficulties with the adoption proceedings." Lotus' voice caught. He started to cry, then breathed deep, from his toes to his mind.

"Go on," Arnica lovingly urged.

"She was dressed in her new dress, the one Pearl had hand embroidered for her adoption day. You should have seen how proud Jewel was. Sunna danced for Jewel. We wanted to call Pearl and tell her but..."

But Pearl was in Verdeville on the Genetricia and Lotus and Jewel were in a hotel in Mill City, their dreams of Sunna legally becoming family with them filling their hearts with such joy. And now...

"Mrs. Miniver was very grandmotherly... She provided play things in the office. And then she said that we could sign the papers. She picked up her office phone and called for her secretary to bring the papers in. But it was Slade Hatchitt and two of his aides .... along with a police officer. And they took Sunna."

191

"They took Sunna?" Arnica's voice was loud, reflecting his shock. How could this even be legal?

"Hatchitt told us 'We cannot approve this adoption by heathen parents and consign this baby to hell. She belongs in the Kristos Arms.'"

"Damn." Arnica never cursed. He was so upset he almost said 'damn him,' but Hatchitt was not worth the 'damn.'

"She'll be O.K." Arnica's mind was already organizing what had to be done. At least they knew Sunna was in the orphanage. "Bring Jewel home. Tell her that Midsummer's Eve we will put the wheel in motion. Sunna will come home. Mother Goddess will provide."

LXI - Lost & Found

Rosetta offered the young unicorn a handful of succulent blueberries. After quickly nibbling them, the hatchling, Dark Star, leaned over and gave Rosetta a blue-lipped kiss on her cheek. Rosetta and the young unicorn were trying to have a 'normal' day. Arnica and Holly, the two men who lived here in this cabin in Merrywood, had made an emergency trip east, across the River Mountains and Rosetta was picking their blueberries for the men. All this chaos was hard for Rosetta. Her life had been simple. She and Carlos worked hard and led uncomplicated lives. Ever since her son Gino had begun studying Earthkin magick and Carlos quit working in the flour mills, Rosetta found herself increasingly drawn to the religion. It had been easier to passively take note of the wheel of the year in the ways handed down by her mother and her mother's mother but now that Rosetta worked at Trillium School, she found her interest in learning more about the Renaissance Tribes and their beliefs tempting.

Dark Star sat back. The hatchling's thoughts turned to her young friend Dagon. Six years ago she and Dagon had quite an adventure into the Realm of the Fairie.

Dagon had hoped to be shopping this weekend. Now seven, he would be starting school. His parents, Jewel and Lotus, had dreams that the local Earthkin people in and around Merrydale might someday have their own Early School. Trillium School, starting only its third year, had been very successful. There was already talk of adding the seventh grade. Then Trillium School would encompass what was both "junior" and "senior" high school in the public system.

Although he had been to Trillium School many times, this would be Dagon's first year in as a student. Dagon was very precocious for his age. The coven believed his unexpected Midsummer's Eve journey into the Realm of the Fairie was part of his magickal heritage. Jewel and Lotus had discussed their concerns with Arnica as coven priest and with Deodar Dolorum, Trillium's principal. In addition to clothing and school supplies, Dagon's father had promised to begin carving the boy's first magickal wand.

Although disappointed that he wasn't shopping with his mother, Dagon knew his parents had good reason to be gone. It was just before Midsummer's Eve that Jewel and Lotus had gone all the way to the Children's Office in Mill City. Located on the same street as the Parliament Building they expected to come home with Sunna, a lovely toddler believed to be two this coming Hallows. Sunna was left at sunrise on Arnica and

Holly's doorstep, much to Dark Star's delight. In a frightening turn of events, rather than the adoption moving forward as promised, Sunna was taken from them as they sat in the office waiting to sign the papers.

Lotus sometimes wondered where Jewel found her strength. At midsummer it seemed as if someone had unkindly stirred the cauldron of their lives but they were working on legal action, believing the courts would find Slade Hatchitt in violation of their rights. Hatchitt was well-known by the coven, a Politico with power who often tried to use it to further his belief that his fundamentalist Kristos views should be imposed upon everyone.

The call came at seven in the morning. Jewel didn't even know who it was. Lotus was carving some wood on the back porch and, when he looked up and saw Jewel's face, his stomach felt as if he'd been kicked. One of the staff from Kristos' Arms orphanage had called at seven in the morning to say that Sunna was lost in the mountains. "I could lose my job for telling you," was all the voice said.

Flying Raven was enjoying seeing her children and her grandchildren again. Oddly, she had expected she would miss the Mothervalley more than she did. She found herself thinking often of the forested regions of Merrydale, missing the 'family' of her coven and looking forward to her 'children' in Trillium School. She was sitting on the front porch of her daughter's house, a granddaughter sleeping on her lap when Holly's call came. Raven took the first flight, heading directly to Mill City. Gino, already in Mill City, promised to meet the rest of the coven who would be on the next train leaving Merrydale.

Jewel had first called Arnica and Holly. Next she called Iris and Dolly. Iris, Merrydale's postmarm, had some connections and the story quickly emerged. One of the Cathedral ministers and his wife had taken a large group of children from Kristos Arms to spend a 'night of prayer' at one of the Cathedral of Thorns' summer retreat centers. When the children assembled for their morning prayer, Sunna was nowhere to be found. The children were to have slept in dormitory tents, each holding ten children and one adult supervisor, but the adults had no idea how the little girl could have left the tent without being noticed.

The news spread quickly. The media loved it and the Conserver Party was quick to use it to their advantage, with news conferences targeting the faults of the Politicos and reiterating their claim that the business-friendly party was actually run by the Users, the right-wing movement growing in strength within the Kristos religion and within the Politicos Party. By the time the coven assembled for a quick Circle in River City, many volunteers had joined the government search party and once again Slade Hatchitt was defending his decisions regarding Sunna.

"Sunna!" Gino's voice was hoarse. The young man had been eager to help search. He only learned of Sunna being lost on the radio playing in the hostel where he was staying. Gino had been in Mill City for two weeks, convincing his parents to let him help Jenny sleuth for information about Sunna's 'legal abduction.' Jenny was working as a page in Parliament again this year. His parents had a long talk with him about dating a Kristos girl. They knew that Gino and Jenny were having increased difficulty holding their young passion in check. Gino hoped for an autumn betrothal. Seventeen was not an uncommon age among the Earthkin.

"Sunna, can you hear me?" Gino pushed aside some branches, his feet tired and arms scratched. Jenny's parents were Kristos, although political events caused Philbert to question some of the fundamentalist values, but the girl had not yet told them she was dating an Earthkin boy and wanted a betrothal. Jenny and Gino planned to talk to her parents this autumn after school was under way. In the meantime they both felt certain that despite their sexual longings they wanted to wait until she wore Gino's ring. For now, their time in Mill City had been secretive. Philbert Flower's daughter was easily recognized among the circle of Politicos. Her father having stood up to some of the unfair policies only made her more visible.

Gino could hear Iris and Dolly calling out further off in the canyon.

Their faces streaked with dust, Iris and Dolly looked and called out for Sunna. As parents, they thought often of Diana, safe at home. Pearl, the only covener not searching, remained in Merrydale to keep the postal shop open and watch Diana. Their voices called out, echoing those of strangers, of the government search party and many staff members from the Cathedral and orphanage who were sincerely distraught and genuinely upset with what had happened.

Amber, who taught history and social studies at Trillium School was working through the higher elevations. Dozens of her tribal sisters and their husbands and brothers were helping in the search. Although not all of the Descendant peoples understood why she would live and work with the Renaissance people, the Loon Tribe was close knit and they were supportive of Amber's work to bring the indigenous and the immigrant Earthkin peoples together. The Loon Tribe knew the high country well and could walk where the "New People" (as the Loon called them) were apt to slip and fall.

Arnica and Holly had just emerged from the brush. Holly sensed Dark Star. Even though the River Mountains separated them, he could feel the hatchling's presence, assuring them that she could sense Sunna and that she was safe. Now to comfort the parents with this 'news.' Arnica was no longer young but he worked hard in the gardens and he and Holly had done their part. Arnica knew that Lotus longed to help search but Jewel needed his support.

"I wish we had good news," Holly said quietly to his partner.

Arnica walked over to the distraught parents. Jewel threw her arms around the older herbalist. Her emotions burst through her restraint and her tears soaked into Arnica's sweaty shirt.

Holly put his arm around Lotus. They stood quietly.

"Put your trust in the Goddess," Arnica said.

His words had an immediate effect upon Jewel. Her inner will strengthened and the four of them formed a circle. Looking to the search parties and workers like a group hug, the four silently called out.

Pearl was holding Diana on one hip and counting out stamps for Maude Graves. "Just a moment," she said, slipping her hand into her pocket to caress a small, carved fluorite token. Pearl sat Diana on the counter and continued the conversation, but her inner voice began the coven chant.

Iris turned to Deodar. "Dolly," she said, pulling some sticker seeds from her sleeve, "they need us." They turned to go back to where Lotus and Jewel were waiting for news.

"Wow," Gino said, his freckles responding to two days in the sun. He'd nearly slid down an escarpment, suddenly distracted by Dark Star's voice speaking to his heart. Gino steadied himself and went running out, leaping over downed trees as only the young can do. He nearly ran into Honey.

C'mon, my friend," Gino called. "Catch me!" Honey, Arnica's new student, went running after Gino, their laughter a welcome break in the tension-filled canyon.

Amber felt the earth shift, even though there was no physical movement. "It's time," she said. "Call them all. Sunna's parents are waiting." The drum sounded calling all of the Loon Tribe.

Flying Raven limped toward the group. This was hard work for her and her feet were sore, her joints ached yet she wanted to do her part.

Within a minute or two the coven was joined, their arms about each other, their chant working silently. Just as they reached the final word, shouting roused them from their subtle trance.

"Look," one woman called out, "he's got the baby!"

Ollis Piper trudged from the woods, a large smile on his face and Sunna riding proudly on his shoulders.

Jewel ran to the toddler, her tears now joy-filled. Arnica felt calm. Once Holly told him that Dark Star was turning her thoughts toward them through the crystal ball, Arnica knew it would be soon over. He also knew that this time Sunna would not be taken from Jewel and Lotus.

He turned to Raven ready with a small joke about Sunna being this year's Lammas Harvest but Raven stood there, her mouth agape.

"Ollis Piper," she said, "it's you again!"

"Aye, m'lady," Ollis said, pleased to be on the threshold of life in Merrydale once again.

Lammas Eve two days later was quiet. Emotions needed resting. The ritual was more of a simple blessing although the berries needed picking and the herbs gathered just the same. Everyone was still tired yet drawn closer by this crisis.

Rather than the usual Sabbat Ritual the coven held a feast in Arnica and Holly's gardens by the cabin. Several of Amber's sisters made a rare trip to Merrywood for the event. Rosetta and Carlos were there, happy to be included. And Ollis Piper and Raven sat quietly beneath the rowan. That man had a lot of explaining to do.

LXII - Pledging Troth

Holly thought of the Nine of Pentacles with its image of an Earth Goddess standing before a grape-arbor, a messenger bird sitting upon her gloved hand. The basket at his feet was quickly filling with grapes and the nearby hawthorne was filled with finch songs. It was a good sign.

The harvest this year was amazing. The weighing of the crops was going to be record-setting for the gardens. Arnica's figures indicated more than enough herbs and fruits and foods for the coming year as well as meeting their annual tithing to the government. In addition, he was certain that the surplus, when sold at the market, would do much for their savings.

Holly's left hand cradled a full, sensuous bunch of grapes as his right reached with the clippers to deftly snip it loose. Setting the grapes into the basket, he stepped back to look at the arbor but just then the hatchling came running past, nearly knocking him over. Holly had just recovered his balance from the scampering of the young unicorn when next came Gino, chasing after her. Although seventeen, Gino could be very much a boy. And, Holly reflected, at seven years, Dark Star was still just a young unifilly. Sometimes Holly found it difficult to remember that Gino was now seventeen and eager to pledge his troth to Jenny Flower.

As the young man and unicorn went running gleefully along the path into the woods, Holly found too many thoughts buzzing in his mind. Arnica was over by the drying shed where the bundles of late-season vervain and rose geranium were newly hung to dry. Holly took a break with his partner of many years.

"Did they say anything of a Handfasting date?" Holly asked.

Arnica was weighing angelica seed into bags, dating them and marking the weights.

"Only indirectly," the herbalist said. He opened a tin, took out a small, foil-wrapped cube and began opening it.

"She just ran into the woods with Gino," Holly said, beginning to laugh. "but you know ..." And both men spoke in unison, "sometimes she's like a puppy."

Earlier this summer Arnica had made borage treats and discovered Dark Star could hear the wrapper being opened from quite a distance. The 'puppy' reference arose from a conversation in Merrydale. While they were waiting in line at the food market checkout the woman in front of them (with dozens of cans of dog food) was happily joking that her puppy could hear the can opener up to a mile away. The first time the men discovered that the hatchling could hear the borage candy wrapper from a great distance, "like a puppy" became their catch phrase.

Arnica came back to the topic. "Flying Raven wants to observe the old customs. She and Ollis figure that, at their ages, living together for a year will pass quickly. They're talking about going back to the Mothervalley to visit her children during the Hallows holiday." Hallows Eve was on a Thursday which gave students and faculty alike a four day Sabbat break. Arnica had offered to sit in on Raven's Monday science classes to give her and Ollis an extra travel day.

Just then a light clopping of hooves scurried up the path through the gardens. The hatchling trotted up to Arnica, her eyes bright and eager. She wanted the treat and quickly kissed his cheek and then nuzzled his hand. Arnica laughed and Holly threw his arms around her neck. What a threesome this family of two men and a young unicorn had become!

Arnica looked at Gino, their young friend brushing some seeds off Dark Star's coat. "Is that a new ring?"

Gino blushed. "Jenny gave it to me."

Gino had been dating the daughter of Becky and Philbert Flower. Philbert was the Deputy of Water, appointed by Slade Hatchitt. For many years a solid conservative, active in a strict Kristos church and a staunch supporter of the User faction of the Politicos, over the past year Philbert had begun questioning the extreme views of the Users and had two magickal visions (Dark Star had done her part) which he attributed to his Kristos god. Whether he would give his approval to Gino and Jenny pledging their troth was questionable. His Kristos beliefs considered the Earthkin religion to be evil.

And yet, their young love continued to grow in depth and who knew what magick a unicorn might work? It would be two years this winter that they'd been seeing each other and this had been the second summer Jenny was away at Mill City working as a page in Parliament. Now, they were busy again with school, trying to work out a plan so they could pledge their troth. Gino and Jenny had put last month's excitement behind them.

It was not so with Jewel. The memory of Sunna being spirited away by Slade Hatchitt who placed her in a Kristos orphanage, was too strong. Sometimes Jewel would waken in the middle of the night, her memory replaying the early morning phone call telling her Sunna was lost in the nearby mountains. It took but a few days after Sunna was found for the Children's Office to complete the adoption. It was near-record time, but now the toddler was legally Sunna Woodfolk. Dagon, now seven, was in his first year of school. Not only was Merrydale's public school a new environment for him, but he was officially a 'big brother' and enjoyed these changes. Dagon had once had his own adventure when a year and a Sabbat old. His journey into the Realm of the Faerie with Dark Star had left its mark upon him. Dagon was writing a magickal story to read to Sunna and Diana on Autumn Eve.

The coven was preparing for the autumn ritual. Dark Star was going to lead the procession through the gardens to the stone circle. Despite the undercurrent of worry over global warming, the warm evening was more comfortable than an early frost!

Dark Star was proudly wearing the new saddle basket, hand woven by Amber's Loon Tribe sisters. Amber took a late-summer trip to her homeland. She traded stories of this unicorn with her tribal grandmother's stories of tribal origins of the Loon Peoples. Amber would read the stories when teaching the history of Lothloriën's indigenous peoples.

Gino and Amber were preparing the saddle basket. The lad placed a bunch of grapes in each side, Amber some colored gourds and a woven grain dolly made in one of Pearl's art classes. As Gino set some bunches of herbs he'd learn to dry in the drying shed, Pearl attached some ribbons to Dark Star. The hatchling was looking very proud.

Lotus Woodfolk and Honey, the new coven member, a recent transplant from Eastborough, would carry the lit torches. The sun was setting early and although it would still be light when they began the procession to the stone circle, it would be quite dark upon their return. Lotus' hand felt the small amulet hanging under his robe. A lock of Jewel's russet hair was tucked in with other treasures: Dagon's first tooth and the first crescent trimmed from Sunna's finger when she was a baby. Although he missed Jewel, Honey was such a fun man and the torchbearers filled the gardens with laughter and light.

Iris teased Ollis. She first learned of him when he appeared three years ago and hadn't fully adjusted to having a father. Iris had been joking that she was losing Raven as a coven sister, wondering if this would make Raven her stepmother?

"You were nervous at Diana's baby blessing," she reminded him.

"But I've come a long way," Ollis mused. And he had. Not only his daughter but the woman he'd come to love, were both Earthkin people. Although Ollis had marked Kristos under religious affiliation in the Merchant Marine, he'd mostly avoided religion all together.

"Are you nervous?" Flying Raven had been pleased when Ollis asked if he might attend the sabbat. Raven didn't feel like Iris' stepmother. She had her own children. But she and Iris did believe that Raven would be a fine grandmother for Diana.

"No," Ollis answered. "Arnica's been a great help." Ollis came out to the cabin and helped clean up some downed branches. He was an eager student and bright when it came to theology. Ollis had seen a lot in his travels around Mother Earth.

Holly sounded the bell. Everyone grew quiet and moved into place behind the torches. Dark Star walked between them and Autumn Eve began. They could sit late around the fire. Tomorrow was Sunday and they could sleep late.

They walked the path toward the stone circle. There was much thanks to give. Lotus and Jewel knew their harvest was Sunna's adoption. Flying Raven's bounty was her troth to Ollis Piper. Honey's bounty was the new family found among the coven. Not only was he enjoying his herbal studies with Arnica but there was talk of him starting a morning day care at the school.

Amber was offering thanks for the many stories she'd collected. What started as a simple idea had grown into a goal to collect as many of the stories from her tribal elders as she could before the Loon Tribe's history was lost as had so often been the case with other Descendant Tribes. Pearl was simply giving thanks. She was only 36 and had been widowed for six years, yet she felt that her life was now growing and changing in so many creative ways.

Iris and Deodar gave thanks that Diana, two last Beltane, was healthy. Iris was concerned that Jewel would be unable to watch the postal shop on the mornings Iris taught citizenship and political theory, but Honey was a charm with the little ones and it worked out just well. Deodar was thankful that the school was going well. When classes began on September 2nd, the school now had 109 students and included grades 7-12, both junior and senior high. What a joyful sound as the students and faculty were gathered in the school hall for the ritual invocation of the new school year. If there was much more growth, the school would need to add faculty.

Gino knew that his harvest was Jenny. They were seventeen, in the eleventh grade. This was the traditional time when Earthkin pledged their troth if they truly believed they were soulmates. But Jenny's father... Did they dare?

Arnica and Holly gave thanks for the harvest of their gardens, for the joy of living with the hatchling. Arnica had been troubled of late, but Holly had helped him with a simple banishing ritual before the coven had arrived.

Henley Schrobbe, Lothloriën's Premier, had recently been holding press conferences and speaking in a worrisome tone about an 'enemy,' always undefined but increasingly blamed for a variety of ills. Schrobbe deflected criticism that the goal of the Users to cut more forests in order to favor industry contributed to global warming because his policy was now essential to protect Lothloriën against 'the enemy.' And on the international stage, when the Politicos were criticized by other world leaders, Schrobbe held a press conference claiming to have proof (which must be kept secret for 'security reasons') that global warming was being caused by 'the enemy.' More and more Schrobbe sounded as radical as Slade Hatchitt.

Those who were complacent about government and those whose nature it was to blame others rather than take responsibility were quick to jump on Schrobbe's bandwagon. This past summer some of the northern forests, usually protected against infestations of tree-loving beetles by Boreas' cold winters, were suffering huge losses of trees. Although ecologists and most within the Conserver Party spoke openly about everyone's contributions toward global warming and the need for changes, even if it required business and industry to scale back, Schrobbe had many followers willing to agree with him that the beetles were being released by this secret enemy, one which desired to undue Lothloriën's peaceful strength.

But the good news was that Loon School had just opened. Mill City, the seat of Parliament, was now home to the second Earthkin school. Encouraged, there was now talk of other schools being formed, Renaissance and Descendant Tribes alike, for many areas of Lothloriën. The future of the land lay truly in the young.

LXIII - No Daughter of Mine

"But Dad," Jenny pleaded for understanding, "he's *not* a devil-worshipper. Gino is honest, he's good, he treats me with respect and I love him." Jenny's blonde hair looked shadowed, reflecting her mood.

"Were you honest with me about this?" Philbert was very angry. Jenny was the darling of his heart. He cared more about her than almost anything but what he learned as she opened her heart to him created more fear than anything, even when he questioned his Politico Party about their ecological decisions and felt Slade Hatchitt's rage.

"Daddy," Jenny's voice trembled, "I never lied, but I did keep Gino a secret."

Why she had ever dreamed that her father might understand seemed beyond belief. There were minutes of silence, moments when both tried to speak at the same time, their voices emotional and strong.

Jenny was, after all, her father's daughter. Philbert Flower was a devout Kristos, active in the Church of the Martyr since he was a boy. As a young man he began volunteering for some of the User's causes, aligning himself with the more conservative faction of the Politico Party. As the religious right grew in strength, Flower's career grew as well - until last year when his growing discomfort with the tactics of some party leaders culminated in him stepping back from the Politico Party. Even so, he was proud that Jenny continued as a page at Parliament again this year. Flower's experiences of visions and voices when walking with Jenny among the trees of Merrywood had left him unsettled, only causing his daily prayer to be more fervent. Facing the knowledge that his daughter, his pride, had been dating an Earthkin boy, left him with a sinking feeling and a sense of dread.

"An *Earthkin* boy? The son of a cook and janitor?" Philbert was hurt to learn that his daughter had kept her romance from him, leaving him out of her life. His words echoed his pain and anger.

Earthkin sounded like a bad, vulgar thing in her father's phrase, but Jenny already knew better. She liked Gino's friends and knew they were honest and honorable, kind and loving. All of her experiences with the Renaissance peoples were very positive. The Kristos religion, unable to convert all of the indigenous peoples, had labeled the Descendant Tribes as evil. And as a growing number of people fell away from the Kristos beliefs and joined the Renaissance Tribes, seeking their pre Kristos roots, the Kristos leadership was quick to condemn them all.

Jenny was crushed. Gino had wanted to be there with her. Right now she wished he was, yet she was so glad he hadn't heard her father's bigotry.

"How can you talk like that?" she challenged her father. "The Earthkin are good. They see all of life as divine. They don't lie like some of your User leaders have." Jenny's emotions were racing. Her complexion glowed red from anger, in contrast to it's usual pale beauty. "Don't you remember what you heard when we were in Merrywood? Didn't you hear god? Don't be a hypocrite like the Users."

There was a slight gasp in the next room. Becky knew that her daughter had gone too far with her father.

"No daughter of mine can date an Earthkin boy." Philbert's voice was strong. "The Krista taught us that the Earthkin are evil. It is the word of God. I read it in the Book of Doom."

"Then I'm no longer your daughter."

Jenny ran to the front door, grabbed her coat, and was gone.

A week had passed since Jenny had left home. Hallows Eve was tomorrow and Jenny was still staying with Pearl Lamina. Becky Flower had brought Pearl enough of her daughter's things. Pearl was a gentle soul, well-loved by all the folk of Merrydale. Widowed for six years, she now taught art and music at Trillium School.

Philbert was not pleased that his daughter was staying with an Earthkin woman but he told himself 'it could be worse.' He respected Pearl. Everyone in Merrydale knew her gentle spirit. Jenny was settled into Pearl's guest bedroom, not knowing how long she would be there. Pearl was unconcerned, glad to have someone about her home. Neither Philbert nor Jenny were ready to apologize. Both were hard-headed and had said things which hurt the other's ego.

Becky cried frequently throughout the day. Yet she was more than a little pleased that Jenny had claimed the freedom to explore other beliefs. The afternoon after Jenny's stormy departure, Becky stood at Pearl's front door, timidly knocking. Walking up the path to the cheery, yellow cottage she was taken with the flower gardens with their charming, little hand-painted signs identifying the different species.

"Why, there are six different species of columbine!" Becky thought to herself. "Aunt Juanita would have loved this!" Becky's aunt had taught her how to make a wish using columbine when she was a teen. Becky still believed it was that wish which brought her and Philbert together. She loved her husband dearly, but sometimes she wished his views were, well, a bit *softer*. "I wonder if Juanita might have been Earthkin?"

Becky enjoyed that first visit so much. Pearl was wonderful. Becky had not been in an Earthkin home before and found it warm and inviting. Looking about, she noticed the absence of images of the Krista. Beneath the north window was a cabinet, holding a statue of a goddess. Becky knew her church considered this evil work, but it was so lovely. There was a candle, it's flame dancing in a blue votive. And flowers, and crystals and Becky thought it just wonderful.

"We women," said Pearl gently seeing where Becky's gaze was held, "we know that creation, *divine* creation, must have a woman's hand in it."

Jenny was flourishing in Pearl's home. Her experience with the Renaissance beliefs had been mostly through Gino. She knew he belonged to a coven and remembered that Gino had first begun studying from Pearl and her husband, before they moved to Cloverville in the hope it might improve Phoenix's health. Several times Jenny found herself wondering if *she* might join the Earthkin religion.

Pearl's gentle ways and creative skills allowed Jenny to be herself and to try new ideas. Jenny offered to tend the littlest ones on Hallows Eve. Diana, daughter of Iris and Deodar, and Sunna, daughter of Jewel and Lotus, were delighted with the offer. The girls loved playing together but were too young for the long ritual in the stone circle. Hallows Day was going to be Sunna's second birthday. When Jewel and Lotus signed her adoption papers this past summer, that became her 'official' birthday. Jenny thought it would be great fun helping the girls color some decorations.

Last Beltane she and Gino found their bodies eager for sex. "I could be expecting a child," she thought to herself, grateful that they'd held back. Jenny's time with Gino's friends helped her understand how valuable her freedom was as a teen.

Spreading her wings, Jenny had gone to Trillium School several evenings. Gino was working with his classmates and a few parents to decorate the school for Hallows Eve. Although most of the faculty and staff would be at the coven's ritual, the young people's sabbat was put together by a committee of parents with help from some of the older students.

Increasingly the need was becoming apparent that Trillium School students looked to the faculty to provide them with Sabbat rituals and experience.

"We've reached a point at which we have to have two Sabbat rituals. One for us, one for Trillium School," Deodar had said at the last faculty meeting. Although Trillium School had provided an environment reflecting the values of the Renaissance Tribes, the coven had not foreseen that the school would become the center of Renaissance Tribe religious life in Merrydale. They knew of several smaller covens but the local Earthkin were mostly a lot of believers who didn't practice much.

"But we grew up rejecting religion," one of the mothers said at a recent school meeting. "We are only now discovering that there are choices for us."

"We need to know what to do," added another student's father.

"And where can we go?" asked yet another.

The coven agreed with Deodar, although they hadn't yet decided how to regularly provide rituals at the community level. As principal, Deodar felt it his duty to be at the school and Iris wanted to be there with him. It was difficult for them not being with the coven.

Raven volunteered to be at the school as well. She had begun seeing Ollis Piper since he had once again turned up in her life. This time he appeared to be around for good and was establishing a good relationship with his daughter Iris as well as learning how to become a grandfather. Raven and the others learned about Ollis as well. The years he spent traveling in the merchant marine brought him world experiences. He had sought out many priests and priestesses of religions native to exotic areas of the world and learned much of geography and politics. Raven was embarrassed when she recalled how surprised she was to learn that he had a Master's Degree.

"Caught again by my stereotypes," she'd blushed.

Ollis was taking charge of the food drive the students were holding in their own version of a Feast for the Dead at the school's Hallows observance.

With lit votives in safe holders on the cabin's altar for Raven and for Iris and Dolly, the coven was dressed warm in the stone circle.

The eight of them were sitting around the circle, each facing one of the standing stones of the circle. The circle well cast, they had moved deep into trance in order to part the veils.

Dark Star sat at the Circle's center. An ethereal mist slid along the ferns and moss, mingling with the wisps of incense which drifted out of the cauldron and hung in the damp air. The air was damp but not uncomfortably cool.

Dark Star's eyes were closed, but if one looked closely, you could see that she was looking at something. Invisible to the others, her grandmare Lillian stood there. "You must be there for them," said her much-loved forebear, "your men have great challenges before them."

Arnica sat near the east stone, his body calmed as he moved himself deep into trance. Sitting before him was the image of Weaver, a dear friend who has passed into the Otherworld nearly a decade before. Weaver's cremated ashes had been placed near the great cedar. Always a pacifist, Weaver gave Arnica good counsel. Arnica's concern was for the young men who would be graduating from Trillium School over the next years. The murmurings of war were growing stronger. Schrobbe was too eager to plunge Lothloriën into war. Arnica often felt the weight of the future upon his shoulders.

Gino sat at the southeast. Phoenix, Pearl's late husband, was there. Gino was pleased to see his teacher again. Gino's counsel was to encourage him to enlist his fellow students' help.

Elstrum, an oak dryad, stood before Lotus, both in the south. "I know I was given leave to take my rest," the tree spirit's voice hummed, "but I'm here to plead for my kindred. You know wood." Lotus was skilled at carving and carpentry. "Can you not speak on our behalf?"

Jewel sat in the southwest. Silverwing, Deodar's grandmother, expressed disappointment that he was not at the Circle but found Jewel's ears to welcome her voice.

Honey knelt in the west, his head gently bowed before the Elvenkin Priestess. She was assuring him that a day care at Trillium School was just as important for peace as political activism.

Pearl, in the northwest, sensed Phoenix behind her back but held fast to her gentle chant to avoid losing her focus. Rebecca Morningstar, the first schoolteacher in Merrydale, wanted her attention. Hung for witchcraft in those pioneer days, Rebecca appeared but rarely.

Amber sat in the north. The daughter of the Descendant Tribes, the being before her was almost without form. The blood rushed through her veins and her mind throbbed with the ancestral war drums. She knew that her ancient ones were fearful of these new people. So many of their people had been killed when the Kristos missionaries first came to Lothloriën, bringing their armies and weapons. Amber's body stirred. It took all of her discipline to sit still and embrace the message.

Holly was at the northeast portal. Ladstar's spirit had appeared. "We hear the murmur of war," the youthful spirit said. Ladstar's ashes had been placed near the two firs nearby. "Are we not peace-loving peoples?" Ladstar asked. The young man's spirit spoke for them all.

LXIV - Students Unite

Arnica and Holly were in the potting shed, enjoying a rare Wednesday afternoon at home. Only its third year since opening, Trillium School had certainly changed their lives. Arnica was passing their pruning shears through incense while Holly sewed a small 'holly dolly,' a charm made of several leaves, a few berries and at least one drop of blood. The men were giving thanks for the day's harvest.

"Your charms have been wildly fertile," Arnica laughed, cutting the long branches of holly apart and stuffing them into large burlap bags. "Judging from the number of seedlings this year, we'll never have a shortage."

"No wonder the birds love the berries," Holly said, holding up a sprig. The berries were so bright they glowed with crimson as if the sun shone inside the shed.

By collecting holly for the school hall they were able to prune the hollies in the wooded area. Arnica worried that the woodruff devas were feeling too crowded and today they'd cut back an area of holly which was trying to overrun the woodruff.

It had been a warm, sunny afternoon. Dark Star romped along the paths, trotting to the shed and nuzzling her men, then off she'd go. There were many more garden days this year than usual but it left the men uncomfortable, thinking of empty mountain reservoirs and worrying about drought.

The weather seemed to be warming everywhere and yet Schrobbe's administration was pushing a resolution through Parliament giving large industry even greater access to Lothloriën's beautiful forests. The dryads had begun pleading with Earthkin able to hear their voices. The Descendant Tribes were growing fearful. What had once been a beautiful, wild land was increasingly turned to factories and it seemed that the growing number of the 'new peoples' were taking more and more from Mother Nature. All of the Earthkin, Descendant and Renaissance Tribes alike, considered themselves Children of the Earth and were working hard to educate the public. At the moment Lothloriën's politics seemed distant.

"Such exuberance," Holly said, watching the young unicorn race off to the woods. "What joy to be such a free spirit. Sometimes I wonder if Dark Star fully grasps how worrisome these times are."

"At least the unicorn realm is safe from war," Arnica's heart was often heavy. Henley Schrobbe, Lothloriën's Premier, seemed to be creating a mindset which could plunge the country into war.

The Hatchling

Dark Star, their hatchling unicorn, was seven and still young in unicorn years. The crisp nights and warm afternoons left her frisky. Arnica and Holly had surprised her with their afternoon away from Trillium School. Arnica's botany classes and Holly's literature classes were decorating the school hall for the weekend. When Dark Star saw her men walking up the lane she raced out to meet them and then scampered all about the property. The grove was filled with laughter, a welcome change for the hatchling who missed the life she'd had as a unicolt when the herbalist and his partner were always at the grove.

What joy she felt. This would be her seventh Yule. The coven would be celebrating Solstice Eve and she felt as much a part of the coven as any.

Just the lightest snow was falling. It was late Yule Eve. Arnica and Holly lay beneath the quilt, snuggled in the cabin. They slept deeply. The Solstice observance at the School was tomorrow. The students had asked that the Circle be used to invoke blessings for Merrywood and the other forested lands of Lothloriën. Other students had asked that the invocations to the renewed Sun be used to also invoke peace and harmony, traditional values during this time of year. There was talk among the students that some of their friends who attended Merrydale High were asking for invitations. It was the young who were willing to work together. Since the first protest to save the forest a few years back, the environmental movement was growing. Among older adults were many who were antiwar in their youth and the peace movement was only beginning to coalesce. The young were weaving them together with renewed vitality.

The other coven members were back in their homes in Merrydale. The ritual had been beautiful, followed by home backed treats and gifts. The gift-exchange had a lot of humor for there were few surprises.

Iris and Deodar Dolorum had brought framed invocations. Iris made most of the ink with formulas from Arnica but she managed to surprise the coven elder with the blue ink. That was Amber's gift, and she gave a tiny bottle to each of ink whose formula was held secret by her sisters in the Loon Tribe. Dolly, as Deodar was known to his friends, had made the frames, but this had meant the principal was spending time in the school woodworking classroom with Lotus. Jewel Woodfolk had made candles on the evenings when Lotus tended their two, but she needed Pearl's help to get them out of the molds.

Flying Raven gave fetishes Ollis had brought back from his travels. Visiting every continent and to hundreds of different countries, the former merchant marine had a rich knowledge of world cultures as well as an enviable collection of artifacts representing the global diversity of beliefs. Not only had he charmed Raven with his proposal, but he was a gifted storyteller and could hold his new students spellbound.

Honey gave one of the best gifts. He created a children's sabbat. Their newest covener had written a Yule ritual for the next generation. Diana Dolorum, two and a half, was there, and the Woodfolks were very happy that Dagon and Sunna would have such a fun night. Dagon loved being the oldest of the coven's children. His adopted sister, Sunna, was two and Dagon loved acting many of the ritual parts as he and Honey kept the little girls in awe of this 'magick.'

Gino, Dark Star's young friend, had asked the coven to bless a ring. He hoped to ask his sweetheart to pledge troth with him at Candlemas and he wanted the ring to spend the coming weeks sitting upon his altar. The hatchling had been so pleased because she was the first Gino had asked to bestow upon the delicate ring, one set with an emerald which once belonged to his great grandmother. He had been speechless when his parents sat him down and his mother offered him the small jeweler's box containing the heirloom. He knew at that moment that they trusted him and had faith in his growth into an adult.

Arnica's arm pulled Holly closer. Their dreaming began to merge. Nearby on a dresser was the hand-embroidered altar cloth Pearl made for them as a Yule gift. In the other room near the fireplace was the new pillow Pearl had made for Dark Star, but the hatchling was not there. Dark Star had quietly stepped out of the cabin, not at all easy. Her hooves made sharp sounds upon the wood floors. She sat in the Stone Circle, invoking the presence of Lillian, her grandmare. The hatchling had been experiencing recurrent dreams and all she could remember was that they had something to do with icicles. She hoped Lillian would solve the riddle.

Dark Star was not the only one up late at night. Jenny Flower knelt before Pearl's altar, learning how to pray to the Lady. Despite some nights of tears knowing she wouldn't share Kristmas with her parents (she and her father had not yet forgiven each other) she was learning to give thanks. She adored Gino and she wanted to take her first Lunar Month. After all, she'd been old enough for several years. She saw some of the girls at Trillium School wearing the mark of the Goddess and saw how it changed them. When she asked them they willingly spoke of the honor - and responsibility - of being old enough to conceive.

In a different area of Merrydale Becky Flower lit a candle. Jenny's mother was quietly pleased at how much her daughter had matured over the past months, and she recognized Jenny's free spirit was tempered with a maturity gained from her new Earthkin friends. Three of Jenny's classmates, members of the Church of the Martyr, had dropped out of school this fall. Despite the moral teachings of the church, Becky knew that many of the teens could not wait to consummate their young love. Becky suspected that Jenny and Gino wanted to pledge their troth but she didn't think it would happen this Kristmas. Or was that Yule? How curious were practices of the Renaissance Tribes, Becky had learned...

Philbert was already asleep. The solstice held no meaning for him and his dreams were of politics. The Users were pressuring him to return to his position as Deputy of Water. The right-wing faction of the Politicos believed him credible and, although Mr. flower had resigned from the Politicos a year ago last summer, the recent turbulence with his daughter had caused him deep trouble. He found solace in reading from the Book of Doom and, when attending the Church of the Martyr, it was his old, conservative friends who seemed the most supportive.

Throughout the land people felt polarized. The Users were growing in strength. Many of the Politicos felt that their party had been coopted by the right wing.

Meanwhile the Conservers, still feeling uncertain about their own future having lost some key seats in the last elections, found that speaking against Schrobbe's hawkish speeches left them tarnished as unpatriotic.

The Descendant Tribes were not much for politics but were discovering that trying to stay out of things only gave the Users the upper hand. Some of the Renaissance Tribes were trying to mobilize their numbers but some of the people expressed concern that their recently won rights (Trillium and Loon Schools) might be taken away. It was the young who got things going. The students at Trillium School and Loon School started petitions. Many of the public school students signed and began asking to join in.

Iris' classes in citizenship and government had become very popular with the students and every day the students were eager to discuss the news. Schrobbe's speeches were woven with threats of layoffs in Mill City and other cities if the forests were not made available to the industrialists. And in truth, people typically felt their jobs more important than the trees. Schrobbe spoke about loyalty to the Land of Lothloriën, weaving this theme with the need to support an increased military.

Jenny didn't know what the future would hold, but she felt that she and Gino were soul mates. Her heart spread its wings as she whispered to the Goddess.

Dark Star sat near Lillian's feet. The sweet, old unicorn began crooning a song to the hatchling. The hatchling began dozing. The snow was comforting and touched with peace.

Jenny tiptoed off to bed, not wanting to wake Pearl. Tomorrow was a big day at Trillium School and Jenny was ready to attend the ritual and to watch Gino performing in a key role. It was already Yule morning in Merrydale and Jenny Flower was the last to sleep.

LXV - Of Horns and Icicles

It was a late January morning when Dark Star discovered an icicle hanging from a cabin eave. It was a crisp, sunny morning following two days of snow. Her men were still in bed as she quietly moved her hooves across the cabin floor and slipped out to romp in the snow. And then, there it was, catching the sun like a slender crystal.

There was something in it's shape which fascinated her and she sat back, entranced with it. She couldn't stop looking at it when suddenly, it all fell into place. This was the answer to her grandmare Lillian's riddle. Dark Star recalled last Yule Eve late at night when she had gone out to the stone circle to seek her grandmare's counsel.

Her mind had slid into the realm between worlds, that place in which the astral reality of unicorns took form. The hatchling's grandmare, Lillian, appeared. The hatchling could hear the beautiful, gray unicorn's voice as her elder bent, stroking Dark Star's mane with her many-spiralled silver horn.

"My dreams, grandmare," Dark Star questioned. As Yule had neared the hatchling had begun having recurrent dreams about icicles and they made no sense. She found herself unable to even turn to Holly with her question and instead spent Yule Eve's midnight out beneath the trees.

Lillian's kind eyes twinkled in the dark and then the hatchling heard her grandmare speak:

"When a unicorn's horn drips down from the sky, meeting one from the earth, growing way up high..."

But Dark Star didn't know what that meant. Since that night, she often spent her quiet time alone at the grove walking back to the stone circle and calling for Lillian, but all she got was the memory of her ancestor's voice. There was something about Lillian's voice that held Dark Star back from asking Holly when they communicated through the orb.

"Look at her," Arnica chuckled. He looked out the kitchen window. Their young unicorn was sitting in the snow, a bewildered look upon her face.

"I wonder what she's thinking," Holly mused. Dark Star had something on her mind but even when the hatchling and Holly opened their thoughts to each other through the crystal ball, there was some secret she kept quiet. Holly and Dark Star had never held back before.

Dark Star was puzzled. A drip of pendulous water hung from the tip of the icicle, then plummeted down. The hatchling looked down and saw that many drips had landed this morning, and a small lump of ice was forming. Suddenly she knew. She jumped up, all four legs suddenly in motion. Why, this was just like the image in Gino's geology book.

Arnica and Holly were glad to see her so wound up. The hatchling had been a little quiet the past two days and, frankly, had seemed distracted since just before Yule.

"It's going to be a fine day."

In her own words, that's what Dark Star was thinking as well. Her riddle had been solved and she looked forward to explaining to Holly and Arnica that this summer would bring an adventure. The hatchling knew that this summer she would be led to a cavern where there were stalactites like icicles and stalagmites like unicorn horns. Yes, it would be a wonderful day she thought, kicking up her heels and trotting to the cabin door.

Later on that same day Gino and Jenny had walked back to the stone circle. There was too much snow in Merrywood for them to walk to their original goal of the Dryad Tree. It was from that tree that the spirit world had so changed Jenny's life. Moving out of her parents' home, she now lived with one of the coven, Pearl, who taught art and music at Trillium School where Gino was a Junior. Jenny was adjusting to the school, but it was an easier transition than she had expected. The classes were just as challenging but she was bright and learned quickly. Since she moved last Hallows she had spent quite a bit of time at Trillium School and was very happy there, feeling strongly that she wanted to convert to the Renaissance Tribal ways. Actually, she secretly hoped that she might some day be invited to join the coven which met at Arnica and Holly's cabin.

Gino spread a braided rug on the leaves in the stone circle. The trees overhead had kept away most of the snow and the ground was mostly bare, but cold. He took a small votive candle and glass holder from his knapsack. There were a few other items as well: some sticks of rose-scented incense, sage for smudging away worrisome feelings, a small bottle of blessed water from the last Full Moon ritual.

Candlemas was only a few days away. Gino had pointed out the swelling buds on many of the trees as they had walked from Merrydale out to the cabin. They stopped to play with Dark Star but after a few minutes the hatchling went running off, as if she needed to gallop in the snow.

Dark Star knew that Gino wanted this time alone. The day before he'd come out and showed her the ring he had now in his pocket.

"Look, munchkin," he said, calling her by her unicolt name, "this once belonged to my great grandmother. It's an emerald."

And it was, a modest but beautifully-cut stone. The color reminded Dark Star of a green she had seen in one of her ancestor's eyes. The stone was passed down mother to daughter. Rosetta, having no daughters, believed that Gino and Jenny were well-suited. She trusted her son's choice. Gino's training with the coven and his growing role at Trillium School had made the Rosario family so proud of their son.

Gino and Jenny sat within the stone circle. It would be nine years ago Candlemas that Dark Star's egg had appeared here. Gino was looking at the ring he'd been wearing these past months as they spoke about their growing commitment. The small ribboned box was in his pocket, just waiting. Their conversation had much to cover.

Gino felt ready to pledge his troth with Jenny. He knew that she wanted to pledge to him as well. Gino and Jenny had spoken with his parents. Rosetta, always concerned about a mother's role in life, worried that Becky Flower might be unhappy with her daughter's engagement. Jenny assured Mrs. Salvia that her mother had told her that she was proud of Jenny's growing independence. Jenny was over sixteen and was of legal age.

Rosetta had felt assured when she met Jenny's mother at Trillium School the day Becky Flower had come to sign the forms so Jenny could change schools. Becky was nervous. She knew that Philbert would be troubled when he learned that his daughter was now going to an Earthkin school. Jenny and her father had not yet spoken but their mutual anger over his disapproval of her choices was cooling.

Rosetta and Becky looked at each other, each knowing the other to be the mother of their child's love. There was some concern but each saw in the other the values reflected in the young. Despite the passion flamed by their young bodies, Gino and Jenny had not yet pledged their troth and their love remained unconsummated. Rosetta walked with Becky to the school's entrance after they left Principal Dolorum's office. They stood quietly by the front doors, curiously holding hands, exchanging support and compassion.

"He's a good son," Rosetta said. They had not even spoken of Gino.

"I know," Becky answered. "She did tell me all about him one afternoon." Becky had visited her daughter at Pearl's home. Philbert had gone over the River Mountains, east to Mill City, to Parliament. His separation from his beloved daughter was nudging him back to involvement in the more conservative wing of the Politicos, even though he had resigned from his position with the Users nearly two years ago.

Their kiss left them breathing heavily, their breath forming small, soft clouds of steam in the cool, afternoon air.

Jenny's first ritual had been completed and she was now ready to take the mark of the Goddess. Last night she had prayed hard, sitting on the floor before Pearl's altar. Pearl's favorite Goddess statue reflected the candle light with a loving glow.

Jenny had learned that her new Earthkin friends called the onset of menses "celebrating their first lunar moon." These girls were honored each year at Candlemas, the "Eve of the Waxing Light." The symbol of the Goddess was drawn upon their foreheads in blue. Jenny wanted this, even though she would be several years older than the other girls.

"I..." Gino's hand was in his pocket with the ring box. He didn't know what to say.

"What?" Jenny asked, uncertain of his unspoken words.

"Oh, Jenny," he said. "You know I think about our pledging troth every day."

"I know that I want to bring our child into the world," Jenny said. "Pearl is teaching me how to meditate and twice this week I've seen him. He's waiting."

Gino wanted this young woman so much, yet he looked startled.

"No, not yet," Jenny said. "First we finish school. Until then..."

Until then Jenny knew they had not formally made their decision. She realized now that Gino wanted to ask her to pledge her troth to him.

"I'm still only learning about our religion," she said. "I don't want to rush our baby's spirit," she added. From what several of the girls at Trillium School had said, a couple, once betrothed, were blessed if they chose to consummate their troth yet both were expected to exercise their knowledge to avoid parenthood. They were believed mature enough to embrace the Great Rite but not yet ready for parenthood. Jenny felt there was too much to learn. She wanted to learn about the herbals Arnica would offer her to help her avoid conception until the timing was good.

Dark Star sat before the altar in the cabin. Holly sat nearby, moving himself down, into a trance. Arnica was at his desk in the other room, quietly working to finalize the preparations for Candlemas Eve for the coven and the next day's Candlemas Sabbat ritual at the school.

The hatchling formed the images of the cavern.

"Where," Holly silently asked.

"She hasn't shown me yet," Dark Star indicated. Lillian would be bringing her more information in the coming months.

Holly could see how the coven's lives were fit together like pieces of mosaic. Jenny would be there, too. The mark of the Goddess was on the girl's forehead in Holly's vision.

Jenny kissed the ring upon her finger. Oh, how she loved the idea of the Goddess. She loved Gino and she loved her new life as well. Somehow, knowing that she was preparing herself for vows as a daughter of the Goddess, her sensual desire was not diminished one bit but her spirit was tempered with the delicious quality of patience.

LXVI - Babies and Eggs

Trillium School's kitchen was bustling with activity. The scents of herbal dyes, Rosetta's home-made vinegar for setting the colors, and wisps of incense were woven with the murmur of chants and lively conversations, filling the school with Magick. Arnica and Holly were having a wonderful time.

Rosetta, Gino Rosario's mother, was the school's cook. This was a major event, and in *her kitchen*. It was filled with students coming and going. When not in the kitchen dying their eggs, they gathered in classrooms and in the hallways, sitting on the floors and working on their eggs, writing words calling for peace.

Pots of bright, herbal dyes raised steam as an offering to the Goddess. Arnica had formulated numerous recipes. Using lore learned from his teacher decades ago, young Gino helped him by taking notes as the elder herbalist recalled the phrases and formulas.

And then the new recipes, based upon a lifetime of experience. All of this was now recorded into his herbal grimoire, safe for future herbalists.

Pearl Lamina, the school's art teacher, had been working with her students to create stencils and transfers. Two rooms were set up with quill pens and water-proof ink for those wanting to write wishes and blessings on the eggs, looking as clear and visible even after the eggs had been dyed. These eggs would be the ones left for all to see following Eostara.

The noisiest room was the crafts room where Lotus taught wood-working and other tools' skills. Their son Dagon would be eight years old in May. Lotus and Jewel had more freedom to be involved in their community. Sunna, their darling adopted daughter, was two this past winter, and having a gleeful time playing in the school's nursery. When Jewel learned that her husband would have eight or nine fathers who volunteered to 'needle the eggs' and then carefully blow out the raw yolk she and the other wives teased the men until there wasn't a 'hot air' joke left in Merrydale. This morning the tool shop was frequently erupting with whoops and bursts of laughter and, as the eggs were emptied, dozens by dozens, the fathers' diaphragm muscles were beginning to whine.

Trillium School echoed with laughter and it was good. This was a troubled time in the Land of Lothloriën. In many ways life had never been better. The coven was working on next fall's curriculum for the school's fourth year. Merrydale was proud of having the first Earthkin School throughout the country.

Loon School, over the mountains in Mill City, offered a curriculum for the Descendant Tribes whereas Trillium School's coven was better trained to teach the Renaissance ways. One would think that the growing religious freedom and prominence of the Earthkin was an indication of a growing enlightenment throughout the Land of Lothloriën. And yet, Henley Schrobbe, Lothloriën's premier for the past two years, had moved the country significantly to the right, sounding a call for military involvement far across the Atlantikos.

The older boys were meeting with the principal, Deodar Dolorum. Deodar and Ollis Piper, the new geography teacher, had met twice with Mayor Browning. When Trillium School first opened, some had expected a rivalry with Merrydale High, yet the opposite had proven true. Iris, Deodar's wife and the local postmarm, had the students in her classes study whether it might be Schrobbe himself who was indirectly promoting unity. At least in the District of Merrydale there was a growing public support for living in harmony with the wonderful forests and mountains of Lothloriën.

Many of Merrydale High's students had come to last December's Solstice observance, wanting to join Trillium's students invoking blessings for Merrywood and other forests, calling for increased peace and harmony for the world.

At a recent faculty meeting Iris commented that "the more Schrobbe's politics call for loyalty and increased military strength, the stronger our young grew in their desire to work together for peace. What a blessing!"

True, there were a few hawks among the Users, as the radical right of the Kristos churches and the Politicos Party were called. They advocated using the forests for financial gain and believe that the earth is theirs to use and dominate.

"I spoke that way once, and believed it," Deodar said. He was once the Church of the Martyr's minister. His conversion to the Renaissance beliefs certainly stirred things up but when he and Iris married and had a baby many of the Kristos saw them as a focal point for all that was good about Merrydale.

"We've got to learn not only about our own Lothloriën but about the world." Jenny Flower was increasingly passionate about global politics. Now enrolled in Trillium, she thrived. She loved the citizenship studies and was getting top grades. Iris taught them to follow the news and learn all they could not only about Lothloriën.

"Did you know the Premier of Atalanta and every one of their barristers voted to go on record against Schrobbe's request for military support?" Jenny asked a former classmate whose grandmother lived just a half day east of the great Motherflow River in a small village.

"Nana wrote me about that," the girl answered.

Jenny had learned so much about the world. Although many of the older generations knew little of life across the Atlantikos, Trillium School's students were urged to learn all they could. Jenny's passion for learning was fueled by her new life. She tried hard to avoid bragging when she showed the girls her ring after she and Gino pledged their troth last month. "But they asked," she assured herself.

Jenny understood the nature of conflict. She no longer felt resentful of her father's disapproval of her Earthkin fiance. She wrote her father a very nice letter, apologizing for storming out her parents' house last autumn. When Philbert made derogatory comments about Gino's parents being the school's cook and custodian, she knew this was his Kristos' belief that all Earthkin were the work of some devil. But it didn't stop her from feeling very hurt. Last summer they were growing close and Philbert even broke away from the Users, caring for the land.

But now Mr. Flower felt that his visions a year and a half ago near the Dryad Tree were the work of evil and that Jenny moving out was a punishment for him having failed his faith. Philbert was once again in Mill City, working hard for the Politicos and his own beliefs were once again toward the far right.

"I'm worried about Honey," Amber, the social studies teacher mentioned to her friend Raven.

"I am too," Raven answered. "One of my grandsons got a conscription notice the other week as well."

"He's got to make his own decision," Holly said, although his heart wasn't in it. Holly and Arnica had given Honey information about filing as a conscientious objector and also the names of some friends living far to the south in Azteca, should he wish to leave the country to avoid the war, if it did come to that.

The three covenmates were carefully wrapping and setting the hollowed eggs into egg flats where they could safely await the Sunday parade.

Merrydale *loved* parades. The User members of the Church of the Martyr planned a prayer service but they knew most of the churches members would be at the festive event. Parades for peace were planned in cities throughout all the provinces.

"I hope you all love scrambled eggs and omelets," Rosetta said, bringing two more finished eggs to the three. A big school breakfast was planned before the parade. Gino's mother loved being able to feed people.

"These eggs were painted by the little ones," Rosetta held them up. "Honey is letting the toddlers make eggs as well."

Throughout Lothloriën the spring festivities had an undertone of anxiety and worry. The peace marches brought comfort and raised peoples' spirits and yet, Schrobbe managed to activate conscription.

Lothloriën's Premier saw Italica as a potential market. Henley had great plans and they seemed to be growing. Schrobbe's vision harvested the trees of Lothloriën. Lumber was a valuable commodity across the seas. Italica, an ancient country, had few forests left. Old-growth lumber brought high prices. But italica wasn't ready to buy. They were distracted with a border skirmish with some Saracenites. This was an old war, one which had never ended. Italica was long ago converted to the teachings of the Krista but the peoples of Saracenia still practiced their old tribal ways, worshipping a male deity they knew as Bawa'al. Bawa'al was a ferocious god, the type which could give people the strength to survive the harsh, desert conditions. Neither religion was particularly loving nor forgiving although both religions taught those values.

Schrobbe saw this as an opportunity. If he could help Italica defeat the Saracenites, the result would be prosperity and a demand for lumber, cheaply freighted across the Atlantikos. The Users had real financial power these days and the Politicos had managed to make many voters fearful of unknown dangers. Schrobbe lobbied Parliament and young men now faced conscription. Lothloriën had not seen conscription since the Great War which took place so long ago there were few elders who were alive when it ended.

But today many of Merrydale's young people were coloring eggs. There would be eggs to bury as "peace for Lothloriën's future" was planted in the parks and in a loose circle surrounding the city limits. The hollowed eggs would be hung from trees to remind people that the birthing of peace was believed by the young more important than Schrobbe's grand vision. The school was alive and filled with vitality and, at least in Merrydale, people were promoting peace and joy.

Many days had passed. The people of Merrydale still spoke of the activities of the past Sunday. Since she was allowed to wear the mark of the Goddess upon her forehead, Jenny had created her own altar. How proud she was, having been given a 'fertility egg' by Gino's coven. It was a gift of love, a blessing for the baby which awaited her and Gino in their future. As she sat in the Stone Circle with Dark Star, the image of the egg flickered in her mind and Dark Star nudged her with her horn, as if the two could share their thoughts.

Jenny and Dark Star often spent time together. Both of them missed their parents. Dark Star knew that she had been sent to Merrywood to fulfill an important destiny. She had come to believe that Gino's young woman might be playing a role in this as well.

A few weeks back, Jenny had a New Moon dream. In it she saw Dark Star wearing a garland of flowers. Although the words weren't clear, Jenny awoke in the middle of the night and knew that somehow, Dark Star was to be the Maiden at her Handfasting.

Two days later she learned from Holly that Dark Star had dreamt of Jenny. Holly didn't share the details, not yet knowing quite how it all fit together. Jenny was standing, skyclad, in a cavern. It may well be the cavern waiting at the end of this summer's quest. This Dark Star communicated to Jenny through Holly.

It was a warm, sunny spring day. Jenny held an orb in her hand. It was a gift from Arnica and Holly who bought it for the girl after seeing the special bond forming between Jenny and Dark Star. She was trying to learn how to communicate with the hatchling but, for now, it seemed to no avail.

Dark Star was pleased. It was too soon for the young human to see the babies in her future.

LXVII - The Expedition Takes Shape

"Dyubkz...." Holly was having some difficulty sounding out the word. "I've never heard of them, have you?"

"I have, actually," Arnica mused. "I remember back in my university days taking a course in world governments. They were a tribal people who invaded many of the countries in Europa. Just the other day," he paused, drinking from his mug of meadowsweet tea, "I looked at my old books. I wanted to better understand the ancient roots of the enmity between the Saracenians and the Italicans."

Dark Star, laying near the hearth, began to doze off. Her horn rested on Holly's knee, but she was tired. The hatching had been studying hard and she was discovering what the young humans must be experiencing at Trillium School. She much preferred being a unicorn.

Pearl and Flying Raven were making ribbons for the Maypole. They took turns ironing the wrinkles out.

"I was so sorry to see him go," Raven said. They were talking about Honey, a young man who had moved to Merrydale from Eastborough just last year. He quickly fit in with the coven and had been planning to open a day care at Trillium School.

"Diana and Sunna will miss him," Pearl answered. Honey was good with children and often tended Diana Dolorum, the almost three year old daughter of Deodar, the school's principal, and Iris, the town's postmarm. Sunna would celebrate her third birthday at Hallows. She was a foundling, left on Arnica and Holly's door on Yule morning but had been adopted and was much loved by Jewel and Lotus Woodfolk.

"He'll do well." The coven had loved Honey. He was cheerful and helpful and they had hoped he would enjoy living in Merrydale, but Honey was often restless. His father had been an adventurer and Honey surprised everyone when he announced he was moving to Delphine, a city in Atalanta, where he hoped to establish his own learning center.

"The Mother Goddess of the planet humans call Earth manifests Herself in three aspects. When She descends to Earth in all three forms at once, the Three will often be seen riding upon the three Dark Lords of our Unicorn Ancestors..."

Arnica and Holly worked hard to translate some of the material Dark Star received from Lillian, the hatchling's grandmare. They had been brought two of the sacred scrolls protected by the Unicorn Elders. Arnica and Holly, sworn to secrecy, found that the only passages they could translate were those relevant to the expedition. All else was beyond any of their skills and magickal knowedge.

Amber's history and social studies students were hard at work. With Honey leaving Merrydale, the future for a day care at Trillium depended upon finding someone. Amber wanted to speak with two widowed sisters, Topaz and Peridot. They might just be interested. But Amber's priority was working in trance with seven of her Loon Tribe sisters in their sacred cavern deep beneath the River Mountains. It took the women nearly two hours to descend down to the ritual space alongside an underground spring.

Arnica sent a small vial of his special formula, the ointment which would make Dark Star's horn temporarily invisible. Amber also carried a small, quartz sphere in a special linen pouch, hand embroidered by Pearl. The quartz provided a link to the Orb Arnica and Holly had used for years. Dark Star communicated to the men through it. This would be a strong link and should assist Amber in scrying the location of the mystical cave Dark Star had seen in her visions.

Seated within the circle of candles with the others, Amber rubbed her drum with the ointment and it seemed to vanish. The women drummed and chanted as Amber journeyed into the womb of Mother Mountain seeking the answer to Dark Star's riddle.

The drumming and chanting echoed in the chamber and the crystalline stone seemed itself to chant and vibrate in response. Amber's drum was completely invisible and she felt herself passing through the portal into the Otherworld.

"Aiyee..." Her voice called out and she swooned. The Loon Tribe women continued to drum and chant, drawing strength from seeing that Amber's quest would be successful.

"That's a hard word," Holly said, stumbling over the phrase *Ghulghul invasion.*

"They were horseriding tribes temporarily united under the first Khan, the one known as Dyubkz Khan, who led them from their mountainous homes with promises of wealth and land if they conquered neighboring countries and then went beyond even those." Arnica remembered the paper Deodar had found, his voice sounding like a university lecture.

"The Ghulghuls were preparing to cross the mountains to enter Europa with a large and barbarous army known for their ability to terrorize villagers with their torching of homes, slaughter of all but the young women whom they would take for slaves..."

Dark Star was gazing at the Orb, not listening closely when suddenly she *saw* images of the event taking place. Her hair bristled and she sat up, now listening with care as Arnica continued his story.

"As the horde neared the mountain pass the sky darkened. Thunder clouds gathered overhead and lightning began to strike. Suddenly, three unicorns appeared at the crest of the pass, rearing up and making fearsome sounds."

The hatchling whinnied in approval, her heart quickening as she saw the three stallions looking fierce and threatening.

The Hatchling

"The Ghulghuls believed the unicorn holy. There was a mention of a unicorn being sacred to their god in one of their religious texts. It was a powerful sign to them and they called off their planned invasion and returned to their homeland. Euoropa was safe."

The coven was collectively working on Dark Star's quest. The images had begun appearing to the hatchling even before Yule. She turned to her grandmare Lillian who had responded cryptically, but that information helped the hatchling realize that it wasn't an icicle in her vision but the stalactites of a cavern.

Trillium School had become the coven's primary service to their community and the importance of the quest brought it into the school in subtle ways. Deodar, once a Kristos minister, thrived since his discovery of his Earthkin heart. Now the school's principal and a proud father and husband, he researched unicorn history. Despite how secretive the astral realm of unicorns had kept their lore, the day he brought the paper to his ethics class which related a documented, historical event which took place nearly a millennium ago in which unicorns had been instrumental in stopping war, the students were fascinated.

Jenny Flower, whose father was a prominent member of the Politico Party, had left home, unable to reconcile her father's close-minded beliefs. Enrolled in Trillium School (her mother secretly pleased at her daughter's maturity and growth into an intelligent, independent young woman) Jenny was thriving. Having taken the mark of the Goddess near Candlemas, she was now studying with Jewel and had begun participating in some of the coven's work. Jenny created a button which read 'wage peace' and had a drawing of a unicorn in the background. She made enough for her classmates in Ethics it was instantly popular. Several classmates had taken over the button-making and selling them as a fund-raiser for the school. Word had it that nearly all the students in Loon School, over the mountains in Mill City, were now wearing the buttons as well.

Pearl was bringing her embroidery skill to her art classes. When the students found out that she was teaching not just the needle's wisdom, but how to do magickal stitching within a cast Circle, the class was rescheduled to meet after hours and had to be moved to the school hall. Rosetta, Gino's mother, was participating. Iris, who also taught geography and citizenship, tried to be there for as many of the classes as her busy life allowed. Unknown to the students, the stitching magick the adults were doing was for a special robe Dark Star would wear into the cavern.

Gino stood behind Jenny. Although not yet an initiate, the coven knew that Jenny was the best choice for the role of the Goddess for this Beltane Eve. Only Jenny could be the Maiden as Gino invoked the Green Man, the role the coven traditionally gave to the newest male initiate. The young lovers remained poised between adolescence and maturity, sometimes wanting to frolic and play like children. Other days their longing to consummate their vows, to unleash the sexual hunger their love kindled was almost more than they could manage.

But they did manage, drawing upon the highest ideals of the Renaissance Tradition of their coven. Although eighteen (well, Jenny would be in less than two weeks) and having pledged their troth it was their own choice. At times, like now as Gino helped her practice invoking the Goddess, Jenny could *feel* the child they would have. In Earthkin ways it was acceptable for them to express their love physically. Gino and Jenny were

215

learning from the coven which herbs would prevent conception and perhaps it was some of Jenny's Kristos upbringing or a desire they both had to prove to Philbert Flower that they were very responsible.

Today, as they prepared for Beltane Eve, Jenny had never been happier. Learning how to live in harmony with the earth, coming to understand how the Renaissance Traditions taught one to be part of all that exists, she felt more religious than she ever had attending the Church of the Martyr. This was what she'd always believed in. She was betrothed. Settling into her new school she was getting top grades. If only her father could be happy for her...

Fighting off distraction, Jenny recalled what Pearl told her one afternoon. "Don't wear the clothing of his sorrow." Those words had often given her strength. This Sabbat would be Jenny's first serious working with the coven. And the following Sabbat? She would be participating with all of them in Dark Star's quest.

The coven was working hard to 'wage peace.' Each of them was working in some way, whether researching and studying and helping the hatchling with her learning or preparing themselves for the journey. Even Ollis, newly studying to become a Novice, was offering his experience from travelling the world as a merchant marine. He had visited those areas of Saracenia where Henley Schrobbe wanted to use military means to further the financial gains of his close advisors. Ollis had several small, unusual stones from the terrain and a small, hand-carved statue of Bawa'al, the Saracenian's god which would prove useful.

Not only the coven, but close friends of theirs were busy at work as well. Although she lived in Highlands, a long distance from Merrydale, Wren planned to join the coven when they accompanied Dark Star on her quest. She was using her skills as a bard to write a song which would weave protection around Dark Star and those who descended into the underworld with her.

Arnica was using the threads of Wren's melody and lyrical imagery to help him as he created a new formula for the hatchling's horn ointment, one which would last throughout the journey to the cavern. Dark Star would step through the veil for counsel from Lillian on Midsummer's Eve and at Lammas as their Earthkin friends celebrated the sun, they would be descending into the Underworld.

As the Descendant Tribes prepared to celebrate the dance of the Great Deer Father and the Corn Maiden and as the Renaissance Tribes of Lothloriën prepared for Beltane, the coven was preparing to use unicorn magick to wage peace on Schrobbe's militaristic desires. When Dark Star found herself wishing she could play with the young humans at Trillium School, she thought of Arnica and Holly, of the humans she knew. Their commitment to this work made her whinny. And she thought of Gino and Jenny, knowing the young lovers would be there as well.

Dark Star returned to the Orb, seeking to commune with the ancients who brought an end to the Ghulgul invasion.

LXVIII - Once Again Through the Veil

Small candles held in glass lanterns were set along the path from the shrine to the goddess Diana, nestled into the base of the old cedar leading back to the stone circle. They had paused at the shrine before taking the path back into the woodland.

Arnica aspurged them with some herbal water, made with a special formula which helped them leave all thought of war behind. Arnica and Holly's cabin and gardens always seemed a place of peace and harmony, yet war clouds continued to loom in the land of Lothloriën as Henley Schrobbe, the Premier, continued to push for war. Thousands of young men from each of the Districts had been conscripted and were now being trained in military camps. Some had already set sail on large ships crossing the Atlantikos for Italica. In his public talks Schrobbe spoke of 'the evil ways' of the Saracenites who were heathens, still worshipping Bawa'al. The possibility of war gave passion and purpose to the Users, the right wing of the Kristos religion yet it was helping give purpose as well to those who did not see war as a reasonable choice.

Blessed at the shrine, they sang a simple chant to banish evil and fear walking to the stone circle, prepared to embrace their ritual work with strength and inner light.

The coven was working the ritual for Midsummer's Eve, seeking to keep open the portal to the realm of the faerie. The hatchling, Dark Star, had just stepped through the stone gate, looking as if she was now sitting just outside the Circle in haze.

Iris stood behind the altar, Deodar behind her, as the words of the Goddess were intoned. There was too much work this summer and Merrydale's postmarm would remain at home come Lammas. Their daughter Diana was now three.

The sound of the voices had changed. Dark Star was familiar with the words her humans used in their ritual work, but it was almost as if their voices were ... "Silly," she reminded herself, "I've just stepped through the veil!"

The scent of the incense clung to her coat but there was another flavor in the air, one she remembered from her first passage into the realm of the faerie, just eight years ago this Sabbat. It also reminded her of her grandmare, Lillian.

Jenny, having been the Maiden to Gino's Green Man this past Beltane found that her understanding of the Wiccan religion had grown. She also felt her resolve to await their handfasting or at least until they were done at Trillium School slipping away. Her desire to be filled with Gino, for their virginity to be an offering to each other and to the Goddess grew with each lunar phase.

As the presence of the Goddess filled the Circle, the young lovers sat in meditation at the east altar, continuing to bring in visions of the element of air. They would be seniors this year. Several of their classmates were being handfasted this summer. The young lovers knew that their desire was more than the lust of teenagers. The rings upon their fingers were a promise. If they did consummate their love, it would be a choice made carefully. Since taking the mark of the Goddess this past Candlemas, Jenny had learned which herbs to bring together in ways which could keep a young woman from conceiving.

Jenny's mother seemed to grow in understanding but her father had been gone to Mill City for many months, now. The rift between father and daughter seemed to grow as

Jenny embraced the Earthkin ways and her father was again enmeshed in the User's politics. Sometimes Jenny wished she could sit and tell her father how wonderful her life was becoming and how much she loved Gino but she knew that he did not approve and took refuge in his religion and politics.

And she *did* love Gino. He was her soul mate and she watched him growing into manhood. Jenny was grateful to have the preparation for Dark Star's quest to keep them busy. Despite the longing within her body, she knew they were building a foundation for their life and that it would be a lasting bond.

Dark Star was looking at both worlds. She could see the forms of her humans and their coven in the stone circle. When the hatchling gazed toward Jenny and Gino she saw their future, saw the baby they would bring into the world.

She felt honored among unicorns to live in the world of humans. But there was another world, the realm of faerie, and the spirits of the trees - dryads, the coven called them - were moving about, and tiny beings of light were playing among the ferns and mushrooms and small plants.

Flying Raven and Ollis Piper were at the south altar. The flames had died out but they kept the spirit of fire flowing with warmth.

Raven has her quill. She will be attempting to journey with Dark Star this Midsummer, her astral quill in hand, not leaving the Circle but catching the hatchling's thoughts and images so they could be recorded on paper.

Ollis, Iris' father, was now studying so he could be a full participant in the coven's rituals. It may have taken some years, but both Raven and Ollis were moving into a new life together. Raven was not going east this summer to visit her family. Her daughter had called a few weeks back to tell Raven she now had a new, seventh grandchild. Claudia told her mother about the planned baptism and it was quickly apparent that Claudia was moving toward the more conservative beliefs of the Users.

Raven was troubled but made light of it. "She's going to 'dunk' my new granddaughter," she joked. More and more Raven felt that she was brought by the Mother to live in Merrydale, to teach at Trillium School and to meet and marry Ollis. The former merchant marine, however, was not thinking of Raven at the moment, but trying to keep the visualizations and words in the order he was learning them.

It looked as if a tunnel had opened into the underworld. The tapping sound of hooves echoed within its depth. Dark Star recognized the gait. "My dearest Lillian..."

Hearing water dripping into a pond, the hatchling looked up and saw a stalactite which had appeared, almost glowing with a pale, golden color. Each drop of water plummeted like a jewel, landing almost at Dark Star's feet. Looking down, she saw Dagon's face reflected in the rippling surface.

Jewel Woodfolk did not want to miss this adventure but she and Lotus had talked at length and felt it best if she stayed in Merrydale. Sunna, only two and a half, wasn't old enough for the Lammas journey nor was she ready to have her entire family gone.

Dagon, now eight, will accompany the coven to the cavern, although this had meant numerous reminders by Jewel that he may *not* head off on any adventures with Dark Star.

Although Dagon was always well-behaved, he was magickally precocious and there had been that incident just seven years ago when he went off with Dark Star into the faerie realm.

"But mom..." Dagon would answer, sounding like all kids his age, then add, "I was only one!"

Lotus looked forward to the trip. He had not been camping in the River Mountain in some years and looked forward to hiking and seeing ancient trees.

Jewel sat, enfolded in Lotus' arms, as they shared mental images of their favorite waterfall, an appropriate visualization for the west altar.

The hatchling sat at her grandmare's hooves, listening. Once again Lillian told her the stories of the three unicorns who halted the Ghulguls as they prepared to invade all of Europa under the leadership of Dyubkz Khan, a fearless and ruthless leader.

"And you have been chosen to bring a halt to this new threat of war, my dear." Lillian's voice was so loving and soothing that Dark Star sensed nothing unusual about the elder unicorn's statement.

Wren and Pearl sat at the north. Wren did not often sit in Circle with the coven, usually working her rituals quietly back in Highlands, a long journey from Merrydale, nestled on the eastern side of the Red Mountains. Her partner, Robin, could not take the time away from her job although she hoped to join the group for Lammas.

Unaccustomed to the coven's usual imagery, she played a song of earth on her lute as Pearl, the coven seamstress and arts teacher at Trillium School, held the image of the fertile soil clearly in her mind.

Pearl had only finished embroidering a pattern into Dark Star's robe this morning. In the lining, it provided an astral cloak of protection. Dark Star had found that the robe, more of a blanket which was buttoned beneath her neck, glowed gently once she had passed through the veil. Fascinated with the glyphs, she didn't know what they meant and, with Holly translating, had posed her question during the last fitting this afternoon in the cabin, shaping her sentences into the orb where Holly could sense them.

"But Dark Star," Pearl laughed, "it's a *mystery*."

Amber often worked as an elemental partner with Pearl, but their Descendant Tribe friend was back in the River Mountains. She was once again journeying to the sound of drumming. As two of her tribal sisters tapped the intricate rhythms which echoed in counterpoint, Amber moved into spirit and joined the flight of a bat, peering into the dark to see where Dark Star's path might be found. This path would lead the hatchling to the gateway to the future, allowing her to pass to the destined mountain pass known as 'The Cauldron' where a terrifying battle was waiting to erupt.

Momentarily distracted from Lillian's narrative, Dark Star pulled her attention back from the orb. Usually sitting in the cabin on an altar, Holly had brought it to the Stone Circle.

Arnica and Holly, the hatchling's much-loved men, stood on either side of the northeast portal through which she had passed. Either was prepared to move into the realm of the faerie if need be to help bring her back.

"Look there," Lillian motioned, pointing her horn toward the very portal. "See the two unicorns who will share your journey?"

Dark Star saw them, just on this side of the thin veil which separated the two worlds. When she looked closer she saw Arnica and Holly, but on this side of the veil were two handsome, strong stallion unicorns.

"They're *gorgeous*," she thought, but quickly remembered that this was a matter of survival for many humans.

"Their names," Lillian spoke, her voice now strong and clear, "are Joachim and Boaz... Do not forget."

LXIX - The Cauldron of Battles

Dark Star became aware that the sound of water dripping from the stalactite into the pool was as steady as a metronome, but its rhythm was much slower than her heart which was very fast. She looked down and saw the glow of her horn reflected in the rippling water. Her image would begin to take shape and then, plunk, another drop of water and it would be scattered. The new magickal formula Arnica had made for her horn helped her to see as she made her way into the earth's depths.

The hatchling recalled how her dreams of icicles last December brought her a riddle from her grandmare, Lillian. "When a unicorn's horn drips down from the sky, meeting one from the earth, growing way up high..." Some weeks later the riddle was solved and now she stood watching. All about her were stalactites which dripped down upon growing stalagmites.

She listened to the next drop of water. The pool sounded very deep. Lost in the reflection and thought, all thought of the Quest was momentarily gone when suddenly, she heard her grandmare Lillian's voice call out, "Jump, Dark Star, jump!"

The hatchling jumped into the pool. It *was* very deep.

Dark Star was in way over her head.

"May the god Neptune watch over the seeker as the Initiate plunges to the depths of knowing..."

Raven held a cobalt blue urn filled with sacred waters. It was a hand-blown glass pitcher Ollis bought years ago when travelling the globe as a merchant marine. He had kept it safe, sensing it would have a special role in his life and now, trothed for nearly a year to Raven, he was continually in awe of how his life fell into place as he learned more of Magick.

She tipped it to pour water down to the glossy stone. The sound of the water from the blue glass splattered lightly but just then the coven was startled by a loud splash echoing throughout the depths of the cavern.

There were twelve of them working the Circle on this Lammas Eve. Robin was not part of the coven but was there as one with Wren, assisting her with the bardic journey. Dark Star was their thirteenth for this ritual. The coven sensed that the splash was their hatchling but, as one, they breathed slowly with great care, staying calm and reaching out to Dark Star with their single mental image.

The hatchling found herself running, galloping along the floor of the cavern's pool, racing through the water as if it was air.

"Run, Dark Star," she heard, but the call was no longer Lillian's voice.

Following the bed of an ancient, underground river, she ran and ran. Without even realizing it she emerged amid valleys and forests. Her heart was thumping loudly but she felt fleet of hoof. Dark Star was swift and exhilarated. Why, she hadn't run like this since ... and the hatchling realized that was in a previous life!

Wren picked up the tempo of the music. She didn't know why and it didn't matter. Her robe was folded beneath her (the coven was skyclad for this ritual), she sat playing her lute. The notes drifted, sounding upon the crystalline spires and, even when unheard, wove protection about Dark Star. Wren was *becoming* the music. Her partner, Robin, stood behind her, keeping her grounded so Wren might unfold her spirit like the petals of a musical flower. Her bardic song was being played into the astral, carried by Magick to the hatchling.

Dark Star's beautiful, embroidered robe flowed behind her like wings. The sound of hooves grew louder and, without looking, she could sense that the two unicorns had joined her. Lillian had told her that their names were Joachim and Boaz. She could feel them drawing near but there was no slowing down. Her heart raced with urgency.

On the hatchling's right Boaz, his glossy black coat deeper than the night and on her right Joachim, so white that he glowed as if lit by the brightest sun. As they neared her the robe spread out in the wind like a sail. Hand-stitched with colored threads, it had been embroidered within many Circles as Pearl, Rosetta and Iris prepared it for Dark Star's quest. None of them knew how its magick would unfold.

The three thundered forward, running like the wind. A large canyon appeared before them, but not a one slowed. Dark Star felt their minds creating an image and as they left the edge of the precipice the abyss fell away from sight below for they were aloft. Her two handsome stallions were carrying the hatchling up, over the huge chasm. Dark Star felt she had become an image from Arnica's tarot deck and hoped that her friend Holly would see it in his orb.

"The Chariot." Holly spoke quietly. The coven was in a deep, collective trance. They didn't hear Wren's music as much as felt it. He sat at the center of the circle. In the darkness beneath the earth they had been surprised how much light their candle lanterns provided.

Their weeks of training and practice brought them an intense and steady focus.

Holly sat at the center of the Circle, holding the orb.

Pearl sat in a full lotus at the East. She and Arnica were the only two who could do so in comfort. She visualized the element of air blowing from behind her, passing through her body and entering the clear, crystal orb.

Dolly worked with a combination of images including the cauldron fire they often used in the stone circle and the raging forest fire which brought terror to the River Mountains just two years ago. Dolly could feel Iris sending him her loving energy from their home altar. There were slight interruptions in its flow which could have been their four year old distracting her mother. It was just four years ago that he and Iris conceived Diana but he thought only of the fire and allowed his wife and daughter to flow through him as he centered the element into the orb.

Hills and forests and open farmland passed beneath. Dark Star thought she had seen the great Motherflow River easing her waters to the south. The urban areas glowed at night, their unnatural light bright against the darkness. And then the vast ocean ("Is that the Atlantikos?" Dark Star wondered). There was a desert and mountains and then, before them, twin peaks framed a mountain pass. Boaz and Joachim slowed and the three landed in a small olive grove. It seemed a beautiful setting, the trees were knowing of many centuries.

But there was a disquiet in the land. Nests were empty, for the birds were flying away from the pass. Several deer went running past. The hatchling heard them crash against a tree, unable to see in the dark and frantic, for this was their time for rest but the land was warning them to flee.

Ahead was the Cauldron Pass and it was here that the armies were gathering.

Lotus held a piece of wood, one of the first he had carved. Upon it were the relief images of stones and mushrooms sprouting from soil, of tree roots reaching beneath the loam. He sensed his son, Dagon, sitting to his right at the northwest spoke of the Circle. Dagon's role was to steady the family connection. Jewel was back in Merrydale with Sunna, only two and a half. It was the stability and fertility of soil which Lotus brought to the orb.

Jeremiah Swarthmann, Henley Schrobbe's top general, slept fitfully in his large tent. Near his cot sat a large icon of his god, the Krista. Swarthmann had prayed that night, asking the Krista that he might bring a victory over the heathen Saracenites, protecting Italica so it could be a Kristos nation. Schrobbe believed Italica would be a fine market for his lumber and for the industry barons who were his major financial supporters. Swarthmann knew they would provide well for him if he was victorious, but he didn't include that in his prayer.

The hint of a soulful note carried through the stillness. Across the pass the Saracenites, a tribal peoples loosely unified by their worship of Bawa'al, began to stir. They were being called to prayer and would soon rise to await the sun. They knew their god would help them defeat the infidels and settle the dispute with Italica which dated back more generations than they could count.

Jenny and Gino stood on either side of Holly. They had pledged their troth just days before Candlemas. Having taken the mark of the Goddess, Jenny loved learning the Renaissance traditions of the coven.

"We are both the Maiden," Jenny spoke. As the Consort, Gino shaped her voice and spiraled it into the orb.

The two teens were working skyclad. Dark Star had seen Jenny's standing freed of her past (her father, Philbert, remained in Mill City helping run the government for Schrobbe and continued to act as if he had no daughter), her nude body looking like the Goddess incarnate as Maiden.

Dark Star felt the Goddess touch her. She looked at the two standing next to her. Black and white, they were looking at the Cauldron Pass and waiting.

"We are both the Mother." Jenny and Dark Star had grown close and both had come to know the spirit of the baby which awaited Jenny's womb. The girl held a small orb in her hand, the gift from Arnica and Holly. It helped her focus her images to Dark Star into Holly's orb.

'It is time,' although no words nor thoughts were shared.

'Perhaps it is the Mother who spoke,' Dark Star wondered. 'I am both,' she heard herself think and the silence was shredded with a terrifying thunder, the darkness torn apart with lightning which appeared to leap back and forth from one side of the Pass to the other.

The hatchling's last thought was the quotation from the scroll Lillian had given her: "Thunder clouds gathered overhead and lightning began to strike. Suddenly, three unicorns appeared at the crest of the pass, rearing up and making fearsome sounds."

Their physical forms remained by the olive trees as they were swept into the air by a torrent of wind. A huge explosion of light and sound shattered the night.

She stood before him but not as a unicorn. She had been given the form of the ancient Goddess, looking so sensual and desirable that a human man would lose self control and looking so terrifying and crone-like that she would stir awe and fear. At her left stood the stallion.

Which one was it? Dark Star could not tell.

He was the leader and his armies were waiting. The man, wearing his military uniform, was kneeling before her, not yet aware of her presence. Before him was the image of his deity.

As she heard his prayer, Dark Star realized that she was on both sides of the Cauldron at once. Before her knelt Swarthmann, Schrobbe's most trusted General, the man who would lead Lothloriën's troops into a savage and murderous battle. Before her the Saracenite, General El-Jabiba, prostrated himself before his image of Bawa'al. Their prayers merged and Dark Star could hear them both praying for the same thing.

The stallion snorted loudly. Each general looked up, startled, believing his god was speaking to him. What they heard and what they saw no one knows and neither would say.

Each man went out to his troops groping in darkness, but the sun had risen. Both generals had been blinded by their vision of their god astride unicorns. There would be no war.

She could see Ollis' head bobbing as he nodded off. The coven had felt a resolution. Light flickered in the orb (Holly almost dropped it he was so surprised) but then it began to emit the gentlest radiance.

She whinnied softly and they turned. The young ones jumped up but the older ones stood more slowly. It had been a long night sitting on cold stone. Arnica knew his 'old bones' would welcome a good night's sleep after they returned to their cabin.

It was time to ascend back from the cavern and trek back to Merrydale. The gardens at the cabin were awaiting the harvest.

LXX - Trillium School and the Harvest

The weather turned very warm following Lammas. Merrydale's youth thought this great for swimming but the rivers lowered themselves and parents grew nervous. Farmers watched the skies and felt anxious. The Loon Tribe elders gathered high in the River Mountains where their ancestors held ceremonies in ice caves. Now a herd of elk grazed upon grasses and alpine flowers on that sacred ground. They shook their heads in sadness, feeling that somehow the factories of the cities and loss of forests had caused Mother Earth pain.

The summer months had been difficult in much of the Land of Lothloriën. The narrowly-avoided war left a divisive political clime. The far right faction of the Politicos, known as Users, resented the failure of their agenda which promoted corporate wealth at the expense of the environment. The Users considered themselves well above the population.

On the other side of the spectrum, the Conservers were apprehensive, having learned just how far Premier Schrobbe was willing to go. The Earthkin were traditionally Conserver in their politics but the Descendant Tribes usually did not bother to vote, very distrustful of a government of people whose ancestors had taken away much of their land. The Conservers had a lot of work before them if things were to change.

Schrobbe and his advisors had committed considerable amounts of money to the planned battle against the Saracenites. They expected a brief war followed by financial reward. "Saving" Italica, with its Kristos population, from the heathen Saracenites would open a large market for Lothloriën's lumber.

After a brief trip to Mill City to file papers for the School, Arnica laughingly told the coven it was "busy as a hive after a storm."

The Users were scrambling. Having pushed through legislation which, without the war, left the country in debt they felt their only choice was to cut public funding, including money for the public schools. Many wanted a 10% increase in the annual tithe yet would exempt those who owned large businesses claiming it would be good for the economy. Despite their majority in Parliament a growing number of the Politicos realized that the people would not tolerate such measures. The Politicos Party was having heated debates within its ranks.

The people of Merrydale were relieved to have the schools start again. Merrydale Junior and Senior High were considering cutting back their marching band and athletics budgets if the local people were unable to provide additional funding.

Trillium school, however, was a source of local pride. Privately funded by Earthkin donations (which rankled some of the Users), the school was steadily growing. This year a library was being added. A small house near the school had been donated and the coven knew, instinctively, that it could make a perfect library. They submitted their plans to the town hall and, in late August, Mayor Browning issued the permits. The work would be done by Lotus' wood-working classes with help from two school fathers who had a small construction company.

Despite everyone's best intentions news of Dark Star's quest quietly circulated within the local Earthkin community. Even before the first day of school the students had made it known that they wanted their Full Moon observance to give thanks to Dark Star. Nearly all of the local Earthkin now knew that Arnica and Holly had a unicorn living with them. To be honest, much of Merrydale had heard the story although many did not believe unicorns existed and the ultra-conservative Users felt certain that any unicorn was surely a manifestation of the the devil.

This year, however, Dark Star is going to school almost every day. Back in the cabin after Arnica and Holly's morning ritual ended ("nothing but good shall come to us, let nothing but good go from us...") one of the men rubbed some of Arnica's newest formula onto her horn which left her horn unseen by those who did not work regular ritual for Mother Earth. The hatchling felt more than ready to share her days with Trillium's students.

Two weeks into the semester, tomorrow Trillium School would observe the Equinox. Each student would bring something from the family's harvest. Home-canned foods, fruits and vegetables would be donated to those in need. Some were bringing jars of coins or books for the library. Several were bringing poems to read. The Sabbat energy permeated the school which was busy with the work of learning.

Holly's classroom was quiet with students busy writing. On the large board was the title "What I Did On My Summer Vacation." As he wrote the words, the students groaned and laughed, all good-natured. Knowing that not everyone had similar summer opportunities, Holly had explained that they could write using reality or fantasy or even both!

In the next classroom, the students studying herbal science from Arnica were also quiet. Learning how to set luscious, black belladonna fruit into apothecary jars, it was important that they keep the juice off their skin as they handled the fruit with care. Arnica had guided them through the study of the belladonna plant as well as the ethical and magickal implications of making a tincture which could either save or end a life. This semester's course started even before the first month of school as the students helped Arnica and Holly harvest goldenseal and echinacea roots, now hanging in the drying shed back at the Grove. Arnica and Holly raised their tithing money from the sale of the root. If Parliament did succeed in the increased taxation, the belladonna tincture might be sold to some of the larger medical firms and would cover the cost.

Deodar, the school's principle, found his class in ethics which was offered for twelfth year students, to be very popular. Several of the younger students who were free that period asked if they could sit in. The underlying theme of this semester's class addressed the ethics of the decisions made by the current administration. Six years ago Deodoar Dolorum was still the Kristos pastor at Church of the Martyr but now, his dark hair grown longer, Merrydale embraced him in his present role as principle of Trillium School. Six years ago he stood up to the Kristos bishop to defend the Earthkin's Maypole tradition. How that changed his life! Although he loved teaching math and philosophy classes, his favorite class was ethics. Dolly, as the coven knew him, believed that change in Lothloriën's voting population began in the classroom. The principle wanted to teach his students how to become informed participants in changing government and was thrilled to learn how much this interested their parents.

Iris Dolorum's teaching schedule was unusual this year. After much discussion Iris' class in world politics was scheduled for three evenings a week. As Merrydale's postmarm, Iris spoke with more people over the course of a week than nearly anyone in Merrydale. The coven realized that many of the parents, and not just Earthkin, wanted to hear what she would be teaching. This year people realized they knew far too little about global politics or the alliances and treaties which Lothloriën held with other countries. Iris was more than willing to set aside some evenings. She liked her duties as postmarm although she also loved being at the school. With their daughter Diana not yet three and a half, being able to spend most of her time working at the postal shop which was attached to their home was a blessing. And Jewel would be there to help which meant Diana's favorite friend, Sunna, would be there as well.

The curtains were drawn in Pearl Lamina's art room. The soft scent of lilac incense drifted through the room. The lights were dimmed and candles lit. Pearl's desk had been transformed into an altar. Jenny, three other senior girls and Bering, a senior boy, were preparing to ritually cleanse and consecrate their sewing tools. Dark Star stood to the side, wearing the robe Pearl had embroidered. The Pictish woman was teaching the five students the skills needed to mend the robe without affecting any of the Magick Pearl had originally stitched into place and without altering any of the Magick now held by the fabric which retained the memories and images of the hatchling's underworld experience.

With Ollis Piper's world geography class not scheduled until next semester, he would be helping with the new library construction but was also enjoying sitting in on Flying Raven's class. Her science students were studying global warming. Having been trothed for a year, they worked well together. Ollis spoke about his travels to tropical islands, describing the climates he experienced as a merchant marine. Raven's students used the scientific information she had given them and tried to calculate what changes would be brought to the peoples of these distant places. They were learning graphic lessons about their planet.

Amber was enjoying this year even more. With two of her tribal sisters now living in Merrydale and working at the school, she was able to feel more connected with her Loon Tribe customs. And, in turn, Peridot and Topaz Crowfeather were enjoying learning about the Renaissance Tribe traditions which Amber worked with the coven. As the sun streamed through a window Amber's history class students were busy writing. The near-war had provided them with a great opportunity in living history. For two weeks they had collected the oral history, interviewing their teachers who had accompanied Dark Star as well as local politicians and, by letter, attempted to gain more information from Parliament about the events. The voices of the preschool children playing in the autumn sun kept them focused on this week's assignment: to write the 'history' of this past summer for the young generation who would be sitting in this class in another decade.

This morning Lotus was teaching the students how to sand the wooden shelves in preparation for the later finishing. "Gently, now, always with the grain." Lotus' dark blond hair had grown long but he taught the students safety and a large bandanna was wrapped around his head. Lotus' wife, Jewel, was helping at the postal shop so she and Iris could watch their daughters together.

Gino, a pencil for marking the boards tucked behind his ear, was having a wonderful time. Working with Lotus on the new library suited him. This was the final year for Gino and Jenny. They wanted to make the best of it so their union would have a solid foundation.

Gino's parents worked at the school. Carlos, the school's maintenance man, needed a break and having a cup of coffee with his wife was a needed respite. With Gino and Jenny in their final year of school, a Handfasting was not that far into the future. But the topic at hand was the activity in the school, now the center of so many Earthkin lives.

"The Daycare Sisters?" Carlos answered Rosetta's question. "They seem to like the room."

The Rosario's had created the affectionate name for Peri and Topi who were tending the School's new daycare. Carlos had put in many hours getting the room and the outdoor play spaces prepared but the time was enjoyable. The Crowfeathers had a wonderful sense of humor and they were hard-workers. Topi Crowfeather loved to cook and was helping Rosetta in the school kitchen.

Dark Star began to doze off. The sewing students were quietly working threads into the robe. The entire school was quietly at work. Tonight the hatchling would be back at the cabin and would help the coven carry harvest blessings out to the Stone Circle and tomorrow would be a full day at school. She drifted into a dream, the images of the handsome unicorn stallions Joachim and Boaz warming her memories.

It had been a long summer.

LXXI - The Mirror In The Log

Leaves drifted down in the warm, sunny breezes of late October. Cold, late-autumn rains kept people indoors for nearly a week and then there were several nights of hard frost. But this weekend a burst of warm, summer-like days brought people out. People were in their gardens and yards, cleaning up small limbs brought down by the autumn weather. Leaves were raked, the last weeding done and the sound of neighbors greeting each other as their children played was music.

Locals called this weather 'pumpkin summer.' Warm days after a cold spell meant an exceptional pumpkin harvest. Indeed, the markets were busy. Pumpkins would be carved for Hallows and even the Kristos children would find pumpkin cookies and pumpkin bars in their treat bags. Despite the Users' complaints (the ultra-conservative members of the Kristos religion), children everywhere loved dressing up as their favorite ancestor and going door-to-door.

Pumpkin summer touched Merrydale with a welcome exuberance. Lothloriën had been through a difficult political season. Although the District of Grainland to the east continued to generate political news (Premiere Schrobbe was incurring a growing national debt for the Land of Lothloriën) most people were eager to turn to the cares at home.

Deodar Dolorum was enjoying life. Once the Kristos Pastor of the Church of the Martyr, he gave daily thanks for having learned the Earthkin ways. Most of his former Kristos congregants seemed to warmly embrace him as principal of Trillium School, the first Earthkin school in Lothloriën. Merrydale was proud of Dolorum and the school. The school brought status and even a small boost to the local Merrydale economy. Deodar, called Dolly by his friends, was romping in a large pile of leaves with the two girls.

His daughter, Diana, and the Woodfolk's daughter, Sunna were almost like sisters. Sunna's mother, Jewel, was helping Iris Dolorum at the postal shop. Trillium School might have these days off for the Sabbat but Merrydale's postmarm followed the civic calendar.

Ollis Piper was busy raking leaves toward the pile. Dagon, Sunna's older brother, had a smaller rake. Already eight and in the second grade, he could be wise beyond his years one moment but then, quickly, still a child. Ollis and Dagon would rake the leaves back into the pile and Dolly, Diana and Sunna would shriek and run and jump right into them, scattering them about.

They were having great fun although Ollis was thinking an afternoon nap might help him through the Sabbat Eve. What a glorious day! Well before the sun rose this morning, Ollis sat before his altar for a long time. Ollis gave thanks for his growing role as a father figure for Iris and for his new life in Merrydale, including his betrothal to Flying Raven. Sitting upon his altar was an old photo of Madrona, Iris' mother, which he would be taking to Trillium School.

"Can you manage this by yourself?" the older man asked the boy.

"Of course I can," Dagon answered, as if there should be no doubt.

Ollis kissed the girls goodbye, and embraced Dolly. "I must take Madrona's photo to the school for the altar," Ollis said. "How I would have enjoyed this when Iris was little," he added wistfully.

Trillium School's doors were open as students and their parents came to visit the ancestral altars. Some brought additional photos of deceased family members. The altar area, set up in the courtyard, had quite a few pictures of dogs and cats, a couple of hamsters and two guppies. Some students had taken photographs and some had created pictures in their art classes.

As the geography teacher, Ollis was able to place his photo on the main altar. It was large and elaborate, created by Lotus' woodworking class and able to hold many candles and pictures. The altar was draped with a beautiful, embroidered cloth created by Pearl's sewing students. Two unicorn statues, one black and one white, flanked the altar. The hatchling, Dark Star, wanted to represent Joachim and Boaz, the two astral stallions from her summer adventure.

Ollis recognized several of the images. Mildora Dolorum, Dolly's mother, had passed over seven years ago. He set Madrona's picture next to Mildora's, the two mothers-in-law. He recognized a photo of Jed, Raven's late husband. He'd seen the photo in Raven's bedroom. There was a small watercolor of Phoenix, Pearl's partner, who passed over seven years ago as well.

Additional small altars had been placed about the courtyard amid large baskets. As the day passed the baskets filled with apples and pears, some with canned goods. People wanted to remember the old customs of leaving food for one's ancestors, but this food would go to Merrydale's food bank for families who could use help. Many were unable to find work. Parliament struggled to pay the debts incurred by Schrobbe's failed attempt to topple the Saracenites. The governments expense caused hardship and many of the mills had laid off workers.

His quiet meditation before the altar ended. Ollis began to make his way to the school kitchen, a slow progress as the students and parents he saw all wanted to talk.

Raven was waiting for Ollis. The kitchen was warmed by the ovens and rich with the scent of pumpkin pie. Rosetta, the school's cook (Ollis liked to call her *Trillium's Chef*), had been baking pumpkin bread for the student lunches. They were joking and talking and having so much fun they hadn't noticed how quiet their Descendant Tribe friends were.

Peridot and Topaz were engaged in a quiet but intense conversation with Amber. Tribal sisters, Peri and Topi had recently moved from the River Mountains to manage the day care at Trillium School.

"I was checking with my fingers the way the nurse showed me," Peri said.

"Where is it?" Amber asked, her voice heavy with concern.

"Right about there," Peri moved her hand toward her left breast.

"I made an appointment for her at Merrydale Clinic," Topi interjected, "It's first thing on Monday."

Amber began telling Peri what she had learned from Jewel, who went for a mammogram and biopsy at the Clinic just four years ago. "Ask her tonight," she urged, encouraging Peri to ask Jewel for information and support.

"Just three drops," Arnica said. Each drop of the reddish brown tincture plummeted into the crystal jar, hand-cut and generations old. The herbalist gently replaced the apothecary style lid. Arnica's formula had been perfected over many years, allowing the coven to part the veils at Hallows. The belladonna tincture had been carefully prepared during this year's harvest. The elixir had only enough atropine to invoke the Crone and not enough to cause any physiological effect. Belladonna was an herb to use with care.

Dark Star lay before the fireplace, dozing. She had gone running with Gino early in the morning and drifted through dreams of the handsome unicorn steeds who had stirred her pulse. She stirred. The hatchling loved having all of her humans about.

Pearl sat near the young unicorn, embroidery floss of all colors at hand. She was sewing a new jar dolly with threads her grandmother, Lady Ellhorn, had sent her from Cloverville. Eighty-one years old, Pearl's grandmother still walked miles every day, thriving in the climate of the Four Deserts. The dry heat had helped Phoenix during his final months but Pearl much preferred the climate back in Merrydale.

Holly was reading through pages of notes, proofreading and making comments. Quietly, Arnica and Holly were teaching an adult class. Several of the parents of Trillium students were working toward initiation and would be forming their own covens. Clearly, the school was bringing many changes to Merrydale.

Rested, the hatchling rose up on her legs and went out into the gardens looking for Gino and Jenny. She found them helping Lotus position his new carving, a mirror in a log. A thick, cedar branch came down in the woods this past winter. Holly cut a large section and he and Arnica took it to school to Lotus who dried and cured it. He'd carved faces of the Crone into it and it now held a large, scrying mirror.

The mirror sat just outside the northeast portal. The sky was clear through the branches, the moon just past her first quarter, resting upon the tree tops. The Circle cast, the elements invoked, the Divine Parents had been asked for blessings. The night was cooling and turning brisk. The moss on the large stones was collecting a light dew. The scrying cauldron, filled with flame, provided some welcome warmth as one by one they went to the altar, poured a measure of elixir into the chalice and prepared to visit the mirror in the log.

Dark Star went after Arnica and Holly. The hatchling was sure she would be able to see Joachim and Boaz. They were so handsome, so muscular... But when she gazed into the mirror she saw herself surrounded by tree spirits. The dryads were chanting a plea. The hatchling could not understand them and sent a question into the mirror. The image moved like reflecting water into which a stone had been dropped. Now she saw her grandmare, Lillian, and knew that she would find her answers later.

Jenny took her turn walking the circle, pausing to chant at each of the eight directions. She kept refocusing her mind. This was her first Hallows Eve and she was just a bit nervous. Would she see Juanita, her mother's aunt, who knew of some magick? As she stepped through the northeast portal Jenny felt the temperature change, yet she couldn't sense whether it was warmer or cooler. She took a deep breath and calmed herself as Jewel was teaching. She reached into her mind and felt Arnica's elixir moving within her blood, then opened her eyes and gazed into the mirror, scrying.

In her arms she was holding a baby... Jenny wondered if this was the baby she would have with Gino but as the question formed in her mind, it wasn't the baby she was holding, it was Peri. A few tears came down Peridot's cheek. Her left breast emanated an eerie light. Jenny was growing uncomfortable but the image shapeshifted and she saw herself sitting with her arm around Dark Star. The hatchling's image assured her that everything would be fine.

LXXII - Seeds of Light

"What do you think about this paper?" Holly held up wrapping paper which was embossed with the images of sun babies. This was the sixth choice of paper, and there was only one remaining.

Dark Star looked uncertain, her head tilted to one side. There was a lack of enthusiasm.

"Do you like this?" Holly said steadily, knowing the hatchling seemed quite picky in choosing paper to wrap her presents for the two unicorn stallions she met last summer. He had saved this for last, feeling certain it would be her choice.

With help from her much-loved men, Dark Star had been weaving two Yule wreaths, one for each of the two handsome unicorns she met during last summer's adventure. Although too young to mate, they were her first crushes and she wanted the paper to be just perfect.

"She likes it!" Holly exclaimed, relieved and happy. The paper was not holiday-like at all, but a pattern of black and white. Dark Star liked it. She'd had her humans weave dried belladonna berries, shiny and black into the wreath for Boaz, and dried snowberries from the *Symphicarpos* in the gardens, dried very carefully to preserve their white color. These had been carefully sewn onto the wreath for Joachim.

Over the days as Holly, Arnica and Gino (when he wasn't in school or with Jenny) did the hand-work for her, the hatchling focused joyful Magick into every bit of each wreath. It had been difficult at times. The images of the tree spirits she saw in the Hallows Eve mirror remained a distraction and she felt certain that they were connected to the Politicos' desire to harvest her beloved forest trees but one way to turn the tide was to work on the Magick for turning the Wheel of the Year.

"What about this for Peri?" Holly held up a small statue of maiden, cradled in a crescent moon.

"Thank the gods it's not another hat." Arnica laughed so hard he dropped the spool of ribbon which unrolled itself across the floor. As he bent to pick up the long thread of ribbon the old herbalist added, "that's amazing."

"I know," Holly said quietly, "it *is* just about like her tattoo design."

"Is she O.K.?" Raven asked.

The women could hear Peri in the bathroom, retching as she vomited once again into the toilet. Peridot was finishing her fourth (and hopefully final) week of chemotherapy.

"The doctor said this should be the last week," her sister Topi answered. "At least we've been able to go to Merrydale Clinic," she added. The Loon Tribe sisters were grateful they no longer needed to travel to Mill City for treatment. It was usually a full day over the River Mountains each way with no time for a short detour to visit their tribal home but some of their relatives had moved from Eagle's Nest to Mill City to teach at the new Loon School. Peri had a lot of support from her tribal family and also from her 'new' family in Merrydale.

Peridot returned to the group looking slightly flushed but otherwise fine. Looking at Raven she asked, "So when's the date?"

Pearl laughed, her needles dancing. She had crocheted and knitted a couple of hats for Peri to wear when her hair fell out. Pearl was growing to love the Crowfeather sisters. Pearl Lamina had moved back from Cloverville after her husband, Phoenix, died seven years ago this past Hallows. With Amber and Raven both settling in to Merrydale for Trillium School and now Peri and Topi, they had a strong bond as older women, able to dote upon the youngest generation and help Iris and Jewel with their children. The coven and school created a joyful family.

Pearl knew that some of her coven family and many of her students were busy at Trillium School working on the collective Yule Magick both the Renaissance and Descendant peoples were bringing to Merrydale.

"He really put the invitation under his pyramid?" Holly was quite amused. He was curling the ends of the bow on the two wrapped parcels he was preparing for the hatchling. Dark Star was curled up on the floor. Despite her long legs she could still be almost coltish at times, although at eight and a half, she was maturing.

Having a small, hand-carved pyramid to help one with personal magick was part of the coven's work. The youngest initiate, Gino was making excellent progress in learning all the skills required in his pathworking.

"Yes, he's done well with it." Arnica was wrapping the package for the Rosarios, Gino's parents. Rosetta loved using the fresh-dried herbs from Arnica's garden in her cooking and Carlos appreciated the ointment which eased the pain in his shoulder. "He and Jenny are handling this quite well."

"I've been meaning to ask you," Holly started, "you know what this is all about, don't you?"

"I ran into Becky a few weeks back when I was at the market. She asked if we could talk. It seems that Jenny has a trust fund due her from her grandparents, and Philbert is the executor." Arnica sat back to relate the story.

"Despite his involvement with the Users," Holly mentioned, referring to Philbert Flower's right-wing political activity, "he seems like a moral and good man... A little stubborn at times." Holly laughed.

"Philbert wants Jenny to have her trust so she and Gino can buy their own house. He definitely does not approve of their lifestyle but he's struggling to accept it." Jenny and her father had not spoken in over a year.

"Do you think she can accept her father?" Holly asked in jest. Sometimes Jenny could be as stubborn as her father. They were not as different as they sometimes thought.

"Becky said that a Kristos chaplain at Parliament had been giving Philbert good advice. I assured her that Gino would be very open-minded about the invitation."

They sat quietly on a bench in the courtyard. Although some parts of the school bustled with activity, it was cool and damp outside with traces of snow sheltered in the corners. Jenny was taking a break, helping her classmates from one of Pearl's classes who were making hats to send to the St. Marian Cancer Center for all those undergoing chemotherapy.

Jenny was still unsettled about going to her parents for Kristmass.

"But remember what he wrote in the invitation," Gino said, "It was 'I may not approve but I love you.' It's time for us to deal with your family..."

Jenny did not look persuaded.

"And I'll be there." Gino's arms drew her close.

"I love you." And Jenny did. She was looking forward to their handfasting and to carrying their first child after they graduated this spring.

"There's a delicious irony in it, isn't there?" Holly mused. He and Arnica had been talking about Lotus. The Church of the Martyr hired him to build a replacement creche for their outdoor manger scene. A few of the right wing members grumbled about it being blasphemy, but this winter there was no one else in Merrydale able to provide quality carpentry on such short notice. Most of Merrydale's Kristos believers were growing in acceptance of the Earthkin, proud of what Trillium School was providing their community.

"It's quite a bit of money," said Arnica. "Lotus wants to fix up their kitchen and now he can."

"Who would have thought that Merrydale would become a role model for the old ways becoming so accepted?"

"Certainly I didn't when we first moved here," Arnica said, momentarily taken back decades in time. "But we're fortunate to have people like Iris and Dolly, both so well respected long before they were known as Earthkin."

Deodar was giving Iris the afternoon off, working in the postal shop for her, much to the amusement of the townfolk. His inner unhappiness as the Kristos Paster of the Church of the Martyr left him dark and brooding and then, before everyone's eyes, he was transformed into the husband of Merrydale's postmarm, the principal of the new Trilium School, a man obviously converted from the conservative Kristos religion to the not-always-accepted Earthkin. And now he was the 'postmarm.' Oh, some of the folk had a great time teasing him.

Iris was sitting back. Ollis was there, playing with his granddaughter. Diana adored him. Although only three and a half, she listened to the stories he told of his years in the merchant marine. Iris had come to terms with his having left her mother but her relationship with him was not really daughter and father.

Diana was standing so still. It was a wonder that Ollis could keep her like that sometimes for more than an hour! He was slowly building a tower around her of wooden blocks and she loved it.

"Have you chosen a date?" Iris asked. She was looking forward to his Handfasting to Raven.

"Not yet," Ollis answered. "We haven't decided whether to wait until school is done this spring or not. It could be great but it could prove too much of a distraction."

"For you or the students?" Iris teased.

"All of us," Ollis' eyes twinkled.

Jewel was packing cookies to take to the cabin in the grove. Dagon was helping Sunna find her favorite toys so she and Diana could play quietly while the adults were working their ritual.

She looked around their kitchen. What a present Lotus was giving her this year. And who could have imagined that the money for the project was coming from the church where Deodar was once a Kristos minister.

Jewel paused for a moment to give thanks. Two healthy children, a loving husband. The Lady had been very good to them. She loved being more 'public' when she helped Iris in the postal shop and Lotus' classes in woodworking had done much for his reputation as a skilled wood worker. Between teaching at Trillium School and all the projects offered to him, their life had never felt so secure.

She caught flame at the gas range, where the pilot light held the spark they brought down each year in ritual, and lit a votive candle.

"Dear Mother," she prayed, "Keep us strong. Thank you for your blessings and for giving us the tools we will need this coming year."

The coven would have much work this year. The political struggles in Parliament would resume when Lothloriën's politicians returned after the holidays. Schrobbe's difficulties seemed only to make the Users stronger and more determined to reap financial reward by harvesting trees. They saw the earth as something for their own gain.

Dark Star held a long stick of incense in her teeth, stepping slowly around the cabin. She loved setting the Magick in place for tonight's Sabbat. "Oh, if they could see her now," her mind danced to the memory of Joachim and Boaz before she returned her focus to the cabin.

She would see them this very Yule Eve. After the coven left and her two men had gone to bed, she would trot out to the Stone Circle and, with her grandmare Lillian's help from the other side, slip through the portal. She was going in skill, learning how to travel in the astral, and knew she would be back to share the Yule sunrise with her beloved humans.

LXXIII - The Sound of Water

"Do you remember the paint?" Holly was pouring some water from a small, cut crystal vial. The water was a gift from Rosetta whose mother had brought it from a famous site in Italica, their homeland in Europa.

"Has it been five years already?" Arnica knew how much time had passed since the ritual painting and blessing of Trillium School, but was still in awe of how fast time sped as the years passed.

The sound of the water danced through the cabin. The men were seated upon the floor, the temple fireplace brightly warming the room. Dark Star, the hatchling unicorn, was now maturing. Come the following Sabbat, she would be eight years in human time.

Dark Star nudged Holly's neck. She wanted *her* water to be next.

"I'm glad we have storm windows on," Raven thought to herself, adding more copal resin to the charcoal disks burning before her. Flying Raven always had a very practical quality, something she felt was part of her heritage. The folk who originally settled in the District of the Mothervalley were primarily farmers, their survival dependant upon keeping their wits about them. Raven wondered what Ollis would think were he at home to hear the drumming.

"O-ne-na-ma," Peri chanted, the drum held between her crossed legs. Propped before the Loon Tribe woman was the image of a maiden sitting in a crescent moon. Peri planned to have this design tattooed on the flat plane of her chest, from which her left breast had been removed. When she asked her doctor how long the skin needed for healing, the way he began his response with 'Miss Crowfeather' was a clear indication that going for breast reconstruction in Mill City was the only *sensible* option.

Topi, Raven and Amber Whitefeather were helping Peri call upon her Loon Tribe grandmothers to speed the healing. Amber smudged the room, the thick grass scent blending with the copal smoke, holding the reverberations of the drum until the trance was fully achieved.

The hatchling was very proud of the water she'd brought for her men. They had small bottles of water in an old, wood cabinet which had been collected from many ancient and sacred sites. Dark Star asked her grandmare, Lillian, to take her back to the underworld where the stalactites dripped their rhythms of crystal clear drops into the pool beneath.

"Travel to the Underworld should never be taken lightly," the kindly, elder unicorn had said, but the hatchling was a favorite of her grandmare. Dark Star was so proud to be able to bring a gift to Arnica and Holly's anniversary party. They hadn't even missed her the night she slipped out of the cabin to meet Lillian in the stone Circle. Dark Star managed a complete surprise!

None of them would have imagined this expedition. Seven men were examining the house, storage building and five acres of land situated midway between Merrydale and the Grove where Arnica, Holly and Dark Star were preparing the water for the Candlemas Eve Ritual.

"What do you think?" Gino turned proudly to his father. Gino and Jenny really liked this house. It was small but they wanted to add a large, family room with a fireplace (large enough for rituals!). There was an old, untended garden which would be perfect for new herb beds, and several apples and a pear. The house was small but surrounded by the trees of Merrywood. On a parcel of five acres there were nearly two full acres cleared.

Carlos was so proud of his son, although he had some misgivings that the money for the property came from Jenny's trust. Carlos was not always comfortable with the shifting roles of these younger people. "Did the Willow Woman find good results?" Carlos asked.

"Yes, she said the well taps into a good and abundant water. She also found a spring on the other side of the clearing." Gino answered.

As Gino and his father talked and began looking at the gardens, Lotus was taking measurements of the house and writing down figures. Dagon, Lotus's son, was helping by holding the end of the measure.

Philbert Flower, Jenny's father, was at a loss. Accustomed to being a moving force within the Politicos he didn't know what to make of this group of Earthkin men. His preconceptions were in disarray. Why, these folk were so giving of their time and help, and they were so knowledgeable. Deodar Dolorum and Ollis Piper were seated on a bench going over the legal and financial paperwork for Gino.

Deodar, sensing Philbert's discomfort, called the man over. They had known each other when Deodar was still the Kristos minister at the Church of the Martyr (before he came to terms with his true religious feelings) and Dolly sensed that the very conservative man might be feeling uncomfortable. Dolly knew this past year or two had been very difficult for Philbert Flower but was pleased that the man was reconciling with his daughter and trying to be supportive of her marriage.

Jenny stood, trying not to move. She drew upon her recent training, holding an image of the Goddess Moon reflected upon a perfectly still pond. Filling herself with this energy she had the energy to remain calm as the women fussed with the fabric.

Becky Flower stood back and watched Pearl pin and adjust the gown. Becky's Aunt Juanita had made the wedding dress for her. In fact, since Jenny had converted to the beliefs of the Renaissance Tribe, Becky thought often of her Aunt Juanita who practiced a type of 'flower magic' in her own, Kristos manner.

Gino's mother, was sitting and crocheting a lace veil. Her fingers fairly danced with the needles. 'What talent she has,' thought Pearl.

"Rosetta, I am so envious," Becky mused, her voice sincere. "I feel so untalented with you women."

"Oh, mom," Jenny wanted her mother to be an integral part of the work. It was her dress she was wearing.

"I just hope I'll have it done by Midsummer Day," said Rosetta. Seeing her son Handfasted to such a fine young woman! Rosetta was very pleased.

Dark Star sat back upon her haunches, the vessel of water on the floor beneath her heart. Arnica and Holly knelt so they could hold hands, forming a circle around the hatchling, invoking the Goddess of Waters.

"I'm glad we have a long weekend for the Sabbat," Diana said. She and Jewel were alone in Merrydale's postal shop. It was more than ten minutes since the last customer and they were grateful for time to talk.

"And they're both asleep," Jewel added with gratitude in her voice that only the mother of a toddler could appreciate. Sunna Woodfolk and Iris and Dolly's daughter, Diana, were sound asleep in their afternoon naps.

"How did it go?" Iris had watched the girls the evening of the ritual. Girls who had begun their menses and participated in their first Lunar Moon since the flow were given the Mark of the Goddess. The courtyard at Trillium School had been prepared for the ritual. Jewel helped Pearl who held the role of the Priestess this year.

"At one point the girls could hear the boys and were quite distracted," Jewel said, "but they settled down again." The boys' ritual of First P'aratem was being held in the school hall. When the coven planned the rituals they forgot just how loud boys could be at that age.

As the door opened, ringing a bell, they turned their attention to several townsfolk who came in to post letters and purchase stamps. After they left Iris checked their daughters. Both were still resting.

"They'll be beautiful flower girls," Iris said. Jenny and Gino had asked that both girls strew the flower petals when the circle was cast. Diana would be four at Beltane and Sunna not until Hallows but they'd be perfect.

"Is it set for Lammas?" Jewel's mind flitted to the other Handfasting. Ollis and Raven were planning a small ceremony. Jewel and Iris had formed a close friendship since Jewel began helping the postmarm. Iris knew right where the conversation had gone.

"The Sunday before Lammas," Iris answered, referring to Raven and Ollis' Handfasting.

"Two this year," Jewel mused. "What a busy coven we are!"

The coven had been very busy with the young families and the creation of Trillium School all in but a couple of years.

"She mailed the letters this morning," Iris said.

"Do none of them approve?" Holly asked.

"I think not," Arnica answered. "Raven is concerned but she knows they're still having difficulty with her move and her active role with Trillium School. Raven was always open about her beliefs but their father was Kristos at heart so religion was never really discussed."

"She told me about Marina." Raven recently learned that one of her grandchildren had converted to an Earthkin group this past year while at university. "Is that for the house?" Holly asked.

Arnica had just set aside a bottle of the Candlemas Eve water for Gino and Jenny's house blessing.

"Oops," Arnica said, moving the bottle further. Dark Star had fallen asleep, her hoof moving during a dream. He wouldn't want the bottle tipping over. If all went well the Eostara Eve Ritual would also be the young couple's new home blessing.

"I heard about Schrobbe," Holly said. They grew quiet. No matter how much joy they had in Merrydale and within their coven and school, the politics of Lothloriën remained troubling.

The news coverage was muted although in some cities the Premier got the media attention he wanted. Henly Schrobbe claimed that the military 'found' an abandoned boat on the coast. "The enemy is at hand," shouted some headlines as the Premier and his advisors claimed the boat to be from the Saracenites. The Users, the right wing faction of the Politicos and Kristos, jumped on the news. The Cathedral of Thorns in Mill City claimed that "the beast shall walk amongst us," a prophecy in the Book of Dooms, was manifesting.

"And Hatchitt was appointed to investigate..." Slade Hatchitt was everything the Earthkin did not want in a politician. It appeared he was recovering from his scandal two years ago and once again gaining power.

"Hey," Arnica shouted. Holly had just 'aspurged' him with the sacred water.

"Let's wash away the politics," Holly laughed.

Their noise woke Dark Star and all three went out to walk to the stone Circle.

The coven usually worked in the privacy of the Grove but Arnica had recommended they use the fountain Lotus had built in the school courtyard for their ritual. Observing the Sabbat in Merrydale made child care easier. The two young girls were at the Rosarios.

The Circle was fully cast and they were taking turns going to the fountain, enacting the ancient ritual in which the Goddess bathed Herself in the sacred spring, restoring her youth and vigor so that She might once again dance upon the land as the Maiden.

Arnica and Holly had visited the fountain together, dipping their fingers into the water and tracing symbols upon each other's hearts.

Peri bathed the healing scar upon her chest.

Jenny held her betrothing ring in the water, asking the Lady to bring healing to her parents.

One by one each of them sought the boon of the Goddess.

Dark Star was last, standing before the fountain and lowering her head. She did not ask favor nor blessing but thanked the Lady that the nights were still dark. She shook her horn, the magickal formula from Arnica's powder washing off. Her horn becoming visible again, she was ready to trot home with her men as a unicorn!

LXXIII - Needles and Pins

Although she was more nervous than she'd expected, the needle's droning buzz was calming in a hypnotic way. The drawing of the maiden goddess cradled by a crescent moon was now drawn upon the new skin where Peri's left breast had been. Topi and Flying Raven were softly creating rhythms on the small hand drums they'd brought with them on the train. Ollis, Raven's betrothed, was in the next chair. Peri felt comforted knowing Ollis was having one of his old tattoos (from his merchant marine years) touched up.

They'd left Merrydale early in the morning, taking the sunrise train over the mountains to Mill City. Ollis' geography students had enough work to do to keep them busy. Raven's classes were working on their individual science projects. The projects counted significantly toward their final grades for the year and Raven felt assured they'd be working hard.

They had a fine ride over. Peri looked radiant. Losing her breast to cancer left her drawing upon the growing integration of her Loon Tribe ways with the more contemporary traditions of the Renaissance beliefs she was learning from the coven. Peri and Topi Crowfeather would stay with a cousin of theirs. They were once all girls living in the River Mountains but, just as the Crowfeather sisters moved west to work at Trillium School in Merrydale, Pippi Proudfeather (her birth name was Pipestone which she *never* really liked) had moved east to teach at the Loon School when it opened the year before.

It was a fine Saturday morning, the sun warming Arnica and Holly's cabin. It was Becky Flower's first visit. She was working with Pearl to tailor the wedding dress, which was now hanging in the Becky's sewing room, the alterations pinned in place.. Becky's Aunt Juanita had sewn it by hand. She never thought she'd see a woman whose skill would match her Aunt Juanita's but Pearl could work, well, *magic*, with a needle.

"Becky," teased Pearl as the women sat sewing small velvet bags, "I *know* that all good Kristos mothers pray that their daughters marry a virile, child-producing man." Pearl and Becky were working on the gifts that Gino and Jenny would give their guests at the Midsummer wedding.

"P-Pearl," Becky Flower glowed with embarrassment but was actually very pleased. She was quite curious and hadn't made a stitch in a several minutes, watching Arnica.

Arnica couldn't resist. "Pearl, would you want to take it to the Church of the Martyr to have it blessed?"

"Arn," Holly said, trying to help Jenny's mother in her embarrassment.

"What kind of oil is that?" Becky was more interested than might have been expected.

Arnica was rubbing an herbal oil into a small stone phallus, hand-carved from quartz. "It's pure rose oil," he answered Becky. "I have to have it sent in all the way from Eastborough." That was the capitol of New Celtria far to the east in the Atlantikos.

"My Aunt Juanita rubbed a fresh rose bud..." With her daughter Jenny having converted from the Kristos religion to the Earthkin, Becky often remembered her Aunt Juanita who would have been pretty comfortable with many of Jenny's new beliefs.

Becky took a deep breath. "She rubbed it between my breasts." Odd, Juanita's flower 'blessing' didn't seem to be such a forbidden gesture among Jenny's coven. *'Coven,'* Becky reminded herself, 'my daughter is part of a *coven* with these people.'

Becky reached into the basket, scooping up lavender to sew into the small, embroidered pouch. She liked working in Arnica and Holly's cabin. Glancing at the small crystal phallus, she thought 'something new.' Something 'blue' were the velvet bags sachets she and Pearl were making, filled with lavender. She liked these people. Becky Flower had made her peace with Jenny's plans to be Handfasted.

Many things about Trillium School caused the local Merrydale folk to ponder. Not only did the school do well scholastically, but the students seemed to love their studies and work. Why, many of them went to school on Saturdays, just for extra learning. Despite some of the grumbling from the Kristos and the political maneuvering from the Users (the right-wing faction of the Politicos) to impose their beliefs upon everyone, Merrydale was proud to have the first Earthkin school in Lothloriën.

The work being done on Jenny and Gino's new home-to-be was a community effort among the Earthkin. Gino's role in the school had been prominent, even though few knew with any certainty that he was active within Arnica's coven. It was the coven who started the school and it was the coven who provided its basic faculty. As Gino grew from a boy into a man his education extended far beyond the typical classroom. His work ethic and friendly ways made him very popular, even though he was often quiet by nature. With the new house he and Jenny purchased (with Jenny's trust fund for the down payment) a mile and a half north of Merrydale the Earthkin found a joyful reason to come together. This was far more fun than the political struggles they had against Henley Schrobbe, Lothloriën's Premier.

Jenny and Rosetta, Gino's mother, were painting the doors of the kitchen cabinets. Rosetta, Trillium School's cook, also taught cooking. With Lotus' help she had designed the remodelling of the kitchen, understanding the plumbing and electrical aspects nearly as well as a contractor. Several of Jenny's classmates from the cooking class were helping.

Lotus was overseeing the framing and sheeting of the new family room which would add considerable space to the small house. Many of the boys from the school were helping, eager to gain practical building experience. Carlos, Gino's father, was helping two of the boys' fathers mix cement. A fireplace was being built with local stone.

Jenny's father, Philbert Flowers, had stopped by earlier in the morning. He was needed back in Mill City where he was working in Parliament for the Politico Party. Once again Philbert was feeling an internal crisis of faith. Seeing how healthy and vibrant these Earthkin folk were, and how strong their moral and family values, it was difficult to reconcile this with Schrobbe's rhetoric. Philbert wondered if his return to the User faction might have been rash, if he hadn't misjudged the Earthkin when he condemned Jenny's dating?

"Dark Star," Gino said, "do you remember when I first saw you?" It was eight years ago this past autumn. The young man would soon be 19 and was to be in Trillium School's first graduating class. Gino had spent so many hours helping with the house that he needed to have a quiet break. It gave him time with Dark Star, who remained one of the coven's 'mysteries,' not often seen by others.

The hatchling nudged Gino's shoulder. She lay beneath a towering cedar and Gino was sprawled out nearby. They'd been working hard. Gino was clearing a path so he and Jenny could walk to Arnica and Holly's cabin, the Grove. Through the woods it would be only a ten minute walk. On the road it was at least twice that.

Nearby were the large, woven saddle baskets into which Gino would pile brush as he cut and cleared a path. The branches would provide fuel for this year's Beltane fire. With the spring sap rising in the trees and the bulbs bursting forth at the Grove's gardens, Gino's young male lust anticipated with hope Beltane. He and Jenny had been waiting... *Two years*, his hormones sang out.

"Ow," Gino laughed. Dark Star had poked him lightly in the tummy with her horn. She knew that he was distracted with his desire for Jenny. "O.K., I'll travel with you," Gino said.

Gino sat up, his legs crossed, postured as he'd learned from Arnica and Holly. He reached into his pocket for the small, clear quartz sphere. Since his first initiation two years ago at Candlemas he was now learning how to work with an orb of his own. Holly had taught him how to share thoughts and images with the hatchling through the sphere.

Gino and Dark Star sensed Merrydale, but as a series of images. There was the park across from Iris and Dolly Dolurum's house. Look how tall the liburnum was growing! Would the Handfasting be there? It was growing in size and, with Philbert's growing approval and comfort, more of the Flowers' friends and family were being invited. There was Iris, Merrydale's postmarm, closing up the postal shop. She paused, looking toward the north. Gino could feel her thinking about Dolly. The school's principal was working at the house with the other men.

Perhaps the Handfasting would be at the school in the courtyard? Trillium School emerged in their shared vision. There was Amber, Peri and Topi's tribal sister, preparing the Equinox altar in the courtyard. Meanwhile Jewel tried to maintain a semblance of order. Dagon, now almost nine ('He's almost as old as I was when we met,' Gino thought at Dark Star), was helping his mother hide eggs around the school for tomorrow's egg hunt. His sister Sunna and her best friend, Diana Dolorum, were not yet four, both wanting to help but not quite old enough to be productive.

Dark Star's stomach rumbled gently and their images shifted to the cabin. Becky was preparing to leave. Holly was in the pantry, preparing the ritual drink for the Eostara Eve.

The hatchling was tugged back into the physical world. "You shouldn't do that," she chided Gino. The reminder of this evening's coven work to invoke fertility for the District of Merrydale turned Gino's thoughts to Jenny, and what he was thinking did not belong in their shared visioning.

Gino hugged the young unicorn and kissed her on her fetlock, then turned to run back toward the new house. There was much to clean up, people to thank, and then he had to hurry home, take his ritual bath, and come back out to the cabin for the ritual.

Dark Star trotted off. She knew that the cabin would be busy but calm as her two men prepared for the coven's arrival.

"Oh, those humans," she mused, for she had so enjoyed growing up with Gino. One more Sabbat after tonight, and then the Handfasting!

LXXV - Beltane Fires

Despite the sunny spring day, Trillium School students were busy at work. In weeks the school's fifth year would come to a close. Students not in class were busy preparing for their finals. Classrooms were as busy as the bees in Lothloriën's orchards, the students collecting new ideas and information as enthusiastically as the pollinators. Not only was summer coming but there would be two Handfastings this summer! Gino and Jenny were popular. Graduating seniors their romance was like a story book, complete with Jenny's disapproving father, her moving out of her parents' home and 'new life' as she converted to the Renaissance Tribe religion.

Pearl Lamina's small, Pictish frame, was lively as she conducted a vocal group during the music class. They would be singing at Gino and Jenny's handfasting, which would be taking place in the courtyard or, if it grew much larger, in the school hall. The song was one Pearl composed as a gift for her young friends. With Jenny in her home, Pearl had found a sense of family missing since the loss of her husband, Phoenix, over seven years ago.

Several classes were meeting together in the school hall. Amber's Social Studies class sat near Ollis Piper's World Geography students. At the moment, Flying Raven (Ollis and Flying Raven would be handfasted at Lammas, the cause of teasing by some of their students) was making a presentation about recent scientific studies, alarming in their implications for global warming. She spoke passionately about melting glaciers, encroaching disease in global forests and the enormous challenge to bring the planet back into balance. Raven avoided the politics of it all. That would be Iris' realm. Iris Dolorum was both Merrydale's postmarm as well as teaching the courses in government and political theory.

There was something special about Trillium School. The school grew out of the coven which was centered at Arnica and Holly's cabin and the faculty were either actively in the coven or closely associated with it through family. The coven's love of wisdom imbued the school with a passion for learning, something which was envied by more than several of Merrydale High's faculty! The special assembly in Trillium School's hall would culminate when the principal, Deodar Dolorum, discussed the ethical implications from the afternoon discussions.

A small group of 11th and 12th graders were sitting quietly with Arnica in the courtyard. A number of medicinal plants were now growing in the few beds and it was a good space for today's Herbal Science class.

"Look at the flower buds and let them guide you through the plant into its roots." Arnica had been showing them how to learn of a plant's strength through communion with its spirit. When the journeying was done he would be discussing herbal birth control.

Jenny found it difficult to journey. She knew how essential learning this herbal knowledge was for her.

The Hatchling

Trillium School was vibrant with the rising energies of the season. All of the classes combined to fill the school with a highly charged environment. The students were attentive in all of their work and yet, Beltane Eve was the next night!

Always precise, Philbert Flower drew the sash brush along the trim around the new, stone fireplace. Jenny's father had taken two days away from his work at Parliament in Mill City, wanting to help prepare the house where she and Gino would be living. Not a drip was to be found on the drop cloth on the floor. He stepped back to admire his work. Philbert Flower's work ethic was always very serious, a quality which had served him well within the conservative faction of the Politicos. He looked out the window. What he saw caused him distress.

Right there in the clearing within sight of his *daughter's* home the men were securing a pile of brush to use in a *Beltane fire*. And *she* - his daughter, was one of them! Flower closed his eyes. It had been a struggle to be adequately accepting of her decision to marry an Earthkin boy and he was trying to be tolerant but there it was, right within sight of the house. The men had seemed so nice and responsible. They worked hard. A banged thumb didn't even provoke blue language. How could they believe in such wanton beliefs? 'Those devil-worshippers,' he muttered to himself.

"Why, Mr. Flower, Sir, do ye not remember your wedding at the Church of the Martyr?" Sam, the plumber, was working in the kitchen. He even did work for Philbert's father, installing the new bathroom when Philbert's father modernized their house nearly fifty years ago. Sam was slow now, but his work was the best.

Philbert hadn't realized he had begun talking out loud to himself.

Sam continued, "Did they not throw rice at ye? It was so yer missus would be fertile and you would have that beautiful daughter. Is it not so different?"

"Sam, I just don't know," Philbert responded honestly. "It's been a struggle. You know what they tell us at church."

Philbert remembered Sam at the Church of the Martyr as long as he could remember.

'Well, is it so different?' Philbert asked himself. Settled for now, he went back to painting. Movement outside caught his eye again. "That is a pretty horse," he thought.

Dark Star, her horn rubbed with Arnica's ointment to keep it unseen by those who did not know, had run over to join the men working with the brush.

The fire would be smaller than originally planned. It was already quite dry this year, with predictions that the forest fire danger would be high. Henley Schrobbe, Lothloriën's Premier, advocated for increased logging as a way to reduce the fire danger and, no matter what global scientists were saying, maintained that 'global warming' was merely a false argument put forth by those who were against his Politicos administration.

Gino and Dark Star, the hatchling, had amassed quite a pile of brush when Gino cleared a path from his new home through Merrydale Forest to Arnica and Holly's cabin, which was Dark Star's home. There was far too much for the Beltane fire so it had been sorted, with select branches chosen for the fire and the rest placed beneath a tarp where it would be kept from the weather.

Gino's father, Carlos, was there, helping Lotus hold the bundle of branches. Ollis was wrapping a braided twine cord around the bundle, then securing it with a sailor's knot he learned to tie when in the merchant marines.

Gino was holding a wax figurine, hand-shaped to represent one of the goddess statues found in ancient caves of Italica across the Atlantikos. Gino and Jenny had saved candle stubs from their personal altars and the coven had saved their candle stubs as well. The waxen offering would be the couple's way of formally asking the Goddess to bless their union.

Although they would have welcomed rain, Saturday evening was warm, the early stars dancing around a low-slung Moon. They looked forward to a lunar eclipse in another three nights. The coven held hands in the Stone Circle. Jenny had Drawn Down the Moon, her first time with the coven, the first time she'd done so in a formal ritual. Jenny would be the Queen of the Meadow for Beltane.

Only Gino and Dark Star were missing from the Circle. Gino was kneeling before Arnica and Holly's altar in the cabin, calling upon the Universe to give him strength. Dark Star gazed upon this young man with pride. She had watched him outgrow his boyhood for nearly nine years and this night he would embrace his manhood.

She whinnied softly. Their thoughts were connected through the crystal orb sitting before them on the altar.

Gino sat back, massaging ointment into the soles of his bare feet. Arnica and Holly had made the mixture over the past lunar months to protect Gino's bare feet as he ran naked through the woods. What fun they'd had, Dark Star and Gino. The hatchling had helped Gino better understand the state of mind needed to run freely, letting instinct know where to place his feet.

Jenny lowered her head. Holly stood behind her, helping fold her arms across her chest. She looked so lovely, wearing a filmy robe, one of Pearl's finest creations this spring! She bowed her head in silent prayer to the Lady. Tomorrow morning she and Gino would awake in each other's arms for the first time. By sunrise on Beltane they would have consummated their troth. 'Finally,' her heart picked up its tempo.

The Goddess invoked, the coven began a joyful procession along the path to the couple's new home. New candle lanterns, matching those which led from the cabin to the Stone Circle, lit the way to the Beltane fire.

"I'm glad I don't have to pursue you naked through the woods," Ollis teased Raven.

"Ah, but if we were their ages?" Raven hadn't felt this wonderful in years.

"It's time." Dark Star nudged Gino. The hatchling could sense the coven gathering around the brush pile.

Gino and Dark Star went outside. It *was* time. Gino put out his lantern and set it on a shelf by the drying shed. He slowed his thoughts, as he had been trained, and brought the images to mind as he moved himself into a deep trance. It was time for the Horned Dance.

Dark Star trotted off to join the coven.

The fire was beautiful, controlled yet wild. The coven held hands as they danced the Rune around it. As the final word spiralled up into the night, Jenny stepped forth. In a single movement the robe was parted and removed, handed to Pearl.

She reached forward, an unlit torch in hand. Catching some flame, she stepped outside the circle of loved ones and began her dance toward the new gardens and remodeled house. The coven sat quietly, Dark Star laying near Arnica and Holly yet turned so she could watch Jenny. This was the first time the hatchling had ever witnessed this human custom!

"Maybe in my next life I could be human," Dark Star thought.

The Goddess was within Jenny. The Maiden was singing and crooning, wailing and sighing. She called out into the wild for her lover. It was time to consecrate the Earth.

A wild howl came from the woods, sending a shiver through the coven, raising heat within Jenny and bringing a smile to Dark Star's heart.

Gino's presence appeared out of the woods, his naked youthfulness a work of art. He didn't see the coven yet Dark Star knew that he sensed them, but all he could see was his betrothed. He whooped through the night, quickly reaching Jenny. He whisked her off her feet and carried her into the house. The torch's light could be seen moving from room to room.

The coven rose. The fire having burnt fast and joyful, was now little more than embers. Dolly (Deodar's name among his friends) and Lotus shoveled a few spadefuls of soil to protect the forest and the coven walked back to the Stone Circle, gathering and putting out the candle lanterns as they went.

Would the magick worked this night protect the Land of Lothloriën?

LXXVI - A Perfect Morning

"Look at them all," Jenny exclaimed. There were baskets of flower petals sitting all about the walkway leading to the entrance to Trillium School. Graduation had been two weeks ago. Since that time no one would allow either Jenny or Gino to set one foot into the school or the hall. She was unprepared for what was only the first of many surprises.

"That's nothing," Peri Crowfeather responded in astonishment. Peri and her sister Topi rose early this Midsummer morning, joining their friends at Trillium School for the Handfasting. "Come, look," the Loon Tribe woman said, taking Jenny by the hand to quickly take her into the school's courtyard.

There were vases of flowers everywhere. Canning jars, gallon jugs, all manner of containers had been covered with paper and fabrics and filled with flowers from local gardens.

"She's been busy," Topi mused when she saw a stunned Jenny brought into the school's courtyard.

When Jenny's mother, Becky Flower, had read through the Handfasting Ritual, she was deeply moved. The passages referring to her daughter's pagan deities were uncomfortable reading, but the ritual poetry was beautiful, romantic and left her with many days of thought. Reading that the Circle would be first strewn with flower petals, Becky offered the flowers in her own garden and, although she understood Arnica's reasoning, Jenny's mother was just a little disappointed to learn that they were being gathered from the sacred gardens from many of the Earthkin homes in Merrydale.

However, Arnica's suggestion was perfect and Becky was thrilled to know she had great freedom to decorate the school, the courtyard and to provide the altar flowers. This would be even more fun! When Becky's friends learned that the flowers in their gardens were welcome as part of their friend's daughter's wedding (it was easier for them to hold onto the conventional word) they began transforming glass containers into creative and exceptionally beautiful works of art.

Topaz and Peridot were decorating a large, school folding table. Draped with fabrics, they were creating a small altar with gems and minerals. Many of the specimens they had gathered themselves from sacred sites in the River Mountains near Eagle's Nest, their tribal village. A beautiful guest book sat waiting.

Nearby was a large basket filled with 'something blue.' Becky and Pearl hand-stitched small, blue velvet bags, each filled with dried lavender flowers from last summer's harvest. There were enough for all of the women and girls who would be attending.

The courtyard was festive with all the scents of flowers and, when near the basket, the pungent lavender aroma. Jenny didn't tarry, for she had much to do on her Handfasting morning, and turned to walk down the corridor to the large school hall.

Jenny had barely made it past the first classroom doors when the sound of hooves lightly tapping alerted her to the next Handfasting surprise. Dark Star, the hatchling, came trotting toward her. It amazed Jenny how lightly the hatchling could be on her hooves when she was indoors. "Perhaps it had something to do with the astral," she mused.

And then, "my Goddess!" the young woman exclaimed, "Look at you!" Jenny was delighted and hugged and kissed Dark Star, who proudly stepped back and turned her head so she could be admired.

"What do you think," asked Pearl. Pictish, small of build and light on *her* feet as well, Pearl moved quickly to give Jenny a warm hug. The girl had become almost like a daughter, living with Pearl for a year and a half since leaving her parents' home.

"It's a horn mask," Jenny oohed. "Dark Star, you're our 'mascot!'" Trillium School's mascot was a unicorn, an obvious choice as the coven provided the founding organization and most of the teaching staff. Pearl had sewn a beautiful, beaded 'horn' which fit snugly over Dark Star's horn and had a conspicuous tie beneath the hatchling's chin.

"What a wonderful illusion," Jenny said, for it did look as if a small, precocious horse was transformed into a 'unicorn' with a tie-on horn.

"Arnica was working to devise a new ointment formula so Dark Star could be here all day without setting off 'unicorn alarm bells' among those who don't know..."

"Almost everyone," Jenny interjected in her enthusiasm.

"Today's the debut of Dark Star as a 'unicorn' for all of Merrydale," Pearl said proudly, "and, if it goes well, the only challenge will be new decorated 'horns' as her real horn grows."

Dark Star had already started down the corridor, whinnying impatiently and pausing at the corner. She wanted Jenny to see the hall.

The school hall was large enough to hold everyone. Although every student in Trillium School and their parents and families would have loved to attend the

Handfasting they knew that this was, after all, for the couple and their immediate friends and family. As it was the guest list had grown and the hall was just large enough.

But the large space no longer looked like the Trillium School Hall. When Jenny last saw it there was a large "Bless Our Graduates" sign hanging at one end and she was proud to have joined this class, the first to have completed all five years of Trillium leading to graduation.

Entering through the double doors, Jenny gasped. The hall had been completely transformed. It appeared that endless bolts of cotton gauze were stretched out and suspended from the rafters, enough so that the entire ceiling was hidden from view. The windows were covered with panels of plywood, blocking out all outdoor light. The walls were draped with fabric remnants of various earth tones and hundreds of house plants were set along the walls creating the feeling of a woodland in the evening.

Eight large papier-mâché 'stones' provided the ritual circle at the center and over the altar a large, filtered flood light shone down, almost like the Moon. Small Yule lights between the gauze and the ceiling looked like stars. Somehow the hall looked like an outdoor Stone Circle beneath a full moon!

Arnica and Holly were arranging their ritual tools upon the altar. The elemental altars stood just before each of their standing stones and the Earthkin family Jenny had found through Gino was busy preparing for her Handfasting. Jenny took a deep breath, calmed herself, and dropped into a light trance. She wanted to walk around the circle but quietly, without disruption.   Iris, both Merrydale's postmarm and Trillium's teacher of political theory and government, had numerous feathers on her robe. Jenny thought she recognized them as some of the feathers Peri and Topi had brought from the Loon Tribe. Iris' husband, Deodar, was the school principal. Dolly, as the coven knew him, was placing some blocks of charcoal upon the large censer which sat upon the east altar.

"May we embrace the fires of longing... No, that's not it." Dagon, at nine, was ten years younger than Jenny and Gino but some unusual magickal events indicated that he would have a strong future as an Earthkin Priest. "May we embrace the fires of learning..." Dagon was a perfectionist, and this would be the first time he had a ritual role in public... And this was a *huge* event for Merrydale. "The fires of learning ... that's it!" Dagon beamed at Jenny, but quickly sensed that she was in mental preparation for her Handfasting and returned to his script. Dagon would be at the south altar with Pearl, but Pearl had gone to the changing room and was waiting to help Jenny into her dress.

Jenny felt the sound of water before she realized it reached her ears. Jewel and Lotus Woodfolk, Dagon's parents, were at the west altar. Lotus had teased about moving the courtyard fountain in for the West so they could *really* have water!

"How lucky I am," Jenny thought. "Gino has some of the best qualities of each of these men." Gino was learning different skills and knowledge from them and, seeing Lotus, she thought "that would be just like him." Lotus was kneeling, holding a large, hand-blown glass bowl as Jewel slowly poured water from a cut crystal pitcher so the sound of it filled the temple space with the music of water. There was music in the air.

"Dear Ones," Jenny said, giving a curtsy at the north altar. Flying Raven was so dear. She made the study of science seem like a love affair with Mother Earth. And Ollis Piper, this curious man, would be joined to Raven at the next Sabbat during a small, quiet Handfasting at the cabin. His unexpected arrival in Merrydale brought Iris her father, a man she'd never known. It was difficult for a time, but Ollis had his daughter, even his granddaughter, Diana who turned four this past Sabbat, and soon he would have his wife.

"Who could have believed it," Ollis thought, "that one so young would be Handfasted even before Raven and I are joined." Ollis was now retired from the merchant marine but his experiences made him ideal as the world geography instructor.

Jenny walked over and quietly kissed Arnica and Holly on their cheeks.

"There is music," she thought, and the question on her face left her thinking Arnica could read her thoughts.

"Wren is here," he said quietly. "You haven't met Wren and Robin Sylphing, yet, but Wren is our coven bard even though she lives in Highlands. She has brought a new Handfasting song to sing as you are brought to the altar."

Jenny looked about for Wren but Holly brought her focus back. "Quickly," he said. "Pearl is waiting for you. Wren will be here for several days. You have time."

Jenny stepped through the doors. There, just outside the Circle, Gino waited. He was wearing a deep, green robe and looked so handsome. Arnica, holding his staff, and Holly stood at the circle's portal waiting for her. Wren's harp filled the hall with the most beautiful of sounds. Her bardic skill had woven all of the friends and family into the illusion that they were among the trees...

"Join me in the woods tonight and sailing go, my love..."

Heads turned to look at her but Jenny's growing ritual skills allowed her to remain focused on the Circle.

The young woman was beautiful in the dress her Aunt Juanita had made for Jenny's mother. "Something borrowed: Pearl's magickal needles made the dress look as if Aunt Juanita had made the dress just for our Jenny." The word 'magickal' had slipped freely through Becky Flower's thoughts.

As she neared the opening in the northeast between the 'standing stones,' she passed between the parents.

What changes their son had brought into their lives. Carlos had once worked in the flour mills in Mill City trying to earn enough money for his family but now he and Rosetta both worked for Trillium School and their son had graduated as one of its top students.

Rosetta was wearing a beautiful, blue velvet dress with small, white beads stitched into it. She had certainly surprised Pearl. Coming from a seamstress as talented as Pearl, the compliments to her own sewing were exceptionally fine.

Amber Whitefeather and Peridot and Topaz Crowfeather began walking to escort Jenny on on her final steps to stand next to Gino at the portal. Holding mountain sagewort braided into cords, they accepted flame from Holly and prepared to smudge the couple once Jenny reached Gino.

Becky Flower was past thinking. The beauty of her daughter, this setting, it was all so different than the big 'church wedding' she once hoped for her daughter and then, after Jenny left home only seventeen with two more years of school... But this, this was beyond belief! Becky was thrilled.

Philbert felt a sense of relief, of inner peace. Seeing the look of joy upon his daughter's face reflected as pure love and respect as Gino looked at Jenny, Philbert knew that this would work. His hand reached to his breast, feeling the envelope in his inner jacket pocket. "It was the tree," he thought. "What did Jenny call it? A 'dryad tree?'" Jenny and her father had shared several mystical experiences at that tree. Whether it was his Kristos or one of Jenny's nature deities didn't really matter, did it? Sam the plumber knew. Philbert's gift to Jenny and Gino was something new. He'd had to pull a lot of strings in Parliament and call in every political favor he could think of. Despite Henley Schrobbe's threat of a veto, Merrywood would now be protected. Its designation as a 'trust forest' meant that the forests surrounding Merrydale, Gino and Jenny's new home and that 'dryad tree' would never be logged.

"Gino, do you take your Lover and your Friend to be your sworn partner..." Arnica was reading the vows as the couple knelt before the altar. On the far side at the north altar Raven and Ollis looked at each other. Their Handfasting was at Lammas!

Gino reached into his pocket for the ring he would place on Jenny's finger. It encircled the quartz phallus Arnica and Holly had given him, one which would be placed within their altar in their new home. "Something old," Holly had said.

LXXVII - The Print in the Center

The Stone Circle suddenly filled with the sound of bells and, as if on cue, chickadees and finches began singing their songs as well. Flying Raven and Ollis Piper, their wrists bound with a red cord, hastened along the path to the House on the Rise.

Just before they hurried through the portal of the Stone Circle, Raven tossed the circlet of flowers from her hair. Wouldn't you know? Dark Star, the beloved unicorn who had hatched in this very Stone Circle nine years ago this spring, caught it with her horn. The hatchling trotted ahead of them, sometimes breaking into a canter and running around the newly married couple. The air was filled with the sounds of glee.

Although Raven glowed with a slight blush ("they all *know*," she thought as she and Ollis went off to celebrate the Great Rite and consummate their Handfasting), she was so happy and grateful that Gino and Jenny offered the privacy of their new home.

Dark Star was so enjoying herself. Although exuberant and happy at Gino and Jenny's Handfasting just this past Midsummer, that was a large event held at Trillium School in Merrydale. She was able to be 'horned,' but wearing the fake horn mask wasn't the same as being herself. Unicorns are very proud of their horns.

"She's filled with the frolics," Holly laughed as he and Arnica began collecting their altar tools.

"May I help?" Marina, Raven's granddaughter and only family member who attended, was a delightful young woman. In her second year of University at Verdeville, she was able to travel to Merrydale without her family knowing. Marina had always been Raven's favorite, if only because she resisted her mother's pressure to conform to Caroline's increasingly conservative Kristos beliefs. Marina was very independent and, upon coming into a small inheritance from her grandfather's trust, upset her parents by announcing her plans to move to Verdeville to attend the University.

"Follow us," Arnica said. "We have everything from the altar but we'll get you some garden scissors from the potting shed and you can work with Holly to fill the vases."

Iris and Deodar had help collecting their things from the East Altar. Diana, four, carefully carried the box of incense resins. She was so careful to avoid any mishap. Gino and Jenny set their altar items from the South outside the ring of stones. They would not take them to their home until later, knowing that it was now sacred space for Raven and Ollis.

Pearl carried her antique, cut glass pitcher, one which was once her grandmother's. Dagon placed his items from the West Altar into a basket and then helped his parents with the North Altar. It had held the ritual cake as well and Jewel and Lotus Woodfolk appreciated his help. Dagon was now nine and growing within the coven. Sunna was already off, her job was to help with the flowers.

"This is heaven," Iris exclaimed. Merrydale's postmarm stretched out, her head laying on Dolly's lap. A Handfasting inevitably gave couples much to muse. How different were their lives. Handfasted just five years ago at Beltane, Iris was now well-known as part of Trillium School's faculty as well as her postal duties. And Dolly! Deodar was a minister at the Church of the Martyr when they met but now, as principle, Dolly had done much to make Trillium School a success and a role model for other Earthkin schools. Their legs stretched out into the sun, but they lay on their blanket in the shade. Ollis sat near them. What an odyssey this had been for him. He would never have imagined himself marrying at this stage of life, and his daughter and her husband at an altar. Ollis was now part of his daughter's coven and married to a wonderful woman!

Lotus and Dagon set up a wooden framework and stretched canvas over the top. They could lounge about in the gardens all afternoon and no one would need worry about the sun. He was proud of Dagon's help. Lotus and Jewel sat on little chairs with Sunna and Diana. The four of them were the 'children's table' much to the delight of the two girls. Jewel had painted it a color she thought of as 'Goddess blue' after Lotus and Dagon gave it a final sanding. When school started it was going to be part of the pre-school program.

"How is your Aunt Claudia?" Raven inquired discreetly. Claudia was, in Raven's mind, the most radical of her Kristos daughters.

All three girls had married Kristos husbands and were aligned with the User faction of the Politicos. Her daughters and their churches saw the political and religious differences between the Earthkin and Kristos as something abhorrent. Claudia had the most difficulty with her mother's life, creating a distance which at first was very painful for Raven. As time passed, Raven accepted their choices and was so happy she had moved across country to Merrydale. And now! Raven looked down at her wrist as she waited Marina's answer, noting the new ring and the absence of the red cord. When they returned a shout of 'the cord's gone' led to a new bell-ringing as she and Ollis approached the gardens. Flying Raven was quite pleased that she was no longer the center of attention.

"My mom and Aunt Claudia had quite a time when I was a senior," Marina said. Without thinking she reached over and caressed Raven's arm. She mad missed her grandmother more than she realized. "When she learned that my parents said I could go to university at Verdeville, she had a fit." Verdeville, the seat of the District of the Mothervalley, was a large, cosmopolitan city. 'Sin city,' is what Claudia called it.

"How is your mom," Raven asked. Perhaps Raven was relieved to be away from their politics but she still missed her daughters. Caroline seemed the most understanding but was not able to stand up to her sister Claudia nor to her own husband. Raven stretched out on the blanket, glad to once again be in comfortable clothing, the beautiful, blue gown Pearl had sown safely hanging in the House on the Rise.

"Sometimes lost in that world of rednecks, as she told me once," Marina answered. "But she does well and she's happy. Daddy treats her well and mom does like the structure of their church. But it's not for me!"

Teasing each other, Jenny slipped an ice cube down the front of Gino's pants. Soon they were rolling in the grass, teasing each other and then off they went, running. What joy their Handfasting had brought the coven!

Arnica and Holly sat over to the side, talking with Carlos and Rosetta, Gino's parents. They had laughed, being the 'old married' couples. Arnica and Holly had been together for over thirty-two years. Even before they met for the first time people they knew among the Earthkin tribes told them they should meet. They were truly soul mates and looked enough alike that, when in the hostile territory of the Users, often were thought of as brothers.

Gino was the Rosario's only child and they were so proud of him. Just over nineteen, he had spent the past eight years studying with the coven and it changed all of their lives. Carlos no longer had to spend most of his time over the mountains in Mill City, working in the flour mills. Both Carlos and Rosetta worked for Trillium School, much respected and deeply loved by all of the community.

"'The House on the Rise,' is that what they're calling it?" Carlos asked no one in particular and all of them in general.

"It seems more that it's what the house is calling itself," Arnica answered and, with Holly off guard, began tickling his lover's ear with a long-stemmed clover.

"Hey," Holly jumped, at first expecting a bug of some type. Holly knew that it was an expression of love. The two men had such a wonderful relationship and were admired by most of Merrydale, even by many of the Kristos who sought out their herbal knowledge. Although their church condemned two men living together in love, how could anyone criticize such a loving, happy partnership. "Who's up for croquet?" Holly called out.

Cries of "I am" and "me" filled the garden. Arnica and Holly had set up the croquet hoops on a relatively level area of grass. It was mowed just for this celebration. The two moms helped their daughters. Iris and Diana would play as one person and Jewel would help Sunna. The moms would wield the mallets and the girls would point at the goals.

Dagon wanted to join in with Holly and the girls as well. "Come on, Ollis, Dad..." he called out.

"He's holding back because he knows I can beat him," Dolly teased Lotus.

Dark Star trotted up, whinnying. Her coat looked more iridescent than ever, the blue tints glimmering in the sun like the wings of a dragonfly.

"*You*," Holly said to the hatchling, scratching her ears, "had better lay down in the shade and cool down." Dark Star nuzzled him in agreement. Still young for a unicorn at nine, some days she didn't feel quite as coltish any more and this year was unseasonably hot.

"Can I pick fresh borage for her?" Marina had already learned what would cool the hatchling and Dark Star *loved* borage.

"Yes, there's some in bloom over near the potting shed," Arnica said.

Just then Pearl came out from the cabin. "Arnica, there's a call for you." Pearl looked a bit worried. "The fire in the River Mountains foothills is spreading in this heat. The marshall has asked if you can make up more of the burn balm and ointment for the crews."

"Go play. Maybe you can give Iris or Jewel a turn with the girls," Rosetta said to Carlos. "I want to go in and work with Pearl and the others." Rosetta was ready to spend some time with the women.

Pearl, the Crowfeather sisters Peri and Topi, and Amber were sitting in Arnica and Holly's cabin, finishing up the final stitches on a large Handfasting quilt they were giving to Raven and Ollis. Each person attending the handfasting had signed their name and the signatures were being embroidered to keep the autographs as a wonderful memory.

And right in the center of the quilt? Dark Star's hoof print, embroidered in beautiful shades of blue and jet black.

LXXVIII - School's In

Trillium School began later this year. Despite a summer drought the harvest was good and the markets busy. Earthkin parents in Merrydale on business were happy to let their young spend time at Trillium School and the building had been a hub of activity for weeks leading up to the New Moon. Two Handfastings during the summer invigorated the coven and they began the school year with enthusiasm. The meetings for faculty and staff proved great fun. The faculty were all part of the coven and the 'staff' either coven or family. This year a small faculty room had been added. There was no room in the school building but the house which had been converted into a library building just a year ago had a large kitchen. It was a lively and loving environment with which to provide a solid education which included religious emphasis on Mother Earth.

This sixth year promised to be the best yet. It had been a long, dry summer which meant the rivers were low and swimming was not easy to find. The students were more than ready to return. As Lammas passed students began turning to the school's library which moved into the converted house just last autumn. It was now open to Trillium students several afternoons a week.

Gino Rosario, nineteen last spring and Handfasted this past Midsummer, was hired as the school's part-time librarian. Recently accepted into one of the top educational programs, Gino was studying by correspondence from Genetricia University in Verdeville, the seat of the District of the Mothervalley. Generally quiet in the mornings, the library was an ideal setting for his schooling. His afternoon library work and his ability to help the school's students would be the foundation for his teaching experience, and would be gaining him academic credits as well.

With the first week of classes behind them, Trillium School was settling down. Arnica felt relief. His Herbal Science classes would begin meeting at the cabin from the

Equinox through Hallowmas, later if the weather gods were kind. This would allow Arnica to tend the gardens and harvest, finishing the bundling of herbs for tithing which was good for the juniors. The seniors would be learning how to create tinctures from fresh roots and rhizomes. The school's principal, Deodar Dolorum (Dolly, to his friends) put together a creative schedule. Arnica's botany class would meet on Thursdays and Fridays but run two periods each day.

Dark Star, the unicorn hatchling, enjoyed occasional trips into Merrydale and enjoyed the school but, frankly, so many young humans were a distraction. Now just nine and a half (in *human* calendar years, she would think), Dark Star enjoyed the days she had the Grove to herself. The hatchling was now studying Unicorn Mysteries from both her father, Andrius and her grandmare, Lillian as well as learning how to journey with care into the Otherlands where she could experience the Land of Faerie more intensely, something she could *not* do when she had humans with her.

At other times she would grow a bit lonely for the excitement of the young and nudge Arnica or Holly into putting her 'horn mask' on her so she could trot in to Merrydale, looking like a smallish horse wearing a false unicorn's horn. Although some of the Earthkin 'knew' of Dark Star's true nature, Merrydale loved the idea of a small horse wearing a unicorn disguise. After all, Trillium School's mascot was a unicorn!

"I heard one of the constables call her 'old frowny face,' and she doesn't seem to like me," Jenny was talking with Dolly about Missy Birches, Mayor Browning's secretary. "My job is perfect and I enjoy it so much. Missy is *polite*, but I don't think she likes me." Jenny had been hired for the opening in the Merrydale Council's permit and license office. She loved having the contact with the public and was very good with filing.

Life was good for the young married couple, Handfasted not even two Sabbats. Their newly remodeled home was paid for and they were able to live simply. Walking down the school corridor to Dolly's office, Jenny reflected on the dramatic changes in her life. Two years ago she was still living with her parents, attending (but not enjoying) the Church of the Martyr with them. There was still occasional discomfort between her and her father and she sometimes wondered if they would *ever* be as close as they were.

There were new banners hanging in the corridor. Pearl, the coven seamstress and Trillium School's art and music teacher, sewed them this summer with help from Rosetta, Gino's mother. The first was the largest and read 'Trillium School.' Beneath that was Merrydale and the background had the embroidered outline of the school's mascot, a unicorn. Dark Star was very proud of that banner. The next banner was for Loon School in Mill City, just starting its third year. Four new Earthkin schools had opened this fall. Yarrow School East and Yarrow School West in Verdeville were the next two banners. Iguana School in Cloverville and The Elm Druids School in Eastborough were the remaining banners. There was some discussion about including The Elm because it was in Atalanta, not in Lothloriën, but for now being an Earthkin school was enough.

"Missy attended the Church of the Martyr when I was still a Kristos minister," Dolly said. "She was not a happy woman. She stayed at home to care for her aging father who was a handful. As his memory went he was increasingly unruly, often throwing tantrums like a child. Missy's was a hard life for a young, attractive woman."

The Hatchling

"It's hard to imagine her any different than I know her." Jenny was thoughtful. "This helps me understand her, but I'm not sure how to deal with her."

"Cautiously. Her service to her widowed father kept her from dating, from continuing her education. And she's heard some of the local children call her 'old frowny face.'"

Jenny giggled. She remembered doing the same when she was little.

"Just remember," the principal continued, "she's jealous of you. When she was your age she abandoned her dreams of marriage and university to care for her father, a man who didn't even know who she was and who acted out his rage at having lost his own memory. Compassion will be your key."

Jenny hurried off so she would have time to stop in at the school library and drop off a sack lunch for Gino before her lunch break was over.

With the promise of a light frost, the coven chose to work their Autumn Eve ritual in the warm sun of the September afternoon. The Circle closed, Gino and Dark Star trotted along the new path from the Stone Circle to the House on the Rise. Gino and Jenny's new home had a larger cleared area with room for fire pit (safely removed from the trees of Merrywood) and this would be their first fire. Gino was quite proud of the stone lined hollow. The hatchling so loved having Gino and Jenny just a short trot through the woods.

Arnica and Holly carried the large basket with their altar tools, walking back to their cabin. "I've been teaching them about the magick of words," Holly was talking about his classes. "Somehow, thinking of them as *magick* has raised their interest in learning to use grammar as a useful tool." Holly loved teaching!

"It's the same with the senior herbal science class," Arnica answered. "Oh, look!" A nuthatch landed nearby on a sunflower and pecked a seed loose. "Understanding that there's a connection between our Mother Earth and botany and herbal magick and medicine makes them so much more interested and appreciative."

"Speaking of connections, do you know what Lillian is teaching Dark Star?" Holly often communicated with the hatchling through the sharing of images in their crystal orb.

"I know that one of the subjects has to do with the Great Rite." Arnica chuckled. "Ever since Lammas of last year the mention of either Joachim or Boaz gets quite a reaction from her." Dark Star was *very* attracted to those two stallions she met in the Otherworld. "I'm not certain that it's actually *blushing*, but it must be as close as a unicorn can come!"

They laughed, happy in knowing that Dark Star was able to run freely between the cabin and the House on the Rise, safe within the magick of Merrywood.

The sun was lowering itself down to the tops of the douglas firs of Merrywood. Two long, make-shift tables were covered with red and white checked picnic cloths and a litter of plates and utensils and numerous covered bowls. The autumn feast had been sumptuous and they enjoyed the bright warmth of the fire.

"You're not serious," Iris said. Merrydale's postmarm had found her 'public' role in Merrydale growing since joining the faculty nearly four years ago. Last year she had begun teaching her World Politics course evenings because so many local adults were interested.

This summer Lothloriën's Premier, Henly Schrobbe, called for elections. The Politico Party hoped to further their agenda which promoted an increased use of natural resources (including cutting vast forests for lumber). The Politicos were dependent upon the votes and financial support of their right-wing faction, the Users, who believed that their fundamentalist approach to the Kristos was the *only* way. A year ago the news was dominated by Schrobbe's attempted battle with the Saracenites and, although that potential war never materialized (Dark Star, Joachim and Boaz had key roles in that solution), Slade Hatchitt, another User spokesman, continued to try and stir fear, claiming that Lothloriën was being infiltrated by 'the enemy,' renegade Saracenites, who would try to overthrow Lothloriën.

The public was confused with conflicting reports. Although many of the Users spoke in Kristos churches and a few even denounced the new Earthkin schools as works of the devil, the coven felt it best to maintain a separation of religion and government, yet so many of Merrydale wanted Iris to teach evening classes this year to help them learn more about the workings of Lothloriën's government.

Holly and Arnica sliced pies they'd brought from the cabin, fresh-baked this very morning. One pear pie and two apple pies, and an oat and borage biscuit for Dark Star!

"Jenny, your preference?" Holly asked.

"A small apple, please." Jenny looked at the others, eager to share the news. "As I walked back to Town Hall I remembered something I learned from all of you. I asked Missy for help and explained that I had a dilemma."

Jenny now had everyone's attention.

"What did she say," asked Amber. Amber's experience with Missy Birches had not been comfortable. When Amber still had the Crystal Emporium she felt Missy's disapproval of any shop owned by a woman from the Loon Tribe. Amber hoped that she had misread Missy's behavior.

"I spoke to the goddess which would be within Missy. She was very ready to help and our being Earthkin did not seem to be an issue at all. And get this..." Jenny looked at Iris, "she immediately called Mildred Poindexter, the president of the Floral Belles."

"Is that really the group's name?" laughed Peri Crowfeather. Sometimes these immigrant peoples had the *strangest* ways of honoring Mother Earth.

"Yes, it's part of Merrydale's 'society,'" answered Arnica.

"Did she have a space for my classes?" asked Iris, who was more than ready to get the classes going. The politicking was strong and the people needed a clear understanding of the election.

"No," Jenny continued, "but Mrs. Poindexter called a friend of hers and ..."

"And?" asked several voices all at once.

"Believe it or not, the reception hall in the Merrydale Hotel is ours for free!" Jenny was just delighted. As voices exclaimed their amazement, Jenny added "Missy lobbied the hotel's owner, after Mrs. Poindexter got things going, and convinced him that it would be good for business. In fact, she reminded him that the reception for our Handfasting," she looked at Gino with the devotion of the young, "was at Trillium School and suggested that he should begin to look forward to the changes taking place in Merrydale. Can you believe it?"

"I can't believe this pie," Lotus said. "Holly, did you make this crust?"

It was a beautiful, latticework crust. "Not I," Holly said. "We have none other to thank than Rosetta."

Gino's mother, Rosetta Rosario, smiled, shy yet proud. Carlos reached over and put his arm around his wife. How good was life. No longer did he have to live part-time across the mountains in Mill City, struggling to earn enough for his family in the flour mills. These people were his coworkers and he loved his job tending Trillium School and its grounds.

Dark Star looked around at her humans. Stars were bright in the dark, clear sky. There would be a frost tonight and, although the fire was toasty, she knew they'd all soon be heading to their homes. Just the other night Lillian had begun showing her how to scry the future upon the surface of a small pool of water found in their secret temple in the Otherworld.

"Enjoy tonight," the hatchling silently wished her humans. "Difficult times are coming."

LXXIX - Hallows Skeletons in the Campaign

The Lodgefellows, owners of the Merrydale Hotel were pleased. Iris' class was drawing a crowd. The dining room and coffee shop were at capacity prior to each class and the snacks offered at the news stand sold briskly.

This was the fifth session in the evening series which explained how Lothloriën's government worked. Iris was a lively speaker. Many of Merrydale's residents knew her as the postmarm and now as the wife of Deodar Dolorum, former Kristos minister but now the principal of the Earthkin's school. What a story that had been!

Iris was a warm, friendly speaker. No wonder the postal shop was always a gathering place for the locals to exchange news. But apart from the faculty and students of Trillium School, where she had been teaching citizenship and government along with political theory for several years, few ever knew she had such a grasp of the political workings of their national government. Word spread.

The second week the reception hall held a standing-room only crowd. The Political Theory students from Trillium School sat on the floor in front, getting credit for attending the series and later writing a thesis on its impact on Merrydale's citizens. Before the third session met Salmond Burnside, Merrydale's fire marshal, intervened, meeting with the faculty and the Hotel's owners, the Lodgefellows, who agreed to repeat the series. The *Merrydale Gazette* put a notice on the front page to let the public know that no more could register but that Iris would repeat the series. The brief article recommended the series, adding that the repeated series would be of great value even with the election already passed.

The first week a few representatives of the Users' faction of the Politicos were outside the hotel, picketing. They had difficulty believing that someone from Trillium School, even Iris who was Merrydale's postmarm, would be objective. John Trouver, the town's Chief Constable, convinced the three men to go up to the reception hall and listen for themselves.

The Users, prepared to respond with animosity, believed that Iris, an Earthkin and the wife of '*that turncoat*,' would be biased against the Politicos Party.

"Well, that was something, wasn't it?" Jewel and Pearl collected food outside the hotel. The price of admission was one non-perishable food item. Unlike Mill City, Merrydale was able to accept home-canned goods.

Gino and Ollis Piper were loading the goods into a large cart so Trouver could drive the cartons of food to The Larder, Merrydale's food bank. Despite the few Users who had never forgiven Dolorum for his resignation from the Church of the Martyr and his becoming not only Earthkin but the principal of Trillium School, the residents of Merrydale were generally quite proud of how well the school was doing. Mayor Browning had suggested the food collection and Iris' classes at the Hotel had done much to help families in need.

The Larder reported that they'd never received so much food outside of the organized Kristos church drives at the holidays!

"Saracenia is a very ancient land. Its inhabitants are primarily a tribal people and there have been border disputes and territorial wars with the country of Italica as far back as recorded time. The Saracenites are a monotheistic people and worship a god they call Bawa'al." Iris had told the audience that she wanted to give them some information about the country which Schrobbe and Hatchitt referred to as 'the enemy.'

A couple of the more right-wing Kristos in the audience were heard muttering. The Kristos believed that their God, Krista, was the only religion and that all other religions would lead to hell. The Users believed that the Earthkin peoples, both the indigenous Descendant Tribes as well as the Renaissance Tribes, would all end up in 'hell.'

"Bawa'al's followers are not tolerant," Iris continued. "They believe that their religion is the only way and that all other peoples are infidels." She took a quick breath, calmed herself, and continued, moving into potentially dangerous territory.

"Marian, the mother of the Krista, lived in ancient times in Italica. Several centuries later the emerging Kristos followers found themselves in a holy war with the Saracenites. Each side believes that their religion is right and that the other is wrong. Even in the best of times any cooperation between the two cultures has been grudging and it takes little for hostility to return."

Iris was relating the history of this culture but in an objective way and, to her relief, not even the Users who intended to protest her classes objected to her material.

"If the abandoned boat discovered last January by the coastal militia was, indeed, left by Saracenites who were attempting to invade Lothloriën, this would be the first time that holy war had ever crossed an ocean. However, the Saracenites believed that the oceans were crossed when our Premier came close to bringing our troops into war against them last summer."

There was some controversy over whether or not this boat had, in fact, originated in Saracenia or if it was a claim Schrobbe's party was using toward their own political goals.

"Is the school open?" John Trouver pulled up in front of Trillium School and leaned out the open window to call to Carlos. Mr. Rosario was sweeping dead leaves off the school's sidewalk.

"No, sir," Carlos answered, "but they're inside working. Can I help you?" Gino's father was always very respectful of the law.

"If Arnica is here, I have a photo I'd like set on the ancestral altar," the Chief Constable replied, surprising Carlos a little.

"It looks like you're on the way to The Larder," Carlos said. "Do you have room for Rosetta's tomato sauces?"

"You bet I do." Trouver loved good food and he's already had some of Rosetta's sauce. "It makes me wish I could go to the food bank for my own groceries," he said, laughing.

Suddenly Carlos realized ... "Just a minute, sir, I need to make sure the men aren't ... in prayer," he stammered, hastening to the school's entrance.

"It's important to understand politics and social conflict without blame," Iris was answering a young woman in the audience whose question clearly placed the Politicos in the role of the 'bad guys' when it came to forest preservation.

"These are simply different views of how humans would relate to their environment." Iris pushed her braid back over her shoulder.

Dolly was so proud of his wife. He'd never seen her speaking before a large group before these classes started and his admiration had grown considerably. Even Diana, their toddler of four and half, seemed to be listening.

"How many of you have been to Europa?" Iris asked. A dozen or so raised their hands. Many looked around to see who had travelled across the Atlantikos.

"How many of you have seen pictures of the countryside in Europa, and marveled at how beautiful and quaint it is?" Iris asked next. It looked as if every hand in the hall went up, including her students.

"Think of this," her voice softened and everyone was drawn in to listen closely. "Once upon a time Europa was all forested, much as the District of Merrydale and the northern Districts of Lothloriën."

"What happened?" a voice called out.

"They chose to cut their trees for lumber and to improve their economies for their people. They expanded their farm land to grow food for their increasing population. They used the wood in their factories and became the leading culture on our planet."

The hall fell silent. Few had ever considered that evolution before. Some reflected on Europa's struggle now that it's populations grew and its countries had, over the centuries, gone to war with each other. Some began to better understand the Politicos' goal, even though they didn't agree. And the more conservative Users felt that Iris gave an argument which explained their party's position better than the Politicos spokesmen!

"Where should I put this photo?" Holly held a wedding photo of Arnica's parents. It was in a beautiful, oval frame, looking old-fashioned with its sepia tones.

"Let's put all wedding photos over here, on the West altars." Arnica was setting up a small, table fountain.

Carlos and Lotus, the wood-working teacher, had set up two cafeteria tables along each of the four sides of the courtyard creating four large, elemental altars.

"Let me guess, great-grandparents in the north?" They were having fun with this.

"What about matriarchs?" Carlos asked. The men all laughed.

A gentle whinny from the hatchling reminded Carlos that he'd best hurry.

"Is her horn visible?" Carlos knew that sometimes it was and sometimes it wasn't. He didn't understand Magick, even though his son, Gino, was now an initiate in Arnica's coven. Carlos scratched Dark Star's ears and she licked his face.

"Constable Trouver is coming in," Carlos added. "He has a photo for your altar and he's going to get Rosetta's tomatoes sauce for The Larder."

"C'mon munchkin," Holly said, "Let's tuck you in a classroom for a minute. I'll brush your coat."

Holly reached in his pocket and brought out a borage biscuit and unwrapped it. The treat was one of Dark Star's favorites.

"When it comes to our forests," Iris continued, "you must form your own opinions. The Descendant Tribes consider them sacred. It is where their ancestors walked and for them the trees are like those in the Kristos cemeteries."

Peridot and Topaz Crowfeather, from the Loon Tribe nodded. This is why they found life in Merrydale fulfilling and what they wanted to explain the next time they visited their families in the River Mountains.

"And there are those who see the forests as the means to lift the poorer parts of our population up out of poverty, to provide jobs and money for schools and health care."

Mayor Browning nodded at this. He loved the forests and mountain trees of Merrydale District but Merrydale's budget had so little money for social needs.

"What can we do," one of the fathers called out.

"Be educated. Be informed. We need forests as a crop. Encourage the industry to examine sustainable forests, although there are many different opinions about what that means."

Iris certainly gave the people much to consider.

John Trouver set a photograph of his Aunt Tibby on one of the altars. "How's that?"

"That looks great," Holly called out, coming back into the courtyard with Dark Star trotting along. She was wearing her cone-shaped 'horn mask' that made it look as if she was a horse disguised as a unicorn.

"Look at them all," Arnica said. "There's Rebecca Morningstar. The historical society lent us her portrait."

"And that's Juanita, Jenny's great aunt," Trouver mentioned. He'd known Jenny's family even before her parents married. "And look at that, some statues of your school mascot ... You're a sweet pony," he said, looking at Dark Star.

The hatchling avoided showing her indignation, knowing that she needed to keep her true nature a mystery.

"We are fortunate to live in a country which elects its government through popular vote," Iris said.

Just then a man entered the hall and quietly slipped down an aisle to whisper something in the mayor's ear. Mayor Browning raised his hand.

"Mayor Browning?"

"May I address the hall?" Mr. Browning said.

He walked up to the front, looking distressed and puzzled all at once. The room grew very quiet, sensing that something must be very important.

"Word has come in about the boat." Mr. Browning looked flushed. "It has been proven to belong to young Malcolm Peters, the oldest son of Edward Peters." Most of the adults gasped and began whispering among themselves. Edward Peters was a prominent radical Kristos clergyman.

"The Peters boy was running drugs to raise money for guns hoping to infiltrate and promote a possible war against the Saracenites."

People were stunned.

"He's under arrest."

Rosetta Rosario was in the school kitchen preparing a large, traditional (for her heritage) feast. The foods represented a tradition dating back to her ancestors in Italica. She was so pleased to be cooking for the coven's Hallows Eve Ritual. Tomorrow the school would finish the week observing the Even of Hallows and tomorrow night she and Carlos would watch the younger children from the coven parents.

Sitting nearby were five dozen quart jars of Rosetta's finest tomato sauce. She canned tomato sauce for the annual tithing as well as for home use and more. This year there had been a late summer project with some of the Trillium School mothers and there was an abundance of sauce to use in the school's lunch program.

"Chief Constable!" Rosetta exclaimed as John Trouver came through the door, followed by laughter and the noises of Dark Star with her two men. Carlos came in as well.

"Please," Trouver smiled, "I'm just John. Carlos mentioned that you had a heavy shipment of food for The Larder and I thought I'd stop by and take it along with tonight's collection.

"I would love to have that counter freed up," Rosetta said.

"I can get the packing boxes, Mom," Gino said.

Just then the back kitchen door flew open. "Mr. Trouver, Arnica." Jenny had been running.

Gino ran to her side and put his arms around her. "What's wrong," he asked. He'd never seen his new wife look so upset.

"You'll never guess what happened at the hall." And Jenny began to relate Browning's announcement.

Arnica sat down in bewilderment. How would this affect the election?

LXXX - Yule Baubles

In the weeks leading to Yule Merrydale was buzzing with the election news. In fact, the election was the main topic for all of Lothloriën. An abandoned boat last January had been a major part of Schrobbe calling for elections as the Users attempted to stir a fear of the unknown enemy. Some had claimed the boat to belong to the Saracenites. Politico strategists believed that an election could give the Politicos solid control of Parliament. Some of the right wing Kristos had been trying to encourage their followers to do whatever possible. With enough Users in power they could guarantee that the Politicos might even be able to pass laws against the Earthkin schools.

Just before the voting day, however, a minor scandal had broken out with the arrest of Malcolm Peters, the son of a prominent Kristos clergyman, one who had come out strongly supporting Lothloriën's Premier, Henly Schrobbe. Polls showed that most of the undecided voters and, in fact, many moderate Politicos, intended to vote for Conserver candidates, their faith in Schrobbe and the User faction of the Politicos shaken.

When not discussing Lothloriën's politics, the members of the coven worked on their plans for the Sabbat. Yule seemed deserving of an exceptional ritual this year. Gino and Jenny's Handfasting was six months before, just this past Midsummer and life at the Grove had changed. The coven's sacred land had expanded, now that Gino and Jenny were living in the house to the south. The path through the woods from the Grove to the Rise was gradually being lined with two rows of large stones, a project Gino was enjoying. There was an unexpected snowfall one day as a an early winter storm came in off the great Protean Ocean. It was appropriate that the vast sea was named for an ever-changing sea deity!

Dark Star so enjoyed the path. It was only a quick gallop for her and a modest walk for her humans. On many brisk mornings before any of the humans were awake she'd quietly leave the cabin and have a wild and exuberant run from the cabin to the house on the Rise and back. Although she'd be ten years old this coming spring (in human years) sometimes she felt as young as she had as a hatchling.

The early results of the election showed the Conservers holding a modest lead but, when the final count was announced, somehow the Politicos had won by a landslide. In Cloverville, the seat of the District of the Four Deserts, people were so upset that thousands turned out in protest. When a contingent of the Users, the radical right of the Politicos, showed up verbal arguments led to a scuffle with a number of black-and-blue eyes and at least several broken noses.

Some of the young voters in Heartland, the seat of the Great Plains, were outraged. Many of the demonstrators were from Jade College, known for its partying. When the constables showed up the Users among the force began taunting some of the young. It was reported that there were hooligans mixed in with the demonstrators, some of whom were always ready to smash a few store windows and set dumpsters on fire. A few believed that they were not hooligans but some young Users who were trying to create a riot and blame it on the Conservers.

Dark Star had so enjoyed one night a couple of weeks ago. Pearl had come to the cabin to work on her ornaments. She was crocheting around a glass sphere working with beautiful silk threads and delicate beadwork. This ornament was to be used for the coven's scrying work and Dark Star was helping. Pearl Lamina was the best in the coven with her needle work. Her reputation as Trillium School's arts teacher had spread and even the public school systems of other Districts knew that Trillium School had one of the best.

"We got this from Rosetta nearly five years ago. Her mother brought it from Astarte's Well in Italica when they emigrated to Lothloriën many years ago." Arnica measured several droplets of water. He and Holly were working at one of their magickal cupboards, this one which held all manner of beautiful, small bottles with water from many sacred places.

The drops plummeted into the depths of the glass sphere. The ornament was the color of smoky quartz. With the sphere filled, Flying Raven sealed it with melted glass. Raven had come out to the cabin just long enough for this step in the scrying sphere. Ollis came with her to carry the small canister of fuel for her torch.

"Those clouds look darkening," Raven said as she hugged her covenmates.

Arnica and Holly worked in the other room on their lesson plans as Pearl's needles created their magick. The men had set the Orb upon their altar and left Pearl and Dark Star in a cast Circle. With Holly's encouragement, Pearl had learned how to join minds with the hatchling, gazing into the depths of the crystal ball. Dark Star shared visions with Pearl of some of the scrying pools which few humans had ever seen, allowing Pearl to keep all stray thoughts from working their way into the crocheted magick.

The cabin was so busy no one had looked out the window until they finished their evening meal. Pearl was about to light a lantern and walk back to Merrydale when the sound of Dark Star's hooves outside the kitchen door sounded odd. When they opened the door, the hatchling *and* the gardens were filled with a surprise snow. Walking back to Merrydale was no longer an option.

Pearl spent the night curled up in the front room with Dark Star. In the morning the sun was bright and the snow already melting but there were hoof prints in the fresh snow!

Merrydale District's voting was clearly in favor of Conservers and some moderate Politicos. Merrydale itself elected two Conserver Speakers and one Politico Speaker of Parliament. Jenny was part of the vote-counting committee as part of her new position working for the Merrydale Council. And then there was the court-ordered recount. It had taken Lothloriën's Supreme Court to settle the dispute. Barristers from both parties had filed suit.

The Court did find, in their emergency ruling, that there was just cause to suspect possible irregularities although the Court stopped short of further findings. Any of those claims could be settled in District Courts. The recount meant some late nights at work but Gino used the time to work hard on his correspondence courses with Genetricia University.

No irregularities were found in Merrydale District's voting.

Beneath the tree waited a few presents near a small creche set depicting Marian holding the baby Kristos. Becky and Philbert had not had a Kristmas tree the past two years. Their home had seemed so empty after Jenny left. Jenny and her father went a year and a half without speaking but now she and her new husband were coming to dinner.

The presents were gaily wrapped. One, a long parcel, held a pair of snowshoes. Mr. Flower had called on Gino's parents in secret to ask what Gino would both use and enjoy.

Snowshoes it was. A small gift for Jenny contained a small, silver necklace, which had belonged to her great-Aunt Juanita. Becky's Aunt Juanita had taught her some simple flower magick but she doubted her Aunt had ever gone beyond simple folk beliefs.

Jenny was another story. Combining her maternal line of magickal belief (she was a *coven* member, after all!) with her father's political background, both parents were so proud of their daughter. On the tree was pinned a small envelope. A gift for their newly remodeled home, it contained a gift certificate that the Flowers had arranged through Lotus... built-in bookshelves!!! Philbert was so impressed with Mr. Woodfolk's work on his daughter's house that he knew this gift would only grow in value as the years passed.

"Oh, my dear, I do so apologize." Becky blushed. She had glanced down at her daughter's stomach, relieved that she did not look pregnant.

Could Merrydale have a riot? No one believed it possible. Merrydale was much smaller than any of the other District Seats, one of Lothloriën's smaller and more modest cities. In fact people still thought of it as a 'town.'

Everyone in Merrydale, including both extremes in both parties, felt that the results for both Merrydale and the District of Merrydale were accurate and fair. But when the news came from Heartland, Mayor Browning asked Iris to temporarily postpone her evening classes at the Merrydale Hotel.

Jenny had caught her mother and wanted to be bothered but, it was still the Yule Sabbat (well, a few days later and the Kristos' version) and time to be mature. "It's all right, Mom," she said. "We're waiting."

Philbert was talking about the gift certificate with his new son-in-law. The more he knew of Gino, the prouder he was. It was difficult to remember how strong had been his prejudices about his daughter marrying an Earthkin boy!

"And I asked him if he could make one section to be a cabinet with a door to protect your jars of herb from the light." Philbert was eager to be friendly with Gino.

Arnica smiled at that. Seeing the expression on Philbert's face he suddenly remembered what Jenny had told him about the her father. Jenny had taken him to the Dryad tree and he heard the tree speak to him. Philbert had never spoken of it with Arnica but the herbalist wondered if that might be behind some of Philbert's changes. First he stood up to the right wing of the Politico Party and told them he would not remain aligned with them but then, following his fight with Jenny, he returned to the ultra-conservative fold. Last spring Philbert helped Gino and Jenny find a house and joined in with his daughter's Earthkin friends in painting and fixing up the house. His views were clearly changing.

Pearl's Yule ornament for the coven was a success. Mother Nature had tipped the balance and Yule Eve was warm enough that the Solstice was observed in the Stone Circle. All twelve adults were there (and Dark Star made thirteen!) as the Yule fire was lit and the scrying ball consecrated.

The glass sphere in its crocheted netting hung from one of the lantern hooks Amber had made several years ago. They held hands, with Dark Star between Arnica and Holly. Suddenly the hatchling started, and snorted a bit, distracting them all.

"I think she's ready for cookies," Holly teased, although he knew *something* troubled her. "I wonder if it was her vision?" he later commented to Arnica. That night Dark Star didn't sleep. She spent the night before the altar, moving into the Otherworld to seek advice from her grandmare, Lillian.

It was a happy household. The Flowers invited Arnica and Holly as well as the Dolorums, Deodar and Iris, to a small dinner on Kristmas. Kristos families traditionally went to church and had large family gatherings. This year, for reasons Jenny did not quite understand, her parents wanted their Kristmas to be a small affair. Jenny was caught off-guard when she learned the Flowers had not attended their services at the Church of the Martyr.

"She's spending the day playing with Sunna at the Woodfolks," Iris answered. Merrydale's postmarm was enjoying going out with Dolly knowing that Diana was having a fun day. Diana and Sunna were almost like sisters and Dagon Woodfolk, now over nine years old, was much like an older brother.

How was your Yule?" It wasn't an easy question for Philbert to ask. He's spent his entire life being told that 'Yule' was a celebration for the devil, but he discovered it wasn't as difficult, either. Deodar had been instrumental in bringing the two holidays together eight years ago for Merrydale. ("Eight years ago? why Jenny was just eleven," Philbert thought to himself.)

Becky brought out coffee and tea. Jenny and Iris helped her, carrying trays of cookies and holiday treats. And they were already stuffed from Becky's wonderful meal!

"Well," Philbert stood. "This has been quite a day." His eyes glistened with a couple of tears of joy. "I know Jenny was wondering why I asked Arnica and Holly, and why the Dolorums are here."

"It will be fine," Lillian assured Dark Star.

"The first time their baby will not be ready to enter this world. The Goddess will call her back so She can continue readying the little one for a challenging world."

Dark Star was still unsettled. She didn't fully understand human birth.

"But when she is ready, the next time around for Gino and Jenny, the baby will arrive happy and healthy."

That was better.

"And there will be a surprise for them as well." Lillian's eyes twinkled. "It's one which will bring you delight and vexation."

'A puzzle,' Dark Star thought, and immediately her mind went off searching for answers.

The room was quiet. The guests had not anticipated an announcement, but it explained what had caused them to wonder.

"There is a quiet but growing moderate presence in the Politicos Party," he said. "Many of us feel that our Party has been taken over by the Users and their right-wing agenda. I agree with many of their goals but much of what they've attempted to do is unacceptable. But let me get to the point. I've been asked to petition the court to be able to run for Parliament in this election. I declined. I believe the court's decision is for a second election without any changes of candidates. But I wish to ask your collective advice before I declare myself for the next election."

"You did well," Holly was impressed at Philbert's acumen.

"We are quietly working with some of the Conservers to create bipartisan support to keep Schrobbe from running Lothloriën into a dark hole. And when the next election is called for, I will be ready."

LXXXI - A Tiny Flame

The winter season throughout the Land of Lothloriën had been controversial. Periodical periods of record-breaking cold slipped down from the north. Many scientists believed that the mass of cold air, usually held in place by the jet stream and the glaciated mass of the Boreal Axis, was now less stable due to global warming. Yet all it took was a few days of blustery cold and many of the Users were quick to claim that global warming was a myth.

Peridot and Topaz shared letters they received from their family, living up in Eagle's Nest in the River Mountains. A small group of hunters had returned from a long trek to the higher elevations and reported that some of the glaciers, long revered by the Elders, were shrinking. Stone cairns had been placed at their edges generations ago which were now surrounded by vegetation. The antelope were higher than ever.

And yet, life moved forward.

The Hatchling had been wearing her horn 'mask.' Most people in Merrydale thought it great fun, and continued to think of her as a horse disguised as Trillium School's mascot. But there were several who had 'the sight.' And not all of those were Earthkin. There were a couple of fundamentalist Kristos who experienced internal discomfort when they saw Dark Star, their instinct telling them that the truth was being veiled.

Merrydale did not see Dark Star that often. The coven learned which route was the least visible and she was able to slip into the Eastside with ease, trotting through a greenbelt early in the morning. This morning she arrived early at Pearl's home, where she was helping. Trillium School's artist was working on a painting which would be offered to the gods on Candlemas Eve. Dark Star was posing. What a fun time this was!

"No, not this morning." There were times Pearl could understand the hatchling although she looked forward to improving her skill with an orb so they could communicate mind-to-mind. "The girls will be here tomorrow morning."

Diana Dolorum would not be five until Beltane and Sunna Woodfolk was four just this past Hallows. Pearl knew they could get restless and when the two girls wanted to play, Dark Star had difficulty sitting still. They could bring out the unifoal in the hatchling! Pearl continued with the pastels, nearly done with the unicorn in her painting. All that remained were the faces of the two faerie spirits.

The Land of Lothloriën was (at last) settling down from the election held not long after Hallows. As the election ended the polls indicated that the Conservers were winning just enough to hold the majority vote in Parliament. When a landslide for the Politicos was announced it went to the courts. The District Court for Heartland found that, indeed, someone had tampered with the voting count. The Court ordered a recount and the Conservers ended in the lead. The Four Deserts District Court found that several large cartons of mail-in votes in Saigaireau Province were concealed, replaced with forged ballots. Cloverville's newspapers had great fun with headlines about the "voting dead!" The District of Great Plains was won by the Politicos, but by a smaller margin. There was no landslide and the Politicos lost seats in Parliament.

Voting now in Parliament would still be close but Parliament would now be in the hands of the Conservers. A new Premier was appointed on January 2nd. Melinda Barkley, Lothloriën's first woman Premier, had a maternal demeanor and Lothloriën seemed calmed.

Her appointment was not a big deal in Merrydale. Merrydale itself had more than one woman mayor in its past.

"I love this space," said Arnica. He leaned back in his chair, one that gave his old bones good lumbar support. A chorus of voices agreed. Nearly all of the coven was present. Pearl was at home, working on her Candlemas painting.

"Close the door," several voices said in unison. Gino came into the faculty room. Several sticks of incense were burning and the coven created endless jokes about their new faculty lounge. Generations ago a teacher's lounge in the public schools was hazy with cigarette smoke. Trillium School's had a light drift of incense smoke meandering through it. Still, they didn't want the smoke to soil the books in the school's library.

"Gino, how's school coming along?" Amber was shuffling the tests she was grading for one of her Social Studies courses.

"I heard you got your first semester grades," Flying Raven was proud of Gino, as were all of the coven.

Gino blushed, his freckles disappearing into the glow of his skin. "Well," he began, always modest and now a little embarrassed, "I got a 4.0." Gino was carrying a full credit load from Genetricia University, studying by correspondence in the school's new library. Once a modest home, the house had been converted into Trillium School's library. The former kitchen was now the faculty lounge. And Gino was the school's librarian, for which he got credit!

"I think it's time to move my night class out of the hotel." Iris had been teaching classes in the workings of Lothloriën's government followed by the history of the Saracenites and their conflicts with the early Kristos. Now, with the election finally past the classes were smaller.

"What about taking the global warming debate to the hotel?" Holly was enthusiastic.

"Think of it!" Lotus added excitedly. "We have Raven's science background, Ollis has toured the world and teaches global geography."

"And for the political aspect both Iris and Amber could bring in their knowledge," Holly added.

"I'm certain the Lodgefellows would like the idea," Iris mused. "When I mentioned that it may be time to move the series back to a school classroom they were definitely disappointed."

"Did you hear about the flight heading north?" Gino asked. The room quieted. "I just learned about this in one of my courses."

"Tell us what you've learned," Arnica asked.

Just then a knock at the back door caught there attention and they turned as it opened. Pearl and Dark Star came into the faculty room. Pearl took a chair around the large kitchen table and the hatchling sat upon her haunches on a thick, latched rug kept there just for her.

"Listen to this," Arnica mentioned to Pearl. "Gino was about to tell us of an air expedition." Air flights were no longer common. Since the advent of the Changing Times people no longer had the glut of fossil fuel squandered by previous generations.

"The countries of Lothloriën, Atalanta and Azteca are negotiating a joint agreement with Italica and other countries in Europa and Asie. Our new Premier (a few voices interrupted with cheers) Barkley just committed Lothloriën. With us there are thirteen governments who pledged to fund the flight." Jet fuel was extremely expensive, particularly for a long flight over the Boreal Axis, a route not much taken in these times.

"A team of scientists and photographers will be photographing the glaciers and mountains to compare them with older photos in the archives of various governments. They plan to cross over the Axis as many as ten times until the entire Boreal Continent is covered."

Dark Star had never been in one of the humans airplanes but she had seen a few of them flying overhead. The very thought made her nervous.

A bell rang, signaling time for the faculty to head back to their classrooms. Pearl had no classes this day, her art and music students all working on preparing the school's hall for a student and parent Candlemas observance.

"I'll see you all tomorrow evening," Pearl hugged those within reach. "The painting is done and will be ready for the ritual."

"Oh, sweet Pearl," Arnica kissed her cheek. "This is wonderful!"

Dark Star sat in the Stone Circle, lost in thought. All the humans were sleeping. Her ears turned as if she could sense the sound, but it was her mind which knew them all to be in the Dreaming.

The image of the two women, just beyond the western stones, was still clear. Lotus had set up a temporary fountain. An orange cord, unbelievably long, snaked along the stones lining the path leading to the house on the Rise, plugged into Gino and Jenny's house which provided the fountain's pump with electricity.

Pearl represented the Old Goddess. She asked for the role of the Crone. Although the second oldest, Pearl wanted the part. She held the painting in her hand and, in a theatrical flourish, let out a chilling cry as she thrust it into the cauldron's flames.

Although everyone knew what was happening, the drama proved a distraction and, as Pearl swept her robe over herself and stepped away, Jenny stepped forward by the fountain looking like the Maiden Goddess emerging from the spring of renewal.

'Jenny was such a lovely Maiden.' Dark Star thought. She was about ready to walk to the Grove. She knew her men were sleeping yet she felt the temptation to try snuggling up on their bed with them. 'It was easier when I was a young hatchling,' she thought.

Ready to take the path east to the cabin, she paused and turned the other way, toward the Rise and there, against the dark shadows of Gino and Jenny's home was the image of a star, a tiny flame in the night.

'Jenny's pregnant,' the hatchling realized.

LXXXII - Rebirth and Loss

"Eostara," Dark Star thought. "When Father Sun rises in the east I will have been here ten years in human time." The coven had left for their homes but this night the hatchling was both joyous and troubled. She had spent many hours these past days, thinking of the anniversary of her hatching and the many memories she held dear, living with her humans.

Yet, underlying this happiness, was Lillian's puzzle. "What was there about Jenny's baby? And what did Grandmare mean?" Dark Star turned toward the north stone. "Grandmare," the hatchling invoked, "Please come to me this Sabbat Eve."

"Didn't she come in?" Arnica was already in bed, waiting for Holly. The coven's elder herbalist was trying to read but it had been a long day and his eyelids were proving the laws of gravity. The words of his book, a history of Culpeper, were being woven into his dreaming, a mixture of tomorrow's work, thoughts of the gardening to do, a lesson plan past due... And, now and then, the image of Jenny's face drifting through like a spring breeze.

"After we put away the ritual things I noticed that she was sitting out near the greenhouse, gazing at the crescent Moon." Holly folded his clothing and set it neatly near his night-stand. He looked out the window toward the woods. "The last I saw she was walking slowly back toward the Stone Circle."

Arnica looked at his partner. Holly stood there wearing just his t-shirt. 'Handsome,' Arnica thought to himself. The flickers of Sabbat lust and his desire for his lover of decades stirred in his blood.

"She seemed well at the ritual." Arnica, one of the most skilled herbalists in the region, reflected on their unicorn.

"Yes, but she's had some occasional quiet times over the past couple of months." Holly turned down the light and slipped under the comforter, snuggling up against Arnica.

Lillian stepped through the northeast portal. It seemed as if she emerged out of the fog, yet there was no fog to be seen. The almost-spring night was cooling and clear. Off in the distance Dark Star could see a light from the cabin's bedroom window. As the tree leaves grew the cabin would be obscured.

Dark Star was sitting in the center of the Stone Circle. She looked at Andrius' mother. "Grandmare," a tear was sliding down toward her nose. "My heart hurts."

"Do you remember, last Yule, that I told you the goddess will call the little one back?"

"Yes, but I realized that I didn't think about that." Dark Star leaned against her grandmare. "I let myself be distracted by the puzzle of a surprise."

"Humans experience pain in ways which are difficult for unicorns to understand," Lillian said, gently. "And that is why you needed to live with humans. It was difficult for your father to let you go, but Andrius is wise and he understood that you needed to learn these mysteries, just as he learned at your mother's passing."

"My mother?" asked Dark Star. "No one ever speaks of her."

"Little mommy," Gino loved teasing Jenny. She could almost hear his speaking aloud, her memory was so clear. She wasn't sleeping well and lay in bed, snuggling against Gino for comfort, not wanting to leave the warm bed.

'Our lives are going so well,' Jenny thought. She reflected on their relationship. Why, they were only in ninth grade when their bond formed. There could never be any other man in her life.

A cloud slipped between the moon and their House on the Rise. The bedroom darkened just slightly. Jenny loved their home. Life in the country was so fulfilling. She'd spent her life in Merrydale and, with her father often at Parliament in Mill City, she had never truly experienced living with Nature as she now did. Their closest neighbors were Arnica and Holly, and even that was a good stroll when taking the shortcut - the new path through the woods and past the Stone Circle.

"But where will the baby be?" The hatchling was feeling better. Lillian's wisdom gave her comfort.

"Among the stars with the Mother Goddess." Grandmare spoke lovingly. She knew that this was a vulnerable time for Dark Star.

"Is that where my mother is?" Dark Star had never thought much about it. Grandmare came to here infrequently, visiting from the Otherworld. Andrius had come to her during a few important times in her life but mostly she was alone. The only unicorn, but surrounded with these wonderful, loving humans. There were no unicorns present when she hatched and she'd grown never really missing her mother. But now, seeing Jenny become pregnant, this was the first Dark Star was old enough to think about love and fertility and birthing as a unicorn.

"Oh!" Jenny felt a sharp pain. It took away her breath and she sat up instantly. 'Was it something I ate at the Sabbat feast?' But then, it tore at her again and she realized it wasn't her stomach, it was her womb. "Gino," Jenny cried out.

Gino sat up, instantly awake and alert. Something was wrong. "What is it?" He reached for the light and turned it on. Jenny was pale. He'd never seen her look so fearful and ashen.

"I'm bleeding." She sobbed. "Something's wrong with the baby."

Gino's stomach sank. Sudden fear left him nauseous.

"Please," Jenny pleaded, "get Arnica as fast as you can."

Gino grabbed his robe and ran from the house. Neither the coolness of the night nor the stones and twigs which cut at his bare feet could get his attention. He ran the path to the herbalist's cabin as fast as he could.

As he passed the Stone Circle he saw only Dark Star, vaguely wondering why she sat alone, meditating in the dark.

And then, the horrible sound carried through the night. Jenny wailed out. Gino fought panic and raced toward the cabin.

The noise crashed into their dreams. Arnica and Holly leaped from their bed, instantly alert. There was a pounding and shouting at the cabin door.

As Arnica rushed to open it, he noted the absence of Dark Star. In a jumble his thoughts wondered if there was a fire, if the hatchling might be in trouble...

"Arnica, Holly!" Gino's voice sounded the energy of panic.

The door opened, Gino nearly fell into Arnica's arms. Holly was there in a moment, his arms around the young man in comfort.

"The baby," Gino panted. "Something's wrong.... Hurry..."

"Grab my things," Arnica said quickly to Holly, and rushed out the door wearing just slippers and nightshirt.

"You knew." Arnica called. He saw both Dark Star and Lillian.

The hatchling nodded. It was obvious she was saddened.

"This moment's sorrow will transform itself into a later joy." Lillian rose and stepped toward the Stone Circle's portal.

Arnica was past, rushing toward the House on the Rise. No matter the future, at this time Jenny was in great need.

As Gino and Holly came running along the path, each carrying a satchel with Arnica's herbs and equipment, Dark Star rose. Lillian had again slipped into the Otherworld. The hatchling shook herself, and went running behind the men toward Jenny.

Spring came to Merrydale. The sun had yet risen but the River Mountains to the east were sharp silhouettes against the lightening sky.

The Dolorums were still in bed, about to be wakened by Diana. Nearing five, she was often up earlier than her parents. Deodar had a full day's work at Trillium School as its principal and Iris loved to have a few minutes of family time in bed before they met the day. This would be a challenging Monday.

The Rosarios slept poorly. Rosetta tossed all night, the dreams of a mother whose son was facing the worst night of his life. Gino didn't want to call his parents this early in the morning. He held back from calling Jenny's parents as well, wondering if the Flowers were sleeping, if Jenny's father, Philbert, was even at home or if he was at Mill City working in the government offices.

Pearl was awake. She had slept poorly and rose just as Jenny began to miscarry. She sat before her altar, a large, flat basin of water before her. Earlier she had gazed into it which calmed her mind and, as her eyes closed and she drifted into trance, she sensed Jenny's distress and understood what was taking place. Once she knew, she set a large, white candle in the center of the basin and sat before her altar as the hours passed into morning, directing peace and emotional healing toward Jenny.

The other coven members would soon learn of Jenny and Gino's sorrow. This would be a day of healing.

LXXXIII - Horned Hunter of the Night

Barely able to stand, he was gasping for air, his body coated with perspiration. It was cool enough that his breath formed quick bursts of steam. Gino dropped to his knees on the wet grass, trying to restore order to his lungs.

Dark Star, by contrast, raced back and forth from the house on the Rise to Merrywood road. This was so much fun! She could run and run and finally had a human to enjoy this great sport.

"No more," Gino panted. "That's ... as much ... as I can ... manage ... this morning."

The hatchling understood. Gino was working to be in condition for Beltane. Dark Star looked up at the house. There were lights on.

Jenny knelt before the altar in their temple, lighting a candle before the statue of the Goddess. She chanted the words, calling upon the Great Mother to bless her. She asked the Crone to protect their baby's spirit. And she called upon the Maiden to be one with her at this year's Horned Dance. Once again would she be the Maiden, invoking the Wild One within Gino.

Deep breathing exercises calmed her as threads of anxiety sought to surface. Jenny had worked hard to take control over her fears, to see the miscarriage on Eostara morning as a simple indication that the baby was not ready to come to this life. 'But what if I conceive?' she worried herself.

As she raised the mug of warm, raspberry leaf tea, Jenny felt the Goddess speak to her. "Trust in me. It is my timing, not thine. When the seed is planted, this time you shall bear fruit."

Pearl also sensed the presence of the Goddess. The Pictish woman had a close bond with Jenny, who had lived with her as she finished high school. Jenny and her father had since mended their painful rift but Pearl was like a parent, not only guiding Jenny in the ways of the coven, but thinking of her as the daughter she'd never had.

Pearl's fingers worked their magick as she embroidered a new design in a corner of the cape. It showed a shooting star above an empty womb, representing the baby's spirit which was called back by the Goddess. The cape was the one Jenny had worn last Beltane when she first took the role of the Maiden. The candles on Pearl's altar were bright as the morning sun shone through the window. Trillium School's art and music teacher had made this her morning ritual ever since the women of the coven, along with the couple's mothers, had worked a healing ritual for Jenny. Even this morning Pearl was not alone in offering healing blessings for Jenny.

The morning hour found Becky Flower quietly slipping out of bed, not wanting to wake Philbert. Becky had attended the healing ceremony Jenny's coven sisters had held. Becky liked the environment of all-women working to help her daughter and found it comforting. Wanting to be there for her daughter in her own way, she held her copy of the *Book of Doom* close to her heart and prayed to Kristos, asking that her god protect her daughter. It was not easy. Becky sometimes struggled with her faith.

Over in the eastside of Merrydale, Carlos was washing up and shaving. Rosetta considered this an ideal time. The Rosarios had a home altar. Gino's mother lit a candle and knelt, praying to Santa Madre. She was raised with such a different view of Kristos than what the Flowers found at their Church of the Martyr. The Kristos was O.K., but it was his sacred mother who moved her heart. Although Rosetta and Carlos worked at Trillium School and were increasingly involved in the ritual cycles of the Earthkin ways, she still had a soft spot for Santa Madre.

Not all of the coven were working ritual. Iris Dolorum was still snuggled in bed. Diana, who would be five tomorrow, had crawled into the warm spot vacated by her father. She adored her parents and had been promised that Dark Star would come to her birthday party!

Dolly was jogging along the quiet streets of Merrydale. Not too many others were out this early.

"Good morning, Mr. Dolorum." Jimmy Rubrum was delivering papers house to house.

"Jimmy," Deodar panted a response. It felt good. With all that had taken place over the past years during his transition from Kristos minister to his role as Trillium School's principal, now well-known as Earthkin, this spring he had taken up running. It was time to balance his academic work with tending his body's needs as well.

"Deo," a voice called out. Lotus Woodfolk was up early.

Dolly stopped, leaning forward to catch his breath. He stretched his legs. There, he wasn't nearly as winded as he'd expected. He was definitely in good condition. "Lote..." Dolly teased in turn. Lotus joked that 'Deo' was a better nickname than Dolly. "How's the Maypole?"

"I'm heading over to the school now," Lotus answered. "Ollis said he'd be there as soon as he finished writing the geography finals."

"This is the first year he's taught geography to seniors," Deodar answered. "I spoke with Raven last night. She said Ollis would be up late with lanterns!"

"Burning late night oil?" Lotus laughed.

Arnica and Holly were unloading a large cart, filled with bags of cedar shavings. Early risers, they enjoyed their quiet morning with mixed feelings. It was like the time before the hatchling arrived in their lives but oddly quiet, even though she was simply out, running with Gino. Numerous large, burlap bags of shavings arrived several days ago on the train from Mill City. Available for the modest shipping cost, two men worked at one of the wood mills and volunteered the labor of bagging the shavings and trucking them to the train. Their wives were both on the faculty at Loon School, Trillium's sister school.

As the two men began wheelbarrowing loads of pungent cedar back to the path which connected their cabin with the Stone Circle and then to the house on the Rise, Dark Star came bustling up to them, her eyes bright, her coat damp from her long, invigorating morning running with Gino.

Arnica scratched her around the ears, which she loved. "Ah, munchkin, it's good for you to run. I enjoyed it when I was young." Arnica knew his running days were well past.

Holly rubbed his forehead against Dark Star's, feeling her joy from mind to mind. "We missed you," he said.

The coven was in various stages of preparation for Beltane Eve. Arnica and Holly would spend the day home at the Grove. With Dark Star's help ('frisky help,' Arnica joked) they would finish spreading the shavings on the path and then prepare the Stone Circle for the Sabbat.

The Woodfolk's house was busy. Jewel was fixing breakfast. Dagon, already thinking of himself as ten years old ("Not for two weeks," Sunna would say), had been dressed and restless. He heard his father leave to set up the Maypole and was eager to take his role. Dagon would be leading Maypole dance tomorrow afternoon. Sunna, only four and a half, was proud of her older brother yet sibling rivalry sparked with him over his role of her 'teacher' tomorrow afternoon.

"No one's leaving without breakfast," Jewel reminded Dagon. The boy was more than ready to run out the door to see how his father was doing with the Maypole at Trillium School. "And Dagon," Jewel added," I know you're wonderful with Sunna but please watch her well at school."

"Mom," Dagon said, sounding like a teenager. But he knew that his responsibilities were part of his work toward being able to join the coven in a few years and his mother needed to work at the postal shop for Iris today.

Iris was padding about their house, Diana following behind. Diana could not sit still. Dolly was in the shower, washing off his morning run. He would be taking Diana with him to the school. Iris needed the quiet time to prepare the house for tomorrow's big day. Not only was it Beltane with the school's Maypole festivities but it was Diana's fifth birthday. And she seemed to think that Beltane happened just for her birthday!

Pearl was unpacking a large, wicker basket. The Crowfeather sisters were oohing and a-ahing at the wonderful lengths of beautiful ribbon.

"I'd best go tend the small ones." Peridot was going to rescue Dagon and any others who had young ones with them, keeping the children busy with fun projects in the day care.

"And I'd better get to the kitchen," her sister Topaz added. "There were delicious smells coming from it when I arrived. Rosetta is such a hard worker." Gino's mother, Rosetta, was taking the first batch of Beltane cookies out of the school ovens. Just as the women left, a group of high schoolers burst into the room, filling it with laughter. The students, both juniors and seniors (eight girls and two boys) in Pearl's art classes were in charge of the ribbons as a class project but help was needed for all of the activities and the school was a hive of activity with all staff and faculty busy at work.

The joyful clamor of the building and grounds raised another level when the adults and students saw Flying Raven and Ollis Piper arriving. Calls of 'stay-a-bed' teased them loudly.

Ollis was quick, "I was adding an extra page of questions to the geography final." The seniors among the boys near the just risen Maypole groaned loudly. Ollis walked over to Lotus and Carlos. "How about if I handle the mowing?"

"Remember last year?" Gino poked his head around the corner of the bedroom door, wearing the ritual horns. Last year had been their first Great Rite.

"Do I!" Jenny adored her young husband.

Gino's demeanor slipped. His inner care suddenly showed.

"Gino!" Jenny admonished. "I'm fine, truly I am. And, as soon as I get back from Merrydale I want to tell you about the dream I had last night!" Instinctively her hands dropped to her stomach.

"You mean?" Gino's asked, his face lighting like the rising sun.

"Yes," Jenny said, "the baby's waiting again. My womb is healed!" Gino started reaching for her but she slipped past his grasp. "I'm already late and I promised your mother I'd help her in the kitchen." Still, Gino's arms found her and he kissed her with passion on her neck.

"We must wait for tonight." Jenny freed herself and headed toward the door. "Besides, you need to finish your ointment.

Gino was making the herbal ointment himself this year. It would protect his feet as he ran through the woods barefoot, wearing the horns as he invoked the God in pursuit of his Maiden for the Beltane Eve Ritual. Once again they would celebrate the Great Rite for the coven, their second year.

Dark Star was unable to sit still. She knew that Arnica and Holly would want some privacy so they, also could celebrate the Great Rite. And she knew it likely that all of the couples were making love, even Iris and Dolly, if they could get Diana to sleep! There was a longing in the Hatchling. She remembered how handsome and virile those two unicorns were. It had been nearly two years and, although either of them could have won her heart, she remembered the white one most often.

Just then a long-tailed meteorite broke into the atmosphere. Dark Star looked up to see the shooting star, arcing toward the house on the Rise and, just then, she 'knew' the seed had been planted and Jenny would conceive.

"Dark Star," a soft voice called her.

Had the veil parted? She hadn't expected her grandmare to be here this night. Lillian stepped through the portal of the Circle.

"Joachim sent me with a message for you."

Could it be? Would she be the maiden for Joachim's chase?

LXXXIV - The Ripening Season

The sun, filtered through the leaves, shone into the Stone Circle. The hatchling, enjoying an afternoon siesta on the warm, late-spring day was in a deep dream state, experiencing anew her Beltane Eve.

The Circle over, Jenny and Gino were enjoying the Great Rite in their house on the Rise. Dark Star was hopeful that Arnica and Holly were making love as well. The unicorn chose to spend some time alone in the Stone Circle when, just as a stunning falling star soared through the sky, her grandmare, Lillian called to her. 'Joachim sent me with a message for you.'

It was nearly two years ago that Dark Star first met the two unicorn steeds. Joachim was as bright as the Midsummer sun. A human might think of him as white.

The sun was now shining upon the hatchling's stomach as a fly landed in her ear, tickling her awake with her dream thoughts still drifting in her mind. She was wondering what a unicolt sired of Joachim will look like.

"And will my next have Boaz as its sire?"

A summer dragonfly darted along the cleared path which connected the Stone Circle with the cabin where Dark Star lived with her men and the House on the Rise. Voices quickly followed. Dark Star felt her ears warm, even though blushing was for humans. None of this world knew, yet, that the hatchling was no longer a 'maiden.' Dark Star's ear could sense Gino pulling a two-wheeled cart as he and Jenny brought their own ritual things to begin preparing the Circle for Midsummer's Eve. Dark Star, not ready to share her thoughts, quietly headed off to the cabin.

"Feel my stomach." Jenny said, as she stretched out upon the soft moss in the Stone Circle.

"I thought..." Gino began but Jenny interrupted him.

"Quietly," she said. "I had my dream again. You won't feel her form yet.."

"It's a girl?" Gino was startled. "Already? How can you tell?"

"I saw her ... and I can *feel* her." Jenny placed Gino's hand upon her stomach. "Listen with your hand for the Goddess."

Gino quieted his mind and moved his perception to the palm of his hand.

Arnica was seated on a stool by the potting shed holding a bundle of lavender stalks. "This cord with which I'll tie them is, for this lavender, not unlike the cords taken by an Initiate." He was explaining the ritual harvesting of herbs to the group of students from Trillium School enrolled in the summer herbal course. Some were watching him intently, some busy taking notes... he could cover so much information so quickly! A young girl noted the hatchling quietly pause across the gardens, nibble at the flowering borage, then slip around the far side of the cabin.

"Is the munchkin O.K?" Holly and Dolly were securing two sheets of plywood upon solid frames to create picnic tables. The coven and their families were having an afternoon picnic followed by siestas.

"I think so," Holly answered, yet she did not seem to be her normal self and Holly's voice showed some concern.

"Go check on her. I can clamp these sheets down easily and when you come back we'll put up the top." Ollis Piper donated the colorful tarp, yet another one of the treasures he'd collected during his life in the merchant marines.

Holly headed off to the cabin, his eye catching Arnica. The momentary exchange of information was imperceptible to Arnica's class.

It was quiet in the cabin. Picking up the large, crystal orb, Holly held it to his heart and filled his lungs with a calm, deep breath. 'Ah, she's at the front door,' he sensed, and soon Holly and Dark Star were seated upon the floor in the front temple.

They knew as soon as their eyes met. The gardens were filled with joyful sounds. Dark Star and Jenny were sitting quietly together over by the greenhouse, removed from the hub of activity. Jenny didn't quite know how to speak with Dark Star, yet they knew. And they knew that they knew. Each was now in transition, leaving maidenhood behind. Jenny could sense that the hatchling knew that this time the Rosario's would be blessed with child. The baby's spirit would complete its journey from the Otherworld. And Jenny knew that Dark Star would become full with unicolt in her own way. Yet she knew almost nothing of unicorn births, other than the coven's story of how Dark Star hatched from an egg ten years ago this past Eostara morning. It was time to rejoin the picnic.

Ollis's brightly covered canopy was the central gathering place, communal shade. Diana and Sunna were playing with their stuffed unicorns. An unspoken agreement among the coven acknowledged the closeness between the two girls. At Diana's fifth birthday last Beltane, Pearl gave them nearly identical unicorns, the differences in color and embroidery yet quite individual. Sunna would not celebrate her fifth birthday until this coming Hallows. They were talking to each other through their unicorns as the adults chatted away.

"How about the weather?" Iris asked. Merrydale's postmarm was both an activist for the local environment but also considered the town's pundit when it came to political matters. Her political theory course at Trillium School was so widely respected that, as Lothloriën's election issues heated up, she was called upon to offer evening classes for the town's voters which filled the hotel's ballroom.

It seemed impossible for any conversation among the Earthkin to continue without global warming coming up and that inevitably led to discussions of politics and government policies.

"Oh, yes, the weather..." Lotus Woodfolk said. The merriment in his voice stimulated laughter. "But it *is* a beautiful day..."

"Even if it has been warmer and sunnier than normal," Amber Whitefeather tossed her almost-subtle global warming comment into the discussion.

The laughter welcomed the sound of a small, brass bell.

"Please," Dagon asked, "could I announce the planning for the Firefly Ritual?" Dagon, Lotus and Jewel's ten-year-old, continued to grow in youthful wisdom. Touched by the Realm of the Faerie when only a year old, he was already wise beyond his years. The influence of his gentle parents as well as the coven taught him at an early age that he could take joy in the wisdom of Magick yet keep his ego from interfering. As a result he was popular and seen as someone who knew the Mysteries even by the older students at Trillium.

Several of Trillium School's honor students were guests at the picnic. They would be taking roles in the evening's Firefly Ritual held at the school. This was the first Midsummer's Eve ritual for the young ones of Merrydale. The students were eager to show their Earthkin neighbors this expanded role for Trillium School. It was hoped that some day the school would expand to include elementary grades, spanning the gap between the day care and the current grades 7-12.

The honor students walked over toward Dagon's tent. There were a number of tents set up along the path connecting the Grove and the Rise.

Dagon was quite proud of his tent. Ollis had found it when looking through his collection for the canopy. The adults would be spending the night following the ritual near the Stone Circle. A few would keep watch, tending the flame they would collect from the setting sun watched from up by Jenny and Gino's house on the Rise, keeping it lit throughout the night in order to set the cauldron aflame during the sunrise ritual.

Dagon had set up his tent just beneath some trees as the path wove under the firs and cedars to the cabin. Pearl's tent was nearby. The lad was feeling quite 'grown up' to be staying on his own. His parents tent was large, and along the cleared path toward the

Rise. In past camping times he'd stayed in his parents' tent along with Diana and he was more than ready to sleep alone.

After they sang a few of their coven songs, Peridot and Topaz stood and, as Amber used her voice to create a percussive rhythm, the sisters chanted one of their sacred calls to the Mother rarely heard outside the Loon Tribe. It was late when the last tent flaps were zipped against any stray mosquitoes.

"I'm glad we're in the cabin," Arnica said. "I think my time for sleeping upon the Earth is well past. My old bones won't sleep that close to the Mother until it's time for me to be compost."

Holly sat up in their bed and began massaging his lover's legs. "Does that help?"

Arnica's arthritis was moving past the point of responding to herbal medicine. The herbalist recognized that he had led a full life, although his time was clearly not yet at hand. "That's wonderful... your hands are like Magick." As Holly's hands brought vigor to his joints, Arnica silently pondered a possible new formula of herbs to help his joints. "Tell me about Dark Star," he said, realizing they'd not had time to discuss Holly's time with the hatchling.

"We communed," Holly said, "but it's what she *didn't* image to me that was interesting."

"What do you mean?"

"Well, I have this feeling that Jenny is not the only one who is pregnant."

Arnica sat up. "Are you serious?"

"I'm uncertain and, with the Sabbat, there's been no quiet time, none for the two of us and none for either of us to sit with Dark Star."

Arnica stretched out and relaxed. "It was a wonderful Ritual, wasn't it?"

"Music and all," Holly answered. Following the late night Sabbat they sat around a small fire, lit from the sunset flame.

Dark Star had gone off once the humans gathered for song. She was ready for some quiet time. She loved her human companions but there were times when she needed unicorn thoughts. She missed having her mother, but Lillian, her mother's mother, had said to meet her by the Dray Tree, over near Fern Hollow. On a Midsummer's Eve it was time for the grandmare to teach Dark Star some of the Mysteries of unicorn birth.

LXXXV - Harvest Thoughts

"Make a large, sweeping arc." Carlos Rosario was holding a scythe nearly as tall as himself. He turned, swinging it around with a strong, steady movement. Tall, golden grain fell to the ground, the stalks laying orderly so it could easily be gathered.

"I'm impressed." Lotus had tried to work the scythe without success. "How ever did you learn that?"

"Back when I worked in the mills..." Carlos paused, gazing off at the River Mountains to the west. "That was over seven years ago," a rush of memories flew through his mind like a dust devil across the prairie. "It was when Kalven was still alive. It must be eight, nine years ago this summer. Kalven was a good man. He took me out to meet a farmer uncle of his. I think his name was Wally? Weather-beaten and colored by the sun, to look at Wally you could see the history of the grain fields."

"Here, you try." Lotus handed the scythe to Ollis.

Ollis Piper laughed. "I have an advantage. I was once in Kan'ai when the ship I was on made a long route all the way around the coast of Afresia with freight from Saracenia on its way up to Hebrides."

"Did you see any of the standing Stone Circles in Hebrides?"

Carlos laughed. "Gentlemen, the Loon Sisters are waiting for the grain."

Pearl Lamina sat cross-legged in the center of the Stone Circle at the Grove. Just beyond the stones, along the edge of the path which ran to Arnica and Holly's cabin to the left and the House on the Rise to the right, was her tent. She may be staying in a tent, but she was so grateful that she could use the bathroom at the House on the Rise!

Pearl was beading her Croning gown, hand stitching each bead into place. A beautiful, wooden pentagon sat on the ground before her, perfectly positioned to be at the exact center of the coven's ritual space. The five triangular pieces which fit around it to create a pentagram were with various members of the coven.

At the Full Moon just over a fortnight ago, all six pieces had been consecrated, then carefully polished with a coating of wax from the altar candles to protect them against moisture during the coven's Quest. When the coven was next together the five triangles, representing the four elements and spirit (Dark Star would carry the piece for spirit!) would be reassembled around the pentagon.

The Lammas Ritual would be worked to harvest protective Magick for the Land of Lothloriën. Grain would be hand harvested as the Ancestors had done. It would be stone-ground into flour in Eagles Nest in the River Mountains and then baked into a loaf in a hand-made brick oven in Merrydale.

Pearl was offering the sacrifice as her contribution. More and more she had come to realize that she felt complete in her life and, with the onset of menopause since her 39th birthday this past March, she wanted to embrace her Cronehood and would take vows before the Crone at Hallows, which would be the ninth anniversary of Phoenix's passing.

"Thank the Mother you stayed here," Holly warmly embraced Amber.

"I can smell it," Rosetta Rosario said excitedly. They were testing the new, brick oven. A week ago Arnica and Holly were in Trillium School's kitchen with Rosetta, talking about transforming it into a temporary temple when Amber, Trillium's history teacher, came in to make a cup of tea.

"Guess what," she'd said. "I stayed in Merrydale to work on some new projects for the fall semester. This year's focus will emphasize how ancient peoples created their own technology. Can I build a brick oven? My grandmother taught me how and many of my Loon Tribe Sisters still use them."

It was like a small kiln. Amber had built it closer to the school's library building. They thought that safer than near the actual school. Arnica had brought some dried branches from the summer pruning of the trees surrounding the herbal gardens at the Grove and the first loaf, a pan of cornbread, was in the brick oven, baking away. A light smoke curled out from various spots like an incense for the Corn Mother, hinting of hawthorne and elder and a few branches of apple from last winter.

The Hatchling

"Should I get the butter and maple syrup?"

"Look who's here," Rosetta was pleased to see her son.

"It was a warm day and the windows were open," Gino laughed. He'd been studying while keeping the library open for Trillium's summer students. Now a sophomore as a correspondence student through Genetricia, Gino was taking one academic course for eight credits but would probably be awarded nearly ten more credits for his summer apprenticeship with Arnica. He loved his herbal studies. He kissed his mother on the cheek.

Arnica looked at his student carefully. "How are things?"

Gino knew what Arnica meant. "It's difficult, but we're using the quartz." Gino looked at Holly for it was Holly who was teaching the young couple how to communicate using their stones. "Just before I woke this morning I felt Jenny. She reminded me that we could draw upon the beginning of our relationship."

"The crystals are working well?" It was Holly who originally showed Gino how to share mental images with Dark Star through the crystal orb.

"They're with the point," Gino referred to one of the five pentagram points. He kept one with him, along with his smoky quartz sphere which was 'linked' to Jenny's, a pale blue piece of 'Lady Quartz.'

"Have you heard from the reapers or the millers?" Rosetta asked her question of everyone.

They all looked briefly around. It appeared that no one had.

"Have you heard from Dad?" Gino asked his mother.

"No, but Carlos had assured me that 'no news is good news.'"

"And that means our flour will arrive right on schedule," Amber added.

"You can turn the wheel yet," Deep River teased, "but not later!"

Jenny had never been in an all-women's village before. The Elder Sisters of the Loon Tribe had their own area at the edge of Eagle's Nest. They were honored by their tribal families but the Loon Tribe had long honored the Crone. They lived the old ways and, despite their aging bones, continued to live in their hovas made of hides, even in the fierce River Mountains winters. The old women would laugh and joke, telling the others of the Loon Tribe that the winters kept them young.

It was not often that a young woman would have the privilege of spending several nights in a hova or live, if but for a few days, within the circle of the Sisters' homes.

Amber had sent an eagle feather, set into a beaded holder. The beads formed an intricate pattern but, when Jenny asked if it had meaning, Amber smiled. "Give it to Deep River. It is my way of asking her to allow you to stay with my Elder Sisters."

It was not an easy journey. Once they left the train in the pass it was a long walk. Although Peridot and Topaz Crowfeather asked Jenny often if she was doing OK, Jenny realized that she was not yet three months pregnant and the exercise was wonderful but Peri and Topi were Elders in their tribe. Perhaps living now in Merrydale they were not as accustomed to long hikes nor the elevation.

And yet, as they reached Eagle's Nest, they found themselves invigorated, eager to embrace their part of the Lammas work the coven had undertaken. Jenny was thoroughly smudged by several women before she stepped from the tribal village into the circle of hovas to be embraced. When the first of the wise women welcomed her, Deep River then

278

stepped back to say "A daughter ... and then she'll have a brother," Jenny broke into tears of joy.

The sound of gentle chanting and soft drumming awoke Jenny. She had slept so well yet she missed Gino so very much. She held her Lady Quartz to her heart and began whispering softly. As Jenny stepped out of the hova the sun had just crested over the mountains. The Elder Sisters seemed to be all up and busy yet a glance beyond the Elder's circle showed Eagle's Nest to be just waking.

The train from Mill City had just stopped at the station. Carlos, Lotus and Ollis were preparing for their walk to Eagle's Nest with the bag of wheat for this year's Grain Man.

Dark Star bowed down before the Mother, laying the fifth of the pentagram's triangles at the Lady's feet. Oh, they were so beautiful! What a journey this had been, perhaps the most exciting yet into the Otherworld.

Pearl had kissed her forehead and, as the hatchling stepped through the Stone Circle's portal into the other Realm her grandmare, Lillian was waiting to lead her to the sacred grotto. Dark Star had had many adventures traveling through the realms of spirit but never, never before had she been honored with personal time with the Mother.

As Lillian guided her into the sacred grotto, Dark Star stumbled more than once. She was so humbled she had difficulty keeping her eyes open!

"You are with foal," the Mother said.

Dark Star looked up. Why, She was so beautiful! The hatchling looked down again, embarrassed by her own desire to stare at the Lady. The Mother sat by Her sacred pool, gazing into the future yet, when Dark Star looked at the waters she saw only stars, as if looking into the night-time sky.

"I'm pregnant," Dark Star thought. She had so many questions, but this was not the time. The Lady caressed the hatchling's ears and mane. Dark Star felt calm, felt the Mother's warmth.

And then the Lady leaned forward to whisper Her magickal word, the one which would manifest the coven's Lammas Magick. What was the scent? Dark Star was reminded of some of the finest perfumes from the flowers at the Grove...

They sat around the center of the Circle. All the coven was present as well as Carlos and Rosetta, Peri and Topi. Dark Star dropped in the last of the five elemental triangles. It was not easy to let go. But she did, thinking, "What my grandmare told me is that next year I'll have a hatchling of my own!"

The Grain Man was passed through the fire. What a magnificent work of baking he was. Various types and colors of seeds had been used to create what could only appear to be a work of art. Each dropped a small piece of bread back into the fire and then ate their portion, washing it down with some of the new blueberry and raspberry juice mixture Holly had canned from this year's harvest.

Now, to see if the Magick worked!

279

LXXXVI - Mothers

"She seemed quiet at the last Full Moon."

"There's something on her mind," Gino answered. "I think Holly and Arnica know, but I have the feeling that it's like a 'mystery' and it's her secret until she's ready to share it with us." Gino Rosario combined his position as Trillium School's librarian with his studies with Genetricia University.

"Several student designers have mentioned that they miss seeing the school's 'mascot' about. That's actually just what I said, that 'it's her *mystery*.' And they accepted that." Pearl had walked over to the school library to get some reference books for the art classes she was teaching.

"Can I see it?" Gino was eager to see how Pearl's Croning robe was evolving.

Pearl carefully unrolled it and lifted the tissue. She spread it out over one of the work tables.

"Oh," Gino exclaimed, "has Jenny seen it like this?"

"She will," Pearl answered, "she's coming by the school on her lunch break. In fact, that's why I came over to the library, to tell you."

"There, that should do it." Holly set down the last of the baskets in the Stone Circle. There were seven of them, each filled with fresh-cut herbs that Arnica personally selected. These would be gifts for Dark Star's quest this morning.

Holly and Dark Star were in the Stone Circle. The sun filtered through the trees and the woodland was kissed with a light fog. It was a most magickal effect provided by the morning sunrise.

Baskets with hoop-handles had been chosen. Arnica always had dozens of baskets of myriad design stored in the drying shed. Arnica and Holly had decorated them with some ribbons, much to Dark Star's pleasure.

Laughter filtered through the fog. Arnica was working this morning with some of his botany and herbal science students. The students loved working with their teacher in the Grove's gardens. Helping Arnica bundle herbs for the tithing was a learning experience. They were also expected to write about the tithing and its role as a type of barter for taxation for their Political Theory classes with Iris.

There was a large cart, as well, filled with apples and early grapes, root vegetables, jars of early honey and fruit juice. Although this year's fruit harvest was greatly depressed due to the drought that affected so much of the Land of Lothloriën, Arnica and Holly always had more than enough and the students had volunteered bring in the cart with the Grove's donation toward Trillium School's harvest food drive.

Lillian appeared at the portal to the Otherworld, her gray coat shimmering in the morning light. Before her sat a basin of water. Dark Star's grandmare was such a beautiful presence. Lillian seemed ageless, yet filled with the wisdom of the ages.

Dark Star bowed down, offering her grandmare a ritual greeting.

Lillian's voice floated into the Stone Circle..."From the deep waters of Her eternal wisdom brings she forth the Mystery of Life..."

The hatchling felt the unspoken instruction. She looked down upon the water's surface. Ripples dance across the water and, as the water stilled, the most beautiful unicorn appeared. Lillian silently told Dark Star who this was.

"M-m-mother," Dark Star was overwhelmed with emotions.

"I was called to be with the Goddess but I did not die, as you would think of my going. Your father Andrius, who lives within the Land of Faerie, and I knew that only when the time was right could you learn of me."

Dark Star picked up the first basket with her teeth, a gift for the Goddess and her court. Lillian had taught her that she must offer gifts for the Realm of Faerie if she was to gain wisdom.

"You must learn to scry in order to commune with me, and it must always be through this portal. The training you have had with Holly was excellent preparation. I chose the placement of your egg with great care."

But what was her mother's name? The hatchling stretched forward to set down a basket of late-summer echinacea before Lillian. Dark Star liked offering the baskets. It gave her the best views of her mother's image.

"Yes, you may ask of me a question."

Dark Star blushed. She had forgotten how clearly her thoughts could be seen.

"You are correct, my love," the reflection answered, "I am the Goddess of Unicorns, now, in the Lady's Court."

"And you are..."

"Yes, I am also your mother. I birthed you."

Dark Star remembered. She set a basket of fresh borage, the third generation this growing season. She wondered if her mother liked borage as much as *she* did.

"You are not bound by human time."

It was time to remember her mother's words. Dark Star was being taught about her pregnancy, about the birthing she would give...

"You are not bound by time in the Realm of the Otherlands."

The last basket was placed. Dark Star began to wonder if she would ever see her mother again.

"Remember to work on your scrying. I am always here for you. You will come to me at the Court when it is time to birth the egg and leave it in my keeping until the day arrives."

And the image disappeared.

"What day? Come to her?"

Lillian pressed her hoof upon the edge of the basin and the water poured over the edge, some streaming down, into the Stone Circle.

The kind grandmare leaned forward and kissed Dark Star upon her forelock. The portal closed itself and Dark Star was alone in the Stone Circle.

Jenny sat back in the chair. She was just over halfway there and always aware of being pregnant. Four and a half more months. Her due date was Candlemas. It had been a wonderful Autumn Eve. Jenny was glad she'd be more than ready to dance when spring's warmth turned to Beltane.

"It's been quite a harvest," Arnica said, following his invocation of blessings for all present. The faculty and staff of Trillium School was gathered, along with Jenny's mom, Becky Flower.

"What about those seniors?" Deodar was so proud of the senior class. This would be the second graduating class which had begun their junior high education through Trillium School, even though the class had grown as Trillium grew.

"I'm so impressed," Iris commented. "They put up posters at the postal shop and in a number of prominent places, requesting food donations."

"And the way they are creating a list of families who need food..." Raven was enthusiastic. "They're so respectful of the families' privacy and pride. Homes will get food without having to announce their needs to the community."

A noise at the door announced Dark Star. She came in with Holly and was wearing her horn mask. Only one person did not know she was truly a unicorn, but Jenny wasn't sure her mother was ready for this.

"I asked for this meeting," Jenny said. Arnica handed her the eagle feather. "I remember not getting much sexual education from my mother ... Sorry Mom," Jenny turned toward her mother. "It wasn't her fault. I also wondered why more girls at Merrydale High School get pregnant and usually have to drop out of school. It's not really talked about among their parents."

"They think of it as shameful," Becky interjected. Becky cared about this discussion.

"When I went to Merrydale High some students whispered that the Earthkin could get an herbal birth control but it wasn't until I was studying for the coven that I realized that the primary difference had to do with knowledge and understanding."

The sounds of approval and self-congratulations filled the faculty room.

"Working for the Merrydale Council," Jenny continued, "I've seen the statistics. It's more than a few girls and it's very hard on their lives. Some are kicked out of their homes..."

"The User faction of the Kristos are taught that a sinful child is better off living elsewhere," Dolly commented. Trillium School's principal, Deodar Dolorum, was the Church of the Martyr's Kristos Pastor before his 'change of life,' as he and Iris sometimes called it.

"When Jenny told me about all of this," Becky took over the presentation, "I was very concerned. I knew I couldn't go to our Pastor. We..." she blushed a little, "don't go to church very much these days and I also knew he would strongly disapprove. I've decided that things must change and it will take a long term, serious plan. I am following Gino's example. I started University long ago but in those days a degree was not that important for a woman, for a Kristos woman, anyway. I'm now enrolled for a nursing degree through Genetricia. In a year, if I work very hard, I'll have my nursing degree. I started this week at Merrydale Clinic where I'll work as a volunteer and gain both education and hands-on experience."

Applause and some cheering filled the room.

"Philbert and I have spoken about it at length. He's doing a lot of legal checking when he's working in Mill City at Parliament. Some how we're going to create a local organization to provide education for all young women. Abstinence and blame are not working. And those who are banned from their families are in need of housing and other help. I'm asking you, the Board of Directors of Trillium School ... and the rest of you, Jenny's coven and all of you ... if you would provide me with encouragement and support."

"Financial support?" Ollis sounded uncertain.

"Oh, no," Becky realized her request was open to interpretation. "I want to work with your day care program and I want to know if any of you who are teachers would help me begin to set up a home-tutoring program to be in place when we have the organization up and running. Philbert can find all the funding, I'm certain. But I need your wisdom."

Nearly done, Becky felt self-conscious.

"And your love." And she sat down.

Dark Star and Jenny caught each other's eyes. Just then, Jenny realized ... *Dark Star, she's expecting...*

Trillium School's courtyard was filling with the harvest. This year's senior class had quickly organized themselves. Even as juniors they had begun to agree on their class project. The mundane visage of their project was a series of food drives but the magickal part was to bake and distribute bread to needy families as well.

Several measures of the coven's Lammas Grain were given to Rosetta. Over the summer a number of the seniors had been accepted into Earthkin apprenticeships. The twins, Jimmy and Yarrow Croffy, had both signed agreements with Arnica to not only be herbal apprentices but both wanted to begin training for the coven. Yarrow would study with Jewel and Pearl. Her brother would study from Arnica and Holly. Dwight and Loretta were so proud of their twins.

Sel Boulanger was in charge of the 'bread committee,' as the students called it. Sel had learned that her great-great grandmother was a Descendant Chieftess, and she was making her apprenticeship with the goal of being accepted into the Loon Tribe after graduation.

Those seniors who had begun apprenticeships of magickal training had been invited to work with the coven as a piece of the Grain Man bread was placed in the receptacle beneath the altar in the school's courtyard, which often served as a ritual space. The grain could draw upon the magick of the Grain Man, and bring wellness to the families when the bread was baked and distributed to the families in and around Merrydale. And the rituals the students were learning would further empower the piece of the Grain Man to continue to protect and inspire the school.

Drought or no drought, the arrival of autumn reminded all of Trillium School that there was great fertility in their lives. This was promising to be the best year ever.

Of that, Dark Star was certain!

LXXXVII - The Croning

"This is some seclusion," Pearl laughed. She had withdrawn from her usually busy life for a week in preparation for her Croning Ritual. Her private ritual, with a few of her coven sisters, would follow the coven's Hallows Eve observance. Earlier that morning Jimmy and Yarrow, the Croffy twins, brought Pearl some herbs from the drying shed for her use. They were all smiles, thrilled to have even a small role in the work of the coven. If, after graduation, they approached their coven studies with as much eagerness, Pearl had told Arnica the other morning, they would do well.

Sel Boulanger was waiting for Pearl now. Sel, like the Croffy twins, was also a senior at Trillium School. Sel was working as an apprentice hoping to move to the River Mountains after graduation, to study with the Elder Mothers of the Loon Tribe.

Sel had carried some hot water from the cabin to the wickiup. The forests of Merrywood, indeed of much of the Land of Lothloriën, remained very dry. Once again there was less rain and the temperatures were above normal. Pearl could not have a fire, even to boil water. The sole fire would be one set in the cauldron when the coven gathered in the Stone Circle tomorrow night.

"It's been, well, *different*." Gino was snuggling Jenny, who sat on his lap. They were taking some quiet time with the library closed for Gino's lunch break. Jenny had walked to Trillium School from the Town Hall. She had a longer lunch break on most Fridays and this being a holiday for her, even her Kristos coworkers happily encouraged her to take some extra time.

"It's hard for me to believe it's real," Jenny said. Gino's hand was on her belly, feeling their growing child, now six months along.

"I walked past the Arts classroom this morning, and seeing your Mother at Pearl's desk was so odd." Becky Flower, Jenny's mother, was filling in as substitute teacher during Pearl's seclusion.

Did you hear what he said?" Jenny still had difficulty believing this. "Mom said Dad told her that if he knew anything about the arts, he would have offered to take Pearl's classes so Mom wouldn't miss her time at Merrydale Clinic."

"Who knows?" Gino said. He kissed Jenny's neck. It would soon be time for her to go back for work and for Gino to open the Trillium School library. He also had a paper due for one of his Genetricia University courses. "Remember, Dolly was once a Kristos minister!" Deodar Dolorum was Trillium School's principal, now a happily married Earthkin father and active in the coven.

Dark Star was laying near the wickiup. She loved the coming and going of the people and she loved having this time with Pearl. Few in the coven knew that Dark Star was in foal. Pearl knew. Jenny seemed to know, but Jenny was not yet able to communicate with her and Gino, well, Gino was so excited about becoming a father that Dark Star had not yet shared those images with her young human friend.

It had been difficult to tell Arnica and Holly. Human births were so ... *different*.

Unicorns, to prepare for the solitary lives they would live when in the incarnate world helping humans, did not give live births as did humans. The unifoal would be birthed into the hands of the Goddess Who would place it safely in an egg. Dark Star's egg had been placed just over there, in the Stone Circle.

Ah, the hatchling loved being out here. It was where she felt connected with her grandmare, where she found the portal that allowed her to move into the other worlds.

Dark Star yawned and stretched. She'd been dozing off, the sun warming her belly. "Life, I have life inside of me!" she thought. Her horn bumped against the wickiup, set at the side of the clearing which connected the path to the cabin and the path to the House on the Rise. Dark Star could hear the Croffy twins working in Arnica and Holly's gardens. They were fun.

Last weekend the hatchling had romped with them in the gardens. Piles of leaves and fir needles had been raked up by the twins for the Grove's compost.

"Remember when we could burn them?" Arnica mused wistfully. The scent was so wonderful, yet the gardens were much happier being enriched. There would be no burning again this year, not even a small fire for nostalgia.

"Is it true?" asked Jimmy.

"We may never have a fall bonfire again?" Yarrow finished.

"That's what our Dad said." They ended in unison.

"Global warming is real, but the climate doesn't change quite that fast," Arnica answered. "Still, the forests of Lothloriën continues to grow warmer and the forests drier."

It felt good knowing that there were hard-working, thoughtful young people who cared about the future.

The hatchling wondered if the small hut would be able to stay when Pearl was done with it. Amber Whitefeather, Peri and Topi Crowfeather had the materials sent by train from the tribal homeland in the River Mountains. Only women could put it up. It was funny. Ollis Piper hadn't seemed so certain that Flying Raven and the other women of the coven knew what they were doing but Lotus, known for his skills at woodworking and construction, knew at a glance that they knew what they were doing. The sounds of Pearl's chanting were so soothing. Dark Star's thoughts drifted once again into dreaming. The sun warmed her womb.

Pearl scratched Dark Star's chin. This was bliss. Pearl felt so close to the unicorn, grateful to have had this time, yet she looked forward to being back with her classes on Monday morning. She wondered what the students would say when they saw her shaved head.

"It'll grow out," and Pearl dozed off as well.

Holly was placing a few carefully chosen gemstones and crystals just underneath the altar. Arnica was sprinkling water around the altar and the courtyard. Earlier, Arnica had infused one of his herbal formulas back at the cabin before they came in to Trillium School to finish setting up the ancestral altar for the school.

"Mph." Arnica continued to be bothered by his 'old bones.' His herbal remedies kept him limber and able to do his work, still, they were not a cure for the arthritis which ran in his family.

"Are you all right?" Holly was always concerned about his partner of decades.

Arnica came around and the two sat on the stone floor. "My hands are a nuisance but sitting works well." He moved into a half lotus.

"I was thinking about Yule gifts," Holly loved giving gifts to their friends. He snuggled closer as he felt Arnica's arm go around him. "for Dark Star," he added.

"Isn't it beautiful" Arnica's other arm stretched out, indicating the entire courtyard.

Trillium School's Hallows Eve was an afternoon event, allowing for those who wished to have the evening for their own ritual work and celebrations.

Set around the perimeter of the courtyard were many smaller altars. Many others were in the school hall. The school's courtyard and the hall would be open to the public all afternoon and for the remainder of the weekend. All were asked to bring donations for the local food bank. One classroom had been vacated for much of the past week to provide storage for the many cartons filling with boxed and canned goods and jars of home-canning, each marked so the empty jar could later be returned to its home.

"It gets dark so early," Holly said. "I know it does it every year, but still..."

It was a perfect night for a Hallows Eve ritual. On this night the coven was glad to have an above-average temperature. Too many years an early frost had moved them into the cabin and this year they definitely wanted to be in the Stone Circle.

"It's pure magick, isn't it?" Arnica put clear images of the view into his mental files. This was not to be forgotten.

The path from the cabin back into the woods and the Stone Circle was lined with gourd and pumpkin lanterns. As the men carried the basket of ritual tools for Hallows Eve back to the stone altar, another string of candle flames came into view. Pearl had lit them, having done a Drawing Down the Sun ritual at noon and saving the flame until sunset.

"Look," Holly said, "who did those?" The men of the coven had carved the gourds and pumpkins as a gift for Pearl as well as an added element for Hallows, but they had only made enough lanterns to reach the Stone Circle.

"They were a gift from the women of the Loon Tribe." Pearl walked toward them. She was wearing her Croning gown, hand beaded over the past months. She looked iridescent, the beads shimmering even in the dim light of the candles, Pearl herself practically glowing from her week in the wickiup. "They sent them to Peri and Topi and they gave them to Gino to bring home. He set them out so early this morning I was still sleeping."

Dark Star came trotting down the hill from the House on the Rise. She had a purple shawl draped around her neck, her head raised high. She and Jenny would both represent the Goddess Mother, later at Pearl's Croning. The color of the silk would be the 'announcement' to the coven that, just as Jenny was expecting, the hatchling was in foal.

"Good evening, sirs." Sel was in a pale blue. "I'm going up to the rise. Jenny and Gino will let me use their bath and temple so I can prepare for Pearl's Croning." Sel would join the women in the Stone Circle after the coven's work had ended. She would be a beautiful Goddess Maiden.

"Halloo," Jewel and Lotus were coming down the path from the cabin. They had shared a horse carriage with Iris and Dolly walking just a short distance behind. Dagon, the Woodfolk's ten-year old was busy explaining the meaning of Hallows to his sister Sunna, turning five this Sabbat, and Diana, Iris and Dolly's daughter, who was five last Beltane.

Other voices soon called out and the sky darkened. There were seventeen of them, including the coven's children. The paths, lit by candles, stretched out in both directions to the cabin and House on the Rise. Dark Star lowered her head, tipping her horn toward the altar.

The Stone Circle brimmed with light and Magick and the voices joined together, "And the Goddess breathed gently into the void..."

LXXXVIII - Surprises for Dark Star

Something was going on and she didn't know what. Dark Star *knew* that it had to do with the wrapped gifts under the Yule tree ... but there were many gifts there every year. Her men and their coven loved to exchange gifts and took great joy in giving and every one of them had included her all these years. But there was some type of magick going on this year and it was like a puzzle she could not set aside.

Just the other night she was almost caught. She was nudging one of the brightly-wrapped parcels. Well, the gift tag said it was for her, a gift from the Woodfolk family. Dagon had placed it under the tree in the front temple just days ago and there was something about the look in his eye.

Dark Star turned and looked toward the cabin's front room - it's temple. There were packages with her name on them! Arnica and Holly were at Trillium School teaching and she was alone in the cabin. Did she dare? 'No, a unicorn's honor is sacred,' she thought to herself and pushed open the door to head out to the Stone Circle. The hatchling had an appointment with her grandmare, Lillian.

"Does she suspect?" Several of the school's faculty were on break. The door between the faculty room and the library was open. Only a few students were working on research in the library which allowed Gino to sit with his coven mates.

It was the Friday before Yule Eve and the school's classes had let out early but the school, itself, would not close.

There was a small Yule tree in the remodeled kitchen, sitting on a folding table. It was simple. Attached to it were hand-made 'wishes' members of the coven made for various students and their family. But beneath it was a mound of wrapped parcels which overflowed, filling nearly the entire space underneath the table as well. Some were expected: the jars of home-harvested maple syrup from the Croffy twins' parents, wrapped from the same paper used last year. The Mason jars were obvious and the syrup was pure joy!

"No, I don't think so." Arnica took another drink from his mug of steaming herbal tea.

"Ms. Munchkin and I were imaging each other last night," Holly added. Holly and Dark Star had the best communication, sending mental images to each other through the crystal orb at the cabin.

"*Ms.* Munchkin?" Pearl was knitting baby things for Gino and Jenny's baby, due in just one more Sabbat.

"Well," Holly laughed. Everyone knew a joke was coming. Pearl's needles paused. "Arnica and I were talking last night and we are doubtful that she's had a hoof-fasting without inviting us."

"I'm late." Iris Dolorum hurried in to the faculty room, kissing her husband, Dolly, on the head. "I've got to relieve Jewel at the postal shop." Trillium's principal quickly stood up, his arm around Iris, pulling her back to the doorway. He swooped her down with a huge kiss.

Everyone, even the students in the library, burst into enthusiastic applause. Iris hadn't noticed the mistletoe tacked overhead.

287

The Hatchling

Dark Star was sitting before the altar, leaning against her favorite teacher, her grandmare, Lillian.

"It is one of the difficulties inherent in their species," the elder unicorn was explaining. "The same qualities which make them so wonderful allow many of them to be caught by the webs of their own egos and senses of self-importance."

"But what about those humans like my coven?" Dark Star was troubled. She wanted to believe that all humans were as caring of Mother Earth as her friends.

"Well, we talk about that in our councils," Lillian answered. "Some of the elders still question whether the Goddess, in Her wisdom, made the best decision when she gave the human species the gift of controlling fire and of language. Humans have the gift of choice but their ability to choose reflects reality, both the joyful light and the terrifying darkness."

This morning brought Dark Star one of the more challenging lessons in her training. The hatchling could easily understand that the growing life within her belly was a gift, one which would bring joy and blessings to her human family.

"They are an earth-bound species," Lillian counseled, "they do not have a unicorn's ability to understand time. They are like children, and only those who understand the Mother's Mysteries seem to grasp the long-term implications of their actions."

"So that is why they prefer to harvest lumber than to live with forests, why their governments seem to support the consumption of fossil fuel rather than teach conservation?"

"Yes, little one," Lillian added. "But what a remarkable species. They have created some of the most amazing wonders of this manifest world, they taught themselves how to amass knowledge, to collect history, to develop technology, but many cannot see past their own lives."

"They are ... mortals," Dark Star said, a new understanding of that word flashing through her mind.

There was not a lot of space in the cabin's front room but it was a beautiful temple. The fireplace was warm and bright and, across the room was the Yule tree. The altar looked beautiful in the candlelight.

The coven were sitting around the room, the Yule Ritual completed. Everywhere, it seemed, except near the fireplace, boxes and bright paper were scattered about. The women were all wearing scarves which were cowl-like. Pearl had made them to be worn at Jenny's birthing ceremony. The coven's women would be there, creating the Circle for Jenny and Gino when their baby would enter the world.

The hatchling realized that her secret had not been as well kept as she'd thought. She'd expected Gino and Jenny to receive all sorts of gifts for their baby, but Dark Star was completely caught by surprise as her human family helped her open her own gifts. 'Yule presents,' she'd told Lillian just the other day, 'what a wonderful, loving and generous custom!'

Dark Star had a long day. She would not birth the egg of her own unicolt for another six months and yet she already sensed that all of her energy was no longer her own. 'How did Jenny manage,' she wondered!

She was laying off to the side, her opened gifts before her. Eggs! They'd given her eggs! The hatchling looked at the beaded egg Pearl had made. It sparkled with the reflection of the fire. And the hand-carved wooden egg from Lotus with the design of a baby unicorn, and the crocheted egg from Raven...

Holly had teased her, "what else could we all give our sweet munchkin... You have everything..."

"Or you will later this year," Arnica had chuckled, scratching her ear.

And she would. She looked over at the small netsuke egg Ollis had given her, one of the many treasures he had collected during his earlier global travels. Dark Star's head dropped. She was tired as well and began to drift, wondering what her own egg would look like ... and what her own unicolt would be when it hatched.

Sunna Woodfolk and Diana Dolorum were both snuggled up with the new quilt Pearl made for Raven and Ollis. When Raven saw her friends' daughter growing sleepy, she put her gift down by Dark Star and the two five-year-old girls dozed off, their arms around their hatchling friend's legs. Diana rolled over, her fingers reaching for Dark Star's neck. Dark Star could not remember feeling so loved.

Several of the coven were in Arnica and Holly's kitchen where Arnica was offering hot toddies to those who wished a little 'spirit' in their Yule spirit.

"I read yet another new report on global warming," Iris Dolorum was agitated. "Scientists have new measurements from the ice shelves of the Boreal Axis. Huge sections of glaciers are calving off. It's very alarming." Merrydale's Postmarm was known for her political activism.

"I've seen them," Ollis Piper spent years in the merchant marines before he reunited with his daughter, Iris. Now a grandfather, married to Raven, the Trillium students found world geography to be vital and fascinating. Few schools had geography teachers who had *seen* nearly all of the lands described in the textbooks. "The vastness of the ice, the fierceness of the cold. It was wild and wonderful and part of our Mother's balance with the steamy tropics."

"The news of our tree friends is no better," Arnica added. "I've had letters from a number of herbalists I know in other lands. Their climates are just a few degrees warmer but that's been enough to bring drastic change."

"Beetles," Holly interjected.

"Vast reaches of forest in regions as diverse as Afresia and Europa are dying off. Even some of the forests in the northern latitudes of Lothloriën are suffering." Arnica looked deeply troubled. "Merrywood is a more temperate forest but if it continues to warm, even our trees may be at risk."

"To a healthier year for our Mother." Deodar raised his mug in a toast.

Mugs and cups clinked together but the sound stirred the adults, waking tired children. It was time to bundle everyone up for a brisk ride back to Merrydale, time for life in the cabin to settle in for the night.

Dark Star lay in the middle of the temple floor on the rug, all her 'eggs' surrounding her as she dreamt of her grandmare and the Goddess and the unknown life within her belly.

Arnica and Holly had quieted down. Despite a long day and the picking-up after the coven left, Holly's surprise of mistletoe hanging over their bed had led to some Yule Eve Magick! If only it might be so simply to bring healing joy to the planet...

LXXXIX - Baby Pains

"Unnh," Jenny reached for her belly, "there's one."

"A contraction?" Gino had a concerned look on his face.

Jenny laughed. Gino seemed more anxious than she was! "No, love, just a good kick. If it's a girl, I bet she'll play soccer."

Gino reached over and placed his hands on her large belly. Just then the baby kicked again ... hard!

"Wow," Gino reacted, "feel that!"

"Trust me," Jenny winced, "I did..."

Dark Star sat in awe of the numerous bottles, many of them cut crystal with ground stoppers, the tops of which sparkled in the light. She was struggling to stay out of the way. More than anything she wanted to poke her horn around the kitchen counter filled with such beautiful magick and yet, even sitting there wasn't comfortable. The growing life in her belly wanted some space as well.

"How long?" the hatchling wondered. *Midsummer is when you may birth your egg*, her grandmare, Lillian had said. Dark Star envied Jenny.

"The water from Lady Ellhorn and the artesian well..." Arnica poured a small amount of water from the beautiful bottle.

"And some from Phoenix's Ritual of Passing..." Holly added a little water from another bottle.

"Water from the Genetricia River..."

"From the Grotto of Our Lady..."

"The 'Pan water' from Bavariana..."

There were dozens of bottles and decanters and vials. Dark Star lay her head down. Her unifoal was sleeping. She could feel the quiet in her womb... Soon, the men spoke quietly as they added more waters into the large container. Dark Star was *snoring* , but very quietly.

"Ah, motherhood," Arnica whispered as he picked up a bottle of water from the River Mountains. Arnica was mixing ritual waters to pour into the birthing tub the afternoon of Candlemas Eve.

The planning for Candlemas had been extensive. Both the house on the Rise and the Grove's Stone Circle had undergone some dramatic changes since the dark moon.

At the New Moon just days after the Yule Sabbat the coven sat in circle sharing their memories of their own initiations. Jenny and Ollis Piper were both studying for Initiation. Peri and Topi were working with the coven often, their Elder Sisters back in the River Mountains too far away. The Crowfeathers were thinking about working toward Initiation, as Amber had done, working in two cultures.

Amber Whitefeather and the sisters Peri and Topi Crowfeather had been brought through the Moon Mother Dance, the Loon Tribe's rite of passage when women were brought into the Circle of Elders as wise women. Although the circumstances of their ceremony had its differences, the coven talked about how they related.

"And you see," Peri said, animated by her train of thought, "our entering the cave touches on the same mystery the coven has through the candidate's being blindfolded and then later, again seeing the light!"

"Ow," Jenny laughed. "The baby is ready to dance the Rune again."

"When will she be due?" Peridot was known for her precognitive skill, certain that the young Rosario's first baby would be a girl.

"The doctor's date puts it close to the Full Moon after Candlemas. Gino and I are hoping for Candlemas, that ... the baby (Jenny didn't want to count on a girl or a boy) was conceived on Beltane Eve." She blushed a little, yet it was obvious that the memory of the Beltane Rite was very powerful and wonderful for her.

"May I scry?"

Peridot's request brought quick and happy affirmations and Holly offered to open a portal to the Circle and bring a shallow basin of water from the kitchen.

"Easy." Philbert Flower, Jenny's father, was helping Carlos, Gino's father, carry in a large birthing tub. Philbert had sent for a fine tub, all the way from Delphine, in Gardenia, east of the Genetricia River. Jenny's mother, Becky, was working to complete her nursing degree so the Flowers could create a healing center for Merrydale's young women. The Flowers wanted to address the problems for young, unmarried women, helping them prevent pregnancy and deal with the issues if they did become pregnant.

When Jenny decided she wanted to be in water when giving birth, Jenny spoke with Clarice Umbat'u, a wonderful woman she'd met at Merrydale Clinic. Clarice had moved to Lothloriën from Afresia, where she'd been a midwife for enough years that she realized she wanted to get a medical degree in Lothloriën. After she graduated (with honors!) from Genetricia University, she moved to Merrydale for her residency. In Afresia Clarice had helped women give birth in a hot spring near her village, one which was sacred to their Mother Goddess. She was perfect ... and Clarice loved the fact that Gino was working toward his teaching degree from Genetricia.

It was two days before Candlemas Eve. Peridot had gazed into the scrying bowl and was certain that Jenny would be in labor that night. This meant time was drawing near.

The birthing tub was beautiful, raised at one end to support the mother's back. Pearl saw it at the Flowers, where it was first uncrated after being shipped from the east coast by train. Pearl's eyes lit up. Her baby blessing gift to Jenny and Gino would be hand-painting the exterior with a design that would have 'hidden blessings' so that not just Jenny, but other young mothers would benefit when the tub was moved to the women's center.

Becky and Jenny were lighting candles in the front room, where Jenny could look out the windows at Merrywood, "if the birth is during daylight," Iris had teased her.

Arnica and Holly had incense ready and were aspurging the floor ahead of the men.

Sometimes Jenny was uncomfortable with the extra concern people showed since her miscarriage last year.

"Mmmh," Jenny said. Another baby pain. And then she let out a sharp noise. It was the first, maybe not yet a contraction, but Jenny was feeling the baby preparing for Candlemas.

The noise woke Dark Star who was sleeping by the young Rosarios' fireplace, dreaming of baby humans and baby unicorns playing in a large field of yellow calendula.

"Men, out!" Clarice said, laughing. "No, not you." She swatted Gino on his rear with her broom, a beautiful hand-made broom she'd brought with her from Afresia. "You can stay, but you must be quiet."

The men chanted, quiet at first but then louder.

Gino stopped, looking at the lit windows of his house, up on the Rise. The candle in the window shone clear.

Arnica and Holly were on either side of him, and gently squeezed his hands in support. Gino thought that sitting and doing nothing was beyond reality. He'd rather be here with the men.

Clarice knew the holy day. She translated her home peoples name for it as "lambs'ad," where it was a women's rite.

The coven women, Jenny and Gino's mothers, Becky and Rosetta, and Clarice were very focused. Jenny lay back in the warm water. Jewel poured a small amount of the sacred waters from Arnica's flask over Jenny's belly each time there was a pause between contraction periods.

"Are you soon to birth?" Clarice asked.

Jenny, holding tightly to her mother's hand with her left and Rosetta's hand with her right, nodded.

"Then, ladies, let us begin."

At Clarice's nod, Raven lit a second candle and placed it in the window alongside the first.

"See that?" Gino said. "We're in labor."

The men chanted, calling upon all of the healing deities they knew. They had passed a long night after closing their Sabbat Ritual, but, warmed by the cauldron fire and strengthened with some of Ollis's special, home-made cider, this was a night to remember.

Gino's father, Carlos, had joined them. Philbert, more comfortable with his daughter's Earthkin ways than ever, was not yet ready to join a Circle, not even a men's circle. Philbert was home, alone, but unable to sleep and trying to focus on prayers for his daughter. Frankly, Philbert was no longer as certain whether he should pray to Kristos or to the deities of all people.

"Ease him out," Clarice urged Jenny.

"It's a *her*," Peridot countered.

"I don't ... care ... right now..." Jenny panted. Becky wiped the perspiration off her daughter's forehead. "Mommy," and she winced as her womb tried, once again, to bring forth the new baby.

Gino was certain he could *feel* Jenny's contractions. It was difficult to stay in the Stone Circle and wait. The camaraderie as the men drummed and chanted, and sat and talked throughout the night had been wonderful. They channeled their collective Magick into him. Gino's work was to send well-grounded Magick to Jenny.

They were very connected.

"Gino!" Jenny cried out.

Dark Star had tried to stay out of the way. This was the first human birth she'd witnessed and it made her anxious about birthing her egg come Midsummer. "Will that be as painful?" she wondered. The hatchling's eyes were wide open.

The sky had grown light and, as Gino saw a third candle appear in the window, the first rays of the sun caught his house as it crested the east.

He went rushing up the path to his house as the men put out the fire and began gathering their things before heading to the Rise.

Dark Star was waiting for him as he rushed through the kitchen.

There, sitting in the rocking chair, wrapped in a large blanket, was his beautiful Jenny, holding the most amazing thing he'd ever seen.

Jenny looked up at Gino. "It's baby Astral, Astral Brigit Rosario," she said. "Isn't she wonderful? She has your hair."

LXXXX - Dark Star's Lessons

The gardens were busy. Jonquils aimed their yellow trumpets toward the waxing sun. The crocuses created brilliant patches of purple and white and yellow. Over toward the potting shed a tall camellia was filled with red blooms. The colchicum and peonies and valerian were all eagerly reaching their new leaves toward the sun. Life and vigor of the coming springtide showed everywhere at the Grove.

Preparations for the Equinox had kept the coven busy, even at Trillium School. What began as a child's question in the day care was brought to the faculty meeting. Peri loved the story. She explained how they were telling the children about egg decorating as something they, as Children of the Earth, could do... "And then Alice said..."

"Why can't all the kids in Merrydale have eggs." Topi finished the sentence for her sister. The idea quickly took hold in the faculty room. The coven (all of whom were part of Trillium School's faculty) discussed the idea. The idea was circulated through several classrooms (of the students able to take this as a special project). It had even gained formal public support. Jenny, still on maternity leave, took the proposal to Merrydale's Town Hall when she took Astra to show her to her coworkers. Only a few weeks old, Astral had her own magick, it seemed.

"No, she's not named for Eostara," Jenny explained to Sara Bellum, a Council secretary who was increasingly interested in the Earthkin beliefs.

"She's named for a very special *Star*." Jenny was uncertain how much Sara knew about Trillium School's mascot and felt it best to keep any unicorn discussions out of the workplace.

Jenny's coworkers oohed and a-ahed over the newborn and were enthusiastic about a Merrydale egg hunt. The idea quickly turned up in the Council meetings, and both the Merrydale Council and the Greater Merrydale Council favored the idea. Only Pastor Evangel voiced opposition, calling an egg hunt "a devilish undertaking."

"Should we serve deviled eggs?" Iris joked later, when Jenny shared the news with the coven that the councils supported the plan and the egg hunt could take place at the town square.

"I'll need more eggs than Mrs. O'Realy can provide!" Rosetta Rosario, Gino's mother and Trillium School's cook offered to be in charge of the egg-boiling to be held at the school. "If even half of the town children turn out..."

"I think most will be there," Iris said. As postmarm, Iris often knew more about Merrydale than anyone.

"Well, we'll need at least fifty dozen," Rosetta said, after a pause for some mental math.

"Oh, my Goddess!" Peri and Topi chimed in unison.

Dark Star had been to the cavern before. The path into the Otherlands from the portal of the Stone Circle was familiar, although it took Lillian's guidance to pass through the portal. Dark Star was surprised that she could not easily pass through the veil as she was accustomed.

"My dear," her grandmare reminded her, "it is but three more months when you will birth the egg. If your young one is as strong-willed as you, it is no wonder you cannot so simply bring its life with you."

Dark Star passed through the veil with great humor and an increased awareness of her own maternal state. As they moved deeper into the Earth, Dark Star grew quiet. Going to speak with The Mother was a rare event. The hatchling wanted to learn all she could from the Lady.

As they entered the Hall of Wisdom, with its soft-glowing stalactites lighting the chamber, the gentle sound of dripping spring water Dark Star saw The Mother. There, with several torches near Her, the Lady sat on Her throne. 'She is so like the High Priestess,' Dark Star thought, remembering Holly's tarot cards.

Then the hatchling saw something so unexpected that she slipped and nearly fell. Over to one side of the chamber were two young unicorns, perhaps the same age or a little older than herself. Both sitting back on their haunches, Dark Star could see that they both had very full bellies. 'Do I look like that?' she wondered.

"You will in two more lunations," the Lady said.

Dark Star blushed. She had forgotten that the Goddess could hear thoughts just like voices!

"Not too hard," Jenny said, "we want her to fall asleep."

Diana, Iris and Deodar's daughter, would soon be six. She and Sunna Woodfolk were taking turns rocking Astra. Several of the coven had gathered at the house on the ridge and the two young friends were feeling very grownup, being able to help with Jenny.

The rocking crib was beautiful, a gift from Jewel and Lotus Woodfolk. Lotus had made it by hand, hand-carving a beautiful, magickal design into the surfaces. Jewel had surprised even herself with her artistic skill, working out the patterns on paper.

Pearl's glasses had slid down her nose. Holding an egg right in front of her eyes, she was using tweezers to apply tiny sequins and beads to an egg. Dagon, Diana's older brother, was helping Pearl, keeping small amounts of strong epoxy ready so Trillium's art teacher could dab at it with a toothpick, applying it just so for each miniature jewel.

As he watched, Dagon was creating mental designs. Dagon attentively watched every motion Pearl made. Now ten ("going on eleven," he would add), Dagon had already skipped one grade. He was a fine student but also enjoyed playing with his classmates. The coven knew he was special, ever since his adventure in the Stone Circle when he entered the Realm of Faerie with Dark Star when but age one. One more year and he could go to Trillium School!

Two of the designs he wanted on his egg were just for that, for school! Dagon's design would be intricate, just like his mind. He had found seeds of many colors but was working in shades of white, off white, and black-like colors, using the smallest seeds he could find in Arnica's herb stock and in town at the garden store. Thank goodness for the poppy seeds!

The lad missed Dark Star. They had an unspoken bond and he often envied Gino's closeness with the unicorn. Dagon felt that his time would be coming. He, too, would have a unicorn as a close friend. Where was Dark Star? Arnica had only mentioned that she was off in the Otherworld studying.

'Is that like when I went to the Faerie?' Dagon wondered to himself.

"It is a *sylvan ovum*," The Mother said, holding a beautiful egg-shaped crystal so Dark Star could see it.

The Hatchling looked up at the Lady. 'What beautiful eyes She has,' Dark Star thought, and then blushed again, remembering that The Mother would have heard that thought.

But The Mother's eyes just sparkled, and She continued the lesson. "This contains all the Mysteries you will need to know when you become one whose role it is to tell My stories to younger unicorns."

"Even my unicolt?" asked Dark Star. Dark Star had been told by the Mother that she would be present when her egg hatched, something which rarely happens among those unicorns chosen to live with humans. Lillian added, that "the situation on this planet is growing dire and we cannot always observe ancient custom." The Mother had nodded in agreement.

"Yes, dear one," The Mother's voice was like music. Planet Earth is facing some fierce changes. The human species has caused such imbalance I do not know that even I can bring things back."

"Global warming?" Dark Star had heard her men speak of it many times.

"Yes," the Lady said, "and more. My forests are now prone to disease. Many of My fish can no longer survive in the oceans. And humans in many countries will grow fearful and turn upon each other in the next generations to come. Your work and the work of other unicorns..." She paused a moment, as Dark Star looked over toward the two other unicorns. "Yes, all of you have much work to do."

A tear slipped from Dark Star's eye. "Will my humans be O.K?"

"Yes, they will. The coven which has created Trillium School, even Merrydale, will make it through these next hard times."

Dark Star was so happy. Her time with Lillian and The Mother had spanned several human days yet it seemed like she had been gone *forever* and it seemed like she hadn't been gone at all... Yet Some of these eggs were dazzling!

The coven's egg preparing had occupied several nights, and the egg-boiling at the school was an entire Saturday.

The Eostara Eve ritual had been so beautiful. Dark Star knew just where she would plant *her* egg. Hers had no human writing on it but Holly had been able to pen two symbols on it as she imaged them to her human friend using their crystal orb. That was her first night back. Arnica had made herbal dyes for their eggs and experimented with some new techniques. The patterns of color were beautiful.

And Pearl! Pearl had surprised her with a little "egg holster," a knit bag just egg-sized with a beautiful strap which fit around her neck. The hatchling was able to carry her own egg throughout the ritual.

It had been difficult to be focused during the ritual. All of them, humans and Dark Star alike, felt the rising sap of Aries. Jenny and Gino were always aware of Astra. Gino thought the vision of his young wife with the baby sling across her heart was the most beautiful thing he'd ever seen.

Iris and Deodar had been reading new government reports. The mountain glaciers, the ice of the Boreal Axis, all were melting at alarming rates.

Each of them found their minds danced from mental seed to mental seed. This would be a very busy year before them.

And Dark Star? Her thoughts continually surrounded the life in her belly yet, at times, she would think about the cold frames that Arnica had planted that very morning... There were many pots planted just for her. Thank goodness The Mother said that eating borage would help bring forth a healthy unicolt.

LXXXXI - Andrius' Tale

It was nearing midnight several nights before Beltane Eve when Dark Star, step by step, headed toward the kitchen door. She needed to be so careful so as not to wake the men. Her hooves could be quite loud on the wooden floor so she paused after each step, breathing with care, even though her heart was pretty active.

Pushing the kitchen door open so slowly (and hoping that some of the early spring moths wouldn't come flying in!), then holding the knob in her teeth to carefully close it. What a slow process this was.

But then, success! Outside, now, with a waxing moon overhead, she wanted to run, to gallop wildly toward the stone circle in joy at having made it out of the cabin with neither Arnica nor Holly even suspecting.

But a full belly kept her from running. It was now nearly a year since she conceived, and her womb was full of a baby unicorn. As she stepped into the Stone Circle, there was her grandmare, Lillian, waiting for her.

The night was so still that, off in the distance, they could hear the first bell tone of midnight from the clock tower of Merrydale's Town Hall.

Just then Dark Star saw an elfin-looking man step into view. "Poppy!"

Gino was yawning as he watched the pan of water gently heating. Sitting in the water was a baby bottle with chamomile tea. It was Gino's turn to make Astral's tea.

"Astral Brigit Rosario," he said, looking out the kitchen window of the House on the Rise. He loved being a new father! Just then he almost thought he saw movement in the Stone Circle but no. Gino yawned again. The kitchen clock indicated it was midnight. He turned off the flame and removed the baby bottle. Just as Jenny had showed him, he squeezed just a few drops onto the inside of his wrist. The temperature was perfect.

"Really, we can just talk?" Andrius was so pleased.

"Yes, Grandmare was waiting at the portal with Poppy, someone I hadn't seen since I was not much more than a hatchling. He held some large flowers filled with some type of dew and poured them over me."

"*Horus indefinus...*" Andrius said, "Clock-stopper vine. It's very rare and doesn't grow in the human world at all."

"You know herbs too?" Dark Star thought of Arnica, her herbalist human.

"Ah, little one," said Andrius gently, "you're not here to talk about me."

Holly had rolled onto his back and was snoring. It wasn't overly loud, but enough to almost waken Arnica, who was always a light sleeper.

Arnica, half-asleep, reached over and jiggled Holly's shoulder. His lover rolled back over onto his side. Just before he drifted back into his dream, one eye looked at the bedside clock. 'Just midnight,' he thought and then slid back into his dreaming.

"She had the prettiest eyes I'd ever seen. Her horn..." Andrius looked away. Sometimes he still missed her so very much. It was not easy to speak about her, even with his offspring.

Dark Star swam a bit, as she waited. They had walked over to this underground hot spring. For the first time in days her belly felt weightless, and the warmth was wonderful.

"Well, it caught the light just so." Andrius looked back at Dark Star. "And when she ran, every muscle was beautiful. Her mane flowed behind her, her tail danced in the air... I was smitten, and determined to win the race."

"The race?"

"Yes, that year for Beltane, the ritual was planned so that whomever won the race would invoke the Horned God. When I saw the Lady place a circlet of flowers upon my Lovely's head - that is what my heart called her from the first moment I saw her - I knew I had to win that race. There were more than two score of us running that year. I've never worked so hard. Later, when my Lovely and I left the Circle to invoke the Divine Mother and Divine Father, I was so tired from the race that you were nearly not conceived." Andrius chuckled at the memory.

"You mean?"

"Yes, munchkin," Andrius like the names the humans called Dark Star, "you were conceived as my Lovely and I were filled with Magick. I doubt there has ever been a more beautiful Goddess. Other than our Lady, of course..."

"Oh, my..." Dark Star was lost in thought...

Dagon Woodfolk was having difficulty sleeping. Although he was still a few weeks short of turning eleven, of all the coven and their families, he had the closest connection with the Realm of Faerie. Ever since Dark Star carried him through the portal at the Full

Moon after Beltane (when he was barely one year old) he had a sense of *knowing*. Dagon stirred during the night, pausing between waking and dreaming. *Something* was taking place, but as he heard the chiming of the bell tower, his reality again became his dreaming.

They were seated beneath a large rowan, its branches spreading wide overhead laden with bloom. Now and then some of the petals would drift down, landing on their food. Andrius had made certain to have some borage cakes ('made by elves') for his offspring.

Andrius loved having this time with Dark Star. Like any devoted daughter, she laughed at his jokes with glee.

"Oh," the hatchling said, "my belly hurts. Please no more jokes or I'll go into labor!"

Andrius looked at her with great affection. It was so good to have this personal time, something rare in the world of unicorns.

"That's just what my Lovely said when she was carrying your egg."

"How..." This was difficult for Dark Star. "How did... how did she pass away? And why? I thought we lived long lives?"

Andrius took a calm, deep breath. He had known this question would be coming. In fact, it was for this very reason the Lady had arranged for them to have this time together.

Pearl's eyes barely opened. Half asleep, she saw the votive candle's flame on her bedroom altar. It was nearing its end, the flame erratic as the wick drew up the final droplets of melted wax. The painting of the Goddess (Pearl had painted that as part of her university juries) glowed and the small photograph of her beloved Phoenix was lit by the dancing light. The sound of the clock tower quickly lulled her back to dreaming.

"Oh, it was many turns of the Wheel ago. Not long after your egg had been placed in the Mother's safekeeping and she had recovered. Your mare was a great lover of all the Mother's creatures."

Dark Star loved hearing that about her mother.

"Unlike you, sweet, my Lovely was not born into the world of flesh. While her egg was in the Underworld, in the Lady's great chamber, warmed with quilts filled with thistledown, hand stitched by the Faeries, a tragic event happened upon planet earth."

Dark Star inhaled. She did not like the turn of events in this story.

Andrius moved just a little closer to her and continued. "A large section of glacier broke loose in the high mountains which separate Dyubkz and Saracenia, some of the tallest in the world."

"Are they much higher than the River Mountains?"

"In truth, if you can imagine and picture it in your mind, they are more than twice as tall. The oldest of the glacier gods have lived there almost as long as humans have muddled about on Mother Earth."

"Twice as tall..." Dark Star closed her eyes and tried to imagine...

Lillian was waiting at the portal for the hatchling. Poppy sat nearby, trying to be still, for he was of a frisky lineage and this was difficult even at times like this.

She turned her head and perked up her ears. The hatchling's grandmare heard the clock bell. Dark Star needed to be back soon. Although several days would seem to have passed in the Otherworld, only a couple of seconds had lapsed in this human world.

They walked among stalagmites, ducked beneath stalactites.

"Here, here is one of her legends." Andrius had taken Dark Star to yet another realm, a beautiful cavern in which the Mother of Time stored her lore and knowledge for future generations of Her magickal creatures. "She made so many trips to the creature's world."

Andrius spoke of his Lovely, and how she cared for all of the Mother's children. From her earliest colthood she was empathic, always knowing just ahead of time when the planet Earth - the goddess Gaia - was about to rearrange herself, when her oceans might flood. And every time she would run to the Mother and beg her.

"The Lady cautioned her. These trips pleased the Lady greatly. Your mother saved thousands upon thousands of lives. Over here..." And Andrius turned his horn toward what looked like a large obsidian tetrahedron, sitting upon the floor, "this is the legend of my Lovely alerting a jungle filled with all manner of species. Her warning gave them nearly two hours to flee before a huge lehar came rushing down from Mount Peturba."

"A lehar?"

"Yes, an eruption of hot lava melted the glaciers at Peturba's heights. Without warning only a few of the feathered ones might have escaped but there were relatively few losses thanks to your mother."

Dark star gazed at the black shining surfaces. 'My mother,' she thought, pondering how wonderful her mother had been. 'Could I ever be as brave a unicorn as she?'

"Each time, your mother lost a little more of her ability to manifest. Each of these quests took a little more of her strength and substance. One night a new star entered the sky. She had become pure spirit."

Andrius sniffled a bit. "No, I'm not crying," he said.

Dark Star was doubtful.

"It was not death as your human world thinks of it, more of a transformation."

Suddenly Andrius' head tilted. His ear cocked, as if he'd heard something. "But now you must return as well. Even the clock-stopper has limits."

Dark Star felt just a bit disoriented. Her mind was still filled with the question which had popped into her head. "Will I become part of this lore?" She was just about to ask her sire when she felt herself swept back in time. There waited her grandmare. And Poppy seemed to have dozed off!

Lillian nuzzled her forelock just as she stepped through the portal, back into the Stone Circle. Dark Star could just barely hear the bell, still chiming midnight. Her belly full, Dark Star hurried toward the cabin as best she could.

Gino looked out the window again as he wiped off his wrist.

Astral was waiting for him, cradled in his sweet Jenny's arms.

LXXXXII - The Birthing

Gino set down his tools and rose to his feet. Gino had an assortment of tools and some beautiful lumber nearby, along with several wheels with rubber tires.

"How many years have I known you?" he asked Dark Star.

"It will be eleven years ago this autumn," the hatchling responded. "You were just a boy ... and look at you now."

"And you were just a hatchling!" Gino laughed. He looked back into the orb to continue the conversation.

"I will miss you, Munchkin..."

As Dark Star nuzzled his neck, she heard the door open. Jenny, looking as radiant as the summer morning, came out, holding Astral Brigit in her arms. Astral cooed when she saw her father.

"Daddy's going to build you a baby wagon today, sweetie," Jenny carried the baby over to Gino and handed her to him.

"And you," Jenny looked at Dark Star. "I am so amazed by this new adventure of yours."

Gino laughed. "Dark Star's only response is that her belly hurts!"

Jenny kissed Gino on the cheek. Astral would be in the playpen watching Gino at work. "Dad said he'd be along shortly. Actually, my mom called and relayed his message. He'd just left the house and he'll probably get here while I'm at the Stone Circle."

Philbert Flower was walking out to the house on the rise from Merrydale. Over the past years he took increasing joy in being among the trees. When the wind blew just right, he often thought he could hear the dryads. Gino, his son-in-law, was learning some excellent carpentry skills from Lotus Woodfolk, but Philbert was eager to share some of his skills learned as an engineering student at university many years ago.

Philbert was in charge of designing the axles for Astral's baby wagon.

"Are you ready?" Jenny nuzzled Dark Star. A special bond had developed between them. Jenny knew what it was like to be filled with baby.

Gino handed Jenny the orb. Dark Star leaned over and gave the young man a unicorn's kiss on his cheek. Yet, she wondered why Gino wasn't the one guiding her to the portal. 'It must be part of the Mysteries of Birth,' she quieted her own question.

Astral fussed in her playpen and Gino turned his attention to the baby as Dark Star and Jenny began walking the path down to the Stone Circle. Not yet able to 'hear' Dark Star through the orb, Jenny could only talk, but knew that the hatchling wanted to know more about giving birth.

"Oh, there were times it hurt so bad, and I'd been told the pain would be intense. Iris and Jewel did their best to prepare me but there I'd be, enjoying the sensations of Astral preparing herself to emerge, feeling warm and happy and embracing motherhood and then. *Oh ... my ... Goddess...* The only good thing is that the labor pains didn't last forever and then, when passed, life was O.K. again."

They walked the path, Jenny sharing her experience with the hatchling. Dark Star wondered if birthing an egg would be much different. She looked forward to being able to walk again with ease, even to trot through the gardens and stretch and feel energetic!

"I can tell your womb is filled with life." Jenny laughed at Dark Star's funny gait. "Do you remember how I waddled?"

"Here we are."

The Stone Circle waited, empty. The hatchling felt a curious energy in the air, but then, nothing felt normal. More than anything she wanted to feel the Lady's touch and birth the egg. It was her destiny and she wanted this experience. She looked at Jenny. The young mother was so beautiful. Dark Star envied her. *She* had given birth up in the house on the rise, with the coven there to support her and lend Magick.

But it was time for the meditation. Lillian would be waiting. Dark Star settled back on her haunches. It was very uncomfortable. How big an egg was this? She closed her eyes and began working with the images as Lillian had taught her.

Was it the wind? Squirrels? What was that noise? Dark Star opened her eyes. Her humans! They were all coming to the Stone Circle. She looked around and there was Gino, running down the hill. Arnica and Holly were entering the circle and all of the coven was arriving.

She struggled up onto her legs, her eyes wide with a look of astonishment. Lillian and Poppy were waiting at the portal, but the meditative quiet of the Stone Circle was quickly replaced with the joyful sounds of her humans.

Gino came running down the hill. Panting, he ran up to stand by Jenny. "Your dad's there... watching Astral... Hullo..." Gino greeted Dark Star and all the coven.

So, thought the hatchling, all of this had been just ... to be a surprise...

They were so connected, that Holly sensed her surprise and made a pun which filled the circle with laughter. "Munchkin, did we keep our 'Dark Star' in the *dark*?"

"Look, my dear," said Pearl. Peri and Topaz were opening a bundle of fabric. Raven and Amber each took the other two corners and there was a beautiful, embroidered quilt. "It's an 'egg blanket,'" Pearl said, "to keep your baby warmed between birthing and when the Mother takes it under Her care."

"Poppy!" Arnica and Holly were so happy to see their elfin friend.

Poppy stepped out of the Otherworld through the portal and hugged his herbal couple. What love the three of them had shared. Then he knelt before Gino, who took his orb from Jenny's hands and kissed it before handing it to Poppy.

Holly brushed the hatchling's forelock away from her eyes. "With this you'll be able to send your thoughts to us. Arnica and I are going to sleep by the altar after tonight's ritual. We'll be there with you, in a way, and we'll know just how you're doing. You can send your thoughts through the orb to us, and Poppy will bring it back when you return."

Dark Star didn't know what to say. She turned and looked at all of these humans. The young ones, Diana and Dagon and Sunna, and all of the adults of the coven. She loved living here with them, sharing in their lives.

Just then a searing pain almost brought her down to her knees. It was definitely time to go. She nodded, whinnied gently. Followed by Poppy, Dark Star stepped through the portal of the Stone Circle to join Lillian and enter the Otherworld.

"I wish I were with my humans." Another spasm gripped her and the thought was torn from her mind.

Calm. Breathe deep. That's what the Mother told her.

Dark Star felt the warm water soothing her tired muscles. Lillian had brought her to this hot spring, deep in some cavern. It was a wonderful place, glowing with light from numerous crystals set about. The Mother had waded right into the water with her, and was soothing her.

The hatchling had never imagined that *She* would be there, right in the water with her.

"Push."

How could a unicorn not respond to that divine voice?

The unicorn's cry echoed throughout the underground chamber, but there it was, floating alongside her. *It seemed so large...* 'That was inside of me?' wondered Dark Star.

"Look," She focused thoughts of relief, of pride, of emotions way beyond the languages she had been taught. Poppy sat over on a rock ledge near Lillian. The elfin man had been holding the orb. At various moments Dark Star had felt images of love flooding her heart, all the way from the cabin's altar in the aboveworld. She hoped they could see the egg. It would be spending time in the Mother's care in the Underworld until the time was right.

Unlike all of her unicorn foremares before, Dark Star was going to have the opportunity to be present when the egg hatched.

"Oh my..." Holly could hardly believe the vision he'd just seen. "Is it true?"

"I saw it also," Arnica said. "The Mother, the egg, all of it. Another day or two of resting..."

"And bathing in that wonderful water..." Holly loved hot baths!

"And she'll be back." Arnica felt a sense of relief, of comfort. More than any of the other coven humans, the old herbalist sensed that Dark Star's offspring would play a key role in the future of their planet.

"And now," Arnica said, kissing the orb where they'd seen images of their munchkin, "summer's here."

"To the gardens," Holly said, eager to tend the borage. He knew Dark Star would love some fresh, flowering borage when she returned.

LXXXXIII - Death and the Harvest

July had been a very warm month with some of the hottest days on record for Merrydale. Even at the Grove the men ended up sleeping outside in a tent, the screened ends zipped against the mosquitoes. Dark Star slept in her new 'summer bed,' as Holly and Arnica called it when they welcomed her home.

It took the hatchling a couple of weeks to recover. Frankly, she was *sore* from birthing the egg. And the only ones who seemed to have any understanding were the women of the coven who had become mothers. Dark Star and Jenny were learning to communicate through a crystal, now, just as she had done these many years with Holly and Arnica and then also with Gino. She and Jenny, both giving birth this year, had found a special bond. And what a surprise to find that it was almost as if some of the vocabulary of images she and Gino developed through that crystal was there, waiting for her and Jenny to use.

"It's like a secret sorority," Jenny had said, holding Astral in her arms. Jenny had walked over from the house on the rise the day after Dark Star's return from the Mother's birthing pool. The young unicorn lay in her new bed, all filled with fresh-cut borage.

Arnica had replenished the borage just yesterday. "Enjoy it while it's still in season," he added. Dark Star knew she'd be very happy sleeping in the cabin with her humans again once the weather cooled again.

Despite the heat, the days were busy at the Grove. It was a warm walk from Merrydale but the trees of Merrywood kept the air cooler than it was among the paved streets of Merrydale. Trillium School's faculty did most of their planning in the shade.

The school building was warm. Carlos was painting some of the classrooms. Rosetta went to school on those days as well. She *said* it was to prepare the kitchen and plan the menus for the coming year, but she'd shared her secret with Raven one afternoon. She brought Carlos frequent glasses of water and iced tea. On the days when Ollis and Lotus helped with some of the summer repair and maintenance Rosetta made the men lunch. She even made two different types of lemonade, one with jasmine in it, satisfying a thirst Ollis developed in his earlier life in the merchant marine.

The women of the coven spoke among themselves in admiration of Rosetta. Although she and Carlos were not part of the coven, they'd learned much about magick from their son, Gino, and from their work with the school and coven. Sometimes the faculty joked about Trillium School's kitchen being 'Rosetta's temple.' And Carlos has asked Arnica for several herbal tinctures he could blend into the paints to bring special magick to the rooms being painted.

Arnica enjoyed making a tincture with herbs which helped control the fire spirits. Some of the students in Flying Raven's chemistry class were a little too enthusiastic with their lab time.

Jimmy and Yarrow Croffy each brought a basket of cut borage to Dark Star's bed. This was one of their favorite tasks.

"Dark Star," Yarrow called. "Do you want some curry?" Yarrow was holding the currycomb. He loved to run it over her coat. It removed loose hair and stimulated the circulation of her skin. The Croffy twins' grandfather had horses, so they learned about currycombs at the family stable. It was one of the 'welcome back' presents, all gift wrapped, waiting for the hatchling when she returned.

Jimmy and Yarrow had returned from their graduation trip, a gift from their other grandparents. They'd traveled on a large steamer all the way across the Atlantikos to visit the homeland of their ancestors. They loved Hebrides, and brought several stones from sacred sites to add to the Stone Circle, but they were glad to be home, more than eager to move forward with their studies.

Their father hoped they would pursue university degrees but they were content to be studying herbal magick from Arnica and took their training very seriously. They were determined to join the coven this Hallows.

Their immediate goal was to be there and help Arnica and Holly with the harvest. Arnica had a long conversation with them - and a longer one with the Croffy parents and the coven. Arnica and Holly offered to pay the boys' tuition for a correspondence program through Genetricia University if they wished to continue working at the Grove.

"I must be honest," Arnica had said.

It was another warm night and Dark Star had difficulty sleeping. Arnica and Holly were dreaming nearby in the tent, aided by an evening cup of passion flower and valerian. But the hatchling had quietly walked to the Stone Circle.

"How are you, my egg?" Her question slipped silently through the portal into the otherworld. She was ever aware of the life force of her offspring. And oh, how she longed to see it. Him? Her? She didn't know. Dark Star wondered what color its coat would be, whether it would run fast like the stallions Boaz and Joachim or be wise like her father, Andrius.

There was also a new connection with the Goddess. "Mother," the hatchling imaged, "I miss you." And she did.

Dark Star remembered Lillian's counsel. Use this time to meditate, to speak with the Lady! This time in the middle of the night, just a couple of days before Lammas, was a gift! She moved her mind into that sacred space and imaged descending down, into the cavern. The hatchling remembered laying her head across the Mother's knee, and recreated that image as vividly as possible, then spoke with the Mother.

The hatchling ran through all of the images, relating what had happened since her return to the above-world. And then, the pleasures of sleeping upon a bed of borage, and how wonderful it was and how magickal and how cooling the scent when...

"You are sleeping on death."

Dark Star stopped breathing. That was the voice of the Mother...

Just then she realized that she had been so focused upon the new life being brought into the world, *her unicolt*, that the pleasure of the borage bed had been a joy and she had not realized. The borage devas were being *sacrificed* for her own comfort. This was very sobering.

"It is a lesson of Lammas," the Lady's voice came to her again.

Just then a shooting star zipped a brief streak of light overhead, catching the hatchling's eye. Now she was ready for sleep. The internal restlessness was calmed.

Iris and Jewel had their hands full of long grain stalks, trying to follow Amber's directions.

"Now, fold them over." Amber was very patient.

"What is this," Iris teased, "grain origami?"

"Perhaps more than you think," Topaz Crowfeather offered.

Several of the women were working on making grain men and dollies, one for the coven's Lammas Eve and a couple to provide harvest magick for Trillium School.

"How do you do it," Iris asked Peri.

The Crowfeather sister answered, "I think it's part of our genetic heritage. We grow up weaving. There are woven baskets at our tables, our babies have woven rugs, are carried in woven slings."

"To weave is to experience life," Topi added, quoting a lesson she'd learned as a girl.

"But look at Sel," Amber said. "She has weaving fingers." Sel Boulanger was studying with the Loon Tribe women who now lived in Merrydale to work at Trillium School. Sel had woven several wheat dollies. Sel was spending the summer months preparing to leave her birth family for the dark half of the year. She would be walking alone up into the River Mountains to Eagle's Nest where she would spend a year and a day studying with the Loon Tribe elders - the 'sacred grandmothers.'

The Lammas fire burned brightly, kept safe in the large, cast cauldron. It was a smallish fire, but Merrywood was very dry again this year. The fire season seemed to once again be worse in many parts of the Land of Lothloriën. More and more people spoke about global warming.

The Circle was cast, the elemental Magick held in place. The Dolorums tended the East altar. Iris, Merrydale's postmarm, had one of the metal dyes used to stamp dates on the letters which passed through her office and Deodar had brought a binder which would hold the first ten years of Trillium School's legal records. Diana, now six, waved a feather fan and sang to the wind.

Flying Raven and Ollis Piper were at the South. Raven had made some special flash paper, soaking tissue in a solution of potassium nitrate, then drying it at a very controlled temperature. Ollis brought quill pens from the Finch Islands, one of the many exotic lands he had visited in earlier times. Each covener had written their wishes upon this paper, which had been first used to invoke the element of fire.

The Woodfolk were at the West. Lotus had created a beautiful waterfall, but it needed Jewel standing at the base, filling cobalt blue pitchers, which she handed to Dagon, who reached up and handed it to Sunna, who sat up at the top. As Lotus played a 'water' melody upon a carved, wooden flute, the family relayed the water and the Stone Circle was filled with the music.

At the north were Pearl, Amber, Peridot and Topaz. They represented the element of Earth with the Lammas feast: baskets of treats stacked near the altar, and the large Grain Man bread who represented continued good crops for Merrydale.

Gino stood at the altar's left, calling upon the God of the Forest and Jenny, with Astral in a silk sling, stood at the right. Arnica and Holly stood with Gino, invoking the elderly aspect of the Horned One.

And Dark Star? She stood with Jenny, the two of them both new Mothers.

Next, as one, all present, adults and children, humans and the hatchling, called out into the night. They placed their papers into the fire, creating bright flashes of flame as their wishes disappeared into the Universe.

Holly put Dark Star's into the fire. It was safer.

Dark Star wished so much that her new unicolt would be a happy hatchling as the Wheel turned.

LXXXXIV - By Degrees

"How do I look?" Becky Flower turned away from the mirror, but looked over her shoulder at the reflection. She was wearing a "Pearl Lamina original," one Pearl designed and made with help from her advance students at Trillium School.

The dress was very smart. "You'll look wonderful." Pearl adjusted a few pins for the final stitching.

"Mom, it's beautiful!" Jenny was so proud of her mother. Jenny came over to Trillium's day care every day on her lunch break. Astral Brigit was only seven and a half months old, but the Earthkin environment was a loving and stimulating environment for the baby. Jenny glanced at her watch, kissed her Mom on the cheek and gave Pearl a quick hug.

"Honey, do you have to go already?" Becky wanted just a little more admiration. It had been hard work. Her project and
thesis for her Master's Degree was based upon the work she'd

done to try and set up an organization for young women. Despite her best efforts - and her husband Philbert had *many* political connections in Parliament, Becky found herself unable to overcome the quiet undertones of fear which came from the more conservative Kristos members of the Church of the Martyr's board of directors.

Undaunted, Becky pursued her goals, working with the parents, single moms and older Earthkin girls. Trillium's Day Care had benefitted from having a nurse (an "almost nurse" as Becky called herself) often present and Becky found she gained the insight she wanted through communicating directly with the young women.

"Mrs. Lamina?" One of the students knocked at the makeshift fitting room. The girls were ready to do the final stitching.

Glancing out the window, Becky saw Jenny quickly walking toward the library building.

Trillium school had been in session a fortnight. Classes began a few days prior to the Full Moon. The student body (or, 'the student bodies,' as some of the coven liked to joke) was now at 158 students and, for now, this was considered to be 'at capacity.'

Arnica, Holly and Deodar Dolorum, the principal, were in the faculty room next to the library. The faculty room was once the large kitchen for the small house which had been remodeled into the school's library.

"Gino," Arnica called out, "can you come in here?"

Arnica, as the coven's head, and Deodar (whom they called Dolly) had been having a serious discussion.

"How much did you say?" Holly felt stunned by the news. This was unbelievable.

"Enough to buy the Beacon Building and convert it into a small elementary school for grades one through six with room to spare." Dolly was meeting with Arnica and Holly. He wanted to put together some plans before the rest of the coven met for their pre-Equinox dinner. "And there's enough to pay off the remaining mortgages on our other buildings."

Arnica exhaled sharply, a quick prayer went off to the Goddess.

"But wait," Dolly added, "there's more. Her daughters have made a donation as well. They are setting up an endowment which will provide school expenses for at least several financially strapped families each year. It will be called 'The Trillium Fund' and, like their mother, their names and identities are to remain completely anonymous. I only know the identity of the attorney functioning as an intermediate."

"Yes, my Dear Sirs?" Gino's eyes sparkled as he called Arnica and Holly by the name he called them when he was but a lad of ten. Now he was twenty-one, married and a father. Trillium School's librarian, he had worked with the Earthkin parents who'd been home-schooling their young ones with the goal of Trillium School as they entered seventh grade.

"I have a teaching offer for you, one you won't want to refuse," Dolly said, chuckling.

Gino's eyes opened wide. This sounded most curious.

Dark Star was wandering about the cabin, feeling a bit lost. When she stepped across the wood floor between the Persian rugs, her hooves made a tapping, restless sound.

"How curious," she thought. "I so miss my egg."

It was a cool but sunny autumn day. "Almost-autumn morning," Holly had said before he and Arnica left for Merrydale. There was just a hint of early frost here and there but it was warming as the sun reached the gardens.

Dark Star nudged the door. This was the fourth time she would walk out to the Stone Circle since the men had left.

The Merrydale Council was in session. This was Jenny's most important task to date. She was the assistant chairwoman for a new Commission on Global Warming. Parliament had issued a ruling that every District must convene a commission. There was still some debate over global warming. Just two weeks ago three scientists spoke out against the ruling, claiming that the rising global temperatures were natural, and "simply part of God's plan." With Lothloriën's forests and the oceans showing clear symptoms of a warming planet, most scientists as well as the majority of Lothloriën's people felt otherwise.

Rap! The sound of the wooden gavel silenced the meeting chamber. "I would like to call this meeting to order." Jenny's voice sounded confident. "Our chairman, Mr. Tabbler, is in Mill City this week.'

Jenny's work was simple this afternoon, calling on one speaker after another. This was the information-gathering stage of the District Commission. For weeks anyone who wished could present her or his views on global warming's effects on the District of Merrydale. There were microphones and later, a secretarial pool of volunteers from Merrydale's Junior and Senior High Schools and Trillium School would type up complete transcripts.

Some of the speakers were more interesting than others. Some of Merrydale's citizens seemed to want no more than to be able to give their opinions. At those times Jenny's mind wandered back to the school, where her love, Gino, was busy at work.

'One more year,' she thought. When Gino got his degree next summer she would be enrolled in Genetricia University. She looked across the room and there were the Croffy twins. Jenny flashed them a big grin. She knew they'd be sharing stories of the meeting during the coven's Equinox gathering. A harvest feast was planned to follow an afternoon ritual.

The Hatchling

Jimmy and Yarrow would formally be entering the coven at Hallows. They were going to speak, representing Arnica's herbal gardens where they were apprentices. Both were enrolled in a premed undergraduate program. Their goal was to provide a combination of traditional medical along with herbal care and open a pediatric clinic in Merrydale.

"Someday," they would add in unison, then laugh as they often did when their thoughts were verbalized in unison.

The Hatchling knew where the egg would be placed. No one had told her, not even the Mother. She just *knew*.

Dark Star sat in the center of the Stone Circle. Her eyes closed, her horn lowered, she slowed her breathing as her grandmother, Lillian, had taught her. As she took control of her conscious mind, she allowed the imagery of the birthing to flow. The warm water ... the radiant crystals ... and the Mother, standing right there by her, in the water ...

And then, there it was ... Dark Star felt the heartbeat.

"It's stronger," she thought. "Candlemas, I so long for Candlemas..."

So taken was the hatchling with her connection with the growing life that not even the flurry of activity in the woodland was a distraction. Merrywood was filled with birds and small creatures preparing for the winter. Several times squirrels brushed against the unicorn. She sat so still they were not aware of her until scampering through the stone circle, cheek pouches filled with seeds and nuts for their winter cache.

Trillium School was every bit as busy as Merrywood. Donna Darling was practicing her folk harp. Donna, a senior, had spent part of the summer in Hebrides. Donna had sent an audition recording to a bardic school and, much to the Darlings' surprise, was accepted. Her parents could barely afford to send Donna, but Donna had so much talent.

Pearl, Trillium's music teacher, recognized Donna's ability. "Frankly," she'd written the faculty at Mill City College, "I'm in awe."

Apparently the music department at the college agreed. They put the Darlings in touch with the music department at West Anglia School of the Arts in Eastborough, way to the east in Atalanta. Spending five weeks overseas was life-changing for the family.

Pearl could help Donna learn composition and music theory but, other than an occasional suggestion about integrating her spirit into her performing, could only arrange school time for Donna to practice.

And it worked perfectly. As Donna practiced, the music gave Astral a wonderful afternoon nap. As the baby slept, the day care children learned how to make paper by hand. They loved creating the pulp with their bare hands, then spreading it onto the screens. The kids had so enjoyed collecting autumn leaves and sorting them by color.

Holly's class was busy taking notes. "Grammar lessons?" a couple of students had groaned, but when he told them that the Commission was looking for a few volunteers to edit the transcripts, the class was instantly attentive and enthusiastic.

"This autumn we're going to study the political process by looking at the history of eco-activism in the District of Merrydale," Iris announced.

"Is it true you've been a protester?" a wide-eyed sophomore asked.

Iris laughed. "I'll get to that, but first let's go back to what I like to call the 'invasions.' Who knows what I mean by this?"

"The arrival of the Europans?"

"And the Asiens and Aztecans..." Another voice added.

"Yet," Iris interjected, "even the First Peoples migrated here from the Continent of Asie during a great Ice Age millennia ago."

"You mean Mother Earth has been invaded by humans all along?" That was a new concept for the students.

"I'm ready for a good Sabbat," Raven was sitting comfortably in a lawn chair, sipping a mug of Arnica's herbal tea.

"How are your classes going?" Amber Whitefeather asked.

"Ollis' new class is very popular," Raven answered. She had worked with Ollis on a new course which studied geography by looking at the ecology of various climates around the planet and how they were currently affected by global warming. Raven was covering the regular geography classes alone, as she did before their Handfasting when they began team teaching.

"Look who's here!" Amber turned. "My tribal sisters."

Peri and Topi Crowfeather came walking around the cabin, carrying a large wicker basket filled with picnic treats. Pearl was with them, a large tablecloth for the picnic table draped over her shoulder.

"Merry Meet" Arnica stood in the kitchen door, holding utensils and wearing an apron. He was making a large kettle of soup. Holly slipped past him, kissed his partner on the cheek, and went out to greet the women with hugs.

It was a fine afternoon. The other men were over near the greenhouse. Some of the Trillium School boys had begun asking if they could put together a couple of teams and try competing with other schools. Tim Fairly, a husky Junior, told the faculty that it was time that the Earthkin boys show that they're good at sports as well.

Gino and Jenny were with the young ones. Gino was showing Diana and Sunna how to make paper. Dagon, already eleven years old, was trying to act uninterested but it was obvious that he wanted to join in. Astral was sleeping in a small, portable crib. Jenny sat in the shade with the baby. She was talking quietly with the Croffy twins. Every so often the twins would giggle when Dark Star, who was sprawled out on the grass with her head on Jenny's lap, sleeping, would snore just every so gently.

Holly went back into the kitchen to help Arnica. They were gathering all of the ritual items to take back to the Stone Circle. What fun to have an afternoon ritual on such a fine autumn day.

The harvest had gone well. They had more than enough for the tithe and herbal medicines tincturing which would be donated to the food bank as well. The Croffy twins had helped Arnica fill the herbal cupboards. By now all the herb bunches were dried and put away. Tomorrow the men would make apple cider for the Yule Ritual.

"It's good, isn't it?" Arnica put his arms around Holly as they looked through the window before setting out toward the Stone Circle.

LXXXXV - Where There's a Will

Dark Star sat in the gardens, looking about. The first frost, just the day after the Equinox, was light but there had been others since then. More and more the gardens were looking barren. Arnica had been busy cutting back the herbs to the ground. In recent years Gino would be here helping, but now Gino was tending his own gardens, up at the House on the Rise. With the trees of Merrywood near the stone circle shedding their leaves as the coloring foliage was tugged by the wind and weighted by rain, the hatchling could see the top of the house with smoke coming from its chimney.

Jimmy and Yarrow Croffy, twin brothers, were now Arnica's primary apprentices. They had been around a lot, lately, and Dark Star enjoyed them. They could run fast and loved racing with her. They had been studying and the hatchling knew their goal was to join the coven soon after Hallows.

Even the borage looked ready for Hallows. There were a few new, baby plants which had come up, but the tall, beautiful furry plants with their blue star-like flowers were all gone. Life was now held down in the roots, safe within the soil.

"Why," thought the hatchling, "just like my baby!"

The hatchling had been restless in recent weeks. She had grown so accustomed to the growing life in her belly. She *knew* that her unicorn baby was being kept safe in its egg with the Mother, but she missed it... Oh, she missed it so much.

There had been a morning fire in the fireplace, but now just a few embers remained. The attorney's office had large, south facing windows and was warm and comfortable in the autumn morning.

"Is this correct?" Robert Barrister was reading from the papers on his desk, "The Grove will be held as a trust, administered by your coven. The land will actually be owned by Trillium School. You have its stated purpose as being for herbal education. It will also serve as a private place where coven initiations might be held?" Barrister looked up, his eyes twinkling over his reading glasses. "May I suggest that you replace some of these words. I don't know how well the courts would understand one's *coven* being the administration."

Holly nudged his partner lightly with his elbow. Looking at Arnica he teased, "See, I thought so."

Arnica was bemused. "All right, how about this?" He proffered an alternate wording he'd worked out with Holly and Trillium School's principal, Deodar Dolorum.

Dark Star stood in the stone circle, facing the north. Nearby on the altar were the two large crystals. The Croffy boys had brought matching smokey quartz crystals which were sitting on the altar, waiting for their Ritual of Dedication.

The hatchling wished them a blessing. Then, as she'd been taught by Lillian, she calmed her mind, began to separate herself from the world of humans, and stepped through the portal into the Otherworld.

"Executor of their estate?" Jenny sounded uncertain about all of this.

"Yes," Gino answered. "Arnica and Holly have both told me for years, now, that I'm sort-of like a son to them. and it's because we live so close to the Grove."

"What did you say?"

"Well, Holly said my face turned white." Gino grinned at his love. "I remember looking at Arnica and sort of mumbling, 'you're O.K., aren't you?'"

"I bet I know what he said," Jenny laughed.

They chanted in unison, "I'm not planning to be compost any time soon..." Arnica often joked about 'there being nothing wrong in being compost,' but when anyone asked if he was talking about himself, all of them knew his answer.

"But you know," Gino said, a little more seriously, "it got me thinking. Maybe we should put our wishes on paper as well..."

"Just the other day Pearl asked me if I'd given any thought to choosing goddessparents for Astral Brigit."

"So what did you say?" Gino asked.

"I was caught by surprise," Jenny answered, "and sort-of joked about Dark Star... but Mom and Dad asked me the same thing."

"You don't suppose..." Gino looked up toward the ceiling and Jenny joined in "it's part of growing up and being parents?" That was something both sets of Astral's grandparents had said to them at various times since their Handfasting, house purchase and, now, being parents!

Dark Star carefully stepped into the large chamber. It was filled with light, as she'd seen before, the cavern walls endless clusters of glowing crystals. But over there, in a rocking chair ('a rocking chair?' she asked herself) was the Goddess, holding the large egg, gently rocking and singing.

The lady looked at the hatchling. "Yes, a rocking chair."

Dark Star blushed. It was always a bit unnerving when the Lady so easily heard her thoughts.

"Come here" The Goddess had such a lovely voice. "She's waiting for you."

"She?" Dark Star's heart raced. "It's a girl?' "

"Well, as Andrius, your Sire would say, a 'unifilly...'"

Dark Star wanted to trot right over but the image of the Mother holding the unicorn egg reminded her of one of the pictures she'd seen, a picture Jenny had from her childhood of the baby Kristos and his mother. A 'madonna,' it may have been called. The hatchling stepped carefully. "Is she sleeping?"

"Yes, but I can sense that she knows you're here," the Lady answered. Dark Star carefully stepped near, her hooves making tiny, light sounds which tapped echoes into the far ends of the cavern.

The Goddess drew back the blanket.

Why, it was the egg blanket that Pearl and Jewel and Raven and the women of the coven had embroidered for her.

There it was! "It is so beautiful... But..." Dark Star was shocked at its size.

Before the question could even form in the hatchling's mind the Lady laughed, and music filled the air. "No, it wasn't this size when you birthed it. She's grown much since Midsummer. This is the fourth basket already, and she's nearly outgrown this one."

There, on the stone floor, was a beautifully woven basket filled with thistledown quilts. The Lady had told her that Her fairies-in-waiting would help her protect and nurture the egg until it was ready to be placed for hatchling.

Dark Star reached forward to kiss it. Her breathing grew rapid. She didn't know if she wanted to cry or to click her hooves together and jump in the air! "My Deorling," she whispered.

"What did you call her?" asked the Lady.

"Deorling..." The hatchling looked puzzled. "And I don't know why. The name just came to me.

"So mote it be," spoke the Goddess, her fingers tracing a curious symbol upon the surface of the shell. "Let this little one be known as Deorling."

The adults sat around the stone circle, shawls, sweaters, warm hats and scarves over their robes to keep them warm. Frost was forecast and everyone present was certain the weatherwoman's prediction on the radio would prove quite accurate. Iris shivered lightly and snuggled against Deodar.

Gino picked up the large horn and trumpeted a note out into the night. He tried to hide how pleased he was to have been given the role of summoning the crone. The Croffy twins, wearing their new, identical robes, were suitably impressed. Gino had been a role model for them.

"Come dear Goddess, come this night..." Gino's voice sang out.

"Join us on this darksome night..." the coven chanted.

Pearl and Jenny were leading a children's ritual up in the House on the Rise.

Arnica prostrated himself before the altar. 'Pretty good for an old man,' he thought to himself. His knees held up well and his trance work kept his body warm despite the night.

"Oh Lady of the Dark Veil..." Holly sang out into the night. Crisp stars dotted the darkened sky. The Moon would not rise through the trees for another two hours.

"It is I..." A dark figure stepped from behind the trees, just beyond the light from the cauldron fire and candles. Her face obscured by a black net veil, three hooded figures walked with her. Yarrow shuddered just a bit, a childhood scary story or two slipping through his memories.

Ollis was surprised. He did not often see Raven taking such a strong ritual role. Having invoked the Crone, her voice sounded other-worldly and, had he not known it was his wife, he would not have recognized the woman behind the Dark Veil.

"We are the Muses of your Ancestors..." The Crowfeather sisters and Amber Whitefeather carried baskets holding mementos, photos, a few heirlooms and other relics of the coven's ancestors.

"I greet you." Arnica walked to the portal and kissed the Lady of the Dark Veil on both cheeks as he welcomed her into the Circle. Holly cleared the altar of all the ritual items and the 'Three Muses' created an ancestral altar upon the large, stone slab.

It was time, now, for contemplation. Lotus added a few pieces of kindling into the large, cast-iron cauldron and they all sat quietly. It was time to extend their spirits out beyond the circle, to commune with their ancestors.

"Ancestors? Dark star thought to herself. "How can I think about Lillian, or my mare Lovely... My mind is on the coming birth, the future generations..."

LXXXXVI - A Star In The Night

"Brrr..." Holly's feet didn't stay on the cold floor very long. He jumped right back into the warm bed.

"Keep them off me!" Arnica laughed.

"I think the fire's out." Holly lay on his back, rubbing his feet on the flannel sheet to warm them.

"Is she out there again?" Arnica reached for his warm, snuggly robe hanging over the chair at his side of the bed.

"Yes. I thought I heard her hooves tapping softly on the floor, then the sound of the kitchen door. You know, she's very good at trying to be quiet..."

"For a unicorn," the men said in unison, laughing.

"And when I got up to pee," Holly continued, "she was nowhere to be seen so I'm sure she's back out there."

Arnica climbed out of bed and pulled on his robe. "I'll go stoke the fire. She's out there almost every night, isn't she?"

"She'll be in tonight. With everyone here for Yule Eve, the kids will be a good distraction."

Dark Star sat in the center of the Stone Circle, so quiet and unmoving that, from a distance, human eyes would not even see her.

The waxing Moon was rising overhead. There were small drifts of snow among the trees. The sky was crispy clear but the hatchling was beyond feeling the night air. Her horn pointed at the Moon, Dark Star opened herself to the connection between the egg and the Lady's light.

"Where are you?" she asked. It wasn't here, yet. Dark Star could feel the soil, she could feel the Goddess. But her own baby was not yet here. There was such a longing. Just the other day she was up at the House on the Rise spending some time with Jenny and Astral Brigit. Seeing the look in Jenny's eyes as she held the baby... Why, it was almost a physical pain. Dark Star looked up at the sky. The stars certainly were bright. Would her unifoal want to nurse from her? Would she have enough milk? Will it really be a unicolt? She'd been thinking so all along, but what if it was a unifilly?

It would be a good Solstice Ritual, filling the cabin. Gino and Jenny were hosting a sleep-over for those with children. It would be snug, but festive.

Iris and Deodar came out with Diana. The first-grader had her mother's dark hair, but preferred it short. She thrived on an active life and just couldn't be bothered and with Iris tending the postal shop *and* teaching at Trillium School, her own long braid sometimes seemed so much work. When Dolly would catch her looking at it in the mirror, he'd snuggle up to her and whisper in her ear, reminding her of the fun they had with her braid when Diana was visiting friends or late at night when they made love a little more quietly but with as much passion. Diana would stay in the house but Iris and Dolly were bringing a tent.

"Not me," Raven laughed. "We're too old for camping."

"I love the kids," Ollis joined in, "but I need our bed at night." In their sixties, they were renting a large, horse-drawn carriage for the evening, "just for fun," Ollis added.

The Hatchling

Jewel and Lotus were also planning a tent. It was the sixth anniversary of Sunna's appearing at the cabin door. They celebrated her birthdays on Hallows Day, but Yule was always an anniversary. The two first-graders were going to be 'big girls,' helping Jenny with Astral Brigit. Sunna had been asking Jewel questions for days. She and Diana were almost like sisters, sitting next to each other in school and spending nights sleeping over. This was their first foray into serious responsibility and they were very excited. Dagon would be sleeping at the cabin.

Peri and Topi were intent upon riding with Ollis and Raven. The Crowfeather sisters loved their time with children but Trillium's daycare was as much as they could manage. Amber Whitefeather, a Loon Tribe 'sister' of theirs had promised them all she'd bring some of her grandmother's "Dark Sun Potion" she'd learned to make growing up in the River Mountains. Her grandmother always made it for the men of the tribe but Amber wondered why the men should have all the fun?

The House on the Rise would also hold Astral Brigit's grandparents Rosario and her maternal grandparents as well, her grandparents Flower.

When Jenny was working out the sleeping arrangements, it suddenly occurred to her, "Mom, did you know that this was destiny?"

Becky Flower looked at her daughter. Jenny always asked such *curious* questions. Becky knew this was just a set-up for something Jenny wanted to say. Becky's eyebrows asked 'what?' as she didn't have to speak a word.

"You know... *Rosario* - rose, and 'flower...'" Jenny was delighted with this. Somehow, it seemed, no one had yet come up with this connection. The two grandmothers would share Gino and Jenny's bedroom. Jenny would sleep on a sleeping pad in the bedroom. Diana Dolorum and Sunna Woodfolk were sharing a sleeping pad in Astral's room. 'Probably none of them will sleep,' Jenny thought, 'but at least I can keep them quiet enough for our Moms.'

Gino and his dad, Carlos, would set up a men's room downstairs, sharing it with Philbert. Mr. Flower was surprisingly happy about all this. More and more he was enjoying his time with his daughter's Earthkin friends.

The Flowers and the Rosarios were growing fond of each other as well. Rosetta and Becky had offered to stay at the House on the Rise during the Yule Eve Ritual. Philbert and Carlos has discovered that they both enjoyed cribbage.

It was a happy foursome household when the coven arrived, singing their way up the hill after their Yule Eve Circle.

"Can I go running with Dark Star, can I?" Dagon's newest passion was running.

"Ask your Dad," Jewel said. Sunna was tired and Jewel was holding her, rocking her in Arnica's chair by the fire.

Dagon's face began to express displeasure but he thought better of it. It was a good thing, too, because his mother wasn't done.

"It's O.K. with me if it's O.K with Dark Star," Jewel continued. Dagon's eyebrows raised in anticipation. "But you need to have your Dad talk to Arnica. I heard Holly saying something about Dark Star having some difficult times lately."

"Daddy!" Sometimes Dagon forgot he was trying to act like a teenager and his boyish ways slipped right through.

The Hatchling

"A mug of Holly's cider for you..." Holly had mulled the cidei with cloves and allspice. There was a small dollop of fresh whipped cream floating on the top with a sprinkle of fresh ground nutmeg. "Oh, and Ollis offered to liven it up with some brandy he brought back from Europa years ago. He said it's aged well."

"Daddy can I..." Dagon realized his parents were still talking. "Oops. Sorry," he added.

"Cider yes, brandy no," Jewel said. "I'd fall sound asleep with Sunna." She glanced at Dagon, then at Lotus. Dagon didn't even see her wink at Lotus. They knew that Dagon inevitably came out of a ritual overflowing with energy.

"I'm off then." Lotus acted as if he needed to leave in haste.

"But Daddy, please..."

"Oh... my... Goddess..." Dark Star was breathing heavy. She and Dagon were running with exuberance. Why, this was what it was like when she was a unifilly, out running with Gino when she was young.

She and Dagon had raced back to the house. It was hard work to win. "And you've got *four* legs! You should be faster!" Dagon had teased.

"You didn't birth an egg last summer," the hatchling thought back at the boy.

Suddenly, her mane bristled. She looked up into the night. Dagon followed her upturned head, let out a whoop, and ran to the house, opening the door and shouting loud enough to wake Astral, "Hey, everybody, come and look!"

The adults, holding cider and hot chocolate (and a few holding hot toddies) came out. Diana and Sunna looked up and were so excited they started trying to turn cartwheels.

"Northern lights," Arnica said, putting his arm around Holly. "It's been years."

"There!" Holly pointed. All eyes followed his finger.

"A falling star!" Gino shouted in excitement.

It was so close. They watched and it plummeted down, landing at the foot of the rise.

Dark Star whinnied and went running.

"What did she say?" Jenny asked.

"It's here," Holly answered.

Dark Star reached the Stone Circle. There, just to the left of the portal, lay a small piece of meteorite in the snow, a wisp of steam curling up.

There was a mound of fresh, upturned soil, just large enough.

Dark Star lay down over it. It was warm. How ever would she return to the cabin. She knew the egg had to spend a Sabbat cycle here, but could she just walk away? 'The Mother *told* me,' she reminded herself. 'And my unicolt needs some time alone, without a doting mommymare at hand.'

She heard the voices nearing. They had all come to see. Holly and Arnica knew. 'I think Gino and Jenny know as well,' Dark Star thought.

Pearl started a lovely round, a lullaby. The humans all sang, softly. Dark Star lay curled up, her happiness so overwhelming her eyes filled with tears.

'Truly,' she thought, 'tonight we birthed the light.'

LXXXXVII - Full Circle the final episode

"Have you ever seen anything like that?" Gino was incredulous. Walking back to the House on the Rise, they had seen a family of deer standing at the edge of the Stone Circle, watching Dark Star, who was laying over her egg.

"There were raccoons and I saw a pair of fox as well." The Crowfeather sisters were thrilled at seeing some of their tribe's totem animals so close. "And did you see the wolf?" Peri chimed in before Topi finished 'pair of fox.' "The wolf was sitting there quietly next to the deer."

"And they all watched together without any fear of each other!!!" Jimmy and Yarrow spoke in unison in counterpoint to the Crowfeathers.

The two pair of siblings laughed. Despite the thirty-plus years difference in their ages, they were the only ones who understood the blood bonding so strong.

It had been quite the scene. The humans paused, standing near the Stone Circle. All the creatures were oblivious to them although Dark Star looked at her human friends and nodded. It was a cool yet sunny day but she looked warm and radiant, a maternal glow radiating from her very being.

As the hatchling's gaze turned toward Gino, her eyes blinked and Gino nodded. No one else seemed to notice their exchange. *I must tell Arnica,* Gino thought to himself.

It was a beautiful late winter morning. Although usually cool and damp this time of year, it had been warm and sunny for several days. Even though the weather suggested global warming, the Sabbat morning was just too beautiful and the Earth was filled with joy.

Last night's ritual was focused upon bringing the gift of Hope to the Land of Lothloriën. All the coven had attended, even though the cabin was a little small now that the coven had grown to be twelve, plus the Croffy twins who were finishing their apprenticeships.

Jewel, in the role of the Mother Goddess, was in charge of consecrating the ritual candles which would be used in Trillium School's rituals over the coming year. The warmer-than-usual evening allowed a procession as the coven carried the candles out to the Stone Circle and back into the cabin's temple.

Arnica and Holly wanted to somehow keep the hatchling connected. The past few days Dark Star had come home only to eat, spending every waking - and sleeping! - hour out at the Stone Circle. Her humans now knew and she loved them for bringing the candles out to the four elemental altars, and to her.

"Will my hatchling go to Trillium School," she wondered?

As they neared the house, the group was a murmur of the conversations stimulated by this morning's faculty meeting at Arnica and Holly's cabin. The planning for the following school year was exciting. When school opened this autumn, Trillium would have a fully-accredited school, from day care through high school. Gino would have his degree and the faculty would be growing to accommodate the burgeoning student enrollment.

"Daddy!" Diana came running down the hill toward them.

"What is it, pumpkin?" Deodar Dolorum asked as the school's principal scooped up his daughter and lifted her to his shoulders to ride.

"They're here!" Diana squealed in glee.

"Who's here?" Dolly (*Papadolly*, as Diana called Dolly as the coven knew him) asked her. This conversation had quickly gained everyone's attention.

"It's a secret..." she giggled.

"Not any more," Arnica said, his ears catching the soft strains of lute music.

"They *are* here!" Holly said, beginning to lope up the hill toward the house, slowing as he realized he didn't run as easily any more.

The house was filled with sound. Wren was playing some new songs for the coven children as Robin Sylphing answered questions in the other room with some of the Trillium faculty. Arnica and Dolly were talking to Robin about a position in the school teaching math as Raven and Ollis tried to talk over the serious conversation, telling Robin that she and Wren 'simply must' look at the house across the street from them which had a new 'for sale' sign.

Jenny was in the kitchen where she and Iris were putting the finishing touches on a birthday cake. Pearl held a candle that she'd brought through last night's ritual, just one candle, perfect for Astral Brigit's first birthday.

The grandmothers, Rosetta Rosario and Becky Flower were in the bedroom, putting the finishing touches on a new blanket. Over the months they'd discovered a friendship which brought them great comfort and together they'd decided to begin a trousseau quilt, one which would grow by another embroidered block each year. Carlos and Philbert were carrying a new cedar chest up the steps.

"Careful," Becky cautioned.

"Dear..." Philbert answered and Becky knew that he was overtaxing himself but needed to be left alone.

"I can hear it," Dark Star thought out loud.

"Really?" asked the deer. "Is it wonderful?"

"I spoke with the Lady just the other day," brooed a snowy owl up in the cedar. "*She* told me that this baby would be very important for the futures of us all.

A soft tapping sounded beneath the mounded soil.

"Is it okay?" barked the fox.

"He's fine," Dark Star answered, speaking from her soul. "I hear his heartbeat."

"You do?" responded the voices of many creatures in their own languages.

This was the most amazing thing which had happened in Merrywood... well, since *Dark Star* was hatched!

"Quick, call the others."

"I'll light the candle."

"Are her gifts wrapped and at the table?"

"Lotus carved her a magick wand."

"Tell them to stop talking about the school and come to sing!"

"It's lit, let's carry it out."

The house was bursting with the sounds of voices and joy.

"Happy birthday to you, happy birthday to you..."

In the distance there was a rumble, an odd sound, almost like the train which headed to Mill City but deeper and more frightening.

The House became instantly silent. No one spoke, no one moved.

Then the sound of glass jiggling gently against glass. A crashing in the distance. Sunna shrieked out loud. "Mommy, hold me!"

The House groaned and shook. The sound of breaking glass or china rattled in counterpoint.

"Stop," Arnica called out, his voice reaching everyone. "Don't panic! It's our Mother Earth. She's cracking her bones and She'll stop."

The house gave one intense shake and the sound passed on into the distance leaving a sigh of relief.

"Happy birthday to you..." As Holly's voice finished the first line, there was laughter and soon everyone chimed in.

All four grandparents came into the room. Becky's face was pale. This had frightened her but they soon saw that everyone was just fine.

As the candle was puffed out, Astral Brigit's cheeks pink and glowing, Arnica quickly looked at Holly and said, "our last earthquake was eleven years ago..."

"This coming Eostara..." Holly interjected.

The men grabbed their hats and rushed out the door shouting to everyone as they headed for the Stone Circle, "It's a Unicolt!"

The Hatchling

The Hatchling

Notes: Who's Who in the Coven

Arnica and Holly
Arnica is an elder of the Renaissance Tribe and the coven elder. He is an herbalist and, together with his partner Holly of many years, maintain herbal gardens surrounding their cabin in the Grove. Arnica is fifty years old when the story opens and Holly is forty-six. The two men are much loved by all who know them. They have lived outside of Merrydale in their cabin for many decades.

The Rosarios
Gino is an Aries. His birthday is April 3rd. When he first appears in the story, is but a boy, ten years old. By the time the series ends, Gino is married, working on his University degree, and has become an initiated priest of the coven. Gino's knowledge and talents all blossom as he grows in the Earthkin religion. Gino is handfasted with his sweetheart Jenny when they are nineteen.

Jenny Flower Rosario becomes Gino's sweetheart, despite her father's strong disapproval of her being involved with an Earthkin boy. Her conflict with her father is so strong she storms out of the house and moves in with Pearl as she begins her studies with the coven and enters Trillium School. A Taurus, Jenny's birthday is May 11th. She is just weeks younger than Gino.

Astral Brigit Rosario is born on Candlemas morning, a most magickal baby, just months before her parents turn twenty-one.

The Dolorums
Iris appears early in the series. She is a central figure in Merrydale, the postmarm. As such she knows much of what takes place in the city. Iris cares much about the environment, organizing as march to Fern Hollow as one of her first major activities we see. Iris is handfasted to Deodar Dolorum four years after the story begins.

Deodar, known as Dolly by his friends, is first known to us as 'Pastor Dolorum,' working with the Church of the Martyr. He is not happy in the Kristos ministry, eventually leaving it to become active within the coven and the principal of Trillium School.

Diana is their baby, both just a year after her parents marriage.

The Woodfolk
Jewel and **Lotus** are already married as *The Hatchling* opens. Jewel is expecting their first child, **Dagon**. Jewel is quiet by nature, but helps Iris in the postal shop. An Aquarius, she is twenty-six as the story opens.

Lotus is known for hiss construction skill, building a fountain for Trillium School, the Diana Shrine in the woods near the cabin, and later teaching wood-working and related skills in Trillium School.

Dagon is a precocious child, something of a 'magickal prodigy,' both little more than four months after *The Hatchling* begins. He quickly bonds with Dark Star who carries him into the realm of the faerie when he is one year old.

Sunna is found at sunrise at the cabin door in the fourth year of the story. She is adopted by the Woodfolk.

Pearl Lamina
When we first meet **Pearl** she is married to **Phoenix**, already known for her skills with arts and with crafts. Phoenix's deteriorating health causes them to move to Cloverville and stay with Lady Ellhorn. After Phoenix passes, Pearl returns and becomes an active and vibrant presence in both the coven and in Trillium School.

Flying Raven and Ollis Piper
Flying Raven lives far away in the Mothervalley. She lives alone, her husband Jed, having passed away some time earlier. Her three daughters, Claudia, Caterina and Caroline are on their own. Claudia is a conservative Kristos and does not approve of her mother. With little to keep her in the Mothervalley, Raven moves to Merrydale to be part of the creation of Trillium School. One summer she becomes involved with a 'dark stranger.' She and Ollis create a very good life together.

Ollis Piper begins as a mysterious figure who turns out to be Iris's father. His experience in the merchant marine provides him with a wealth of information. He and Raven are handfasted and Ollis brings his experience to Trillium School teaching world geography.

Amber Whitefeather
Amber once owned a little Merrydale shop, '*Amber's Crystal Emporium*,' but it was subject to prejudice and pressure from the local Kristos. She moved back to the River Mountains to her family and kin, the Loon Tribe. She becomes increasingly connected with the coven and joins, after moving back to Merrydale to work with Trillium School.

Peridot and Topaz Crowfeather
Peri and **Topi** are blood sisters who find that moving to Merrydale to be near their tribal sister, Amber, opens a wonderful life through the coven and Trilliam School. With Amber they are able to maintain their Loon Tribe ways.

Jimmy and Yarrow Croffy
The **Croffy twins** appear as young students. By the end of the story we see that they will be part of the next generation of the coven and life in Merrydale.

Who's Who: Keeping Track of the Others

Carlos and Rosetta Rosario
When we first read of **Gino's parents**, Carlos is working in the flour mills in Mill City. Several years pass before he returns home. With Gino's involvement in the coven, both Carlos and Rosetta find great joy in being part of Trillium School. Although never formally part of the coven, their lives are intrinsically part of the coven and of Trillium School.

Philbert and Becky Flower
Jenny's parents undergo an interesting revolution during the story. Philbert struggles with his religious and political beliefs yet has his own mystical experiences. Becky begins to discover herself. Philbert and Jenny undergo major changes in their lives and truly, could be a story of their own.

Lillian
Lillian is Dark Star's grandmare. She is very wise and has a close interaction with the Goddess. Unicorns do not need last names.

Wren and Robin Sylphing
Wren is a Bard. She and her partner Robin live in Highlands but sometimes travel to Merrydale to participate in coven events. Were they to live in the same city they would be active coven members.

Minor Characters

On a first name basis:
Amethyst and Crystal - a couple who are involved with the coven in the first two years until they move some distance away

Echo - Lives in the Red Mountain Plateau near the Highlands where she explores Bardic work with Wren

Elstrum - A dryad living in an oak

Juanita - Becky Flowers' aunt

Lupine - Spends a few months in Merrydale to study for the Renaissance Priesthood but then moves on

Madrona - Iris Dolorum's mother

Marco - A friend of Amber's cousin, lives in Azteca

Marina - Flying Raven's granddaughter and attends university in Verdeville. Her mother is Caroline. She is the only member of Raven's family who likes the Earthkin ways.

Nettie - A busybody who loves to gossip

Poppy - Of an elven mother and Earthkin father, he spends a short time in Merrydale

Quicksilver - Lives in the River Mountains, a steelsmith who dates Amber for a time

Rhymer - A Renaissance Tribe Elder and Bard

Sam - A plumber living in Merrydale

Silverwing - Deodar Dolorum's great-great-great-grandmother, of the Descendant Tribe

Tibby - Jouhn Trouver's aunt

Alphabetically by last name:

Thurifera Amberson - Known as 'Honey,' he moves from Eastborough to study with the coven for a time and then moves on to Delphone.

Missy Birches - Mayor Brown's secretary, Jenny's coworker

Jacob Browning - Merrydale's Mayor

Samuel Burnside - Merrydale's fire marshall

Lady Ellhorn - Pearl's grandmother, in her 70s when the stories begin. She lives in Cloverville in the Saigaireau Province.

Maude Graves - An older, local woman who helps a fund-raising event. Her father is **Jinko Graves**.

Slade and Glenda Hatchitt - A right wing conservative of the Politico party later caught by his own hypocrisy; and his wife

Rebecca Morningstar - One of the earliest settlers of Merrydale, she was hung for witchcraft.

Mrs. O'Realy - An elderly widow living on a two acre farm, she sells eggs and produce and also sews for income.

Mildred Poindexter - Head of the Floral Belles, Merrydale's gardening club

John Pounds - The tithing agent

Pipestone Proudfeather - 'Pippi' is the Crowfeathers' cousin. She moves to Mill City to teach at the Loon School.

Mr. & Mrs. Lodgefellows Owners of the Merrydale Hotel

Henley Schrobbe - A Politico politician who is ultra-conservative

Shadow Tail - Member of the Loon Tribe who spends a little time in Merrydale

John Trouver - Merrydale's law enforcement figure, the Constable

Politics, Geography and Other Information

The Land of Lothloriën
We learn of Lothloriën primarily from the perspective of Merrydale and the coven. These are difficult times. Many believe that the lands are growing warmer and are alarmed by the changing climate. The life of Lothloriën's people has become more polarized, with the Users on one side favoring the use of all natural resources to further their wealth and the Conservers trying to gain enough power to protect the land.

The Earthkin
This is a name used in Lothloriën which refers to all people of the earth, who see the natural world as sacred. Most of these peoples are polytheistic and/or pantheistic and sometimes called the Children of the Earth. They are not thought of kindly by the majority of Kristos, who see them as a dark force.

The **Descendant Tribes** are those who lived in Lothloriën and Atalanta before the great migrations from Europa began. They hold to their old ways. They have bonded with the Renaissance Tribe to work toward mutual goals.

The **Renaissance Tribes** are those who are primarily descended from the their families who came to this land from other countries. They love the old ways and learned that the pre-Kristos ways of their ancestors in Europa were very similar to the ways of the Descendant Tribes. It is not unusual for the Renaissance young to become engaged even before they complete their education. Girls celebrate the onset of menses with a rite of passage called the First Lunar Moon which dedicates them to the Goddess. Boys celebrate their First P'aratem after the onset of puberty and are dedicated to the God.

Although sexual, couples who are trothed practice birth control. It is rare for a couple to conceive a child until after their handfasting.

Once Trillium School has been established, it is soon followed by Loon School in Mill City, Yarrow School East and Yarrow School West, Iguana School in Cloverville and The Elms Druids School in New Celtria.

The Kristos are a large religious following of the Krista. They are, generally, a good and loving people, tolerant and open to their neighbors (including the Earthkin). Over recent generations the political life of Lothloriën along with the more powerful churches of Kristos have moved increasingly toward the perspective of the Users, the right-wing faction of the Politicos. The Users believe that natural resources are there for humans to use (hence their popular name). They also tend to see the Earthkin as under the influence of the devil.

Merrydale

Merrydale is about two-and-a-half miles from the cabin, usually considered walking distance. The city has grown around a village square where the Merrydale Hotel and Town Hall are located. The Town Hall is where the Merrydale Council - the city government - and the District of Merrydale's Greater Council meet.

Merrydale, still a 'town' in the minds of most locals, has grown. The Eastside is the quieter side of town. The Grove and cabin are east of the Eastside. It is here where the postal shop and Trillium School are located.

The Westside is where Merrydale High School and Merrydale Junior High School are located. The Church of the Martyr and many of its followers live in the Westside as well.

Merrydale Clinic is the primary location for medical care.

Merrywood

The forest and woodlands between the cabin and Merrydale are known as Merrywood although that forest land is far larger. **Fern Hollow** is a favorite location, one considered very beautiful and near sacred by the Earthkin. The Dryad Tree is a sacred oak near Fern Hollow.

The River Mountains

Part of a large, north-to-south mountain range reaching nearly to Azteca, the River Mountains separate the District of Merrydale from the District of Grainland. The Loon Tribe live in The River Mountains, many of them in Eagle's Nest which is on the eastern slopes of the mountains.

Lothloriën is the western region of the continent and **Atalanta** is the eastern side. They are separated by the great Genetricia River. The southern territory is the country of **Azteca**. The Land of Lothloriën is bordered to west by the **Protein Ocean** and on the east by the **Genetricia River**.

The District of Merrydale is seated in Merrydale.

The District of Grainland is east of The River Mountains. It is centered in **Mill City** and is where Parliament is located as well. Mill City is named for its many mills.

Mill City is also home to the **Cathedral of Thorns** and the **Kristo's Arms**, the largest source of right-wing Kristos activity, headed by their Bishop.

The District of the Mothervalley has its seat in **Verdeville**. It is east of the District of Grainland.

The District of the Four Deserts is south of the Merrydale District. It's seat is **Cloverville**. It includes the Saigaireau Province.

East of the Four Deserts is the **District of the Red Mountains**. It's government seat is in **Highlands**. Red Mountain Plateau is a suburb of Highlands.

And east of the Red Mountains District is the **District of Great Plains**, bordered on its east by the Genetricia River. The seat of government is **Heartland**.

Atalanta is the country between the Genetricia River and the Atlantikos Ocean. Atalanta and Lothloriën often think of themselves as 'sister countries,' sharing much in the way of trade and economy. Their Parliament is located in **Eastborough**, a major city and port on the Atlantikos. Eastborough is also the seat of **New Celtria**.

We don't read much about Atalanta. **Delphine** is the governmental seat of **Gardenia**.

Azteca is a country found south of both Lothloriën and Atalanta.

Europa is a continent on the other side of the Atlantikos Ocean. The Rosarios come originally from **Italica** which, today, is mostly Kristan. Italica has been at war with Saracenia off and on since ancient times.

Hebrides is the country which was the primary source of immigrants to Lothloriën and Atalanta and from where the language spoken by most non-Descendants originated. **Keltavia** is a distant country on the eastern side of Europa.

Saracenia is a somewhat tribal country which has worshipped the god Bawa'al for countless ages. The wars between Saracenia and Italica are, as a consequence, territorial and political but also religious. Saracenia is located on the continent of **Asie**. Much further to the east in Asie is **Dyubkz**.

Kan'ai is a country on the continent of **Afresia**, also across the Atlantikos.

about the author:

Well-known throughout the neo-pagan and Wiccan world, Beyerl's columns and articles have appeared in many publications beginning in the 1970s. *The Master Book of Herbalism,* first published in 1984, remains popular today. Beyerl has been teaching workshops and courses since 1976.

Beyerl is the founder of The Rowan Tree, a Wiccan Church, which obtained legal recognition in 1980. He is the creator of The Tradition of Lothloriën. *A Wiccan Bardo, Revisited* describes this Tradition and Beyerl's view of ritual theology. Within the Rowan Tree, The Mystery School is the educational forum for its inner teaching, combining The Tradition of Lothloriën with a broad-based metaphysical curriculum, including the Tarot. Originally centered in Minneapolis, The Rowan Tree Church moved west with Beyerl.

In addition to his work as herbalist and astrologer, Beyerl is known for his presentations on aspects of ritual, death and dying, ethics, alchemy, initiation, meditation and visualization techniques, and for his performances of ritual which incorporate skills of theatre and music. Beyerl's work has reached a vast number of students over the past thirty years. Many of his former students have moved on to become reputable teachers.

In 1989 Beyerl moved to Dallas and began a circuitous journey which would return him to a northern climate. His work completed in Texas, he moved to Los Angeles to teach for three years. It was while there that he and gerry became partners. In 1994 the Beyerls returned to their roots, opening their herbal gardens. Their home became a religious and educational center known as The Hermit's Grove in Kirkland (a Seattle suburb). The gardens and land were a project begun over twenty years ago by gerry on land known for its stone circle and herbal dreams. Today, Beyerl teaches courses in herbal medicine, horticulture and other studies at two Community Colleges and is the administrator of a Master Herbalist Program.

For further information:
paul@thehermitsgrove.org

The Rowan Tree Church
P.O. Box 0691, Kirkland, WA 98083-0691
www.therowantreechurch.org

The Hatchling is a reflection of The Tradition of Lothloriën. If you would like more information on The Tradition of Lothloriën or to express your comments to the author, you can do so by writing to us directly.

The Rowan Tree Church is an earth-focused network of communities and solitary practitioners dedicated to the study and practice of the Wiccan Tradition we call Lothloriën. We encourage spiritual growth through support, resources and educational opportunities for our Members. We also offer formal pathworking to an understanding of the Inner Mysteries.

The Rowan Tree Church was founded by Rev. Paul Beyerl and legally established in 1979. In 1994 it relocated its publishing and administrative work to The Hermit's Grove in Kirkland, Washington.

The Tradition of Lothloriën works with universal archetypes as depicted in The Holy Books. Although Wiccan, our Tradition is derived not only from European roots but sees itself as part of a global movement toward enlightened wisdom.

To help people better understand The Tradition of Lothloriën and Beyerl's work, we offer books, published rituals, including many written by Beyerl, newsletters and Membership in our Church.

The Mystery School, a traditional form of self-disciplined training, is the equivalent of working toward graduate degrees in Wiccan theology and religious studies. Founded by Rev. Paul, those who work within the Church as Initiates are among the best teachers to be found.

The Unicorn, a newsletter begun by Beyerl in 1977, arrives to celebrate the eight religious holidays containing artwork, letters, reviews, fiction, poetry and other works to promote inspiration. The Unicorn continues under Rev. Paul's editorship.

If you would like information about our work with a price listing of our publications and books, send a business sized, self-addressed stamped envelope to The Rowan Tree Church.

You might also be interested in our 'sample packet' which includes samples of The Unicorn, the catalog describing our Church and a copy of our Member newsletter, *The Rowan Tree News*, are also included. Send $4.00 to The Rowan Tree Church.

The Hatchling

The Hermit's Grove
P.O. Box 0691, Kirkland, WA 98033-*0691*
www.thehermitsgrove.org

The Hermit's Grove is a non-profit organization dedicated to the healing of body, soul and planet. Founded by Rev. Paul and gerry Beyerl in 1994, our educational programs include many related fields, ranging from herbal medicine to herbal magick and many other disciplines. We teach the traditional sciences used by healers, including astrology and spiritual wisdom. The Hermit's Grove offers workshops and classes, over an acre of gardens with hundreds of species and other resources. Its publishing program makes the books of Paul Beyerl available to you, as well as offering a monthly journal.

Through the Hermit's Grove you may study by correspondence, or purchase dried herbs and botanicals (nearly two hundred are offered). The Hermit's Grove is centered in the Beyerls' private home. To protect the gardens and sacred spaces and to respect the needs of our students, we are open by appointment only.

The Memorial Grove: A small woodland at the east end of our gardens is the Memorial Grove. A path through the sacred woodland brings you to a small, stone circle, a safe, private place for meditation and prayer. The Circle has stones from many sacred sites all about our planet. Bells hang from the trees, their sound ringing out in memory of those passed into the Otherworld. Sitting around on the stones is a small herd of Unicorns... If you wish to have a bell hung or a unicorn placed in our garden in memory of a loved one, please contact The Hermit's Grove to make arrangements. Weatherproof unicorns are always welcome!

Do you want a magickal stone??? Magickal stones from our garden are available, tumbled and polished. Send one from your home garden or sacred space for our Stone Circle and we will send one to you. Because The Hermit's Grove is definitely non-profit (sometimes too non-profit for its own good) this project will welcome any donations. The cost of a stone (including postage, mailer, and the tumbling grits and polishes) runs one or two dollars for stones sent within North America and more when the stones are honored by becoming foreign travellers.

The Hermit's Lantern A monthly publication for those concerned with wellness of body and of spirit. Features include our garden journal and an 'herb of the month. More reading includes herbal lore, tarot, gem and mineral lore, an astrological guide for ritual work during the coming month and more.

For a current price list, catalog and a sample issue of *The Hermit's Lantern*, send $5.00 to The Hermit's Grove.

329